PENGUIN  CLASSICS

THE CHARTERHOUSE OF PARMA

MARIE-HENRI BEYLE, known through his writings as Stendhal, was born in 1783 in Grenoble. In 1799 he moved to Paris, where the patronage of a cousin in the War Ministry got him a commission in the Napoleonic army. A year later he joined his regiment in northern Italy, a country he much preferred to his own. He then served intermittently on the administrative side of the army, which he accompanied in 1812 on its disastrous invasion of Russia. After Napoleon fell, Stendhal settled in Milan and started to write, but in 1821, suspected by the Austrian authorities of being a French spy, he returned to Paris. There he published a psychological study, *De l'amour* (*On Love*), a first, unsuccessful novel, *Armance*, and in 1830 his first masterpiece, *Le Rouge et le noir* (*The Red and the Black*). Following the 'revolution' of that year, he solicited the new regime for an official post and was appointed French consul in Civitavecchia, near Rome. On an extended leave back in Paris in 1838 he wrote his second great masterpiece, *La Chartreuse de Parme* (*The Charterhouse of Parma*). His health having begun to fail, he returned to Paris for the last time in 1841 and died there the following year. Various autobiographical works, his *Journal*, his *Souvenirs d'égotisme* (*Memoirs of an Egotist*) and notably an account of his early life, *La Vie de Henry Brulard*, all appeared posthumously.

JOHN STURROCK has been a literary journalist since the late 1960s. He was deputy editor of *The Times Literary Supplement* from 1972 to 1984 and is currently consulting editor of the *London Review of Books*. He has published critical books on the French New Novel, the stories of Jorge Luis Borges, autobiography and Structuralism, and has previously translated books by Victor Hugo, Stendhal and Marcel Proust for Penguin Classics.

STENDHAL

The Charterhouse
of Parma

Translated with an Introduction and Notes by
JOHN STURROCK

PENGUIN BOOKS

PENGUIN BOOKS

Published by the Penguin Group
Penguin Books Ltd, 80 Strand, London WC2R ORL, England
Penguin Group (USA) Inc., 375 Hudson Street, New York, New York 10014, USA
Penguin Group (Canada), 90 Eglinton Avenue East, Suite 700, Toronto, Ontario, Canada M4P 2Y3
(a division of Pearson Penguin Canada Inc.)
Penguin Ireland, 25 St Stephen's Green, Dublin 2, Ireland
(a division of Penguin Books Ltd)
Penguin Group (Australia), 250 Camberwell Road,
Camberwell, Victoria 3124, Australia (a division of Pearson Australia Group Pty Ltd)
Penguin Books India Pvt Ltd, 11 Community Centre,
Panchsheel Park, New Delhi – 110 017, India
Penguin Group (NZ), cnr Airborne and Rosedale Roads, Albany,
Auckland 1310, New Zealand (a division of Pearson New Zealand Ltd)
Penguin Books (South Africa) (Pty) Ltd, 24 Sturdee Avenue,
Rosebank, Johannesburg 2196, South Africa

Penguin Books Ltd, Registered Offices: 80 Strand, London WC2R ORL, England

www.penguin.com

First published in French 1839
This translation first published in Penguin Classics 2006
2

Translation, introduction and editorial material copyright © John Sturrock, 2006
All rights reserved

The moral right of the translator has been asserted

Set in 10.25/12.25 pt PostScript Adobe Sabon
Typeset by Rowland Phototypesetting Ltd, Bury St Edmunds, Suffolk
Printed in Great Britain by Clays Ltd, St Ives plc

ISBN-13: 978-0-140-44966-2
ISBN-10: 0-140-44966-3

Contents

Chronology

1783 23 *January*: Marie-Henri Beyle, the future Stendhal, born in Grenoble, to Chérubin Beyle, a lawyer, and Henriette Gagnon.

1790 Death of his mother in childbirth.

1792–4 Two years of domestic 'tyranny' at the hands of a tutor, Father Raillane, and his aunt, Séraphie Gagnon.

1796 Enters the newly founded École Centrale in Grenoble.

1799 Wins first prize in mathematics. *November*: Goes to Paris to take the entrance exam for the École Polytechnique, which he never attends. Becomes the protégé of a cousin, Pierre Daru, a senior figure on the administrative side of the army.

1800 *May*: Leaves for north Italy and the army there, arriving in Milan a month later. Given a commission in a regiment of dragoons.

1801 Returns to Grenoble on sick leave.

1802 Back in Paris. Resigns his army commission. Obsessed with the theatre; learns English so as to be able to read Shakespeare.

1804–5 Affair with a young actress Mélanie Guilbert, whom he follows to Marseille.

1806 *October*: Attached to the Grande Armée, works in the military commissariat in Germany. Posted to Brunswick.

1807–9 Becomes the 'intendant' of the German department of the Ocker. Lives in Brunswick for two years before returning briefly to Paris.

1809 *Spring*: Follows the army into Austria and spends six months in Vienna. Attends Haydn's funeral.

1810 *August*: Returns to Paris. Appointed to the Conseil d'État, made responsible for the upkeep of Crown buildings and furnishings.

1811 Spends his leave in Italy. Visits Parma, Florence, Rome, Naples. Translates Luigi Lanzi's *History of Painting in Italy*.

1812 Sent as a courier to Russia, following Napoleon's invasion of that country. *14 August*: Arrives in Moscow, then, following the burning of the city by its inhabitants, forms part of the Grande Armée's catastrophic winter retreat. Succeeds in getting back to Paris, sufficiently drained to liken himself to 'a dead man', but proud of having acted bravely and honourably throughout.

1813 *May*: Sent to army headquarters in Dresden. Present at the battle of Bautzen, where he sees 'all you can see of a battle, to wit nothing'. Falls ill and convalesces in Milan. *December*: Organizes frontier defences in his native Dauphiné.

1814 Writes *Lives of Haydn, Mozart and Metastasio*, which is published the following year. *July*: Leaves for Milan, travels widely in Italy.

1816 Milan. Meets Byron at La Scala.

1817 Finishes writing his *History of Painting in Italy* (based on his earlier translation of Lanzi), which is published in August. Spends a fortnight in England, the first of three visits. Publishes a travel book, *Rome, Naples and Florence in 1817*. Starts work on a life of Napoleon, which will never be finished.

1818 Develops a violent passion for Métilde Dembowski (née Viscontini), the wife of a Polish general in the Napoleonic army.

1819 Writes *On Love (De l'amour)*. Father dies, leaving a much reduced inheritance.

1821 *June*: Finally leaves Italy for Paris, fearful of being arrested by the Austrian authorities, who believe him to be a 'supremely dangerous man'. *October*: Spends a month in London.

1822 *August*: *On Love* is published, but ignored by the literary world. Starts contributing on French subjects to English literary reviews.

1823 Writes first version of a polemical anti-classical pamphlet, *Racine and Shakespeare*. Writes a *Life of Rossini*.

1825 Second version of *Racine and Shakespeare* published. Métilde Dembowski dies in Milan.

1826 Starts his first novel, *Armance*. Spends two and a half months in England.

1827 New version of *Rome, Naples and Florence* published. *August*: *Armance* is published, mystifying its few readers, who fail to realize its true subject is its unhappy hero's impotence. Extensive travels in Italy, ending in Milan.

1828 Ordered to leave Austrian territory without delay. Lives, heavily in debt and in search of employment, in Paris.

1829 Publishes *Promenades in Rome*. *September*: Travels widely in southern France.

1830 *July*: The 'Three Glorious Days' of insurrection in Paris lead to the abdication of King Charles X. Starts writing *The Red and the Black* (*Le Rouge et le noir*), together with several novellas. *November*: *The Red and the Black* goes on sale (ahead of publication). Austria refuses to authorize Stendhal's appointment as consul in Trieste.

1831 Appointed consul in Civitavecchia.

1832 Takes charge of the finances of a French expeditionary force sent to Ancona. Writes *Memoirs of an Egotist* (*Souvenirs d'égotisme*), an autobiographical account of his life between 1821 and 1830.

1833 Discovers some Italian manuscripts, on which he bases the stories in his *Italian Chronicles* (*Chroniques italiennes*), published posthumously. Three months' leave in Paris.

1834 Starts writing *Lucien Leuwen*, his longest novel, published posthumously.

1835 Receives the Légion d'honneur. Abandons *Lucien Leuwen*, starts writing an autobiographical account of his early life, *The Life of Henry Brulard* (*La Vie de Henry Brulard*).

1836 *March*: Granted a leave that is to last three years. Abandons *Henry Brulard* and leaves for Paris.

1837 Starts another novel, *The Pink and the Green* (*Le Rose et le vert*), never finished. Travels in the centre and west of France.

1838 Travels extensively in southern France, Switzerland, Germany and the Low Countries. Publishes *Memoirs of a Tourist* (*Mémoires d'un touriste*). *November*: Starts writing *The Charterhouse of Parma* (*La Chartreuse de Parme*).

1839 Publishes *The Abbess of Castro* (*L'Abbesse de Castro*), a novella. *April*: The *Charterhouse* published. *June*: Returns to Civitavecchia.

1841 *March*: First attack of apoplexy. Granted sick leave, returning to Paris in November.

1842 After second attack of apoplexy during the evening of 22 March, dies early the following morning. Buried in the Montmartre cemetery.

Introduction

An astonishing fact about *The Charterhouse of Parma* is that this magnificent novel of nearly five hundred pages (in the present edition) was written within the space of fifty-three days. We have a date and an address for when it was begun: in rented lodgings at no. 8, rue Caumartin in Paris, on 4 November 1838. In his journal for that year, Stendhal kept regular note of the number of pages to which the manuscript was growing: '10 november 38. 177 of the *Charterhouse*'; '15 november 1838. The manuscript of the *Charterhouse* is at page 270';[1] and so on. A draining tempo of composition, it might be thought, but one favoured by an author who believed that writing should be as direct as talking. His ideal was prose that would be as urgent and free from artifice as he could make it (something his translator should try to bear in mind).

On 26 December 1838, he was able to hand his old friend Romain Colomb six 'enormous exercise-books' containing the finished text, with instructions to go off and find a publisher. This Colomb did, without any great difficulty, for Stendhal was well known to publishers even if they would not have expected to make money from publishing him. But the *Charterhouse* was, by his lights, a success: it came out in April 1839 in an edition of 1,200 copies and sold out within eighteen months – good enough going for the time.

Stendhal, by nature the most footloose of men, had returned to Paris from a tour of north-west France two days before he sat down to write. He then closed his door to callers, suspending the sociability that normally ordered his day, gave instructions that anyone who came should be told he had gone off to the country to shoot, and wrote. That what he wrote in such haste should have turned out to be a great masterpiece is evidence that in this book, as his foremost biographer, Michel Crouzet, has written, he 'for the first time in his life perhaps, had imagination, imagination in its pure and happy state'.[2] The writer was by now fifty-five years old and the *Charterhouse* was the book in which the experiences he had lived through in that time, and the fantasies he had always relied on to make up for those experiences when they disappointed him, came more or less seamlessly together. The principal setting of the story is that part of southern Europe which he had known the most intimately and liked above all others, northern Italy; the period is the bourgeois nineteenth century, in the wake of the Napoleonic Wars, which he scorned for its tameness and its obsession with money, with, smoothly stitched into it, a more heroic Italian past that he admired for the passions to which it had given free rein; and, poised as the fiction is between a recognizably real world and a lovingly imagined one, its mood shifts engagingly between the satirical and the romantic. Small wonder that Stendhal thought that *Don Quixote*, in which the delusions of the knightly hero are sabotaged by the gross realism of his squire, Sancho Panza, was the most perfectly pitched of all great novels.

The cult of Italy that shows through in the *Charterhouse* has a lot to do with Stendhal's circumstances at the time when he wrote it. In the autumn of 1838, he was on extended leave from his post as French consul in Civitavecchia, a drab and unhealthy – by his own sour account of the place – seaport thirty-odd miles from Rome. 'Extended' is an understatement: he had originally been granted a month's leave of absence back in the spring of 1836, so that by now he had been away from his duties not for a month but for two and a half years. A congé of these proportions was, to say the least, exceptional and Stendhal owed its perpetuation to ministerial favour, a favour that even stretched to the absentee consul receiving his full salary throughout, when by the rules he should have gone down to half pay. Stendhal spent his adult life chronically in debt, so he had extra cause to be grateful for this enlightened patronage. He knew, however, that his leave could not last indefinitely, and the sorry prospect of having to return to a town he disliked and work that bored him can but have sharpened the desire to create a more appealing and infinitely more dramatic version of Italy in the novel that he decided to write while he still had the opportunity.

So how, in his fifties, did a committed hedonist and craver after amusing company such as Stendhal find himself serving reluctantly as a consul somewhere like Civitavecchia? To earn some money would be the obvious answer, something he had never been able to do from his writing. But we need to know more about his earlier life, or at least those elements in it that have a bearing on the present novel. Stendhal was not the writer's real name. He was born in 1783, in Grenoble, in south-eastern France, as Marie-Henri Beyle, the son of Chérubin Beyle, a lawyer by profession. Stendhal, the pseudonym he used for the first time in his mid-thirties – Stendal was the name of a small town in northern Germany he had passed through years before – was only one of an extraordinary number of disguises he amused himself by adopting at different stages of his life. Biographers fail to agree on the precise total but their estimates have climbed as high as three hundred and fifty. For this was someone who relished the idea of secrecy, even if he was never fully serious when it came to practising it: one story has him sending a coded dispatch back to Paris in the course of his consular duties and enclosing the key to the code he had used along with the dispatch. Inevitably, and happily, codes and disguises have their part to play in the *Charterhouse*, whose protagonist, Fabrizio del Dongo, goes more than once in disguise and is to be found exchanging coded signals by lantern with his aunt from on top of a tower.

To shelter beneath pseudonyms was, other considerations aside, pleasing to Stendhal for denying the public evidence of his paternity. For young Henri Beyle did not like his father. In the wonderfully mordant account of his childhood and adolescence that he wrote in the winter of 1835–6 (thought shocking, it was first published only in 1890) under the title of *The Life of Henry Brulard*, he displays nothing but contempt for his parent: too serious a man for his son's taste, too much the royalist for a boy who claims to have been a Jacobin, or revolutionary extremist, almost from the cradle, and too mean with his money. Thus the one name Stendhal never wrote under was Beyle. To get away from the joyless household of Chérubin Beyle, and from Grenoble, became, as he tells it in *Henry Brulard*, the main purpose of his stultifying youth.

And get away he did, as soon as it was practicable. He was a fiercely competitive and hence unpopular schoolboy, especially strong in mathematics, a subject he extolled on the typically Stendhalian ground that it offers no scope for hypocrisy: in mathematics you are either right or wrong, you cannot lie or practise deception. It was thanks to mathematics that he finally made his escape. In 1799, aged sixteen, he was sent up to Paris to take the entrance exam for the École Polytechnique, the elite school founded six years before to train engineers for the public service. While he was on the road, the thirty-year-old Napoleon Bonaparte came to power in France in a coup d'état; he was appointed First Consul, a large step along the way to being crowned as Emperor five years later. From that moment on, Stendhal was a Napoleonist, unbounded in his admiration for this visionary upstart and strategist, who had come from no-where and by his energy and genius was to conquer half of Europe. The glorious Napoleonic moment in European history and the anti-climax that followed it are crucial to the scheme of the *Charterhouse*.

Stendhal never sat the exam and never meant to attend the École Polytechnique. Instead, after being taken in hand by a family of cousins, the Darus, he set off over the Alps in the spring of 1800 to join the French army in northern Italy, where it was once again in action against the Austrians. Stendhal in fact chooses to begin this novel four years earlier, when Napoleon had conducted a particularly brilliant and successful campaign in Lombardy. In *Henry Brulard*, whose narrative ends with his arrival in Italy, he makes fun of his naive, hopeful but incurably diffident seventeen-year-old self. That arrival was, however, to be the most important displacement of his life. It exposed him for the first time to the lakes and mountains of

Lombardy, whose great beauty he celebrates in the *Charter-house*; to what struck him as the free and easy habits – the sexual habits especially – of Italians; to their love of music, opera above all; and to spirited, well-born Italian women, with whom he was very ready to fall unsuccessfully in love. This whole life-changing experience is reflected obliquely in the opening pages of the *Charterhouse*, which describe the liberating effects on the local population of the arrival of the French army in Milan in 1796. In Stendhal's version, that army does northern Italy the high service of releasing it from the tutelage of a politically repressive imperial power in Vienna and a morally repressive clerical one. These liberating effects, now transferred on to a whole population, are the selfsame ones that Italy had had on the adolescent Stendhal, finally released into independence and manhood from the tutelage of his family.

Once in uniform, and even though he was a clumsy horseman, he was given a commission in a regiment of dragoons. He saw little or no action, however, during the two years that he spent in Italy. Garrison duty was disillusioning for a young man dreaming all the while of military and amatory glory, and in July 1802 he resigned his commission to return to Paris. In October 1806, bored once more and hard up, Stendhal was taken on as an assistant auditor or commissioner in the Commissariat of Wars in Brunswick. This was a bureaucratic role that he performed well; he proved most efficient and soon rose to the higher rank of intendant, with responsibilities for the logistics of the district where he was stationed. He spent two years in Germany, returned for a short time to Paris, then left in the army's wake once more, this time for Vienna. On the way, he for the first time witnessed some of the horrors of war. He was not in action but came near enough to it to see the blackened corpses of French and German soldiers in the field. 'I admit that this whole scene made me sick to my stomach,' he wrote in his journal for 5 May 1809, a nauseous reaction to be found reflected in that of Fabrizio del Dongo when he is caught up in the aftermath of the slaughter at Waterloo.

Back in Paris, Stendhal continued as a member of the Imperial bureaucracy, though not much was asked of him by way of work or even attendance: forty hours a month seems to have satisfied superiors who acknowledged his abilities while fault-ing his lack of dedication. The standard of living that he thought was his right remained out of reach, however. He had a small allowance from his father and he had his pay, but his income lagged well behind his outgoings. For all that he says in the present novel about vanity being the besetting sin of the French nation, he appears to have been as vain as any other Frenchman: to try to cut a dash socially, he overdressed, overspent and tried to conceal the unhappy fact that he was both overweight and losing his hair. In August 1811, he spent a period of leave back in Italy, a 'traveller' there for the first time, as he himself put it, a free agent, that is, able to go and to do as he liked. The prime draw was a Milanese woman for whom he had fallen eleven years earlier, Angela Pietragrua, 'dark-haired, proud, voluptuous'.[3] In 1811, he at last became her lover. Pietragrua was notoriously promiscuous but this long-delayed conquest still meant much to him, to the point where he inked the date of its accomplishment on his braces.

In July 1812, Stendhal embarked on what was to be the most terrible experience of his life. Napoleon had set off on the invasion of Russia with the Grande Armée, and Stendhal was one of the auditors given the task of carrying dispatches to him from Paris. Having reached the Emperor's headquarters in the east a month later, he remained with him as part of his entour-age, entering Moscow in mid-September. He was thus caught up in the catastrophe that met the Grande Armée once it was forced by the inhabitants' burning of the city to start on its midwinter retreat. The extreme cold, starvation and the unre-lenting depredations of marauding Russian troops saw to it that in the end a bare tenth part of the army's original manpower of seven hundred thousand got back to France. Stendhal per-formed stoically and well in these awful conditions, in charge at one time of provisioning a significant sector of the broken army. But the awful things he had witnessed were an extreme test for his *beylisme*, or that philosophy of amused and ego-tistical detachment whereby the world and whatever went on in it for good or ill became pure spectacle, undeserving of any sympathetic involvement by the superior self. He continued to keep a journal throughout the Russian debacle but the experience did not find its way directly into his novels, resisting as it did ready assimilation into the fundamentally ironic texture of Stendhal's fiction.

That ironic texture nowhere shows to finer advantage than in the justly celebrated sequence here in which Fabrizio witnesses the battle of Waterloo. Or does he witness it? The question is one that he puts to himself after it is over, since he cannot be sure that what he has witnessed was in fact a battle, so far did it fall short of what he had imagined in his callow excitement a battle might be like. He has heard and seen gunfire, has observed units of an army losing their discipline and spirit of comradeship in defeat, been sickened by the sight of violent death and mutilation: has had, in short, an experience of battle appropriate not to an all-seeing novelist but to a private soldier who has actually taken part in one. Stendhal may never, strictly speaking, have taken part in a battle, but his wartime experiences had certainly qualified him to portray a battle in the inglorious terms he chooses in the *Charterhouse*.

Least of all did he experience the battle of Waterloo. He was left indifferent by the Emperor's fall and exile in 1814, and by the time Napoleon had returned to France and then lost his final battle the next year, Stendhal was comfortably back in Italy, though not without having made overtures to the provisional government in hopes of being offered a post that might help him pay off his debts. To any resumption of warfare, he preferred to stay on in Milan, perpetuating as best he could his affair with the unreliable Pietragrua. Milan, indeed, was to remain his base right up until 1821. He broke quite soon with Pietragrua, only to become lastingly smitten in 1818 with the glamorous wife of a Polish general, Métilde Dembowski. She belonged to the politically progressive or liberal faction in Milanese society, at a time when there were widespread stirrings against the authoritarian Austrian regime. The conflict between the two camps, of pro-Austrian reactionaries and pro-French liberals, plays a large part in the plot of the *Charterhouse*, which should be read, as should all of Stendhal's major novels, as a political book, even if the squalid politics of the principality of Parma are shown in a sardonic light, not a seriously ideological one. It has been said that had Machiavelli wanted to write a novel, it would have read like this one, and, certainly, there is no more Machiavellian a character in all of fiction than Count Mosca, Stendhal's supreme political operator, a man in whom principle is forever being cynically betrayed in the interests of pragmatism. Ever the spectator, Stendhal did not get mixed up in any conspiracies during his Milan years, but he sympathized with the liberals and left no one in any doubt as to his subversive opinions. The authorities had no reason to like or to trust him and it was his fear of being arrested as a French spy and agitator that in the end led him to leave Milan, and Italy, in 1821, to his lasting resentment.

He was to spend the next nine years in Paris. Soon after he returned, in 1822, he published *On Love*, his first truly original work, an acute analysis of the psychology of a lover, drawn much of it from his own torturous involvement with Métilde. The book was not understood and was a flop: it sold forty copies in two years, helping to persuade its author that he was ahead of his time, that the twentieth century would appreciate him even if the nineteenth did not – as the twentieth century emphatically did. He became in these years a frequenter of liberal salons, and his conversation grew more and more risqué in his desire to shine socially: the most entertaining talker in Paris, no one denied, but too extreme in his opinions for the taste of many. The money problem remained. His father had finally died in 1819, but the size of his inheritance was a severe disappointment; the detested Chérubin Beyle had been speculating in land and property and had frittered away the greater part of his wealth. This rankled with his needy son, whose great hope had been that his father's death would at last ensure his financial independence.

He did not in fact prosper in these Parisian years. His love life seldom went as he would have liked and he contemplated suicide at intervals, how seriously it is hard to know. He indulged in a certain morbidity: in 1827 alone, he wrote no less than thirty-six different versions of his last will and testament, even though he had little if anything to leave. But the decade ended promisingly for him, with the uprising in Paris subsequently known as the Trois Glorieuses, or the 'Three Glorious Days' (27–9 July 1830), which succeeded in ridding the country of the last Bourbon king. The Bourbons were a dynasty the ten-year-old Henri Beyle had so hated that he crowed at the guillotining of Louis XVIII, if only to give offence to his father; and he could but welcome the potentially more liberal regime of Charles X's successor, King Louis-Philippe. Stendhal thought he saw his chance of returning into the employ of a more tolerable government in a senior and above all well-paid job. He had his sights on a pleasant, undemanding prefectship somewhere in provincial France; but the ministry had other ideas.

In November 1830, he was appointed French consul in Trieste, on the Adriatic, not quite his beloved Italy but close enough. Trieste, however, was part of the Austrian domains and the Austrians had neither forgotten nor forgiven him for his real or presumed subversions in Milan ten years before. They refused to sanction his appointment and so it was that he found himself in March the following year taking up his post in Civitavecchia. This was not an agreeable alternative. For a start, Civitavecchia formed part of the Papal States, which meant that the Vatican played the predominant role in its governance. Priestly rule was anathema to Stendhal, just as his political liberalism and disdainful atheism were anathema to the Vatican, which had placed his books on the Index of forbidden reading two years before. And, for a crowning disadvantage, the consulship in Civitavecchia paid a third less than that in Trieste. Stendhal was back in Italy, but not as happy about it as he should have been.

THE CHARTERHOUSE OF PARMA

Stendhal had been in Paris during the excitements of the Trois Glorieuses, but not down in the streets with the insurrectionaries. He was indoors, attending to the proofs of the novel he had been writing. This was *The Red and the Black*, the first of his two great masterpieces, which was published early the next year. It was well received, and that was a new experience for him, even if the critical stir it made in Paris was lost on a writer by now many hundreds of miles away in central Italy. *The Red and the Black* is a French novel and a contemporary one, set that is to say in Restoration France, in Stendhal's native south-east to start with and later in Paris. Its protagonist, Julien Sorel, is nothing socially, the son of a carpenter, but he is a clever and ambitious young man, a devotee of Napoleon who means to rise in the world like his hero. His ascent, from tutor to a bourgeois family in the country to seminarian to private secretary of an aristocratic ultra in Paris, enables Stendhal to paint an unforgiving picture of post-Napoleonic society in France, as one ruled by money, rank and hypocrisy. Julien Sorel succeeds in that society but in the end it rejects him, as he rejects it, after he has been condemned to be guillotined for shooting at the first of his two mistresses while she is praying in church. The novel ends in an unexpectedly macabre scene, with the second of Julien's mistresses, the arrogant yet vulnerable daughter of his aristocratic employer, driving off in a carriage clutching the severed head of her young lover.

This bizarre concluding image must strike all but the most accepting reader of the novel as an anachronism, an act of extreme passion belonging to an age very different from that in which Stendhal was living and about which he might have appeared up until then to be writing. As such, it serves very well to link *The Red and the Black* with its great successor, *The Charterhouse of Parma*, written eight years later, pointing as it does to the degree of alienation from which Stendhal suffered in respect both of his native country and the passionless modern age in which he was obliged to live. The episode of the severed head he had come across when reading – as he was fond of doing – about the Italian Renaissance, a time when he believed life had been lived as it should be and now wasn't: dangerously, generously and in haughty disregard of polite convention.

That certainly is how the favoured characters in the *Charterhouse* choose to live their lives, as though they had found themselves back in the lawless setting of the sixteenth century, and not in the respectable society of the nineteenth. A few years before he wrote this novel, Stendhal had unearthed in Italian libraries a number of manuscripts recounting violent tales of Renaissance life, typically full of blighted love, murder, revenge and banditry; and he had contracted to write a series of novellas based on them for a Paris publisher. (Some of these were collected and published in a volume after his death as the *Chroniques italiennes*.) More than a little of the atmosphere to be found there is preserved in the *Charterhouse*, transposed now into the principality of Parma, a principality which should not be mistaken for the real Duchy of Parma (which was annexed to France from 1802 to 1816, and thereafter ruled over by Marie-Louise, formerly the consort of the Emperor Napoleon). In Stendhal's nineteenth-century Parma political faction has replaced family as the source of animosities that may at any moment lead to violent death, and where the superior individuals who are led by their passions and not by their reason – Fabrizio del Dongo, his aunt, the Duchess Gina Sanseverina, the outlaw Ferrante Palla – serve by their courage, their high-handedness and their impulsiveness to condemn the timid, calculating souls around them. Behind the character of Fabrizio lay for Stendhal the sixteenth-century figure of Alessandro Farnese, who in 1534 became Pope Paul III and about whose celebrated family Stendhal had read in one of his manuscripts, so that the bare plot of the fiction has its source in a document, even if the document itself was far from trustworthy. Alessandro Farnese it was who created the duchy of Parma and members of his family provided its dukes for almost two hundred years. The two rulers of Parma who appear in the novel can only be seen, one in his fear of revolutionaries, the other in his extreme diffidence, as laughably inadequate substitutes for the historical Farnese.

AFTER THE *CHARTERHOUSE*

Stendhal's unduly prolonged leave came to an end at last in the summer of 1839, and he was forced to return from the pleasures of Paris to the desert of Civitavecchia, the boredom of which could be mitigated only by regular escape to Rome, where there was better company to be had and better music to be heard. In September 1840, he was both astonished and gratified when Honoré de Balzac, by then generally recognized as France's greatest living novelist, published a very positive and admiring review of the *Charterhouse*, describing it as 'a great and beautiful book' (in the *Revue Parisienne* for 25 September 1840). He admired especially the Waterloo sequence in the first part of the novel, and thought indeed that Stendhal should have begun with it. It is a sequence that later on Tolstoy, too, admired hugely as introducing a new truthfulness into the description of warfare, and kept in mind as a model when writing the battlefield scenes in *War and Peace* (1868–9). In his review, perceptive and generous though it was, Balzac had also allowed himself certain criticisms of Stendhal's book, and Stendhal took these comments so much to heart that he – the writer who preferred never to waste time on second thoughts – actually sat down and started on a revision. He eventually abandoned it, partly because his health was now starting to fail.

In March 1841, he suffered a first apoplectic fit. He survived it, continuing to work and to travel, but in October was granted sick leave and returned to Paris. There, in March 1842, he suffered a second attack when walking in the street one evening. This time, he never recovered consciousness and died the next morning, leaving posterity to recognize – and posterity took its time in doing so – that in him France had lost one of its four or five very greatest writers of fiction.

HISTORICAL BACKGROUND

The Charterhouse of Parma should not be read as a historical novel in any strict sense; it is a highly personal work of imagination. A broad idea of what was happening in France and northern Italy during the years Stendhal is concerned with helps when reading the novel, however.

France had first gone to war against an imperialist Austria in 1792, in defence of the republican principles of the Revolution of 1789. In 1795, a three-pronged attack on Austria and its territories was planned, with the southernmost campaign, in northern Italy, to be led by the twenty-six-year-old General Napoleon Bonaparte (1769–1821). Napoleon's invasion of Piedmont and Lombardy was brilliantly conducted and in 1796 the French army entered Milan in triumph. In 1798, the French government declared that the areas it now controlled in Italy constituted the Cisalpine Republic. With Napoleon having gone, however, French forces suffered reverses, and in 1800 he returned, to lead another lightning campaign, whose culmination was the resounding defeat of the Austrians at Marengo. Thereafter, what became known as the Napoleonic Wars were conducted either further north, in Austria itself, Germany and Russia, or else in Spain and Portugal. After Napoleon's final defeat, at Waterloo, in 1815, the peace settlement reached at the Congress of Vienna awarded what was now to be recognized as the kingdom of Lombardy-Venice to the Austrians.

The duchy of Parma meanwhile, previously part of the possessions of the Spanish Bourbon dynasty, had been annexed to the Cisalpine Republic in 1802. In 1815 it was awarded to Marie-Louise (1791–1847), a daughter of the Austrian Emperor, who had married Napoleon (himself crowned as French Emperor in 1804) in 1810 but left Paris in 1814 and was never reunited with him.

NOTES

1. *Oeuvres intimes II* (Paris 1982), p. 339.
2. Michel Crouzet, *Stendhal ou monsieur moi-même* (Paris, 1990), p. 687.
3. Cited without any reference in Crouzet, ibid., p. 173.

Translator's Note

This new translation follows the text of the novel as given in the Bibliothèque de la Pléiade edition of 1948, an edition that has, surprisingly, not been updated, even though this would not have involved any significant alterations to the text, and itself follows, bar a few very minor corrections, the text of the first, 1839 edition of the *Charterhouse*.

A point worth making about the translation concerns the form of the hero's name. As I have indicated above, the *Charterhouse* is a novel set in Italy but which keeps the contemporary history and condition of France constantly in view, for purposes of contrast. Stendhal uses certain French forms where he should have used Italian ones: in the case of aristocratic titles, for example, he prefers the French Marquise to the Italian Marchesa, the French Comte to the Italian Conte, and so on. In the case of proper names, he switches from a French form to an Italian one at random, from Ascagne to Ascanio, for instance. In this respect, the novel's hero, Fabrizio del Dongo, poses a problem of translation. He is referred to as Fabrice throughout the novel, not once as Fabrizio, as though he were a born Frenchman, not an Italian. I was strongly tempted to leave him in this English version as Fabrice, because I feel sure that he is intended as the representative in the book of the novelist, who liked to look on himself as a hybrid, as either an Italian Frenchman or else a French Italian – he claimed that his mother's family had its roots in Italy, but there's no evidence that it did. This wilful mongrelism is supported by the quiet hint that is dropped early on in the story that the boy Fabrizio

is in fact illegitimate, his birth having taken place at a gynaeco-
logically appropriate interval of time following the billeting on
the del Dongo family of a gallant and personable French officer,
Lieutenant Robert (whom Fabrizio actually encounters on the
field of Waterloo, the lieutenant having by now become a general and a count). To leave Fabrizio as Fabrice would make a
valuable point about the novel, therefore. But precedent in the
end was too strong, previous translators of the *Charterhouse*
into English seem all of them to have settled on Fabrizio as the
right form of the name, and I have done the same.

Sums of money are specified all the way through the novel in
terms of French currency, whether historical or modern: in
francs, écus, livres, louis and napoleons. The écu is here taken
as being worth five francs, the livre is used simply in place of
the franc when annual incomes are being calculated, the louis
and the napoléon were both gold coins with a value of twenty
francs. (Very occasionally, Stendhal also introduces sequins,
another anachronistic but this time Italian coin, worth ten
francs.) For a rough indication of what the franc was worth in
the early nineteenth century: Stendhal once declared that he
dreamt of living in Italy with thirty thousand francs a year;
but also admitted, more realistically, that he could just about
manage on six thousand a year.

JOHN STURROCK

Further Reading

Stendhal's other fictional masterpiece, *Le Rouge et le noir*, has been newly, and well, translated three times in the past fifteen years:

The Red and the Black, translated by Catherine Slater (Oxford World Classics, 1991)

The Red and the Black, translated by Roger Gard (Penguin Classics, 2002)

The Red and the Black, translated by Burton Raffel (Random House, 2004)

His third major work of fiction, *Lucien Leuwen*, the most directly political of all his novels in its second half, was never finished, but is very well worth reading. A translation by H. L. R. Edwards appeared in Penguin Classics in 1991; it is now out of print but can be found second-hand.

Two volumes of his autobiographical writings exist in new translations:

The Life of Henry Brulard, translated by John Sturrock (New York Review of Books, 2002)

Memoirs of an Egotist, translated by Andrew Brown (Hesperus Press, 2003)

His psychological study of love exists in English as *Love*, translated by Gilbert and Suzanne Sale (Penguin Classics, 1975).

For biographies in English, there are Robert Alter's excellent *A Lion for Love: A Critical Biography of Stendhal* (Basic Books, 1979); and Jonathan Keates's *Stendhal* (Sinclair-Stevenson, 1991). Three very accessible critical books on the novelist are: Margaret Tillett, *Stendhal: The Background to the Novels*

(Oxford University Press, 1971); Geoffrey Strickland, *Stendhal: The Education of a Novelist* (Cambridge University Press, 1974); and Roger Pearson, *Stendhal's Violin: A Novelist and His Reader* (Oxford University Press, 1988).

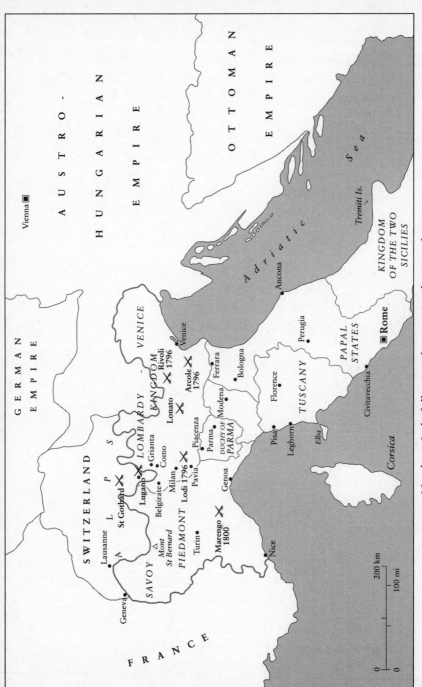

Northern Italy following the peace settlement of 1815

THE CHARTERHOUSE
OF PARMA

I

Gia mi fur dolci inviti a empir le carte
I luoghi ameni.

Ariosto,[1] Satire IV

[Once, favourite places were a sweet invitation to me
To fill sheets of paper.]

FOREWORD

This short novel was written in the winter of 1830[1] and three hundred leagues from Paris; hence no reference to the affairs of 1839.

Many years before 1830, in the days when our armies were marching across Europe, chance handed me a billeting order for the house of a canon; it was in Padua, a charming town in Italy. My stay being prolonged, we became friends.

Passing through Padua once more towards the end of 1830, I hurried to the good canon's house; he was no more, I knew that, but I wanted to revisit the parlour where we had spent a great many pleasant evenings, missed so frequently since. I found the canon's nephew and the nephew's wife, who received me as an old friend. A few people came by, and it was very late when we broke up; the nephew sent out for an excellent zabaglione from the Caffè Pedroti.[2] What kept us from bed above all was the story of the Duchess Sanseverina to which somebody alluded and that the nephew was kind enough to recount in its entirety, in my honour.

'In the country I'm going to,' I told my friends, 'I shan't meet with many evenings such as this one, and to pass the long evening hours I shall turn your history into a novel.'

'In that case,' said the nephew, 'I'm going to give you my uncle's records which, under the heading of Parma, cite some of the amorous intrigues in that court, in the days when the duchess ruled the roost there; but be warned! The story is anything but moral and now that you pride yourselves on your evangelical purity in France, it may earn you a reputation as an assassin.'

I am publishing this novel without altering anything in the manuscript of 1830, which may have two disadvantages:

The first for the reader: the characters being Italians they will perhaps interest him less, hearts in that country are somewhat different from French hearts. Italians are genuine, good people and not scared to say what they think. They display vanity only in fits and starts; then it becomes a passion and goes under the name of *puntiglio*.[3] Lastly, among them, poverty is not seen as ridiculous.

The second disadvantage has regard to the author.

I will admit that I have been rash enough to leave the characters with the asperities of their nature; but in return, I say it loud and clear, I heap the most moral censure on many of their actions. What would be the point of giving them the lofty morality and attractions of French natures, which love money above all else and hardly ever sin out of hatred or love? The Italians in this novel are more or less the opposite. It seems to me in any case that whenever one progresses two hundred leagues, from the south to the north, there is a case for a new landscape as for a new form of romance. The canon's amiable niece had known and even been very fond of the Duchess Sanseverina and has asked me not to alter anything in her adventures, which are open to criticism.

23 January 1839

CHAPTER I
MILAN IN 1796

On 15 May 1796, General Bonaparte made his entry into Milan at the head of the youthful army which had just crossed the bridge at Lodi and let the world know that after all these centuries, Caesar and Alexander had a successor. The miracles of valour and of genius of which Italy was the witness within a few months reawoke a slumbering people; a week before the arrival of the French, the Milanese still saw them only as a bunch of brigands, used always to taking flight faced by the troops of His Imperial and Royal Majesty:[1] that anyway was what a small newspaper the size of a human hand, printed on filthy paper, repeated to them three times a week.

In the Middle Ages, the republican Lombards had given proof of a valour equal to that of the French, and deserved to see their town razed to the ground by the emperors of Germany. Since they had become 'loyal subjects', their main business was printing sonnets on little pink taffeta handkerchiefs whenever a girl belonging to some noble or wealthy family happened to get married. Two or three years after this great moment in her life, the girl would take a *cavaliere servente*: sometimes, the name of the cicisbeo[2] chosen by the husband's family occupied an honourable place in the marriage contract. Which effeminate customs were a far cry from the profound emotions aroused by the unforeseen arrival of the French army. Soon new and passionate customs arose. An entire people realized, on 15 May 1796, that everything it had respected hitherto was supremely ridiculous and sometimes odious. The departure of the last Austrian regiment signalled the fall of the old ideas: to risk one's life became the fashion; they could see that in order to be

happy after centuries of increasingly lukewarm sensations, they
needed to feel a genuine love of their homeland and go in quest
of heroic deeds. They had been plunged into blackest night by
the continuation of the jealous despotism of Charles V and
Philip II;[3] their statues were thrown down and they suddenly
found themselves flooded with light. For some fifty years past,
and while the *Encyclopédie* and Voltaire[4] were bursting out in
France, the monks had been dinning it into the good people of
Milan that learning to read or learning anything at all was a
great waste of effort, but that by paying one's tithe without fail
to the priest, and faithfully recounting to him all one's petty
sins, one was more or less certain of getting a good place in
paradise. To complete the enervation of this people, once so
terrible and so fond of reasoning, Austria had sold it at a
bargain price the privilege of not furnishing any recruits to the
army.

In 1796, the Milanese army consisted of twenty-four ruffians
dressed in red, who guarded the town in concert with four
magnificent regiments of Hungarian grenadiers. Morals were
lax in the extreme, but passion was very uncommon. Moreover,
apart from the unpleasantness of having to recount everything
to the priest, on pain of ruination even in this world, the good
people of Milan were still subject to certain minor monarchical
impediments which could not fail to vex them. For example,
the archduke,[5] who resided in Milan and governed in the name
of the Emperor, his cousin, had had the lucrative idea of dealing
in corn. As a consequence, the peasants were forbidden to sell
their grain until His Highness should have filled his granaries.

In May 1796, three days after the entry of the French, a
young painter of miniatures, a little mad, by the name of Gros,[6]
celebrated subsequently, who had come with the army, hearing
tell of the exploits of the archduke, a huge man as it happens,
in the grand Caffè Servi (fashionable at the time), took up the
list of ice creams advertised on a sheet of wretched yellow
paper. On the reverse side he drew the gross archduke; a French
soldier was sticking a bayonet into his belly and instead of
blood an unbelievable quantity of corn was coming out. What
are called jokes or caricatures were unknown in this land of a

wary despotism. The drawing left behind by Gros on the café table in the Servi seemed like a miracle come down from heaven; it was engraved during the night and twenty thousand copies were sold the following day.

On the same day, bills were posted advising of a war tax of six million, imposed for the needs of the French army, which, having just won six battles and conquered twenty provinces, lacked only shoes, trousers, jackets and hats.

So great was the mass of happiness and pleasure that irrupted into Lombardy with these impoverished Frenchmen that the priests alone and a few noblemen noticed how onerous this tax of six million was, which was soon followed by many more. The French soldiers laughed and sang all day long; they were not yet twenty-five and their commanding general, who was twenty-seven, passed for being the oldest man in his army. This gaiety, youthfulness and insouciance made an agreeable response to the furious preachings of the monks who, for the past six months, had been announcing from on high in their pulpits that the French were monsters, obliged, on pain of death, to burn everything and cut off the head of all and sundry. To this end, each regiment marched with a guillotine at the head.

In the countryside, in the doorways of the cottages, a French soldier was to be seen busy rocking the mistress of the house's small child, and almost every evening some drummer would improvise a dance, playing on the violin. The quadrilles proving much too learned and complicated for the soldiers, who hardly knew them in any case, to be able to teach them to the local women, it was the latter who showed the young Frenchmen the Monferina, the Sauteuse[7] and other Italian dances.

As far as possible, the officers had been quartered on the rich; they had great need of recuperation. For example, a lieutenant by the name of Robert got a billeting order for the palazzo of the Marchesa del Dongo. When he entered the palace, the worldly goods of this officer, a somewhat unscrupulous young conscript, amounted to a six-franc écu which he had just received in Piacenza. After the crossing of the Lodi bridge, he took a magnificent pair of brand-new nankeen breeches off a

handsome Austrian officer killed by a cannonball, and never
was an item of clothing more timely. His officer's epaulettes
were of wool and the material of his jacket had been sewn up
with the lining from the sleeves so that the pieces might hold
together. There was a sadder particular still: the soles of his
shoes had been made from bits of a hat likewise taken from the
field of battle, beyond the Lodi bridge. These improvised soles
were held on above the shoes by highly visible laces, so that
when the majordomo of the house presented himself in Lieutenant Robert's room to invite him to dine with the marchesa, he
was plunged into a mortal embarrassment. He and his voltigeur[8]
spent the two intervening hours until this fateful dinner by
attempting to patch the jacket up a bit and dye the wretched
shoelaces black with ink. The terrible moment finally arrived.
'Never in my life had I felt more ill at ease,' Lieutenant Robert
told me; 'the ladies thought I was going to frighten them, and I
was shaking more than they were. I looked at my shoes and
didn't know how to walk gracefully. The Marchesa del Dongo,'
he added, 'was then in the full flower of her beauty; you've met
her, with those lovely eyes of hers and her angelic sweetness,
and her pretty hair of a dark blonde which brought out so well
the oval of that charming face. In my room I had a *Salome* by
Leonardo da Vinci,[9] which could have been her portrait. By
God's grace, I was so taken with that supernatural beauty that
I forgot my costume. For the past two years I had seen only
ugliness and poverty in the Genoese mountains. I dared to
address a few words to her about the rapture that I felt.

'But I had too much sense to dwell for long in the complimentary vein. As I spun my phrases, I could see, in a dining room
all in marble, a dozen lackeys and footmen dressed in what
seemed to me at the time the height of magnificence. Just
imagine, these rascals not only had good shoes but even silver
buckles. Out of the corner of my eye I could see all those stupid
stares fixed on my jacket, and perhaps also on my shoes, which
cut me to the quick. I could have struck fear into the lot of
them with a single word; but how to put them in their place
without running the risk of scaring the ladies? For to give herself
a bit of courage, as she has told me a hundred times since, the

marchesa had sent to the convent where she was then boarding for Gina del Dongo, her husband's sister, who was later to become the charming Contessa Pietranera; no one in the days of prosperity surpassed her in gaiety or the spirit of geniality, just as no one surpassed her in courage or serenity of soul when adversity struck.

'Gina, who could then have been thirteen but who looked eighteen, lively and outspoken, as you know, was so much afraid of bursting out laughing in the presence of my costume, she didn't dare eat. The marchesa, to the contrary, smothered me in forced compliments; she could easily see the stirrings of impatience in my eyes. In short, I cut a foolish figure, I bit back my contempt, something said to be impossible for a Frenchman. Finally, I had a brilliant thought, sent down from heaven. I started to recount to these ladies how penniless I was and what we had suffered these last two years in the mountains around Genoa, where we'd been detained by imbecilic old generals. There, I said, we were given assignats[10] that couldn't be exchanged locally, and three ounces of bread a day. I hadn't been speaking for two minutes before the good marchesa had tears in her eyes and Gina had become serious.

' "What, signor lieutenant," the latter said, "three ounces of bread!"

' "Yes, signorina; but on the other hand the distribution failed three times a week, and since the peasants we were billeted on were even more poverty-stricken than ourselves, we gave them some of our bread."

'On leaving the table, I offered the marchesa my arm as far as the door of the salon, then quickly retracing my steps, I gave the servant who had served me at table the one six-franc écu on the spending of which I had built so many castles in Spain.'

'A week later,' Robert continued, 'once it was established beyond doubt that the French weren't guillotining anyone, the Marchese del Dongo came back from his castle at Grianta on Lake Como, where he had valiantly taken refuge on the army's approach, abandoning his very beautiful young wife and his sister to the hazards of war. The hatred that the marchese had for us was equal to his fear, that's to say immeasurable; his great pale, sanctimonious face was an amusing sight when he was paying me compliments. The day following his return to Milan, I received three aunes[11] of cloth and two hundred francs out of the six million of taxes; I grew new feathers and became the ladies' escort, for the balls were beginning.'

Lieutenant Robert's history was that of more or less all the Frenchmen. Instead of making fun of these brave soldiers' poverty, people took pity on them and took them to their hearts.

This period of unforeseen happiness and intoxication lasted only two short years. So excessive and so widespread was the madness that it would be impossible for me to convey any notion of it, unless through this profound historical observation: this people had experienced a hundred years of boredom.

In the old days, the sensuality natural to the countries of the south had reigned at the courts of the Viscontis and the Sforzas,[12] those famous dukes of Milan. But since the year 1624, when the Spanish had taken possession of the duchy, and taken possession of it as masters who were taciturn, suspicious, arrogant and perpetually fearful of revolt, gaiety had fled. The population, adopting the customs of their masters, thought more about avenging the least insult with a thrust from a dagger than about enjoying the present moment.

The wild delight, the gaiety, the sensual pleasure, the shutting off of all sad or even reasonable feelings, were carried to such an extreme, from 15 May 1796, when the French entered Milan, until April 1799, when they were driven out following the battle of Cassano, that old millionaire merchants can be cited, old moneylenders, old notaries, who, during this interregnum, had forgotten to be morose or to make money.

It would have been possible at most to number a few families belonging to the upper nobility, who had withdrawn into their palazzi in the country, as if to turn their backs on the general cheerfulness and opening up of every heart. It is a fact also that these wealthy noble families had been singled out in a disagreeable manner when the war taxes demanded for the French army were being allotted.

The Marchese del Dongo, put out by the sight of so much merriment, had been one of the first to get back to his magnificent castle at Grianta, beyond Como, to which the ladies took Lieutenant Robert. The castle, situated in a position like no other in the world perhaps, on a plateau a hundred and fifty feet above that sublime lake, a large portion of which it dominates, had been a fortress. The del Dongo family had had it built in the fifteenth century, as was evidenced on all sides by the marble escutcheons; one could still see drawbridges and deep moats, though empty of water it has to be said. But with walls eighty feet high and six feet thick, the castle was safe from any sudden assault, which was why the suspicious marchese was so fond of it. Surrounded by twenty-five or thirty servants whom he supposed to be devoted, apparently because he never addressed them without an insult on his lips, he was less tormented by fear than in Milan.

That fear was not altogether gratuitous: he was very actively engaged in correspondence with a spy whom Austria had stationed on the Swiss border three leagues from Grianta, in order to aid the escape of prisoners captured on the field of battle, something the French generals might have looked decidedly askance at.

The marchese had left his young wife in Milan. There, she managed the family's affairs, with responsibility for facing up to the taxes imposed on the *casa del Dongo*, as they say in those parts. She had been trying to get them reduced, which forced her to call on those members of the nobility who had accepted public office, and even some highly influential non-noblemen. A great event supervened in the family. The marchese had arranged a marriage between his young sister Gina and a very wealthy personage of the highest birth. But he powdered his hair, on which score Gina received him with peals of laughter, and soon committed the folly of marrying Count Pietranera. He was in truth a most good-natured gentleman, well set up physically, but ruined from father to son and, what was the ultimate stigma, an ardent supporter of the new ideas. To crown the marchese's despair, Pietranera was a junior officer in the Italian legion.[13]

After these two years of happiness and folly, the Directory in Paris,[14] adopting the attitudes of a firmly established sovereign, displayed an undying hatred for anyone who was not mediocre. The inept generals it gave to the army in Italy lost a succession of battles on these same plains of Verona, the scene two years before of the prodigies of Arcole and Lonato. The Austrians neared Milan; Lieutenant Robert, having become a battalion commander and been wounded at the battle of Cassano, came to lodge for the last time with his friend the Marchesa del Dongo. The farewells were sad. Robert left together with Count Pietranera, who followed the French in their retreat on Novi. The young countess, whose marriage portion her brother refused to pay, followed the army riding on a farm cart.

There then began that period of reaction and of a return to the old ideas that the Milanese call *i tredici mesi* (the thirteen months), because their happiness demanded indeed that this return to stupidity should last for only thirteen months, up until Marengo.[15] Everything that was old, sanctimonious, morose, reappeared at the head of affairs, and resumed control of society. Soon, those who had remained loyal to the right teachings let it be known in the villages that Napoleon had been hanged by the Mamelukes in Egypt,[16] as he had merited on so many grounds.

Among the men who had gone off to sulk on their estates and who returned thirsting for revenge, the Marchese del Dongo was remarkable for his frenzy. His extremism carried him naturally to the head of the party. These gentlemen, perfectly respectable fellows when they were not afraid, but forever fearful, succeeded in outwitting the Austrian general: a decent enough fellow, he let himself be convinced that severity was high politics and had a hundred and fifty patriots arrested; at that time, they were all that was best in Italy.

They were soon taken off to the Bocche di Cattaro[17] and thrown into underground caves, where the damp and above all the lack of bread promptly put paid to all these scoundrels.

The Marchese del Dongo held a high position, and combining as he did a sordid avarice with a host of other fine qualities, he boasted publicly of not sending a single écu to his sister, the Countess Pietranera; still madly in love, she refused to leave her husband and was dying of hunger with him in France. The kindly marchesa was in despair; she finally managed to purloin a few small diamonds from her jewel-case, which her husband took back from her each evening to lock it away under his bed, in an iron chest. The marchesa had brought her husband a dowry of eight hundred thousand francs, and received eighty francs a month for her personal expenses. During the thirteen months the French spent away from Milan, this most timid of women found excuses and did not leave off wearing black.

We will admit that, following the example of many serious authors,[18] we have begun our hero's story a year before he was born. This essential personage is none other, in fact, than Fabrizio Valserra, *Marchesino* del Dongo, as they say in Milan.* He had just taken the trouble of being born when the French were driven out and found himself, by the accident of birth, the second son of the Marchese del Dongo, that very great lord, of whose fat waxen face, false smile and unbounded hatred for the new ideas you already know. The house's entire fortune had been entailed to the elder son, Ascanio del Dongo, the fitting portrait of his father. He was eight years old, and Fabrizio two, when all of a sudden General Bonaparte, whom all well-born persons thought had long since been hanged, came down from Mont Saint-Bernard.[19] He entered Milan; the moment is still unique in history. Picture to yourselves a whole population madly in love. A few days later, Napoleon won the battle of Marengo. Of the rest there is no need to tell. The intoxication of the Milanese was at its height, but this time it was mixed in with thoughts of revenge: this good people had been taught hatred. Soon what remained of the patriots deported to the Bocche di Cattaro were seen arriving. Their return was celebrated by a national holiday. Their pale faces, their great astonished eyes, their wasted limbs, made a strange contrast with the joy that was bursting forth on every side. Their arrival was the signal for the more compromised families to depart. The Marchese del Dongo was among the first to flee

---

* It is pronounced *markaizeen*. In the local usage, borrowed from Germany, this title is given to all the sons of a marquis; *contine* to all the sons of a count, *contessina* to all the daughters of a count, etc.

to his castle in Grianta. The heads of the great families were filled with hatred and fear; but their wives and their daughters recalled the delights of the Frenchmen's first stay, and missed Milan and the festive balls, which were organized at the Casa Tanzi straight after Marengo. A few days after the victory, the French general responsible for ensuring that Lombardy remained peaceful noticed that all the nobility's tenant farmers and all the old women of the countryside, very far from still having their minds on the astonishing victory of Marengo, which had changed Italy's destiny and retaken thirteen strong-holds in one day, had their souls occupied only with a prophecy of St Giovita, the foremost patron of Brescia. According to this sacred pronouncement, the French and Napoleon would cease to prosper exactly thirteen weeks after Marengo. What partly excuses the Marchese del Dongo and all the noblemen sulking in the countryside is that they were not play-acting but genuinely believed in the prophecy. None of these people had read four books in their entire lives; they made their preparations openly to return to Milan at the end of thirteen weeks; but as time went by, it brought fresh successes for the French cause. On his return to Paris, Napoleon's sensible decrees saved the revol-ution internally, just as he had saved it against foreigners at Marengo. The Lombard nobility, holed up in their country houses, then discovered that they had at first misunderstood the holy patron of Brescia's prediction; it was a matter not of thirteen weeks but rather thirteen months. The thirteen months went by and France seemed increasingly successful day by day.

We shall glide over ten years of progress and happiness, from 1800 to 1810. Fabrizio spent the early ones at the castle in Grianta, giving and receiving a good many blows amidst the young peasants in the village, and learning nothing, not even to read. Later on, he was sent to the Jesuit college in Milan. His father the marchese demanded that he be shown Latin, not as found in those old authors who are always talking about republics, but in a magnificent volume illustrated with more than a hundred engravings, masterpieces by artists of the seven-teenth century. This was the Latin genealogy of the Valserra, Marchesi del Dongo, published in 1650 by Fabrizio del Dongo, the archbishop of Parma. The Valserras' fortunes being above all military, the engravings represented a great many battles, and one was forever coming upon some hero of the name laying about him with his sword. The book greatly pleased the young Fabrizio. His mother, who adored him, got permission from time to time to come and visit him in Milan; but since her husband never offered her any money for these journeys, it was her sister-in-law, the amiable Countess Pietranera, who lent it to her. After the return of the French, the countess had become one of the most brilliant women at the court of Prince Eugène, the viceroy of Italy.[20]

Once Fabrizio had made his first communion, she obtained permission from the marchese, still in voluntary exile, to take him out now and again from his college. She found him odd, lively minded, very serious, but a pretty boy, and by no means out of place in the salon of a fashionable woman; for the rest, as ignorant as you like and scarcely able to write. The countess, whose enthusiastic nature was displayed in all that she did, promised the head of the establishment her patronage if her nephew Fabrizio made astonishing progress, and won a lot of prizes at the end of the year. To give him the means of earning them, she sent for him every Saturday evening, and often returned him to his masters only on the Wednesday or Thursday. The Jesuits, although much cherished by the prince viceroy, had been driven from Italy by the laws of the kingdom, and the superior of the college, an astute man, was aware of all the advantages he might derive from his dealings with a woman all-powerful at court. He took good care not to complain about Fabrizio's absences, who, more ignorant than ever, won five first prizes at the end of the year. On which understanding, the brilliant Countess Pietranera, followed by her husband, a general commanding one of the divisions of the guard, and by five or six of the leading figures in the viceregal court, came to the Jesuits to attend the prize-giving. The college head was complimented by his superiors.

The countess took her nephew to all the brilliant festivities that marked the too short reign of the amiable Prince Eugène. On her own authority she had made him an officer in the hussars and, at the age of twelve, Fabrizio wore the uniform. One day, enchanted by how pretty he looked, the countess asked the prince to give him a position as page, which would mean that the del Dongo family's resistance was weakening. The next day, she had need of all her credit to ensure that the viceroy was good enough not to remember this request, for which all that was lacking was the consent of the future page's father, consent which would have been resoundingly withheld. Following on this act of folly, which caused the sulking marchese to shudder, he found an excuse to recall the young Fabrizio to Grianta. The countess was supremely contemptuous of her brother; she thought him a sad sort of fool, who would turn nasty if ever he had the power. But she was mad about Fabrizio and, after a ten-year silence, wrote to the marchese to reclaim her nephew: her letter went unanswered.

On his return inside that formidable palazzo, built by the most warlike of his ancestors, Fabrizio knew nothing, only how to drill and to ride a horse. Count Pietranera, as mad about the boy as his wife, often made him get up on horseback and took him with him on parade.

When he arrived at the castle in Grianta, Fabrizio, his eyes still very red from the tears shed on leaving his aunt's splendid salons, found only the passionate caresses of his mother and his sisters. The marchese was shut away in his study with his elder son, the Marchesino Ascanio. There, they manufactured letters in cipher which had the honour of being sent to Vienna; father and son appeared only at mealtimes. The marchese affected repeatedly to be teaching his natural successor to keep accounts, in double entry, of the yield from each of his estates. But in actual fact, the marchese was too jealous of his own authority to discuss such matters with a son, the necessary heir to all these entailed estates. He put him to work encoding dispatches of fifteen or twenty pages which two or three times a week he sent on into Switzerland, whence they were forwarded to Vienna. The marchese claimed to be informing his legitimate sovereign of conditions inside the kingdom of Italy, of which he had no knowledge. His letters were highly successful all the same, and here is why. As one or another French or

Italian regiment went along the road to relieve the garrison, the marchese would have them counted by some trustworthy agent and, when reporting on the event to the court in Vienna, was careful to reduce the number of soldiers present by a good quarter. These letters, which were anyway ridiculous, had the virtue of contradicting other, more truthful ones, and they gave pleasure. Thus, shortly before the arrival of Fabrizio at the castle, the marchese had received the star of a renowned order: it was the fifth one to adorn his chamberlain's jacket. It pained him indeed not to show off this jacket outside his study; but he never allowed himself to dictate a dispatch without having put on the embroidered costume, decorated with all his orders. He thought it would be lacking in respect to behave otherwise.

The marchesa was struck with amazement at her son's charming ways. But she had maintained the habit of writing two or three times a year to General Count A***: the present name of Lieutenant Robert. The marchesa shrank from telling lies to the people she liked; she questioned her son and was appalled by his ignorance.

If I find him uneducated, she told herself, I who know nothing, Robert, who is so learned, would find his education completely lacking; but nowadays you have to have ability. Another detail which surprised her almost as much was that Fabrizio had taken all the religious things he had been taught by the Jesuits seriously. Although very devout herself, she shuddered at the boy's fanaticism; if the marchese has the wit to detect this means of influencing him, he'll take my son's love away from me. She wept freely and her passion for Fabrizio grew.

Life in the castle, populated by thirty or forty servants, was very dreary; thus Fabrizio spent all his days hunting or going about the lake on a boat. He had soon become good friends with the coachmen and the stable boys. All were madly pro-French and made fun openly of the sanctimonious valets attached to the persons of the marchese or his elder son. The great subject of the jokes directed at these solemn personages was that they powdered their hair, in imitation of their masters.

CHAPTER 2

... When the Evening Star comes to darken our eyes,
Taken up with the future, I contemplate the heavens,
Where God writes, in notes that are not obscure,
The lots and destinies of every creature.
For, watching a human being from deep in the heavens,
Moved sometimes by pity, He shows him the way;
Through the stars in the sky that are his characters,
Predicts for us both the good and the adverse things;
But men, weighed down by the earth and by death,
Scorn such writings and do not read them.

RONSARD[1]

The marchese professed a vigorous hatred of enlightenment; it is ideas, he said, that have ruined Italy. He did not really know how to reconcile this sacred horror of education with the wish to see his son Fabrizio complete the schooling begun so brilliantly with the Jesuits. In order to run as few risks as possible, he charged the good Father Blanes, the parish priest of Grianta, with making Fabrizio go on with his study of Latin. The priest himself would have needed to know that language, but for him it was an object of contempt. His knowledge in that sphere was limited to reciting by heart the prayers in his missal, whose meaning he was more or less able to convey to his flock. But for all that, the priest was greatly respected and even feared in the canton; he had always said that it was certainly not in thirteen weeks or even thirteen months that they would see the patron of Brescia, St Giovita's celebrated prophecy being fulfilled. He added, when talking to trusted friends, that the number *thirteen* needed to be interpreted in a way that would astonish a great many people, were everything allowed to be said (1813).[2]

The fact is that Father Blanes, a person of a *primitive* honesty and virtue, and an intelligent man what was more, spent every night at the top of his bell-tower: he was mad about astrology. Having used up all his days working out conjunctions and the positions of stars, he employed the better part of his nights following them in the sky. As a consequence of his poverty, his one instrument was a long telescope with a cardboard tube. One can easily imagine the contempt felt for the study of languages by a man who spent his life discovering the precise epoch of the fall of empires and of the revolutions that change the face of the world. What more do I know about a horse, he would say to Fabrizio, for being taught that in Latin it's called *equus*?

The country people feared Father Blanes as a great magician; for his part, with the help of the fear instilled by his spells in the tower, he stopped them from stealing. His fellow priests round about, very jealous of his influence, detested him. The Marchese del Dongo quite simply despised him, because he reasoned too much for a man of such humble origins. Fabrizio adored him: in order to please him, he would sometimes spend whole evenings doing additions or enormous multiplications. Then he would go up into the tower; this was a great favour, which Father Blanes had never granted anyone. But he loved the boy for his innocence. If you don't become a hypocrite, he told him, perhaps you will be a man.

Two or three times a year, Fabrizio, who was passionate and fearless in his pleasures, came close to drowning in the lake. He was the leader in all the big expeditions of the young peasant boys in Grianta and La Cadenabia. These boys had got hold of a few small keys, and once the night was pitch black, they tried to undo the padlocks on the chains attaching the boats to some large stone or tree near the shore. You need to know that on Lake Como the ingenious fishermen set standing lines a long way out from the water's edge. The top end of the line is attached to a small cork-lined board, and a very flexible hazel branch, which is fastened to the board, supports a small bell which tinkles when the fish is caught and sets the line jerking.

The main objective of these nocturnal expeditions, on which Fabrizio was commander-in-chief, was to go and visit the standing lines before the fishermen had heard the warning given off by the little bells. They chose days when it was stormy and embarked on these hazardous trips in the morning, an hour before dawn. What was admirable about these exploits was that, as they climbed into the boat, the boys believed they were rushing headlong into the greatest danger and, following the example of their fathers, they would devoutly recite an Ave Maria. Now it frequently happened that at the moment of departure, and immediately after the Ave Maria, Fabrizio was struck by an omen. Such were the fruits he had come away with from the astrological studies of his friend Father Blanes, in whose predictions he did not at all believe. In accordance with his youthful imagination, he took this omen as undoubtedly heralding either success or failure. And since he was more resolute than any of his comrades, the whole band became so accustomed to the omens that if, just as they were embarking, they saw a priest on the shore, or if a crow was seen taking flight to their left, they made haste to replace the padlock on the chain of the boat and all went back home. Thus Father Blanes had not passed on his somewhat difficult science to Fabrizio but had, unknowingly, inoculated him with a boundless confidence in the signs which can foretell the future.

The marchese was aware that any accident befalling his coded correspondence could put him at the mercy of his sister, and so every year, on the feast of St Angela, Countess Pietranera's patron saint, Fabrizio got permission to go and spend a week in Milan. He lived the whole year looking forward to or back on this week. On this great occasion, so that this diplomatic journey might be accomplished, the marchese handed his son four écus but, as was his custom, gave nothing to his wife, who was taking him. But one of the cooks, six lackeys and a coachman with two horses left for Como on the eve of the journey and every day, in Milan, the marchesa found a coach at her disposal, and a dinner service for twelve.

The Marchese del Dongo's sullen way of life contained few amusements for sure; but it had the advantage of permanently enriching the families who were good enough to give themselves up to it. The marchese, who had more than two hundred thousand livres a year, did not spend the fourth part of it; he lived off hopes. Over the thirteen years from 1800 to 1813, he believed consistently and firmly that Napoleon would be overthrown within six months. Imagine how overjoyed he was when, early in 1813, he learnt of the disasters at the Beresina![3] He all but went out of his mind at the capture of Paris and the fall of Napoleon, permitting himself to say the most outrageous things to his wife and sister. Finally, after fourteen years of waiting, he had the inexpressible delight of seeing Austrian troops re-enter Milan. Following orders sent from Vienna, the Austrian general received the Marchese del Dongo with a consideration bordering on respect; they hastened to offer him one of the leading positions in the government, which he accepted as the repayment of a debt. His elder son got a lieutenancy in one of the monarchy's finest regiments; but the second son refused ever to accept the offer of a place as a cadet. This triumph, which the marchese enjoyed with rare insolence, lasted only a few months, and was followed by a humiliating reverse. He had never had any gift for public affairs, and fourteen years spent in the countryside, among his footmen, his attorney and his doctor, combined with the ill humour of old age, which had now set in, had made him altogether incapable. But in the Austrian domains, it is not possible to hold on to an important post without having the kind of talent demanded by the slow, complicated but very rational administration of that old monarchy. The Marchese del Dongo's lapses scandalized the clerks and even brought business to a halt. His ultra-monarchical remarks inflamed a population that they wished to see fast asleep and uncaring. One fine day, he learnt that His Majesty had graciously condescended to accept the resignation he had handed in from his post in the administration, and at the same time conferred on him the position of 'second high majordomo major' in the kingdom of Lombardy-Venice. The marchese was indignant at the atrocious injustice of which he was the victim;

he had a letter to a friend printed, he who so execrated the freedom of the press. Finally, he wrote to the Emperor that his ministers had betrayed him, and were nothing but Jacobins.[4] All of which having been done, he returned sadly to his castle in Grianta. He had one consolation. After the fall of Napoleon, certain powerful figures in Milan had Count Prina, a former minister of the king of Italy and a man of great ability, assaulted in the streets.[5] Count Pietranera risked his own life to save that of the minister, who was killed by blows from an umbrella, and whose agony lasted for five hours. A priest, the Marchese del Dongo's confessor, might have been able to save Prina by opening the grille of the church of San Giovanni, in front of which the unfortunate minister had been dragged, to be left for a moment even in the gutter in the middle of the street. But he jeered at him, refused to open the grille and, six months later, the marchese had the pleasure of obtaining a fine promotion for him.

He execrated Count Pietranera, his brother-in-law, who, without having even fifty louis a year, dared to be quite contented, took it upon himself to display his loyalty to what he had loved all through his life, and was insolent enough to extol this spirit of justice without respect of persons, which the marchese called wicked Jacobinism. The count had refused to serve under the Austrians. This refusal was made much of and, a few months after the death of Prina, the same personages who had paid the assassins managed to get General Pietranera thrown into prison. Upon which, the countess, his wife, took a passport and asked for posthorses so as to go to Vienna and tell the Emperor the truth. Prina's murderers took fright and one of them, a cousin of Mme Pietranera's, came and brought her at midnight, one hour before she left for Vienna, the order setting her husband free. The next day, the Austrian general sent for Count Pietranera, received him with all possible distinction, and assured him that his retirement pension would shortly be liquidated on the most advantageous terms. The good General Bubna,[6] a feeling and intelligent man, appeared quite ashamed of Prina's murder and the count's imprisonment.

After this squall, averted by the firmness of the countess's

character, the couple lived, as best they could, off the retirement pension, which was not slow in coming, thanks to the
recommendation of General Bubna.

Fortunately, it happened that, for the past five or six years,
the countess had been on the friendliest of terms with a very
wealthy young man, who was also a close friend of the count,
and did not fail to put at their disposal the finest team of English
horses then to be found in Milan, his box at La Scala and
his house in the country. But the count knew himself to be
courageous, his soul was generous, he was easily carried away
and would then permit himself strange comments. One day
when he was out hunting with some young men, one of them,
who had served under other flags from him, started to joke
about the valour of the soldiers of the Cisalpine Republic;[7] the
count slapped his face, they immediately fought and the count,
isolated in the midst of all these young men, was killed. There
was much talk about this duel of sorts, and those individuals
who had been present chose to go travelling in Switzerland.

The absurd form of courage known as resignation, the courage of a fool who allows himself to be hanged without protest,
was not at all the countess's style. Furious at her husband's
death, she would have liked Limercati also, the wealthy young
man, her close friend, to take it into his head to go travelling
in Switzerland, and shoot Count Pietranera's murderer with his
carbine or slap his face.

Limercati found this plan totally absurd and the countess
realized that her contempt had killed her love. She redoubled
her attentions towards Limercati; she wanted to reawaken his
love and then drop him, and cause him to despair. In order to
make this project of revenge intelligible in France, I shall say
that in Milan, a country far distant from our own, love can still
drive people to despair. The countess who, in her widow's
weeds, far outshone all her rivals, flirted with the young men
most in view and one of them, Count N***, who had always
said that he found Limercati's qualities somewhat heavy, somewhat stiff for so spirited a woman, fell madly in love with the
countess. She wrote to Limercati: 'Will you act for once like a
man of spirit? Imagine that you have never met me. I am, with

a little bit of contempt perhaps, your most humble servant,
Gina Pietranera.'

On reading this note, Limercati left for one of his country
houses. His love took fire, he became wild and talked of blowing
out his brains, which is uncommon in countries where they
believe in hellfire. The very next day after his arrival in the
country, he had written to the countess to offer her his hand
and his income of two hundred thousand livres. She returned
his letter unopened via Count N***'s groom. Whereupon,
Limercati spent three years on his estates, returning every two
months to Milan, but without ever having the courage to remain
there, and boring all his friends with his passionate love for the
countess and detailed account of the kindnesses she had once
shown him. In the early stages, he would add that she was
destroying herself with Count N*** and that such a liaison
dishonoured her.

The fact is that the countess felt no love of any kind for
Count N***, which is what she declared to him once she was
quite sure Limercati was in despair. The count, versed in the
ways of society, asked her not to divulge the sad truth she had
entrusted him with: 'If you have the extreme indulgence,' he
added, 'to continue to receive me with all the outward distinction granted to the reigning lover, I shall perhaps find a suitable
position.'

After which heroic declaration, the countess would have
nothing more to do with Count N***'s horses or his box at
the opera. But for the past fifteen years she had been accustomed
to a very fashionable way of life: she needed to resolve the
difficult, or, rather, impossible problem of living in Milan off a
pension of fifteen hundred francs. She left her palazzo, rented
two rooms on a fifth floor, dismissed all her people and even
her maid, who was replaced by an old woman who did house-
work. This sacrifice was in point of fact less heroic and less
arduous than we might think. In Milan poverty is not the
subject of ridicule and hence does not strike frightened souls as
the worst of evils. After a few months of this noble poverty,
besieged by continual letters from Limercati, and even from
Count N***, it chanced that the Marchese del Dongo, normally

execrably tightfisted, came to reflect that his enemies might well crow over his sister's poverty. What, a del Dongo reduced to living off the pension that the court in Vienna, which he had reason to complain of, grants to the widows of its generals!

He wrote to her that an apartment and treatment befitting his sister awaited her at the castle in Grianta. The countess's inconstant soul embraced the idea of this new style of life with enthusiasm. Not for twenty years had she lived in that venerable castle rising majestically amidst the old chestnut trees planted in the days of the Sforzas. There, she told herself, I shall find repose and, at my age, is that not happiness? (Because she was thirty-one, she thought it was now time to retire.) On that sublime lake where I was born, a happy, peaceful life finally awaits me.

I do not know whether she was deceiving herself, but what is certain is that this passionate soul, who had just so unceremoniously rejected the offer of two immense fortunes, brought happiness to the castle in Grianta. Her two nieces were wild with delight. 'You have given me back the good days of my youth,' the marchesa said, embracing her. 'The day before you arrived, I was a hundred years old.' The countess began, together with Fabrizio, to revisit all the enchanting spots in the vicinity of Grianta so greatly celebrated by travellers: the Villa Melzi on the far side of the lake, opposite the castle and serving it as a viewpoint; up above, the sacred wood of the Sfondrata, and the bold promontory which separates the two branches of the lake, the voluptuous Como branch and that which runs towards Lecco, full of severity: sublime, graceful prospects that the world's most renowned beauty spot, the Bay of Naples, may equal but does not surpass. It was with rapture that the countess rediscovered the memories of her early youth and compared them to her present feelings. Lake Como, she said to herself, is not surrounded, like Lake Geneva, by large tracts of land, tightly enclosed and cultivated using the best methods, things that remind you of money and speculation. Here on every side, I see hills of unequal height covered with clumps of trees planted by chance, which the hand of man has not yet spoilt and forced to *yield an income*. In the midst of these hills

with their admirable contours, which slope so strangely and
rapidly down towards the lake, I can preserve all the illusions
in the descriptions of Tasso and Ariosto.[8] Everything is noble
and tender, everything speaks of love, nothing recalls the ugliness of civilization. The villages situated halfway up are hidden
by tall trees, and above the tops of the trees there rises the
charming architecture of their pretty church towers. If some
small field fifty paces across happens to interrupt the clumps of
chestnuts and wild cherry now and again, the satisfied eye sees
happier, more vigorous plants growing there than elsewhere.
Beyond the hills, whose summits display hermitages, all of
which one would like to live in, the astonished eye perceives
the peaks of the Alps, always covered in snow, and their severe
austerity recalls all that is needed of life's calamities to enhance
one's present intense delight. The imagination is touched by the
distant sound of the bell in some small village hidden beneath
the trees; these sounds, carried across the water that softens
them, take on a note of gentle melancholy and resignation, and
seem to be saying to man: life is escaping, don't look askance
therefore at the happiness that offers itself, make haste to enjoy
yourself. The language of these ravishing places, which have
their like nowhere else in the world, gave the countess back her
sixteen-year-old's heart. She could not imagine how she had
been able to go so many years without revisiting the lake. Has
happiness then taken refuge in the onset of old age? she asked
herself. She bought a boat which Fabrizio, the marchesa and
she decorated with their own hands, for they had no money for
anything, in the midst of a household maintained with great
splendour. Since his fall from favour, the Marchese del Dongo
had become even more the ostentatious aristocrat. For example,
in order to reclaim ten yards of land from the lake, near the
famous avenue of plane trees, beside La Cadenabia, he had a
dyke built the estimate for which came to eighty thousand
francs. At the far end of the dyke could be seen rising, from the
designs of the famous Marchese Cagnola, a chapel built entirely
from enormous blocks of granite, and, in the chapel, Marchesi,[9]
the fashionable sculptor from Milan, was building him a tomb

on which numerous bas-reliefs would represent the noblest exploits of his ancestors.

Fabrizio's older brother, the Marchesine Ascanio, wanted to be part of the ladies' excursions, but his aunt threw water on his powdered hair, and every day found some fresh practical joke to aim at his solemnity. In the end, he spared the merry band, who did not dare laugh in his presence, the sight of his great pallid face. They fancied he was his father the marchese's spy, and that stern despot, furious ever since his enforced resignation, required careful handling.

Ascanio swore to be revenged on Fabrizio.

There was a storm in which they ran risks. Although they had hardly any money, they paid the two boatmen generously not to say anything to the marchese, who had already displayed much ill temper at their taking out his two daughters. They encountered a second storm. These are terrible and unexpected on that beautiful lake: squalls of wind emerge without warning from two mountain gorges running in opposite directions, and do battle on the water. The countess wanted to disembark in the midst of the hurricane and the claps of thunder. She argued that, were she set down on an isolated rock in the middle of the lake, the size of a small bedroom, she would enjoy a singular spectacle. She would find herself besieged on every side by raging waves; but, in jumping from the boat, she fell into the water. Fabrizio threw himself in after her to rescue her, and both were dragged some way off. To drown is not pleasant for sure, but tedium had been taken by surprise and banished from the feudal castle. The countess had become enthused by the primitive character and the astrology of Father Blanes. The little money remaining to her after the acquisition of the boat had been used to buy a small, makeshift telescope, and almost every evening, together with her nieces and Fabrizio, she installed herself on the platform of one of the castle's Gothic towers. Fabrizio was the savant of the band, and they spent several hours there very cheerfully, far away from the spies.

It has to be admitted that there were days when the countess did not address a single word to anyone. She was to be seen walking beneath the tall chestnut trees, sunk in a gloomy reverie. She was too lively minded not sometimes to sense the tedium there is in not changing one's ideas. But the next day she would be laughing like the day before: it was the grievances of the marchesa, her sister-in-law, which had produced these gloomy impressions in a soul so very active by its nature. 'So are we going to spend what's left of our youth in this dreary castle!' the marchesa would exclaim.

Up until the arrival of the countess, she had not even had the courage to feel such regrets.

Thus did they live through the winter of 1814–15. Twice, despite her poverty, the countess came and spent a few days in Milan. She needed to see a sublime ballet by Vigano,[10] performed at La Scala, and the marchese did not forbid his wife from accompanying her sister-in-law. She was about to draw her small quarterly allowance, and it was the poor widow of the Cisalpine general who lent the ultra-rich Marchesa del Dongo a few sequins. These trips were delightful: they invited old friends to dinner and consoled themselves by laughing at everything, just like children. This Italian gaiety, full of brio and the unforeseen, made them forget the gloomy sadness that the looks of the marchese and his elder son spread around them at Grianta. Fabrizio, aged barely sixteen, represented the head of the family very well.

On 7 March 1815, the ladies had been back for two days from a delightful short journey to Milan. They were walking in the beautiful avenue of plane trees, recently extended on to the extreme edge of the lake. A boat appeared, coming from the direction of Como, and made peculiar signals. One of the marchese's factors jumped on to the jetty: Napoleon had just landed in the Golfe de Juan.[11] Europe was good-natured enough to be surprised by this event, which in no way surprised the Marchese del Dongo. He poured out his heart in a letter to his sovereign: he offered him his talents and several million, and repeated that his ministers were Jacobins, in league with the ringleaders in Paris.

On 8 March, at six in the morning, the marchese, clad in his insignia, was having dictated to him, by his elder son, the draft of a third political dispatch. He was busy solemnly transcribing it, in his very elegant hand, on paper bearing in filigree the effigy of his sovereign. At the same moment, Fabrizio was having himself announced to Countess Pietranera.

'I'm leaving,' he told her, 'I'm going to join the Emperor, who is also king of Italy; he was such a good friend to your husband! I shall go via Switzerland. Last night, in Menagio, my friend Vasi, who sells barometers, gave me his passport. Now give me a few napoleons, for I've only two of my own. But if I have to, I shall go on foot.'

The countess wept for joy and anxiety. 'Great heaven, why do you have to have had that idea!' she exclaimed, taking Fabrizio by the hands. She got up and went to fetch a small purse decorated with pearls from the wardrobe, where it had been carefully hidden away. It was all she possessed in the world.

'Take it,' she told Fabrizio, 'but in God's name, don't get yourself killed. What will your unhappy mother and I have left, if we don't have you? As for Napoleon succeeding, it's out of the question, my poor love. Our gentlemen will be well able to finish him off. Didn't you hear, a week ago in Milan, the story of the twenty-three assassination plots, all very well planned and which he escaped only by a miracle? And at the time he was all-powerful. And you've seen that it's not the will to destroy him that our enemies lack. France was nothing any more after his departure.'

It was in tones of the liveliest emotion that the countess spoke to Fabrizio of Napoleon's future destiny. 'By allowing you to go and join him, I'm sacrificing to him what I hold dearest in all the world,' she said. Fabrizio's eyes moistened, he shed tears as he embraced the countess, but his determination to leave was not shaken for an instant. He explained effusively to this very dear friend all the reasons that had decided him, and which we shall take the liberty of finding very pleasing.

'Yesterday evening, it was seven minutes to six, we were walking, as you know, along the edge of the lake in the avenue of plane trees, below the Casa Sommariva, and we were walking to the south. There, for the first time, I noticed in the distance the boat that was coming from Como, the bearer of such great news. As I was watching the boat, without thinking about the Emperor, merely envying the lot of those who are able to travel, I was suddenly gripped by a profound emotion. The boat touched land, the agent spoke in a low voice to my father, who changed colour and took us aside to announce the *terrible news*. I turned towards the lake with no other aim but to hide the tears of joy with which my eyes were flooded. Suddenly, at an immense height and on my right I saw an eagle, Napoleon's bird; it was flying majestically in the direction of Switzerland, and consequently towards Paris. And I, too, I told myself at that instant, I shall cross Switzerland with the rapidity of the eagle, and go and offer that great man nothing very much but all anyway that I'm able to offer, the aid of my feeble arm. He wanted to give us a fatherland and he was fond of my uncle. At that moment, when I could still see the eagle, by some strange design my tears dried up. And the proof that this idea has come from on high is that, at the same instant, without any argument, I reached my decision and saw the means of effecting the journey. In a flash, all the dreariness that, as you know, poisons my life, on Sundays especially, was as if removed by a divine breath. I saw that great image of Italy rising up from the slough in which the Germans have kept it covered.* She was stretching forth her bruised arms, still half weighed down by chains, towards her king and liberator. And I, I told myself, the as yet unknown son of that unhappy mother, I shall leave, I shall go either to die or to conquer with that man marked by destiny, who sought to cleanse us from the contempt cast at us by even the most servile and base among the inhabitants of Europe.

'You know,' he added dropping his voice, coming closer to the countess, and fixing her with eyes that blazed fire, 'you know that young chestnut tree that my mother planted herself, in the winter I was born, on the edge of the big pool in our forest two leagues from here. Before doing anything, I wanted to go and visit it. The spring isn't too far advanced, I told

---

* It is someone of passion speaking, he is translating into prose a few lines from the celebrated Monti.[12]

myself. Well, if my tree has leaves on it, that will be a sign for me. I, too, must come out from the state of torpor in which I've been languishing in this cold and dreary castle. Don't you think that these blackened old walls, the symbols nowadays and once the means of despotism, are a true image of the dreary wintertime? They are for me what the winter is for my tree.

'Would you believe it, Gina? Yesterday evening at half past seven I got to my chestnut tree. It had leaves on, pretty little leaves already quite big! I kissed them without harming them. I hoed the earth respectfully around my darling tree. Filled with a new excitement, I at once crossed the mountain. I reached Menagio. I needed a passport to get into Switzerland. Time was flying, it was already one o'clock in the morning when I found myself at Vasi's door. I thought I'd need to knock for a long time to wake him; but he was up and about with three of his friends. At my first words: "You're going to join Napoleon," he cried and threw his arms around my neck. The others too embraced me excitedly. "Why am I married?" said one of them.'

Countess Pietranera had become pensive. She thought she should raise a few objections. Had Fabrizio had the least experience, he could easily have seen that the countess herself did not believe in the good reasons she hastened to give him. But, in the place of experience, he had determination: he did not even deign to listen to the reasons. The countess was soon reduced to getting him at least to let his mother into his plan.

'She'll tell my sisters, and the women will give me away without realizing!' cried Fabrizio, with a sort of heroic hauteur.

'So show more respect when you speak of the sex that will make your fortune,' said the countess, smiling amidst her tears. 'Because you'll always upset men, you've too much fire in you for prosaic souls.'

The marchesa burst into tears on learning of her son's strange plan. She was blind to its heroism and did everything she could to hold him back. Once she was persuaded that nothing at all, bar the walls of a prison, could stop him from leaving, she handed him the little money she possessed. Then she remembered that since the day before she had had eight or nine small diamonds worth perhaps ten thousand francs, which the

marchese had entrusted to her to have mounted in Milan.
Fabrizio's sisters came into their mother's room as the countess
was sewing the diamonds into our hero's travelling coat. He
gave these poor women back their paltry napoleons. His sisters
were so enthused by his plan, they embraced him joyfully and
so noisily that he took the few diamonds that still remained to
be concealed in his hand and wanted to leave there and then.

'You'll give me away without your realizing,' he told his
sisters. 'Since I've got so much money, there's no point in taking
any old clothes; you can find them anywhere.' He embraced
these people who were so dear to him and left that same instant
without looking to go back to his own room. He walked so
quickly, still afraid of being pursued by men on horseback, that
he entered Lugano that same evening. Thank God, he was in a
Swiss town and no longer feared being roughed up on the lonely
road by gendarmes in the pay of his father. From this place, he
wrote him a splendid letter, a childish weakness that reinforced
the marchese's anger. Fabrizio caught the stage, crossed the
St Gothard. His journey was rapid and he entered France by
Pontarlier. The Emperor was in Paris. There, Fabrizio's troubles
began. He had set off firmly intending to speak to the Emperor;
it had never crossed his mind that this might prove difficult. In
Milan, he saw Prince Eugène ten times a day, and would have
been able to address him. In Paris, he went every morning
into the courtyard of the Tuileries Palace to watch Napoleon
inspecting the troops; but he was never able to approach the
Emperor. Our hero thought all Frenchmen were as profoundly
moved as himself by the extreme danger the fatherland was in.
At table in the hotel where he was staying, he made no secret
of his plans and his devotion. He met quiet, friendly young men
even more enthusiastic than himself who, within a few days,
had not failed to steal all the money he possessed. Luckily,
purely out of modesty, he had not mentioned the diamonds
given him by his mother. On the morning when, following a
night of excess, he found he had been well and truly robbed,
he bought two good horses, took on an ex-soldier and horse-
dealer's stableboy as a manservant and, in his contempt for the
honey-tongued young Parisians, left for the army. He knew

nothing, except that it was assembling near Maubeuge. No sooner had he reached the frontier than he found it absurd to remain inside a house, busy warming himself in front of a good hearth, while soldiers were bivouacking. Whatever his manservant, who did not lack good sense, might find to say, he wasted no time rashly intruding himself in among the bivouacs right on the frontier, on the road into Belgium. Hardly had he reached the first battalion, positioned next to the road, before the soldiers began eyeing this young civilian, whose attire carried no suggestion of a uniform. Night was falling, a cold wind was blowing. Fabrizio went up to a fire, and offered to pay for hospitality. The soldiers looked at one another in astonishment, especially at the idea of payment, and kindly accorded him a place at the fire; his manservant made him a shelter. But an hour later, the regimental sergeant-major going past within range of the bivouac, the soldiers went to recount the arrival of this stranger speaking bad French. The sergeant-major questioned Fabrizio, who spoke of his enthusiasm for the Emperor in a highly suspect accent; whereupon the warrant officer asked that he go with him to the colonel, installed in a nearby farmhouse. Fabrizio's servant came up with the two horses. The sight of them seemed to make such a keen impression on the sergeant-major that he at once changed his mind and began questioning the servant also. The latter, a former soldier, guessing straight away what his interlocutor's plan of campaign was, spoke of the protection his master enjoyed, adding that he would not for sure let his fine horses be 'pinched'. A soldier summoned by the sergeant-major at once laid a hand on his collar, another soldier took charge of the horses, and the sergeant-major sternly ordered Fabrizio to follow him without answering back.

After having made him cover a good league, on foot, in a darkness made to seem denser by the fires of the bivouacs that lit up the horizon on every side, the sergeant-major handed Fabrizio over to an officer from the gendarmerie who, wearing a serious expression, asked him for his papers. Fabrizio showed his passport, which described him as a dealer in barometers 'carrying his merchandise'.

'How stupid can they get,' exclaimed the officer, 'it's going too far!'

He put questions to our hero, who spoke of the Emperor and of liberty in terms of the liveliest enthusiasm, whereupon the officer broke into fits of laughter. 'You're not so very clever, I must say!' he cried. 'It's a bit much, their daring to send us novices of your sort!' And despite all that Fabrizio was able to say, as he strove to explain that he was not in fact a dealer in barometers, the officer sent him to the prison in B***, a small town in the vicinity where our hero arrived around three in the morning, beside himself with anger and dead tired.

Fabrizio, astonished at first, then furious, and understanding absolutely nothing of what was happening to him, spent thirty-three long days in this wretched prison. He wrote letter after letter to the commandant of the place, and it was the gaoler's wife, a good-looking Flemish woman of thirty-six, who undertook to see that they reached him. But since she had no wish to get such a nice-looking boy shot, and because moreover he paid well, she never failed to throw all these letters into the fire. In the evenings, very late, she deigned to come and listen to the prisoner's grievances. She had told her husband that the greenhorn had money, upon which the prudent gaoler had given her a free hand. She made use of this licence and received a few gold napoleons, for the sergeant-major had taken away only the horses, and the gendarmerie officer had not confiscated anything at all. One June afternoon, Fabrizio heard a loud cannonade quite a long way off. So they were finally fighting! His heart leapt with impatience. He also heard a lot of noise in the town. In fact, a large troop movement was being carried out, three divisions were passing through B***. When, around eleven at night, the gaoler's wife came to share his sufferings, Fabrizio was even friendlier than usual. Then, taking her by the hands: 'Get me out of here, I give you my word of honour I'll come back into prison as soon as they've stopped fighting.'

'That's complete rubbish! Have you got the "shekels"?' He looked anxious, he did not understand the word 'shekels'. The gaoler's wife, seeing this expression, adjudged that the waters were low and, instead of talking in terms of gold napoleons as she had been resolved to do, now spoke only of francs. 'Listen,' she said, 'if you can give me a hundred francs, I'll put a double napoleon on each of the eyes of the corporal who'll be coming to relieve the guard during the night. He won't be able to see you leave the prison, and if his regiment has to get on the move during the day, he'll accept.'

The bargain was soon concluded. The gaoler's wife even agreed to hide Fabrizio in her bedroom, from where he would be able to escape more easily in the morning.

The next morning, before dawn, the woman said to Fabrizio, full of pity: 'You're still very young to be going in for this filthy trade, young man; believe me, don't come back again.'

'What!' repeated Fabrizio. 'Is it a crime then to want to defend your country?'

'That'll do. Always remember I saved your life, your case was a foregone conclusion, you'd have been shot. But don't tell a soul, because you'd lose my husband and me our place. Above all, don't ever repeat your false story about a gentleman from Milan disguised as a dealer in barometers, it's too stupid. Listen to me carefully, I'm going to give you the clothes off a hussar who died two days ago in the prison. Open your mouth as little as possible. But if a sergeant or an officer questions you in such a way as to force you to answer, say you were left behind sick in the house of a peasant who took you in out of charity because you were trembling with fever in a ditch along the road. If that answer doesn't satisfy them, add that you're going to rejoin your regiment. They'll arrest you perhaps because of your accent; then say you were born in Piedmont, that you're a conscript who remained in France last year,' etc., etc.

For the first time, after thirty-three days in a rage, Fabrizio grasped the explanation of all that had been happening to him. He had been mistaken for a spy. He reasoned with the gaoler's wife who, that morning, was very affectionate. And in the end, as she, armed with a needle, was taking in the hussar's uniform, he told the astonished woman his full story. She believed it momentarily. He had such an innocent expression and he looked so pretty, dressed as a hussar!

'Since you're so full of the desire to fight,' she finally said to

him, half convinced, 'you needed to enlist in a regiment when
you got to Paris. Buy a sergeant a drink, and the deal would
have been done!' The gaoler's wife added much good advice
for the future and finally, just as day was breaking, she put
Fabrizio out of the house, having made him swear over and
over again that he would never reveal her name, whatever might
befall. As soon as Fabrizio had left the small town, swaggering
along with the hussar's sabre underneath his arm, he felt a
qualm. Here I am, he said to himself, with the uniform and the
movement order of a hussar who died in prison, where he'd
been taken, they say, for stealing a cow and some silver spoons!
You could say I've inherited his existence ... and without
wanting to or at all foreseeing it! Beware of prison! The omen's
clear, I shall have to suffer a lot in prison!

It was less than an hour since Fabrizio had left his benefac-
tress when the rain began to fall with such force that the new
hussar could scarcely walk, hampered by badly made boots
that had not been intended for him. He encountered a peasant
riding a sorry-looking horse, he bought the horse, explaining
himself by signs. The gaoler's wife had recommended that he
spoke as little as possible, because of his accent.

That day the army, which had just won the battle of Ligny,[13]
was marching straight on Brussels; it was the eve of the battle
of Waterloo. Around midday, the torrential rain still continuing, Fabrizio heard the sound of cannon. This happiness made
him quite forget the awful moments of despair brought on by
his unjust imprisonment. He walked until the night was well
advanced and as he was beginning to have some common sense,
he went and found a billet in a peasant's house a long way from
the road. The peasant was weeping and claimed that they had
taken everything from him. Fabrizio gave him an écu and found
some oats. My horse doesn't look much, Fabrizio told himself;
but never mind, he could well turn out to be to the liking of
some sergeant-major, and he went and slept in the stable next
to him. An hour before first light, the next day, Fabrizio was
on the road and, by dint of patting him, managed to make his
horse break into a trot. At around five o'clock he heard the
cannonade: it was the lead-up to Waterloo.

CHAPTER 3

Fabrizio soon met with some vivandières, and the extreme gratitude he felt towards the gaoler's wife in B*** led him to address them. He asked one of them where the 4th Regiment of Hussars was, to which he belonged.

'You'd do well not to be in so much of a hurry, young soldier,' said the canteen-woman, touched by Fabrizio's pallor and his beautiful eyes. 'You haven't got the grip yet for all the sabreing they're going to be doing today. Though if you had a gun, I don't say but you could loose off a ball as well as the next man.'

Fabrizio did not like this advice. But however hard he urged his horse on, he could not go any faster than the canteen-woman's wagon. From time to time, the sound of the cannon seemed to come closer and prevented them from hearing one another, for Fabrizio was so beside himself with enthusiasm and happiness that he had resumed the conversation. The canteen-woman's every word increased his happiness by making him understand it. With the exception of his real name and of his escape from the prison, he ended by telling this woman who seemed so kind-hearted everything. She was greatly surprised and understood not the first thing that this handsome young soldier was recounting.

'I've got it,' she exclaimed at last with a triumphant expression, 'you're a young civilian in love with the wife of some captain in the 4th Hussars. Your sweetheart has given you the uniform you're wearing as a present and you're running after her. It's as true as that there's a God above that you've never been a soldier. But like the brave lad you are, because your

regiment's under fire you want to show up and not go down as
a yellow-belly.'

Fabrizio agreed with everything, it was the one means he had
of receiving some sound advice. I don't know at all how the
French go about things, he told himself, and if I don't get any
guidance, I'll manage to have myself thrown into prison again,
and they'll steal my horse.

'First of all, young man,' said the canteen-woman, who was
becoming more and more friendly, 'admit you're not twenty-
one. You can't be a day over seventeen.'

This was the truth, and Fabrizio confessed as much with
good grace.

'So, you're not even a conscript, it's purely on account of
madame's lovely eyes that you're going to get yourself shot to
pieces. She's not squeamish, I must say! If you've still got a few
of those nice yellow coins she handed over, you need first of
all to buy another horse. Look how your nag pricks up its
ears when the rumbling of the cannon gets too close; that's a
peasant's horse that'll get you killed the moment you're in the
line. That white smoke that you see there above the hedge,
that's the infantry firing, young man! So be ready to get the
wind up all right once you hear the shot whistling past. You'd
do well to eat something too while you've still got time.'

Fabrizio took this advice, handing the vivandière a napoleon
and asking her to pay herself. 'I weep to see it,' the woman
exclaimed. 'The poor lad doesn't even know how to spend his
money! It'd serve you right if after pocketing your napoleon I
set Cocotte off at a smart trot. Damned if your nag'd be able to
follow me. What would you do, you booby, when you saw me
clear off? You need to learn that when the guns are growling, you
never show your gold. Here,' she said, 'here's eighteen francs
fifty centimes, and your dinner's costing you thirty sous. Now
we're soon going to have horses to resell. If the animal's small,
give ten francs, in any case never more than twenty francs, not
even if it were the horse of the four brothers Aymon.'[1]

Dinner over, the vivandière, who was still holding forth, was
interrupted by a woman who was coming over the fields and
crossed on to the road.

'Ho there,' the woman shouted. 'Ho there, Margot! Your 6th Light are on the right.'

'I have to leave you, young man,' the vivandière told our hero. 'But the truth is I feel sorry for you. I've taken a liking to you, dammit all! You don't know anything about anything, you're going to learn the hard way, as sure as God is God! Come to the 6th Light with me.'

'I realize perfectly well I don't know anything,' Fabrizio said 'but I want to fight and I'm determined to go over towards that white smoke there.'

'Look how your horse is twitching his ears! As soon as he's over there, however little energy he's got, he'll force your hand and start galloping, and God knows where he'll take you. Don't you believe me? As soon as you're with the young soldiers, pick up a gun and a cartridge pouch, get next to some soldiers and do exactly the same as they do. But dear God, I bet you don't even know how to tear open a cartridge.'

Fabrizio bristled but admitted all the same to his new friend that she had guessed correctly.

'Poor young lad! He's going to get killed straight off. As God's my witness, it won't be long. You absolutely must come with me,' the canteen-woman went on, with an air of authority.

'But I want to fight.'

'You'll fight too. Come on, the 6th Light is famous, and there'll be enough for everyone today.'

'But will we soon be at your regiment?'

'In quarter of an hour at the outside.'

With this good woman's advice, Fabrizio told himself, my ignorance of everything won't get me mistaken for a spy and I'll be able to fight. At that moment, the sound of the cannon grew louder, one report not waiting for the next. 'It's like a rosary,' said Fabrizio.

'We're beginning to make out the infantry firing,' said the vivandière, applying her whip to her small horse, which seemed all excited by the gunfire.

The canteen-woman turned to the right and took a side road through the fields; there was a foot of mud; her little wagon was on the point of remaining there; Fabrizio pushed on a wheel. His horse fell twice. Soon the road, less waterlogged, was nothing more than a track in the midst of the grassland. Fabrizio had not gone five hundred paces before his nag stopped dead: there was a corpse, lying across the track, which filled both horse and rider with horror.

Fabrizio's face, naturally very pale, went a pronounced shade of green. The canteen-woman, having looked at the dead man, said, as if talking to herself: 'He's not from our division.' Then, looking up at our hero, she burst out laughing. 'Ha ha, young man,' she exclaimed, 'a dish fit for a king!' Fabrizio remained frozen. What struck him above all were the filthy feet of the corpse, which had already been stripped of its shoes and left with only a wretched pair of blood-soaked trousers.

'Come closer,' said the canteen-woman. 'Get off your horse, you've got to get used to it. Look,' she cried, 'he got it in the head.' A bullet had entered beside the nose and come out through the opposite temple, disfiguring the corpse in a hideous fashion. He still had one eye open.

'So get off your horse, young man,' said the canteen-woman, 'and shake him by the hand to see if he returns it.'

Even though he was ready to give up the ghost with disgust, Fabrizio did not hesitate but threw himself down from his horse, took the corpse's hand and gave it a firm shake. Then he remained as if prostrated; he felt he did not have the strength to get back on his horse. What horrified him above all was the open eye.

The vivandière is going to think I'm a coward, he told himself bitterly. But he felt any movement was out of the question; he would have fallen over. It was a ghastly moment; Fabrizio was on the verge of actually being sick. The vivandière saw, jumped nimbly down from her little vehicle, and handed him, without a word, a glass of brandy, which he swallowed in a single gulp. He was then able to get back on his nag and continue on his way without saying a word. The vivandière looked at him now and again out of the corner of her eye.

'You'll fight tomorrow, young man,' she said to him at last, 'today you'll stay with me. You can easily see you've got to learn the soldier's trade.'

'On the contrary, I want to fight straight away,' cried our hero with a sombre expression, which the vivandière thought was a good omen. The sound of the cannon increased and seemed to be coming closer. The reports were beginning to form a sort of running bass. There was no interval separating one from the next, and against this running bass, reminiscent of the sound of a distant torrent, the firing of the infantry could be clearly heard.

At that point, the road ran into the middle of a clump of trees. The vivandière saw three or four of our soldiers come running towards her at full tilt. She jumped nimbly down from her vehicle and ran and hid fifteen or twenty paces from the road. She cowered in a hole that had been left after a large tree had just been uprooted. So, Fabrizio told himself, I'm going to see if I'm a coward! He stopped near the little vehicle the canteen-woman had abandoned and drew his sabre. The soldiers paid no attention to him but went running past alongside the wood, to the left of the road.

'They're some of ours,' the vivandière said calmly, returning all out of breath to her little vehicle ... 'If your horse was capable of galloping, I'd say push on ahead as far as the end of the wood, see if there's anyone in the open.' Fabrizio did not need to be told twice, he snatched a branch off a poplar tree, stripped it of leaves and began to beat his horse as hard as he could. The nag broke into a gallop momentarily then reverted to its customary easy trot. The vivandière had set her horse galloping. 'So stop, will you!' she shouted to Fabrizio. Soon, both of them were out of the wood. On reaching the edge of the open country, they heard a frightful din, the cannon and the muskets were sounding on every side, to the right, to the left, behind them. And because the clump of trees from which they had emerged occupied a mound raised eight or ten feet above the plain, they had a clear enough view of one corner of the battle. But there was no one in the field beyond the wood. This field was bordered, a thousand paces away, by a long line of very bushy willow trees. Above the willows there appeared a white smoke that now and again rose swirling into the sky.

'If only I knew where the regiment is,' said the vivandière in embarrassment. 'We mustn't go straight across this big field. Incidentally,' she said to Fabrizio, 'if you see an enemy soldier, stick the point of your sabre into him, don't go having fun hacking him down.'

At that moment, the canteen-woman caught sight of the four soldiers of whom we have just spoken. They were issuing from the wood into open country to the left of the road. One of them was on horseback.

'Now's your chance,' she said to Fabrizio. 'Hey there, ho!' she shouted to the one on horseback. 'So come over and drink a glass of brandy.' The soldiers came up.

'Where's the 6th Light?' she shouted.

'Over there, five minutes away, before the canal that runs along the willows. And Colonel Macon's just been killed.'

'You, do you want five francs for your horse?'

'Five francs, come off it, dearie, an officer's horse I'm going to be selling for five napoleons before quarter of an hour's up.'

'Give me one of your napoleons,' the vivandière said to Fabrizio. Then, going up to the soldier on horseback: 'Quickly, get down,' she said to him, 'here's your napoleon.'

The soldier got down, Fabrizio leapt joyfully up into the saddle, the vivandière untied the small portmanteau that was on the nag.

'So help me, you lot!' she said to the soldiers, 'do you think a woman should do all the work!'

But hardly had the captured horse felt the portmanteau before it began to rear up, and Fabrizio, good horseman though he was, needed all his strength to restrain it.

'A good sign,' said the vivandière, 'this gentleman isn't used to being tickled by a portmanteau.'

'A general's horse,' exclaimed the soldier who had sold it, 'a horse that's worth ten napoleons if he's worth a sou.'

'Here's twenty francs,' said Fabrizio, who was not altogether delighted at having a restless horse between his legs.

At that moment, a cannon ball struck the line of willows at an angle, and Fabrizio enjoyed the curious spectacle of all the small branches flying this way and that as if mown down by a scythe.

'Here, that's the artillery advancing,' said the soldier, taking his twenty francs. It might have been two o'clock.

Fabrizio was still enthralled by this curious spectacle when a troop of generals, followed by a score of hussars, galloped across one corner of the huge open expanse on the edge of which he was halted. His horse whinnied, reared two or three times in succession, then tossed its head violently against the bridle restraining it. All right, so be it! Fabrizio said to himself.

Given its head, the horse went off full tilt and joined the escort that was following the generals. Fabrizio counted four hats with braid on. Quarter of an hour later, from a few words spoken by a hussar next to him, Fabrizio understood that one of these generals was the celebrated Marshal Ney.[2] His happiness was at its height. He could not work out, on the other hand, which of the four generals was Marshal Ney. He would have given all he possessed to know, but remembered that he must not speak. The escort stopped in order to get over a wide ditch filled with water from the previous day's rain. It was lined by tall trees and marked the end on the left of the open country at the entrance to which Fabrizio had bought the horse. Almost all the hussars had dismounted. The side of the ditch was precipitous and very slippery, and the water was a good three or four feet below the level of the field. Fabrizio, in his delight, had his mind elsewhere, he was thinking more about Marshal Ney and about fame than about his horse, which was very excited and jumped into the canal, which caused the water to come spurting up to a considerable height. One of the generals was soaked through by the sheet of water and let out an oath: 'God damn the f****** animal!' Fabrizio felt deeply wounded by this insult. Can I demand satisfaction? he asked himself. Meanwhile, in order to prove that he was not so clumsy, he set his horse to climbing the opposite bank of the ditch. But it was precipitous and five or six feet high. He had to give up. He then went upstream, with his horse up to its neck in the water, and at last found a sort of watering place. By its gentle slope, he easily made his way into the field on the far side of the canal. He was the first man of the escort to appear there. He began to trot proudly along the bank. In the bottom of the canal the hussars were thrashing about, somewhat hampered by their situation, for in many places the water was five feet deep. Two or three horses took fright and sought to swim, which produced a terrible splashing. A sergeant saw the manoeuvre just executed by the raw recruit, who did not look much like a soldier. 'Upstream, there's a watering place to the left!' he cried, and gradually they all got across.

On reaching the far bank, Fabrizio had found the generals on their own. The sound of the cannon seemed to be getting louder. He could hardly hear the general he had soaked to the skin, who shouted in his ear: 'Where did you get that horse from?'

Fabrizio was so confused he replied in Italian: 'L'ho comprato poco fa.' (I bought it just now.)

'What did you say?' shouted the general.

But the din became so loud just then that Fabrizio was unable to answer. We will admit that our hero was very far from heroic at that moment, even if fear was only a secondary concern. He was shocked above all by the noise, which hurt his ears. The escort broke into a gallop. They were crossing a large stretch of ploughland, situated beyond the canal, and this field was strewn with corpses.

'The redcoats! The redcoats!' the hussars of the escort shouted joyfully, and at first Fabrizio did not understand. Finally he observed that, indeed, nearly all the corpses were dressed in red. One detail made him shudder in horror. He observed that many of these unfortunate redcoats were still alive. They were crying out, manifestly asking for succour, and no one was stopping to give them any. Our hero, very humanely, took all possible care to stop his horse from treading on any redcoats. The escort halted. Fabrizio, who was not paying sufficient attention to his soldierly duty, kept on galloping, his eye still on some wounded unfortunate.

'Halt will you, were you born yesterday!' the sergeant shouted. Fabrizio realized he was twenty paces ahead of the generals on the right, in the very direction where they were aiming their eyeglasses. Coming back to join the line of the other hussars who had remained a few paces to the rear, he

saw the fattest of the generals talking to his neighbour, likewise
a general, with an air of authority and almost of reprimand; he
was swearing. Fabrizio could not contain his curiosity and,
despite the advice never to speak, given him by his friend the
gaoler's wife, he arranged a very French, very correct short
sentence, saying to his next-door neighbour: 'Who is he, the
general who's giving his neighbour a piece of his mind?'

'That's the marshal, for God's sake!'

'What marshal?'

'Marshal Ney, you imbecile! I don't know, where've you
been serving up till now?'

Fabrizio, highly susceptible though he was, did not think to
be angered by this insult. Lost in childlike admiration, he gazed
on the famous prince of Moskova, the bravest of the brave.[3]

Suddenly, they set off at a fast gallop. A few moments later,
Fabrizio saw, twenty paces ahead, a ploughed field that was
being disturbed in a peculiar fashion. The bottoms of the furrows were full of water, and the very damp soil, which formed
the crest of the furrows, was flying off in small black lumps
going three or four feet up into the air. Fabrizio noticed this
odd effect as he passed. Then his thoughts reverted to the
marshal and his fame. He heard a sharp cry close beside him:
it was two hussars who had fallen, hit by grapeshot. By the
time he looked, they were already twenty paces from the escort.
What he found horrible was a horse all covered in blood that
was struggling on the ploughed soil, its feet caught up in its
own entrails. It was trying to follow the others; the blood was
flowing into the mud.

Ah, so I'm under fire at last! he told himself. I've seen firing!
he repeated with satisfaction. Now I'm a real soldier. At that
moment, the escort was going hell for leather, and our hero
realized that it was grapeshot that was making the earth fly
about in all directions. He looked in vain to see where the shots
were coming from; he could see the white smoke of the battery
a long way off but, in the midst of the regular, continuous
rumble the cannon were making, he seemed to be able to hear
shooting from much closer by. He could not understand it at all.

At that moment, the generals and the escort went down into

a narrow lane full of water, which was five feet lower down.

The marshal stopped, and looked through his eyeglass again. This time Fabrizio could inspect him at his leisure. He found that he had very fair hair, and a large red face. We don't have faces like that in Italy, he told himself. I, who am so pale and have chestnut hair, I shall never be like that, he added sadly. For him, these words meant: I shall never be a hero. He looked at the hussars. With only one exception, they all had yellow moustaches. If Fabrizio was staring at the hussars of the escort, they too were all staring at him. Their stares made him go red, and, to put an end to his embarrassment, he turned his head towards the enemy. There were strung-out lines of men in red, but what greatly surprised him was that these men seemed quite small. Their long files, which were regiments or divisions, seemed no taller than hedges. A line of red horsemen was trotting to get closer to the sunken lane that the marshal and escort had begun slowly to follow, splashing through the mud. The smoke prevented anything being made out in the direction in which they were advancing. At times, galloping men could be seen outlined against the white smoke.

Suddenly, from the direction of the enemy, Fabrizio saw four men arriving hell for leather. Ah, we're being attacked, he told himself. Then he saw two of the men speak to the marshal. One of the generals in the latter's retinue left at a gallop in the direction of the enemy, followed by two hussars from the escort and the four men who had just arrived. After a small canal which everyone got over, Fabrizio found himself next to a sergeant-major who looked a decent sort. I must talk to this one, he told himself, perhaps they'll stop looking at me. He pondered for a long while.

'Monsieur, this is the first time I've been present at a battle,' he said at last to the sergeant-major. 'But is this a real battle?'

'Sort of. But you, who are you?'

'I'm the brother of the wife of a captain.'

'And what's his name, this captain?'

Our hero was horribly embarrassed, he had not foreseen this question. Luckily, the marshal and escort were leaving again at the gallop. What French name shall I say? he thought. Finally, he remembered the name of the owner of the hotel he had lodged at in Paris. He moved his horse up to the sergeant-major's and shouted at the top of his voice: 'Captain Meunier!'

The other, not hearing properly because of the rumble of the cannon, replied: 'Oh, Captain Teulier? Well, he's been killed.' Bravo! said Fabrizio to himself. Captain Teulier: I have to show I'm upset. 'Oh, dear God!' he cried, and adopted a pitiful expression. They had left the sunken lane, they were crossing a small field, they went hell for leather, the grapeshot was coming down again, the marshal was making for a division of cavalry. The escort found itself among corpses and the wounded. But the sight of them no longer had the same effect on our hero; he had other things on his mind.

While the escort was halted, he caught sight of the canteen-woman's little vehicle and his fondness for that respectable body coming before anything else, he left at a gallop to join her.

'Stay here, you little s***!' shouted the sergeant-major.

What can he do to me here? thought Fabrizio, and continued galloping towards the canteen-woman. As he spurred on his horse, he had some hope that it was his kind-hearted canteen-woman from that morning. The horses and the little wagons bore a strong resemblance, but the proprietor was quite different, and our hero thought she looked decidedly nasty. As he came up, Fabrizio heard her saying: 'He was a fine-looking man though!' A thoroughly unpleasant spectacle awaited the new soldier. They were sawing through the thigh of a cuirassier, a good-looking young man of five feet ten. Fabrizio closed his eyes and drank four glasses of brandy one after the other.

'You're going at it, you young devil!' the canteen-woman exclaimed. The brandy gave him an idea: I need to buy the goodwill of my comrades, the hussars in the escort.

'Give me the rest of the bottle,' he said to the vivandière.

'But you know the rest costs ten francs,' she replied, 'on a day like today?'

As he rejoined the escort at a gallop: 'Ah, you're bringing us back a swig!' cried the sergeant-major. 'Is that why you deserted? Give it here.'

The bottle went round. The last one to take it tossed it into the air after drinking. 'Thanks, comrade!' he shouted to Fabrizio. Every eye looked at him benevolently, looks that lifted a hundred-pound weight from off Fabrizio's heart: it was one of those hearts too delicately made which have need of the friendship of those around them. At last, his companions no longer looked askance at him, there was a bond between them! Fabrizio took a deep breath, then in an easy tone said to the sergeant-major: 'So if Captain Teulier's been killed, where shall I be able to join my sister?' He saw himself as a young Machiavelli for saying Teulier so neatly instead of Meunier.

'That's what you'll find out this evening,' answered the sergeant-major.

The escort set off again, making for the infantry divisions. Fabrizio felt completely drunk; he had drunk too much brandy, he was rolling about on his saddle. He remembered very aptly a remark that his mother's coachman used to repeat: when you've been lifting your elbow, you need to look between your horse's ears and do as your neighbour is doing. The sergeant-major halted for a long time near several groups of cavalrymen, whom he made to charge. But for an hour or two our hero was scarcely aware of what was going on around him. He felt very weary and when his horse galloped he fell back into the saddle like a lump of lead.

Suddenly, the sergeant-major shouted to his men: 'Can't you see the Emperor then, you s***!' Immediately, the escort cried 'Vive l'Empereur!' at the tops of their voices. As may be imagined, our hero strained his eyes, but saw only generals galloping, they too followed by an escort. The long horse-tails that hung from the helmets of the dragoons in the retinue prevented him from making out the faces. So I wasn't able to see the Emperor on a field of battle, because of those accursed glasses of brandy! This reflection brought him fully awake.

They went down again into a lane filled with water; the horses wanted to drink.

'So was that the Emperor who went past?' he asked his neighbour.

'It certainly was, the one who didn't have braid on his coat.

How come you didn't see him?' his comrade replied good-
naturedly. Fabrizio felt a strong urge to gallop after the
Emperor's escort and join up with it. What happiness actually
to make war in the retinue of that hero! It was for that that
he'd come to France. I'm perfectly at liberty to, he told himself,
for after all I've no other reason for doing the service I am
doing than the will-power of my horse, who began galloping
to follow the generals.

What determined Fabrizio to remain was that his new comrades the hussars were looking well-disposed towards him. He
was beginning to see himself as the boon companion of all the
soldiers with whom he had been galloping for several hours
past. Between them and him he saw the noble fellowship of the
heroes of Tasso and Ariosto. If he joined the Emperor's escort,
there would be new acquaintances to be made. Perhaps they
would be hostile even, for these other horsemen were dragoons
and he was wearing a hussar's uniform, like everyone who was
following behind the marshal. The manner in which they were
now looking at him made our hero as happy as could be; he
would have done anything at all for his comrades; his soul and
his mind were in the clouds. Everything seemed to wear a
different look now that he was with friends, he was dying to
ask questions. But I'm still a bit drunk, he told himself, I must
remember the gaoler's wife. As they left the sunken lane he
noticed that the escort was no longer with Marshal Ney. The
general they were following was tall and thin, with a gaunt face
and terrifying eyes.

This general was none other than Count d'A***, the Lieutenant Robert of 15 May 1796. How happy he would have
been to find Fabrizio del Dongo!

For a long time now, Fabrizio had no longer been noticing
the earth flying up in black clods from the effects of the cannon
balls. They arrived behind a regiment of cuirassiers, he could
distinctly hear the case-shot striking the cuirasses and he saw
several men fall.

The sun was already very low, and was about to set when
the escort, emerging from a sunken lane, climbed a short slope
of three or four feet to enter ploughland. Fabrizio heard a

peculiar small noise quite close; he turned his head, four men
had fallen with their horses. The general himself had been
knocked over, but was getting up all covered in blood. Fabrizio
looked at the hussars who had been thrown to the ground.
Three were still twitching convulsively, the fourth was shouting:
'Pull me out from under here!' The sergeant-major and two or
three men had dismounted to help the general who, leaning
on his aide-de-camp, was trying to take a few steps. He was
attempting to get away from his horse, which was struggling
upside down on the ground and lashing out furiously with its
hooves.

The sergeant-major came up to Fabrizio. At that moment
our hero heard someone say behind him and right next to his
ear: 'It's the only one that can still gallop.' He felt himself seized
by the feet. They were raised at the same time as his body was
being supported underneath the arms. He was passed over the
rump of his horse, then allowed to slide down to the ground,
where he fell sitting.

The aide-de-camp took Fabrizio's horse by the bridle. The
general, aided by the sergeant-major, mounted and galloped
off. He was quickly followed by the six remaining men. Fabrizio
got up in a fury and began running after them shouting 'Ladri!
Ladri!' (Thieves! Thieves!) It was comic, to be running after
thieves in the middle of a battlefield.

The escort and the general, Count d'A***, soon vanished
behind a line of willow trees. Fabrizio, in a blind rage, also
came to the line of willows. He found himself hard up against
a very deep channel, which he crossed. Then, having got to the
other side, he began swearing when again catching a glimpse,
though a long way off, of the general and escort disappearing
into the trees. Thieves, thieves! he shouted, this time in French.
In despair, much less at the loss of his horse than at having
been betrayed, he let himself drop down on the bank of the
ditch, tired and dying of hunger. If his splendid horse had been
taken by the enemy, he would not have given it a thought, but
to find himself betrayed and robbed by the sergeant-major he
had liked so much and by the hussars he had looked on as his
brothers, that is what broke his heart. He could not be consoled

for such infamy and, leaning against a willow tree, he began weeping hot tears. He rid himself one by one of all his beautiful dreams of a sublime brotherhood of knights, like that of the heroes of *Jerusalem Delivered*.[4] To see death arriving was nothing, surrounded by heroic and tender souls, noble companions who shake you by the hand as you draw your last breath; but to preserve your enthusiasm surrounded by worthless scoundrels!!! Fabrizio was exaggerating, like any man roused to indignation. After a quarter of an hour of self-pity, he observed that the shot was beginning to come as far as the row of trees in whose shade he was musing. He stood up and tried to get his bearings. He looked at the fields bordered by a wide canal and the row of leafy willows: he thought he knew where he was. He noticed a body of infantrymen who were crossing the ditch and entering the fields, a quarter of a league ahead of him. I was about to fall asleep, he told himself. The thing is not to be taken prisoner. And he began to walk very quickly. As he advanced, he was reassured. He recognized the uniform, the regiments he feared being cut off by were French. He veered to the right to rejoin them. After the moral hurt of having been so shamefully betrayed and robbed, another hurt was making itself felt more keenly by the minute: he was dying of hunger! So it was with extreme delight that after having walked, or rather run for ten minutes, he noticed that the body of infantry, which was also going very quickly, had halted as if to take up position. A few minutes later, he found himself in the midst of the first soldiers.

'Comrades, can you sell me a morsel of bread?'

'Here, this one takes us for bakers!'

This cruel remark and the general guffawing that followed it crushed Fabrizio. So war was no longer the shared and noble impulse of souls in love with glory that he had imagined from Napoleon's proclamations! He sat down, or rather let himself drop on to the grass. He went very pale. The soldier who had spoken to him, and had stopped ten paces away to clean the percussion-lock of his gun with his handkerchief, came up and tossed him a piece of bread. Then, seeing that he did not pick it up, the soldier put a bit of the bread into his mouth. Fabrizio opened his eyes and ate the bread without having the strength to speak. When at last he looked about for the soldier to pay him, he found himself alone, the nearest soldiers had drawn a hundred paces off and were on the march. He got up automatically and followed them. He entered a wood. He was on the point of dropping with fatigue and was already looking around for a convenient spot. But to his immense pleasure, he recognized first the horse, then the vehicle and finally the canteen-woman from that morning! She ran up to him and was alarmed by his appearance.

'Keep walking, young man,' she said. 'Are you wounded then? And your beautiful horse?' So speaking, she led him towards her vehicle, into which she made him climb, supporting him under the arms. Hardly was he in the vehicle before our hero, overcome by tiredness, fell fast asleep.

CHAPTER 4

Nothing could wake him, not the musket-shots let off right next to the little wagon, nor the trotting of the horse, which the canteen-woman was whipping with all her might. The regiment, attacked without warning by swarms of Prussian cavalry, after having believed all day long in victory, was beating a retreat, or rather fleeing in the direction of France.

The colonel, a handsome young man, nicely 'got up', who had just succeeded Macon, was cut down. The major who replaced him in command, an old man with white hair, ordered the regiment to halt. 'F*** it all!' he said to the soldiers, 'in the days of the republic we waited to be forced by the enemy before we cleared off. Defend every inch of ground and get yourselves killed!' he cried, with an oath. 'It's the soil of the fatherland these Prussians are looking to invade now!'

The little wagon stopped, Fabrizio suddenly awoke. The sun had long since set; he was astonished to find it was almost dark. The soldiers were running this way and that in a confusion that greatly surprised our hero. He thought they looked shamefaced.

'So what's going on?' he said to the canteen-woman.

'Nothing at all. The fact is we're done for, young man. It's the Prussian cavalry that's cutting us down, that's all. That imbecile of a general thought it was our cavalry at first. Come on, look lively, help me repair Cocotte's trace, it's broken.'

A few musket-shots were loosed off ten yards away. Our hero, fresh and in good spirits, said to himself: But I haven't actually fought the whole day. I've only escorted a general. 'I have to fight,' he told the canteen-woman.

'Don't worry, you'll fight and more than you want! We've had it.'

'Aubry, my boy,' she shouted to a corporal who was passing, 'keep an eye on the little wagon from time to time.'

'Are you going to fight?' Fabrizio asked Aubry.

'No, I'm going to put my pumps on to go to the ball!'

'I'll follow you.'

'Take good care of the little hussar,' shouted the canteen-woman, 'the young townie's got guts.' Corporal Aubry walked without saying a word. Eight or nine soldiers joined him at a run, he led them behind a big oak tree surrounded by brambles. Once there, he positioned them on the edge of the wood, still without speaking, in a very extended line. Each one was a good ten paces from his neighbour.

'Now then, you lot,' said the corporal, and it was the first time he had spoken, 'don't go firing before the order, remember you've only got three cartridges.'

But what's going on then? Fabrizio wondered. Finally, when he found himself alone with the corporal, he said: 'I haven't got a gun.'

'Shut it! Go forward there, fifty paces in front of the wood, you'll find one of the poor soldiers from the regiment who've just been cut down. Take his cartridge-pouch and his gun. Don't go stripping one of the wounded, mind, take the cartridge-pouch and gun of one of them that's good and dead, and hurry, or you'll have our own men shooting at you.' Fabrizio ran off and quickly returned with a gun and cartridge-pouch.

'Load your gun and get over there behind that tree, and above all don't fire before I give the order ... God almighty!' said the corporal, breaking off, 'he doesn't even know how to load his weapon!' He helped Fabrizio while keeping on speaking. 'If an enemy horseman gallops up to cut you down, go around your tree and shoot only at point-blank range, once your horseman's three paces away. Your bayonet needs to be almost touching his uniform.'

'Throw away that great sabre,' exclaimed the corporal, 'do you want it to trip you up, for God's sake! What soldiers they're giving us these days!' So speaking, he took hold of the sabre himself and threw it angrily off into the distance.

'Clean the flint of your gun with your handkerchief. Haven't you ever fired a gun before?'

'I go hunting.'

'God be praised!' resumed the corporal with a deep sigh. 'Above all don't fire before I've given the order,' and he went off.

Fabrizio was overjoyed. At last, I'm actually going to fight, he told himself, to kill an enemy! This morning they were sending over grapeshot and all I did was expose myself to being killed: a mug's game. He looked all around him with an extreme curiosity. After a moment, he heard seven or eight musket-shots go off quite near by. But not receiving any order to fire, he kept still behind his tree. It was almost dark. He fancied he was lying in wait, hunting bears, in the Tramezzina mountains above Grianta. A huntsman's thought occurred to him. He took a cartridge from his pouch and removed the ball. If I see him, he said, I mustn't miss, and he poured this second ball into the barrel of his gun. He heard two shots fired right beside his tree. At the same time, he saw a horseman dressed in blue gallop past in front of him, going from right to left. He's not three paces away, he said to himself, but at that range I'm sure of my aim; he followed the rider carefully with the end of his gun and finally pressed the trigger. The horseman fell together with his horse. Our hero thought he was out hunting: he ran delightedly towards the game he had just brought down. He was already touching the man, who seemed to be dying, when, with incredible rapidity, two Prussian cavalrymen arrived to cut him down. Fabrizio fled at top speed towards the wood; to help him run, he threw away his gun. The Prussian cavalrymen were no more than three paces away when he reached a fresh plantation of small oak trees as thick as an arm and growing straight up, which bordered the wood. These small oaks halted the cavalrymen for a moment, but they got past and resumed their pursuit of Fabrizio into a clearing. They were once again on the verge of catching him, when he slipped between seven or eight large trees. At that moment, he almost had his face scorched by the flame of five or six musket-shots that went off in front of him. He lowered his head. As he was raising it again, he found himself face to face with the corporal.

'Did you kill yours?' Corporal Aubry said.

'Yes but I lost my gun.'

'It's not guns we're short of. You've done well, you old b***. You may look wet behind the ears but you've earnt your keep, and these soldiers here have just missed the two who were chasing you and coming straight at them. I didn't see them myself. And now we've got to be on our way and no hanging about. The regiment must be quarter of a league away and what's more there's a little bit of open country where we could be rounded up in a semicircle.'

As he spoke, the corporal was marching rapidly at the head of his ten men. Two hundred paces further on, on entering the small open field he had spoken of, they encountered a wounded general being carried by his aide-de-camp and a servant. 'You'll give me four men,' he said to the corporal in a feeble voice, 'I've got to be transported to the ambulance. My leg is shattered.'

'Go and f*** yourself,' replied the corporal, 'you and all the generals. You've all betrayed the Emperor today.'

'What,' said the general, enraged, 'you're ignoring my orders! Do you know I'm General Count B***, commanding your division,' etc., etc. The speech-making continued. The aide-de-camp threw himself on the soldiers. The corporal thrust his bayonet into his arm, then went off with his men at the double. 'Would they were all like you,' the corporal said repeatedly, swearing, 'with their arms and legs shattered! Conceited pipsqueaks! All sold out to the Bourbons[1] and betraying the Emperor!' Fabrizio was stunned to hear this terrible accusation.

Around ten in the evening, the little band rejoined the regiment at the entrance to a large village which formed several very narrow streets, but Fabrizio observed that Corporal Aubry avoided speaking to any of the officers. 'There's no going on!' the corporal exclaimed. All the streets were choked with infantry, horsemen and above all artillery wagons and trailers. The corporal reported to where three of the streets emerged. After going twenty paces he had to stop. Everyone was swearing and getting angry.

'One more traitor giving orders!' exclaimed the corporal. 'If the enemy has the wit to encircle the village we'll all be taken prisoner like dogs. Follow me, you men.' Fabrizio looked. There were now only six soldiers with the corporal. Through a large open doorway they entered a vast farmyard; from the farmyard they passed into a stable, whose small door gave them entry to a garden. They were lost in it for a moment, wandering this way and that. But finally, getting through a hedge, they found themselves in a vast expanse of buckwheat. In less than half an hour, guided by shouts and the general hubbub, they had regained the high road beyond the village. The ditches alongside the road were full of abandoned guns. Fabrizio chose one. But the road, although very wide, was so choked with fleeing men and carts that in half an hour the corporal and Fabrizio had barely advanced five hundred paces. It was said the road led to Charleroi. As the village clock was striking eleven: 'Let's cut across country again,' cried the corporal. The little band was now made up of only three soldiers, the corporal and Fabrizio. When they were a quarter of a league from the high road:

'I can't go any further,' said one of the soldiers.

'Me neither,' said another.

'Just what I want to hear! We're all in the same boat,' said the corporal. 'But obey me and you'll be all right.' He saw five or six trees along a small ditch in the middle of an immense expanse of wheat. 'To the trees!' he said to his men. 'Lie down here,' he added when they got there, 'and above all not a sound. But before we go to sleep, who's got any bread?'

'I have,' said one of the soldiers.

'Give it here,' said the corporal, authoritatively. He divided the bread into five pieces and took the smallest.

'Quarter of an hour before daybreak,' he said as he ate, 'you'll have the enemy cavalry on your backs. The main thing is not to let yourselves be cut down. One man on his own is done for with cavalry on his back in these great open spaces, five on the other hand can get away. Stay with me, close

together, fire only at point-blank range, and tomorrow evening
I undertake to get you to Charleroi.' The corporal woke them up
an hour before first light. He made them reload their weapons,
the din on the high road was continuing and had lasted throughout the night: it was like the sound of a torrent heard in the
distance.

'They're like sheep running away,' said Fabrizio to the corporal, with an innocent air.

'Shut it, will you, what d'you know!' said the indignant
corporal; and the three soldiers who comprised his whole army
along with Fabrizio looked at the latter angrily, as if he had
blasphemed. He had insulted the nation.

That's rich! thought our hero. I've already noticed that with
the viceroy in Milan. Oh no, they don't run away! You're not
allowed to speak the truth with these French when it upsets
their vanity. But let them give me dirty looks, I don't care, and
I have to make them understand that. They were still marching
five hundred paces from the torrent of fugitives that covered
the high road. A league further on, the corporal and his band
crossed a lane that was about to rejoin the high road, where a
lot of soldiers were lying down. Fabrizio bought quite a good
horse which cost him forty francs, and from among all the
sabres thrown away higgledy-piggledy he carefully chose a long
straight one. Since we're told to stick it into them, he thought,
this one here's the best. Thus equipped, he set his horse at a
gallop and soon rejoined the corporal, who had gone on ahead.
He braced himself on his stirrups, took the scabbard of his
straight sabre in his left hand and said to the four Frenchmen:
'Those men running away on the high road look like a flock of
sheep . . . they're marching like frightened sheep . . .'

It was no good Fabrizio emphasizing the word *sheep*, his
comrades no longer remembered having been provoked by the
word an hour before. And here is revealed one of the contrasts
between the French and the Italian character: the Frenchman is
no doubt the more fortunate, he glides over life's events and
does not bear grudges.

We shall not hide the fact that Fabrizio was very pleased with
himself after having talked about *sheep*. They exchanged small

talk as they went on. Two leagues further on, the corporal, still greatly surprised at not seeing the enemy cavalry, said to Fabrizio: 'You're our cavalry, gallop to that farm on the little hillock, ask the peasant if he's willing to *sell* us some breakfast, make it clear there are only five of us. If he hesitates, give him five francs in advance out of your money but don't worry, we'll take the silver back after breakfast.'

Fabrizio looked at the corporal, saw he was imperturbably serious and wore an air of true moral superiority; he obeyed. Everything transpired as the commander-in-chief had foreseen, except that Fabrizio insisted they did not take back by force the five francs he had given the peasant. 'The money's mine,' he told his comrades, 'I'm not paying for you, I'm paying for the oats he gave my horse.'

Fabrizio's French pronunciation was so bad that his comrades thought they detected a tone of superiority in his words. They were deeply offended and from then on a duel loomed in their minds for the end of the day. They found him very different from themselves, which offended them. Fabrizio on the other hand was beginning to feel very friendly towards them.

They had been advancing without saying anything for two hours when the corporal, looking at the high road, exclaimed delightedly: 'Here's the regiment!' They were soon on the road, but alas, there were not even two hundred men around the eagle. Fabrizio's eye soon lighted on the vivandière. She was advancing on foot, red-eyed and weeping from time to time. Fabrizio looked in vain for the little wagon and Cocotte.

'Looted, lost, stolen,' cried the vivandière in answer to our hero's glances. The latter, without a word, got down from his horse, took it by the bridle and said to the vivandière: 'Get up.' She did not have to be told twice.

'Shorten the stirrups,' she said.

Once firmly established on the horse, she began to recount to Fabrizio all the night's disasters. After an account that lasted for ever, but was listened to avidly by our hero who, truth to tell, understood not the first thing, but felt a fondness for the vivandière, the latter added: 'And to think it was Frenchmen who ransacked me, beat me, injured me . . .'

'What, not our enemies?' said Fabrizio with an innocent air that lent charm to his pale, serious, handsome face.

'You're so stupid, my poor boy!' said the vivandière, smiling in the midst of her tears, 'But for all that, you're very nice.'

'And such as you see him, he brought down his Prussian all right,' said Corporal Aubry, who, in the midst of the milling crowd, found himself by chance on the other side of the horse the canteen-woman was riding. 'But he's proud,' the corporal went on . . . Fabrizio made a gesture. 'And what's your name?' the corporal went on, 'For after all, if there's a report I shall want to name you.'

'My name is Vasi,' replied Fabrizio, pulling a strange face, 'that's to say *Boulot*,' he added, hastily catching himself up.

Boulot had been the name of the owner of the movement order the gaoler's wife in B*** had handed him. Two days earlier, he had studied it carefully on the march, for he was beginning to use his head a little and was no longer so surprised by things. Apart from the hussar Boulot's movement order, he had kept safe the Italian passport according to which he could aspire to the noble name of Vasi, dealer in barometers. When the corporal reproached him for being stuck-up, he had been on the point of answering: 'Me, stuck-up! Me, Fabrizio Valserra, Marchesino del Dongo, who consents to bear the name of a Vasi, a dealer in barometers!'

While he was reflecting and telling himself: I really have to remember my name is Boulot, or watch out for the prison that threatens to be my fate, the corporal and the canteen-woman had exchanged a few words on his account.

'Don't accuse me of sticking my nose in,' said the canteen-woman, ceasing to address him by the familiar *tu*. 'It's for your own good I'm asking you questions. Who are you, really?'

Fabrizio did not at first reply. He reckoned that he would never be able to find more devoted friends to ask for advice, and he had a pressing need of advice. We're about to enter a place of war, the governor will want to know who I am, and beware the prison if I let them see by my answers I don't know anyone in the 4th Regiment of Hussars whose uniform I'm wearing! In his capacity as an Austrian subject, Fabrizio knew all about the importance that was attached to a passport. The members of his family, although of the nobility and religious, and although they belonged to the winning side, had been harassed a score of times over the matter of their passports. He was thus not in the least offended by the question addressed to him by the canteen-woman. But as, before answering, he was searching for the clearest French expressions, the canteen-woman, spurred on by a keen curiosity, added, in order to get him to speak: 'Corporal Aubry and I are going to give you some good advice on how to go about things.'

'I don't doubt it,' replied Fabrizio. 'My name is Vasi and I'm from Genoa. My sister, a celebrated beauty, married a captain. Since I'm only seventeen, she made me come to join her, to show me France and educate me a little. Not finding her in Paris, and knowing that she was with the army, I came here, I searched for her everywhere without being able to find her. The soldiers were surprised by my accent and had me arrested. I had money at that time, I gave some to the gendarme, who handed me a movement order and a uniform and told me: "Clear off and swear you'll never mention my name."'

'What was his name?' asked the canteen-woman.

'I gave my word,' said Fabrizio.

'He's right,' said the corporal. 'The gendarme's a wretch, but our comrade mustn't name him. And what's the name of the captain, your sister's husband? If we know his name we'll be able to look for him.'

'Teulier, captain in the 4th Hussars,' replied our hero.

'So,' said the corporal, with a certain shrewdness, 'from your foreign accent, the soldiers mistook you for a spy?'

'An infamous word!' cried Fabrizio, eyes aflame. 'I who so love the Emperor and the French! It was that insult that annoyed me the most.'

'It was no insult, that's where you're wrong. The soldiers' mistake was quite natural,' replied Corporal Aubry gravely.

He then explained with much pedantry that in the army you must belong to a unit and wear a uniform, failing which you will quite simply be taken for a spy. 'The enemy lets lots of them loose on us; everyone's a traitor in this war.' The scales fell from Fabrizio's eyes, he realized for the first time that he had been in the wrong in everything that had happened to him these past two months.

'But the lad must tell us everything,' said the canteen-woman, whose curiosity was being more and more strongly aroused. Fabrizio obeyed. Once he had finished: 'In fact,' the canteen-woman said to the corporal, wearing a serious expression, 'this child isn't a soldier at all. We're going to fight a filthy war now we've been beaten and betrayed. Why should he risk his neck *gratis pro Deo*?'

'Especially when he doesn't even know how to load his gun,' said the corporal, 'either for a volley or in his own time. It was me that loaded the shot that brought the Prussian down.'

'What's more, he lets all and sundry see his money,' added the canteen-woman. 'He'll have the whole lot stolen the moment he's no longer with us.'

'The first cavalry NCO he meets will confiscate it for his own benefit,' said the corporal, 'to treat himself to a glass, and maybe they'll recruit him for the enemy, because everyone's a traitor. The first person to come along is going to order him to follow, and he'll follow. He'd do better to come into our regiment.'

'No thanks, corporal!' cried Fabrizio quickly. 'It's more comfortable on horseback, and anyway I don't know how to load a gun, and you've seen I can handle a horse.'

Fabrizio was very proud of this little speech. We shall not give any account of the long debate concerning his future destiny which took place between the corporal and the canteen-woman. Fabrizio noticed that as they debated these people repeated all the particulars of his history three or four times: the suspicions of the soldiers, the gendarme selling him a movement order and a uniform, the way in which the day before he had found himself forming part of the marshal's escort, the Emperor seen galloping, the slaughtered horse, etc., etc.

With a woman's inquisitiveness, the canteen-woman kept returning to the manner in which he'd been dispossessed of the fine horse she'd made him buy. 'You felt yourself gathered up by the feet, they passed you gently over your horse's tail, and they sat you down on the ground!' Why go on repeating what we all three of us know perfectly well? Fabrizio said to himself. He did not yet know that in France this is how the common people go in search of ideas.

'How much money have you got?' the canteen-woman said all of a sudden. Fabrizio did not hesitate to answer; he was confident of this woman's nobility of soul: that is the good side of France.

'In all, I may have thirty gold napoleons and eight or nine five-franc écus left.'

'In that case, you're as free as air!' exclaimed the canteen-woman. 'Get yourself out from among this rabble of an army. Jump off to one side, take the first road you find that's been cleared a bit on your right hand. Keep your horse going hard, away from the army all the time. The first opportunity you get, buy some civilian clothes. Once you're eight or ten leagues away and can no longer see any soldiers, take the stage and go and rest for a week and eat steak in some nice town. Don't tell anyone you were with the army. The gendarmes'll pick you up as a deserter. And though you're very nice, young man, you're not yet smart enough to answer the gendarmes. As soon as you've got some town clothes on your back, tear your move-ment order into a thousand pieces and go back to your real name. Say you're Vasi. And where should he say he comes from?' she asked the corporal.

'From Cambrai on the Escaut, it's a nice town, quite small, d'you understand, where there's a cathedral and Fénelon.'[2]

'That's it,' said the canteen-woman. 'Never say you were at the battle, don't breathe a word about B***, or the gendarme who sold you the movement order. When you want to go back into Paris, make for Versailles first of all and go through the Paris tollgate on that side, strolling, on foot, like someone out walking. Sew your napoleons into your trousers. And above all, when you have to pay for something, don't let them see anything except the money you need for paying with. What makes me sad is that they're going to fleece you, they'll pinch everything you have. And what will you do once you've no money, you who don't know how to go about things,' etc.

The good canteen-woman went on speaking for a long time yet. The corporal backed up her advice with nods of the head, unable to get a word in. All of a sudden, the crowd that had been covering the high road first quickened its pace, then, in a trice, crossed the small ditch that lined the road on the left and began fleeing as fast as their legs could carry them. 'The Cossacks! The Cossacks!'[3] the cry went up all around.

'Take your horse back!' cried the canteen-woman.

'God forbid!' said Fabrizio. 'Gallop! Fly! I'm giving it to you. Do you want the wherewithal to buy a small wagon? Half of what I have is yours.'

'Take your horse back, I tell you!' cried the canteen-woman angrily, and she began preparing to dismount. Fabrizio drew his sabre: 'Hold on tight!' he shouted, and he applied the flat of his sabre two or three times to the horse, causing it to break into a gallop and follow the fugitives.

Our hero looked at the high road. Previously, three or four thousand individuals had been swarming there, pressed together like peasants following a procession. After the word *Cossacks*, he could see precisely no one. The fugitives had abandoned shakos, guns, sabres, etc. The astonished Fabrizio climbed into a field to the right of the path, twenty or thirty feet higher up. He looked along the road in both directions and across the open country; he saw no sign of any Cossacks. Funny people, these French, he said to himself. Since I have to go to the right, I might as well get going here and now. It's possible these people have a reason for running off that I don't know about. He picked up a gun, checked that it was loaded, stirred the powder in the cartridge-cap, cleaned the flint, then chose a well-stocked cartridge-pouch and looked again in every direction. He was absolutely alone in the middle of this plain previously covered with people. In the far distance, he could see the fugitives who were beginning to disappear behind the trees, still running. It's all very strange! he said to himself. And recalling the manoeuvre employed by the corporal the day before, he went and sat down in the middle of a wheat-field. He did not move off because he wanted very much to see his good friends, the canteen-woman and Corporal Aubry, again.

In the wheat, he confirmed that he was now down to eighteen
napoleons, instead of thirty as he had thought. But he still had
some small diamonds that he had put into the lining of his
hussar's boots that morning, in the gaoler's wife's room in
B***. He concealed the napoleons as best he could, while
pondering this very sudden disappearance. Is it a bad omen for
me? he asked himself. What mainly upset him was not having
put the question to Corporal Aubry: have I really been present
at a battle? He fancied that he had, but his happiness would
have been at its height had he been sure.

All the same, he told himself, I was present bearing the name
of a prisoner, I had a prisoner's movement order in my pocket
and, what's more, his coat on my back! That's what bodes ill
for the future; what would Father Blanes have said? And the
wretched Boulot died in prison! It's all very ominous; destiny
will lead me into prison. Fabrizio would have given anything
to know whether the hussar Boulot was in fact guilty. Summoning up his memories, he fancied that the gaoler's wife in B***
had told him that the hussar had been picked up not only for
some silver spoons, but also for having stolen a peasant's cow
and beaten the peasant mercilessly. Fabrizio did not doubt that
he would one day be put in prison for a misdemeanour having
some connection with that of the hussar Boulot. He thought of
his friend, Father Blanes; what would he not have given to be
able to consult him? Then he remembered that he had not
written to his aunt since leaving Paris. Poor Gina! he said to
himself, and had tears in his eyes, when he suddenly heard a
slight noise close by. It was a soldier feeding corn to three horses
whose bridles he had removed and who looked dead from
hunger. He was holding them by the snaffle. Fabrizio rose like
a partridge, the soldier took fright. Our hero saw this and
yielded to the pleasure of playing the role of hussar for a
moment.

'One of those horses belongs to me, you f***!' he cried. 'But
I'm willing to give you five francs for your trouble bringing it
to me here.'

'What do you take me for?' said the soldier. Fabrizio took
aim at him from six paces away.

'Let go of the horse or I'll blast you!'

The soldier had his gun slung across his shoulder, and he twisted round so as to recover it.

'The slightest movement and you're a dead man!' cried Fabrizio running at him.

'All right, give me the five francs and take one of the horses,' said the soldier in confusion, after casting a longing glance at the high road where there was absolutely no one. Fabrizio, holding his gun up high with his left hand, threw him three five-franc coins with his right.

'Get down or you're a dead man . . . Put a bridle on the black one and move away with the others. I'll blast you if you stir.'

The soldier obeyed, muttering. Fabrizio went up to the horse and passed the bridle into his left hand, without taking his eyes off the soldier, who was slowly moving away. Once Fabrizio saw he was fifty paces away, he leapt nimbly on to the horse. Hardly was he up and fumbling for the right-hand stirrup with his foot, when he heard a musket-ball whistle close beside him. It was the soldier who had fired at him. Beside himself with anger, Fabrizio began to gallop at the soldier, who fled as fast as his legs would carry him, and soon Fabrizio saw him mounted on one of the two horses and galloping off. Good, he's out of range, he told himself. The horse he had just bought was magnificent, but seemed to be dying of hunger. Fabrizio returned on to the high road, where there was still not a living soul. He crossed it and set his horse at a trot in order to reach a small fold in the ground on the left where he hoped to find the canteen-woman. But once at the top of the small rise, he could see, more than a league away, only a few isolated soldiers. It's written I shan't see her again, he told himself with a sigh, a brave and good woman! He reached a farm that he had caught sight of in the distance to the right of the road. Without dismounting, and having paid in advance, he got them to give his poor horse, so famished that he was gnawing the manger, some oats. An hour later, Fabrizio was trotting along the high road, still in the vague hope of meeting with the canteen-woman again, or at least Corporal Aubry. Keeping going and looking to this side and that, he came to a marshy river crossed by quite a narrow wooden bridge. Before the bridge, to the right of the road, was an isolated house bearing the sign Le Cheval Blanc. There I shall dine, Fabrizio told himself. There was a cavalry officer with his arm in a sling at the entrance to the bridge. He was on horseback and wore a very unhappy expression. Ten paces away, three cavalrymen on foot were filling their pipes.

This lot look as if they'd certainly want to buy my horse for even less than it cost me, Fabrizio told himself. The wounded officer and three pedestrians watched him come up and seemed to be waiting for him. I shouldn't cross by this bridge, but follow the line of the river to the right, that would be the route the canteen-woman would advise to keep out of trouble ... Yes, our hero said to himself, but if I turn tail, tomorrow I shall feel thoroughly ashamed. Besides, my horse has good legs, the officer's is probably tired. If he tries to get me off I shall gallop. So arguing, Fabrizio *gathered* his horse and advanced at as slow a pace as possible.

'Come forward then, hussar,' shouted the officer authoritatively.

Fabrizio advanced a few paces and halted.

'Do you want to take my horse from me?' he shouted.

'Not in the least. Forward.'

Fabrizio looked at the officer: he had white moustaches and the most honest expression imaginable. The handkerchief that supported his left arm was soaked in blood, and his right hand too was wrapped in a bloodstained bandage.

It's the ones on foot that are going to jump at my horse's bridle, Fabrizio told himself. But taking a closer look, he saw that the ones on foot also were wounded.

'In the name of honour,' said the officer, who wore a colonel's epaulettes, 'stay here on sentry-go, and tell all the dragoons, chasseurs and hussars you see that Colonel Le Baron is in the inn you see there, and that I order them to come and join me.' The old colonel appeared broken-hearted. His very first words had won over our hero, who made a sensible reply: 'I'm very young, monsieur, for them to be willing to listen to me. I'll need a written order signed by you.'

'He's right,' said the colonel looking hard at him. 'Write the order, La Rose, you've got a right hand.'

Without speaking, La Rose pulled a small parchment notebook from his pocket, wrote a few lines and, tearing the sheet out, handed it to Fabrizio. The colonel repeated the order to the latter, adding that after two hours on duty he would be relieved, as was proper, by one of the three wounded cavalrymen who were with him. Having said which, he went into the inn with his men. Fabrizio watched them go and remained motionless at the end of his wooden bridge, so struck had he been by the mournful and silent grief of these three individuals. They're like genii who've been enchanted, he told himself. Finally, he unfolded the piece of paper and read the order couched as follows:

'Colonel Le Baron of the 6th Dragoons, commanding the 2nd Brigade of the 1st Cavalry Division of the 14th Corps, orders all cavalrymen, dragoons, chasseurs and hussars not to cross the bridge, but to join him at the Cheval Blanc inn, near the bridge, where his headquarters are.

'From headquarters, next to the La Sainte bridge, 19 June 1815.

'Pp Colonel Le Baron, wounded in the right arm, and on his orders, Sergeant-Major La Rose.'

Fabrizio had been standing sentry at the bridge for barely half an hour when he saw six mounted chasseurs arrive and three on foot. He conveyed the colonel's order to them. 'We'll be back,' said four of the mounted chasseurs and passed over the bridge at a smart trot. Fabrizio then spoke to the two others. During the discussion, which grew heated, the three men on foot crossed the bridge. One of the two mounted chasseurs who had stayed ended by asking to see the order again, and carried it off, saying: 'I'm going to take it to my comrades, who won't fail to come back. Hold on and wait for them.' And he galloped off; his comrade followed him. All this was done in a flash.

Fabrizio, furious, called one of the wounded soldiers, who appeared at one of the Cheval Blanc's windows. The soldier, on whom Fabrizio could see a sergeant-major's insignia, came down and shouted as he approached: 'Sabre in your hand, there, you're standing sentry!' Fabrizio obeyed, then said: 'They've taken away the order.'

'They're in an ugly mood after yesterday's affair,' answered the other, with a mournful expression. 'I'm going to give you one of my pistols. If they force you again, fire into the air, I'll come, or the colonel himself will appear.'

Fabrizio had clearly seen the sergeant-major's start of surprise at the announcement that the order had been taken away. He realized he had suffered a personal insult and promised himself he would not be taken advantage of a second time.

Armed with the sergeant-major's saddlebow pistol, Fabrizio had proudly resumed his sentry duty when he saw seven mounted hussars coming up: he had placed himself so as to block the bridge, he passed on the colonel's order, they appeared very annoyed and the boldest of them attempted to get across. Fabrizio, following the sensible precept of his friend the vivandière who, the previous morning, had told him to thrust and not hack with his long straight sword, lowered the point and made as if to jab it into the man who was trying to force a passage.

'Aha, he wants to kill us, the boy soldier!' cried the hussars; 'as if they hadn't killed enough of us yesterday.' They all drew their sabres at once and fell upon Fabrizio. He gave himself up for dead. But he remembered the sergeant-major's surprise and did not want to be held in contempt a second time. As he fell back on his bridge, he attempted to use the point of his sword. He looked so comical as he brandished this big cavalryman's long straight sword, which was far too heavy for him, that the hussars soon realized who they had to deal with. They then tried, not to wound him, but to cut his jacket away from his body. In this way, Fabrizio received two or three light sabre blows on his arms. As for him, still faithful to the canteen-woman's precept, he went at them as hard as he could with his sword-point. Unfortunately, one of these thrusts wounded a hussar in the hand. Exceedingly angry at being caught by such a soldier, he countered with a fierce thrust which caught Fabrizio in the top of the thigh. The blow only carried because our hero's horse, far from fleeing the skirmish, seemed to take pleasure in it and threw itself at the assailants. The latter, seeing Fabrizio's blood running down his right arm, were afraid of having taken the game too far and, pushing him towards the left-hand parapet of the bridge, they galloped off. As soon as Fabrizio had a moment of respite, he fired his pistol into the air to alert the colonel.

Four mounted hussars and two on foot, from the same regiment as the others, were coming towards the bridge but were still two hundred paces away when the pistol shot went off. They stared long and hard at what was happening on the bridge, and imagining that Fabrizio had fired at their comrades, the four on horseback swooped down on him at a gallop, sabres held high. It was a veritable charge. Colonel Le Baron, alerted by the pistol shot, opened the door of the inn and dashed on to the bridge just as the galloping hussars arrived, and notified them of the order to halt himself.

'There are no colonels here any more,' cried one of them and urged on his horse. The exasperated colonel broke off from remonstrating with them and, with his wounded right arm, seized the horse's reins on the near side.

'Halt, you're no sort of soldier,' he said to the hussar. 'I know you, you're from Captain Henriet's company.'

'Well, let the captain himself give me the order! Captain Henriet was killed yesterday,' he sniggered, 'and you can go and f*** yourself!'

Saying which, he tried to force his way past and pushed the old colonel, who fell sitting on the roadway on the bridge. Fabrizio, who was two paces further on on the bridge, but facing in the direction of the inn, urged on his horse, and as the breast of the assailant's horse knocked the colonel down, he not having let go of the reins on the near side, the indignant Fabrizio thrust at the hussar with the point of his sword. Luckily, the hussar's horse, feeling itself being tugged towards the ground by the bridle that the colonel had hold of, made a sideways movement, so that the long blade of Fabrizio's heavy cavalry sword slid along the hussar's waistcoat and its full length passed beneath his eyes. Furious, the hussar turned round and, with all his strength, dealt Fabrizio a blow that slashed his sleeve and went deep into his arm. Our hero fell.

One of the dismounted hussars, seeing the two defenders of the bridge on the ground, saw his chance, jumped on Fabrizio's horse and tried to take charge of it, setting it at a gallop on to the bridge.

The sergeant-major, running from the inn, had seen his colonel fall and believed he was seriously wounded. He ran after Fabrizio's horse and plunged the point of his sword into the small of the thief's back. The latter fell. Seeing only the sergeant-major now on the bridge on foot, the hussars crossed at the gallop and made rapidly off. The one who was on foot ran off into the countryside.

The sergeant-major came up to the wounded men. Fabrizio had already got up. He was not in much pain but he had lost a great deal of blood. The colonel got up more slowly. He was dazed by his fall, but had not received any wound.

'The only thing that's giving me pain,' he told the sergeant-major, 'is the old wound in my hand.'

The hussar wounded by the sergeant-major was dying.

'Devil take him!' cried the colonel. 'But,' he told the sergeant-major and the two other cavalrymen who had run up, 'spare a thought for this young fellow whom I put at risk when I shouldn't have. I'm going to remain on the bridge myself to try to stop these madmen. Take the young fellow to the inn and dress his arm. Take one of my shirts.'

CHAPTER 5

This whole episode had lasted less than a minute. Fabrizio's wounds were nothing; they bound up his arm in strips cut from the colonel's shirt. They wanted to arrange a bed for him on the first floor of the inn: 'But while I'm there being spoilt on the first floor,' Fabrizio said to the sergeant-major, 'my horse, which is in the stables, will be bored all on its own and will go off with another master.'

'Not bad for a conscript,' said the sergeant-major; and Fabrizio was installed on good fresh straw in the same manger to which his horse was attached.

Then, since Fabrizio felt very weak, the sergeant-major brought him a bowl of mulled wine and engaged him briefly in conversation. A few compliments included in this conversation sent our hero into a seventh heaven.

Fabrizio did not wake until the following day at first light. The horses were giving long whinnies and making a terrible din. The stables were filling with smoke. At first, Fabrizio could not begin to understand what all the noise was about and did not even know where he was. Finally, half suffocated by the smoke, he got the feeling that the house was ablaze. In the twinkling of an eye he was out of the stables and on horseback. He looked up. The smoke was coming billowing out from the two windows above the stables, and the roof was covered by swirling black smoke. A hundred or more fugitives had arrived during the night at the Cheval Blanc; all of them were shouting and swearing. The five or six whom Fabrizio could see close by seemed completely drunk. One of them tried to stop him and shouted: 'Where are you taking my horse?'

Once he was a quarter of a league away, Fabrizio looked back. No one was following him, the house was in flames. Fabrizio recognized the bridge, he thought of his wound, and his arm, gripped tightly by the bandages, felt very hot. And what will have become of the old colonel? He gave up his shirt to dress my arm. Our hero was as cool as could be this morning. The quantity of blood he had lost had rid him of the entire romantic side of his nature.

To the right! he told himself, and on our way. He began quietly to follow the course of the river which, after passing under the bridge, flowed towards the right of the road. He remembered the good canteen-woman's advice. She was so friendly, he said to himself, and so open a nature!

After keeping going for an hour, he felt very weak. Oh lord, am I going to pass out? he asked himself. If I pass out, they'll steal my horse and perhaps my clothes, and with my clothes my jewels. He no longer had the strength to guide his horse and he was trying to keep his balance when a peasant, hoeing in a field beside the road, saw how pale he was and came to offer him a glass of beer and some bread.

'Seeing you so pale, I thought you were one of the wounded from the big battle,' said the peasant. Never was succour more timely. Just as Fabrizio was munching on the piece of black bread, his eyes began to hurt when he looked ahead of him. Once he had recovered somewhat, he thanked him. 'And where am I?' he asked. The peasant informed him that three quarters of a league further on was the market town of Zonders, where he would be very well looked after. Fabrizio arrived in the town, not really knowing what he was doing, and thinking only at each step of not falling from his horse. He saw a large open door. He entered, it was the Étrille inn. The good mistress of the house at once hurried forward, an enormous woman. She called for help in a voice faltering with pity. Two young girls helped Fabrizio to set foot on the ground. Hardly was he off his horse before he fainted clean away. A surgeon was called, he was bled. On that day and those that followed, Fabrizio had no clear idea of what they were doing to him, he slept almost without a break.

The sword wound in his thigh was threatening to become infected. Once he had his wits about him, he asked them to look after his horse and repeated over and over that he would pay them well, which gave offence to the good mistress of the inn and her daughters. For a fortnight he had been well looked after and was beginning to think straight once again when one evening he saw that his hostesses wore a very concerned expression. Soon a German officer came into the room. To answer him, they used a language Fabrizio did not understand. But he could easily see that they were talking about him. He feigned sleep. A little time later, once he thought that the officer might have left, he called his hostesses: 'Didn't that officer come to put me on a list and take me prisoner?' The innkeeper agreed that he had, with tears in her eyes.

'Right, there's money in my dolman!' he exclaimed, sitting up on his bed. 'Buy me some civilian clothes and tonight I will leave on my horse. You've already saved my life once by taking me in just as I was about to fall dying in the street. Save it again by giving me the means to join my mother.'

At that moment, the innkeeper's daughters started to burst into tears. They were fearful for Fabrizio and, since they scarcely understood French, they approached his bed to ask him some questions. They debated in Flemish with their mother, but their eyes were forever turning pityingly to our hero. He thought he understood that his escape might put them seriously at risk but that they were very willing to take the chance. He thanked them effusively, holding their hands in his. A local Jew supplied a complete suit of clothes, but when he brought it round, towards ten in the evening, the young ladies recognized, comparing the coat with Fabrizio's dolman, that it would need to be much shortened. They at once got down to work; there was no time to be lost. Fabrizio pointed out a few napoleons hidden in his clothes, and asked his hostesses to sew them into the garments that had just been bought. As well as the clothes, a fine pair of new boots had been brought. Fabrizio did not hesitate to ask these kind girls to cut the boots unceremoniously open at the point he indicated, and they hid the small diamonds in the lining of the new boots.

By a singular effect of the loss of blood and the resulting weakness, Fabrizio had almost completely forgotten French. He addressed his hostesses in Italian, who themselves spoke a Flemish dialect, so that they understood one another almost solely by signs. When the girls, perfectly disinterested though they were, saw the diamonds, their enthusiasm for him knew no bounds. They thought he was a prince in disguise. Aniken, the younger and more naive of the two, embraced him without being asked. Fabrizio, for his part, found them charming. And towards midnight, when the surgeon had allowed him a little wine, on account of the journey he was about to undertake, he almost did not feel like leaving. Where could I be better off than here? he said. Nevertheless, at around two in the morning, he got dressed. Just as he was leaving his room, the good innkeeper informed him that his horse had been led away by the officer who had come and inspected the house a few hours earlier.

'Ah, the swine!' cried Fabrizio, with an oath. 'From a wounded man!' He was not enough of a philosopher, this young Italian, to remember at what price he himself had bought the horse.

A tearful Aniken informed him that they had hired a horse for him. She would rather he was not leaving; the farewells were tender. Two tall young men, relatives of the good inn-keeper, lifted Fabrizio on to the saddle. During the journey they supported him on horseback, while a third went a few hundred paces ahead of the little procession, to see whether there might not be a suspect patrol in the lanes. After advancing for two hours, they stopped at the house of a cousin of the innkeeper of the Étrille. No matter what Fabrizio might say, the young men who were accompanying him refused steadfastly to leave. They claimed they knew the paths through the woods better than anyone.

'But tomorrow morning, when they find out I've escaped, and you're not to be seen in the neighbourhood, your absence will put you at risk,' said Fabrizio.

They set off once more. Luckily, once it began to get light, the plain was covered in thick fog. At around eight in the

morning, they arrived near a small town. One of the young
men went off separately, to see whether the posthorses had
been stolen. The postmaster had had time to get them out of
sight, and to recruit some broken-down nags with which he
equipped his stables. They went to fetch two horses from the
marshes where they had been hidden and, three hours later,
Fabrizio climbed into a small cabriolet, dilapidated but drawn
by two good posthorses. Some of his strength had returned.
The moment of separation from the young men, the innkeeper's
relatives, was truly pathetic. No matter what friendly pretext
Fabrizio was able to invent, they refused to accept any money.

'In your state, monsieur, you have greater need of it than us,'
these brave young men kept replying. Finally, they went off
with letters, in which Fabrizio, somewhat fortified by the jolting
along the road, had tried to let his hostesses know all that he
felt for them. Fabrizio wrote with tears in his eyes, and there
was certainly love in the letter addressed to the young Aniken.

Nothing untoward occurred during the remainder of the
journey. When he reached Amiens, the sword wound in his
thigh was causing him great pain. The country surgeon had not
thought to open up the wound and, despite the bleedings, an
infection had formed. During the fortnight that Fabrizio spent
in the inn at Amiens, kept by a fawning and avaricious family,
the allies[1] invaded France, and Fabrizio became like another
man, so profoundly did he reflect on the things that had been
happening to him. He remained a child on only one point: was
what he had seen a battle? And, secondly, was that battle
Waterloo? For the first time in his life he took pleasure in
reading. He was always hoping to find in the newspapers, or in
the accounts of the fighting, some description that would enable
him to recognize the places he had passed through in the retinue
of Marshal Ney, and later with the other general. During his
stay in Amiens, he wrote nearly every day to his good friends
at the Étrille. As soon as he was healed, he went to Paris. At his
old hotel he found twenty letters from his mother and his aunt,
begging him to come back as soon as possible. A last letter
from Countess Pietranera struck a certain enigmatic note that
worried him greatly, and this letter rid him of all his tender

daydreams. His was a nature that required only a few words to start foreseeing the worst disasters. His imagination then undertook to depict these disasters in the most dreadful detail.

'Be very careful not to sign the letters you write giving us your news,' the countess had told him. 'On your return, you mustn't come to Lake Como straight away. Stop in Lugano, on Swiss territory.' He was to arrive in that small town under the name of Cavi. At the principal inn he would find the countess's footman, who would indicate what he needed to do. His aunt ended with these words: 'Hide the folly you have committed by every means possible, and above all don't keep any papers on you, printed or written. In Switzerland you will be surrounded by the friends of Santa-Margarita.* If I have enough money,' the countess told him, 'I shall send someone to Geneva, to the Hôtel des Balances, and you will have details that I can't write but which you need to know before you arrive. But in God's name, not one day more in Paris, you'd be recognized there by our spies.' Fabrizio's imagination began to picture the strangest things and he was incapable of any pleasure other than that of trying to guess what his aunt might have to tell him that was so strange. Twice, while crossing France, he was stopped; but he was able to extricate himself. He owed these uncomfortable moments to his Italian passport and to the strange profession of dealer in barometers, which scarcely fitted with his youthful face and with having his arm in a sling.

Finally, in Geneva, he found one of the countess's men who told him, for his part, that he, Fabrizio, had been denounced to the police in Milan as having taken to Napoleon proposals drawn up by a vast conspiracy organized in the former kingdom of Italy. If such had not been the object of his journey, said the denunciation, what was the point of adopting an assumed name? His mother would try to prove what was true, i.e.:

1. That he had never left Switzerland;
2. That he had left the castle without warning following a quarrel with his older brother.

* M. Pellico[2] has made this name European; it is that of the street in Milan where the palace and prisons of the police are to be found.

Fabrizio derived a feeling of pride from this account. So I was a sort of ambassador to Napoleon! he told himself. I had the honour of speaking to that great man. Would it were so! He remembered that his grandfather seven times removed, the grandson of the one who came to Milan as a follower of the Sforzas, had the honour of having his head cut off by the duke's enemies, who surprised him as he was on his way to Switzerland bearing proposals for recruiting soldiers from the cantons that were for hire. In his mind's eye he could see the engraving referring to this exploit, set into the family genealogy. Questioning the footman, Fabrizio discovered he had been outraged by a circumstance which he finally let slip, despite the countess's express order several times repeated not to mention it. It was Ascanio, his older brother, who had denounced him to the Milan police. This cruel piece of information sent our hero into something like a fit of madness. To get into Italy from Geneva one goes via Lausanne. He wanted to set off there and then, on foot, and do ten or eleven leagues, even though the stage from Geneva to Lausanne was due to leave in two hours' time. Before leaving Geneva, he got into a quarrel in one of the cheerless local cafés with a young man who was, so he claimed, giving him strange looks. Which was only too true, the young Genevan, phlegmatic, reasonable and with money alone on his mind, thought he was mad. On entering, Fabrizio had cast furious glances in every direction, then spilt the cup of coffee he had been served over his trousers. As they quarrelled, Fabrizio's first impulse came straight out of the sixteenth century: instead of raising the question of a duel with the young Genevan, he drew his dagger and hurled himself at him to stab him with it. In this moment of passion, Fabrizio forgot all he had learnt about the rules of honour and reverted to instinct, or, rather, to memories of his earliest childhood.

The confidential agent whom he found in Lugano enraged him further by giving him fresh details. Because Fabrizio was popular at Grianta, no one would have named him and but for the loveable conduct of his brother, everyone would have pretended to believe he was in Milan, and the attention of the police in that town would never have been drawn to his absence.

'There's no doubt the customs men have your description,' his aunt's envoy said, 'and if we follow the main road, you'll be arrested at the Lombardy–Venice frontier.'

Fabrizio and his men knew every narrowest path in the mountains separating Lugano fron Lake Como. They disguised themselves as hunters, that is to say as smugglers, and since there were three of them and they wore an air of considerable determination, the customs men they encountered thought only of saluting them. Fabrizio so arranged things as to reach the castle only towards midnight. At that hour, his father and all the footmen who wore powder had long been in bed. He climbed down without difficulty into the deep moat and got into the castle through the small window in a cellar. There, he was awaited by his mother and his aunt; soon his sisters came hurrying in. The outbursts of affection and the tears followed one another at length, and they were only just starting to talk sense when the first glimmerings of dawn came to warn these people who saw themselves as unfortunate that time was flying.

'I hope your brother won't suspect you've arrived,' said Signora Pietranera. 'I've hardly spoken to him since his fine escapade, and his self-regard did me the honour of being greatly piqued. This evening at supper I condescended to address him. I needed to find an excuse to conceal the wild delight that might have made him suspicious. Then, once I'd realized he was as proud as could be of this supposed reconciliation, I took advantage of his delight to make him drink to excess, and he certainly won't have thought of setting an ambush so as to keep on plying his trade as a spy.'

'Our hussar must be hidden in your apartment,' said the marchesa, 'he can't leave straight away. At this early stage, we're not sufficiently in command of our reason, and the important thing is to find the best way of throwing the terrible Milan police off the scent.'

This idea was taken up. But the marchese and his elder son noticed, the next day, that the marchesa was constantly in her sister-in-law's room. We shall not pause to describe the transports of tenderness and of joy which that day still excited these happy individuals. Italian hearts are, far more than our own, tormented by suspicion and the wild ideas presented to them by a fiery imagination, but in return their joys are more intense and last longer. On that day, the countess and marchesa were not in their right minds. Fabrizio was obliged to begin all his stories over again. Finally, it was decided to go and hide their common joy in Milan, so difficult did it seem to elude for any longer the marchese and his son Ascanio's police.

They took the household's usual boat to go to Como. To have acted otherwise would have aroused endless suspicion. But on arriving at the harbour in Como, the marchesa remembered that she had left papers of the highest importance at Grianta. She hurriedly sent the boatmen back for them, who were thus unable to pass any comment on how the two ladies employed their time in Como. Hardly had they arrived before they hired at random one of the carriages which wait conveniently near the tall medieval tower that rises above the Milan gate. They left that same instant, without the coachman having had time to speak to anyone. A quarter of a league from the town, they came across a young man of the ladies' acquaintance who was out shooting and who, obligingly, since they did not have a man with them, was very willing to act as an escort as far as the gates of Milan, to which his shooting would take him. All went well, and the ladies were engaged in the most cheerful conversation with the young traveller, when at a detour which the road makes in order to go round the charming hill and wood of San Giovanni, three policemen in disguise jumped at the horses' bridle. 'Oh, my husband has betrayed us!' cried the marchesa, and fainted. A sergeant-major who had hung back somewhat stumbled up to the carriage, and said in a voice that seemed to be coming from the tavern: 'The commission I must execute pains me, but I'm arresting you, General Fabio Conti.'

Fabrizio thought the sergeant-major was playing a bad practical joke on him by calling him 'general'. You'll pay for this, he told himself. He kept his eye on the disguised policemen, looking for the right moment to jump down from the carriage and take off across country.

The countess smiled, on the off-chance, as I believe, then said to the sergeant-major: 'But my dear sergeant-major, is it this child of sixteen you're taking to be General Conti?'

'Aren't you the general's daughter?' said the sergeant-major.

'There you see my father,' said the countess, pointing at Fabrizio. The policemen burst into uncontrollable laughter.

'Show your passports and no arguing,' replied the sergeant-major, riled by the general merriment.

'These ladies never take them to go to Milan,' said the coachman, with a cool, philosophical expression. 'They've come from their castle in Grianta. This is Signora the Countess Pietranera, that's Signora the Marchesa del Dongo.'

The sergeant-major, thoroughly disconcerted, moved to the head of the horses and conferred there with his men. The conference had been going on for a good five minutes when Countess Pietranera asked the gentlemen to allow the carriage to be moved forward a few paces and placed in the shade; the heat was stifling, although it was only eleven o'clock in the morning. Fabrizio, who was looking very attentively all around him, seeking for the means of escape, saw, emerging from a small cross-country track and arriving covered in dust on the high road, a young girl of fourteen or fifteen who was crying shyly under her handkerchief. She came forward on foot between two uniformed policemen and, three paces behind her, also between two policemen, walked a tall, gaunt man affecting a dignified attitude like a prefect following a procession.

'Where did you find them then?' said the sergeant-major, now completely drunk.

'Escaping across the fields, and not a passport to be seen.'

The sergeant-major seemed to lose his head completely. He had five prisoners in front of him instead of the two he needed. He drew a few paces off, leaving only one man to guard the prisoner, who was trying to look dignified, and another to stop the horses from moving forward.

'Stay,' the countess told Fabrizio, who had already jumped to the ground, 'it's all going to be sorted out.'

A gendarme was heard to exclaim: 'What's it matter if they don't have passports, they're a good prize all the same!' The sergeant-major did not seem quite so sure. The name of Countess

Pietranera was causing him some concern, he had known the general, of whose death he was unaware. The general's not the man not to take his revenge if I arrest his wife out of turn, he said to himself.

During this long-drawn-out deliberation, the countess had got into conversation with the young girl who was on foot in the dust on the roadway beside the barouche. She had been struck by her beauty.

'The sun will be bad for you, signorina. This good soldier,' she added, speaking to the gendarme placed at the head of the horses, 'will certainly allow you to get into the carriage.'

Fabrizio, who was prowling round the carriage, came up to help the girl get in. The latter was already jumping on to the footrest, her arm supported by Fabrizio, when the imposing man, who was six paces behind the carriage, shouted in a voice made gruff by the wish to be dignified: 'Stay on the roadway, don't get into a carriage that does not belong to you.'

Fabrizio had not heard this order. The girl, instead of getting into the barouche, sought to get down again, and, Fabrizio continuing to support her, she fell into his arms. He smiled, she blushed scarlet. They stayed looking at each other for a moment after she had disengaged herself from his arms.

She would be a charming prison companion, Fabrizio told himself. What profound thoughts beneath that brow! She would know how to love.

The sergeant-major approached with an air of authority: 'Which of these ladies is named Clelia Conti?'

'I am,' said the girl.

'And I,' exclaimed the elderly man, 'I am General Fabio Conti, chamberlain to His Highness monsignor the prince of Parma. I find it quite out of order that a man of my sort should be hunted down like a robber.'

'The day before yesterday, on embarking in the harbour at Como, did you not send the inspector of police who had asked you for your passport packing? Well, today he's preventing you from taking an excursion.'

'I was already moving off with my boat, I was in a hurry, there was a storm coming; a man without a uniform shouted to me from the jetty to return to harbour, I told him my name and continued on my way.'

'And this morning, you escaped from Como?'

'A man like myself does not take a passport to go from Milan to visit the lake. This morning, in Como, I was told I'd be arrested at the gate; I came out on foot with my daughter. I was hoping to find some vehicle along the road that would take me as far as Milan, where my first call for sure will be to lodge my complaint with the general commanding the province.'

The sergeant-major seemed relieved of a great burden. 'Very well, general, you have been arrested, and I'm going to take you to Milan. And you, who are you?' he said to Fabrizio.

'My son,' answered the countess. 'Ascanio, son of Major-General Pietranera.'

'Without a passport, signora countess?' said the sergeant-major, much mollified.

'At his age he's never taken one. He never travels alone, he's always with me.'

During this exchange, General Conti was standing more and more on his injured dignity with the policemen.

'Cut the speeches,' said one of them, 'you're under arrest, that's enough.'

'You'll be very lucky,' said the sergeant-major, 'if we agree to your hiring a horse from some peasant or other. Otherwise, despite the dust and the heat, and the title of chamberlain of Parma, you'll march very well on foot, in the middle of our horses.'

The general began swearing. 'Will you shut up!' the gendarme went on. 'Where's your general's uniform? Can't the first man who comes along claim to be a general?'

The general became all the angrier. Meanwhile, things were going much better inside the barouche.

The countess had got the policemen behaving as if they were her own people. She had just given one of them an écu to go and fetch some wine and especially some cold water, from a hut that could be seen two hundred paces away. She had found the time to calm Fabrizio down, who had wanted at all costs to run off into the woods that covered the hill. 'I've got good pistols,' he said. She persuaded the irritated general to let his daughter get up into the carriage. The general, who liked to talk about himself and his family, took the opportunity to inform the ladies that his daughter was only twelve years old, having been born in 1803, on 27 October. But so much good sense did she have, everyone took her to be fourteen or fifteen.

An altogether common man, the countess's eyes said to the marchesa. Thanks to the countess, everything was sorted out after an hour's discussion. A gendarme, who it turned out had business to attend to in the nearby village, hired out his horse to General Conti after the countess had told him: 'You'll get ten francs.' The sergeant-major left on his own with the general. The other policemen remained under a tree accompanied by four enormous bottles of wine, a kind of small demi-john, which the gendarme sent to the hut had brought back, aided by a peasant. To return to Milan, Clelia Conti was authorized by the worthy chamberlain to accept a place in the ladies' carriage, and no one had any thought of arresting the son of the gallant General Count Pietranera. After the first few moments given over to courtesies and to comments about the minor incident that had just ended, Clelia Conti remarked the barely suppressed enthusiasm with which a lady as beautiful as the countess spoke to Fabrizio: she was certainly not his mother. Her attention was excited above all by repeated allusions to something heroic, foolhardy and in the highest degree dangerous that he had recently done. But for all her intelligence, the young Clelia could not guess what it was.

She looked with astonishment on the young hero, whose eyes seemed still to be radiating all the heat of the action. He for his part was a little inhibited by the very singular beauty of this twelve-year-old girl, and his glances made her blush.

A league before arriving in Milan, Fabrizio said that he was going to visit his uncle, and took his leave of the ladies.

'If ever I extricate myself from this affair,' he told Clelia, 'I shall come to see the beautiful paintings in Parma, and then will you deign to remember this name, Fabrizio del Dongo?'

'Wonderful!' said the countess; 'so that's how you go about preserving your incognito! Signorina, deign to remember that this scapegrace is my son and his name is Pietranera, not del Dongo.'

That evening, very late, Fabrizio re-entered Milan by the Renza gate, which leads to a fashionable promenade. The dispatching of the two servants into Switzerland had exhausted the marchesa and her sister's very sparse savings. Fortunately, Fabrizio still had a few napoleons and one of the diamonds, which it was decided they should sell.

The ladies were much liked and knew everyone in the town. The personages of most weight in the Austrian and religious party went and spoke in Fabrizio's favour to Baron Binder, the chief of police. These gentlemen could not imagine, they said, how anyone could take seriously the escapade of a child of sixteen who quarrels with an older brother and abandons the paternal home.

'My job is to take everything seriously,' Baron Binder, a sensible and unhappy man, answered mildly. He was at that time setting up the famous Milan police force, and had pledged to prevent a revolution like that of 1740, which drove the Austrians out of Genoa. The Milan police, which has since become so celebrated through the adventures of Messrs Pellico and Andryane,[3] were not cruel exactly, they merely executed severe laws rationally and without mercy. The Emperor Francis II[4] wished to strike terror into these overbold Italian imaginations.

'Give me,' Baron Binder repeated to Fabrizio's protectors, '*proven* indications day by day of what the young Marchesino del Dongo has been doing. Let us take him from the moment of his departure from Grianta, on 8 March, up until his arrival, yesterday evening, in this town, where he has been hiding in one of the rooms of his mother's apartment, and I am ready to treat him as the friendliest and most mischievous of the young men in the town. If you cannot supply me with the young man's itinerary for every day following his departure from Grianta, however distinguished his birth and whatever the respect I bear towards the friends of his family, is my duty not to have him arrested? Must I not hold him in prison until he has given me proof that he did not take messages to Napoleon on behalf of

a few malcontents who may exist in Lombardy among the
subjects of His Imperial and Royal Majesty? Observe further,
gentlemen, that if the young del Dongo succeeds in justifying
himself on that score, he will remain guilty of having gone
abroad without a regularly issued passport, and moreover of
adopting a false name and knowingly making use of a passport
issued to a mere workman, that's to say from a class so far
below that to which he belongs.'

This cruelly reasonable declaration was accompanied by all
the marks of deference and respect that the chief of police owed
to the Marchesa del Dongo's high position, and to that of the
important personages who had come to intervene on her behalf.

The marchesa was in despair when she learnt of Baron
Binder's response.

'Fabrizio is going to be arrested,' she exclaimed, weeping,
'and once in prison, God knows when he will come out! His
father will disown him!'

Signora Pietranera and her sister-in-law held counsel with
two or three close friends and, for all that they could say, the
marchesa was quite insistent that her son should leave the very
next night.

'But you can easily see,' said the countess, 'that Baron Binder
knows your son is here. He's not an unkind man.'

'No, but he wants to please the Emperor Francis.'

'But if he thought it would do his career good to throw
Fabrizio into prison, he'd be there already. Making him run
away shows we're defying him and will be damaging.'

'But admitting to us that he knows where Fabrizio is is saying
to us: make him leave! No, I shan't live as long as I'm able to
repeat to myself: in a quarter of an hour's time my son may be
between four walls! Whatever Baron Binder's ambitions,' added
the marchesa, 'he thinks it useful to his personal position in
this country to make a show of consideration for a man of my
husband's rank, I see proof of that in the singular open-
heartedness with which he admitted that he knows where to
lay his hands on my son. What's more, the baron obligingly
spelt out the two contraventions of which Fabrizio stands
accused following his brother's ignominious denunciation. He

explained that those two contraventions carry a prison sentence. Isn't that saying to us that if we prefer exile, the choice is ours?'

'If you choose exile,' the countess went on repeating, 'we shall never see him again as long as we live.' Fabrizio, present throughout the whole of this exchange, along with one of the marchesa's old friends, now a counsellor at the court set up by Austria, was very much of the opinion that he should get away. And in fact, that same evening, he left the palace hidden in the carriage that was taking his mother and his aunt to La Scala. The coachman, whom they did not trust, went to spend some time as usual in the tavern and while the lackey, a trustworthy man, was looking after the horses, Fabrizio, disguised as a peasant, slipped out of the carriage and left the town. The next morning he crossed the frontier with the same good fortune, and a few hours later was installed on an estate his mother owned in Piedmont, near Novara, to be precise at Romagnano, where Bayard[5] was killed.

It may be imagined how attentively the ladies listened to the performance once they had arrived in their box at La Scala. They had gone there only so as to be able to consult several of their friends belonging to the liberal party, whose appearance at the Palazzo del Dongo might have been misinterpreted by the police. In the box, it was decided to make a fresh approach to Baron Binder. There could be no question of offering this magistrate a sum of money, he was a perfectly honest man and in any case the ladies were very poor; they had forced Fabrizio to take all that remained from what they had got for the diamond.

It was most important none the less to know what the baron's final word was. The countess's friends reminded her about a certain Canon Borda, a most amiable young man, who in the old days had sought to pay court to her, and in a somewhat crude fashion. Finding himself unsuccessful, he had denounced her friendship with Limercati to General Pietranera, whereupon he had been chased away as a scoundrel. But these days the canon played games of tarot every evening with Baroness Binder, and was naturally a close friend of the husband. The countess determined on the horribly painful step of going to see the canon; and early the next morning, before he left home, she had herself announced.

When the canon's one servant uttered the name of the Countess Pietranera, the man was affected to the extent of losing his voice. He made no attempt to repair the untidy state of his very casual attire. 'Show her in and leave us,' he said in a faint voice. The countess entered; Borda went down on his knees.

'It's in this position that an unhappy madman must receive your orders,' he said to the countess, who that morning, carelessly dressed in her semi-disguise, was irresistibly appealing. Her deep unhappiness at Fabrizio's exile, the violence she was doing herself by appearing at the house of a man who had behaved treacherously towards her, all conspired to give her eyes an unbelievable brilliance.

'It's in this position that I wish to receive your orders,' exclaimed the canon, 'for it's clear that you have some service to ask of me, otherwise you would not have honoured the poor house of an unhappy madman with your presence. Once upon a time, transported by love and jealousy, he behaved towards you like a coward, when he saw he could hold no attraction for you.'

The words were sincere and all the better for the canon now being a man of great influence. The countess was touched to the point of tears. Fear and humiliation had frozen her soul, but instantly pity and a degree of hope succeeded them. In a twinkling, she passed from a state of deep misery into one almost of happiness.

'Kiss my hand,' she told the canon, holding it out to him, 'and get up.' (One needs to know that in Italy, the familiar form of address can indicate simple friendship, just as easily as tenderer feelings.) I have come to ask for a pardon for my nephew Fabrizio. Here is the complete, unvarnished truth, such as one tells it to an old friend. At sixteen and a half he has just committed a notable act of folly. We were at the castle in Grianta, on Lake Como. One evening, at seven o'clock, we learnt, via a boat from Como, of the Emperor's having landed in the Golfe de Juan. The next morning, Fabrizio left for France, after having got them to give him the passport of one of his friends among the common people, a dealer in barometers called Vasi. Since he doesn't exactly look like a dealer in barometers, he'd hardly gone ten leagues in France before he was arrested on account of his appearance. His impulsive enthusiasm in bad French seemed suspicious. After some time, he escaped and managed to reach Geneva. We sent to meet him in Lugano . . .'

'Meaning Geneva,' said the canon with a smile.

The countess finished her story.

'I shall do everything that is humanly possible for you,' the canon went on, effusively. 'I place myself entirely at your disposal. I will even do what I shouldn't,' he added. 'Tell me, what am I to do the moment my poor parlour is deprived of this heavenly apparition, which marks an epoch in my life's history?'

'You must go to Baron Binder's and tell him that you have loved Fabrizio since he was born, that he was born in the days when you used to come to us and that in short, in the name of the friendship he accords you, you must beg him to set all his spies to verifying whether, before his departure for Switzerland, Fabrizio had even the briefest of meetings with any of the liberals he's having watched. Provided the baron is being well served, he'll see that all we have here is sheer youthful silliness. You know that, in my beautiful apartment in the Palazzo Dugnani, I had engravings of the battles won by Napoleon. It was from reading the captions on those engravings that my nephew learnt to read. From the age of five, my poor husband explained those battles to him. We put my husband's helmet on his head, the boy dragged around his big sabre. Well, one fine day he learns that my husband's god, the Emperor, is back in France. He sets off to join him, hare-brained as he is, but he didn't manage it. Ask the baron what penalty he wishes to impose for that moment of madness.'

'I was forgetting one thing,' exclaimed the canon, 'you will see that I am not altogether undeserving of the pardon you are

granting me. Here,' he said, searching among his papers on the
table, 'is the denunciation of that infamous *col-torto*,* see,
signed Ascanio Valserra del Dongo, who started this whole
business. I took it yesterday evening from the police bureau and
went to La Scala, in the hope of finding someone who normally
goes into your box, through whom I could get it to you. A copy
of this document has been in Vienna long since. There's the
enemy we have to combat.' The canon read the denunciation
together with the countess, and it was agreed that, in the course
of the day, he would get a copy made for her by someone
trustworthy. It was with a joyful heart that the countess
returned to the Palazzo del Dongo.

'That one-time villain couldn't have been more of a gentleman,' she told the marchesa. 'This evening at La Scala, at ten
forty-five by the theatre clock, we shall send everyone out of
our box, we shall extinguish the candles, we shall close our
door and, at eleven, the canon himself will come and tell us
what he's been able to do. That's what we thought was the
least risky for him.'

The canon was a highly intelligent man. He took good care
not to miss his appointment. At it, he displayed unfailing kindness and a complete openness of heart rarely to be met with
except in countries where vanity does not dominate every other
feeling. His denunciation of the countess to General Pietranera,
her husband, was one of the great sources of remorse in his life,
and he had found a means of cancelling out that remorse.

That morning, once the countess had left his house: there she
is, making love with her nephew, he had told himself bitterly,
for he was far from cured. Haughty though she is, to have come
to me here! ... When that poor Pietranera died, she rejected
my offers of service with horror, though they were very courteous and very well presented to her by Colonel Scotti, her
former lover. For the lovely Pietranera to be living on fifteen
hundred francs! added the canon, walking vigorously about the
room. Then to go and live in the castle at Grianta with an
abominable *seccatore*,[6] that Marchese del Dongo! It all becomes

* A hypocrite.

clear now! It's a fact that the young Fabrizio is very attractive, tall, well built, always a smile on his face . . . and better than that, a certain look, full of soft sensuality . . . a Correggio[7] face, added the canon bitterly.

The difference in age . . . not too great . . . Fabrizio born after the entry of the French, around '98 I fancy. The countess may be twenty-seven, twenty-eight, couldn't be prettier or more adorable. In this land so fertile in beauty, she beats the lot. Marini, Gherardi, Ruga, Aresi, Pietragrua,[8] she wins out of all those women. They were living happily, hidden away on beautiful Lake Como, when the young man wanted to go off and join Napoleon . . . There are still souls in Italy! Whatever they may do! My beloved country! . . . No, continued this heart inflamed by jealousy, impossible otherwise to explain her being resigned to go off and vegetate in the country, with the distasteful sight every day, at every mealtime, of the terrible face of the Marchese del Dongo, plus the vile, pasty countenance of the Marchesino Ascanio, who'll be worse than his father! . . . Very well, I shall serve her honestly. At least I'll have the pleasure of seeing her other than at the end of my lorgnette.

Canon Borda explained the matter very clearly to the ladies. Basically, Binder could not have been better disposed. He was charmed that Fabrizio should have made off before the orders that might come from Vienna; for Binder did not have the authority to decide anything, he was awaiting his orders concerning this affair as for all the others. He sent every day to Vienna an exact copy of all the information, then he waited.

It was necessary that during his exile in Romagnano, Fabrizio:

1. Should not fail to go to Mass every day, take for his confessor a man with his wits about him, devoted to the cause of the monarchy, and confess at the bar of penitence to only the most irreproachable sentiments;

2. Was not to associate with any man passing as intelligent and, should occasion arise, must speak of rebellion with horror and as never being permissible;

3. Was never to let himself be seen at the café, must never read any newspapers other than the official gazettes of Turin

and Milan. In general, to show a dislike of reading, never to read, especially anything published after 1720, with the exception at most of the novels of Walter Scott;

4. Finally, added the canon with a hint of malice, he must above all pay court openly to one or other of the pretty women in those parts, from among the nobility obviously. That will show that he does not have the gloomy, discontented temperament of a budding conspirator.

Before going to bed, the countess and the marchesa wrote two interminable letters to Fabrizio in which they explained with a charming anxiety all the advice given them by Borda.

Fabrizio had no desire at all to conspire. He loved Napoleon and, in his capacity as a nobleman, thought himself intended to be happier than other men and found the bourgeoisie ridiculous. He had not opened a book since schooldays, when he had read only books provided by the Jesuits. He installed himself a short distance from Romagnano, in a magnificent palace, one of the masterpieces of the architect San Micheli.[9] But it had not been lived in for thirty years, so the rain came into all the rooms and not one window would close. He took over the horse of the steward, which he rode unceremoniously all day long. He never spoke but he thought. The advice to take a mistress from a family of ultras he found amusing and he followed it to the letter. He chose for confessor a scheming young priest who wanted to become a bishop (like the confessor at the Spielberg[10]).* But he did three leagues on foot and wrapped himself in a mystery he believed was impenetrable, in order to read the *Constitutionnel*,[11] which he found sublime. 'It's as good as Alfieri and Dante!' he would often exclaim. Fabrizio had it in common with the youth of France that he paid more attention to his horse and his newspaper than to his bien-pensant mistress. But there was no room as yet in that firm and innocent soul for 'the imitation of others', and he made no friends in the society of the stolid market town of Romagnano.

* See the curious memoirs of M. Andryane, as entertaining as a work of fiction and which will survive, like Tacitus.

His simplicity was taken for haughtiness; they did not know what to say about his character. 'He's a younger son fed up with not being the older one,' said the parish priest.

CHAPTER 6

We shall admit in all sincerity that Canon Borda was not altogether wrong to feel jealousy. On his return from France, Fabrizio appeared to Countess Pietranera's eyes as a handsome stranger whom she had once seen a lot of. Had he spoken of love, she would have loved him. Did she not already have a passionate and as it were boundless admiration for his conduct and his person? But Fabrizio had embraced her with such an effusion of innocent gratitude and simple affection that she would have been horrified at herself had she looked for some other sentiment in this almost filial affection. The fact is, the countess told herself, a few friends who knew me six years ago at the court of Prince Eugène may still find me pretty or even young, but for him I am a respectable woman ... and, if we must stop shilly-shallying and not spare my self-esteem, an old woman. The countess was under an illusion as to the stage of her life she had reached, but not in the way that women of the common sort are. At his age, anyway, she added, one somewhat exaggerates the ravages of time. A man further on in life ...

The countess, who was walking about in her salon, stopped in front of a mirror, then smiled. One needs to know that for the past few months Signora Pietranera's heart had come under serious attack from a singular personage. Shortly after Fabrizio's departure for France, the countess, who, without altogether admitting it to herself, was becoming much preoccupied with him, had fallen into a profound melancholy. All her occupations seemed unrewarding, and, dare I say it, to lack savour. She told herself that Napoleon, in his desire to attach the peoples of Italy to him, would take Fabrizio for an aide-de-camp. 'He's lost to me!' she exclaimed, weeping. 'I shan't see him again. He will write to me, but what shall I be to him ten years from now?'

It was in this frame of mind that she made a trip to Milan; she was hoping to find there more direct news of Napoleon and, who knows, perhaps as a by-product news of Fabrizio. Without admitting it to herself, this active soul was becoming very weary of the monotonous life she led in the country. It's stopping oneself from dying, it's not living, she told herself. To see those *powdered* figures every day, her brother, her nephew Ascanio, their footmen! What would the excursions on the lake be like without Fabrizio? Her sole consolation she had derived from the affection that joined her to the marchesa. But for some time now, she had begun to find this intimacy with Fabrizio's mother, older than she was and despairing of life, less agreeable.

Such was the peculiar situation of Signora Pietranera. With Fabrizio gone, she hoped for little from the future. Her heart had need of consolation and of novelty. Once in Milan, she developed a passion for the fashionable opera. She went and shut herself away alone, for hours on end, at La Scala, in the box of General Scotti, her former lover. The men whom she tried to meet with so as to get news of Napoleon and his army seemed to her vulgar and coarse. Having returned home, she improvised on her piano until three o'clock in the morning. One evening at La Scala, in the box of one of her woman friends, where she had gone in search of news from France, she was introduced to Count Mosca, a minister in Parma. He was an agreeable man who talked about France and Napoleon in such a way as to give her heart fresh reasons to hope or to fear. She went back to the box the next day. This intelligent man reappeared and throughout the performance she enjoyed talking to him. Not since Fabrizio's departure had she had such an animated evening. The man who had amused her, Count Mosca della Rovere Sorezana, was at that time minister of war, police and finance to the famous prince of Parma, Ernest IV, so celebrated for his severities, which the liberals of Milan called cruelties. Mosca might have been forty or forty-five. He had large features, no trace of self-importance and a simple, cheerful expression which told in his favour. He would have been very handsome too, had a quirk of his prince not forced him to wear powder in his hair as a guarantee of his having the right political ideas. Because they have little fear of offending anyone's vanity, people are soon on intimate terms in Italy and making personal remarks. For which usage, the corrective is not to see one another again if offence has been given.

'Why then, count, do you wear powder?' Signora Pietranera asked him the third time she met him. 'Powder! A man like you, agreeable, still young, and who went through the war in Spain with us!'

'The fact is, I never stole anything in Spain, and one has to live. I was mad for glory. One complimentary word from the French general, Gouvion-Saint-Cyr,[1] who was in command of us, meant everything to me in those days. When Napoleon fell, it so happened that while I was squandering my worldly goods in his service, my father, a man of imagination who already saw me as a general, was building me a palazzo in Parma. In 1813, I found that all I possessed was a large, unfinished palazzo and a pension.'

'A pension; three thousand five hundred francs, like my husband?'

'Count Pietranera was a major-general. My pension, as a poor company commander, was never more than eight hundred francs, and I've only been paid that since I became finance minister.'

Because the only other person in the box was the lady of very liberal opinions to whom it belonged, the conversation continued with the same frankness. Questioned, Count Mosca spoke of his life in Parma. 'In Spain, under General Saint-Cyr, I faced musket-fire in order to win a medal and then a little renown, now I dress up like a character in a play so as to earn a fine domestic establishment and a few thousand francs. Once embarked on this sort of chess game, and shocked by the insolence of my superiors, I wanted to occupy a leading position. I have got there, but my happiest days are always those I can come and spend in Milan from time to time. There, I fancy, there still lives the heart of your army in Italy.'

The frankness, the *disinvoltura*, with which this minister of a prince who was greatly feared spoke pricked the countess's curiosity. From his title she had expected to meet with a pedant full of self-importance, but she found a man who felt shame at the gravitas of his position. Mosca had promised to pass on to her all the news from France he was able to gather: a major indiscretion in Milan, in the month preceding Waterloo. It was then a question for Italy of to be or not to be. Everyone in Milan was in a fever, of hope or of fear. In the midst of this universal agitation, the countess questioned people concerning this man who spoke so irreverently of so greatly envied a position, which was his sole resource.

Curious, interestingly bizarre things were reported to Signora Pietranera. Count Mosca della Rovere Sorezana, it was said, is on the point of becoming the first minister and acknowledged favourite of Ranuce-Ernest IV, the absolute ruler of Parma and, what was more, one of the wealthiest princes in Europe. The count would already have attained to that supreme position had he been willing to appear more serious. It was said the prince often lectured him on that subject.

'What difference does my manner make to Your Highness,' he would answer unapologetically, 'if I conduct his affairs successfully?'

'This favourite's good fortune is not without its pitfalls,' they would add. 'He has to please a sovereign who is a man of good sense and intelligence no doubt but who, since he ascended to an absolute throne, seems to have lost his head and shows suspicions, for example, worthy of an old woman.'

Ernest IV is brave only in war. On the field of battle he's been seen a score of times leading a column into the attack, brave general that he is. But after the death of his father, Ernest III, on his return to his States, where, as ill fortune would have it, he possesses unlimited power, he began declaiming wildly against liberty and the liberals. Soon he was imagining they hated him. Finally, in an ill-tempered moment, he had two liberals hanged, not very guilty perhaps, but advised to it by a wretch called Rassi, a sort of minister of justice.

From that fatal moment on, the prince's life was changed.

He was seen to be tormented by the weirdest suspicions. He's not yet fifty, but fear has so diminished him, if one can so put it, that, the minute he gets on to the Jacobins and the plans of the ruling committee in Paris, his features seem to become those of an old man of eighty. He relapses into the fanciful fears of early childhood. His favourite, Rassi, the public prosecutor (or chief justice), is influential only thanks to his master's fears. And the moment he's afraid for his own position, he hurries to uncover some new conspiracy of the blackest, most fanciful kind. If thirty rash individuals come together to read an issue of the *Constitutionnel*, Rassi declares them to be conspirators and sends them as prisoners to the famous citadel of Parma, the terror of the whole of Lombardy. Since it's very tall, a hundred and eighty feet, it's said, it can be seen from a long way off in the middle of that immense plain. And the physical form of the prison, of which terrible things are recounted, makes it the queen, through fear, of the whole of the plain that stretches from Milan to Bologna.

'Would you believe it?' another traveller told the countess; 'at night, on the third floor of his palace, guarded by eighty sentries who, every quarter of an hour, shout out a whole sentence, Ernest IV is shaking with fear in his room. All the doors have ten bolts on them, and the neighbouring rooms, both above and below, are full of soldiers, he's afraid of Jacobins. Should one of the floorboards happen to creak, he leaps for his pistols and thinks there's a liberal hiding under the bed. Immediately, all the bells in the castle are set going and an aide-de-camp goes to wake Count Mosca. Once at the castle, the minister of police is careful not to deny the conspiracy, quite the reverse. Alone with the prince and armed to the teeth, he searches every corner of the apartments, looks under the beds and, in short, indulges in a host of ridiculous actions worthy of an old woman. All these precautions would have seemed highly degrading to the prince himself in those happy times when he was waging war and had only killed anybody by shooting them. As he's a man of the highest intelligence, he's ashamed of these precautions. They strike him as ridiculous even as he's giving in to them, and the source of Count Mosca's immense standing is that he applies all his skill to ensuring that the prince need never become embarrassed in his presence. It's Mosca who, in his capacity as minister of police, insists on looking under the furniture and, it's said in Parma, even inside the double-bass cases. It's the prince who protests and teases his minister on his excessive diligence. It's a wager, is Count Mosca's answer. Think of the satirical sonnets the Jacobins would be showering on us if we let you be killed. It's not only your life we're defending, it's our honour. But it seems that the prince is only half taken in, because if anyone in the town should take it into his head to say that the day before they spent a sleepless night in the castle, the prosecutor Rassi sends the prankster to the citadel. And once inside that lofty abode, *in the fresh air*, as they say in Parma, it would take a miracle for anyone to remember the prisoner. It's because he's a military man who in Spain, in the midst of all the surprises, saved himself a score of times, pistol in hand, that the prince prefers Count Mosca to Rassi, who's much more pliable and more obsequious. The wretched prisoners in the citadel are kept in the most rigorous solitary confinement and stories are told concerning them. The liberals claim that, thanks to an inspiration of Rassi's, the gaolers and confessors are under orders to persuade them that, just about every month, one of them is taken off to be executed. On that day, the prisoners have permission to go up on to the esplanade of the huge tower, a hundred and eighty feet up, from where they can see a procession go by, with a spy playing the role of some poor devil going to his death.'

These tales, and twenty more of the kind, no less authentic, keenly interested Signora Pietranera. The next day, she asked Count Mosca for details, teasing him spiritedly. She found him amusing and put it to him that, without his suspecting it, he was basically a monster. One day, on returning to his inn, the count said to himself: Not only is Countess Pietranera a charming woman, but when I spend the evening in her box, I manage to forget certain things about Parma the memory of which cuts me to the heart. 'This minister, for all his light-hearted air and brilliant ways, did not have a soul *à la française*. He did not know how to *forget* his sorrows. When there was a thorn in his bolster, he was obliged to snap it in two and wear it out by sticking it into his throbbing limbs.' I beg forgiveness for these words, translated from the Italian. The day following this discovery, the count found that, despite the business that had brought him to Milan, the day dragged most dreadfully. He could not remain still. He wore out his carriage horses. At around six o'clock, he got on his horse to go to the Corso. He had some hopes of running into Signora Pietranera there. Not having seen her, he remembered that at eight o'clock La Scala opened. He went in and found fewer than a dozen people in that vast auditorium. He felt some embarrassment at finding himself there. Is it possible, he said to himself, that at the age of forty-five I should be committing acts of folly that would make a subaltern blush? Luckily, no one suspects them. He fled and tried to use up the time by walking in the very charming streets that surround La Scala. They are occupied by cafés which, at that hour of the day, are overflowing with people. In front of each of these cafés, crowds of the inquisitive are installed on chairs in the middle of the street, eating ice creams and criticizing the passers-by. The count was a passer-by of note and so had the pleasure of being recognized and accosted. Three or four importunates, of the sort who are not to be brushed off, took the opportunity of gaining an audience with so influential a minister. Two of them handed him petitions. The third contented himself with giving him very lengthy advice on his political conduct.

One doesn't sleep, he said, when one has this much intelligence. One doesn't take a walk when one has so much influence. He returned to the theatre and had the idea of taking a box in the third tier. From there, he could look down, without anyone noticing him, on the box in the second tier where he hoped to see the countess arrive. Two whole hours of waiting did not seem too long for this man in love. Confident of not being seen, he happily surrendered himself to his folly. Does old age, above all, he asked himself, mean no longer being capable of such delightful acts of childishness?

The countess finally appeared. Armed with his lorgnette, he examined her, enraptured: young, brilliant, light as a bird, he told himself, she's not twenty-five years old. Her beauty is the least of her attractions. Where else to find such a soul, always sincere, which never does the *prudent* thing, which gives itself up totally to the impression of the moment, which asks only to be carried away by some new purpose? I can understand why Count Nani was so besotted.

The count could find excellent reasons for his madness, just so long as he thought only of conquering the happiness he could see in front of him. He could not find such good ones once he came to consider how old he was and the sometimes very dreary concerns that took up his life. An astute man whose fears take away his intelligence gives me a splendid existence and a great deal of money for being his minister. But if tomorrow he dismisses me, I shall be left old and poor, that's to say the most contemptible thing on earth. What an agreeable person to be offering the countess! These thoughts were too black; he came back to Signora Pietranera. He could not tire of watching her, and to think about her all the more clearly, he did not go down into her box. She took Nani, so I've just been told, only so as to thwart that imbecile of a Limercati, who wouldn't hear of taking a sword or a dagger to her husband's murderer. I would fight twenty times over for her, exclaimed the count, transported. Moment by moment he consulted the theatre clock which, with its brilliantly lit figures standing out against a dark background, alerted the spectators, every five minutes, to the moment when it is permitted to enter the box of a friend. The count said to himself: I'd only be able to spend half an hour at most in her box, recent acquaintance that I am. If I stay longer, I shall draw attention to myself, and thanks to my age and even more this accursed powdered hair, I shall have all the attractions of a Cassandra. But one reflection suddenly decided him: if she was about to leave her box to pay a visit, I shall be well rewarded for the avarice with which I've been storing up this pleasure. He got up to go down into the box in which he could see the countess. Suddenly, he no longer felt any real desire to appear there. Oh, that's charming, he exclaimed, laughing at himself, and pausing on the stairs. An impulse of genuine shyness, it's a good twenty-five years since any such adventure befell me.

He almost had to force himself to enter the box. But, intelligent man that he was, he took advantage of the accident that had befallen him, he made no attempt to appear at his ease or display his wit by launching into some amusing anecdote. He had the courage to be shy, he employed his intelligence to let his agitation be glimpsed without seeming ridiculous. If she gets the wrong end of the stick, I'm done for once and for all, he told himself. Shy, when my hair is covered in powder, and would look grey if it weren't for the powder! But anyway it's a fact so it can seem ridiculous only if I exaggerate it or glory in it. The countess had so often been bored at the castle in Grianta, confronted by the powdered figures of her brother, her nephew and a few tedious bien-pensants from round about, that she did not think to concern herself with her new adorer's hair style.

The countess's mind being shielded against the laughter that burst out on his entering, she was attentive only to the news from France, which Mosca always had to give her in detail on arriving in her box. Doubtless he made it up. Discussing it with him this evening, she remarked the kindly and appealing expression in his eyes.

'I imagine that in Parma,' she said, 'among your slaves, you won't be wearing that agreeable expression; it would spoil everything and give them some hope of not being hanged.'

The complete absence of self-importance in a man who passed for being the leading diplomat of Italy struck the countess as strange. She found him attractive even. In short, since he spoke well and animatedly, she was in no way offended that he should have thought it appropriate to adopt for the evening, without any thought for the consequences, the role of admirer.

It was a major step to take, and very perilous. Happily for the minister, who, in Parma, did not come across cruel women, the countess had only just arrived from Grianta in the last few days. Her mind was still stiff from the tedium of rural life. It was if she had forgotten how to tease. And all those things that belong to a fashionable and light-hearted way of life had taken on as it were a tinge of novelty for her which made them sacred. She was not inclined to make fun of anyone, not even of a lover who was forty-five years old, and shy. A week later and the count's temerity might have met with a very different reception.

At La Scala, it is customary to restrict these little visits that are made to the boxes to some twenty minutes or so. The count spent the whole evening in the box where he had had the good fortune to meet Signora Pietranera. This is a woman who is giving me back all the foolishness of my youth, he told himself. But he was well aware of the danger. Will my rank of all-powerful pasha forty leagues from here earn me forgiveness for this folly? I'm so bored in Parma! Nevertheless, every quarter of an hour he promised himself he would leave.

'It has to be confessed, signora,' he said laughingly to the countess, 'that in Parma I am dying of boredom, and I have to be allowed to become intoxicated with pleasure when I meet with it along the way. And so, without consequence and for one evening, allow me to play the role of lover in your presence. In a few days' time, alas, I shall be far away from this box which makes me forget all my vexations and, you will be saying, all the proprieties.'

A week after this mammoth visit to the box at La Scala, and following several minor incidents an account of which would perhaps be found long-winded, Count Mosca was head over heels in love and the countess was already thinking that age did not have to be an objection, when she found him so agreeable. Such were her thoughts when Mosca was recalled by a courier from Parma. It was as if his prince were afraid on his own. The countess returned to Grianta. Her imagination no longer embellishing that lovely spot, she found it a desert. Can I have become attached to that man? she asked herself. Mosca wrote and had no need for pretence, absence had removed the source of all his thoughts. His letters were amusing and, thanks to a small peculiarity which was not taken amiss, in order to avoid the comments of the Marchese del Dongo, who did not like paying the postage on letters, he sent out couriers who put his own in the post in Como, Lecco, Varese or some other of the charming small towns in the vicinity of the lake. The intention was to get the courier to bring back the replies; it succeeded.

Soon the couriers' days became an event for the countess. These couriers brought flowers, fruit and small, trifling gifts which amused her, as they did her sister-in-law. The memory of the count was mixed in with the idea of his great power. The countess had become curious about all that was said of him; the liberals themselves paid homage to his abilities.

The principal source of the count's bad reputation was that he passed for being the leader of the ultra party at the court in Parma, while the liberal party had at its head a scheming woman who was capable of anything, even of success, the Marchesa Raversi, who was immensely rich. The prince was very careful not to discourage whichever of the two parties was not in power. He knew very well that he would always be the master, even with a minister drawn from the salon of Signora Raversi. Grianta was given countless details about these intrigues. The absence of Mosca, whom everyone portrayed as a minister of the highest abilities and a man of action, enabled them to stop thinking about the powdered hair, the symbol of all that is slow and dreary. It was a detail of no consequence, one of the obligations of the court, where he played after all so splendid a role. A court is ridiculous, the countess told the marchesa, but it's fun. It's a game that is interesting, but whose rules you have to accept. Who has ever taken it into their heads to complain that the rules of whist are ridiculous? Yet once you're accustomed to the rules, it's nice to make a slam against your opponents.

The countess's mind often turned to the author of so many agreeable letters. The day she received them was a pleasant one for her. She would take her boat and go to read them at the beauty spots on the lake, at the Pliniana, at Belan, in the Sfondrata woods. The letters seemed to console her somewhat for the absence of Fabrizio. She could not at least deny the count his being very much in love. A month had not gone by before she was thinking of him with fond affection. For his part, Count Mosca was very nearly sincere when he offered to hand in his resignation, to leave the ministry and to come and spend his life with her in Milan or elsewhere. 'I have four hundred thousand francs,' he added, 'which will still give us an income of fifteen thousand livres.' A box once again, horses, etc.! the countess told herself. These were pleasant dreams. The sublime beauty of the views on Lake Como had begun to delight her again. She went to daydream on its shores of this return to the brilliant and exceptional life which, against all odds, had again become possible for her. She could see herself on the Corso in Milan, happy and cheerful as in the days of the viceroy. Youth, or an active life at least, would begin all over again for me!

At times, her ardent imagination concealed things from her, but she never had any of those wilful illusions born of cowardice. She was above all a woman who was sincere with herself. If I'm a little too old to be doing silly things, she told herself, envy, which creates illusions just as love does, could poison my stay in Milan. After my husband's death, my noble poverty was a success, as was my rejection of two large fortunes. My poor dear Count Mosca hasn't the twentieth part of the wealth that those two nincompoops Limercati and Nani laid at my feet. The paltry widow's pension I struggled to obtain, the servants given notice, which caused a stir, the little room on the fifth floor which brought twenty carriages to the door, all that once made a strange spectacle. But I shall have disagreeable moments, however cleverly I go about it, if a widow's pension is still my only fortune and I come back to Milan to live a life of bourgeois ease on the fifteen thousand livres that Mosca will have left after he resigns. A powerful objection, which envy will turn into a terrible weapon, is that the count, although long since separated from his wife, is married. They know about the separation in Parma but in Milan it will be news and it will be put down to me. And so, my lovely La Scala, my heavenly Lake Como . . . farewell, farewell!

Despite all these misgivings, if the countess had had the least fortune, she would have accepted Mosca's offer to resign. She looked on herself as an old woman and the court frightened her. But what will seem wildly improbable on this side of the Alps, is that the count would have been happy to hand in his resignation. That at least is what he succeeded in convincing his mistress. In all his letters he solicited with ever increasing desperation a second meeting in Milan; it was granted. 'To swear that I am passionately in love with you,' the countess told him one day in Milan, 'would be to tell a lie. I would be only too happy to love today, at past thirty, as once I loved at twenty-two! But I've seen so many things collapse that I believed were everlasting! I have the deepest affection for you, I have a boundless confidence in you, of all men you are the one I prefer.' The countess thought she was being perfectly sincere, yet towards the end this declaration contained a small falsehood. Perhaps, had Fabrizio wanted it, he would have reigned supreme in her heart. But Fabrizio was only a child in Count Mosca's eyes. The latter arrived in Milan three days after the young hothead's departure for Novara, and made haste to go and plead his case with Baron Binder. The count considered exile to be an irremediable matter.

He had not arrived in Milan alone, he had in his carriage Duke Sanseverina-Taxis, a pleasant little old man of sixty-eight, dapple-grey, very polished, very proper, immensely rich but insufficiently noble. It was his grandfather only who had amassed millions from his role as farmer-general of the State of Parma. His father had had himself appointed the prince of Parma's ambassador to the court of ***, the reasoning being as follows: 'Your Highness grants thirty thousand francs to his envoy to the court of ***, who cuts a very insignificant figure there. If he deigns to give me the post, I shall accept six thousand francs of emoluments. My expenditure at the court of *** will never fall below a hundred thousand francs a year, and my steward will remit each year twenty thousand francs to the coffers of the foreign ministry in Parma. With that sum, such secretary to the embassy as you care to appoint may be put in alongside me, and I shall not be in the least curious to learn the diplomatic secrets, if there are any. My aim is to lend lustre to my still new lineage, and lend it distinction by one of the country's great offices.'

The present duke, the son of this ambassador, had been tactless enough to reveal himself as something of a liberal, and for the past two years had been in despair. In the time of Napoleon, he had lost two or three million by his insistence on remaining abroad, but since order had been re-established in Europe he had still not been able to obtain a certain grand order which adorned the portrait of his father. The absence of this order had sent him into a decline.

At the point of intimacy that follows on love in Italy, vanity no longer posed any objection between the two lovers. It was with the utmost simplicity therefore that Mosca said to the woman he adored: 'I have two or three plans of action to offer you, all rather well thought out. I've dreamt of nothing else these past three months.

'1. I hand in my resignation, and we live as simple citizens in Milan, Florence, Naples, or wherever you like. We will have an income of fifteen thousand livres, independently of the prince's beneficence, which will continue more or less.

'2. You condescend to come and live in the country where I can do things, you buy an estate, Sacca, for example, a charming house in the middle of a forest, overlooking the course of the Po, you can have the sale contract signed in the next seven days. The prince will attach you to his court. But here a huge objection arises. You will be well received at the court. No one would dare bat an eyelid in front of me. In any case, the princess believes herself to be unhappy and I have just done her a few favours with you in mind. But I will remind you of one crucial objection. The prince is religious in the extreme and, as you know, as fate would have it, I am married. Whence an infinite number of troublesome particulars. You are a widow, which is a fine title needing to be changed for another, and that is the subject of my third proposal.

'We might find a new husband who won't get in the way. But first of all he would need to be well on in years, for why would you refuse me the hope of replacing him one day? Well, I've come to a peculiar agreement with Duke Sanseverina-Taxis, who of course doesn't know the name of the future duchess. He knows only that she will make him an ambassador and will give him the grand order that his father had, the absence of which makes him the most unfortunate of mortals. That aside, the duke isn't too imbecilic; he has his clothes and his wigs sent from Paris. He's not at all a man given to harbouring malice, he seriously believes that honour consists in having an order, and is ashamed of his worldly wealth. A year ago he came and proposed founding a hospice in order to earn the order. I laughed at him, but he didn't laugh at me when I suggested a marriage. My first condition, naturally, was that he would never again set foot in Parma.'

'But you do know that what you are proposing there is most immoral?' said the countess.

'No more immoral than everything else that's done in our court and in twenty others. What's convenient about absolute power is that it sanctifies everything in the eyes of the popu-lation. So what is an absurdity that nobody notices? For the next twenty years, our policy is going to consist of being afraid of the Jacobins, and afraid is the word! Every year we shall think we're just coming up to '93.[2] You will I hope hear how eloquent I become on that subject at my receptions. It's very fine! Anything that may lessen that fear somewhat will be *supremely moral* in the eyes of the nobility and the pious. And in Parma, anyone who isn't either a nobleman or pious is in prison, or packing up his things to go there. You can rest assured that this marriage will seem strange in my country only on the day I fall from favour. The arrangement won't do anyone any mischief, that's the main thing, it seems to me. The prince, for whose favour we are making this bargain, has laid down only one condition for giving his consent, which is that the future duchess must be of noble birth. Last year, my position, when all the sums are done, was worth a hundred and seven thousand francs. My income must have come to a hundred and twenty-two thousand in all. I invested twenty thousand of it in Lyon. Very well, choose! 1. A splendid existence based on having a hundred and twenty thousand francs to spend, which, in Parma, is worth at least four hundred thousand in Milan; but with this marriage which gives you the name of a tolerable man whom you will only ever set eyes on at the altar. 2. Or else the humble life of a citizen with fifteen thousand francs in Florence or Naples, because I'm of your opinion, you've been too much admired in Milan. Envy would persecute us there and would perhaps succeed in putting us in an ill temper. The splendid existence in Parma will have, I hope, a few hints of novelty, even in your eyes, which have seen the court of Prince Eugène. It would make sense to experience it before shutting the door on it. Don't think I'm trying to influence your opinion. As for me, my choice is made. I prefer to live on the fourth floor with you rather than going on with my splendid existence alone.'

The possibility of this peculiar marriage was debated daily between the two lovers. The countess saw Duke Sanseverina-Taxis at the ball and found him very presentable. In one of their last conversations, Mosca summed up his proposal thus: 'We must come to a definite decision, if we want to spend the rest of our lives in a cheerful fashion and not be old before our time. The prince has given his approval. Sanseverina is a good rather than a bad person. He possesses the finest palazzo in Parma and a bottomless fortune. He's sixty-eight years old and is obsessive about the grand order. But one major blemish is spoiling his life: in the old days he bought a bust of Napoleon by Canova[3] for ten thousand francs. His second sin, which will be the death of him if you don't come to his aid, is to have lent twenty-five napoleons to Ferrante Palla, a madman in our country, but also a bit of a genius, whom we have since sentenced to death, in absentia fortunately. This Ferrante has written two hundred lines of poetry in the course of his life, which are without equal. I will recite them to you, they're as fine as Dante. The prince will send Sanseverina to the court of ***, he will marry you the day he sets out, and in the second year of his journey, which he will call an embassy, he will receive the order of ***, without which he can't live. In him you'll have a brother who won't be at all difficult, he'll sign in advance all the papers I want, and in any case you will see him seldom or never, as it suits you. He asks for nothing better than not to show himself in Parma, where his grandfather the tax-farmer and his purported liberalism are an embarrassment. Rassi, our executioner, claims that the duke subscribed secretly to the *Constitutionnel* through Ferrante Palla the poet, and that calumny was for a long time a serious obstacle to the prince giving his consent.'

Why would the historian who is following faithfully every

least detail of the account that was given to him be guilty? Is it
his fault if the characters, seduced by passions which he does not
share, unfortunately for him, lapse into profoundly immoral
actions? It is true that things of this sort are no longer done in
a country where the one passion that has survived all the rest
is money, the means of vanity.

Three months after the events recounted hitherto, the Duchess Sanseverina-Taxis astonished the court of Parma by her
easy affability and the noble serenity of her mind. Her house
was, without compare, the most agreeable in the town. This was
what Count Mosca had promised his master. Ranuce-Ernest IV,
the reigning prince, and the princess, his wife, to whom she was
presented by two of the greatest ladies in the land, accorded
her a most distinguished welcome. The duchess was curious to
set eyes on this prince who was master of the fate of the man
whom she loved, she wanted him to like her and she succeeded
only too well. She found a man tall in stature but somewhat
thickset. His hair, his moustaches and his enormous whiskers
were, according to his courtiers, of a beautiful golden shade.
Elsewhere, their colour would have earnt them the ignominious
description of flaxen. In the middle of a large face, there rose,
just, a very small, almost feminine nose. But the duchess
observed that, in order to notice all these grounds for finding
him ugly, one needed to try to itemize the prince's features.
Overall, he had the air of a man of intelligence and a firm
character. The prince's bearing, his way of holding himself,
did not lack majesty, but he frequently sought to impress his
interlocutor. At those times he would himself grow embarrassed
and lapse into an almost continual shifting from one leg on
to the other. For the rest, Ernest IV had a penetrating and
domineering gaze. There was nobility in the movements of his
arms and his words were at once measured and concise.

Mosca had warned the duchess that, in the large cabinet
where he held audience, the prince had a full-length portrait of
Louis XIV, and a very fine scagliola table from Florence. She
found the imitation striking. He was obviously striving for the
expression and the noble delivery of Louis XIV, and he leant
on the scagliola table in such a way as to give himself the

attitude of Joseph II. He sat down immediately after the first words he addressed to the duchess, so as to give her the opportunity of making use of the *tabouret*[4] that went with her rank. In this court, duchesses, princesses and the wives of Spanish grandees alone sit down, the other women wait until invited to do so by the prince or princess. And to mark the difference in rank, these august personages are always careful to allow a brief interval to pass before asking the ladies who are not duchesses to be seated. The duchess felt that at certain moments the prince rather overdid the imitation of Louis XIV: for example, in the way he had of smiling benevolently while throwing back his head.

Ernest IV wore a dress-coat in the style then coming in from Paris. Each month he was sent from that town, which he abhorred, a dress-coat, a frock-coat and a hat. But, in a bizarre mixture of garments, on the day when the duchess was received, he had put on red knee-breeches, silk stockings and well-covered shoes, the models for which may be found in the portraits of Joseph II.

He received Signora Sanseverina graciously. He said witty and acute things to her. But she could easily see that there was nothing excessive about her good reception. 'Do you know why?' Count Mosca said on returning from the audience; 'it's because Milan is a bigger and finer town than Parma. He'd have been afraid, had he given you the welcome I was expecting and which he had led me to hope for, of seeming like a provincial going into ecstasies over the attractions of a beautiful lady coming from the capital. No doubt also he's still put out by a particularity I don't dare tell you about: the prince can't see in his court a single woman to rival you where *beauty* is concerned. Yesterday evening, at his *petit coucher*,[5] that was the one topic of his conversation with Pernice, his head valet, who is well disposed towards me. I foresee a small revolution in etiquette. My biggest enemy in this court is an idiot by the name of General Fabio Conti. Picture to yourself an original who has perhaps seen one day of military action in his whole life and thinks that means he can go around behaving like Frederick the Great. On top of which, he insists also on reproducing the upper-class affability of General Lafayette,[6] and that because here he's the leader of the liberal party (God knows what sort of liberals!).'

'I have met Fabio Conti,' said the duchess. 'I had sight of him near Como. He was arguing with the gendarmerie.' She recounted the small adventure which the reader will perhaps recall.

'You will learn one day, signora, if your mind ever succeeds in penetrating the profundities of our etiquette, that young ladies appear at court only after their marriage. Well, so ardent is the prince's patriotism, for the superiority of his town of Parma to all others, that I'd wager he will find a way of having the young Clelia Conti, our Lafayette's daughter, presented to him. She's charming I will say, and a week ago still passed for being the loveliest person in the prince's States.

'I don't know,' the count went on, 'whether the horrors that the sovereign's enemies have put abroad about him have reached as far as the castle of Grianta. They have turned him into a monster, an ogre. The fact is that Ernest IV was full of minor virtues, and one might add that, had he been invulnerable like Achilles, he would have continued to be a model among potentates. But in a moment of boredom and anger, and partly too in order to imitate Louis XIV cutting off the head of some hero or other of the Fronde who was discovered living quietly and insolently on an estate next to Versailles, fifty years after the Fronde,[7] Ernest IV one day had two liberals hanged. It seems that these rash individuals used to meet together on an appointed day to speak ill of the prince and address their ardent vows to heaven, that the plague might come to Parma and rid them of the tyrant. The word *tyrant* was proved. Rassi called that conspiring. He had them sentenced to death and the execution of one of them, Count L***, was ghastly. It took place before my time. Ever since that fateful moment,' the count added, lowering his voice, 'the prince has been subject to attacks of fear *unworthy of a man*, but which are the one source of the favour I enjoy. But for the sovereign's fearfulness, my abilities would be of too brusque a kind, too harsh for this court, which is awash with imbeciles. Would you credit that the prince looks under the beds in his apartment before going to sleep, and spends a million, which in Parma is like four million in Milan, to have a good police force, and you see before you, signora duchess, the head of that terrible police force. Thanks to the police, that's to say to fear, I have become minister of war and of finance. And since the minister of the interior is my nominal chief, inasmuch as he numbers the police among his responsibilities, I've had that portfolio given to Count Zurla-Contarini, an imbecile but a glutton for work, who indulges himself in writing eighty letters every day. I've just received one this morning on which Count Zurla-Contarini has had the satisfaction of writing with his own hand the number 20,715.'

The Duchess Sanseverina was presented to the unhappy princess of Parma, Clara-Paolina, who, because her husband had a mistress (rather a pretty woman, the Marchesa Balbi), thought herself the most unfortunate person in the universe, which had made her perhaps the most tedious. The duchess found a very tall, very thin woman, who was not yet thirty-six but looked fifty. Her regular and noble features might have passed for beautiful, even if somewhat marred by large round eyes that could hardly see, had the princess herself not given up the struggle. She received the duchess with so marked a diffidence that a few courtiers hostile to Count Mosca dared to say that the princess had the air of the woman being presented and the duchess of the sovereign. The duchess, surprised and almost disconcerted, did not know where to find the words that would put her in a position inferior to that which the princess had given herself. To restore a certain composure to this poor princess, who was by no means unintelligent underneath it all, the duchess could find nothing better than to launch out on and sustain a long dissertation on botany. The princess was genuinely knowledgeable on the subject. She had some very fine hothouses with a great many tropical plants. Merely by seeking to extract herself from an awkward situation, the duchess made a permanent conquest of Princess Clara-Paolina, who, from having been diffident and tongue-tied at the start of the audience, found herself so much at ease towards the end that, contrary to all the rules of etiquette, this first audience lasted no less than five quarters of an hour. The following day, the duchess had exotic plants bought and emerged as a great lover of botany.

The princess spent her life with the venerable Father Landriani, the archbishop of Parma, a man of learning, a man of intelligence even, and a perfectly worthy man, but who presented a singular spectacle when he was sitting on his chair of crimson velvet (which his office entitled him to), facing the princess's armchair, surrounded by her ladies-in-waiting and her two *lady companions*. The aged prelate with his long white hair was even more diffident, if that is possible, than the princess. They saw one another daily, and every audience began with a silence lasting a full quarter of an hour, to the point where Countess Alvizi, one of the lady companions, had became a sort of favourite because she had the art of encouraging them to speak to one another and getting them to break the silence.

To bring this series of presentations to an end, the duchess was admitted to the presence of His Most Serene Highness the hereditary prince, a personage taller in stature than his father and more diffident than his mother. He was an expert in mineralogy and sixteen years old. He went exceedingly red on seeing the duchess enter and was so disoriented that he was quite unable to come up with anything to say to this beautiful lady. He was a very good-looking man and spent his life in the woods, hammer in hand. Just as the duchess was getting up to put an end to this silent audience: 'Good heavens, signora, how very pretty you are!' exclaimed the hereditary prince, which the lady being presented did not consider to be in wholly bad taste.

The Marchesa Balbi, a young woman of twenty-five, could still pass for the most perfect example of *Italian prettiness*, two or three years before the arrival of the Duchess Sanseverina in Parma. Still today she had the most beautiful eyes imaginable and the most fetching little expressions, but, viewed from close to, her skin was strewn with countless small fine lines, which made the marchesa seem like a young old woman. Seen from a certain distance, at the theatre say, in her box, she was still a beauty; and the audience in the pit considered that the prince had very good taste. He spent all his evenings at the Marchesa Balbi's, but frequently without opening his mouth, and the boredom she could see in the prince had caused the poor woman to grow extraordinarily thin. She aspired to a subtlety that knew no bounds and was always smiling mischievously. She had the most beautiful teeth imaginable and sought on the off-chance, by a sly, more or less meaningless smile, to give people to understand something quite other than what her words seemed to say. Count Mosca used to say that it was these perpetual smiles, when inwardly she was yawning, that had given her all those lines. Balbi was involved in every business arrangement, and no thousand-franc State contract could be signed without there being a 'memento' (that was the respectable term in Parma) for the marchesa. Public rumour had it that she had invested six million francs in England, but in reality her fortune, of recent origin truth to tell, amounted to less than fifteen hundred thousand francs. It was in order to be shielded from her tricks, and have her dependent on him, that Count Mosca had had himself made minister of finance. The marchesa's one passion was fear, disguised as a sordid avarice: 'I shall die a pauper,' she sometimes told the prince, who found the remark infuriating. The duchess observed that the anteroom in the Palazzo Balbi, with its resplendent gilding, was lit by a solitary candle overflowing on to a table of precious marble, and the doors of her salon were black from the fingers of the lackeys.

'She received me,' the duchess told her lover, 'as if she'd been expecting a fifty-franc tip.'

The duchess's triumphal progress was somewhat interrupted by the reception she was given by the most astute woman at the court, the celebrated Marchesa Raversi, a consummate schemer who found herself at the head of the party opposed to that of Count Mosca. She was seeking to topple him, all the more so over the past few months because she was the niece of Duke Sanseverina and feared that the new duchess's charms might threaten her inheritance. Raversi is certainly not a woman to be despised, the count told his mistress, I hold her to be such a menace that I separated from my wife solely because she insisted on taking for a lover the Cavaliere Bentivoglio, one of Raversi's friends. The lady in question, a tall virago with very black hair, notable for the diamonds she wore from first thing in the morning and for the rouge with which she covered her cheeks, had declared herself in advance to be the duchess's enemy, and on receiving her at her house, she made a point of starting the war. In the letters that he wrote from ***, Duke Sanseverina seemed so enchanted by his embassy, and above all his hopes of the great order, that his family were afraid that he might leave part of his fortune to his wife, on whom he had heaped small gifts. Uniformly ugly though she was, Raversi had for a lover Count Baldi, the best-looking man at court: generally speaking, she succeeded in everything she undertook.

The duchess maintained a very splendid household. The Palazzo Sanseverina had always been one of the most magnificent in the town of Parma, and, on the occasion of his ambassadorship and future order, the duke had spent very large sums on embellishing it. The duchess had directed the improvements.

The count had guessed correctly: a few days after the duchess had been presented, the young Clelia Conti came to court and was made a canoness. In order to counter the blow which this favour might have seemed to strike at the count's standing, the duchess gave a party on the pretext of inaugurating the gardens of her palazzo, and, in her charming way, made Clelia, whom she called her young friend from Lake Como, the queen of the soirée. Her monogram was to be found, as if by chance, on the principal transparencies.[8] Although a little pensive, the young Clelia spoke charmingly of the small adventure near the lake, and of her keen gratitude. She was said to be very devout and a great lover of solitude. I would wager, said the count, that she has wit enough to feel ashamed of her father. The duchess made a friend of this young girl, she felt drawn to her. She did not want to appear jealous and included her in all her amusements. In short, her system was to seek to reduce all the hatred of which the count was the object.

Everything smiled on the duchess. She was amused by this existence at court, where storms are always to be feared; she felt she was beginning life over again. She had a fond attachment for the count, who was literally madly happy. This pleasant situation had procured for him a complete imperturbability where anything not having regard to the realizing of his ambitions was concerned. Thus barely two months after the arrival of the duchess, he obtained the letters patent and honours of first minister, which come very close to those paid to the sovereign himself. The count held his master in the palm of his hand; proof of which was about to strike everyone in Parma.

Ten minutes from the town, to the south-east, there rises the famous citadel, greatly renowned in Italy, whose huge tower is a hundred and eighty feet high and can be seen from a long way off. This tower, built on the model of the mausoleum of Hadrian in Rome, by the Farnese, the grandsons of Paul III, around the beginning of the sixteenth century,[9] is so thick that on the esplanade that rounds it off they were able to build a palazzo for the governor of the citadel and a new prison known as the Farnese Tower. The locals hold this prison, built in honour of Ranuce-Ernest II, who had become the much-loved lover of his mother-in-law, to be both beautiful and singular. The duchess was curious to see it. On the day of her visit, the heat was crippling in Parma, but up here, in this elevated position, she found a breath of air, which so delighted her that she spent several hours there. They hurried to open up the large rooms in the Farnese Tower for her.

On the esplanade of the big tower the duchess encountered a poor liberal prisoner, who had come to enjoy the half-hour's exercise that he was accorded every three days. Once back down in Parma, and not yet possessing the discretion necessary in an absolute court, she spoke of this man, who had recounted his entire history to her. The Marchesa Raversi's party seized on the duchess's remarks and repeated them freely, very much hoping the prince would find them offensive. Indeed, Ernest IV had repeatedly declared that what was essential above all was to impress people's imaginations. *Perpetual* is a big word, he used to say, and more terrible in Italy than elsewhere. As a result, never in his life had he granted a pardon. A week after her visit to the fortress, the duchess received a letter of commutation, signed by the prince and the minister, with the name left blank. The prisoner whose name she wrote in would have his property restored to him and be given permission to go and spend the rest of his days in America. The duchess wrote in the name of the man who had spoken to her. Unfortunately, the man turned out to be more or less a scoundrel and a feeble character; it was following his confession above all that the famous Ferrante Palla was sentenced to death.

The rarity of this pardon was the crowning pleasure of Signora Sanseverina's situation. Count Mosca was wildly happy, this was a good period of his life and it had a decisive influence on Fabrizio's destiny. The latter was still in Romagnano, near Novara, making his confession, hunting, reading nothing and paying court to a noblewoman, as per his instructions. The duchess was still a little shocked by this last necessity. Another sign that did not bode well for the count was that, although she was as candid as could be about everything, and thought aloud in his presence, she never spoke about Fabrizio without having weighed her words.

'If you like,' the count said to her one day, 'I will write to that agreeable brother of yours on Lake Como, and, with some small difficulty for myself and my friends in ***, will force the Marchese del Dongo to ask for a pardon for your charming Fabrizio. If it's true, as I certainly wouldn't wish to doubt, that Fabrizio is a cut above the young men who parade their English horses in the streets of Milan, what sort of life is it, that of an eighteen-year-old who does nothing and has the prospect of never doing anything! If heaven had granted him a genuine passion for anything at all, for fishing even, I would respect it. But what will he do in Milan even after he's got his pardon? He will ride the horse he'll have had sent from England at a certain hour of the day, and at another idleness will lead him to his mistress, whom he'll love less than his horse ... But if you give me the order, I shall attempt to procure that style of life for your nephew.'

'I'd like him to be an officer,' said the duchess.

'Would you advise a sovereign to entrust a post which, on any given day, may be of some importance, to a young man: 1. given to enthusiasm; 2. who has displayed enthusiasm for Napoleon, to the extent of going to join him at Waterloo?

Think where we'd all be if Napoleon had won at Waterloo! We wouldn't have any liberals to fear, it's true, but the sovereigns from ancient families would be able to reign only by marrying the daughters of his marshals. So for Fabrizio a military career would be the life of a squirrel going round and round in a cage: a lot of movement in order to get nowhere. He'll be chagrined at finding himself losing out to all those dedicated plebeians. The prime quality in a young man today, that's to say for the next fifty years perhaps, for as long as we're afraid and religion is not re-established, is not to be given to enthusiasm and not to have any brains.

'I've had one thought, but it's going to have you shouting your head off for one thing, and is going to put me to an endless amount of trouble and not just for twenty-four hours; it's a folly I'm willing to commit for you. But tell me what follies I wouldn't commit to obtain a smile.'

'Well?' said the duchess.

'Well, we've had three members of your family as archbishops in Parma. Ascanio del Dongo, who wrote, in 16**, Fabrizio in 1699, and a second Ascanio in 1740. If Fabrizio is willing to enter the prelacy and display virtues of the highest order, I shall make him a bishop somewhere, then the archbishop here, if, that is, my influence endures. That's where the real objection lies: shall I remain minister long enough to realize this beautiful plan which requires several years? The prince may die, he may have the bad taste to dismiss me. But in the end it's the one means I have of doing something for Fabrizio which is worthy of you.'

There was a lengthy discussion: the duchess found the idea wholly repugnant.

'Prove to me again,' she said to the count, 'that any other career is out of the question for Fabrizio.' The count proved it.

'What you are regretting is the dazzling uniform,' he added. 'I don't know what I can do about that.'

After the month that the duchess had requested in order to consider, she sighed and gave in to the minister's sensible views. 'To ride snootily about on an English horse in some large town,' repeated the count, 'or to adopt a profession that doesn't jar with his birth. I see no middle way. Unfortunately, a gentleman can't become a doctor, or a lawyer, and the century belongs to the lawyers.

'Always remember, signora,' the count repeated, 'that you are offering your nephew, on the streets of Milan, the lot enjoyed by the young men of his age who are deemed to be the most fortunate. Once he has his pardon, you give him fifteen, twenty, thirty thousand francs. It hardly matters to you, since neither you nor I aim to save.'

Fame meant something to the duchess. She did not want Fabrizio to be a mere squanderer of money. She came back to her lover's plan.

'Note,' the count told her, 'that I'm not aiming to make Fabrizio into the sort of exemplary priest you see so many of. No, first and foremost he's a great nobleman. He can remain perfectly ignorant if he so wishes, he'll still become a bishop and archbishop, if the prince continues to look on me as someone of use.

'If your orders deign to turn my proposal into an immutable decree,' added the count, 'Parma mustn't on any account see our protégé living unobtrusively. His good fortune will be thought shocking if he's been seen here as a mere priest. He must appear in Parma only with the purple stockings* and with a suitable equipage. Then, everyone will guess that your nephew is to be a bishop and no one will be shocked.

'If you trust me, you'll send Fabrizio to do his theology and spend three years in Naples. During the holidays from the ecclesiastical academy, he can go to visit Paris and London if he wants. But he will never show himself in Parma.' At this the duchess seemed to shudder.

She sent a courier to her nephew, arranging to meet him in Piacenza. Needless to say, this courier was the bearer of all the monetary resources and passports that he needed.

---

* In Italy, young men of learning or who have patrons become a *monsignore* or *prelate*, which does not mean a bishop. One then wears purple stockings. One does not take vows in order to be a *monsignore*, one can leave off the stockings and get married.

Having been the first to arrive in Piacenza, Fabrizio hurried to find the duchess, embracing her so passionately that she burst into tears. She was fortunate that the count was not present; since they had become lovers, this was the first time she had experienced this sensation.

Fabrizio was deeply affected, and then distressed by the plans the duchess had made for him. His hope had always been that, the Waterloo affair having been sorted out, he would end up as a soldier. One thing struck the duchess and enhanced still further the romantic opinion she had formed of her nephew: he absolutely refused to lead the café life in one of the great towns of Italy.

'Do you see yourself on the Corso in Florence or Naples,' said the duchess, 'with English thoroughbreds! For the evening, a carriage, a pretty apartment,' etc. She relished insisting on describing this vulgar form of happiness, which she could see Fabrizio scornfully rejecting. He's a hero, she thought.

'And after ten years of that agreeable life, what would I have done?' said Fabrizio. 'What would I be? A *mature* young man who has to step aside for the first handsome adolescent making his debut in society, who's also on an English horse.'

At first Fabrizio rejected the choice of the Church out of hand. He talked of going to New York, of becoming a republican citizen and soldier in America.

'What a mistake you're making! You won't have any war and you'll fall back into the café life, only unfashionable, without music, without love affairs,' replied the duchess. 'Believe me, for you as for me, life in America would be dreary.' She explained to him the worship of the *god* dollar, and the respect you have to have for the artisans in the street, who decide everything by their votes. They returned to the idea of the Church.

'Before you get worked up,' said the duchess, 'you must understand what the count is asking from you. It's not at all a question of being a more or less exemplary and virtuous poor priest, like Father Blanes. Remember what your uncles the archbishops of Parma were. Read the accounts of their lives again, in the supplement to the genealogy. Above all, it's proper for a man with your name to be a great lord, noble, generous, a defender of justice, destined in advance to find himself at the head of his order . . . and doing only one dastardly thing in his entire life, but that one to very good effect.'

'So there go all my illusions down river,' said Fabrizio with a deep sigh. 'A cruel sacrifice! I'll admit I hadn't considered this horror for enthusiasm and for brains, even when exercised to their advantage, which is to be the rule from now on among absolute sovereigns.'

'To think that a proclamation, a caprice of the heart may propel the enthusiastic man into the party opposed to the one he's been serving all his life!'

'Me an enthusiast,' Fabrizio repeated. 'A strange accusation, I can't even fall in love!'

'What?' exclaimed the duchess.

'When I have the honour of paying court to a beauty, even one of good family, and devout, I can think of her only when I see her.'

This admission created a strange impression on the duchess.

'I ask for one month,' resumed Fabrizio, 'to take my leave of Signora C. of Novara and, what's still harder, of the castles in Spain of my whole life. I shall write to my mother, who will be kind enough to come and see me at Belgirate, on the Piedmontese shore of Lake Maggiore, and on the thirty-first day from today, I shall be incognito in Parma.'

'You'll do nothing of the sort!' cried the duchess. She did not want Count Mosca to see her talking to Fabrizio.

The same two people met again in Piacenza. This time, the duchess was much troubled. A storm had blown up at court. The Marchesa Raversi's party was on the verge of triumphing. It was possible that Count Mosca would be replaced by General Fabio Conti, the leader of what in Parma was known as the *liberal party*. Except for the name of the rival who was growing in the prince's favour, the duchess told Fabrizio everything. She debated once again the possibilities for his future, even in the event of his lacking the count's all-powerful protection.

'I shall spend three years in the ecclesiastical academy in Naples,' exclaimed Fabrizio. 'But since I have above all else to be a young gentleman, and you're not constraining me to living the austere life of a virtuous seminarist, my stay in Naples in no way alarms me; life there will be just as good as that in Romagnano. Good society there was beginning to see me as a Jacobin. In my exile, I discovered that I know nothing, not even Latin, not even how to spell. I had planned to do my education over again in Novara; I shall willingly study theology in Naples. It's a complicated science.' The duchess was overjoyed. 'If we're expelled,' she told him, 'we shall come and see you in Naples. But since you accept until further orders the path of the purple stockings, the count, who knows present-day Italy well, has charged me with a thought to pass on. Believe what they will teach you or not, *but never raise any objections*. Imagine they're teaching you the rules of whist. Would you raise objections to the rules of whist? I told the count you are a believer, and he was gratified by that. That's useful in both this world and the next. But if you believe, don't succumb to the vulgarity of speaking with horror of Voltaire, Diderot, Raynal and all those hare-brained Frenchmen who were the precursors of the two chambers.[10] Let those names come rarely to your lips. But in the end, when you have to, speak of these gentlemen calmly and with irony. They're people refuted long since whose attacks are no longer of any consequence. Believe unquestioningly everything they tell you at the academy. Bear in mind that there are people who will take faithful note of your least objections. You'll be forgiven for the odd amorous intrigue, if it's well conducted, but not for a doubt. Age suppresses amorous intrigues and increases doubts. Act on this principle in the confessional. You will have a letter of recommendation for a bishop who's the factotum of the cardinal archbishop of Naples. You must confess your escapade in France, and your presence on 18 June in the neighbourhood of Waterloo, to him alone. Otherwise cut it short, play down that adventure, confess to it only so that you can't be criticized for having concealed it. You were so young at the time!

'The second idea the count sends you is this. If a brilliant argument occurs to you, a victorious retort that alters the course of the conversation, don't give in to the temptation to shine;

remain silent. The shrewd ones will see your intelligence in your eyes. It'll be time to display it once you're a bishop.'

Fabrizio made his debut in Naples with a modest carriage and four servants, good Milanese, whom his aunt had sent him. A year into his studies and no one was saying that he was an intelligent man; he was looked on as a great lord, diligent, very generous, but something of a libertine.

The year was rather amusing for Fabrizio, and terrible for the duchess. Two or three times the count was on the brink of disaster. The prince, more fearful than ever because he was unwell that year, believed, if he dismissed him, that he would rid himself of the odium of the executions carried out before the count entered the ministry. Rassi was the cherished favourite who had to be kept on at all costs. The duchess became all the more passionately attached to the count in his hour of need; she no longer gave Fabrizio a thought. To make their possible withdrawal seem plausible, it transpired that the air in Parma, which was indeed somewhat humid, like everywhere in Lombardy, did not at all suit her health. Finally, after intervals of disfavour, which led to the count, the first minister, going up to three whole weeks without seeing his master in private, Mosca won the day. He had General Fabio Conti, the purported liberal, appointed governor of the citadel where the liberals convicted by Rassi were imprisoned. If Conti displays indulgence towards his prisoners, Mosca told his mistress, he will be disgraced, as a Jacobin whose political ideas are making him forget his duties as a general. If he shows himself to be severe and ruthless, and that's the direction he's likely to lean in I fancy, he will cease to be the leader of his own party and will alienate all the families who have one of their number in the citadel. The poor man knows how to ooze respect when approaching the prince. If need be, he changes his dress four times a day. He can debate a question of etiquette, but he hasn't the head on him to be capable of following the difficult path by which alone he might save himself. And in any case, I'm there.

On the day following General Fabio Conti's appointment, which put an end to the ministerial crisis, it was learnt that Parma was to have an ultra-monarchist newspaper. 'It's going to give rise to a whole lot of quarrelling, this paper!' said the duchess.

'The idea of the paper is perhaps my masterpiece,' replied the count, laughing. 'I shall gradually, and with the greatest reluctance, allow the raging ultras to take over the running of it from me. I have assigned handsome remuneration to the editorial posts. They'll be soliciting those posts on all sides. The whole affair will get us through a month or two, and the danger I've just been in will be forgotten. Those weighty personages P. and D. are already lining up.'

'But the paper will be quite disgustingly ridiculous.'

'I'm certainly banking on it,' replied the count. 'The prince will read it every morning and will admire the doctrine of the man who started it, me. As for the details, he will either approve or be shocked. That's two of the hours he devotes to work taken care of. The paper will cause a fuss, but by the time the serious complaints come in, in eight or ten months' time, it will be entirely in the hands of the raging ultras. It'll be the party that gets in my way that will have to reply and I shall raise objections against the paper. Basically, I would rather have a hundred ghastly absurdities than a single man being hanged. Who remembers an absurdity two years after the issue of the official newspaper? Whereas the sons and family of the hanged man vow a hatred for me which will last as long as I do and may shorten my life.'

The duchess, forever passionate for something, forever active, never idle, was more intelligent than the whole court of Parma. But she lacked the patience and the impassiveness to intrigue successfully. None the less, she had managed to follow with passion the interests of the various coteries, and she was even beginning to enjoy some personal credit with the prince. Clara-Paolina, the reigning princess, swathed in honours but imprisoned within the most outdated etiquette, saw herself as the most unfortunate of women. The Duchess Sanseverina courted her and undertook to prove that she was by no means so unfortunate. One needs to know that the prince saw his wife only at dinner. This meal lasted thirty minutes and the prince went whole weeks without addressing a word to Clara-Paolina.

Signora Sanseverina tried to change all that. She amused the prince, all the more so because she had been able to preserve all her independence. Even had she wanted, she would not have been able never to tread on the toes of any of the fools who pullulated in the court. This complete incapacity on her part led to her being execrated by the common run of courtiers, all counts and marchesi, generally enjoying an income of five thousand livres a year. She appreciated this misfortune from the first and applied herself exclusively to pleasing the sovereign and his wife, who dominated the hereditary prince absolutely. The duchess knew how to amuse the sovereign and took advantage of the rapt attention he paid to her every word to point up the absurdities of the courtiers who hated her. Since the follies that Rassi had made him commit, and follies involving bloodshed are not to be repaired, the prince was sometimes afraid, and frequently bored, and this had led to his being sadly envious. He felt that he got very little amusement and became gloomy when he thought he could see that others were enjoying themselves. The sight of happiness made him furious. 'We must conceal our love,' the duchess told her lover, and she gave the prince to suppose that she was no longer so very greatly smitten by the count, estimable man though he be.

This discovery had given His Highness a happy day. From time to time, the duchess would let slip a few words about the plan she had of giving herself a break of several months each year that she would use to see Italy, which she did not know. She would go and visit Naples, Florence, Rome. Now, nothing could have caused the prince more distress than this apparent act of desertion: this was one of his most marked weaknesses, actions that might be ascribed to a contempt for his capital city pierced him to the heart. He felt that he had no means of holding Signora Sanseverina back, and Signora Sanseverina was by far the most brilliant woman in Parma. Something unique given how lazy Italians are: they returned from the surrounding countryside to be present at her Thursdays. These were veritable entertainments; the duchess nearly always offered something new and piquant. The prince was dying of envy to witness one of these Thursdays; but how to go about it? To go to the house of a mere private individual! That was something neither he nor his father had ever done.

On a certain Thursday it was raining, it was cold. All evening long, the prince could hear carriages rattling over the paving in the palace square, on their way to Signora Sanseverina's. He felt an impatient urge. Others were having fun and he, the sovereign prince, the absolute master, who ought to be having more fun than anyone else, he was experiencing boredom! He rang for his aide-de-camp; it took time for a dozen trustworthy men to be stationed in the street leading from His Highness's palace to the Palazzo Sanseverina. Finally, after an hour that seemed like a century to the prince, during which he was tempted twenty times to brave the daggers and go recklessly out without taking any precautions, he appeared in Signora Sanseverina's first salon. Had the room been struck by a thunderbolt, the surprise would not have been any greater. In the blink of an eye, and as the prince came forward, a stupefied silence settled on these very noisy, very cheerful rooms. All eyes were fixed on the prince and opened to their very widest. The courtiers appeared taken aback. The duchess alone did not look astonished. Once they had finally recovered the power of speech, the main preoccupation of all those present was to settle this important question: had the duchess been warned of this visit, or was she as much taken by surprise as everyone else?

The prince enjoyed himself, and one may judge of the duchess's thoroughly spontaneous character, and of the infinite power that her vague ideas of departure, adroitly let drop, had allowed her to acquire.

As she was escorting the prince out, he having addressed some very amiable words to her, a singular idea occurred to her which she ventured to put to him quite simply, as though it were something not at all out of the ordinary. 'If Your Most Serene Highness were willing to address two or three of the charming phrases he has been lavishing on me to the princess, that would make for my happiness much more surely than by telling me here that I am pretty. The fact is, I wouldn't at all want the princess to look askance at the signal mark of favour with which Your Highness has just honoured me.' The prince stared fixedly at her and answered curtly: 'I am, it would seem, in a position to go wheresoever I please.'

The duchess reddened. 'I only wanted,' she at once went on, 'not to expose His Highness to making a fruitless excursion, for this Thursday will be the last. I shall be going to spend a few days in Bologna or in Florence.'

As she returned to the reception rooms, everyone thought her at the pinnacle of favour, and she had just hazarded what in living memory no one had ventured in Parma. She signalled to the count, who left his whist table and followed her into a small salon, brightly lit but deserted.

'What you did was very daring,' he told her. 'I wouldn't have advised it. But in hearts that are truly smitten,' he added, laughing, 'happiness enhances love, and if you leave tomorrow morning, I shall follow you tomorrow evening. I shall be delayed only by the thankless labours at the ministry of finance I was foolish enough to saddle myself with, but in four hours that are well spent one can hand over a good many cash-boxes. Let us go home, my own love, and play the self-satisfied minister to our heart's content and without restraint. It's perhaps the last performance we shall give in this town. If he thinks he's being defied, the man's capable of anything. He'll call it "making an example". Once this crowd has gone, we'll advise on the ways of barricading you in for the night, the best thing perhaps would be for you to leave without delay for your house in Sacca, near the Po, which has the advantage of being only half an hour away from the Austrian States.'

For the duchess's love and her amour propre this was a delightful moment. She looked at the count and her eyes were moist with tears. For a minister with so much power, and surrounded by this crowd of courtiers heaping compliments on him the equal of those they addressed to the prince himself, to give it all up for her sake and so nonchalantly!

On her return to the reception rooms she was wild with delight. Everyone bowed low before her.

How happiness alters the duchess, said the courtiers on every side, you wouldn't recognize her. That Roman soul that looks down on everyone has finally deigned to appreciate the exorbitant favour of which she's just been the object on the part of the sovereign!

Towards the end of the soirée, the count came to her: 'I have some news I must give you.' The people who happened to be next to the duchess at once moved away.

'When he got back to the palace,' the count went on, 'the prince had himself announced to his wife. Imagine the shock! "I've come to give you an account of the very agreeable evening I have been spending at Sanseverina's," he told her. "It was she who asked me to describe to you in detail the way in which she has arranged that smoky old palazzo." Then, having sat down, the prince began to describe each of your reception rooms.

'He spent more than twenty-five minutes with his wife, who was weeping for joy. Quick though she is, she was unable to find a single word to keep the conversation going in the light-hearted tone that His Highness wanted to give it.'

The prince was not a spiteful man, whatever Italy's liberals may have said. It was true he had had a fair number of them thrown into prison, but that was out of fear, and he sometimes repeated, as if to console himself for certain memories: 'Better to kill the devil than have the devil kill us.' The day after the soirée of which we have just been speaking, he was as merry as could be, he had performed two good deeds: going to the Thursday and speaking to his wife. At dinner, he actually addressed her. In short, Signora Sanseverina's Thursday brought about a domestic revolution with which the whole of Parma was buzzing. Raversi was stunned and the duchess doubly joyful: she had been able to be of service to her lover and had found him more enamoured than ever.

'All this because of a very rash idea that came to me!' she told the count. 'I shall no doubt be freer in Rome or in Naples, but shall I find a game as absorbing as this? No, the truth is I won't, my dearest count, and you make my happiness.'

CHAPTER 7

It is with small court details as trivial as those we have been recounting that the story of the next four years must be filled. Each spring, the marchesa came with her daughters to spend two months at the Palazzo Sanseverina or on the Sacca estate, on the banks of the Po. They enjoyed pleasant moments and they talked of Fabrizio. But the count would not allow him a single visit to Parma. The duchess and the minister had to make amends for a few thoughtless actions, but overall Fabrizio stuck quite sensibly to the line of conduct laid down for him: a great nobleman who is studying theology and is not relying wholly on his virtue to ensure his advancement. In Naples, he had developed a very strong liking for the study of antiquity, he went excavating; this passion had almost replaced that for horses. He had sold his English horses so as to continue excavating at Misena, where he had found a bust of the still youthful Tiberius, which had taken its place among the finest relics of antiquity. The bust's discovery was almost the keenest pleasure he had met with in Naples. He was too lofty of soul to seek to imitate the other young men, to want, for example, to play the role of lover with any great seriousness. He did not for sure lack mistresses, but they were of no possible consequence to him and, his age notwithstanding, it could be said of him that he had had no experience of love. He was all the more loved for that reason. Nothing stopped him from acting with the most admirable sangfroid, because for him one pretty young woman was no different from the next. He merely found the latest one the most enticing. One of the most admired ladies in Naples had committed follies in his honour during the last year of his stay, which had begun by amusing him and ended by proving exceedingly tiresome, so much so that one of the good things about his departure was that it released him from the attentions of the charming duchess of A***. It was in 1821 that, having done tolerably well in all his examinations, his director of studies or tutor got a cross and a present and he himself left finally to visit the town of Parma, which had been often in his thoughts. He was monsignore and his carriage had four horses. At the posthouse preceding Parma, he took on only two, and in the town made them stop in front of the church of San Giovanni. There was to be found the ornate tomb of Archbishop Ascanio del Dongo, his great-great-uncle, the author of the *Latin Genealogy*. He prayed beside the tomb, then arrived on foot at the palazzo of the duchess, who had not been expecting him until several days later. She had a large gathering in her salon but was soon left on her own.

'Well, are you satisfied with me?' he said, throwing himself into her arms. 'Thanks to you, I have spent four quite happy years in Naples, instead of being bored in Novara with a mistress authorized by the police.'

The duchess could not get over her astonishment, she would not have recognized him had he passed her in the street. She found that he was, in fact, one of the best-looking men in Italy; it was the cast of his features that was especially attractive. She had sent him to Naples looking like some bold desperado, the riding whip he always carried seemed in those days to form an inherent part of his being. Now, he wore a nobler, more restrained air in front of strangers, even if in private she found he still had all the fieriness of his early youth. He was a diamond who had lost nothing by being polished. Fabrizio had not been there an hour before Count Mosca appeared. He arrived a little too soon. The young man spoke to him in such warm terms of the Parma cross awarded to his tutor, and expressed his keen gratitude for other benefits of which he did not dare speak so openly, with such perfect restraint, that from the start the minister formed a favourable opinion of him. 'This nephew,' he said under his breath to the duchess, 'is made to grace all the high offices to which you will want to raise him later on.'

Everything had gone beautifully up until now, but when the minister, very satisfied with Fabrizio, and attentive up until now solely to his doings, looked at the duchess, he found she wore a peculiar expression. This young man is creating a strange impression here, he told himself. This was a bitter reflection. The count had turned *fifty*, which is a very cruel word whose full reverberations can perhaps be felt only by a man who is hopelessly in love. He was the best of men, well worthy of being loved, except for his severities as a minister. But in his own eyes, the cruel word *fifty* cast a dark shadow over his whole life and would have been capable of making him cruel on his own account. In the five years since he had persuaded the duchess to come to Parma, she had often excited his jealousy, in the early days especially, but she had never given him genuine cause for complaint. He believed indeed, and he was right, that it was in the intention of making more certain of his heart that the duchess had resorted to appearing to single out for her favours several handsome young men of the court. He was certain, for example, that she had rejected the attentions of the prince, who had even, on that occasion, said something instructive. 'But were I to accept Your Highness's attentions,' the duchess had said to him, laughing, 'how would I ever be able to face the count again?'

'I should be almost as much out of countenance as you. The dear count! My friend! But that little difficulty could be easily got round, I've given it some thought. The count would be put in the citadel for the remainder of his days.'

At the moment of Fabrizio's arrival, the duchess was so transported by happiness that she had no thought at all for the ideas her eyes might be putting into the count's head. The effect was profound and the suspicions irremediable.

Fabrizio was received by the prince two hours after his arrival. The duchess, foreseeing the good effects that this impromptu audience would produce among the public, had been soliciting it for the past two months. The favour put Fabrizio on a different footing from the very first. The pretext had been that he would only be passing through Parma on the way to see his mother in Piedmont. At the moment when a charming brief note from the duchess came to tell the prince that Fabrizio was awaiting his orders, His Highness was bored. I'm about to see a very simple-minded young saint, he told himself, looking either obsequious or sly. The local commander had already reported the first visit to his uncle the archbishop's tomb. The prince saw a tall young man enter who, but for the purple stockings, he would have taken for some young officer.

This minor surprise drove away his boredom. Here's a strapping young fellow for whom I'm going to be asked Lord knows what favours, he said to himself, all those I have at my disposal. He's just arrived, he must be feeling excited. I'm going to play at Jacobin politics and we'll just see what his answer is.

After the first gracious words on the prince's part: 'Well, monsignore,' he said to Fabrizio, 'are the people of Naples happy? The king, is he loved?'

'Most Serene Highness,' replied Fabrizio without a moment's hesitation, 'as I passed down the street, I admired the excellent turnout of the soldiers of H. M. the King's various regiments. Good society is respectful towards its masters, as it should be. But I will confess that never in my life have I suffered members of the lower orders to speak to me of anything other than the work for which I pay them.'

'I'll be damned!' said the prince, 'we've got a well-trained bird of prey here, sharp like the Sanseverina.' Eager for the fray, the prince employed great skill in getting Fabrizio to talk on this most scabrous of topics. Spurred on by the danger, the young man was lucky enough to hit on some admirable rejoinders: 'It is insolence almost to flaunt one's love for one's king,' he said, 'what one owes him is blind obedience.' Faced with such wariness, the prince all but lost his temper. It seems here we have a sharp-witted man arriving from Naples, and I don't like the species. An intelligent man may live by the highest principles and even be sincere, but there's always some side of him that makes him second cousin to Voltaire and Rousseau.

The prince felt as though he were being challenged by the very correct manner and quite unassailable replies of the young refugee from college. What he had foreseen had not happened. In the blink of an eye, he adopted a tone of bonhomie and,

going back, within the space of a few words, all the way to the
great principles of societies and of government, he brought out,
adapting them to current circumstances, a few sentences from
Fénelon that he had been made to learn by heart as a child for
public audiences.

'These principles may surprise you, young man,' he said to
Fabrizio (he had called him *monsignore* at the start of the
audience and was reckoning on giving him another *monsignore*
when dismissing him, but as the conversation proceeded he
thought it more adroit and more favourable to the emotive
turn it was taking, to use a friendlier form of address); 'these
principles surprise you, young man, I will admit that they hardly
resemble the *absolutist gush* [that was the word] that can be
read every day in my official newspaper. But good Lord, why
would I be quoting you that? Those newspaper writers are quite
unknown to you.'

'I beg Your Most Serene Highness's pardon, but not only do
I read the Parma newspaper, which I find rather well written,
but I also hold, as does it, that everything that has been done
since the death of Louis XIV, in 1715, was at once criminal
and stupid. Man's highest concern is his salvation, there can be
no two ways of thinking about that, and that is a happiness that
is to last for an eternity. The words *liberty*, *justice*, *happiness of
the greatest number* are wicked and criminal. They instil in
people's minds the habit of debate and mistrust. A Chamber of
Deputies *mistrusts* what those people call the *ministry*. Once
this fatal habit of *mistrust* has been contracted, human weakness applies it everywhere, man comes to mistrust the Bible, the
orders of the Church, tradition, etc., etc. From that moment on
he is lost. Even if, and it is horribly false and a crime even to
utter it, this mistrust towards the authority of princes *established by God* were to bring happiness during the twenty or
thirty years of life to which each of us may aspire, what would
half a century or even a whole century be, compared to an
eternity of torment, etc.?'

From the manner in which Fabrizio spoke, it could be seen
that he was trying to arrange his thoughts in such a way as to

let them be grasped as easily as possible by his listener, it was clear that he was not reciting a lesson.

Soon, the prince no longer cared to wrestle with this young man, whose grave and simple manner bothered him. 'Goodbye, *monsignore*,' he said brusquely, 'I can see that they give one an excellent education at the ecclesiastical academy of Naples, and it is self-evident that when these good precepts meet with so distinguished a mind, one obtains brilliant results. Goodbye.' And he turned his back on him.

That oaf didn't take to me at all, Fabrizio said to himself.

It now remains to be seen, said the prince as soon as he was alone, whether this handsome young man is capable of being passionate about something. In that case he would be complete . . . Could the aunt's lessons have been repeated more cleverly? I seemed to hear her speaking. If there was a revolution here, she it would be who would edit the *Moniteur*, like the San-Felice woman once did in Naples![1] But twenty-five years old and beautiful though she was, la San-Felice was hanged I fancy! A warning to women with too many brains. In believing Fabrizio to be his aunt's pupil, the prince was mistaken. Men of intelligence who are born on the throne or beside it soon lose all sense of tact. They proscribe around them any freedom of expression that they consider to be coarse. They want to see only masks and aspire to judge beauty by the complexion. The amusing thing is that they fancy they are full of tact. In the present instance, for example, Fabrizio believed more or less everything we have heard him say. It is true that he did not think about these great principles twice in a month. He had lively tastes, he was intelligent, but he was a believer.

The taste for liberty, the fashion and cult of the *happiness of the greatest number*, with which the nineteenth century is infatuated, were in his view only a *heresy* that will pass like all the others, but only after killing many souls, just as pestilence kills many bodies while it is prevalent in a country. Yet despite all this, Fabrizio read the French newspapers with delight, and even went to imprudent lengths to get hold of them.

When Fabrizio returned, all dishevelled, from his audience at the palace, and was recounting to his aunt the prince's various attacks: 'You must go this minute to Father Landriani, our excellent archbishop. Go there on foot, go up the stairs quietly, don't make much noise in the anterooms. If you're made to wait, so much the better, so very much the better! In a word, be *apostolic*!'

'I understand,' said Fabrizio, 'our man is a Tartufe.'[2]

'Not in the least, he is virtue itself.'

'Even after what he did,' Fabrizio went on, astonished, 'at the time of Count Palanza's execution?'

'Yes, my love, after what he did then. Our archbishop's father was a clerk in the finance ministry, a petty bourgeois, which explains everything. Monsignor Landriani is a man of a lively intelligence, extensive, profound. He is sincere, he loves virtue. I'm convinced that if an Emperor Decius were to return to the world, he would suffer martyrdom like Poliuto in the opera[3] they gave us last week. That's the good side of the medal and here is the obverse. The moment he's in the presence of the sovereign, or merely the first minister, he's dazzled by so much grandeur, he becomes agitated, he goes red in the face. It's physically impossible for him to say no. Whence the things he has done and which have earnt him that cruel reputation right throughout Italy. But what people don't know is that, when public opinion enlightened him about the proceedings against Count Palanza, he imposed a penitence on himself of living off bread and water for thirteen weeks, as many weeks as there are letters in the names Davide Palanza. We have at this court a villain by the name of Rassi, as clever as they come, a chief justice or chief prosecutor, who on the occasion of Count Palanza's death bewitched Father Landriani. At the time of the thirteen-week penitence, Count Mosca, out of pity and a little mischievously, invited him to dine once or even twice a week. The good archbishop, to curry favour, dined like everyone else. He'd have thought it constituted a rebellion or Jacobinism to flaunt an act of penitence for an action approved by the sovereign. But it was learnt that, for every dinner at which his duty as a loyal subject had obliged him to eat like everyone else, he imposed a penitence on himself of two days of living off bread and water.

'Monsignor Landriani, a superior mind, a savant of the front rank, has only one weakness, *he wants to be loved*. So, feel pity when you look at him and, on your third visit, love him thoroughly. Coupled with your birth, that will get you adored straight away. Don't show any surprise if he escorts you out all the way to the stairs, make it look as though you're used to such ways. He's a man born on his knees before the nobility. For the rest, be simple, apostolic, nothing clever, nothing brilliant, no ready repartee. If you don't alarm him, he'll enjoy himself with you. Remember, he's got to make you his vicar-general of his own accord. The count and I will be surprised or even angry at this over-hasty promotion, that's essential vis-à-vis the sovereign.'

Fabrizio hastened to the archbishop's palace. By a singular piece of good fortune, the good prelate's footman, who was slightly deaf, did not hear the name *del Dongo*. He announced a young priest named Fabrizio. The archbishop happened to be with a parish priest of less than exemplary morals, whom he had sent for in order to upbraid him. He was in the middle of issuing a reprimand, something he found very painful, and did not want this discomfort weighing down on him any longer. He therefore made the great-nephew of the great Archbishop Ascanio del Dongo wait for three quarters of an hour.

How to portray his apologies and his despair when, after escorting the priest as far as the second antechamber, and once he had, as he came back, asked the man who was waiting 'how he could be of service to him', he noticed the purple stockings and heard the name Fabrizio del Dongo? Our hero found the situation so droll that, at this very first visit, he dared to kiss the hand of the saintly prelate, in an outburst of affection. One should have heard the archbishop repeating despairingly: 'For a del Dongo to wait in my antechamber!' He felt himself obliged, by way of an apology, to recount the whole tale of the parish priest, his faults, his replies, etc.

Is it really possible, Fabrizio asked himself as he returned to the Palazzo Sanseverina, that that was the man who hurried along the execution of poor Count Palanza!

'What does Your Excellency think?' Count Mosca asked him,

laughing, on seeing him return to the duchess (the count would not let Fabrizio call him Excellency).

'I'm astounded. I know nothing of men's characters. If I hadn't known his name, I'd have wagered he was someone who can't bear to see a chicken being bled.'

'And you'd have won,' returned the count. 'But when he's in front of the prince, or even of me, he can't say no. Truth to tell, if I'm to produce my full effect, I have to have the big yellow sash on over my tunic. In a frock-coat he'd contradict me, so I always put on a uniform to receive him. It's not for us to destroy the prestige of power, the French newspapers are demolishing it quite fast enough. The *obsession with deference* is hardly going to survive as long as we do, and you, nephew, will outlive deference. You will simply be a man!'

Fabrizio took great pleasure in the count's company. He was the first superior man who had condescended to speak to him without playing a part. Moreover, they had a taste in common, that for antiquities and for excavating. On his side, the count was flattered by the extreme attentiveness with which the young man listened to him. But there was one crucial objection: Fabrizio occupied an apartment in the Palazzo Sanseverina, spent his life with the duchess, let it be seen in all innocence that his happiness derived from this intimacy, and Fabrizio had eyes and a complexion of a freshness to make one despair.

Ranuce-Ernest IV, who seldom encountered women who were cruel, had for a long time now been piqued by the fact that the duchess's virtue, which was well known at court, had not made an exception in his favour. As we have seen, Fabrizio's quickness and presence of mind had shocked him from the very first day. He was put out by the excessive affection that he and his aunt displayed so thoughtlessly. He lent a very close ear to the comments of his courtiers, which were never-ending. This young man's arrival and the extraordinary audience he had obtained were the talk of an astonished court for a month. Whereupon the prince had an idea.

He had in his guard a private soldier with an admirable head for wine. This man spent his life in the tavern and reported on the army's morale directly to his sovereign. Carlone was uneducated, but for which he would long since have gained promotion. Now, his instructions were to find himself in front of the palace every day when the great clock struck noon. The prince went himself a little before noon to make a certain adjustment to the blind of an entresol adjoining the room in which His Highness got dressed. He returned to this entresol shortly after it had struck noon and found the soldier there. In his pocket the prince had a sheet of paper and an inkhorn, and he dictated the following letter to the soldier:

'Your Excellency is a most intelligent man, for sure, and it is thanks to your profound wisdom that we find the State so well governed. But my dear count, such great successes do not go without giving rise to a modicum of envy, and I very much fear that they may be laughing a little at your expense, if in your wisdom you have not divined that a certain handsome young man has had the good fortune to inspire, in spite of himself it may be, a most singular love. This fortunate mortal is, they say, no more than twenty-three years old, and what complicates the issue, dear count, is that you and I are much more than double that age. In the evenings, from a certain distance, the count is charming, sparkling, a man of ready wit, as agreeable as could be. But in the mornings, close to, all things considered, the newcomer may perhaps be found the more attractive. Now we women lay great store by the freshness of youth, especially once we are past thirty. Is there not already talk of installing this charming adolescent in our court, in some desirable position? And who is the individual who raises this matter the most frequently with Your Excellency?'

The prince took the letter and gave the solider two écus.

'This is on top of your pay,' he told him, with a mournful air. 'Absolute silence all round, or else the dampest dungeon in the citadel.' In his bureau the prince had a collection of envelopes bearing the addresses of most of the people in his court, in the hand of this same soldier, who passed for not being able to write and never did write, not even his police reports. The prince chose the one that he needed.

A few hours later, Count Mosca received a letter through the post. The time when it might arrive had been calculated, and just as the postman, who had been seen entering holding a small letter in his hand, left the ministry building, Mosca was summoned to His Highness. Never had the favourite appeared so deeply depressed. To enjoy it in all the more leisurely a manner, the prince cried when he saw him: 'I need to relax by chewing the fat with a friend, not to work with the minister. I've got a splitting headache this evening, and am having the blackest thoughts, what's more.'

Need we speak of the abominable ill humour at work inside the first minister, Count Mosca della Rovere, by the time he was permitted to leave his august master? Ranuce-Ernest IV was highly skilled in the art of torturing a heart, and I might make here, without any great injustice, a comparison with the tiger that loves to toy with its prey.

The count had himself driven home at the gallop. He shouted out en route that not a living soul was to be allowed to come up, had the duty secretary told he was free to go (hating the idea that a human being might be within earshot), and made haste to shut himself away in the great picture gallery. There finally, he could give free rein to his fury. There he spent the evening without any lights on, walking aimlessly about, like a man distraught. He sought to impose silence on his heart, so as to concentrate the full force of his attention on debating the course he should follow. Plunged in an anguish to excite the compassion of his cruellest enemy, he said to himself: The man I abhor is lodging in the duchess's house, spends all his time with her. Should I try to get one of her women to talk? Far too risky. She's so good to them. She pays them well! She's adored by them! (By whom, great God, is she not adored!) The question is, he continued, raging: Must I let people guess at the jealousy that's eating me up, or keep quiet about it?

If I remain silent, they won't hide from me. I know Gina, she's a woman who acts purely on impulse, her behaviour is unpredictable even to her. If she tries to lay down a role for herself in advance, she gets into a muddle. Always, when it's time to act, some new idea occurs to her and she gets carried away, thinking it's far and away the best and it ruins everything. Don't say a word about my martyrdom and they won't hide anything from me and I'll see everything that may be going on . . .

Yes, but by speaking out, I shall bring about different circumstances. I shall start them thinking. I shall forestall many of the horrible things that may happen . . . Perhaps he'll be sent away (the count breathed a sigh), then I've all but won the day. Even if there's a bit of bad temper for a time, I'll soothe it . . . and what could be more natural? . . . she's loved him like a son these fifteen years. That's where all my hopes lie: *like a son* . . . but she stopped seeing him after he ran off to Waterloo. But coming back from Naples, he's another man, for her especially. *Another man*, he repeated in fury, and an attractive man at that. Above all he has that fond and innocent expression and those smiling eyes that promise so much happiness! And the duchess can't be used to seeing eyes of that sort in our court! . . . there, they're replaced by expressions that are either mournful or sardonic. And what must my expression not often be like, harassed by state business, prevailing only thanks to my influence over a man who'd like to make me look absurd? However much care I take, it has to be my expression that is old in me! Is my gaiety not always close to irony? . . . I'd go further: here I must be sincere, does my gaiety not let people glimpse, as something very close to it, absolute power . . . and viciousness? Don't I sometimes say to myself, especially when I'm annoyed: I can do what I want? And I'd even add something silly: I must be happier than the next man because I possess what others don't: supreme authority over seventy-five per cent of things . . . Well, let's be fair: having that thought all the time must spoil my smile, must make me look like an egotist . . . self-satisfied . . . And how attractive his smile is! He breathes the easy happiness of early youth and produces it in others.

Unhappily for the count, the weather that evening was warm, stuffy, heralding a storm: the kind of weather, in a word, which in those parts encourages extreme decisions. How to report all the arguments, all the ways of looking at what had been happening to him which, for three mortal hours, put this passionate man on the rack? In the end, prudence prevailed, solely as the result of this reflection: I'm mad, probably. I think

I'm being rational and I'm not being rational. I'm simply turning round and round looking for a less agonizing position, I'm by-passing some decisive reason without seeing it. Since I'm blinded by extreme pain, let's follow the rule, approved by all sensible men, known as *prudence*.

In any case, once I've uttered the fatal word *jealousy*, my role is marked out once and for all. On the other hand, by saying nothing today, I can speak tomorrow, I remain in full control. The crisis was too much, the count would have gone mad had it lasted. He felt relief for a few moments, his attention coming to dwell on the anonymous letter. From which side could it have come? There was a searching for names and an assessment of each one, which provided a distraction. Finally, the count recalled the malicious glint that had flashed from the sovereign's eye when he had come to say, towards the end of the audience: 'Yes, dear friend, let us agree, the pleasures and cares of the most fortunate ambition, even of power without limit, are as nothing compared to the inner happiness that derives from relationships of tenderness and love. I am a man before I am a prince, and when I have the good fortune to love, my mistress addresses the man and not the prince.' The count set this moment of malevolent enjoyment against this sentence in the letter: 'It is thanks to your profound wisdom that we find the State so well governed.' The wording is the prince's, he exclaimed, in a courtier it would be a gratuitous piece of rashness. The letter comes from His Highness.

This problem once resolved, the small pleasure he derived from his successful guesswork was quickly erased by the cruel apparition of Fabrizio's attractions, which returned once more. It was like an enormous weight falling back on the unhappy man's heart. What does it matter who the anonymous letter is from! he exclaimed in a fury, is the fact it proclaims not still a fact? This caprice may change my life, he said, as if to excuse himself for being so distraught. The minute she can, if she loves him in a certain way, she'll go off with him to Belgirate, to Switzerland, to some other corner of the world. She's rich and in any case, even if she had to live on a few louis each year, what would that matter to her? Did she not admit to me, not even a week since, that her palazzo, so well arranged, so splendid, bores her? That very youthful soul has to have novelty. And how simply this new happiness offers itself! She'll be borne off before she's thought about the dangers, before she's thought of feeling sorry for me! Yet I'm so unhappy! cried the count, bursting into tears.

He had sworn he would not go to the duchess's that evening, but he could not stick to it. Never had his eyes so craved the sight of her. He presented himself around midnight; he found her alone with her nephew. At ten o'clock she had sent everyone away and closed her door.

At the sight of the fond intimacy that reigned between these two people, and the duchess's artless joy, an awful difficulty loomed before the count, and without warning, one he had given no thought to during his long deliberations in the picture gallery: how to hide his jealousy?

Not knowing what pretext to resort to, he claimed that that evening he had found the prince exceptionally prejudiced against him, contradicting all his assertions, etc., etc. He had the grief of seeing that the duchess was hardly listening to him and paying no attention at all to circumstances which, two days before, would have set her off arguing endlessly. The count looked at Fabrizio. Never had that handsome Lombard face appeared so simple and so noble! Fabrizio was paying more attention than the duchess to the difficulties he was recounting.

Truly, he told himself, that face combines extreme goodness with the expression of a certain innocent and tender joy which is irresistible. It seems to be saying: love and the happiness it brings are the only serious things in this world. Yet should you get to some detail where intelligence is required, his gaze comes awake and astonishes you, and you're left confounded.

Everything is simple in his eyes because everything is seen from on high. Dear God, how to combat such an enemy? And after all, what is life without Gina's love? With what raptures she seems to listen to the charming sallies of that youthful spirit, which, for a woman, must seem unique in the world.

An atrocious thought seized hold of the count like a cramp: to stab him there in front of her, and kill myself afterwards?

He circled the room, his legs barely able to support him, but with his hand clutched convulsively around the handle of his dagger. Neither of the two was paying attention to what he might be doing. He said he was going to give an order to his lackey; they did not even hear him. The duchess was laughing fondly at a remark Fabrizio had just addressed to her. The count went up to a lamp in the outer salon and looked to see whether the point of his dagger was sufficiently sharp. I must be gracious and show this young man every respect, he told himself as he returned and went up to them.

He was going mad. He fancied that as they leant forward they were giving one another kisses, there in front of him. That's not possible, not in my presence, he told himself; my mind is wandering. I must calm down. If I'm uncivil, the duchess is capable, simply out of injured vanity, to follow him to Belgirate. And there, or during the journey, chance may lead to a word that will give a name to what they feel for one another. And then, instantly, all that follows.

Solitude will make that word decisive and, moreover, once the duchess is far away, what will become of me? If, having got over a great many difficulties where the prince is concerned, I go and show my old, careworn face in Belgirate, what role shall I play among these people who are deliriously happy?

Even here, what am I if not the *terzo incomodo* (the beautiful Italian language is simply made for love)! *Terzo incomodo* (a third person who is in the way)! How painful for a man of intelligence to feel that he's playing that execrable role and to be unable to do anything about it except to get up and go!

The count was about to burst out or at least betray his grief by the distortion of his features. As he circled the room he found himself near the door and he took flight, crying out with a good-natured, friendly expression: 'Goodbye, you two!' We must avoid bloodshed, he told himself.

On the day following this terrible evening, after a night spent at one moment listing to himself Fabrizio's advantages, at another in the cruel throes of the most agonizing jealousy, the count had the idea of summoning a young manservant. The man in question was courting a girl called Chekina, one of the duchess's lady's maids and her favourite. Fortunately, the young domestic led a very orderly, even miserly life, and hankered after a post as concierge in one of the public establishments in Parma. The count ordered the man to get Chekina, his mistress, to come to him there and then. The man obeyed and an hour later, the count appeared without warning in the bedroom where the girl was to be found with her suitor. The count frightened the two of them by the quantity of gold he gave them, then addressed these few words to the trembling Chekina, staring straight into her eyes: 'Does the duchess make love with monsignore?'

'No,' said the girl, making up her mind after a moment's silence . . . 'No, *not yet*, but he often kisses the signora's hands, laughing it's true, but rapturously.'

This testimony was enlarged on by a hundred replies to the same number of questions from the furious count. His impassioned anxiety meant that these poor people certainly earnt the money he had tossed them. He ended by believing what he had been told, and felt less unhappy. 'If the duchess ever suspects this conversation,' he told Chekina, 'I shall send your intended to spend twenty years in the fortress, and he'll have white hair when you next see him.'

A few days went by, during which Fabrizio in turn lost all his gaiety. 'I assure you,' he told the duchess, 'that Count Mosca feels antipathy towards me.'

'So much the worse for His Excellency,' she replied, with a sort of ill humour.

This was not the real source of the anxiety that had caused Fabrizio's gaiety to vanish. The situation in which chance has placed me is untenable, he told himself. I'm quite sure she'll never speak out, to say anything too meaningful would be like committing incest, she'd be horrified. But if one evening, after a wild and reckless day, she should happen to examine her conscience, if she thinks I've managed to divine the liking she seems to have for me, what role shall I be playing as she sees it? *Casto Giuseppe* no less (an Italian proverb, alluding to the ridiculous role of Joseph with the wife of the eunuch Potiphar[4]).

Let her into a fine secret and make her understand I'm

incapable of loving seriously? I don't have the mental composure to announce the fact without making it seem for all the
world like an impertinence. The one recourse left to me is a
great passion left behind in Naples, in which case, go back there
for twenty-four hours. That's the sensible course but it's a lot
of trouble! There remains maybe a small, below-stairs affair in
Parma, which she may not like. But anything rather than the
awful role of the man who refuses to understand. This last
course might, it's true, compromise my future. I'd have to lessen
the danger by being prudent and buying people's discretion.
What was cruel in the midst of all these thoughts, was that in
point of fact Fabrizio was far fonder of the duchess than of any
other human being. One must be very gauche, he told himself
angrily, to dread not being able to persuade her of what is so
very true! Lacking the skill to extricate himself from this situation, he became sombre and morose. Where would I be, dear
God, if I was to fall out with the one person in the world to
whom I feel passionately attached? On the other hand, Fabrizio
could not resolve to spoil this delightful piece of good fortune
by an indiscreet word. His situation had so much to commend
it! His intimacy with so agreeable and so pretty a woman was
so comforting! So far as the more commonplace aspects of his
life were concerned, her protection had created a very pleasant
position for him at court, where all the big intrigues amused
him as if he were at the theatre, thanks to her, who explained
them to him! But at any minute I may be woken up by a
thunderbolt, he told himself. These gay and tender evenings,
spent all but tête-à-tête with a very desirable woman, if they
lead on to something better, she'll think she's found a lover in
me. She'll want passion from me, madness, and all I shall ever
have to offer her will be the warmest affection, but without
love. Nature has deprived me of that sort of sublime madness.
How many reproaches have I not had to endure on that score!
I fancy I can still hear the Duchess of A***, and I laughed at
the duchess! She'll think I'm lacking in love for her, whereas
it's love that is lacking in me. She'll never be willing to understand me. Often, after she's retailed some anecdote about the
court, with the charm and exuberance that she alone possesses,

and is necessary for my education moreover, I kiss her hands and sometimes her cheek. What will happen if that hand squeezes mine in a certain fashion?

Fabrizio appeared daily in the most highly regarded and least gay houses in Parma. Guided by the duchess's clever advice, he paid expert court to the two princes, father and son, to Princess Clara-Paolina and to monsignore the archbishop. He had his successes, but they did not console him for the mortal fear of quarrelling with the duchess.

CHAPTER 8

Thus, less than a month after his arrival at court, Fabrizio knew all the vexations of a courtier's life, and the intimate friendship that was the source of his life's happiness had been poisoned. One evening, tormented by these thoughts, he left the duchess's salon where he had too much the air of a reigning lover. Wandering aimlessly through the town, he passed the theatre, which he saw was lit up. He went in. This was a gratuitous piece of rashness in a man of the cloth, one that he had promised himself indeed he would avoid in Parma, which is after all only a small town of forty thousand inhabitants. It is true that right from the start, he had cast off his official costume. In the evenings, when he was not going into the very best society, he dressed simply in black, like a man in mourning.

In the theatre he took a box in the third tier, so as not to be seen. They were doing Goldoni's *La Locandiera*.[1] He took in the architecture of the auditorium; he hardly had eyes for the stage. But the large audience was forever bursting out laughing. Fabrizio turned to look at the young actress playing the role of the innkeeper, he found her comic. He looked at her more closely, he found her decidedly pretty and above all completely natural. She was an artless young girl who was the first to laugh at the amusing things Goldoni was putting into her mouth and which she seemed quite surprised to be saying. He asked what her name was. He was told: Marietta Valserra.

Ah, he thought, she's taken my name, that's odd! Despite his plans, he left the theatre only at the end of the play. The following day he returned. Three days later, he knew Marietta Valserra's address.

On the evening of the day on which he had, with some difficulty, obtained this address, he remarked that the count received him with a broad smile. The poor jealous lover, who had had the greatest difficulty remaining within the bounds of prudence, had set spies to follow the young man, and his expedition to the theatre had pleased him. How to describe the count's delight when, on the day following that when he had managed to bring himself to look kindly on Fabrizio, he learnt that the latter, half disguised it was true in a long blue top-coat, had gone all the way up to the wretched apartment that Marietta Valserra occupied on the fourth floor of an old house behind the theatre? His joy was renewed when he learnt that Fabrizio had introduced himself under a false name, and had had the honour of exciting the jealousy of a bad lot by the name of Giletti, who in the town played walk-on roles as a valet and in the villages danced on the tightrope. This noble lover had heaped abuse on Fabrizio and said he wanted to kill him.

Operatic troupes are formed by an *impresario*, who takes on individuals from here, there and everywhere whom he can pay or finds are free, and the haphazardly assembled troupe stays together for one or two seasons at most. It is not the same with 'theatre companies'. They may go from town to town and change their place of residence every two or three months, but they nevertheless constitute something like a family, all of whose members love or loathe one another. These companies include established ménages that the young bloods in the towns where the troupe is going to perform often have the greatest difficulty in splitting up. Which is precisely what happened to our hero. Little Marietta was in love with him right enough, but she was horribly afraid of Giletti, who meant to be her sole master and kept close watch on her. He went around protesting that he would kill the *monsignore*, because he had followed Fabrizio and had managed to discover his name. This Giletti could hardly have been uglier or less cut out for love. Disproportionately tall, he was also horribly thin, heavily pockmarked and had a slight squint. For the rest, full of the attractions of his métier, he usually entered the wings where his fellow actors were gathered, turning cartwheels, walking on his hands, or performing some other party trick. He triumphed in roles where the actor has to appear with his face whitened with flour and receive or give out endless blows with a stick. Fabrizio's worthy rival was paid a wage of thirty-two francs a month and thought himself very well off.

Count Mosca felt he had been brought back from death's door when his watchers assured him that all these details were in fact the case. His affability returned. He seemed more cheerful and better company than ever in the duchess's salon, and was very careful not to breathe a word to her of the small adventure that had restored his life to him. He even took precautions so that she should be informed of all that was going on at the last possible moment. Finally, he plucked up the courage to listen to reason, which had been crying out to him in vain for the past month that whenever a lover's credit is on the wane, that lover must go on a journey.

An important matter summoned him to Bologna, but twice a day couriers from his office brought him, not so much official papers from his desk as news of little Marietta's amours, of the terrible Giletti's anger and of Fabrizio's amorous advances.

One of the count's agents asked several times for 'Harlequin skeleton and pie', one of Giletti's triumphs (he emerges from the pie just as his rival Brighella is cutting it open and takes a stick to him). It was an excuse to slip him a hundred francs. Giletti, crippled by debts, took good care not to talk about this handsome windfall, but became astonishingly vain.

Fabrizio's caprice turned into injured amour propre (his worries had already reduced him to having *caprices*, at his age!). Vanity had led him to the spectacle; the young girl had performed very spiritedly and had amused him; on coming out from the theatre he was in love for an hour. The count returned to Parma on hearing that Fabrizio was running real risks. Giletti, who had been a dragoon in the splendid Napoleon regiment of dragoons, was talking seriously about killing Fabrizio, and taking steps to flee afterwards into Romagna. If the reader is very young, he will be scandalized by our admiration for this fine evidence of courage. It was on the other hand no small effort of heroism on the count's part to return from

Bologna, when after all, in the mornings, he frequently looked drawn with fatigue, while Fabrizio appeared so fresh, so untroubled! Who would have dreamt of holding Fabrizio's death against him, had it happened in his absence and for so foolish a reason? But he had one of those rare souls that are eternally remorseful for a generous action that they might have taken but failed to take. He could not moreover bear the thought of seeing the duchess made unhappy, and through his fault.

On arrival, he found her silent and melancholy. Here is what had happened. The young lady's maid, Chekina, racked by remorse, and judging the gravity of her fault by the enormity of the sum she had received for committing it, had fallen sick. One evening, the duchess, who was fond of her, went all the way up to her room. The young girl could not resist this mark of kindness. She burst into tears, sought to give her mistress back what she still possessed of the money she had received, and finally found the courage to confess to the questions the count had put to her and her replies. The duchess hurried to the lamp, which she extinguished, then told the young Chekina that she forgave her, but on condition that she not breathe a word of this strange scene to anyone at all. The poor count, she added, casually, is afraid of ridicule. All men are that way.

The duchess hurried back down to her own apartment. Scarcely had she shut herself away in her room before she burst into tears. She found something horrible in the thought of making love with the Fabrizio she had known from birth. Yet, what did her behaviour mean?

Such had been the principal cause of the black melancholy in which the count found her sunk. Once he had arrived, she burst out impatiently against him, and almost against Fabrizio. She would have liked not to see either of them again. She was upset by the ridiculous role, as she saw it, that Fabrizio was playing with little Marietta. For, like a true lover incapable of keeping a secret, the count had told her everything. She could not grow accustomed to this unhappiness: her idol had a defect. Finally, feeling suddenly affectionate, she asked the count for his advice. For the latter this was a delectable moment and a fine reward for the honourable impulse that had brought him back to Parma.

'What could be simpler!' said the count, laughing. 'Young men want to have all the women, then the next day they've forgotten all about them. Shouldn't he go to Belgirate, and visit the Marchesa del Dongo? Well, let him go. While he's away, I shall ask the theatre troupe to take their talents elsewhere, I'll meet their travelling expenses. But we shall soon see him falling for the first pretty woman that chance puts in his way. That's in the order of things, and I wouldn't want to see him otherwise . . . If it's necessary, get the marchesa to write to him.'

This idea, proffered with an air of complete indifference, was a shaft of light for the duchess; she was afraid of Giletti. That evening the count announced, as if by chance, that there was a courier who, en route to Vienna, would go through Milan. Three days later, Fabrizio received a letter from his mother. He left, much put out at not having yet been able, thanks to Giletti's jealousy, to take advantage of the excellent intentions of which little Marietta had assured him, via a *mammacia*, an old woman who acted as her mother.

Fabrizio found his mother and one of his sisters in Belgirate, a large Piedmontese village on the right bank of Lake Maggiore. The left bank belongs to the duchy of Milan and thus to Austria. This lake runs parallel to Lake Como, also north–south, but is situated some sixty miles further west. The mountain air, the tranquil and majestic aspect of this magnificent lake, which reminded him of that near to which he had spent his boyhood, all helped to turn Fabrizio's vexation, which was close to being anger, into a gentle melancholy. It was with an infinite tenderness that the memory of the duchess now presented itself to him. It seemed as if, from a distance, he was acquiring that love for her that he had never felt for any woman. Nothing would have been more painful for him than to be forever separated from her, and in this frame of mind, had the duchess deigned to resort to the least flirtatiousness, she would have conquered that heart by, for example, setting up a rival for it. But, very far from adopting so positive a course, it was not without blaming herself severely that she found her thoughts forever attaching to the young voyager's footsteps. She blamed herself for what she still called a whim, as if it had been an atrocity. She became doubly attentive and considerate towards the count who, seduced by so much charm, paid no heed to the voice of reason that prescribed a second trip to Bologna.

The Marchesa del Dongo, hard pressed by the nuptials of her elder daughter, whom she was marrying to a Milanese duke, could spare only three days for her beloved son. Never had she found him so fondly affectionate. In the midst of the melancholy that had more and more taken hold of Fabrizio's soul, a bizarre, even absurd idea had occurred to him and had suddenly been acted on. Dare we say that he wanted to consult Father Blanes? That excellent old man was quite incapable of understanding the troubles of a heart torn between childish passions of almost equal force, and it would anyway have taken a week to give him even an inkling of all the self-interest Fabrizio had to negotiate in Parma. But by thinking of consulting him, Fabrizio rediscovered the freshness of his sensations aged sixteen. Is it to be believed? It was not simply as a wise man, as a truly devoted friend, that Fabrizio wanted to speak with him. The object of the course he was taking, and the sentiments that were agitating our hero during the fifty hours it lasted, are so absurd that no doubt it would have been better to suppress them; for the sake of our story, I fear that Fabrizio's credulity may rob him of the reader's sympathy. But then, that is how he was, why flatter him, any more than the others? I have not been flattering either the count or the prince.

Fabrizio therefore, since there's no hiding it, Fabrizio escorted his mother back as far as the port of Laveno, on the left shore of Lake Maggiore, the Austrian shore, where she landed around eight in the evening. (The lake is regarded as neutral territory, and anyone not going ashore does not have to show a passport.) But hardly had it got dark before he had himself set down on that same Austrian shore, in the middle of a small wood which runs out into the water. He had hired a *sediola*, a sort of rapid rural tilbury, with the help of which he was able to follow, some five hundred paces behind, his mother's carriage. He was disguised as a servant from the Casa del Dongo, and not one of the numerous police or customs officers thought of asking him for his passport. A quarter of a league from Como, where the marchesa and her daughter were to halt in order to spend the night, he took a track on the left which, skirting the market town of Vico, then merged with a narrow road constructed recently on the extreme edge of the lake. It was midnight and Fabrizio could hope not to encounter any policemen. The black outlines of the foliage of the trees in the clumps of woodland through which the road kept passing stood out against a sky that was starlit but veiled in a light mist. The water and the sky were profoundly tranquil. Fabrizio's soul was unable to resist this sublime beauty. He stopped, then sat down on a rock that stuck out into the lake, forming something like a small promontory. The universal silence was disturbed, at regular intervals, only by the little waves on the lake coming to expire on the strand. Fabrizio had an Italian heart; I ask that he be forgiven. This failing, which will make him less likeable, consisted above all in this: he was vain only in fits and starts, and he felt moved at the mere sight of such sublime beauty, which took away the keen, hard edge of his afflictions. Sitting on his isolated rock, no longer needing to keep on his guard against the police, protected by the darkness of the night and the immense silence, soft tears moistened his eyes and he experienced, at small cost, the happiest moments he had tasted for a long time past.

He resolved never to tell the duchess any untruths, and it is because he loved her to the point of adoration at that moment that he swore never to tell her that he *loved* her. Never would he utter the word *love* in her presence, since the passion so named was a stranger to his heart. In the upsurge of generosity and courage that had led to his supreme happiness at that moment, he made a resolution to tell her everything at the first opportunity: his heart had never known love. Once this courageous course had been adopted, he felt as though released from an enormous weight. She will perhaps have a few words to say about Marietta. Very well, I shall never see little Marietta again, he answered himself cheerfully.

The crippling heat that had prevailed during the day was

beginning to be tempered by the morning breeze. Already the dawn's faint white glow was picking out the summits of the Alps which rise to the north and east of Lake Como. Their mass, white with snow even in June, stands out against the pure azure of a sky forever cloudless at those immense altitudes. One branch of the Alps advancing southwards towards Italy the Blessed divides the slopes of Lake Como from those of Lake Garda. Fabrizio followed with his eye each branch of these sublime mountains and as the dawn grew brighter, it came to mark out the valleys which divide them, lighting up the faint mist which rose from the bottom of the defiles.

For the last few moments, Fabrizio had been on the move again. He passed the hill which forms the peninsula of Durini and finally there came in sight the bell-tower in the village of Grianta, where he had so often made observations of the stars with Father Blanes. How ignorant I was in those days! I couldn't understand, he said to himself, even the ridiculous Latin of the astrological treatises my mentor used to leaf through, and I fancy I respected them above all because I understood only a few words here and there and my imagination took it on itself to lend them a meaning, and the most romantic one possible at that.

Gradually, his reverie took another direction. Could there be something real in that science? Why would it be different from the others? A certain number of imbeciles and the artful agree among themselves that they know *Mexican*, for example. In that capacity, they impose themselves on the society that respects them and the governments that pay them. They are showered with favours precisely because they are unintelligent, and authority doesn't have to fear that they will stir nations up or play on people's emotions with the help of their generous sentiments. Father Bari, for example, to whom Ernest IV has just granted a pension of four thousand francs and the cross of his order for having restored nineteen lines of a Greek dithyramb!

But good God, do I really have the right to find these things ridiculous? Is it really for me to complain? he asked himself, coming to a sudden halt, hasn't that selfsame cross just been given to my tutor in Naples? Fabrizio felt a sense of profound unease. That noble enthusiasm for virtue that had just now set his heart racing had turned into the ignominious pleasure of playing a leading role in a theft. Well, he said to himself finally, with the lacklustre eyes of a man dissatisfied with himself, since my birth gives me the right to profit from these abuses, it would be a notable piece of deception on my part not to take my share of them. But I mustn't decide to speak ill of them in public. This reasoning was not altogether wrong. But how far Fabrizio had fallen from the sublime heights of happiness on to which he had found himself transported an hour before. The thought of privilege had caused that most delicate of plants which we call happiness to wither.

If we are not to believe in astrology, he went on, seeking to break his train of thought, if that science is, like three quarters of the non-mathematical sciences, a coming together of enthusiastic halfwits and astute hypocrites paid by the people they serve, how is it that I reflect so often, and with feeling, on this fateful circumstance? In the past, I got out of the prison in B***, but with the clothes and the movement order of a soldier who'd quite rightly been thrown in gaol.

Fabrizio's arguments could never reach any further. He circled this way and that around the difficulty without succeeding in surmounting it. He was still too young. In his unoccupied moments, his soul busied itself sampling with delight the sensations produced by romantic circumstances that his imagination was ever ready to supply. He was very far from employing the time looking patiently at the actual particularities of things so as then to divine their cause. The real he still found flat and muddy. I can understand not liking to look at it, but then one shouldn't theorize about it. Above all, one should not raise objections to it based on the diverse testimony of your ignorance.

Thus it was that, though not without intelligence, Fabrizio could not manage to see that his half-belief in omens was for him a religion, a profound impression received on his entry into life. To think about this belief was to feel; it was a form of happiness. And he persisted in searching for how it might be a *proven* science, real as geometry is real, for example. He searched eagerly in his memory for all the situations in which omens he had observed had not been followed by the happy or unhappy event they seemed to be foretelling. But even as he believed he was following the argument and progressing towards the truth, his attention would dwell happily on the memory of instances where the omen had broadly speaking been followed by the happy or unhappy accident it had seemed to be predicting, and his soul was awestruck and moved to tears. He would have felt an insurmountable repugnance for the person who denied omens, especially were they to employ irony.

Fabrizio was walking oblivious of distances, and had reached this point in his fruitless reasonings when, looking up, he saw the wall of his father's garden. This wall, which supported a beautiful terrace, rose more than forty feet above the road, on the right. A course of dressed stone at the very top, next to the balustrade, lent it a monumental appearance. It's not bad, Fabrizio told himself impassively, that's a good bit of architecture, almost in the Roman style. He was applying his new expertise in antiquities. Then he turned away in disgust. His father's severities, and above all his brother Ascanio's denunciation on his return from his expedition to France, came back into his mind.

That unnatural denunciation was where my present life originated. I may hate it, I may despise it, but there it is, it altered my destiny. What would have become of me once I'd been packed off to Novara and been just about tolerated by my father's factor, if my aunt hadn't made love with an influential minister? If that aunt, who loves me with a sort of enthusiasm that astonishes me, had happened to have only a commonplace, dried-up soul instead of that tender, passionate, soul? Where would I be now if the duchess had had the soul of her brother, the Marchese del Dongo?

Oppressed by these cruel memories, Fabrizio's steps had now begun to falter. He reached the edge of the moat directly opposite the magnificent façade of the castle. He barely even glanced at this great edifice, blackened by time. The noble language of its architecture left him unmoved. The memory of his brother and his father closed his soul to any sensation of beauty, his one concern was to remain on his guard in the presence of hypocritical and dangerous enemies. He looked for a moment, but with a marked distaste, at the little window of the third-floor room he had occupied before 1815. His father's character had robbed the memories of his early childhood of all attraction. I haven't been back there, he reflected, since the 7th of March at eight o'clock in the evening. I left to go and get Vasi's passport and the next day my fear of spies made me speed up my departure. When I came back after the journey in France, I didn't have time to go up, not even to see my engravings again, and that thanks to my brother's having given me away.

Fabrizio turned his head away in abhorrence. Father Blanes is more than eighty-three years old, he told himself sadly, he hardly comes to the castle any more, according to what my sister has told me. The infirmities of old age have had their effect. That steadfast and noble soul has been frozen by age. God knows how long it is since he stopped going to his tower! I shall hide in the storeroom, under the vats or under the wine-press, until it's time for him to wake up. I shan't go and disturb the worthy old man's sleep. He'll probably have forgotten what I look like even. Six years is a long time at that age. I shall find only the tomb of a friend! And it's sheer childishness, he added, to have come here to confront the distaste my father's castle produces in me.

Fabrizio was just entering the little square by the church. It was with an astonishment verging on delirium that he saw, on the second storey of the ancient bell-tower, the tall, narrow window lit by Father Blanes's little lantern. The priest was in the habit of setting it down there when he went up to the cage of planks which formed his observatory, so that the glare did not prevent him from reading from his planisphere. This map of the heavens was stretched over a large terracotta urn that had once belonged to an orange tree at the castle. In the opening, at the bottom of the urn, burnt the most exiguous of lamps, the smoke from which was carried out from the urn through a small tin pipe, the pipe's shadow indicating north on the map.

All these memories of such simple things flooded Fabrizio's soul with emotion and filled it with happiness.

Almost without thinking, and using both his hands, he gave the short, low whistle that in the old days had been the signal to let him in. He at once heard several tugs being given on the cord which, from up in the observatory, lifted the latch on the door into the tower. He dashed up the stairs, quite transported. He found the priest on his wooden armchair in his accustomed place. His eye was fixed on the small eyepiece of a quadrant on the wall. With his left hand, the priest signed to him not to interrupt him in his observation. A moment later, he wrote down a figure on a playing card, then, turning round on his chair, opened his arms to our hero, who threw himself into them in floods of tears. Father Blanes was his true father.

'I was expecting you,' said Blanes, after the first words of outpouring and affection. Had the priest been practising his scientific trade or, since he often thought about Fabrizio, had some astrological sign, purely by chance, announced his return?

'And now my death is at hand,' said Father Blanes.

'What!' cried Fabrizio, greatly moved.

'Yes,' the priest went on, in a serious but by no means unhappy tone, 'five and a half or six and a half months after seeing you again, my life, having met with its full complement of happiness, will be extinguished, *Come face al mancar dell'alimento*[2] (like the little lamp when it runs out of oil). Before that supreme moment, I shall probably go one or two months without speaking, after which I shall be received into the bosom of our Father. If, that is, he finds that I have fulfilled my duty in the post where he placed me as a sentinel.

'As for you, you are overcome by fatigue, your emotion disposes you to sleep. Since I have been awaiting you, I have hidden a loaf and a bottle of brandy in my big instrument box. Take those for sustenance and try to gather enough strength to listen to me for a few moments longer. It is within my power to tell you several things before the night has been altogether replaced by the day. I see them much more distinctly now than I shall perhaps see them tomorrow. For, my child, we are always weak, and one must always take that weakness into account.

Tomorrow perhaps the old man, the earthly man in me, will be taken up with the preparations for my death, and tomorrow evening at nine o'clock, you must leave me.'

Fabrizio having obeyed him in silence, as was his habit: 'So, it's true,' the old man went on, 'that when you tried to see Waterloo, you first of all found only a prison?'

'Yes, father,' replied an astonished Fabrizio.

'Well, that was a rare piece of good fortune, for, warned by my voice, your soul can prepare itself for another prison, a far harsher one, far more terrible! You will probably leave it only by way of a crime, but, thank heaven, that crime will not be committed by you. Never fall into crime however violently you may be tempted. I think I can see that it will involve killing an innocent man who, unknowingly, has usurped your rights. If you resist the violent temptation that will seem justified by the laws of honour, your life will be very happy in the eyes of men . . . and reasonably happy in the eyes of the sage,' he added, after a moment's reflection. 'You will die like me, my son, sitting on a wooden seat, far from all luxury, undeceived by luxury, and like me having nothing serious with which to reproach yourself.

'And now the things of the future state are ended between us, I would be unable to add anything of much importance. It is in vain that I have sought to see of what duration that imprisonment will be. Is it a matter of six months, or a year, or ten years? I have not been able to discover. It appears I have committed some fault, and heaven has wanted to punish me with the disappointment of this uncertainty. I have seen only that after the prison, but I do not know whether it is at the very moment of leaving it, there will be what I call a crime, but happily I think I am sure it will not be committed by you. If you are sufficiently weak to have a hand in that crime, all the rest of my calculations are no more than one long error. In that case, you will not die with your soul at peace, on a wooden seat and dressed in white.' As he spoke these words, Father Blanes tried to get up and it was now that Fabrizio observed the ravages of time. It took him almost a minute to stand up and turn towards Fabrizio. The latter remained where he was, neither moving nor speaking. The priest threw himself several times into his arms; he clasped him with an extreme affection. After which he went on, with all the cheerfulness of old: 'Try to arrange yourself among my instruments so you can sleep comfortably for a bit, take my fur pelisses. You will find several expensive ones that the Duchess Sanseverina sent me four years ago. She asked me for a prediction on your account, which I took good care not to send her, while keeping her pelisses and her beautiful quadrant. Any announcement of the future is an infringement of the rules, and runs the risk that it may alter the event, in which case the whole science falls to the ground just like a child's game, and there were in any case harsh things to say to a duchess who is still so pretty. By the way, don't be frightened when you're asleep by the bells, which are going to make an awful din next to your ear when they come to ring for seven o'clock Mass. Later, on the floor below, they'll set the big bass bell swinging, which shakes all my instruments. Today is the feast-day of St Giovita, martyr and soldier. The little village of Grianta has the same patron, you know, as the great town of Brescia, which, incidentally, misled my illustrious mentor Giacomo Marini of Ravenna in a very amusing way. He announced to me several times that I would enjoy a very prosperous ecclesiastical career; he thought I would be the priest of the magnificent church of St Giovita in Brescia. I have been the priest of a small village of seven hundred and fifty hearths! But everything has been for the best. I realized, not ten years since, that if I had been a priest in Brescia, my destiny would have been to be put in gaol on a hill in Moravia, in the Spielberg. Tomorrow I shall bring you all manner of delicacies stolen from the grand dinner I give to all the priests from round about who come and sing at my high Mass. I shall bring them down below, but don't try to see me, don't come down to take possession of these good things until you've heard me go out again. You mustn't see me again *in the daylight*, and the sun setting tomorrow at seven twenty-seven, I shall come and embrace you only around eight, and you must leave while the hours are still measured from nine, that's to say, before the clock has struck ten. Take care you're not seen at the windows in the tower.

The police have your description and they are to some extent under the orders of your brother, who is a regular tyrant. The Marchese del Dongo is in decline,' added Blanes with a sad expression, 'and if he saw you again, perhaps he would put something into your hand. But benefits tainted by stealth in that way are not proper for a man such as you, whose strength will one day lie in his conscience. The marchese abhors his son Ascanio, and it is to that son that the five or six million he possesses will devolve. That is justice. At his death, you for your part will have an allowance of four thousand francs, and fifty aunes of black cloth for your people's mourning.'

CHAPTER 9

Fabrizio's soul had been exalted by the old man's disquisition, by the close attention he had paid and by extreme fatigue. He had great difficulty in getting to sleep, and his sleep was disturbed by dreams, perhaps omens of the future. In the morning, at ten o'clock, he was woken up by the shaking of the whole tower, a terrifying noise seemed to be coming from outside. He got up in bewilderment and fancied it was the end of the world, then thought he was in prison. It took him a little while to recognize the sound of the great bell that forty peasants had set in motion in honour of the great St Giovita; ten would have sufficed.

Fabrizio sought for a convenient spot from which to see without being seen. He realized that from this great height he could look down into the gardens, and even into the inner courtyard of his father's castle. He had forgotten it. The thought of that father nearing the term of his life altered all his feelings. He could even make out the sparrows hunting for a few crumbs of bread on the big balcony of the dining room. They're the descendants of the ones I tamed in the old days, he told himself. This balcony, like all the other balconies in the palazzo, carried a large number of orange trees in terracotta urns of varying sizes. The sight moved him. The aspect of the inner courtyard, thus adorned with its shadows, their edges sharply defined by the brilliant sunlight, was truly imposing.

His father's failing health came back into his mind. But it's really strange, he told himself, my father is only thirty-five years older than me; thirty-five and twenty-three make only fifty-eight! His eyes, fixed on the windows of the bedroom of that unyielding man who had never loved him, filled with tears. He shivered and a sudden chill ran through his veins when he thought he recognized his father crossing a terrace graced by orange trees, which was on the same level as his room. But it was only a footman. Right underneath the tower, a number of young girls dressed in white and divided into various groups were busy laying out patterns of red, blue and yellow flowers on the ground in the streets where the procession was due to pass. But there was one spectacle which spoke more keenly to Fabrizio's soul: from the tower, he could look down on to the two arms of the lake several leagues away, and this sublime view quickly made him forget all the others. It awoke the loftiest feelings in him. All the memories of his childhood came crowding in to lay siege to his mind; and this day spent imprisoned in a bell-tower was perhaps one of the happiest of his life.

This happiness bore his thoughts up to a height somewhat foreign to his nature. Young though he was, he contemplated the events of his life as though he had already arrived at its ultimate limit. It has to be agreed, he said to himself at last, after several hours of delectable daydreaming, that since I arrived in Parma, I have known no peaceful and unalloyed joy, like that I found in Naples galloping along the roads of Vomero or roaming the shores of Misena. All the very complicated interests in a spiteful small court have made me spiteful . . . I get no pleasure from hating, I even think it would be a sad kind of happiness to humiliate my enemies if I had any. But I have no enemies . . . Hold on, he suddenly said to himself, I have Giletti for an enemy . . . That's strange, he said to himself, the pleasure I would get from seeing that ugly fellow go to the devil has survived the faint liking I felt for little Marietta. She doesn't come near the duchess of A***, whom I was obliged to love in Naples because I'd told her I was in love with her. Good God, how bored I often used to get during the long assignations the beautiful Duchess granted me. Not like in that shabby room serving as a kitchen where little Marietta received me twice, and for two minutes each time.

Good God, what do those sort of people eat? It's enough to

make you weep! I ought to have given her and the *mamma-cia* an allowance of three beefsteaks, payable daily ... Little Marietta, he went on, took my mind off the unkind thoughts being near that court gave me.

Perhaps I'd have done better to take up the café life, as the duchess puts it. She seemed to be leaning in that direction and she has far more of a genius for it than I do. Thanks to her beneficence, or even just simply with the allowance of four thousand francs and the forty thousand of capital invested in Lyon that my mother intends for me, I'd always have a horse and a few écus to go excavating and start a collection. Since it seems I'm not to experience love, those will always be the great sources of happiness for me. I'd like, before I die, to go and revisit the battlefield of Waterloo, and try to identify the plain where I was so cheerfully removed from my horse and set down on the ground. That pilgrimage fulfilled, I'd often come back to this sublime lake. There's nothing so beautiful to be seen in the world, for my heart at least. What's the point of going all that way in search of happiness; it's here in front of me!

But, Fabrizio told himself, as an objection, the police will chase me away from Lake Como, but I'm younger than the people who are setting the police on me. Here, he added, laughing, I certainly shouldn't find a duchess of A***, but I'd find one of those young girls down there arranging flowers on the roadway, and the truth is I'd love her just as much. Hypocrisy makes me freeze even in love, and our great ladies aim at effects that are too sublime. Napoleon has given them ideas about how to behave and about constancy.

Curse it! he suddenly said to himself, withdrawing his head from the window, as if he were afraid of being recognized despite the shadow of the enormous wooden screen that protected the bells from the rain, here's the police making their entrance, in full dress uniform. Indeed, ten policemen, four of them warrant officers, had appeared at the top of the main village street. The sergeant was distributing them every hundred paces, along the route the procession was due to follow. Everyone knows me here. If I'm seen, I shall take one jump straight from the shores of Lake Como into the Spielberg, where I shall have a chain weighing a hundred and ten pounds attached to each leg. And how the duchess will grieve!

It took Fabrizio two or three minutes to remind himself that first of all he was situated more than eighty feet up, that the place where he found himself was relatively dark, that the people who might be watching him had a blinding sun in their eyes, and lastly that they were walking with their eyes opened wide in streets all of whose houses had been whitewashed in honour of the festival of St Giovita. Despite which lucid reasoning, Fabrizio's Italian soul would from then on have been in no state to experience any pleasure, if he had not interposed between himself and the policemen a scrap of old cloth which he nailed against the window and in which he made two holes for his eyes.

The bells had been shaking the air for the past ten minutes, the procession was coming out from the church and the *mortaretti*[1] were making themselves heard. Fabrizio turned his head and recognized the little esplanade graced by a parapet and overlooking the lake where so often, in his young days, he had run the risk of having the *mortaretti* go off under his feet, which meant that on feast-day mornings his mother wanted to see him at her side.

One needs to know that *mortaretti*, or little mortars, are nothing more than gun barrels sawn down in such a way as to leave them no more than four inches long. This is why the peasants are avid collectors of the gun barrels which, since 1796, the politics of Europe has sown in profusion over the plains of Lombardy. Once reduced to a length of four inches, these little barrels are filled right to the muzzle and set down vertically on the ground, with a trail of gunpowder leading from one to another. They are arranged in three ranks like a battalion, to the tune of two or three hundred, in some emplacement close to the spot where the procession has to go past. When the Holy Sacrament approaches, they set the trail of powder alight, and there then begins the most irregular and ridiculous running fire of brief explosions. The women go berserk with delight. Nothing could be merrier than the sound of the *mortaretti* heard in the distance on the lake, muffled by the plash of the water. This singular sound, which had so often been the delight of his childhood, drove away the rather too solemn thoughts by which our hero had been besieged. He went to fetch the priest's big astronomical telescope and recognized most of the men and women who were following the procession. Many pretty little girls who Fabrizio had left behind at the age of eleven or twelve were now proud young women, in the full flowering of a very vigorous youth. They caused our hero's courage to revive and he would gladly have braved the policemen to talk with them.

The procession having passed and re-entered the church, through a side door that Fabrizio could not see, the heat soon became extreme, even at the top of the tower. The inhabitants went back home and a great silence fell on the village. Several boats took on board peasants returning to Belagio, Menagio and other villages situated on the lake. Fabrizio could make out the sound of each stroke of the oars, a simple detail which sent him into raptures. His present joy came from all the unhappiness, all the difficulties he had found in the complicated life of the courts. How happy he would have been at that moment to do a league on that beautiful, very tranquil lake, which reflected with such clarity the depth of the heavens! He heard the door open at the foot of the tower. It was Father Blanes's old serving woman, who had brought a large basket. He had the utmost difficulty in stopping himself from speaking to her. She has almost as great an affection for me as her master, he told himself, and moreover I'm leaving this evening at nine o'clock. Would she not keep the secret she'd swear she would, just for a few hours? But, Fabrizio told himself, my dear friend wouldn't like it. I might put him at risk from the police. And he let Ghita go without speaking to her. He made an excellent dinner then settled down to sleep for a few minutes. He did not wake up until half past eight in the evening; Father Blanes was shaking him by the arm and it was dark.

Blanes was extremely tired, he was fifty years older than the day before. He no longer spoke of serious matters. Sitting on his wooden armchair, embrace me, he told Fabrizio. He took him back into his arms several times. 'Death,' he said at last,

'which is about to end this long, long life, will have nothing as
painful as this separation. I have a purse which I shall leave on
trust with Ghita, with the order to draw on it for her needs,
but to hand over to you what remains if ever you come and ask
for it. I know her. After that injunction, she is capable of
economizing for your sake and not buying meat four times in
a year, if you don't give her very precise orders. You may
yourself be reduced to penury and your old friend's obol will
be of service. Expect nothing from your brother except conduct
of the most atrocious kind and try to earn money by work
which renders you useful to society. I foresee strange storms; in
fifty years' time perhaps they will no longer want anything to
do with men who are idle. Your mother and your aunt may be
taken from you, your sisters will have to obey their husbands
. . . Be off, be off! Fly!' cried Blanes eagerly. He had just heard
a faint noise in the clock which gave notice that it was about
to strike ten; he refused even to allow Fabrizio to embrace him
for one last time.

'Hurry, hurry!' he cried. 'It'll take you a minute at least to
get down the stairs. Mind you don't fall, that would be an awful
omen.' Fabrizio dashed down the stairs and, having reached the
square, began to run. He had hardly arrived in front of his
father's castle before the bell sounded ten o'clock. Each stroke
echoed in his chest and produced a strange disturbance there.
He stopped to reflect, or rather to give himself up to the passionate feelings inspired in him by the contemplation of that majestic building that he had judged so impassively the day before.
In the midst of his reverie, men's footsteps came to arouse him.
He looked and found himself in the midst of four policemen.
He had two excellent pistols whose primers he had renewed as
he ate. The faint sound he made arming them drew the attention
of one of the policemen, and was on the point of getting him
arrested. He recognized the danger he was in and thought of
being the first to fire. That was his right, for it was the one
means he had of resisting four well-armed men. Luckily, the
policemen, who were going round clearing the taverns, had
not shown themselves altogether unresponsive to the courtesies
they had received in several of those agreeable places. They did

not make up their minds quickly enough to do their duty. Fabrizio turned tail, running as fast as he could go. The policemen took a few paces, also at a run, shouting: 'Halt, halt!', then the silence returned. Three hundred paces away, Fabrizio stopped to recover his breath. The sound my pistols made almost got me caught. It's exactly what the duchess would have said, if ever it had been given to me to see her lovely eyes again, that my soul finds pleasure in contemplating what will happen in ten years' time and forgets to look at what is going on here and now right in front of me.

Fabrizio shuddered when he thought of the danger he had just avoided. He quickened his pace, but soon could not stop himself from running, which was not very sensible, for he got himself noticed by several peasants returning to their houses. He could bring himself to stop only in the mountains, a league or more from Grianta, and even once he had stopped, he broke out in a cold sweat at the thought of the Spielberg.

A fine time to be afraid, he told himself, on hearing the sound of which words, he was almost tempted to feel ashamed. But doesn't my aunt say that the thing I need most is to learn to forgive myself? I'm always comparing myself to some ideal figure, who can't exist. Very well, I forgive myself for being afraid, for on the other hand I was quite ready to defend my freedom, and certainly they wouldn't all four have remained standing to take me to prison. What I'm doing at this moment, he went on, is not military. Instead of retreating rapidly, having achieved my objective, and perhaps put my enemies on the alert, I'm amusing myself by a fancy more ridiculous perhaps than all the good priest's predictions.

Indeed, instead of retreating by the shortest route, and making for the shores of Lake Maggiore, where his boat was waiting for him, he made an enormous detour to go and visit *his tree*. The reader will perhaps remember the love Fabrizio bore a chestnut tree planted by his mother twenty-three years earlier. It would have been just like my brother, he told himself, to have had the tree cut down. But anything delicate passes creatures of that sort by, it won't have crossed his mind. And in any case, it wouldn't be a bad omen, he added firmly. Two hours later, a disconcerting sight met his gaze: some vandals or else a storm had broken one of the main branches of the young tree, which was hanging down, withered. Fabrizio cut it off reverently, with the help of his dagger, and trimmed the cut, so that water could not get inside the trunk. Then, although time was very precious, because it was about to get light, he spent a good hour hoeing the soil around his beloved tree. All of which foolishness accomplished, he quickly resumed his journey to Lake Maggiore. All in all, he was not unhappy, the tree was doing well, more vigorous than ever, and in five years it had almost doubled in size. The branch was simply an accident of no consequence. Once cut off, it was no longer damaging the tree, which would be all the more graceful for its limbs starting higher up.

Fabrizio had not gone a league before the peaks of the Resegon di Lek, a mountain celebrated in those parts, stood outlined against a dazzling band of white in the east. The road he was following was covered with peasants, but, instead of having military ideas, Fabrizio allowed himself to be moved by the sublime or affecting aspect of the forests in the vicinty of Lake Como. They are perhaps the most beautiful in the world. I do not mean those that bring in the most *shiny new écus*, as they would say in Switzerland, but those which speak loudest to the soul. To listen to such language in the situation in which Fabrizio found himself, exposed to the attentions of signori the police of Lombardy-Venice, was truly childish. I'm half a league from the frontier, he told himself at last, I'm about to encounter customs men and policemen on their morning rounds. They'll have their suspicions about this broadcloth coat, they're going to ask me for my passport. But that passport bears in so many letters a name destined for a prison. Here I am in the agreeable necessity of committing a murder. If, as usual, the police are walking in pairs, I can't simply wait to fire until one of them tries to grab me by the collar. He only has to hold on to me for an instant as he falls and I'm in the Spielberg. Seized by horror at the necessity of being the first to fire, perhaps at one of his uncle Count Pietranera's former soldiers, Fabrizio ran and hid in the hollow trunk of an enormous chestnut tree. He was renewing the primers in his pistols when he heard a man advancing through the wood singing, and singing very well, a delightful aria from Mercadante,[2] then in vogue in Lombardy.

That's a good omen! Fabrizio told himself. The aria, which he listened to religiously, took the edge off the anger that had begun to interfere with his thought processes. He looked closely at both sides of the high road; he saw nobody. The singer will arrive by some side road, he told himself. At almost the same instant, he saw a footman very correctly dressed in the English style, trotting slowly forward on one horse and leading another, a beautiful thoroughbred that was perhaps a little too scrawny.

Ah, were I to reason like Mosca, Fabrizio said to himself, when he dins it into me that the dangers a man incurs are always the measure of his rights over his neighbour, I'd crack this footman's skull open with my pistol and once up on the scrawny horse laugh at all the world's policemen. No sooner back in Parma and I'd send the man or his widow some money . . . but it would be terrible to do that!

CHAPTER 10

As he was reading himself a lecture, Fabrizio jumped down on to the high road that goes from Lombardy into Switzerland. At this point, it is a good four or five feet below the level of the forest. If my man takes fright, Fabrizio told himself, he'll be off at the gallop, and I shall be left rooted here looking like a complete idiot. At that moment, he found himself ten paces away from the footman, who was no longer singing. He could see from his eyes that he was afraid. He was perhaps going to turn his horses round. Without having yet decided on anything, Fabrizio leapt forward and seized hold of the scrawny horse's bridle.

'My friend,' he said to the footman, 'I'm no ordinary robber, because I'm going to start by giving you twenty francs, but I'm obliged to borrow your horse off you. I'm going to be killed if I don't get out of here pretty f****** quick. I've got the four Riva brothers after me, those mighty hunters whom you no doubt know. They've just surprised me in their sister's bed-room, I jumped out of the window and here I am. They came out into the forest with their dogs and their guns. I hid in that big hollow chestnut, because I saw one of them crossing the road, their dogs are going to pick up my scent. I'm going to get on your horse and gallop up to a league the other side of Como. I'm going to Milan to throw myself at the viceroy's feet. I'll leave your horse at the posthouse with two napoleons for you, if you agree with a good grace. If you put up the slightest resistance, I shall kill you with the pistols you see here. If, once I'm gone, you set the police on my trail, my cousin, the brave

Count Alari, the Emperor's equerry, will make it his job to break your neck.'

Fabrizio was making this speech up as he went along, while looking perfectly peaceable. 'What's more,' he said laughing, 'my name is no secret. I am the Marchesino Ascanio del Dongo, my castle is very near here, in Grianta. So let go of the f******* horse,' he said, raising his voice. The stunned footman did not breathe a word. Fabrizio changed his pistol over to his left hand, grabbed the bridle that the other man had let go of, jumped up on to the horse and left at a smart trot. When he was three hundred paces away, he realized he had forgotten to give the twenty francs he had promised. He stopped. There was still no one on the road but the footman, who was galloping after him. He signalled to him with his handkerchief to come forward and once he saw he was fifty paces away, threw a handful of small change down on the roadway and set off again. From the distance, he saw the footman picking up the coins. There goes a truly reasonable man, said Fabrizio to himself, laughing, not one unnecessary word. He pressed rapidly on, stopped around noon in a house away from the road, then resumed his journey a few hours later. At two in the morning, he was on the banks of Lake Maggiore. Soon he saw his boat churning up the water, it came at the agreed signal. He could not see a peasant to hand the horse back to. He gave the noble animal its freedom, and three hours later he was in Belgirate. There, finding himself in friendly territory, he relaxed somewhat. He was very joyful, he had managed it perfectly. Do we dare to point out the true causes of his joy? His tree had done superbly well and his soul had been refreshed by the deep emotion he had found in the arms of Father Blanes. Does he really believe in all the predictions he made? he asked himself. Or, because my brother has given me the reputation of a Jacobin, of a man who fears neither God nor man, capable of anything, did he simply want to make me pledge not to succumb to the temptation of cracking open the skull of some individual who's done the dirty on me? Two days later, Fabrizio was in Parma, where he greatly amused the duchess and the count by narrating the entire story of his journey, in every last particular, as he always did.

On arrival, Fabrizio found the porter and all the servants at the Palazzo Sanseverina bearing the insignia of the deepest mourning. 'Who have we lost?' he asked the duchess.

'That excellent man known as my husband has just died in Baden. He has left me this palazzo. It was something we'd agreed on, but as a token of his affection he has added a legacy of three hundred thousand francs, which is a great embarrassment. I refuse to give it up in favour of his niece, the Marchesa Raversi, who plays vile tricks on me every day. You know about art, you must find me some good sculptor. I shall raise a tomb to the duke costing three hundred thousand francs.' The count began to retail gossip about Raversi.

'I've tried to soften her up by doing her good turns but it's no good,' said the duchess. 'As for the duke's nephews, I've made them all colonels or generals. In return for which, not a month goes by without them addressing some abominable anonymous letter to me. I've been forced to take on a secretary to read letters of that sort.'

'And the anonymous letters are the least of their sins,' Count Mosca went on. 'They run a factory turning out wicked denunciations. I could have had the whole gang up before the courts a score of times, and Your Excellency may well ask himself,' he added addressing Fabrizio, 'whether my worthy judges would have convicted them.'

'Well, for me that spoils all the rest,' replied Fabrizio, with a naivety quite comical in a court, 'I'd rather have seen them convicted by magistrates judging according to their consciences.'

'You would do me a favour, you who travel in order to educate yourself, if you were to give me the address of any such magistrates, I shall write to them before I go to bed.'

'Were I a minister, my self-respect would suffer, if I didn't have judges who were honest.'

'It seems to me,' replied the count, 'that Your Excellency, who is so fond of the French, and who even once lent them the aid of his invincible arm, is forgetting at this moment one of their great maxims: better to kill the devil than have the devil kill you. I should like to see how you would govern these fervent souls, who read the history of the French Revolution all day long, with judges who would acquit the men I'm accusing. They'd end up failing to convict scoundrels who were patently guilty and saw themselves as so many Brutuses.[1] But I have a bone I want to pick: does that very delicate soul of yours not feel any remorse concerning that handsome, rather lean horse that you have just abandoned on the shores of Lake Maggiore?'

'I'm certainly counting,' said Fabrizio, with the greatest seriousness, 'on seeing that the horse's owner gets what it takes to reimburse him for the cost of putting up bills and so on, which will result in it being returned to him by the peasants who will have found it. I'm going to read the Milan newspaper assiduously, to look for the advertisement of a lost horse. I know that one's description very well.'

'He is truly *primitive*,' the count told the duchess. 'And what would have become of Your Excellency,' he went on, laughing, 'if when you were galloping flat out on that borrowed horse, it had taken it into its head to stumble? You'd have been in the Spielberg, my dear young nephew, and all my influence would scarcely have managed to get thirty pounds knocked off the weight of the chain attached to each of your legs. You'd have spent a dozen years in that pleasure palace. Your legs would perhaps have swollen up and gone gangrenous, then they'd have cut them neatly off . . .'

'Oh, please, that sad piece of fiction's gone far enough,' cried the duchess, with tears in her eyes. 'We have him back . . .'

'And you can well believe that I'm more delighted by that than you are,' replied the minister, entirely seriously. 'But then why did this cruel child not ask me for a passport under a suitable name, since he wanted to get into Lombardy? At the first news of his arrest I'd have left for Milan, and the friends I have in those parts would have been happy to turn a blind eye and assume that their police had arrested a subject of the prince of Parma. The account of your horse race is charming and amusing, I'm willing to give you that,' replied the count, resuming a less ominous tone. 'Your emerging from the wood on to the high road I rather like. But between ourselves, since that footman held your life in his hands, you had the right to take his. We're going to ensure that Your Excellency has a brilliant future, or so the signora here has commanded me at least, and I don't fancy my worst enemies can accuse me of ever having disobeyed her commands. What a mortal disappointment for her and for me if, during that sort of race against the clock you've just had with that scrawny horse, it had stumbled! It would almost have been better,' the count added, 'if the horse had broken your neck.'

'You're being very tragic this evening, my love,' said the duchess, much affected.

'The fact is we're surrounded by tragic events,' replied the count, feelingly also. 'We're not in France here, where everything ends in a song or a year or two in prison, and it's truly wrong of me to laugh when I talk of these matters. Well there, young nephew mine, I suppose I must find room to make you a bishop, for obviously I can't begin with the archbishopric of Parma, as, very reasonably, the lady duchess here present would like. Give us some idea perhaps of what your policy will be in that bishopric, where you'll be far removed from our wise counsel?'

'Kill the devil rather than have him kill me, as my friends the French so rightly say,' replied Fabrizio, eyes ablaze. 'To preserve by every means possible, the pistol included, the position you will have made for me. I've read in the del Dongo genealogy the story of that ancestor of ours who built the castle at Grianta. Towards the end of his life, his good friend Galeas, the duke of Milan, sent him on a visit to a fortress on our lake. They were afraid of a fresh invasion on the part of the Swiss. "But I must write a polite note to the commander," the duke of Milan said on dismissing him. He wrote and handed him a letter two lines long. Then he asked for it back, to seal it: "That will be more polite," said the prince. Vespasian del Dongo left, but as he navigated the lake, he recalled an old Greek tale, for he was a man of learning. He opened his good master's letter and found an order addressed to the commander of the castle to put him to death the moment he arrived. The Sforza, over-attentive to the comedy he was playing with our ancestor, had left a gap between the bottom line of the note and the signature. Vespasian del Dongo wrote in the order to acknowledge him as governor-general of all the castles on the lake, and erased the heading on the letter. Having arrived at the fortress and been acknowledged, he threw the commander into a dungeon, declared war on the Sforzas, and a few years later exchanged his fortress for the immense estates which have created the wealth of all the branches of our family, and which will one day bring me in four thousand francs a year.'

'You talk like an academician,' exclaimed the count with a laugh. 'That's a splendid piece of ingenuity you've been recounting, but it's only once every ten years that you get the pleasant opportunity to do these stimulating things. A half-stupid individual who's watchful, and prudent day by day, very often has the pleasure of triumphing over men of imagination. It was by letting his imagination run riot that Napoleon surrendered to prudent John Bull, instead of trying to get to America. John Bull in his counting-house roared with laughter at the letter in which he quotes Themistocles.[2] The ignominious Sancho Panzas are always going to win in the long run over the sublime Don Quixotes. If you're willing to agree to do nothing extraordinary, I don't doubt that you'll be a highly respected bishop, if not a very respectable one. Nevertheless, I stick by my comment: Your Excellency behaved thoughtlessly in the affair with the horse, he came within a hair's breadth of an everlasting prison cell.'

These words made Fabrizio shudder, he remained lost in profound astonishment. Was that the prison I'm threatened with, he asked himself? Is that the crime I was not to commit? Blanes's predictions, which he had laughed to scorn as prophecies, were acquiring all the significance of genuine omens in his eyes.

'Well, what is it?' asked the duchess, in surprise. 'The count has filled your head with dark pictures.'

'I've been illuminated by a new truth, and instead of rebelling against it, my mind had adopted it. It's true, I came very close to imprisonment without end. But that footman looked so handsome in his English-style livery! It would have been a shame to kill him!'

The minister was delighted by his air of quiet good sense.

'He's very good in every way,' he said, looking at the duchess. 'I must tell you, my friend, that you've made a conquest, and the most desirable of all perhaps.'

Ah, thought Fabrizio, here comes a joke about little Marietta. He was wrong. The count went on: 'Your *evangelical* simplicity has won the heart of our venerable archbishop, Father Landriani. One of these days we're going to make you a vicar-general, and what's amusing about that is that the three current vicars-general, capable men, hard-working, two of whom, I fancy, were vicars-general before you were born, will ask, in a splendid letter addressed to their archbishop, that you be ranked first among them. These gentlemen will base themselves first of all on your virtues, and then on the fact that you are the great-nephew of the celebrated Archbishop Ascanio del Dongo. When I learnt of the respect that was felt for your virtues, I at once made the nephew of the senior of the vicars-general a captain. He'd been a lieutenant since Marshal Suchet's siege of Tarragona.[3]

'Go straight away, dressed casually, the way you are now, to pay a heartfelt call on your archbishop,' exclaimed the duchess. 'Tell him of your sister's marriage. Once he knows she's going to be a duchess, he will find you much more apostolic. Moreover, you know nothing of what the count has just confided to you about your future appointment.'

Fabrizio hurried to the archbishop's palace. There, he was both simple and modest, an attitude that came all too easily to him. Contrariwise, he had to try very hard to play the great nobleman. As he listened to Monsignor Landriani's somewhat long-winded stories, he asked himself: Should I have shot the footman who was holding the lean horse by the bridle? His reason told him yes, but his heart could not accustom itself to the bloody image of the handsome young man falling disfigured from his horse.

The prison I was going to be swallowed up by, if the horse

had stumbled, was that the prison I'm threatened with by all these omens?

This question was of the utmost importance for him, and the archbishop was pleased by the close attention he appeared to be paying him.

CHAPTER II

On leaving the archbishop's palace, Fabrizio hurried to little Marietta's. From some way off he could hear the loud voice of Giletti, who had sent out for wine and was indulging himself along with his friends, the prompter and the candle-snuffers. The *mammacia*, who filled the role of mother, alone responded to his signal.

'Things have been happening since you,' she exclaimed; 'two or three of our actors have been accused of having celebrated the great Napoleon's feast-day with an orgy, and our poor troupe, which they call Jacobin, has been ordered to clear out of the States of Parma, and long live Napoleon! But the minister's coughed up, so they say. What's certain is that Giletti has money, I don't know how much, but I've seen him with a fistful of écus. Marietta got five écus from our manager as travelling expenses to Mantua and Venice, and me one. She's still very much in love with you, but Giletti frightens her. Three days ago, at the last performance we gave, he was really out to kill her. He gave her a right pair in the face and, what's an outrage, tore her blue shawl. If you wanted to give her a blue shawl, you'd be a good lad, and we could say we won it in a lottery. The drum-major of the carabinieri is giving an assault-at-arms tomorrow, you'll find the time posted up on all the street corners. Come and see us. If he's left for the assault, so that we might hope he'll be out for quite a long time, I'll be at the window and will signal to you to come up. Try and bring us something really pretty, and Marietta will be all over you.'

Descending the winding stairs of this filthy hovel, Fabrizio was full of compunction. I haven't changed a bit, he told himself. All the good resolutions I made on the shore of our lake, when I took such a philosophical view of life, have flown away. My soul had come loose from its usual foundations, it was all a dream and has vanished in the face of the harsh reality. This would be the time to act, Fabrizio told himself, returning to the Palazzo Sanseverina around eleven o'clock in the evening. But it was in vain that he searched in his heart for the courage to speak with the sublime sincerity that had seemed to come so easily on the night he had spent on the shores of Lake Como. I'm going to annoy the person I love best in the world. If I speak, I shall seem like a bad actor. I'm only really worth anything at certain moments of exaltation.

'The count has been admirable to me,' he told the duchess, after giving her an account of his visit to the archbishop's. 'I appreciate his conduct all the more because I think I can see he doesn't altogether like me. So I must act correctly towards him. He is still mad about his excavations at Sanguigna, judging at least by his trip two days ago. He did twelve leagues at a gallop to spend two hours with his workmen. If they find fragments of statues in the ancient temple whose foundations he's just discovered, he's afraid they may get stolen. I want to propose that I should go and spend thirty-six hours at Sanguigna. Tomorrow, at around five, I am to see the archbishop again; I shall be able to leave in the evening and take advantage of the cool night air to make the journey.'

The duchess did not at first answer. 'It might be thought you were looking for excuses to get away from me,' she then said, with extreme tenderness. 'Hardly are you back from Belgirate before you find a reason for leaving.'

This is a good opportunity to talk, Fabrizio told himself. But I was a little mad on the lake, I didn't notice in my passion for sincerity that my compliment ended with an impertinence. What I would need to say is: I'm devoted to you, I couldn't be fonder of you, etc., etc., but my soul is not susceptible to love. Is that not to say: I can see that you feel love for me, but take care, I can't pay you back in the same coin? If she feels love, the duchess may be angry at being found out, and she'll be repelled by my impudence if she feels no more than a simple affection for me ... and those are the unforgivable offences.

While he was pondering these important ideas, Fabrizio, without realizing it, had been walking about the room, with the grave and lordly air of a man who sees disaster very near at hand.

The duchess watched him admiringly. He was no longer the child she had known from birth, no longer the nephew always ready to obey her. He was a serious man by whom it would be delectable to have oneself loved. She got up from the ottoman where she was sitting, and threw herself rapturously into his arms: 'So you want to run away from me?' she said.

'No,' he replied, with the air of a Roman emperor, 'but I was trying to be sensible.'

The remark was open to various interpretations. Fabrizio had not the courage to go any further and run the risk of hurting this adorable woman. He was too young, too liable to become emotional. His mind could not supply him with any agreeable form of words to make her understand what he meant. On a natural impulse and despite all his arguments, he took this attractive woman in his arms and covered her with kisses. At that same moment, they could hear the sound of the count's carriage entering the courtyard, and at almost the same time he himself appeared in the room. He seemed greatly excited.

'You inspire the most singular passions,' he said to Fabrizio, who was left almost speechless by the remark.

'This evening the archbishop had the audience that His Most Serene Highness grants him every Thursday. The prince has just recounted to me how the archbishop, looking greatly agitated, began with a speech got by heart and very learned, of which the prince at first understood nothing. Landriani ended by declaring that it was important for the church in Parma that Monsignor Fabrizio del Dongo be appointed his senior vicar-general and, subsequently, as soon as he had attained his twenty-fifth year, his coadjutor and *future successor*.

'Those words frightened me, I will admit,' said the count. 'That's going rather too fast and I was afraid of some intemperate comeback from the prince. But he looked at me laughing and said in French: "This is some of your doing, sir!"'

'"I can swear an oath before God and before Your Highness," I cried, as unctuously as I knew how, "that I had absolutely no knowledge of the words *future successor*." Then I told the truth, what we were repeating here even a few hours ago. I added, enthusiastically, that, consequently, I should see myself as overwhelmed by His Highness's favours were he to deign to grant me a minor bishopric to start with. The prince must have believed me, for he thought it appropriate to do the gracious thing: he told me, with all possible simplicity: "This is an official matter between the archbishop and myself, you don't come into it. The good man gives me a very long and fairly tedious report of sorts, after which he arrives at an official proposal. I replied very coldly that the subject was very young, and above all a newcomer to my court. That I would almost look as if I were settling a bill of exchange drawn on me by the Emperor, by setting the prospect of so high an office before the son of one of the great officers of his kingdom of Lombardy-Venice. The archbishop protested that there had not been any recommendation of that kind. It was very foolish telling *me* that. It surprised me coming from so well-informed a man. But he always loses his bearings when he addresses me and that evening he was more agitated than ever, which gave me the idea that this is something he wanted passionately. I told him that I knew better than he did that there had been no high recommendation in favour of del Dongo, that no one in my court denied his capabilities, that his morals were not too ill-spoken of, but that I feared he might be liable to *enthusiasm*, and that I had promised myself never to raise to high office madmen of that sort, whom a prince can't begin to trust. Then," His Highness went on, "I had to endure a second dose of pathos almost as long as the first one. The archbishop went into raptures about enthusiasm in the house of God. Ill-advised, I said to myself, you're going astray and risking the nomination that had almost been granted. He should have cut it short and thanked me effusively. Not a bit of it, he went on with his homily with a fearlessness that was absurd. I was looking for a response that was not too unfavourable to young del Dongo. I found it, and rather a happy one, as you are about to judge. 'Monsignore,' I said to him, 'Pius VII was a great pope and a great saint. Of all the sovereigns, he alone dared to say "no" to the tyrant who saw Europe at his feet! Well, he was liable to enthusiasm, which led him, when he was bishop of Imola, to write his famous pastoral letter as the "citizen cardinal Chiaramonti" in favour of the Cisalpine Republic.'[1]

' "My poor archbishop was left dumbstruck and, to strike him even dumber, I said, looking very solemn: 'Farewell, monsignore, I shall take twenty-four hours to reflect on your proposal.' The poor man added a few ill-phrased and somewhat inopportune supplications after I had uttered the word 'farewell'. And now, Count Mosca della Rovera, I charge you with telling the duchess that I do not wish to delay by twenty-four hours something she may find agreeable. Sit down there and write the archbishop the letter of approval which will bring the whole affair to an end." I wrote the letter, he signed it, he said: "Take it this very minute to the duchess." Here is the letter, signora, a letter that has given me the excuse to have the happiness of seeing you again this evening.'

The duchess read the letter, enraptured. During the count's long narration, Fabrizio had had time to recover. He did not appear at all surprised by this incident, he accepted it as a true *grand seigneur* who has naturally always believed that he had a right to promotion of this extraordinary kind, to strokes of good fortune that would have made a bourgeois lose his head. He spoke of his gratitude, but in the correct terms, and ended by saying to the count: 'A good courtier must flatter the dominant passion. Yesterday you displayed your fear that your workmen in Sanguigna could steal the fragments of antique statues they might discover. I love excavating. If you're willing to allow it, I will go and visit the workmen. Tomorrow evening, after the appropriate thank-yous, to the palace and at the archbishop's, I shall leave for Sanguigna.'

'But can you guess where the good archbishop's sudden passion for Fabrizio has come from?' the duchess asked the count.

'I don't need to guess. The vicar-general whose brother is a captain told me yesterday: "Father Landriani starts from the sure principle that the titular is superior to the coadjutor, and he feels no joy at having a del Dongo under his orders and of having obliged him." Everything that draws attention to Fabrizio's high birth adds to his inner happiness: he has a man like that for an aide-de-camp! In the second place, Monsignor Fabrizio appeals to him, he doesn't feel shy in his presence. Lastly, for the past ten years he has been nursing a very healthy hatred for the bishop of Piacenza, who makes no secret of aspiring to succeed him in the see of Parma, and who is what's more a miller's son. It was with this future succession in mind that the bishop of Piacenza has allied himself very closely with the Marchese Raversi, and now that connection is causing the archbishop to fear for the success of his favourite scheme, of having a del Dongo on his headquarters staff and giving him orders.'

Two days later, early in the day, Fabrizio was directing the work of excavation at Sanguigna, facing Colorno (the princes of Parma's Versailles). These excavations extended into the plain right beside the high road that leads from Parma to the bridge of Casal-Maggiore, the first town in Austria. The workmen were cutting a long trench across the plain eight feet deep and as narrow as possible. They were busy looking, along the ancient Roman road, for the ruins of a second temple which, local word had it, had still existed in the Middle Ages. Despite the prince's orders, several peasants could but feel jealous of these long ditches crossing their land. Whatever they might have been told, they imagined they were searching for treasure, and Fabrizio's presence was useful above all to prevent any minor disturbance. He was far from bored, he kept an enthusiastic eye on the work. From time to time they turned up some medal or other, and he refused to allow the workmen time to get together to smuggle it away.

It was a beautiful day, it might have been six o'clock in the morning. He had borrowed an old single-barrelled gun, he fired at some larks. One of them was winged and fell on the roadway. Going in pursuit of it, Fabrizio noticed in the distance a carriage coming from Parma and making for the frontier at Casal-Maggiore. He had just reloaded his gun when, the very decrepit carriage approaching at a gentle trot, he recognized little

Marietta. At her side she had the great beanpole, Giletti, and the old woman she passed off as her mother.

Giletti imagined that Fabrizio had stationed himself in the middle of the road like this, his gun in his hand, in order to abuse him and perhaps even to abduct little Marietta. Being a man of spirit, he jumped down from his carriage. In his left hand he had a big, very rusty pistol, and in his right held a sword still in its scabbard, which he used when the troupe's requirements forced them to entrust the role of some marchese to him.

'Ho there, you brigand!' he cried, 'I'm glad to find you here a league from the frontier. I'm going to settle your nonsense. You're no longer protected by your purple stockings here.'

Fabrizio was smiling at little Marietta and paying little or no heed to Giletti's jealous shouts, when he suddenly saw the muzzle of the rusty pistol three feet from his chest. He just had time to strike out at the pistol, using his own gun as a stick. The pistol went off, without wounding anyone.

'So stop, f*** you!' shouted Giletti to the coachman. At the same time he was agile enough to leap at the muzzle of his adversary's gun and keep it pointing away from his body. He and Fabrizio each tugged at the gun with all their strength. Giletti was much the stronger and by placing one hand after the other was advancing towards the percussion-lock, and was on the verge of getting possession of the gun, when Fabrizio, to stop him from using it, let it off. He had clearly seen beforehand that the end of the gun was more than three inches above Giletti's shoulder; the detonation took place right beside the latter's ear. He was left somewhat startled but recovered in a trice.

'Oh, so you want to blow my brains out, you scum! I'm going to put paid to you!' Giletti threw aside the scabbard from his marchese's sword and fell on Fabrizio with admirable rapidity. The latter had no weapon and thought he was done for. He ran off towards the carriage, which had stopped a dozen paces behind Giletti. He passed to the left of it, then taking hold of the vehicle's springs, he spun rapidly right round it and came back close beside the right-hand door, which was open. Giletti, having set off on his long legs, had not thought of restraining himself by the vehicle's springs and took several paces in his original direction before being able to stop. Just as Fabrizio was going past the open door, he heard Marietta say to him in a low voice: 'Watch out for yourself. He'll kill you. Here!'

At the same instant, Fabrizio saw a sort of long hunting-knife fall from the door. He bent to pick it up but, at that same moment, was caught on the shoulder by a blow from the sword wielded by Giletti. As he straightened up, Fabrizio found himself six inches from Giletti, who struck him a furious blow in the face with the pommel of his sword. Such was the force with which the blow was delivered that Fabrizio was quite unable to think straight. At that moment, he was on the point of being killed. Fortunately for him, Giletti was still too close to be able to use the point of the sword. Once he had come to his senses, Fabrizio turned tail, running as fast as he could. As he ran, he threw away the sheath of the hunting-knife and then, turning quickly round, found himself three paces away from Giletti, who was pursuing him. Giletti was coming at him, Fabrizio thrust at him with the knife. With his sword, Giletti had time to deflect the hunting-knife slightly upwards but he received the point full in the left cheek. He passed right beside Fabrizio, who felt something pierce his thigh; it was Giletti's knife, which he had had time to open. Fabrizio jumped to his right. He turned about and at last the two adversaries found themselves the right distance apart to fight.

Giletti was swearing like one of the damned. 'I'm going to cut your throat, you filthy priest!' he repeated over and over. Fabrizio was out of breath and could not speak. The blow in the face from the pommel of the sword was very painful and his nose was bleeding copiously. He parried several blows with his hunting-knife and kicked out several times without any clear idea of what he was doing. He had a vague sense he was at a public assault-at-arms. This idea had been prompted by the presence of his workmen who, to the number of twenty-five or thirty, had formed a circle round the combatants, but at a very respectful distance, for they could see the latter forever running and throwing themselves at one another.

The combat seemed to be slowing down somewhat. The blows were no longer succeeding one another with the same rapidity, when Fabrizio said to himself: judging by how much my face hurts, he must have disfigured me. Seized with rage at this idea, he leapt at his enemy, with the point of the hunting knife to the fore. The point went into the right side of Giletti's chest and came out near the left shoulder. At that same instant, the full length of Giletti's sword penetrated the top of Fabrizio's arm, but the sword slid under the skin and the wound was trivial.

Giletti had fallen. Just as Fabrizio was moving towards him, looking at his left hand, which was holding a knife, that hand opened automatically and let the weapon drop.

The villain's dead, Fabrizio told himself. He looked at his face, there was a lot of blood coming from Giletti's mouth. Fabrizio ran to the carriage.

'Have you got a mirror?' he shouted to Marietta. Marietta, white-faced, looked at him without answering. The old woman very coolly opened a green needlework bag, and offered Fabrizio a small mirror with a handle, the size of a hand. Fabrizio looked at himself, feeling his face. The eyes are safe, he said to himself, that's a good start. He looked at his teeth: they were not broken. 'So how come it hurts so much?' he asked himself under his breath.

The old woman answered: 'It's because the top of your cheek was squashed between the pommel of Giletti's sword and the bone we've got there. Your cheek is horribly swollen and blue. Put some leeches on it straight away and it'll be nothing.'

'Ah, leeches, straight away,' said Fabrizio with a laugh, and recovered all his composure. He saw that the workmen had surrounded Giletti and were looking at him, not daring to touch him.

'Help the man then!' he shouted. 'Take off his coat . . .' He was about to go on but, looking up, he saw five or six men three hundred paces away on the high road advancing steadily on foot towards the scene of the action.

They're policemen, he reflected, and because a man's been killed, they're going to arrest me, and I shall have the honour of making a solemn entry into the town of Parma. What a story for Raversi's courtier friends, who detest my aunt!

Instantly, at lightning speed, he tossed all the money he had in his pockets to the gaping workmen, and threw himself into the carriage.

'Stop the police from pursuing me!' he shouted to the workmen, 'and I'll make you rich. Tell them I'm innocent, that that man *attacked me and wanted to kill me.*

'And you,' he said to the coachman, 'set your horses to gallop, you'll get four golden napoleons if you cross the Po before those men there can catch up with me.'

'Right!' said the coachman. 'But never fear, the men there are on foot, and even a trot's enough for my horses to leave them way behind.' Saying which, he set them to galloping.

Our hero was offended by the word *fear* that the coachman had used. The truth was he had felt extreme fear after the blow from the pommel he had got in the face.

'We may meet men on horseback coming towards us,' said the prudent coachman, thinking of his four napoleons, 'and the men that are following us may shout to them to stop us.' This meant: reload your weapons . . .

'You're so brave, my little priest!' cried Marietta hugging Fabrizio. The old woman was looking out through the carriage door. After a short while she brought her head back in.

'No one is pursuing you, signore,' she told Fabrizio, very composedly. 'And there's no one on the road ahead of us. You know how officious the Austrian police clerks are. If they see you arrive at the gallop like this, on the dyke along the Po, they'll arrest you, don't be in any doubt.'

Fabrizio looked out of the door. 'At a trot,' he told the coachman. 'What passport do you have?' he asked the old woman.

'Three instead of one,' she replied. 'Each of which cost us four francs. Isn't it dreadful for poor stage performers who travel all year round! Here's the passport of Signor Giletti, stage performer, that'll be you. Here are our two passports, Marietta's and mine. But Giletti had all our money in his pocket, what'll become of us?'

'How much did he have?' said Fabrizio.

'Forty beautiful five-franc écus,' said the old woman.

'That's to say six and some small change,' said Marietta, laughing. 'I won't have my little priest being tricked.'

'Is it not quite natural, signore,' the old woman went on, not turning a hair, 'that I should try and screw thirty-four écus out of you? What are thirty-four écus to you? Whereas us, we've lost our protector. Who's going to be responsible for finding us lodgings, for haggling over the price with the coachman when we're on the road, and for frightening everyone? Giletti wasn't handsome but he certainly came in handy, and if the little one there hadn't been a stupid, and then fallen head over heels for you, Giletti would never have noticed a thing and you'd have been giving us lovely écus. I assure you we're very poor.'

Fabrizio was touched. He pulled out his purse and gave the old woman a few napoleons. 'You can see,' he said, 'that I've only got fifteen left, so there's no point in pulling any more fast ones from now on.'

Little Marietta threw her arms round his neck and the old woman kissed his hands. The carriage was still moving forward at a slow trot. When they saw the yellow barriers with black stripes in the distance announcing the Austrian possessions, the old woman said to Fabrizio: 'You'd do better to enter on foot, with Giletti's passport in your pocket. As for us, we'll stop here a while, and say we want to smarten ourselves up. Anyway, the customs will go through our things. If you want my advice, cross Casal-Maggiore casually. Go into the café even and drink a glass of brandy. Once outside the village, get going. The police are vigilant as the devil in these Austrian parts. They'll soon find out a man's been killed. You're travelling with a passport that isn't yours, that's more than enough to spend two years in prison. Get to the Po to the right on leaving the town, hire a boat and take refuge in Ravenna or Ferrara. Get out of the Austrian States as quickly as you can. For two louis, you'll be able to buy another passport off some customs man, that one would be fatal. Remember you've killed the man.'

As he approached the pontoon in Casal-Maggiore on foot, Fabrizio carefully reread Giletti's passport. Our hero was very much afraid, he remembered vividly all that Count Mosca had told him of the danger there was for him in re-entering the Austrian States. And now, two hundred paces ahead of him, he could see the terrifying bridge that would give him access to them, whose capital as he saw it was the Spielberg. But what else could he do? The duchy of Modena, which borders the State of Parma to the south, handed back fugitives by virtue of an explicit convention. The State frontier that extends into the mountains in the direction of Genoa was too far away. His misadventure would be known about in Parma long before he might have been able to reach those mountains. There remained therefore only the Austrian States on the left bank of the Po. By the time they were able to write to the Austrian authorities to get them to arrest him, thirty-six hours or two days perhaps would have elapsed. After which due reflection, Fabrizio burnt his own passport with his lighted cigar. It was better that he should be a vagrant on Austrian soil than Fabrizio del Dongo, and it was possible that he would be searched.

Quite apart from the very natural repugnance that he felt at entrusting his life to the wretched Giletti's passport, this document presented material difficulties. Fabrizio's height was at most five feet five, not the five feet ten listed on the passport. He was nearly twenty-four and looked younger, Giletti had been thirty-nine. We will admit that our hero walked for a good half-hour on one of the dykes of the Po near the pontoon before making up his mind to go down. What advice would I give to someone else finding himself in my situation? he asked himself finally. To go across obviously. There's danger in remaining in the State of Parma, a policeman may be sent in pursuit of the man who's killed another man, even if it was in self-defence. Fabrizio went through his pockets, tore up all his papers and kept precisely nothing bar his handkerchief and his cigar case. It was important to cut short the examination he would undergo. He thought of a terrifying objection that might be raised and to which he could think only of the wrong answers: he was going to say his name was Giletti and all his linen bore the initials F. D.

As may be seen, Fabrizio was one of those unfortunate people who are tormented by their imagination, which is rather the defect of the intelligent in Italy. A French soldier equal or even inferior in courage would have presented himself at the bridge to go across straight away, without dwelling in advance on any difficulty. But he would also have carried with him all his composure, and Fabrizio was very far from feeling any composure, when, at the end of the bridge, a small man, dressed in grey, said to him: 'Go into the police office for your passport.'

The office had filthy walls equipped with nails on which the clerks' pipes and filthy hats were hanging. The big pine desk behind which they were entrenched was covered with ink and wine stains. Two or three fat registers bound in green leather bore stains of every shade, and the cut edge of their pages was black from being handled. On the registers, piled one on top of the other, were three magnificent laurel wreaths, which had served two days previously for one of the Emperor's feast-days.

Fabrizio was struck by all these details, they clutched at his heart, this was the price to be paid for the magnificent, pristine and sparkling luxury of his lovely apartment in the Palazzo Sanseverina. He was being forced to go into this filthy office and appear there as an inferior. He was about to undergo an interrogation.

The clerk who stretched out a yellow hand to take his passport was small and dark, and wore a brass pin in his neckerchief. Here's some bad-tempered civilian, Fabrizio told himself. The personage in question seemed excessively surprised on reading the passport, and the reading lasted a full five minutes.

'You've had an accident,' he said to the stranger, pointing to his cheek.

'The coachman tipped us out below the dyke on the Po.' Then the silence resumed and the clerk cast hostile glances at the traveller.

I'm for it, Fabrizio told himself, he's going to tell me he's sorry, he's got some bad news for me, that I'm under arrest. All sorts of wild ideas came into our hero's head, who at that moment was not very logical. He thought, for example, of taking to his heels through the office door which had remained open. I get rid of my coat, I throw myself into the Po, I'll surely be able to swim across. Anything's better than the Spielberg. The police clerk was watching him closely as he was calculating what the chances were of such an escapade succeeding; which made for two fine facial expressions. The presence of danger endows the reasonable man with genius, it raises him above himself, so to speak. In the man of imagination, it inspires romantic fantasies, daring it is true, but often absurd.

It made a fine spectacle, our hero's look of indignation under the inquisitorial glare of the police clerk, adorned by his brass jewellery. Were I to kill him, Fabrizio told himself, I'd be sentenced to twenty years' penal servitude or to death for murder, which is far less terrible than the Spielberg with a one-hundred-and-twenty-pound chain on each foot and living on eight ounces of bread a day, and that lasts twenty years. So I wouldn't get out until I was forty-four. Fabrizio's logic was overlooking the fact that since he had burnt his passport, there was nothing to indicate to the clerk that he might be the rebel, Fabrizio del Dongo.

Our hero was not a little afraid, as may be seen. He would have been much more so had he known the thoughts that were troubling the police clerk. This man was a friend of Giletti and you may judge of his astonishment at finding his passport in the hands of someone else. His first impulse was to have this someone else arrested, then he reflected that Giletti might well have sold his passport to this handsome young man who had to all appearances just been up to some mischief in Parma. If I arrest him, he told himself, Giletti will be at risk. They'll easily find out that he sold his passport. On the other hand, what will my superiors say if they happen to ascertain that I, a friend of Giletti, stamped his passport being carried by someone else? The clerk got up with a yawn and said to Fabrizio: 'Wait, signore.' Then, out of a policeman's habit: 'A difficulty has arisen.' Fabrizio said aside: 'My escape's about to arise.'

In fact, the clerk had gone from the office leaving the door open, and the passport was still on the pine table. The danger is obvious, thought Fabrizio. I'm going to take my passport and go slowly back across the bridge, I'll tell the gendarme, if he questions me, that I forgot to get my passport stamped by the police commissioner in the last village in the States of Parma. Fabrizio already had his passport in his hand when, to his inexpressible surprise, he heard the clerk with the brass jewellery saying: 'I've had enough, I must say. The heat's suffocating me. I'm going to the café for a coffee. Go into the office when you've finished your pipe, there's a passport to be stamped. The stranger's there.'

Fabrizio, who was creeping out, found himself face to face with a good-looking young man who said to himself as he hummed: 'All right, let's stamp the passport, I'll put my signature on it.

'Where does the signore wish to go?'

'Mantua, Venice and Ferrara.'

'Let's say Ferrara,' replied the clerk, whistling. He took up a die stamp, impressed the visa in blue ink on the passport and rapidly wrote in the words 'Mantua, Venice and Ferrara' in the space left blank by the stamp, then waved his hand around several times in the air, signed it and took more ink for the final flourish, which he executed slowly and taking infinite pains. Fabrizio was following every movement of the pen. The clerk looked contentedly at his signature, added five or six dots, and finally handed the passport back to Fabrizio, saying casually, 'Have a good trip, signore.'

Fabrizio was walking off at a pace the rapidity of which he was trying to disguise, when he felt himself held back by the left arm. Instinctively, he put his hand on the hilt of his dagger, and had he not seen he was surrounded by houses, he would perhaps have given way to some piece of foolhardiness. The man who was touching his left arm, seeing how startled he looked, said to him by way of an apology: 'I called the signore three times, without him answering. Has the signore anything to declare to the customs?'

'All I have on me is my handkerchief. I'm on my way to a relative's house close by to go hunting.'

He would have been in some difficulty if he had been asked to name this relative. What with the great heat and his own emotions, Fabrizio was as soaking wet as if he had fallen into the Po. I don't lack courage among play-actors, but clerks adorned with brass jewellery make me frantic. With which thought I shall write a comic sonnet for the duchess.

No sooner had Fabrizio entered Casal-Maggiore before he took a roughly paved street leading down to the Po. I'm in great need of help from Bacchus and Ceres, he told himself, and he went into a shop outside which hung a grey kitchen cloth tied to a stick. On the cloth was written the word *Trattoria*. A cheap bedsheet supported by two very thin wooden hoops, hanging down to within three feet of the ground, shielded the door of the trattoria from the direct rays of the sun. There, a half-naked and very pretty woman received our hero respectfully, which gave him the keenest pleasure. He hastened to tell her he was dying of hunger. As the woman was preparing the breakfast, a man of about thirty came in, who had not given any greeting on entering. He suddenly got up from the bench on which he had thrown himself down with a familiar air and said to Fabrizio: 'Eccellenza, la riverisco' (I salute Your Excellency). Fabrizio was very cheerful at that moment and, instead of forming some sinister plan, he answered, laughingly: 'And how the devil do you know I'm an excellency?'

'What! Your Excellency doesn't recognize Lodovico, one of signora the Duchess Sanseverina's coachmen? At Sacca, the country house where we used to go each year, I always caught a fever. I asked the signora to pension me off and I retired. And now I'm rich. Instead of the pension of twelve écus a year which was the most I could have had a right to, the signora told me that to give me the leisure to write sonnets, because I'm a poet in the "vulgar tongue", she was granting me eighty écus, and the signor count told me that if ever I fell on hard times, I had only to go and talk to him. I had the honour of driving monsignore for one stage when he went like a good Christian to make his retreat at the charterhouse in Velleja.'

Fabrizio looked at the man and vaguely recognized him. He was one of the more stylish coachmen in the Sanseverina household. Now that he was rich, he said, his only clothing was a torn rough shirt and linen breeches, once dyed black, which barely reached his knees; a pair of slippers and a cheap hat completed his outfit. He had not, moreover, trimmed his beard for a fortnight. While eating his omelette, Fabrizio engaged him in conversation absolutely as between equals. He thought he could see that Lodovico was the café-woman's lover. He quickly finished his breakfast, then said to Lodovico, lowering his voice: 'A word with you.'

'Your Excellency can speak freely in front of her, she's a really good woman,' said Lodovico affectionately.

'Well, my friends,' resumed Fabrizio unhesitatingly, 'I'm in trouble, and I need your help. First of all, the business doesn't involve politics in any way. I've quite simply killed a man who tried to murder me because I was talking to his mistress.'

'Poor young man!' said the café-woman.

'Your Excellency can count on me!' cried the coachman, his eyes ablaze with the fiercest devotion. 'Where does His Excellency want to go?'

'To Ferrara. I have a passport but I'd rather not talk to the police, who may have had wind of the affair.'

'When did you dispatch this fellow?'

'This morning, at six o'clock.'

'Your Excellency doesn't have any blood on his clothes?' said the café-woman.

'I was wondering about that,' the coachman went on, 'and anyway, the stuff they're made from is too good. You don't see a lot like those in these country parts, it would attract attention. I'll go and buy some things from the Jew. Your Excellency is roughly my height, but thinner.'

'Please, don't go on calling me Excellency, it may attract attention.'

'Yes, Excellency,' replied the coachman, leaving the shop.

'Hey,' shouted Fabrizio, 'what about the money? Come back!'

'What do you mean, money!' said the café-woman. 'He's got sixty-seven écus that are entirely at your disposal. And I,' she added lowering her voice, 'I've got forty écus that I'm only too glad for you to have. You don't always have money on you when these accidents happen.'

Fabrizio had taken off his coat because of the heat on entering the trattoria: 'You've got a waistcoat there which might get us into trouble if anyone came in. That beautiful English cloth would attract attention.' She gave our fugitive a linen waistcoat dyed black belonging to her husband. A tall young man entered the shop through an interior door, he was dressed with a certain elegance.

'This is my husband,' said the woman. 'Pierantonio,' she said to the husband, 'this gentleman's a friend of Lodovico. He had an accident this morning on the other side of the river, he wants to get away to Ferrara.'

'Well, we'll take him across,' said the husband very politely, 'we've got Carlo-Giuseppe's boat.'

Thanks to another of our hero's weaknesses, which we will admit to as naturally as we have told of his fear in the police office at the end of the bridge, he had tears in his eyes. He was deeply moved by the perfect devotion he had met with from these peasants. He thought also of his aunt's characteristic kindness. He would have liked to be able to do something for these people's future fortunes. Lodovico came back carrying a bundle.

'So much for the other fellow,' said the husband, in the friendliest manner.

'That's not the point,' replied Lodovico, sounding a note of alarm, 'they're beginning to talk about you, they noticed that you hesitated before coming into our passageway, and leaving the main street like a man looking for somewhere to hide.'

'Quickly, up into the bedroom,' said the husband.

The bedroom, a very large, very handsome room, had grey canvas instead of panes of glass in the two windows. There were four beds to be seen, each six feet wide by five feet high.

'Quick, quick!' said Lodovico. 'We've a new conceited fool of a policeman who tried to make up to the pretty woman downstairs, and I've predicted that when he's off patrolling along the road he may well stop a bullet. If that cur hears talk of Your Excellency, he'll want to do the dirty on us, he'll try and arrest you here so as to get Theodolinda's trattoria a bad name.

'Aha!' Lodovico went on, seeing the bloodstained shirt and the wounds bound up with handkerchiefs, 'so the *porco* defended himself? This is enough to get you arrested a hundred times over. I didn't buy a shirt.' He opened the husband's wardrobe unceremoniously and gave one of his shirts to Fabrizio, who was soon dressed as a prosperous country bourgeois. Lodovico took down a net hanging on the wall, put Fabrizio's clothes into the basket where the fish go, ran downstairs and went quickly out through a back door. Fabrizio followed him.

'Theodolinda,' he shouted passing close to the shop, 'hide what's upstairs, we're going to wait in the willows. And Pierantonio, send us a boat and quickly, we'll pay well.'

Lodovico made Fabrizio cross more than twenty ditches. Very long and very springy planks served as bridges over the widest of them. Lodovico withdrew the planks after they had crossed. Having reached the last channel, he pulled the plank off with alacrity. 'We can breathe freely now,' he said. 'That cur of a policeman would have to go more than two leagues to catch up with Your Excellency. You're white as a sheet,' he said to Fabrizio. 'I didn't forget the little bottle of brandy.'

'It's just what I need, I'm beginning to feel the wound in my thigh. What's more, I was scared stiff in the police office at the end of the bridge.'

'I can well believe it,' said Lodovico. 'With a shirt covered in blood like yours was, I can't imagine how you even dared go into such a place. As for the wounds, I'm an expert on those. I shall put you in a nice cool spot where you can sleep for an hour. The boat will come and fetch us there, if there's some way of getting hold of a boat. If not, once you've rested a bit we'll do another couple of leagues or so and I'll take you to a mill where I can get a boat myself. Your Excellency knows many more people than I do. The signora is going to be in despair when she hears about the accident. She'll be told you were mortally wounded, perhaps even that you killed the other man in some underhand way. The Marchese Raversi won't fail to spread all those ugly rumours that might distress the signora. Your Excellency could write.'

'But how to get a letter to her?'

'The boys at the mill where we're going earn twelve sous a day. In a day and a half they're in Parma, so four francs for the journey. Two francs for wear and tear on their shoes. If the journey was made for a poor man like me, it'd be six francs. As it's in the service of a lord, I shall give twelve.'

Once they had reached the resting-place in a wood of alders and willow trees, very dense and very cool, Lodovico went off more than an hour away to fetch ink and paper. Heavens, talk about comfortable! exclaimed Fabrizio. Fortune farewell, I shall never be an archbishop!

On his return, Lodovico found him fast asleep and did not want to wake him. The boat did not arrive until around sunset. As soon as Lodovico saw it appear in the distance, he called Fabrizio, who wrote two letters.

'Your Excellency knows a lot more than I do,' said Lodovico with a pained expression, 'and I'm much afraid of displeasing him deep down, whatever he may say, if I add one thing.'

'I'm not the simpleton you may think me,' replied Fabrizio, 'and, whatever you may say, I shall always look on you as one of my aunt's loyal retainers, and a man who's done everything in his power to get me out of a very nasty situation.'

It took many more protestations for Lodovico to decide to speak, and once he was finally resolved to do so, he began with a preamble which lasted a good five minutes. Fabrizio grew impatient, then said to himself: Whose fault is it? The fault of our vanity, which this man has had a good view of from up on his driving seat. Lodovico's devotion finally led him to run the risk of speaking out.

'How much would the Marchese Raversi not give to the man you're going to send on foot to Parma to have those two letters! They're in your handwriting and because of that could be used as evidence against you in court. Your Excellency's going to think me indiscreet and inquisitive. Or there again, he'd perhaps be ashamed to lay my poor coachman's handwriting before the eyes of the duchess. But in the end your safety opens my mouth, even if you do find me impertinent. Could Your Excellency not dictate those two letters to me? Then I'd be the only one at risk, but only very slightly, I'd say if need be that you appeared in the middle of a field with an inkhorn in one hand and a pistol in the other, and that you ordered me to write.'

'Give me your hand, my dear Lodovico,' cried Fabrizio, 'and to prove to you that I don't wish to have any secrets from a friend such as you, copy the two letters just as they are.' Lodovico understood the full extent of this mark of confidence and was extremely appreciative of it, but after a few lines, as he saw the boat advancing rapidly along the river: 'The letters will be finished sooner,' he told Fabrizio, 'if Your Excellency is willing to take the trouble of dictating them.' The letters once finished, Fabrizio wrote an A and a B on the bottom line and, on a small scrap of paper which he then screwed up, he wrote in French: 'Believe A and B.' The messenger was to hide this crumpled piece of paper in his clothing.

The boat having come within earshot, Lodovico called to the boatmen by names which were not theirs. They made no reply and touched land five hundred fathoms lower down, looking all around them to see whether they might not have been spotted by some customs officer.

'I'm yours to command,' Lodovico said to Fabrizio. 'Do you want me to take the letters to Parma myself? Do you want me to go with you to Ferrara?'

'To go with me to Ferrara is a service I hardly dared ask of you. We'll need to land and try to enter the town without showing the passport. I must tell you I feel the greatest repugnance for travelling under the name of Giletti, and I can't think of anyone except you who might buy me another passport.'

'Why didn't you say something in Casal-Maggiore? I know a spy who'd have sold me an excellent passport, and not expensive, for forty or fifty francs.'

One of the two boatmen, who had been born on the right bank of the Po and consequently had no need of a passport to go abroad to Parma, undertook to carry the letters. Lodovico, who knew how to handle an oar, undertook to steer the boat with the other boatman.

'Lower down the Po, we shall find several armed boats belonging to the police,' he said, 'but I shall know how to avoid them.' More than a dozen times they were obliged to hide among the small, low-lying islands, covered in willow trees. On three occasions they went on land, so that the boats would be empty as they passed the police craft. Lodovico took advantage of these long moments of leisure to recite several of his sonnets to Fabrizio. The sentiments were appropriate enough, but as if blunted in the expression, and were not worth the trouble of being written down. What was odd was that this former coachman had lively and picturesque enthusiasms and ways of looking at things, yet became cold and commonplace as soon as he wrote. It's the opposite of what we find in society, Fabrizio told himself. We know nowadays how to express everything gracefully, but our hearts have nothing to say. He realized that the greatest pleasure he could give this loyal retainer would be to correct the spelling mistakes in his sonnets.

'They make fun of me when I lend them my notebook,' said Lodovico. 'But if Your Excellency were to condescend to spell the words out to me letter by letter, those envious folk would no longer know what to say. Genius isn't knowing how to spell.' It was not until two days later, and in the darkness, that Fabrizio was able to disembark in perfect safety in an alder grove, a league before coming to Ponte Lago Oscuro. He stayed hidden throughout the day in a field of flax, and Lodovico went ahead of him into Ferrara. There, he took lodgings in the house of a poor Jew, who realized right away that there was money to be made if he could keep his mouth shut. In the evening, as the daylight faded, Fabrizio entered Ferrara riding a small horse. He had great need of this assistance, the heat having got to him on the river. The knife wound in his thigh, and the sword thrust he had received from Giletti in the shoulder, at the beginning of the fight, had become inflamed and made him feverish.

CHAPTER 12

The Jewish owner of the lodgings had procured a discreet surgeon who, realizing in his turn that there was money in the purse, told Lodovico that his 'conscience' obliged him to put in a report to the police concerning the injuries to the young man whom he, Lodovico, referred to as his brother.

'The law is clear,' he added. 'It's perfectly obvious that your brother didn't injure himself, as his story has it, by falling from a ladder at the very moment when he had an open knife in his hand.'

Lodovico's icy reply to this law-abiding surgeon was that, should he take it into his head to yield to the promptings of his conscience, he, Lodovico, would have the honour, before leaving Ferrara, of falling upon him with the selfsame open knife in his hand. When he reported this incident to Fabrizio, the latter was highly critical, but there was not a moment to be lost in decamping. Lodovico told the Jew that he wanted to try to get his brother out into the fresh air. He went to look for a carriage and our friends left the house, not to return. The reader will no doubt find the account of all the steps needing to be taken in the absence of a passport very long-drawn-out: this sort of preoccupation no longer exists in France. But in Italy, and in the vicinity of the Po in particular, everyone talks about passports. Once having left Ferrara without any obstruction, as if he were taking a drive, Lodovico dismissed the cab, then re-entered the town through another gate, and came back to pick up Fabrizio in a *sediola* that he had hired to do twelve leagues. Having arrived close to Bologna, our friends had themselves driven across country on the road leading from Florence to Bologna. They spent the night in the most rundown inn they could find, and the next day, Fabrizio feeling sufficiently strong to walk a little, they entered Bologna as if out for a stroll. They had burnt Giletti's passport. The actor's death must have been known about, and there was less danger in being arrested as people without passports than as the bearers of the passport of a man who had been killed.

In Bologna, Lodovico was acquainted with two or three domestics in the big houses. It was agreed that he would go and make contact with them. He told them that, coming from Florence and travelling with his young brother, the latter, feeling the need to sleep, had let him go off alone an hour before sunrise. He was to rejoin him in the village where he, Lodovico, would pause to spend the hottest part of the day. But Lodovico, finding that his brother had not come, had decided to retrace his steps. He had found him injured by a blow from a stone and with several knife wounds and, what was more, robbed by some men who had picked a quarrel with him. This brother was a nice-looking boy, knew how to groom and handle horses, could read and write, and would very much like to find a position in some good household. Lodovico was ready to add, should occasion arise, that after Fabrizio had fallen, the robbers had fled, carrying off the small bag which held their change of clothing and their passports.

On reaching Bologna, Fabrizio felt very tired and, not daring to present himself at an inn without a passport, had gone into the immense church of San Petronio. He found it deliciously cool; he soon felt revived. Ingrate that I am, he told himself suddenly, I come into a church but only so I can sit down, like in a café! He dropped to his knees and thanked God effusively for the protection he had patently been accorded since he had been unfortunate enough to kill Giletti. The danger that still made him shudder was that of having been recognized in the police station in Casal-Maggiore. How could the clerk, he asked himself, whose eyes betrayed so much suspicion and who reread my passport as many as three times, not notice that I'm not five feet ten, that I'm not thirty-eight, that I'm not heavily pock-marked? How many mercies I owe you, oh God! And I've managed to wait until now before laying my nothingness at your feet! My pride wanted to believe that it was to futile human prudence that I owed the good fortune of escaping the Spielberg, which was already opening to swallow me up!

Fabrizio spent more than an hour in this state of high emotion, in the presence of God's immense goodness. Lodovico approached without being heard and placed himself opposite him. Fabrizio, whose face was buried in his hands, looked up and his faithful retainer saw the tears that were furrowing his cheeks.

'Come back in one hour,' Fabrizio told him somewhat harshly.

Lodovico excused the tone of voice on grounds of piety. Fabrizio recited the seven psalms of penitence, which he knew by heart, several times. He paused at length on the verses that had a bearing on his present situation.

Fabrizio asked forgiveness of God for many things, but what is remarkable is that it did not enter his head to number among his sins the plan of becoming an archbishop, purely because Count Mosca was first minister and considered that position and the grand existence that went with it appropriate for the nephew of the duchess. He had wanted it, it is true, but dispassionately, seeing it as in no way different from a position as minister or general. It had not entered his head that his conscience might be implicated in this plan of the duchess's. This is a remarkable characteristic of the religion he owed to the teachings of the Jesuits in Milan. That religion *takes away the courage to think about unaccustomed things* and above all forbids *self-examination*, as the most grievous of sins: it is a step in the direction of Protestantism. To know what one is guilty of, one must question one's priest, or read the list of sins, such as it is to be found printed in the books entitled *Preparation for the Sacrament of Penitence*. Fabrizio knew by heart the list of sins drawn up in the Latin tongue, which he had learnt at the ecclesiastical academy in Naples. Thus, when reciting this list, having come to the article of murder, he had indeed accused himself before God of having killed a man, but in defence of his own life. He had passed rapidly over, without paying them the least heed, the various articles relating to the sin of *simony* (procuring ecclesiastical office for oneself in return for payment). Had they proposed giving him a hundred louis to become senior vicar-general to the archbishop of Parma, he would have rejected the idea in disgust. But though he lacked neither intelligence nor above all logic, it never once entered his head that for Count Mosca's standing to be employed for his benefit was a form of *simony*. Such is the triumph of a Jesuit education: to instil the habit of disregarding things which are as clear as day. A Frenchman, brought up amidst the self-interest and irony so characteristic of Paris, would have been able, without being guilty of bad faith, to accuse Fabrizio of hypocrisy at the very moment when our hero was opening his soul to God with the most extreme sincerity and the most profound emotion.

Fabrizio did not leave the church before having prepared the confession he proposed making the very next day. He found Lodovico sitting on the steps of the vast stone peristyle which rises on the large square in front of the façade of San Petronio. Just as after a great storm the air is purer, so Fabrizio's soul was at peace, happy and as if refreshed.

'I feel very well, I'd hardly know I'd been wounded,' he told Lodovico as he came up to him. 'But first and foremost I must ask your forgiveness. I answered you gruffly when you came and spoke to me in the church. I was examining my conscience. Well, how are things looking?'

'They couldn't be better. I've taken some lodgings, far from worthy of Your Excellency if the truth be told, in the house of the wife of one of my friends, who's very pretty and what's more is close friends with one of the senior policemen. Tomorrow I shall go and make a declaration to the effect that our passports have been stolen. The declaration will be taken in good part. But I shall pay the carriage on the letter the police will write to Casal-Maggiore, to find out whether there exists in that commune someone by the name of Lodovico San-Micheli, who has a brother, by the name of Fabrizio, in the service of madame the Duchess Sanseverina, in Parma. It's all over, *siamo a cavallo*.' (An Italian proverb: we are safe.)

Fabrizio had suddenly started to look very serious. He asked

Lodovico to wait for him for a moment and almost ran back into the church. Hardly was he inside before he dropped quickly to his knees. He kissed the flagstones humbly. 'It's a miracle, Lord,' he cried, with tears in his eyes. 'When you saw my soul disposed to return to its duty, you saved me. Great God, it's possible that one day I shall be killed in some affair or other, remember at the moment of my death the state in which my soul finds itself at this moment.' It was in transports of the most heartfelt joy that Fabrizio again recited the seven psalms of penitence. Before leaving, he went up to an old woman who was sitting in front of a big Madonna and next to an iron triangle set vertically on a stand of the same metal. The sides of the triangle bristled with a large number of spikes, intended to carry the small candles which the faithful in their piety light before the celebrated Madonna of Cimabue.[1] Seven candles alone had been lit as Fabrizio came up. He committed this detail to memory intending to reflect on it at greater leisure.

'How much do candles cost?' he said to the woman.

'Two baiocchi[2] each.'

In fact, they were hardly any thicker than a penholder and not even a foot long.

'How many candles is there still room for on your triangle?'

'Sixty-three, since there are seven lit.'

Ah, said Fabrizio to himself, sixty-three and seven come to seventy. I must make a note of that too. He paid for the candles, placed and lit the first seven himself, then knelt to make his offering and said to the old woman as he got up: 'This is for favours received.'

'I'm dying of hunger,' Fabrizio said to Lodovico, on rejoining him.

'Let's not go into a tavern, let's go to the lodgings. The landlady will go and buy you what you need for breakfast. She'll steal twenty sous and will be all the more deeply attached to the new arrival.'

'Which means I'll be dying of hunger a whole hour longer,' said Fabrizio, laughing with the serenity of a child, and he went into a tavern next to San Petronio. To his extreme surprise, at a table next to the one at which he had sat down, he saw Pepe, his aunt's first footman, the same one who had once come all the way to Geneva to meet him. Fabrizio signalled to him to remain silent. Then, having rapidly breakfasted, with a smile of pleasure playing on his lips, he got up. Pepe followed him and, for the third time, our hero entered San Petronio. Out of discretion, Lodovico remained walking in the square.

'Good Lord, monsignore, how are your wounds? The signora duchess has been horribly anxious. For one whole day she thought you were dead, abandoned on some island in the Po. I shall dispatch a courier to her this very minute. I've been looking for you for six days, I spent three in Ferrara, scouring all the inns.'

'Do you have a passport for me?'

'I've got three different ones. One with Your Excellency's names and titles. The second with your name only, and the third under an assumed name, Joseph Bossi. Each passport is in duplicate, according to whether Your Excellency wants to have arrived from Modena or Florence. All you need do is to take a trip outside the town. The signor count would be happy to see you putting up at the Pelegrino, the owner is his friend.'

Fabrizio, looking as though he were walking aimlessly, advanced into the right-hand aisle of the church as far as the place where his candles had been lit. His eyes fixed themselves on the Cimabue Madonna, then he said to Pepe as he knelt down: 'I have to give thanks for a moment.' Pepe imitated him. On leaving the church, Pepe noticed that Fabrizio gave a twenty-franc piece to the first poor man who asked him for alms. The beggar let out cries of gratitude, which drew swarms of the poor of every kind who normally grace the square of San Petronio to follow behind this charitable individual. They all wanted their share of the napoleon. The women, despairing of breaking into the scrum that surrounded him, swooped on Fabrizio, shouting whether it wasn't true that he had wanted to give his napoleon to be shared out among the Good Lord's poor. Pepe, brandishing his gold-knobbed cane, ordered them to leave His Excellency alone.

'Oh, Excellency,' the women all went on, more shrilly still, 'give the poor women a gold napoleon too.' Fabrizio increased his pace, the women followed him shouting, and many poor beggarmen, flocking in from every street, created something like a small uprising. The whole of this horribly dirty, animated crowd was shouting 'Excellency'. Fabrizio had great difficulty extricating himself from the mob. The scene brought his imagination back to earth. I'm only getting what I deserve, he told himself, I've been associating with the riff-raff.

Two women followed him as far as the Saragozza gate, by which he left the town. Pepe stopped them by threatening them sternly with his cane and tossing them some loose change. Fabrizio climbed the charming hill of San Michele in Bosco, circled one part of the town outside the walls, took a path, came out five hundred paces away on the Florence road, then re-entered Bologna and solemnly handed the police clerk a passport in which his own description was very accurately registered. The passport gave his name as Joseph Bossi, student of theology. Fabrizio noticed a small red ink stain made, as if by accident, at the foot of the page near the right-hand corner. Two hours later he had a spy on his heels on account of the title of Excellency that his companion had given him in front of the beggars at San Petronio, although his passport bore none of the titles that give a man the right to be called Excellency by his servants.

Fabrizio saw the spy and thought him a joke. He was no longer thinking either of passports or of the police and was amused by everything, like a child. Pepe, who had orders to stay close to him, seeing that he found Lodovico quite sufficient, preferred to go and carry the good news to the duchess himself. Fabrizio wrote two very long letters to the persons who were dear to him. Then he had the idea of writing a third, to the venerable Archbishop Landriani. This letter created a splendid impression, it contained a very exact account of the set-to with Giletti. The good archbishop was much moved and did not fail to go and read the letter to the prince, who was very willing to listen, quite curious to learn how the young monsignore went about excusing himself for so terrible a murder. Thanks to the Marchesa Raversi's numerous friends, the prince, along with the whole town of Parma, believed that Fabrizio had had the help of twenty or thirty peasants in knocking down a bad actor who had been insolent enough to compete with him for little Marietta. In despotic courts, the first adroit intriguer dictates the *truth*, as does fashion in Paris.

'But damn it all,' said the prince to the archbishop, 'one gets that sort of thing done by someone else; doing it oneself is unseemly. And then you don't kill an actor like Giletti, you buy him.'

Fabrizio could never have suspected what was going on in Parma. The fact was that the question being discussed was whether the death of this actor, who in his lifetime had earnt thirty-two francs a month, would lead to the fall of the ultra ministry and its leader, Count Mosca.

On learning of Giletti's death, the prince, piqued by the duchess's independent ways, had ordered the chief prosecutor Rassi to treat the whole case as though it had involved a liberal. Fabrizio, for his part, believed that a man of his rank was above the law. He had not taken into account the fact that in countries where the great names are never punished, intrigue can achieve anything, even against them. He often spoke to Lodovico of his perfect innocence, which would soon be proclaimed. His overriding reason was that he was not culpable. Whereupon Lodovico said to him one day: 'I can't imagine why Your Excellency, clever as he is and so well educated, should be troubling to say these things to me, who am his devoted retainer. Your Excellency is taking too many precautions, it's right to say that sort of thing in public or in a court of law.' The man believes I'm a murderer and likes me no less for being so, Fabrizio told himself, coming down to earth.

Three days after Pepe's departure, he was greatly surprised to receive an enormous letter sealed with a plait of silk, as in the days of Louis XIV, addressed to *His Excellency the Very Reverend Monsignor Fabrizio del Dongo, First Vicar-General in the Diocese of Parma, Canon*, etc.

But am I still all that? he asked himself, laughing. Archbishop Landriani's epistle was a masterpiece of logic and clarity. It filled no less than nineteen long pages and recounted very clearly all that had happened in Parma as a consequence of Giletti's death.

'A French army commanded by Marshal Ney and marching on the town would have produced no greater effect,' the good archbishop told him. 'With the exception of the duchess and myself, my dear son, everyone believes that you killed the histrion Giletti for your own pleasure. Should that misfortune have befallen you, these are matters that are suppressed with two hundred louis and a six-month absence. But Raversi wants to use the incident to bring down Count Mosca. It is not the frightful sin of murder that the public blames you for, but solely the *clumsiness* or rather the insolence of not having deigned to resort to a *bulo* (a sort of thuggish underling). Here I am translating into unequivocal terms what is being said around me, for since this forever to be deplored calamity, I go each day into three of the most highly respected houses in the town so as to have the opportunity to make your case. Never have I believed I was making a more sacred use of the little eloquence that heaven has deigned to grant me.'

The scales were falling from Fabrizio's eyes. The duchess's numerous letters, full of outbursts of affection, never condescended to tell him anything. The duchess swore she would leave Parma for good, if he did not soon return in triumph. 'The count will do all that is humanly possible for you,' she told him in the letter which accompanied that from the archbishop. 'As for myself, you have changed my character by this noble escapade. I'm as grasping now as Tombone the banker. I have dismissed all my workmen, I've gone further, I have dictated an inventory of my fortune to the count, which turns out to be far less substantial than I thought. After the death of the excellent Count Pietranera which, incidentally, you would have done better to avenge, instead of risking your life against a creature of Giletti's sort, I was left with an income of twelve hundred livres and five thousand francs of debts. I remember, among other things, that I had two and a half dozen pairs of white satin shoes coming from Paris, and only one pair of shoes for walking in the street. I've almost decided to take the three hundred thousand francs the duke left me, which I wanted to use in its entirety to erect a magnificent tomb for him. Anyway, your, that's to say my, principal enemy is the Marchesa Raversi.

If you're bored on your own in Bologna, you have only to say the word, I shall come and join you. Here are four new bills of exchange,' etc., etc.

The duchess said nothing to Fabrizio of the view being taken in Parma about his affair; she wanted above all to console him, and in any case, the death of a ridiculous creature such as Giletti did not seem to her something for which a del Dongo might seriously be taken to task. 'How many Gilettis have our ancestors not dispatched into the next world,' she said to the count, 'without anyone taking it into their head to blame them.'

Greatly astonished, Fabrizio began to glimpse the true state of affairs for the first time and set to studying the archbishop's letter. Unfortunately, the archbishop thought him better informed than he in fact was. Fabrizio realized that where the Marchesa Raversi had triumphed first and foremost was in the fact that it was impossible to find any eye-witnesses to the fatal combat. The footman who had first brought the news to Parma was at the village inn in Sanguigna when it was taking place. Little Marietta and the old woman who acted as her mother had vanished, and the marchesa had bought the coachman who had been driving the carriage, and who had now supplied an outrageous statement. 'Although the procedure is wrapped in the most profound mystery,' wrote the good archbishop, in his Ciceronian vein, 'and is directed by the prosecutor Rassi, of whom Christian charity alone can stop me from speaking ill, but who has made his fortune by the zealous pursuit of those unfortunate enough to stand accused, like a hound going after the hare; although, as I say, Rassi, whose turpitude and venality your imagination could never exaggerate, has been charged with the direction of the case by an infuriated prince, I have been able to read the coachman's three statements. By a signal stroke of good fortune, the wretch contradicts himself. And I shall add, since I am speaking to my vicar-general, to the man who, after me, is due to have charge of this diocese, that I have sent word to the priest of the parish where this errant sinner lives. I will tell you, my dear son, but under the seal of confession, that this priest already knows, through the coachman's wife, the number of écus he has received from the Marchesa

Raversi. I shall not venture to say that the marchesa is requiring of him that he slander you, but that is probably the case. The écus were handed over by a wretched priest who fulfils no very elevated a function for the marchesa, and whom I have been obliged to forbid to say Mass for the second time. I shall not weary you with the account of several other steps which you would have expected me to take and which moreover fall within my duty. A canon, your colleague at the cathedral, who, let it be said, remembers rather too readily on occasion the influence deriving from the assets possessed by his family, of whom he remains, by divine permission, the sole heir, having taken the liberty of saying at Count Zurla's, the minister of the interior, that he regarded this bagatelle as having been proved against you (he was speaking of the murder of the unfortunate Giletti), I had him called before me and there, in the presence of my almoner and my three other vicars-general, and of two priests who chanced to be in the waiting room, I asked him to share with us, his brothers, the elements of the complete proof of guilt he said that he had acquired against one of his colleagues in the cathedral. The wretched man was able to articulate only inconclusive reasons. Everyone rose up against him and, although I saw fit to add only a very few words, he burst into tears and gave us to witness his full confession of having been completely mistaken, whereupon I promised to keep it a secret in my name and that of all those who had been present at this meeting, on the condition, however, that he should apply all his zeal to rectifying the false impressions which may have been given by the remarks he had been proffering for the past two weeks.

'I shall not repeat to you, my dear son, what you must long have known, that is to say, that of the thirty-four peasants employed on the excavations undertaken by Count Mosca, whom Raversi claims were in your pay to assist you in a crime, thirty-two were in the bottom of their trench, wholly occupied with their labours, at the time when you seized the hunting knife and used it to defend your life against the man who attacked you without warning. Two of them, who were outside the trench, shouted to the others: "The monsignore's being murdered!" That cry alone demonstrates your innocence most vividly. Well, the prosecutor Rassi claims that those two men have disappeared. What is more, they have found eight of the men who were in the bottom of the trench. When first questioned, six declared having heard the shout "The monsignore's being murdered!" I know, indirectly, that at their fifth interrogation, which took place yesterday evening, five declared that they could not remember very clearly whether they had heard the shout directly or had only heard tell of it by one of their fellow-workers. Orders have been given that I be informed where these labourers have their homes, and their priests will make them understand that they are risking damnation if, in order to earn a few écus, they allow themselves to tamper with the truth.'

The good archbishop had gone into endless detail, as may be judged by what we have just reported. Then he added, employing the Latin tongue:

'This affair is nothing less than an attempt at a change of ministry. If you are condemned, it can only be to penal servitude or to death, in which case I shall intervene by declaring, from on high in my archiepiscopal pulpit, that I know you to be innocent, that you quite simply defended your life against a brigand, and that in fact I have forbidden you to return to Parma for as long as your enemies are triumphant there. I even propose to stigmatize the prosecutor, as he deserves. Hatred of that man is as widespread as esteem for his character is rare. But in any case, on the day before the prosecutor pronounces this very unjust charge, the Duchess Sanseverina will leave the town and perhaps even the States of Parma. In that event, no one is in any doubt that the count will hand in his resignation. Then, very probably, General Fabio Conti will succeed to the ministry and the Marchesa Raversi will have triumphed. The real trouble with your affair is that no man of competence is in overall charge of taking the steps needed to reveal your innocence and foil the attempts that have been made to suborn the witnesses. The count believes he can fill that role, but he is too much the *grand seigneur* to stoop to certain details. Moreover, in his capacity as minister of police, he has had to issue the most severe orders against you right from the start. Finally, dare I tell you? Our sovereign lord believes you to be guilty, or at least feigns to so believe, and has introduced a certain acrimony into the affair.' (The words corresponding to 'our sovereign lord' and 'feigns to so believe' were in Greek, and Fabrizio felt infinitely grateful to the archbishop for having dared to write them. He cut that line out from the letter with a penknife, and destroyed it there and then.)

Fabrizio broke off twenty times from reading this letter. He was stirred to an outpouring of the most heartfelt gratitude. He replied instantly with a letter of eight pages. Frequently, he was obliged to look up so that his tears should not fall on the paper. The next day, just as he was sealing the letter, he found its tone too worldly. I shall write to him in Latin, he told himself, the worthy archbishop will find it more appropriate. But as he sought to construct beautiful long Latin sentences, in a faithful imitation of Cicero, he recalled that one day the archbishop, speaking to him of Napoleon, had affected to call him Buonaparte. Instantly, all the emotion that the day before had all but moved him to tears vanished. 'Oh king of Italy,' he cried, 'that loyalty that so many others swore to you in your lifetime I shall preserve after your death. He likes me, no doubt, but because I'm a del Dongo and he the son of a bourgeois.' So that his fine Latin letter might not be wasted, Fabrizio made a few necessary changes and addressed it to Count Mosca.

On that same day, Fabrizio encountered little Marietta in the street. She flushed with pleasure and signed to him to follow her without approaching her. She quickly reached a deserted doorway. There she pulled forward the black lace which, following the local fashion, covered her head, so that she could not be recognized. Then, turning quickly around: 'How come,' she said, 'you're walking freely about in the street?' Fabrizio recounted his story.

'Good Lord, you've been in Ferrara! And I who hunted for you everywhere there! You must know I've fallen out with the old woman because she wanted to take me to Venice, where I knew very well you'd never go because you're on the Austrians' black list. I sold my gold necklace to come to Bologna, a presentiment warned me of the good fortune I've had of meeting you. The old woman arrived two days after me. So I won't make you promise to come to the house, she'll make more of those sordid demands for money that make me so ashamed. We've lived very properly since the fatal day you know about, and haven't spent the quarter of what you gave her. I wouldn't want to come and see you at the Pelegrino, that would get around. Try and rent a small room in a back street, and at the Ave Maria (nightfall) I'll be here, under the same doorway.' Which having said, she took to her heels.

CHAPTER 13

All serious thoughts were forgotten on the unexpected appearance of this agreeable young person. Fabrizio began to live in Bologna with deep enjoyment and in total safety. This innocent readiness to derive pleasure from everything that filled his life came out in the letters he addressed to the duchess; to the point where she was disgruntled by it. Fabrizio hardly noticed. He merely wrote, in a form of shorthand, on the dial of his watch: 'When I write to the d. never say "when I was a prelate, when I was a man of the Church"; it makes her angry.' He had bought two small horses with which he was very satisfied. He harnessed them to a hired barouche each time little Marietta wanted to go to visit one or other of the ravishing beauty spots in the vicinity of Bologna. Almost every evening, he took her to the Reno falls. On the way back, he would stop at the house of the affable Crescentini, who rather saw himself as a father to Marietta.

I must say, if this is the café life that seemed so ridiculous for a man of some worth, I was wrong to reject it, Fabrizio told himself. He was forgetting that he only ever went to the café to read the *Constitutionnel* and that, completely unknown as he was to Bologna society, the joys of vanity played no part at all in his present happiness. When he was not with little Marietta, he was to be seen at the observatory, where he followed lectures on astronomy. The professor had shown himself very friendly and Fabrizio lent him his horses on Sundays so that he could go and show off with his wife on the Corso della Montagnola.

He loathed the idea of bringing down misfortune on anyone at all, however contemptible. Marietta refused absolutely to let him visit the old woman. But one day when she was at church, he went up to the *mammacia*'s, who flushed angrily on seeing him enter. Now's the time to act like a del Dongo, Fabrizio told himself.

'How much does Marietta earn a month when she gets an engagement?' he asked, with the air of a self-respecting young man entering the dress circle at the Bouffes in Paris.[1]

'Fifty écus.'

'You're lying as usual. Tell me the truth, or as God's my witness you won't get one centime.'

'Very well, she was getting twenty-two écus in our company in Parma, when we were unlucky enough to meet you. Myself, I was getting twelve écus, and we each gave Giletti, our protector, a third of what was coming in. Out of which, just about every month, Giletti gave Marietta a present. The present may have been worth two écus.'

'You're lying again. You yourself got only four écus. But if you're nice to Marietta, I shall engage you as if I were an impresario. Every month you'll receive twelve écus for yourself and twenty-two for her. But if I see her with red eyes, I shall declare bankruptcy.'

'You're the proud one. Very well, your fine generosity will ruin us,' replied the old woman furiously. 'We shall lose the *avviamento* (goodwill). Once we've suffered the enormous misfortune of being deprived of Your Excellency's protection, none of the troupes will know us any longer, they'll all be full right up. We shan't get an engagement, and thanks to you we will die of hunger.'

'Go to the devil,' said Fabrizio as he went out.

'I shan't go to the devil, you wicked blasphemer, but quite simply to the police station, who will learn from me that you're a *monsignore* who's thrown his cassock into the bushes, and that you're no more Joseph Bossi than I am!' Fabrizio had already gone down several stairs; he came back.

'First of all, the police know better than you what my real name may be. But if you choose to give me away, if you're that wicked,' he said, with great seriousness, 'Lodovico will come and have a talk with you, and you won't get a knife stuck into your old carcass six times but two dozen, and you'll be six months in the hospital, and without any tobacco.'

The old woman went pale and dashed at Fabrizio's hand, which she tried to kiss.

'I accept with gratitude the future you're making for us, Marietta and me. You look so kind, I took you for a simpleton. And bear it in mind that others may make the same mistake. My advice is, get used to looking more like a great nobleman.' Then she added with an admirable impudence: 'Just think about that good advice, and since winter isn't too far away, you must make Marietta and me a present of two nice coats of that lovely English material that the big fat merchant sells outside San Petronio.'

The pretty Marietta's love offered Fabrizio all the attractions of the sweetest friendship, which set him to thinking of the same kind of happiness that he might have found with the duchess.

But it's a very droll circumstance, is it not, he sometimes said to himself, that I'm not susceptible to that exclusive and impassioned preoccupation that they call love? Among the liaisons that chance found for me in Novara or in Naples, did I ever meet a woman whose presence, even in the early days, I preferred to riding out on a good-looking horse that I didn't know? So can what they call love be one more falsehood? he added. I no doubt love just as I have a good appetite at six o'clock! Could it be that rather vulgar propensity that the liars have turned into the love of Othello or Tancred?[2] Or must I believe I am differently constituted from other men? Why should my soul lack one passion? What a singular destiny that would be!

In Naples, towards the end especially, Fabrizio had encountered women who, proud of their rank, their beauty and the social standing of the adorers they had given up for his sake, had aspired to keep him on a leash, faced with which intention, Fabrizio had broken with them in the most abrupt and scandalous fashion. But, he told himself, if ever I let myself be carried away by the pleasure, very keen for sure, of being close to the pretty woman known as the Duchess Sanseverina, I shall be exactly like the featherbrained Frenchman who one day killed the goose that laid the golden eggs. It's to the duchess I owe the one happiness I've ever experienced from feelings of tenderness. My affection for her is my life and anyway, what am I without her? A poor exile reduced to a painful existence in a dilapidated country house outside Novara. I remember that during the great autumn rains I was obliged in the evenings, for fear of an accident, to fix an umbrella above the canopy of my bed. I used to ride the factor's horses, who was quite willing to put up with it out of respect for my *blue blood* (my great influence), but he was beginning to find my stay somewhat protracted. My father had assigned me an allowance of twelve hundred francs, and thought himself damned for putting bread into the mouth of a Jacobin. My poor mother and my sisters let themselves go without dresses so that I might be in a position to give a few presents to my mistresses. That kind of generosity pierced me to the heart. Moreover, they were beginning to suspect my poverty, and the young nobility round about were on the point of feeling sorry for me. Sooner or later, some coxcomb would have displayed his contempt for a poor Jacobin whose plans had miscarried, for, as those sorts of people see it, that's all I was. I'd have given or received some nice thrust from a sword which would have led me to the fortress of Fenestrelle, or else I'd have gone and sought refuge again in Switzerland, still with my allowance of twelve hundred francs. I have the good fortune to owe the absence of all these evils to the duchess. What's more, it's she who feels for me the transports of affection that I should be feeling for her.

Instead of that ridiculous, mediocre life that would have made a sorry creature of me, a fool, for four years I have been living in a big town and I have an excellent carriage, which has stopped me from experiencing envy and all the mean sentiments of the provinces. My over-generous aunt is forever scolding me for not taking enough money from the banker's. Do I want to spoil this admirable position once and for all? Do I want to lose the one woman friend I have in the world? It would be enough to utter a *falsehood*, enough to say to a charming and perhaps unique woman, for whom I feel the most passionate affection,

'I love you', I who don't know what real love is. She would spend the day turning the absence of those transports that are foreign to me into a crime. Marietta on the other hand, who can't see into my heart and who takes a caress to be a transport of the soul, thinks I am madly in love, and judges herself to be the most fortunate of women.

In point of fact, I've experienced a little of that tender pre-occupation known, I believe, as *love*, only for that young Aniken in the inn at Zonders, near the Belgian frontier.

It is with regret that we are going to set down here one of Fabrizio's very worst actions. In the midst of this tranquil existence, a miserable *stab* of vanity possessed the heart that was unreceptive to love and carried it far away. At the same time as himself, the famous Fausta F*** happened to be in Bologna, unquestionably one of the first singers of our day and perhaps the most capricious woman who ever lived. Burati,[3] that excellent Venetian poet, had written a famous satirical sonnet about her, which was at that time to be heard on the lips of princes as well as the scruffiest street urchin.

'To want and not to want, to adore and to detest in a single day, to be content only in inconstancy, to despise what the world adores, even as the world is adoring it, Fausta has these defects and many more besides. So never let your eyes light on this serpent. If you are unwise enough to look on her, you will forget her caprices. If you have the good fortune to hear her, you will forget yourself and love will turn you, in an instant, into what Circe long ago turned the companions of Ulysses.'[4]

For the time being, this miracle of beauty was under the spell of the enormous whiskers and haughty insolence of the young Count M***, to the point of not being repelled by his abomin-able jealousy. Fabrizio saw the count in the streets of Bologna, and was scandalized by the air of superiority with which he occupied the roadway and deigned to show off his attractions to the public. This young man was very rich, believed he could do as he liked, and since his *prepotenza* (arrogance) had led to his receiving threats, he seldom showed himself unless sur-rounded by eight or nine *buli* (a sort of ruffian) dressed in his livery, whom he had brought from his estates around Brescia.

Fabrizio's glances had once or twice met those of the terrible count, when he had chanced to go and hear Fausta. He was astonished by the angelic sweetness of that voice; he had not imagined anything of the kind. To it he owed sensations of a supreme happiness, which made a splendid contrast with the *placidity* of his present life. Can this be love at last? he asked himself. Greatly curious at experiencing this sentiment, and amused moreover by the act of defying Count M***, whose expression was more forbidding than that of any *drum-major*, our hero succumbed to the childishness of passing over-frequently in front of the Palazzo Tanari, which Count M*** had rented for Fausta.

One day, as it was getting dark, Fabrizio, trying to get himself noticed by Fausta, was greeted by strident guffaws issuing from the count's *buli*, who happened to be in the doorway of the Palazzo Tanari. He hurried home, armed himself well, and went past the palazzo once more. Fausta, hidden behind her window blinds, was awaiting his return, and took good note of it. M***, who was jealous of the entire world, became especially jealous of M. Joseph Bossi and heaped ridicule on him. Upon which our hero had a letter delivered to him every morning containing only the following words: 'M. Joseph Bossi destroys unwelcome insects, and is lodging at the Pelegrino, 79 via Larga.'

Count M***, accustomed to the respect ensured him on every side by his vast wealth, his blue blood and the bravery of his thirty servants, refused to stand for the form taken by this brief missive.

Fabrizio wrote others to Fausta. M*** set spies on his rival, who had not perhaps been found unappealing. He learnt first of all his real name, and then, that for the time being he could not show himself in Parma. A few days later, Count M***, his *buli*, his magnificent horses and Fausta left for Parma.

Fabrizio, stung into action, followed them the next day. The good Lodovico's touching remonstrations were in vain. Fabrizio sent him packing and Lodovico, himself a very brave man, admired him. The journey would in any case take him closer to the pretty mistress that he had in Casal-Maggiore. Thanks to Lodovico's endeavours, eight or nine former soldiers

from Napoleon's regiments entered M. Joseph Bossi's household in the guise of domestic servants. Provided I don't come
into contact with either the minister of police, Count Mosca,
or the duchess, Fabrizio told himself, as he committed the folly
of following Fausta, I am risking only myself. I shall tell my
aunt later on that I was going in search of love, that beautiful
thing which I have never met with. The fact is, I think of Fausta,
even when I don't see her . . . But is it the memory of her voice
that I love, or her person? No longer having an ecclesiastical
career in mind, Fabrizio was sporting a moustache and whiskers
almost as terrible as those of Count M***, which formed a
partial disguise. He established his headquarters not in Parma,
which would have been too risky, but in a neighbouring village,
in the middle of the woods, on the road to Sacca, where his
aunt's country house was. Following Lodovico's advice, he
announced himself in the village as being the manservant of a
great English milord, highly eccentric, who spent a hundred
thousand francs a year on the pleasures of the chase, and who
would shortly be coming to Lake Como, to which he was drawn
by the trout fishing. Fortunately, the charming little palazzo
that Count M*** had rented for the lovely Fausta was situated
at the southernmost limit of the town of Parma, on the selfsame
road to Sacca, and Fausta's windows looked out on to the
beautiful avenues of tall trees that extend beneath the tall tower
of the citadel. Fabrizio was not known in this solitary district.
He did not fail to have Count M*** followed, and one day,
after the latter had just emerged from the beautiful singer's, he
had the audacity to appear in the street in broad daylight. Truth
to tell, he was riding an excellent horse and was well armed.
Musicians, of the kind who roam the streets in Italy and are
often first-rate, came and set down their double basses underneath Fausta's windows. After playing a prelude, they sang,
quite competently, a cantata in her honour. Fausta came to the
window and had no difficulty in noticing a very courteous
young man who, having stopped on horseback in the middle of
the street, first of all bowed, then began giving her looks that
were not hard to interpret. Despite the exaggeratedly English
costume Fabrizio had adopted, she soon recognized the author

of the passionate letters that had led to her departure from Bologna. What a strange person, she said to herself, I fancy I'm going to love him. I have a hundred louis here in front of me, I can easily send the terrible Count M*** packing. The fact is, he's dull and never unpredictable, the only even faintly amusing thing about him is how gruesome his men look.

The next day, having learnt that Fausta went every day, at around eleven, to hear Mass in the centre of the town, in the same church of San Giovanni where the tomb of his great-uncle, the Archbishop Ascanio del Dongo was, Fabrizio ventured to follow her. Truth to tell, Lodovico had procured for him a fine English wig of the most handsome red hair. He wrote a sonnet that Fausta found charming on the colour of this hair, which was that of the flames that were scorching his heart. An unknown hand had undertaken to place it on her piano. This small war lasted for a whole week, but Fabrizio found that, despite all manner of initiatives, he was not making any real progress. Fausta refused to receive him. He had overdone the suggestions of strangeness: she has since said she was frightened by him. Fabrizio was kept going only by what remained of hopes of succeeding in feeling what is known as *love*; but he often felt bored.

'Let's be off, signore,' Lodovico said repeatedly, 'you're not in love. I can see, you're hopelessly composed and full of good sense. Moreover, you're not making any progress. If only out of shame, let's be gone.' Fabrizio was about to leave at this first moment of ill humour when he learnt that Fausta was due to sing at the Duchess Sanseverina's. Perhaps that sublime voice will at last set my heart on fire. And he went so far as to introduce himself in disguise into that palazzo where every eye knew him. The duchess's emotions may be imagined when, right near the end of the concert, she observed a man in footman's livery, standing near the door into the great salon. His attitude reminded her of someone. She looked for Count Mosca, who only then told her of Fabrizio's notable and truly unbelievable foolishness. He was taking it well enough himself. This love for someone other than the duchess pleased him greatly. The count who, outside of politics, was a perfect gentleman, acted in accordance with the maxim that he could find happiness only for as long as the duchess was happy. 'I will save him from himself,' he told his mistress. 'Imagine how delighted my enemies would be if he were arrested in this house! So I have more than a hundred of my own men here, which is why I got them to ask you for the keys to the big water tower. He passes for being madly in love with Fausta, but up until now hasn't been able to get her away from Count M***, who has given that crazy woman the existence of a queen.' The duchess's features betrayed the most acute hurt: so Fabrizio was no better than a libertine, quite incapable of any tender or serious feelings. 'And not to come and see us, that's what I'll never be able to forgive him for!' she said at last. 'And I who write to him every day in Bologna!'

'I very much appreciate his reticence,' replied the count, 'he doesn't want us to be compromised by his escapade, and it'll be amusing to hear him recount it.'

Fausta was too wayward to be able to keep quiet about what was filling her thoughts. On the day following the concert, at which her eyes had directed all her arias at this tall young man dressed as a footman, she spoke of an attentive stranger to Count M***.

'Where do you see him?' asked the count in a fury.

'In the streets, at church,' replied Fausta, taken aback. She at once tried to atone for her rashness or at least steer well clear of anything that might recall Fabrizio. She launched into an interminable description of a tall young man with red hair; he had blue eyes. It was no doubt some very rich, very gauche young Englishman, or some prince or other. At this, Count M***, whose powers of insight were not his strong suit, started imagining, which was very pleasing to his vanity, that this rival was none other than the hereditary prince of Parma. That poor, melancholic young man, watched over by five or six governors, under-governors, tutors, etc., who let him go out only after they had met in conference, cast strange looks at all the passable women whom he was permitted to approach. At the duchess's concert, his rank had placed him in front of the whole audience, on an isolated armchair, three paces from the lovely Fausta, and Count M*** had found his stares extremely shocking. The exquisite vanity of his foolishly supposing he had a prince for a rival amused Fausta, who took pleasure in confirming it by a great many artlessly furnished details.

'Is your lineage as ancient as that of the Farnese, to which this young man belongs?' she asked the count.

'What do you mean, as ancient? I have no illegitimacy in my family.'*

As chance would have it, Count M*** could never get a good look at this purported rival, which confirmed him in the flattering idea that he had a prince for an antagonist. Indeed, whenever Fabrizio's enterprise did not require him to be in Parma, he remained in the woods near Sacca and the banks of the Po. Now that he believed he was in a fair way to be competing for Fausta's heart with a prince, Count M*** became more arrogant still, but also more cautious. He begged her very earnestly to show the greatest restraint in all her actions. After throwing himself at her knees like a jealous and impassioned lover, he declared quite simply that his honour required that she should not become the dupe of the young prince.

'If you'll allow me, I would not be his dupe if I loved him. For my part, I've never seen a prince at my feet.'

'If you succumb,' he went on, with a haughty expression, 'I shan't perhaps be able to take my revenge on the prince. But revenge myself I certainly shall.' And he left, slamming the doors behind him. Had Fabrizio presented himself at that moment, his case would have been won.

'If you value life,' he told her that evening, taking leave of her after the performance, 'see that I never learn that the young prince has got inside your house. I have no power over him, more's the pity, but don't make me remember I have total power over you!'

'Oh Fabrizio, my love,' cried Fausta, 'if only I knew where to find you.'

---

* Piero-Lodovico, the first sovereign from the Farnese family, so highly celebrated for his virtues, was, as is well known, the illegitimate son of the sainted Pope Paul III.

Injured vanity can carry a young man with money, and surrounded by flatterers since the cradle, a very long way. The very genuine passion that Count M*** had felt for Fausta was furiously revived. He was not given pause by the dangerous prospect of doing battle with the only son of the sovereign of the country he happened to find himself in. In the same way, he did not have the wit to try to get sight of the prince, or at least have him followed. Unable to attack him by any other means, M*** ventured to think of making him look ridiculous. I shall be banished for ever from the States of Parma, he told himself, but what does that matter? Had he sought to reconnoitre the enemy's position, Count M*** would have learnt that the poor young prince never went out without being followed by three or four old men, the tiresome guardians of etiquette, and that the one pleasure of his own choosing that he was permitted, was mineralogy. By day as by night, the small palazzo occupied by Fausta, where Parma's high society congregated, was surrounded by watchers. M*** knew hour by hour what she was doing and especially what was being done around her. What is commendable about this jealous man's precautions is that this very capricious woman had no idea to start with that the surveillance had been increased. All the agents' reports told Count M*** that a very young man, wearing a wig of red hair, made frequent appearances before Fausta's windows, but always with a fresh disguise. It's obviously the young prince, M*** told himself, why otherwise disguise himself? And confound it, a man such as myself is not the kind to make way for him. But for the usurpations of the Venetian Republic, I too would be a sovereign prince.

On San Stefano's day, the spies' reports took on a more sombre tone. They seemed to indicate that Fausta was beginning to respond to the stranger's assiduousness. I can leave with the woman this instant, M*** told himself. But dammit, in Bologna I ran away from del Dongo, here I'd be running away from a prince! And what would that young man say? He might think he's succeeded in frightening me! And confound it, I'm from as good a family as him. M*** was enraged but, to make his wretchedness complete, was anxious above all not to make

himself look ridiculous by letting Fausta, sardonic as he knew
her to be, see that he was jealous. On San Stefano's day therefore, having spent an hour with her, and having been received
there with an enthusiasm that struck him as the height of falsity,
he left her at around eleven o'clock, getting dressed to go and
hear Mass at San Giovanni. Count M*** returned home, put
on the threadbare black coat of a young theology student and
hurried to San Giovanni. He chose a spot behind one of the
tombs that adorn the third chapel on the right. He could see
everything that was going on in the church under the arm of a
cardinal who has been represented kneeling on his tomb. This
statue took away the light from the back of the chapel and
offered sufficient concealment. Soon, he saw Fausta arrive, love-
lier than ever. She was dressed in all her finery and twenty
adorers belonging to the very best society formed her retinue.
A joyful smile sparkled in her eyes and on her lips. It's obvious,
the poor jealous wretch told himself, she's counting on meeting
the man she loves here, who, thanks to me, she perhaps hasn't
seen for quite some time. Suddenly, the happiness shining in
Fausta's eyes seemed to grow more marked. My rival is present,
M*** told himself, and his outraged vanity knew no bounds.
What kind of figure am I cutting here, serving as a pendant to
a young prince who wears a disguise? But however hard he
tried, he was unable to discover this rival, whom he searched
for hungrily on every side.

Fausta, having let her eyes stray all over the church, finally
rested her gaze, charged with love and with happiness, on the
dark corner where M*** had hidden himself. In a passionate
heart, love is apt to exaggerate the faintest of hints and draw
the most ridiculous conclusions, and so poor M*** ended by
persuading himself that Fausta had spotted him, that having
become aware, despite all his efforts, of his mortal jealousy, she
wanted to reproach him for it and at the same time console him
by these fond glances.

The cardinal's tomb behind which M*** had taken up his
vantage-point was raised three or four feet above the marble
pavement of San Giovanni. The fashionable Mass having ended
at around one o'clock, the majority of the faithful went out,

and Fausta dismissed the town beaux, on the pretext of her devotions. She had remained kneeling at her seat, her eyes, more brilliant now and more tender, were fixed on M***. Since there were only a few people left behind in the church, her eyes no longer took the trouble of inspecting the whole of it, before coming to rest with delight on the statue of the cardinal. Such tact, the count told himself, believing he was being looked at! Finally, Fausta stood up and went abruptly out, having made a few peculiar movements with her hands.

M***, intoxicated with love and almost wholly disabused of his mad jealousy, was leaving his place to fly to his mistress's palazzo and pour out his gratitude, when, as he passed in front of the cardinal's tomb, he noticed a young man dressed all in black. This funereal figure had remained kneeling up until now, right up against the tomb's epitaph, in such a way that, as he searched for him, the jealous lover's gaze might pass over his head and not pick him out.

The young man got up, walked quickly and was instantly surrounded by seven or eight somewhat awkward, odd-looking figures, who seemed to belong to him. M*** dashed after him but, without it being made to look too obvious, he was stopped in the defile formed by the wooden vestibule at the entrance by the awkward men who were protecting his rival. In the end, once he arrived in the street behind them, all he could see was the door of a rickety-looking carriage closing, which, by a bizarre contrast, was harnessed to two excellent horses, and was instantly out of sight.

He returned home, panting with rage. Soon his watchers arrived, who reported coolly that that day, the mysterious lover, disguised as a priest, had knelt very devoutly right up against a tomb placed at the entrance to an unlit chapel in the church of San Giovanni. Fausta had remained in the church until it was all but deserted and had then rapidly exchanged certain signals with the stranger. She had seemed to be making crosses with her hands. M*** hurried to the faithless one's house. For the first time she was unable to conceal her agitation. She told him, with the false innocence of a passionate woman, how she had gone to San Giovanni as usual, but had not seen the man who had been pestering her there. At this, M*** was beside himself, called her a great many names, told her all he had himself seen and, her lies becoming bolder as his accusations grew fiercer, he took up his dagger and hurled himself on her. Showing great composure, Fausta told him: 'All right, everything you're complaining about is the simple truth, but I've tried to keep it from you so you don't go launching recklessly out on senseless schemes of revenge which could be the undoing of both of us. For let me tell you once and for all, my surmise is that the man who's pestering me with his attentions is the sort who won't let anything stand in the way of his wishes, in this country at any rate.' Having very astutely reminded him that, after all, M*** had no rights over her, Fausta ended by saying that she probably would not be going again to San Giovanni. M*** was madly in love, and a certain flirtatiousness may have been mixed in with the wariness in the young woman's heart; he felt himself disarmed. He thought of leaving Parma. However powerful he might be, the young prince would not be able to follow him, or if he did follow him would be no more than his equal. But vain as he was, this departure would still have the appearance for him of a flight, and Count M*** forbade himself to even consider it.

He doesn't suspect the presence of my dear Fabrizio, the enraptured singer told herself, and now we'll be able to have some priceless fun at his expense!

Fabrizio had no inkling of his good fortune, finding the singer's windows firmly closed the following day and, not seeing her anywhere, the joke began to wear a bit thin. He felt remorse. What sort of situation am I putting poor Count Mosca, the minister of police, in? They'll think he's my accomplice; I will have come to this country to ruin his career! But if I abandon a scheme I've been following all this time, what will the duchess say when I tell her of my amorous endeavours?

One evening when, ready now to give the game up, he was lecturing himself in this way and prowling beneath the tall trees that separated Fausta's palazzo from the citadel, he noticed he was being followed by a spy very small in stature. To shake him off, he went in vain down several streets; this microscopic

creature seemed tied to his heels. He became impatient and ran
into a deserted street situated along the Parma, where his men
were waiting in ambush. At a sign from him, they leapt on the
poor little spy, who threw himself down at their knees. It was
Bettina, Fausta's lady's maid. After three days of tedium and
seclusion, and disguised as a man in order to escape Count
M***'s dagger, of which she and her mistress were very much
afraid, she had undertaken to come and tell Fabrizio that he
was loved to distraction and that someone was yearning to see
him. But there could be no more visits to the church of San
Giovanni. It was high time, Fabrizio told himself, persistence
pays!

The young lady's maid was very pretty, which lifted Fabrizio
out of his moral musings. She informed him that the promenade
and all the streets he had been down that evening were being
carefully watched, without it being apparent, by M***'s spies.
They had rented rooms on the ground floor or first floor and,
hidden behind the blinds and maintaining a total silence, they
were observing all that went on in that seemingly most solitary
of streets and could hear what was being said there.

'If those spies had recognized my voice,' said young Bettina,
'I'd have had a knife in me and no mistake when I got back to
the house, and my poor mistress with me perhaps.'

Fabrizio found her terror most appealing. 'Count M*** is in
a fury,' she went on, 'and the signora knows he's capable of
anything . . . She charged me with telling you she'd like to be a
hundred leagues off with you!'

She then recounted the scene on San Stefano's day and
M***'s fury, who had not missed a single one of the glances
and signs of love that Fausta, mad for Fabrizio on the day in
question, had directed at him. The count had drawn his dagger,
had grabbed hold of Fausta by the hair, and had it not been for
her presence of mind she would have been lost.

Fabrizio made the pretty Bettina go up into a small apartment
he had close by. He told her he was from Turin, the son of a
great personage who happened for the time being to be in
Parma, which obliged him to be very circumspect. Bettina
replied, laughing, that he was far more of a great nobleman

than he wanted to appear. It took a little while for our hero to realize that this charming girl mistook him for no less a personage than the hereditary prince himself. Fausta was beginning to be afraid and to love Fabrizio. She had taken it on herself not to tell her maid his name, but to talk about the prince. Fabrizio ended by confessing to the pretty girl that she had guessed correctly. 'But if my name gets around,' he added, 'in spite of the great passion of which I've given your mistress so many proofs, I shall be forced to stop seeing her, and my father's ministers, those wicked people I shall one day remove, won't fail to send her an order to vacate the country, which she has up until now embellished by her presence.'

Towards morning, Fabrizio hatched various schemes with the young lady's maid for securing a meeting with Fausta. He sent for Lodovico and one of his most enterprising men, who conferred with Bettina, while he wrote Fausta the most extravagant of letters. The situation contained all the exaggerations of tragedy, and Fabrizio denied himself none of them. Only at first light did he separate from the young lady's maid, who was very satisfied with the young prince's way of doing things.

It had been repeated over and over, now that Fausta had come to an agreement with her lover, that the latter would no longer go past beneath the windows of the palazzo, except when he could be received, and then there would be a signal. But Fabrizio, who was in love with Bettina and thought the denouement was close at hand in the case of Fausta, could not bear to remain in his village two leagues from Parma. The next day, around midnight, he came on horseback to sing, to a good accompaniment, a then fashionable aria beneath Fausta's windows, having altered the words. Is this not how gentlemen who are in love behave? he asked himself.

Now that Fausta had manifested a desire for a rendezvous, Fabrizio found this whole pursuit to be very protracted. No, I don't love her, he told himself, singing rather badly beneath the windows of the little palazzo. Bettina strikes me as a hundred times preferable to Fausta, and it's by her I'd like to be received at this moment. Fabrizio, somewhat bored, was on his way back to his village, when five hundred paces from Fausta's palazzo, fifteen or sixteen men threw themselves on him, four of them seizing the bridle of his horse while two others grabbed him by the arms. Lodovico and Fabrizio's *bravi* were assailed but were able to make their escape. They fired off a few pistol shots. The whole affair took only a moment. Fifty lit torches appeared in the street in the blink of an eye and as if by magic. All the men were heavily armed. Fabrizio had jumped down from his horse, in spite of the men who were restraining him. He tried to make a space for himself. He even wounded one of the men who was holding his arms in a vice-like grip. But he was greatly surprised to hear this man say to him in the most respectful tones: 'Your Highness will grant me a good pension for that wound, which will be better for me than sinking to the crime of lese-majesty, by drawing my sword against my prince.'

This is simply my punishment for being foolish, Fabrizio told himself, I shall have damned myself for a sin I didn't even find appealing.

Hardly was the brief apology for a battle over before several lackeys in full livery appeared with a sedan chair, gilded and painted in a bizarre fashion: it was one of those grotesque chairs masques use during the carnival. Six men, daggers in hand, begged His Highness to get into it, telling him that the cool night air might harm his voice. They affected the most respectful attitudes, the name of prince was constantly being repeated, and practically shouted. The procession began to move off. Fabrizio counted more than fifty men in the street carrying lit torches. It might have been one o'clock in the morning, everyone had come to their windows, the affair was passing off with a certain solemnity. I was afraid of having a dagger stuck into me on Count M***'s behalf, Fabrizio told himself. He's contenting himself with making fun of me, I didn't think he had such good taste. But does he really believe he's dealing with the prince? If he finds out I'm only Fabrizio, watch out for the daggers!

After a lengthy pause beneath Fausta's windows, the fifty men carrying torches and the twenty armed men went and paraded in front of the finest palazzi in the town. Majordomos stationed on either side of the sedan chair asked His Highness from time to time whether he had any orders to give them. Fabrizio did not lose his head. With the help of the bright light shed by the torches, he could see that Lodovico and his men were following the procession as closely as they were able. Fabrizio told himself: Lodovico has only nine or ten men and doesn't dare attack. From inside the sedan chair, Fabrizio could see very clearly that the men entrusted with this practical joke were armed to the teeth. He affected to laugh with the major-domos charged with looking after him. After more than two hours of this triumphal progress, he saw that they were about to go past the end of the street in which the Palazzo Sanseverina stood.

As they were turning into the street that leads to it, he quickly opened the door let into the front of the chair, jumped over one of the poles, and knocked down one of the ruffians who was thrusting a torch into his face with a blow from his dagger. He received a knife thrust in the shoulder. A second ruffian singed his beard with his burning torch, and at last Fabrizio reached Lodovico, to whom he shouted: 'Kill! Kill everyone who's carry-ing torches!' Lodovico laid about him with his sword and rescued him from two men who were doing their best to pursue him. Fabrizio reached the door of the Palazzo Sanseverina run-ning. Out of curiosity, the doorman had opened the small three-feet door set into the big one and was gazing open-mouthed at the huge number of torches. Fabrizio leapt inside and shut the miniature door behind him. He ran to the garden and escaped through a gate that gave on to a deserted street. One hour later, he was outside the town; by first light he had crossed the frontier into the States of Modena and was in safety. That evening, he entered Bologna. That was quite an expedition, he told himself, I wasn't even able to speak to my beauty. He hastened to write letters of apology to the count and to the duchess, cautious letters which, while depicting what had been going on in his heart, would give nothing away to an enemy. I was in love with love, he told the duchess. I did everything in my power to experience it, but it seems that nature has denied me a heart for loving and feeling melancholy. I can rise no higher than common-or-garden pleasure, etc., etc.

It would be hard to give any idea of the brouhaha that this adventure caused in Parma. The mystery had excited curiosity: countless people had seen the torches and the sedan chair. But who was the man who had been kidnapped and whom they had affected to treat with all manner of respect? The next day, no well-known figure in the town was missing.

The common people who lived in the street from which the prisoner had escaped said they had certainly seen a corpse, but in the daylight, once the inhabitants had dared to emerge from their houses, they found no other traces of the battle than a lot of blood spilt on the roadway. More than twenty thousand sightseers came to visit the street during the day. Italian towns are accustomed to strange spectacles but they always know the *why* and the *how*. What shocked Parma in this instance was that even a month later, once the torchlit procession had ceased to be the sole topic of conversation, no one, thanks to the precautions taken by Count Mosca, had been able to guess the name of the rival who had sought to take Fausta away from Count M***. This jealous and vindictive lover had taken flight as soon as the parade started. On the count's orders, Fausta was put into the citadel. The duchess laughed loudly at this small injustice, which the count had to permit himself in order to put an end once and for all to the inquisitiveness of the prince, who might otherwise have arrived at the name of Fabrizio.

A scholar was seen to arrive in Parma from the north to write a history of the Middle Ages. He was looking for manuscripts in the libraries, and the count had given him every possible authorization. But this scholar, who was still very young, proved to be irascible. He thought, for example, that everyone in Parma was looking to make fun of him. It is true that the street urchins sometimes followed him because of his huge mop of bright red hair, which he showed off with pride. The scholar thought that at the inn they were overcharging him for everything, and he refused to pay the merest bagatelle without looking up the price in the travel guide of a Mrs Starke,[5] which has gone into a twentieth edition because it lists for the prudent Englishman the price of a guinea-fowl, an apple, a glass of milk, etc., etc.

On the evening of the same day as Fabrizio had gone on his enforced promenade, the scholar with the red mane lost his temper at his inn, and took some *small pistols* from his pocket in order to revenge himself on the *cameriere* who had demanded two sous for a not very good peach. He was arrested, for carrying small pistols is a big crime!

Because this irascible scholar was long and thin, the count had the idea, the next morning, of passing him off to the prince as the hothead who had aspired to take Fausta away from Count M*** and been made the butt of a practical joke. The carrying of pocket pistols is punishable by three years' penal servitude in Parma, but this penalty is never applied. After a fortnight in prison, during which the scholar had seen only a lawyer, who filled him with a terrible fear of the atrocious laws directed by the pusillanimity of the powers that be against those bearing concealed weapons, another lawyer visited the prison and told him of the promenade inflicted by Count M*** on a rival whose identity remained unknown. The police did not want to admit to the prince that they had been unable to discover who this rival was. Admit that you wanted to please Fausta, that fifty brigands abducted you as you were singing beneath her window, that you were paraded about for an hour in a sedan chair without anyone addressing you other than correctly. There is nothing humiliating about such a confession, you are being asked to say a few words only. As soon as, by uttering them, you have extricated the police from their difficulty, they will put you into a post-chaise and take you to the border, where they will wish you a good evening.

The scholar held out for a month. Two or three times the prince was on the point of having him brought to the ministry of the interior and of being present himself at the interrogation. But in the end he abandoned that idea when the historian became fed up, resolved to admit everything and was taken to the border. The prince remained convinced that Count M***'s rival had a forest of red hair.

Three days after the procession, as Fabrizio, who was hiding in Bologna, was organizing with the faithful Lodovico the means of locating Count M***, he learnt that he, too, was hiding in a mountain village on the road to Florence. The count had only three of his *buli* with him. The next day, just as he was returning from an outing, he was abducted by eight masked men who pretended to be sbirri[6] from Parma. Having blind-folded him, they took him to an inn two leagues deeper into the mountains, where he met with all possible courtesy and a very ample supper. He was served the best Italian and Spanish wines.

'So am I a State prisoner?' said the count.

'Not at all!' replied the masked Lodovico, most politely. 'You've given offence to a private individual simply, by under-taking to have him paraded about in a sedan chair. Tomorrow morning, he wishes to fight a duel with you. If you kill him, you will find two good horses, money and relays ready on the road to Genoa.'

'What's the name of this braggart?' asked the count in irri-tation.

'His name is Bombace. You will have the choice of weapons and good, very loyal seconds. But one or other of you must die!'

'But that's murder!' said the terrified Count M***.

'God forbid, it's quite simply a duel to the death with the young man whom you paraded through the streets of Parma in the middle of the night, and who would remain dishonoured were you to remain alive! One of you is de trop on this earth, so try to kill him. You will have swords, pistols, sabres, all the weapons we've been able to procure in a few hours, because we needed to be quick. The police in Bologna are very diligent, as you may know, and we mustn't let them prevent this duel, which is necessary to the honour of the young man of whom you made fun.'

'But if the young man is a prince . . .'

'He's a private individual, like yourself, and much less wealthy than you, but he wants to fight to the death, and he will force you to fight, I must warn you.'

'I fear no man on earth!' cried Count M***.

'It's what your adversary desires most passionately,' replied Lodovico. 'Tomorrow, early in the morning, be ready to defend your life. It will be under attack from a man who has reason to be very angry and who won't go easy on you. I repeat that you will have the choice of weapons. And make your will.'

The next day, at around six in the morning, Count M*** was served breakfast, then a door opened in the room where he was being guarded and he was asked to go out into the yard of a country inn. The yard was surrounded by hedges and quite high walls, and the doors had been carefully shut.

In one corner, on a table that Count M*** was invited to approach, he found a few bottles of wine and brandy, two pistols, two swords, two sabres, paper and ink. A score or so of peasants were at the windows of the inn overlooking the yard. The count implored their commiseration. 'They want to murder me!' he cried. 'Save my life!'

'You're deceiving yourself, or you want to deceive them!' shouted Fabrizio, who was at the opposite corner of the yard, next to a table laden with weapons. He had removed his coat and his face was hidden by one of the wire masks to be found in fencing schools.

'I advise you to take the wire mask which is beside you,' Fabrizio went on, 'then advance towards me with a sword or pistols. As you were told yesterday evening, you have the choice of weapons.'

Count M*** raised numerous objections and seemed very put out to be fighting. For his part, Fabrizio dreaded the arrival of the police, although they were in the mountains a good five leagues from Bologna. He ended by directing the most appalling insults at his rival. Finally, he was fortunate enough to send Count M*** into a rage, who seized hold of a sword and marched on Fabrizio. Battle was joined somewhat limply.

After a few minutes, it was interrupted by a loud noise. Our hero had been well aware that he was embarking on an action which, for the rest of his life, might be the subject of blame or at least slanderous imputations. He had dispatched Lodovico into the countryside to recruit witnesses. Lodovico gave money to some strangers who were working in a nearby wood. They ran up letting out shouts, thinking it was a matter of killing an enemy of the man doing the paying. Having reached the inn,

Lodovico asked them to keep their eyes peeled to see whether one of the two young men who were fighting was cheating or taking illicit advantage of the other.

The fight that had been broken off for a moment by the peasants' war-cries was slow in starting again. Fabrizio aimed further insults at the count's self-conceit. 'Signor count,' he cried, 'when one is insolent one needs to be brave. I sense that's a hard condition for you, you prefer paying men who are brave.' The count, once again aroused, began shouting that he had long frequented the famous Battestin fencing school in Naples, and that he was about to punish him for his insolence. Count M***'s anger had finally resurfaced and he fought stoutly enough, which did not stop Fabrizio from thrusting his sword neatly into his chest, which kept him in bed for several months. As he gave the wounded man first aid, Lodovico said into his ear: 'If you report this duel to the police, I'll have you stabbed in your bed.'

Fabrizio escaped to Florence. Because he had remained in hiding in Bologna, only in Florence did he receive all the duchess's reproachful letters. She could not forgive him for having come to her concert without having tried to speak to her. Fabrizio was delighted by Count Mosca's letters, they breathed open friendship and the noblest sentiments. He guessed that the count had written to Bologna, so as to deflect the suspicions that might fall on him in relation to the duel. The police behaved entirely properly. They confirmed that two foreigners, only one of whom, the one who had been wounded, was known (Count M***) had fought with swords in front of more than thirty peasants, among whom, towards the end of the contest, there happened to be the village priest, who had made vain attempts to part the duellists. Since the name of Joseph Bossi had not been mentioned, less than two months later, Fabrizio ventured to return to Bologna, more convinced than ever that his destiny had condemned him never to experience the noble, intellectual part of love. This is what he gave himself the pleasure of explaining at great length to the duchess. He was very weary of his solitary life and desired passionately to rediscover the charming evenings he had spent between the count and his aunt. He had not experienced the solace of good company since.

'I became so bored with the love I wanted to find for myself, and with Fausta,' he wrote to the duchess, 'that even were that capricious woman still to look favourably on me, I wouldn't go twenty leagues to hold her to her word. So don't be afraid, as you say you are, that I might go to Paris, where I see she's had a wildly successful debut. I'd cover all the leagues there are to spend an evening with you and with the count, who is so good to his friends.'

II

By its constant shouting, this republic might stop us enjoying the best of monarchies.

The Charterhouse of Parma, Chapter 23

II

CHAPTER 14

While Fabrizio went in pursuit of love in a village near Parma, the chief prosecutor Rassi, who did not know he was so close by, continued to treat his case as though he were a liberal. He pretended to be unable to find, or rather he intimidated, the witnesses for the defence. And at last, after all but a year of very skilful efforts, and some two months after Fabrizio's final return to Bologna, on a certain Friday, the Marchesa Raversi, wild with delight, said publicly in her salon that, the following day, the sentence that had been handed down in the last hour on the young del Dongo would be presented to the prince for his signature, and approved by him. A few minutes later, the duchess learnt of her enemy's comment.

The count must be very ill served by his agents, she told herself. Only this morning he believed the sentence couldn't be handed down for another week. Perhaps he wouldn't be upset to see my young vicar-general being sent away from Parma, but, she added, singing, we shall see him return. And one day he will be our archbishop. The duchess rang the bell.

'Gather all the servants together in the waiting room,' she told her footman, 'even the cooks. Go and get the necessary permit from the local commandant for four posthorses, and have the horses harnessed to my landau in the next half an hour.' All the women of the household were busy packing the trunks, the duchess quickly put on her travelling habit, all without having said anything to the count. She was carried away by the thought of scoring a point off him.

'My friends,' she told the assembled domestics, 'I've learnt that my poor nephew is going to be sentenced in absentia for having had the audacity to defend his life against a madman. It was Giletti who was looking to kill him. Every one of you has been able to see how gentle and inoffensive Fabrizio is by nature. Rightly indignant at this awful wrong, I am going to Florence. I am leaving each one of you your wages for ten years. If you fall on hard times, write to me, and as long as I have a sequin, there will be something for you.'

The duchess meant exactly what she said, and at her final words, the servants burst into tears. She too was moist-eyed. She added in an emotional voice: 'Pray to God for me and for Monsignor Fabrizio del Dongo, first vicar-general of the diocese, who will tomorrow be sentenced to penal servitude or, which would be less stupid, to be executed.'

The servants' tears were renewed and gradually turned into more or less seditious shouting. The duchess got into her carriage and had herself driven to the prince's palace. In spite of the unseemly hour, she solicited an audience through the duty aide-de-camp, General Fontana. She was not wearing court dress, which caused stupefaction in the aide-de-camp. As for the prince, he was not at all surprised, and even less annoyed by this request for an audience. We're going to see two lovely eyes shedding tears, he said to himself, rubbing his hands. She has come to ask for mercy. That proud beauty is finally going to abase herself! She was quite unbearable with her independent airs. Those very expressive eyes always seemed to be telling me, at the slightest thing that offended her: Naples or Milan would be a far pleasanter place to live than your little town of Parma. It's true I don't reign over Naples or Milan. But finally this great lady has come to ask me for something that depends solely on me and that she's desperate to obtain. I always thought that the arrival of that nephew would provide me with a way of getting at her.

While the prince was smiling at these thoughts and indulging himself in all these agreeable predictions, he was walking about his large cabinet-room, at the door of which General Fontana had remained standing, as stiff as a soldier at the present arms. Seeing the gleam in the prince's eyes, and recalling the duchess's travelling habit, he fancied the monarchy was about to be dissolved. His amazement knew no bounds when he heard the prince say to him: 'Ask the signora duchess to wait perhaps for quarter of an hour.' The general aide-de-camp turned half about like a soldier on parade. The prince smiled again: Fontana isn't used to seeing the haughty duchess kept waiting, he said to himself. The look of astonishment on his face when he goes and says 'perhaps quarter of an hour to wait' will prepare the way for the affecting tears this room is going to see shed. How the prince savoured that quarter of an hour. He paced firmly and regularly about, he was *reigning*. It's a matter of saying nothing that isn't absolutely appropriate. Whatever my feelings towards the duchess, it mustn't be forgotten that she's one of the greatest ladies of my court. How did Louis XIV talk to his daughters the princesses when he had cause to be displeased with them? And his eyes paused on the portrait of the great king.

The funny thing was that the prince never thought to ask himself whether he would grant Fabrizio a pardon, or what sort of pardon it would be. Finally, at the end of twenty minutes, the faithful Fontana presented himself at the door once more, but without saying anything. 'The Duchess Sanseverina may enter!' cried the prince theatrically. The tears are going to start, he told himself, and, as if to prepare himself for such a spectacle, he drew out his handkerchief.

Never had the duchess been so alive or so pretty. She was not even twenty-five years old. Seeing her quick, light steps barely brushing the carpets, the poor aide-de-camp was on the verge of losing his reason. 'I must beg Your Most Serene Highness's pardon,' said the duchess, in her light, gay little voice, 'I have taken the liberty of appearing before you in a costume that is not exactly appropriate, but Your Highness has so accustomed me to his kindnesses that I ventured to hope he would be willing to grant me this favour too.'

The duchess spoke quite slowly, in order to give herself time to enjoy the prince's face. It was a delight because of its profound surprise and the vestiges of the haughty attitude still to be detected in the position of his head and his arms. The prince remained as if thunderstruck, exclaiming from time to time in his shrill, agitated little voice, though he could barely articulate: 'What! What!' Her complimentary remarks at an end, the duchess, as if out of respect, allowed him plenty of time to reply. Then she added: 'I dare to hope that Your Most Serene Highness will deign to forgive me for the incongruity of my costume.' But as she spoke, so brilliant was the sardonic gleam in her eyes that the prince could not endure it. He looked at the ceiling, which with him was an ultimate sign of the most extreme embarrassment.

'What! What!' he said once more. Then he was fortunate enough to hit on a whole sentence: 'So be seated, signora duchess.' He himself pulled a chair forward with a certain good grace. The duchess was not insensitive to this courtesy, she tempered the petulance in her expression.

'What! What!' the prince again repeated, wriggling about on his chair, as if he were unable to get firmly seated.

'I am going to take advantage of the cool night air to travel post-haste,' the duchess went on, 'and since my absence may be of some duration, I did not wish to leave Your Most Serene Highness's States without thanking him for all the kindnesses he has deigned to show me over these past five years.' At which words, the prince at last understood. He turned pale. He was a man who suffered more than most at finding his expectations were mistaken. Then he adopted an expression of grandeur altogether worthy of the portrait of Louis XIV that he had in front of him. Good, the duchess said to herself, here we have a real man.

'And what is the reason for this sudden departure?' asked the prince in a steady enough voice.

'I've been planning it for a long time,' replied the duchess, 'and a small insult being offered to *Monsignor* del Dongo, who tomorrow is going to be sentenced to death or to penal servitude, has made me hasten my departure.'

'And to which town are you going?'

'To Naples, I rather think.' She added, getting up: 'All that remains is for me to take my leave of Your Most Serene Highness and thank him most humbly for his *past* kindnesses.' In her turn, she was leaving looking so determined that the prince could clearly see that in two seconds it would all be over. The scandal of her departure having occurred, he knew that any compromise was impossible. She was not a woman to go back on her actions. He ran after her.

'But you know very well, signora duchess,' he said, taking her hand, 'that I have always been fond of you, with a fondness to which it was entirely up to you to give another name. A murder has been committed, that is not to be denied. I have entrusted the investigation of the case to my best judges . . .'

At these words, the duchess drew herself up to her full height. Any semblance of respect or even urbanity vanished in the blink of an eye. The outraged woman appeared without disguise, an outraged woman addressing someone whom she knew to be acting in bad faith. It was in tones of the sharpest anger and even contempt that she said to the prince, laying stress on each of her words: 'I am leaving Your Most Serene Highness's States for ever, so as never to hear mention again of the prosecutor Rassi or of the other wicked murderers who have condemned my nephew and so many others to death. If Your Most Serene Highness does not wish to introduce a feeling of bitterness into the last moments I shall spend in the company of a prince who is courteous and intelligent when he is not being deceived, I request him very humbly not to call back to mind the thought of those wicked judges who sell themselves for a thousand écus or a cross.'

The admirable and above all truthful tone in which these words were uttered caused the prince to shudder. He feared for a moment finding his dignity endangered by an even more direct accusation, but overall his reaction soon turned into one of pleasure: he admired the duchess. Her whole person had attained a sublime beauty at that moment. Great heaven, how beautiful she is! the prince said to himself. One must grant something to a unique woman such as perhaps hasn't her equal in the whole of Italy . . . Very well, if I play my cards right it wouldn't be impossible perhaps to make her my mistress one day. It's a far cry from such a creature to that stuffed doll of a Marchesa Balbi, who still steals three hundred thousand francs a year from my poor subjects . . . But did I hear her aright? he suddenly reflected. She said 'condemned my nephew and so many others'. Anger then came to the surface and it was with a haughtiness worthy of his sovereign rank that the prince said, after a silence: 'And what must be done in order for the signora not to leave?'

'Something you are not capable of,' replied the duchess in tones of the bitterest irony and undisguised contempt.

The prince was beside himself; that he was strong enough to resist a first impulse he owed to the habits of his role of absolute sovereign. I have to have this woman, he told himself, I owe myself that, and then I have to kill her with contempt . . . If she leaves this room, I shall never see her again. But, drunk with rage and hatred as he was at that moment, where to find the words which could both satisfy what he owed himself and lead the duchess not to desert his court there and then? One can't repeat or make fun of a gesture, he said to himself, and he went and placed himself between the duchess and the door to his cabinet-room. Shortly afterwards, he heard a scratching at the door.

'Who's the cretin,' he cried, swearing with the full force of his lungs, 'who's the cretin coming to inflict his idiotic presence on me?' Poor General Fontana showed his pale, utterly cowed features, and it was with the air of a man in his death throes that he spoke these poorly articulated words: 'His Excellency Count Mosca solicits the honour of being admitted.'

'Let him enter!' shouted the prince. And as Mosca was bowing: 'Well, here's the Duchess Sanseverina who's intending to leave Parma this instant to go and settle in Naples, and who's being impertinent to me into the bargain.'

'What!' said Mosca, turning pale.

'What, you didn't know about this planned departure?'

'Not a word. I left the signora at six o'clock joyful and contented.'

These words had an unbelievable effect on the prince. First of all he looked at Mosca, whose growing pallor showed he had been speaking the truth and was not an accomplice in the duchess's headstrong action. In that case, he told himself, I am losing her for good. Pleasure, revenge, it's all vanishing at once.

In Naples she'll make up epigrams with her nephew Fabrizio about the silly little prince of Parma's great anger. He looked at the duchess. The most violent contempt and anger were doing battle in her heart. Her eyes were fixed at that moment on Count Mosca, and the very delicate lines of that lovely mouth expressed the most bitter disdain. Her whole face said: Vile courtier! And so, thought the prince, having scrutinized her, I'm losing that means of getting her back to this country. Still at this moment, if she leaves my room she is lost to me. God knows what she'll say about my judges in Naples . . . And with the sharp wits and the divine powers of persuasion that heaven has given her, she'll get everyone to believe her. I shall owe to her the reputation of an absurd tyrant who gets up at night to look under the bed . . . Then, in an astute manoeuvre and as if seeking to pace about in order to lessen his agitation, the prince again placed himself in front of the door to the room. The count was to his right three paces away, pale, drawn and shaking so much that he was obliged to look for support from the back of the chair which the duchess had occupied at the start of the audience, and which the prince had pushed away in a fit of anger. The count was in love. If the duchess goes, I shall follow her, he was telling himself. But will she want me going after her? That is the question.

To the prince's left, the duchess, standing, her arms crossed and held against her chest, gazed at him with an admirable insolence. A total, deathly pallor had succeeded the bright colour that had previously animated those sublime features.

In contrast to the other two, the prince was red in the face and wore an anxious expression. His left hand was toying convulsively with the cross attached to the great ribbon of his order that he wore beneath his coat. With his right hand, he was stroking his chin.

'What's to be done?' he said to the count, without much idea of what he was doing himself but impelled by his habit of consulting him on everything.

'The truth is, I've no idea, Most Serene Highness,' replied the count, with the look of a man drawing his last breath. He was barely able to bring out the words of his reply. The tone of his voice afforded the prince the first consolation that his wounded pride had experienced during the audience, and this small comfort supplied him with a form of words flattering to his self-esteem.

'Very well,' he said, 'I am the most reasonable of the three. I'm quite ready to leave my position in the world completely out of account. I am about to speak *as a friend*,' and he added, with a beautifully condescending smile imitated from the halcyon days of Louis XIV, '*as a friend talking to friends*. Signora duchess,' he went on, 'what must be done to make you forget an untimely resolution?'

'The truth is, I've no idea,' replied the duchess, with a deep sigh, 'the truth is, I've no idea, I find Parma so abhorrent.' The remark was not intended as an epigram, it could be seen that hers was the voice of sincerity itself.

The count turned quickly aside: the courtier's soul was shocked. Then he directed an imploring glance at the prince. With great dignity and composure, the prince allowed a moment to pass. Then, addressing himself to the count: 'I can see,' he said, 'that your charming friend is quite beside herself. It's quite simple: she *adores* her nephew.' And, turning towards the duchess, he added, with the most gallant of expressions and at the same time the attitude one adopts when quoting a line from a play: 'What must I do to appeal to those beautiful eyes?'

The duchess had had time to reflect. In a slow, firm voice, and as if she were dictating her ultimatum, she replied: 'His Highness could write me a gracious letter, as he knows very well how to do. It would say that, not being convinced of Fabrizio del Dongo, the archbishop's first vicar-general's guilt, he will not sign the sentence when they come to present it to him, and that these unjust proceedings will not lead to any further consequences in the future.'

'What do you mean, *unjust*!' cried the prince, going red right up to the whites of his eyes, and his anger returning.

'That is not all!' replied the duchess, with a Roman arrogance. '*As from this evening*, and,' she added, looking at the clock, 'it is already a quarter past eleven, as from this evening, His Most Serene Highness will send to tell the Marchesa Raversi that he advises her to go to the countryside in order to rest from the strain that must have been caused by a certain lawsuit of which she was speaking in her salon at the start of the evening.' The prince was pacing about his cabinet-room like a man in a rage.

'Did you ever see such a woman?' he exclaimed. 'She shows me no respect.'

The duchess replied with perfect good grace: 'Never in my life have I thought to lack respect for His Most Serene Highness. His Highness has had the extreme condescension to say that he was speaking *as a friend to friends*. I have, in any case, no desire to remain in Parma,' she added, looking at the count with the utmost contempt. That look decided the prince, hitherto quite uncertain, although the words might have seemed to announce a pledge. He laid no store by words.

A few more words were exchanged, but finally Count Mosca received the order to write the letter of pardon solicited by the duchess. He left out the phrase 'these unjust proceedings will not lead to any further consequences in the future'. It's enough, the count told himself, that the prince should promise not to sign the sentence that will be presented to him. The prince thanked him by a quick glance as he signed it.

The count had made a serious error, the prince was tired and would have signed anything. He thought he had come well out of the episode, and the whole affair had been dominated as he saw it by the words: 'If the duchess leaves, I shall be bored stiff at court before the week's out.' The count noticed that his master had corrected the date and put that of the following day. He looked at the clock, it showed close to midnight. The minister saw in this correction of the date only a pedantic desire to give proof of exactitude and good governance. As for the banishment of the Marchesa Raversi, that was plain sailing. The prince took a particular pleasure in banishing people.

'General Fontana!' he cried, half opening the door.

The general appeared with so much astonishment and curiosity written on his face that the duchess and the count exchanged an amused glance, a glance which made peace between them.

'General Fontana,' said the prince, 'you are going to get into my carriage which is waiting under the colonnade. You will go to the Marchesa Raversi's, you will have yourself announced. If she is in bed, you will add that you have come on my behalf, and once in her room, you will say these exact words, and no others: "Signora Marchesa Raversi, His Most Serene Highness invites you to leave tomorrow, before eight in the morning for your country house in Velleja. His Highness will let you know when you are able to return to Parma."'

The prince's eyes sought out those of the duchess, who, without thanking him as he had expected, made him an extremely respectful curtsy and quickly left.

'What a woman!' said the prince, turning towards Count Mosca.

The latter, overjoyed at the exiling of the Marchesa Raversi, which made all his actions as minister easier, spoke for a good half-hour like the consummate courtier he was. He sought to pour balm on the sovereign's self-esteem and took his leave only once he saw he was firmly persuaded that the anecdotal history of Louis XIV contained no passage more splendid than that which he had just furnished for his future historians.

On returning home, the duchess closed her door, and told them no one should be admitted, not even the count. She wanted to be alone with herself, and to work out what view to take of the scene that had just occurred. She had acted without premeditation, pleasing herself as she went along, but she would have stuck firmly by whatever steps she had let herself be drawn into taking. She would not have found fault with herself once she recovered her composure, still less have repented. Such was the character to which she owed it that, at thirty-six, she was still the prettiest woman in the court.

She was musing now about what Parma might have to offer that was agreeable, as she might have done on returning from a long journey, so firmly had she believed from nine o'clock until eleven that she would be leaving this country for good.

The look on the poor count's face when he learnt of my departure in the presence of the prince! . . . He's a loveable man indeed, and with a heart of gold. He'd have left his ministers to follow me . . . But then for five whole years he's had no distractions to reproach me with. How many women married at the altar could say the same to their lord and master? It has to be agreed that he's not self-important, not a pedant. He doesn't at all make you want to be unfaithful. In front of me he always seems ashamed of his power . . . He cut such a comic figure in the presence of his lord and master. If he was here, I'd put my arms round him. But not for anything would I undertake to amuse a minister who's lost his portfolio, that's a sickness you're cured of only when you die, and . . . which causes you to die. What a misery to be a young minister! I must write to him, that's one of the things he needs to know officially before he quarrels with his prince . . . But I'm forgetting my good servants.

The duchess rang. Her women were still busy packing trunks. The carriage had been brought forward under the portico and was being loaded up. All the domestics who had no work to do had surrounded the carriage, with tears in their eyes. Chekina, who on great occasions came in alone to the duchess, gave her all these details.

'Send them up,' said the duchess. A moment later, she went into the waiting room. 'I've been promised,' she told them, 'that the sentence against my nephew will not be signed by the *sovereign* [this is how they talk in Italy]. I am suspending my departure. We shall see whether my enemies have sufficient influence to get this decision changed.'

After a short silence, the domestics started shouting: 'Long live the signora duchess!' and applauding furiously. The duchess, who was already in the next room, reappeared like an actress responding to the applause, made a small, very gracious curtsy to her people and said: 'My friends, I thank you.' Had she given the word, all of them at that moment would have marched on the palace to attack it. She signalled to the postilion, a former smuggler and devoted servant, who followed her.

'You are to dress up as a prosperous peasant, get out of Parma as best you can, hire a *sediola* and go as quickly as possible to Bologna. You will enter Bologna on foot through the Florence gate, and hand Fabrizio, who is at the Pelegrino, a package that Chekina will give you. Fabrizio is in hiding and is known there as M. Joseph Bossi. Don't go and give him away by being thoughtless, don't make it look as if you know him. My enemies may set spies on you. Fabrizio will send you back here after a few hours or a few days. It's when you return above all that you must take extra precautions not to give him away.'

'Ah, the Marchesa Raversi's men!' cried the postilion. 'We're waiting for them, and if the signora wanted, they'd soon be exterminated.'

'One day maybe! But don't do anything without an order from me, or on your head be it.'

What the duchess wanted to send Fabrizio was the copy of the prince's letter. She could not resist the pleasure of amusing him, and added a few words about the scene that had produced the letter. These few words became a letter of ten pages. She sent for the postilion again.

'You can't leave until four o'clock,' she told him, 'when the gate opens.'

'I was counting on going by the big drain, I'll have water up to my chin, but I'll get out.'

'No,' said the duchess, 'I don't want to risk one of my most loyal servants catching a fever. Do you know anyone at monsignor the archbishop's?'

'The second coachman is my friend.'

'Here's a letter for that saintly prelate. Enter his palace without making a sound, have yourself taken to the valet. I wouldn't want monsignore to be woken up. If he's already shut away in his bedroom, spend the night in the palace and, as he's in the habit of getting up with the sun, tomorrow morning, at four o'clock, have yourself announced as coming from me, ask the saintly archbishop for his blessing, hand over the package you see here, and take the letters he will perhaps give you for Bologna.'

The duchess had addressed the actual original of the prince's letter to the archbishop. Since the letter concerned his first vicar-general, she requested him to place it in the archbishopric's archives, where she hoped that the vicars-general and canons, her nephew's colleagues, would be good enough to go and acquaint themselves with it. All on condition of the utmost secrecy.

The duchess had written to Monsignor Landriani with a familiarity that was bound to charm that worthy bourgeois. The signature alone was three lines long. This very friendly letter was followed by the words: 'Angelina-Cornelia-Isota Valserra del Dongo, Duchess Sanseverina.'

I haven't written that much, I don't think, the duchess said to herself with a laugh, since my marriage contract with the poor duke. But this sort of thing's the only way you can lead such people on, to the bourgeois eye, a caricature is a thing of beauty. She was unable to end the evening without yielding to the temptation of writing a bantering letter to the poor count. She announced officially, for his *guidance*, as she put it, *in his dealings with crowned heads*, that she did not feel herself capable of amusing a minister who had fallen from favour. 'The prince frightens you; when you are no longer able to see him, will it be up to me to frighten you?' She had this letter taken round straight away.

For his part, as early as seven o'clock the next morning, the prince sent for Count Zurla, the interior minister.

'Once again,' he told him, 'give the strictest orders to all the podestàs¹ to have Signor Fabrizio del Dongo arrested. The word is, he will perhaps venture to reappear in our States. This fugitive being in Bologna, where he seems to be defying the procedures of our courts, station sbirri who know him personally: 1. in the villages on the road from Bologna to Parma; 2. in the vicinity of the Duchess Sanseverina's country house at Sacca and her house in Castelnovo; 3. around Count Mosca's country house. I dare to hope that in your great wisdom, signore count, you will know how to keep all knowledge of these orders from your sovereign secret from Count Mosca. You must know that I wish for Signor Fabrizio del Dongo to be arrested.'

As soon as the minister had left, a secret door admitted the chief prosecutor Rassi, who came forward bent double and bowing at every step. This scoundrel's face was a picture, it did justice to the full infamy of his role and, while the rapid and

erratic movements of his eyes revealed that he was aware of his
own worth, the arrogant assurance of his smirk showed he
knew how to make a stand against contempt.

As this personage will be having quite a significant influence
on Fabrizio's destiny, a word or two about him is in order. He
was tall, he had fine, very intelligent eyes, but a face badly
marked by smallpox. He had wits in plenty, and of the subtlest.
It was allowed that he possessed a perfect knowledge of the
law, but he excelled above all in the spirit of resourcefulness.
Whatever the form in which a case might be presented to him,
he easily found, and instantly, the means, firmly based in the
law, of coming to either a conviction or an acquittal. He was
the king above all of the subtle arts of the prosecutor.

This man, whom great monarchies would have envied the
prince of Parma, was known to have only one passion: of
holding intimate conversations with great personages and
currying favour by his buffoonery. It mattered little to him
whether the man of power laughed at what he said, or at his
person, or made revolting jokes about Signora Rassi. Provided
he saw him laugh and was treated with familiarity, he was
content. The prince, no longer knowing how to violate the
dignity of this great judge, would sometimes start kicking him.
If the kicks were painful, he began to cry. But the clown's
instinct was so strong in him that he was seen daily to prefer
the salon of a minister who jeered at him to his own salon,
where he reigned despotically over every black-robed lawyer in
the land. This Rassi had above all created a position all his own
for himself, in that even the most insolent nobleman found it
impossible to humiliate him. His way of getting his own back
for the insults he endured all day long was to retail them to the
prince, with whom he had acquired the privilege of being able
to say anything. It is true that the response was frequently a
resounding slap in the face, which was painful, but he never
took the least umbrage. The presence of this great judge diverted
the prince in his moments of disgruntlement, at which times he
amused himself by abusing him. As may be seen, Rassi was just
about the perfect member of the court: without honour and
without humour.

'Secrecy's what we need above all!' the prince shouted, without any greeting and treating him quite as if he were some yokel, he who was so courteous with everyone. 'When does your sentence date from?'

'From yesterday morning, Most Serene Highness.'

'How many judges is it signed by?'

'All five.'

'And the punishment?'

'Twenty years in the fortress, as Your Most Serene Highness told me.'

'The death penalty would have caused ructions,' said the prince, as if talking to himself, 'more's the pity! The effect on that woman! But he's a del Dongo and that name is revered in Parma, because of the three archbishops almost in succession . . .

'You said twenty years in the fortress?'

'Yes, Most Serene Highness,' the prosecutor Rassi went on, still standing bent double, 'with, beforehand, a public apology in front of His Most Serene Highness's portrait. Plus fasting on bread and water every Friday and the day before each of the main public holidays, *the subject being of a notorious impiety.* This for the future and to put an end to his career.'

'Write,' said the prince: ' "His Most Serene Highness having condescended in his goodness to hear the very humble supplications of the Marchesa del Dongo, mother of the guilty man, and of the Duchess Sanseverina, his aunt, who have represented that at the time of the crime their son and nephew was very young and led astray moreover by a wild passion he had conceived for the wife of the unfortunate Giletti, has seen fit, despite the revulsion inspired by such a murder, to commute the punishment to which Fabrizio del Dongo has been sentenced to twelve years in the fortress." '

'Give it here for me to sign.'

The prince signed it with the previous day's date. Then, handing the sentence back to Rassi, he told him: 'Write immediately below my signature: "The Duchess Sanseverina having for a second time thrown herself at His Highness's feet, the prince has given permission that each Thursday the guilty man may walk for an hour on the platform of the square tower commonly known as the Farnese Tower."

'Sign that,' said the prince, 'and above all lips sealed, whatever you may hear given out in the town. You will tell Counsellor De Capitani, who voted for two years in the fortress and who even made a speech in favour of that ridiculous opinion, that I ask that he reread the laws and regulations. Once again, silence and good night.' The prosecutor Rassi made three deep, very slow bows, which the prince ignored.

This had taken place at seven o'clock in the morning. A few hours later, news of the Marchesa Raversi's banishment had spread through the town and the cafés, and everyone was talking at once about this great event. For some while, the marchesa's banishment rid Parma of that implacable enemy of small towns and small courts, boredom. General Fabio Conti, who had seen himself as a minister, did not emerge from his fortress for several days, on the pretext of an attack of gout. The bourgeoisie and in their wake the lower orders concluded, from what was going on, that it was clear that the prince was determined to give the archbishopric of Parma to Monsignor del Dongo. The shrewd politicians in the cafés even went so far as to claim that Father Landriani, the current archbishop, had been advised to feign illness and to hand in his resignation. He would be granted a fat pension out of the tobacco tax, they were certain of that. This rumour travelled all the way to the archbishop, who was much alarmed, and for several days his enthusiasm for our hero was largely paralysed. Two months later, this good news was to be found in the Paris papers, with one minor alteration, to the effect that it was Count Mosca, the Duchess Sanseverina's nephew, who was about to be made an archbishop.

The Marchesa Raversi was fuming in her country house at Velleja. She was certainly not one of those feeble women, the sort who think they are getting their own back simply by passing scurrilous remarks about their enemies. On the very next day following her fall from favour, the Cavaliere Riscara and three other of her friends called on the prince on her orders, and asked him for permission to go and visit her at her country house. His Highness received these gentlemen with perfect good grace, and their arrival in Velleja was a great consolation for the marchesa. By the end of the second week, she had thirty people in the house, all those for whom a liberal ministry would find places. Each evening, the marchesa held a regular council with the best informed of her friends. One day, when she had received a great many letters from Parma and Bologna, she retired early. Her favourite lady's maid admitted first of all the reigning lover, Count Baldi, a fine figure of a young man and utterly insignificant; and later on, the Cavaliere Riscara, his predecessor. The latter was a small man, dark both physically and morally, who, having begun as a geometry tutor in the school for the nobility in Parma, could now see himself as a counsellor of state and a knight of several orders.

'I have the excellent habit,' the marchesa told these two men, 'of never destroying any piece of paper, and it serves me well. Here are nine letters that the Sanseverina woman has written me on different occasions. You will both of you leave for Genoa, you will search among the convicts for a former notary called Burati, like the great Venetian poet, or Durati. You, Count Baldi, sit yourself down at my desk and write what I shall dictate to you:

'"I have had an idea so I am writing you this note. I am going to my cottage near Castelnovo; if you're willing to come and spend twelve hours with me, I shall be very happy. There's no great danger, I fancy, after what has just happened. The clouds are lifting. Stop before you enter Castelnovo, however. You will find one of my men on the road. They are all tremendously fond of you. Keep the name of Bossi for this short journey, naturally. They say you have a beard, like the best kind of Capuchin, and you've only been seen in Parma in the decent guise of a vicar-general."

'You understand, Riscara?'

'Perfectly. But travelling to Genoa is an unnecessary luxury. I know a man in Parma who isn't inside yet, admittedly, but who can't fail to end up there. He'll forge Sanseverina's signature admirably.'

At which words, Count Baldi's beautiful eyes opened ever wider; only now did he understand.

'If you know this worthy personage in Parma, for whom you are hoping for some advancement,' said the marchesa, 'it's obvious he knows you also. His mistress, his confessor and his friend may have sold out to the Sanseverina woman. I prefer to defer this little practical joke by a few days, and not expose myself to any mischance. Leave in two hours, like good little lambs, don't call on a living soul in Genoa and return quickly.' The Cavaliere Riscara ran off laughing, and talking through his nose like Punchinello: 'We must pack our things,' he said, running in a burlesque manner. He wanted to leave Baldi alone with the lady. Five days later, Riscara brought the marchesa her Count Baldi back all saddle-sore: in order to save twenty miles, he had been made to cross the mountains on a mule. He swore they wouldn't get him making any more *long journeys*. Baldi handed the marchesa three copies of the letter she had dictated, and five or six other letters in the same handwriting, of Riscara's own composition, of which use might perhaps be made later on. One of these letters contained some excellent jokes about the prince's nocturnal fears and about how lamentably thin the Marchesa Balbi, his mistress, was, who, it was said, left the impression of a pair of tweezers behind on the cushions of the bergère after having sat down there momentarily. Anyone would have sworn that all these letters were in the hand of Signora Sanseverina.

'I now know beyond any doubt,' said the marchesa, 'that the love of her life, that Fabrizio, is in Bologna, or close by . . .'

'I'm too unwell.' exclaimed Count Baldi, breaking in. 'I beg to be spared from a second journey, or at least I'd like to be given a few days' rest to restore my health.'

'I shall plead your cause,' said Riscara. He got up and spoke in a low voice to the marchesa.

'Very well, so be it, I agree,' she replied, smiling.

'Don't worry, you won't be going,' the marchesa told Baldi, with a somewhat scornful expression.

'Thank you,' exclaimed the latter, in heartfelt tones. Indeed, Riscara got into the post-chaise alone. He had hardly been in Bologna two days before he saw Fabrizio and little Marietta in a barouche. Well I'm damned! he said to himself, it seems our future archbishop is none too bothered. I must see the duchess gets to hear about this, she'll be charmed. Riscara needed only to follow Fabrizio to find out where he was lodging. The following morning, the latter received by courier a letter of Genoese manufacture. He thought it rather abrupt but was otherwise unsuspecting. The thought of seeing the duchess and count again sent him into ecstasies, and for all that Lodovico was able to say, he took a horse at the staging post and left at the gallop. Without suspecting it, he was being followed a short distance behind by Cavaliere Riscara who, on reaching the stage before Castelnovo, six leagues from Parma, had the pleasure of seeing a large gathering in the square in front of the local gaol. Our hero had just been taken inside, having been recognized at the posthouse, as he was changing horses, by two sbirri chosen and dispatched by Count Zurla.

The Cavaliere Riscara's small eyes shone with delight. He ascertained with an exemplary patience all that had just happened in the little village, then sent a messenger to the Marchesa Raversi. After which, walking the streets as if to go and visit a very interesting church, and then to look for a painting by Parmigiano[2] he had been told existed locally, he finally encountered the podestà, who was quick to pay his respects to a counsellor of state. Riscara appeared astonished that he had not sent the conspirator he had been fortunate enough to arrest straight to the citadel in Parma.

'One might have feared,' Riscara added coldly, 'that his numerous friends, who were trying two days ago to aid and abet his passage through His Most Serene Highness's States, would encounter the police. There were a good fourteen or fifteen of the rebels, on horseback.'

'Intelligenti pauca!'[3] exclaimed the podestà with a cunning expression.

CHAPTER 15

Two hours later, poor Fabrizio, wearing handcuffs and attached by a long chain to the actual *sediola* into which he had been made to climb, left for the citadel in Parma, escorted by eight policemen. The latter had had orders to take with them all the policemen stationed in the villages through which the cortège was to pass. The podestà himself followed this important prisoner. At around seven in the evening, the *sediola*, escorted by all the street urchins of Parma and by thirty policemen, crossed the beautiful esplanade, passed in front of the small palazzo where Fausta had been living a few months earlier, and finally presented itself at the gateway to the citadel at the very moment when General Fabio Conti and his daughter were about to emerge. The governor's carriage stopped before reaching the drawbridge in order to allow the *sediola* to which Fabrizio was attached to enter. The general at once shouted for the gates of the citadel to be closed, and hurried down to the office in the gateway to try to get some idea of what all this was about. He was no little surprised when he recognized the prisoner, who had become very stiff, after being chained to his *sediola* throughout so long a journey. Four policemen had lifted him out and were carrying him to the gaolers' office. So, the governor told himself with great self-satisfaction, I have in my power the famous Fabrizio del Dongo, with whom Parma's high society seems to have sworn to concern itself exclusively for close on a year now!

The general had met him a score of times at court, at the duchess's and elsewhere. But he was careful not to let it be seen that he knew him. He would have feared putting himself at risk.

'Draw up a detailed report of the handing over of the prisoner by the worthy podestà of Castelnovo,' he cried to the prison clerk.

Barbone[1] the clerk, a fearsome figure thanks to the size of his beard and his warlike appearance, adopted an even more self-important expression than usual, for all the world like a German gaoler. Believing he knew that it was largely the Duchess Sanseverina who had prevented his master, the governor, from becoming minister of war, he was more than ordinarily insolent towards the prisoner. He addressed him as 'Voi', which in Italy is the way one addresses servants.

'I am a prelate of the Holy Roman Church,' Fabrizio told him firmly, 'and vicar-general of this diocese. My birth alone gives me a right to consideration.'

'I know nothing about that!' replied the clerk impertinently. 'Prove your assertions by showing the letters patent that give you the right to those highly respectable titles.' Fabrizio had no letters patent and did not answer. General Fabio Conti, standing next to his clerk, watched him writing without looking up at the prisoner, so as not to be obliged to say that he really was Fabrizio del Dongo.

All of a sudden, Clelia Conti, who was waiting in the carriage, heard a fearful uproar in the guardroom. In drawing up an insolent and very lengthy description of the prisoner's person, the clerk Barbone ordered him to undo his clothing, so that they could verify and register the number and condition of the scratches he had received at the time of the Giletti affair.

'I can't,' said Fabrizio, with a bitter smile. 'I'm not in a position to obey the signore's orders, the handcuffs are stopping me!'

'What!' cried the general, with an innocent expression. 'The prisoner is handcuffed inside the fortress, that's against the rules, an ad hoc order is required. Take off his handcuffs.'

Fabrizio looked at him. A right Jesuit! he thought. He's seen these handcuffs hampering me for the past hour and now he plays at being astonished!

The handcuffs were removed by the policemen. They had just learnt that Fabrizio was the nephew of the Duchess

Sanseverina, and hastened to show him a mealy-mouthed politeness that contrasted with the rudeness of the clerk. The latter appeared to resent this and said to Fabrizio, who remained motionless: 'Come on then, get a move on, show us the scratches you got from poor Giletti at the time of the murder.' Fabrizio leapt at the clerk and struck him so hard across the face that Barbone fell off his chair against the general's legs. The policemen seized hold of Fabrizio's arms, who remained without moving. The general himself and two policemen who were at his side hurriedly picked up the clerk, whose face was bleeding profusely. Two policemen standing further off ran to close the door of the office, thinking that the prisoner was looking to escape. The sergeant in charge did not believe that young del Dongo could be making a serious attempt at escape when he was after all inside the citadel. None the less, with a policeman's instinct, he went over to the window to prevent any disorder. Facing this open window, two paces away, the general's carriage had been drawn up. Clelia was huddled well back so as not to witness the unhappy scene going on in the office. When she heard all the noise she looked out.

'What's happening?' she asked the sergeant.

'Signorina, it's the young Fabrizio del Dongo, who's just given Barbone one in the face for being insolent.'

'What, it's Signor del Dongo who's being taken to prison?'

'Yes indeed,' said the sergeant. 'All the fuss is because of that poor young man's high birth. I thought the signorina knew about it.' Clelia did not now leave the door. Once the policemen who were surrounding the table had moved aside slightly, she could see the prisoner. Who could have told me, she thought, that I would see him again for the first time in this unhappy situation, when I met him on the road at Lake Como? . . . He gave me his hand to get into his mother's carriage . . . He was already with the duchess. Had they begun their love affair at that time?

The reader needs to be told that in the liberal party led by the Marchesa Raversi and General Conti, they affected to be in no doubt as to the amorous liaison that had to exist between Fabrizio and the duchess. Because he had been duped, Count

Mosca, whom they abhorred, was the butt of never-ending jokes.

So, thought Clelia, now he's a prisoner, and the prisoner of his enemies! For deep down, Count Mosca, though they'd like you to think he's an angel, is going to be overjoyed at this capture.

A burst of coarse laughter came from the guardroom.

'So what's going on, Jacopo?' she asked the sergeant, in an emotional voice.

'The general asked the prisoner straight out why he'd struck Barbone. Monsignor Fabrizio answered coolly, "He called me *murderer*, so let him show the documents and letters patent that authorize him to bestow that title on me." And they laughed.'

A gaoler who could write replaced Barbone. Clelia watched the latter emerge, wiping away with his handkerchief the blood that was pouring from his frightful injury. He was swearing like a heathen: 'That f****** Fabrizio,' he said at the top of his voice, 'will die by my hand alone. I'll rob the executioner,' etc., etc. He had paused between the window of the office and the general's carriage to watch Fabrizio, and the oaths resumed.

'On your way,' the sergeant told him. 'You don't swear like that in front of the signorina.'

Barbone raised his head to look into the carriage, and his eyes met those of Clelia, who let out a cry of horror. Never had she seen so terrible a facial expression from so close to. He will kill Fabrizio! she said to herself, I must warn Don Cesare. This was her uncle, one of the most highly respected priests in the town. General Conti, his brother, had obtained for him the position of treasurer and senior chaplain in the prison.

The general climbed back into his carriage. 'Do you want to go home,' he asked his daughter, 'or wait for me, for some time maybe, in the courtyard of the palace? I must go and give an account of all this to the sovereign.'

Fabrizio came out of the office escorted by three policemen. They were taking him to the room that had been allotted to him. Clelia watched through the door of the carriage, the prisoner was very close to her. At that moment, she replied to her father's question with the words: 'I will follow you.' Fabrizio, hearing these words spoken close beside him, looked up and met the gaze of the young girl. He was struck above all by the expression of melancholy on her face. How much more beautiful she has become since our encounter near Como! That expression, so profoundly thoughtful! . . . They're right to compare her to the duchess. The face of an angel! Barbone, the bloodied clerk, who had not placed himself next to the carriage without reason, gestured to the three policemen who were conducting Fabrizio to halt and, going round the back of the carriage, so as to get to the door near which the general was sitting: 'Since the prisoner has committed an act of violence inside the citadel,' he said, 'by virtue of article 157 of the regulations, is there not good cause to apply the handcuffs for three days?'

'Go to the devil!' cried the general, for whom this arrest could not fail to create difficulties. For him, it was a question of not pushing the duchess or Count Mosca too far. And how was the count going to take the affair anyway? Basically, the murder of a Giletti was a bagatelle, and intrigue alone had succeeded in making something of it.

During this brief exchange, Fabrizio looked splendid in the midst of the policemen, wearing his proudest, most aristocratic expression. His fine and delicate features, and the disdainful smile that played on his lips, contrasted pleasingly with the coarse features of the policemen surrounding him. But all this formed only the external part of his physiognomy, so to speak. He was enraptured by the heavenly beauty of Clelia, and his eye betrayed all his surprise. She was deeply pensive and had not thought to withdraw her head from the carriage door. He bowed to her with the most respectful half-smile. Then, after a moment: 'I fancy, signorina,' he said, 'that I have already had the honour of meeting you in the past, near a lake, with an accompaniment of policemen.'

Clelia reddened and was so taken aback she could find nothing to say in reply. How noble he looks in the midst of those coarse creatures! she had been telling herself just as Fabrizio addressed her. The deep compassion and we might almost say tenderness into which she had been plunged, took away the presence of mind required to find any words at all; she became aware of her silence and reddened even more. At that moment, the bolts on the great door of the citadel were violently drawn back, for had His Excellency's carriage not been waiting for at least a minute already? The noise was so violent underneath the vaulting that even had Clelia found some word of reply, Fabrizio would not have been able to hear what it was.

Borne off by the horses, which had broken into a gallop immediately after the drawbridge, Clelia told herself: He will have found me quite ridiculous! Then she suddenly added: Not just ridiculous. He'll have thought he saw in me an abject soul; he will have thought I didn't respond to his greeting because he is a prisoner and I am the daughter of the governor.

The thought made this high-souled girl despair. What makes my behaviour thoroughly demeaning, she added, is that back then, when we encountered one another for the first time, also with 'an accompaniment of policemen', as he says, it was I who found myself a prisoner and he rendered me a service and rescued me from a very awkward predicament ... Yes, there's no two ways about it, my behaviour was a disgrace, it was both rude and ungrateful. Alas, the poor young man! Now that he's in trouble everyone is going to be unpleasant towards him. He said to me then: 'Will you remember my name in Parma?' How he despises me at this minute! A polite word would have cost nothing. I have to admit it, yes, I behaved atrociously towards him. Back then, but for the generous offer of his mother's carriage, I'd have had to follow the policemen on foot in the dust, or, even worse, ride pillion behind one of those men. It was my father that time who'd been arrested and I was defenceless. Yes, my behaviour was a disgrace. And how keenly someone like him must have felt it! What a contrast between his noble features and my behaviour! Such nobility, such serenity! He looked so much the hero, surrounded by his ignominious enemies. I can now understand the duchess's passion. If he's like that when things go against him and may have awful consequences, what must he not look like when his soul is happy!

The governor of the citadel's carriage remained in the palace courtyard for more than an hour and a half, but none the less, when the general came down from the prince's, Clelia did not consider that he had stayed too long.

'What are His Highness's wishes?' asked Clelia.

'His words said "prison!" and his looks "death!"'

'Death, dear God!' cried Clelia.

'Come on, none of that!' the general went on, bad-temperedly. 'I'm a fool, responding to a child.'

Meanwhile, Fabrizio was climbing the three hundred and eighty steps that led to the Farnese Tower, a new prison built on the platform of the big tower, at a prodigious altitude. He did not reflect once, distinctly at least, on the great change in his fortunes that had just occurred. That look, he said to himself, what did it not express! Such profound compassion! She seemed to be saying: Life is woven out of such misfortunes! Don't be too distressed by what happens to you! Are we not here below to be unfortunate? How those loveliest of eyes remained fixed on me, even when the horses were making all that noise advancing under the vaulting!

Fabrizio had quite forgotten to be unhappy.

Clelia followed her father into several salons. At the beginning of the evening, no one had yet heard the news of the arrest of the 'great criminal', for that was the name the courtiers were bestowing two hours later on this poor, rash young man.

People noticed that Clelia's expression was more animated than usual on that particular evening, and animation, the seeming to be participating in what was around her, was what this lovely young person mainly lacked. When her beauty was compared to that of the duchess, it was above all the appearance of being moved by nothing, this way of seeming to be above it all, which tipped the balance in favour of her rival. In England or in France, a land of vanity, they would probably have been of the opposite opinion. Clelia Conti was still rather too slender a young girl to be able to be compared with the beautiful figures of Guido Reni.[2] We will not conceal the fact that, were we to adopt the Greek ideal of beauty, her features might have been faulted for being a little too well defined; the lips, for example, fetching and graceful though they were, were a little too full.

What was so admirably individual about this face, in which

there shone an innocent grace and the celestial impress of the noblest of souls, is that, although it was of the rarest and most individual beauty, it in no way resembled the heads of Greek statues. The duchess on the other hand had a little too much of the *familiar* beauty of the ideal, and her Lombard features recalled the voluptuous smile and tender melancholy of one of Leonardo's beautiful Salomes. Where the duchess was effervescent, sparkling with wit and with mischief, attaching herself passionately, if one may so put it, to all the topics that were set before the eyes of her soul in the course of a conversation, Clelia showed herself calm and slow to be moved, either from disdain for what was around her, or from regret for some absent fancy. It had long been thought that she would end by embracing the life of a religious. At twenty, they could see that she was repelled by the idea of going to a ball, and if she followed her father there, it was simply out of obedience and so as not to prejudice his ambitions.

So I shall find it impossible, the general's vulgar soul repeated too frequently, heaven having given me for a daughter the most beautiful person in our sovereign's States, and the most virtuous, to derive any advantage from it in advancing my career. My life is too isolated, I have only her in the world, and what I desperately need is a family that can be a support socially, which gives me a certain number of salons, where my abilities and especially my aptitude for the ministry are posited as the unassailable foundations of all political argument. Well, my daughter, so very beautiful, so very sensible, so very pious, takes it amiss the minute a young man solidly established at court undertakes to make her accept his attentions. That aspirant having been sent packing, her character becomes less gloomy and I see her almost cheerful, until some other suitor enters the lists. The best-looking man in the court, Count Baldi, presented himself but was not found attractive. The wealthiest man in His Highness's States, the Marchese Crescenzi, took his place; she claims he would make her unhappy.

My daughter's eyes are definitely more beautiful than the duchess's, the general would say at other times, mainly in as much as on rare occasions they are able to be more profoundly expressive. But when do we actually see that magnificent expression? Never in a salon where it might do her honour, but rather when we are on an excursion, alone with me, when she lets herself become all sentimental, for example, over the misfortunes of some hideous villager. Keep some memory of that sublime expression, I sometimes tell her, for the salons where we shall be appearing this evening. But not a bit of it: if she condescends to follow me into society, her pure and noble face offers the rather haughty and far from encouraging expression of passive obedience. The general had, as can be seen, taken all possible steps to find himself a suitable son-in-law, but what he said was true.

Courtiers, who have nothing to look at in their own souls, are attentive to everything. They had observed that it was above all on the days when Clelia could not bring herself to launch out from her cherished daydreams and feign an interest in something that the duchess liked to stop beside her and try to make her speak. Clelia had ash-blonde hair that formed the softest of contrasts with her cheeks, delicate in their colouring if generally a little too pale. The shape of her brow alone might have told an attentive observer that the nobility of her expression and her bearing, so superior to any mere common gracefulness, stemmed from a profound disregard for all that is commonplace. It was the absence, not the impossibility of being interested in something. Since her father had been governor of the citadel, Clelia found she was happy, or at least immune from vexations, in her lofty apartment. The frightening number of stairs one needed to climb to reach the governor's palazzo, situated on the esplanade of the great tower, kept unwelcome visitors away, and for this physical reason, Clelia enjoyed the freedom of a convent. This was very nearly the ideal happiness that she had thought at one time of seeking in the religious life. She was seized by a kind of horror at the mere thought of putting her cherished solitude and intimate thoughts at the disposal of a young man whom the title of husband would authorize to disturb this whole inner life. If by her solitude she had not attained to happiness, she had at least succeeded in avoiding sensations that were too painful.

On the day Fabrizio was taken to the fortress, the duchess encountered Clelia at a soirée given by Count Zurla, the interior minister. Everyone formed a circle around them. That evening, Clelia's beauty prevailed over that of the duchess. The young girl's eyes wore an expression so singular and so profound that they were almost indiscreet. There was pity, there was also indignation and anger in her gaze. The duchess's gaiety and her brilliant ideas seemed to plunge Clelia into moments of grief bordering on horror. How the poor woman will cry out and lament, she told herself, when she learns that her lover, that young man with so great a heart and so noble a countenance, has just been thrown into prison! And those looks of the sovereign's that have condemned him to death! Oh absolute power, when will you cease to weigh down on Italy? Oh base and venal souls! And I am the daughter of a gaoler! And I didn't belie that noble character by not deigning to respond to Fabrizio! And he was once my benefactor! What does he think of me at this moment, alone in his room and in conversation with his little lamp? Revolted by this thought, Clelia cast horrified glances at the magnificent illuminations in the interior minister's reception rooms.

Never, it was being said, among the ring of courtiers that had formed around these two fashionable beauties and was trying to intervene in their conversation, never have they talked to one another looking so animated and at the same time so intimate. Had the duchess, ever on the lookout to ward off the hatred excited by the first minister, thought up some great marriage for Clelia's benefit? This conjecture was based on a circumstance that had hitherto never been observed at the court: the girl's eyes had more fire, more passion even, if one can so express it, than those of the beautiful duchess. The latter, for her part, was astonished, and, it may be said to her credit, delighted by the new attractions she was discovering in the young solitary. For the past hour, she had been watching her with a pleasure that is very seldom felt at the sight of a rival. So what is going on? the duchess asked herself. Never has Clelia looked so lovely and one might also say so affecting. Can her heart have spoken? ... But in that case, it is certainly an unhappy love, there is sorrow beneath that new animation. But an unhappy love keeps silent. Could it be a matter of bringing back an inconstant lover by her success in society? And the duchess made a close inspection of the young men who were surrounding them. She nowhere saw any untoward expression, it was always a more or less contented self-conceit. But we have a miracle here, the duchess told herself, piqued at being unable to guess. Where is Count Mosca, that shrewdest of mortals? No, I'm not mistaken, Clelia is watching me closely, as if I were the object of some new concern for her. Is it the effect of some order given her by her father, that abject courtier? I believed that young and noble soul incapable of stooping to any concern about money. Can General Fabio Conti have some crucial request to put to the count?

At around ten o'clock, one of the duchess's friends came up and spoke two words to her in a low voice. She went excessively pale. Clelia took her hand and dared to squeeze it.

'I thank you and now I understand you ... You have a beautiful soul!' said the duchess, trying to regain control of herself. She barely had the strength to utter these few words. She directed many smiles at her hostess, who stood up to go with her as far as the door of the last reception room: such honours were due only to princesses of the blood and for the duchess were a cruel contradiction of her present situation. And so she smiled broadly at Countess Zurla, but for all the extraordinary efforts she made was unable to address a single word to her.

Clelia's eyes filled with tears, seeing the duchess go past in the midst of these rooms now peopled by all that was most brilliant in society. What will it be like for the poor woman, she asked herself, when she finds herself alone in her carriage? It would be tactless on my part to offer to go with her; I daren't ... What a consolation for the poor prisoner, sitting in some awful room, alone with his little lamp, if he knew he was loved to that extent! How awful, the solitude he's been cast into! And here we are in these dazzling rooms! How horrible! Can there be a way of getting word to him? Great heaven, that would be betraying my father. His situation is so delicate between the two camps. What will happen to him if he exposes himself to the passionate hatred of the duchess, the first minister is at her beck and call, and he's the master in three quarters of the affairs of state! On the other hand, the prince occupies himself constantly with what is going on in the fortress, and won't stand for any raillery on that count. Fear makes people cruel ... In any event, Fabrizio (Clelia no longer said Signore del Dongo) is far more to be pitied. There's much more at stake for him than the danger of losing a lucrative position! ... And the duchess! ... What a terrible passion love is! ... Yet all those liars in society talk about it as though it were a source of happiness! They feel sorry for old women because they can no longer feel or inspire love! ... I shall never forget what I have just seen. What a sudden alteration! The duchess's eyes, so lovely, so radiant, how mournful, how lifeless they became after the fateful words the Marchese N*** came and spoke to her. Fabrizio must be very deserving of being loved! ...

In the midst of these very solemn reflections, which occupied the whole of Clelia's soul, the flattering remarks that always surrounded her seemed even more disagreeable than usual. To be free of them, she went up to an open window, half screened by a taffeta curtain. She hoped that no one would make so bold as to follow her into what was like a refuge. The window looked out over a small plantation of orange trees out in the open; indeed, each winter they were obliged to put a roof over them. Clelia breathed in the scent of these flowers with delight, and her pleasure seemed to restore a little calm to her soul ... I thought he had a very noble expression, she thought, but to inspire such passion in a woman of such distinction! ... She is renowned for having spurned the attentions of the prince, and had she deigned to want it, could have been the queen of his States ... My father says that the sovereign's passion went as far as marrying her if ever he became free to! ... And this love for Fabrizio has endured for so long, because it's a good five years since we encountered them near Lake Como ... Yes, five years ago, she told herself after a moment's thought. I was struck by it even then, when so much went unnoticed by my child's eyes. How those two ladies seemed to admire Fabrizio! ...

Clelia was delighted to observe that none of the young men who had been talking to her so eagerly had dared to approach the balcony. One of them, the Marchese Crescenzi, had taken a few steps in that direction but had then stopped, beside a gaming table. If I could at least see, she said to herself, underneath my little window in the palazzo in the fortress, the only one that gets any shade, some pretty orange trees like those, my thoughts would not be so sad! But when my one prospect is the huge stone blocks of the Farnese Tower ... Oh, she exclaimed, making to move, perhaps that's where they will have put him! It's high time I was able to speak to Don Cesare, he'll be less severe than the general. My father certainly won't tell me anything when we return to the fortress, but I'll find everything out from Don Cesare ... I have money, I could buy a few orange trees which, placed underneath the window of my aviary, would stop me seeing that big wall of the Farnese Tower. It's going to be more hateful still now that I know one of the people it is hiding from the light of day! ... Yes, that was certainly the third time I have seen him. Once at court, at the ball on the princess's birthday. Today, surrounded by three policemen, while that horrible Barbone was asking for him to be manacled, and lastly near Lake Como ... That was a good five years ago. What a harum-scarum he looked in those days! The way he looked at the policemen, and the strange looks his mother and aunt were giving him! There was certainly some secret that day, something private between them. At the time, I had the idea he too was afraid of the policemen ... Clelia shuddered. But how ignorant I was! The duchess was surely taking an interest in him even then. How he made us laugh after a moment or two, once the ladies, despite being so obviously preoccupied, had become more or less used to the presence of a stranger ... And this evening I wasn't able to answer a single word when he spoke to me! ... I'm so ignorant, so timid! How often you resemble all that's blackest! And to be this way now I'm past twenty! ... I was quite right to be thinking of the cloister. All I'm good for really is a refuge. Just like a gaoler's daughter! they'll say. He despises me and as soon as he's able to write to the duchess, he'll talk about my lack of consideration, and the duchess will think me a very false young girl. Because this evening, after all, she may have thought I was very understanding over her calamity.

Clelia saw that someone was approaching, obviously with the intention of placing himself next to her on the iron balcony at the window. She felt annoyed, even as she reproached herself. The reverie out of which she was being snatched was not without a certain sweetness. Here's some importunate person who's going to get a nice reception! she thought. She was turning round with a haughty stare, when she saw the timid figure of the archbishop, who was approaching the balcony with brief, barely perceptible movements. This holy man doesn't know the etiquette, thought Clelia; why come and disturb a poor girl like me? My peace and quiet is all I possess. She was greeting him respectfully, but wearing a haughty expression also, when the prelate said: 'Signorina, have you heard the dreadful news?'

The girl's eyes had already taken on another expression altogether, but following the instructions repeated over and over by her father, she answered with a show of ignorance that was starkly at odds with the language of her eyes: 'I have heard nothing, monsignore.'

'My first vicar-general, poor Fabrizio del Dongo, who is as guilty as I am of the death of Giletti, that brigand, has been abducted in Bologna, where he was living under the assumed name of Joseph Bossi. He has been locked up in your citadel. He arrived there *chained* to the very vehicle that had brought him. A gaoler of sorts called Barbone, who was once pardoned after murdering one of his brothers, tried to do Fabrizio a personal injury, but my young friend is not a man to suffer insults. He threw this wicked adversary down, whereupon they took him down to a dungeon twenty feet below ground, having handcuffed him.'

'Not handcuffs, no.'

'Oh, so you know something!' exclaimed the archbishop, and the old man's features lost their expression of profound dismay. 'But first and foremost, someone may come over to this balcony and interrupt us. Would you be so charitable as to give Don Cesare my pastoral ring you see here yourself?'

The girl had taken the ring but did not know where to put it so as not to run the risk of losing it.

'Put it on your thumb,' said the archbishop, and placed it there himself. 'Can I rely on you to give him the ring?'

'Yes, monsignore.'

'Will you promise to keep secret what I am going to add, even in the event that you don't think it proper to accede to my request?'

'Of course, monsignore,' replied the girl, tremulously, on seeing the sombre, serious expression that the old man had suddenly adopted. 'Our esteemed archbishop can but give me orders worthy of himself and of me,' she added.

'Tell Don Cesare that I commend my adoptive son to him. I know that the sbirri who abducted him did not give him time to take his breviary, I ask Don Cesare to let him have his, and if the signore your uncle would like to send tomorrow to the archbishop's palace, I undertake to replace the book he has given to Fabrizio. I ask Don Cesare similarly to let Signor del Dongo have the ring being worn on that pretty hand.' The archbishop was interrupted by General Fabio Conti, who had come to fetch his daughter to take her to his carriage. There was a brief moment of conversation that was not without its astuteness on the part of the prelate. Without referring in any way to the new prisoner, he so managed things that certain moral and political maxims should come appropriately to his lips in the course of the conversation. For example, there are moments of crisis in the life of courts which determine the lives of the most exalted personages for a long time to come; or, it would be signally unwise to turn the state of political alienation which is often the quite simple consequence of opposing points of view into *personal hatred*. Allowing himself to be carried away somewhat by the profound annoyance caused by so unforeseen an arrest, the archbishop went so far as to say that while one needed assuredly to preserve the positions one enjoyed, it would be quite gratuitously unwise to draw down furious hatred on oneself as a consequence by lending oneself to certain things that are not forgotten.

Once the general was in his carriage with his daughter: 'Those might be called threats,' he told her ... 'threats, to a man of my kind!' No further words were exchanged between father and daughter for twenty minutes.

On receiving the pastoral ring from the archbishop, Clelia had indeed promised herself to speak to her father once she was in the carriage, about the small service that the prelate had asked of her. But after the word *threats*, uttered in anger, she took it as certain that her father would intercept the commission. She covered the ring with her left hand and clutched it passionately. During the whole time it took to get from the interior ministry to the citadel, she asked herself whether it would be criminal of her not to speak to her father. She was very pious, very timorous, and her heart, ordinarily so tranquil, was beating with an unaccustomed violence. But in the end the 'Halt, who goes there?' of the sentry posted on the ramparts above the gate had rung out at the carriage's approach before Clelia could find a suitable form of words such that her father would not refuse, so fearful was she of being refused. As she climbed the three hundred and sixty steps that led to the governor's palazzo, Clelia could think of nothing.

She hastened to speak to her uncle, who scolded her and refused to be party to anything.

CHAPTER 16

'Well,' exclaimed the general, catching sight of his brother Don Cesare, 'here's the duchess going to spend a hundred thousand écus to make me look a fool and rescue the prisoner!'

But for the time being, we are obliged to leave Fabrizio in his prison, at the very summit of the citadel of Parma. He is well guarded and we shall meet him again there, perhaps somewhat altered. We are going to occupy ourselves mainly with the court, where very complicated intrigues, and especially the passions of an unhappy woman, are going to decide his fate. As he climbed the three hundred and ninety steps to his prison in the Farnese Tower, under the eyes of the governor, Fabrizio, who had so dreaded this moment, found that he had no time to reflect on his ill fortune.

Returning home after Count Zurla's soirée, the duchess dismissed her women with a gesture. Then, allowing herself to drop fully clothed on to her bed: 'Fabrizio,' she exclaimed out loud, 'is in the hands of his enemies, and because of me perhaps, they will give him poison!' How to depict the moment of despair which followed this summing-up of the situation in a woman who was so irrational, so much prey to the feelings of the moment and, without admitting it to herself, so hopelessly in love with the young prisoner? There were inarticulate cries, outbursts of rage, convulsive movements, but not a single tear. She sent her women away in order to hide them, she thought she was going to burst out sobbing the moment she was alone. But tears, that first source of solace in all great sorrows, failed her completely. Anger, indignation, the sense of her inferiority vis-à-vis the prince, were too dominant in that proud soul.

'How I've been humiliated!' she exclaimed over and over. 'I've been insulted and, what's worse, Fabrizio's life has been put at risk! And I shan't take my revenge! Whoa there, my prince. You can kill me, so be it, you have the power. But then I, I shall have your life. Alas, poor Fabrizio, what good will that do you? How different from the day when I wanted to leave Parma. Yet I thought I was unhappy then ... how blind I was! I was about to smash all the habits of a pleasant life. Alas, without knowing it, I was on the verge of an event that was going to decide my fate once and for all. But for the count's evil habits, contemptible courtier that he is, he would not have suppressed the words "unjust proceedings" in that fatal letter the prince accorded me in his vanity, and we'd have been saved. It was good fortune on my part rather than skill, it has to be allowed, my exciting his amour propre when it comes to his beloved town of Parma. At that moment I was threatening to leave, at that moment I was free. Good God, now I'm a complete slave! Here I am now stuck in this foul cesspit and Fabrizio in chains in the citadel, the citadel that has been death's ante-chamber for so many men of distinction. And I can no longer hold that tiger at bay with the fear of seeing me abandon his lair!

'He's too intelligent not to sense that I shall never move far from the infamous tower where my heart is in chains. And now the man's pricked vanity may put the strangest ideas into his head. Their bizarre cruelty would act only as a spur to his astonishing vanity. If he goes back to his former mawkish gallantries, if he says: "Accept the homage of your slave or Fabrizio perishes ..." Well, there's the old story of Judith.[1] Yes, but if for me it's only suicide, it's murder for Fabrizio. His half-witted successor, our prince royal, and the evil executioner Rassi will have Fabrizio hanged as my accomplice.'

The duchess let out loud cries. This dilemma, from which she could see no way of escaping, was tormenting that unhappy heart. Her troubled head could see no other likelihood in the future. For ten minutes she tossed about like a madwoman. Finally, this terrible state of mind gave way to a brief exhausted sleep; she was drained of her vitality. A few minutes later, she awoke with a start and found herself sitting on her bed. She had been imagining that the prince wanted to cut Fabrizio's head off in her presence. The duchess looked all around her utterly distraught. Once she had finally convinced herself that neither the prince nor Fabrizio was to be seen, she fell back on the bed and was on the point of losing consciousness. So weak was she physically, she did not feel strong enough to alter her position. Dear God, if only I could die! she said to herself ... But that's sheer cowardice! To abandon Fabrizio in his misfortune! My mind is wandering ... Come, let's get back to what's true. Let's take a dispassionate look at the execrable situation into which I've been plunged for no good reason. What a fatal piece of thoughtlessness to come and live at the court of an absolute prince! A tyrant who knows all his victims. Every time they look at him, he takes them to be challenging his authority. That, alas, is what neither the count nor I realized when I left Milan. I was thinking of the attractions of a friendly court. Something inferior, it's true, but something in the style of the good times under Prince Eugène!

From a distance, we can have no idea of what the authority of a despot who knows all his subjects by sight is like. Seen from outside, despotism is the same as other forms of government: there are judges, for example, but they are Rassis. That monster would find nothing extraordinary in having his own father hanged should the prince order it ... he would call it his duty ... To suborn Rassi! Unfortunate woman that I am, I don't have any means of doing it. What can I offer him? A hundred thousand francs perhaps. And they claim that at the time of the last dagger thrust from which heaven's wrath against this unfortunate land allowed him to escape, the prince sent him ten thousand gold sequins in a chest! Anyway, what sum of money could suborn him? That slimy soul, who has never seen anything except contempt in men's eyes, now has the pleasure of seeing fear, or even respect. He may become minister of police, and why not? Then three quarters of the country's inhabitants will be his abject courtiers and will tremble before him, as servilely as he trembles before the sovereign.

Since I can't flee this loathsome place, I must be of use to

Fabrizio. To live alone, solitary, despairing! What good could I do for Fabrizio then? Come on, forward march, you unhappy woman; do your duty; go into society, pretend not to be thinking about Fabrizio any longer . . . Pretend to forget you, dear angel!

At which point, the duchess burst into tears. At last, she was able to weep. After an hour given over to human weakness, she saw with a measure of consolation that her thoughts were becoming clearer. To have a magic carpet, she said to herself, to abduct Fabrizio from the citadel, and take refuge with him in some happy land, where we can't be pursued, Paris for example. We would live there to start with on the twelve hundred francs which his father's factor passes on with such agreeable regularity. I could easily get a hundred thousand francs together out of the wreckage of my fortune. The duchess's imagination surveyed, with moments of inexpressible delight, all the details of the life she would lead three hundred leagues from Parma. There, she told herself, he could enter the service under an assumed name . . . Placed in a regiment of those brave Frenchmen, the young Valserra would soon make a name for himself. Finally, he would be happy.

These blessed images brought the tears back for a second time, but these were gentle tears. Happiness still existed somewhere then. This state lasted for a long time. The poor woman shrank from going back to contemplating the ghastly reality. Finally, as the dawn light was beginning to mark the tops of the trees in her garden with a white line, she did violence to her feelings. In a few hours' time, she said to herself, I shall be on the field of battle. It will be a question of taking action, and if something happens to provoke me, if the prince takes it into his head to address a few words concerning Fabrizio to me, I'm not confident of being able to retain my composure. I must therefore *come to a decision* here and now.

If I am declared a criminal of State, Rassi will have everything in this palazzo seized. On the first of this month, the count and I burnt, as is the custom, all the papers the police might put to any wrong use, and he's the minister of police, that's the nice part. I have three diamonds of some value. Tomorrow, Fulgenzio, my former Grianta boatman, will leave for Geneva, where he'll put them somewhere safe. If Fabrizio ever escapes (God, look favourably on me! and she made the sign of the cross), the Marchese del Dongo in his bottomless cowardice will decide it's a sin to send bread to a man being persecuted by a legitimate prince, then at least he'll find my diamonds, he will have bread.

I must send the count away ... to find myself alone with him, after what has just happened, that's out of the question. The poor man! He's not malicious, on the contrary; he's only weak. That commonplace soul is not the equal of ours. Poor Fabrizio! Why can't you be here for a moment with me, so we could confer together about the dangers?

The count's such a stickler, so cautious, he'd get in the way of all my plans, and anyway I mustn't drag him down with me ... For why would that tyrant not throw me into prison, vain as he is? I would have conspired ... what could be easier to prove? If he were to send me to his citadel and I was able to bribe my way into speaking with Fabrizio, if only for a moment, how courageously we would walk together to our deaths! But enough of such foolishness. His Rassi would advise him to put an end to me by poisoning. My presence in the streets, riding on a tumbril, might arouse the sensibilities of his dear Parmigiani ... But there, I'm romancing again. But a poor woman whose actual predicament is so unhappy must be forgiven for such foolishness, alas! What's true in all this is that the prince won't send me to my death. But nothing could be simpler than to throw me into prison and keep me there. He'll have all manner of suspicious papers hidden in some corner of my palazzo, as they did with that poor L***. Then three not too rascally judges, for there'll be what they call *conclusive proof*, and a dozen false witnesses are enough. I can then be sentenced to death as having conspired. And in his infinite clemency, the prince, taking into account that I once had the honour of being admitted to his court, will commute my punishment to ten years in the fortress. And I, so as not to depart from the violent nature that has led the Marchesa Raversi and my other enemies to say so many stupid things, I shall bravely poison myself. The populace will be kind enough to believe that at least. But I wager that Rassi will gallantly appear in my dungeon to bring me, on behalf of the prince, a small phial of strychnine or Perugia opium.

Yes, I must be seen to quarrel with the count, because I don't want to drag him down with me, that would be wicked. The poor man has loved me so openly! It was foolish of me to believe that enough soul could remain in a true courtier to make him capable of loving. The prince will very probably find some pretext for throwing me into prison. He'll be afraid that I may pervert public opinion concerning Fabrizio. The count is thoroughly honourable. He will instantly commit what the country bumpkins at court, in their profound astonishment, will call a folly; he will abandon the court. I defied the prince's authority on the evening of the letter, I can expect anything from his wounded vanity. Will a man who was born a prince ever forget the sensation I gave him that evening? Anyway, the count will be in a better position to be useful to Fabrizio if we've quarrelled. But supposing the count, who will be in despair at my decision, were to take his revenge? . . . But that thought will never even occur to him. He doesn't have the fundamentally abject soul of the prince. He may groan and countersign a wicked decree, but he's an honourable man. And anyway, revenge himself for what? For the fact that, after loving him for five years, without once transgressing against his love, I am saying to him: dear count, I had the good fortune to love you. Well, that flame has gone out. I no longer love you. But I know your heart through and through, I shall continue to hold you in the highest regard and you will always be the best of friends.

What answer can an honourable man make to so sincere a declaration?

I shall take a new lover, or at least they'll believe that in society. I shall tell that lover: basically, the prince is right to punish Fabrizio's bit of recklessness. But on his feast-day our gracious sovereign will surely give him back his freedom. In that way I shall gain six months. Prudence would suggest that the new lover be that venal judge and infamous executioner Rassi . . . he'd find himself being ennobled and, in the event,

I would be giving him an entrée into the best society. Forgive me, Fabrizio dear! For me any such effort is out of the question. What, that monster, still covered with the blood of Count P. and D.! He would make me pass out from revulsion if he ever came near me, or rather I would grab a knife and plunge it into his wicked heart. Don't ask me to do the impossible!

Yes, above all forget Fabrizio, and no smallest suggestion of anger against the prince, be my normal gay self again, which will seem all the more pleasing to those slimy souls, firstly because I shall be appearing to submit with good grace to their sovereign. Secondly, because, very far from laughing at them, I shall be sure to make the most of their charming small talents. For example, I shall compliment Count Zurla on the beautiful white plume on the hat he's just had brought by courier from Lyon, which is his pride and joy.

Choose a lover from the Raversi party . . . If the count goes, it will be the ministerial party. That's where the power will lie. It will be a friend of Raversi who reigns over the citadel, because Fabio Conti will enter the ministry. How will the prince, a man of breeding, an intelligent man, used to the count's delightful way of working, be able to do business with that ox, that king of fools who's been preoccupied his whole life long with the crucial problem: should His Highness's soldiers have seven buttons or nine on the front of their tunics? They're animals, brutes who are very jealous of me; that's where the danger lies for you, Fabrizio dear. They're brutes who are going to decide your fate and mine! So don't allow the count to hand in his resignation. Let him stay, even if he has to suffer humiliations! He always imagines that to hand in one's resignation is the greatest sacrifice a first minister can make. And every time his mirror tells him he's getting old, he offers me that sacrifice. So a complete rupture. Yes, and a reconciliation only in the event that that's the one means of stopping him from going. I shall send him packing in as friendly a manner as possible, of course, but after the courtier-like omission of the words *unjust proceedings* in the prince's letter, I feel that if I'm not to hate him I need to go several months without seeing him. On that decisive evening, I had no need of his sharp wits. He only needed to have written at my dictation, he had only to write those words, *which I had obtained* thanks to my character. His obsequious courtier's habits ran away with him. He told me the next day that he couldn't have made his prince sign an absurdity, that *letters of pardon* would have been needed. Dear God, with people like that, with those monsters of vanity and rancour known as the Farnese, you take what you can get.

At this thought, all the duchess's anger revived. The prince has deceived me, she told herself, and in what a cowardly fashion! . . . The man can't be excused. He has brains, subtlety, powers of reason. The only mean thing about him is his passions. The count and I have noticed it a score of times: his mind becomes vulgar only when he imagines someone has sought to offend him. Very well, Fabrizio's crime has nothing to do with politics, it was a small murder such as there are a hundred a year of in these fortunate States, and the count swears he's had the most exact inquiries made, and that Fabrizio is innocent. That Giletti didn't lack courage. Finding himself all but on the frontier, he suddenly felt the temptation to rid himself of a rival who had been found pleasing.

The duchess paused at length to examine whether it was possible to believe in Fabrizio's guilt. Not that she thought it a very great sin, in a gentleman of her nephew's rank, to rid himself of an impertinent play-actor. But in her despair she was beginning vaguely to sense that she was going to be obliged to fight to prove Fabrizio's innocence. No, she told herself at last, the conclusive proof is this: he is like poor Pietranera, he always has a weapon in every pocket, and on that particular day he was carrying only a wretched single-barrelled gun, and that borrowed from one of his workmen.

I hate the prince because he has deceived me, and deceived me in the most cowardly fashion. After his letter of pardon, he had the poor boy abducted in Bologna, etc. But that account will be settled. At around five in the morning, the duchess, exhausted by this prolonged fit of despair, rang for her women. They let out a cry. Seeing her on her bed, fully dressed, with her diamonds, as pale as her sheets and with her eyes closed, they fancied they were seeing her lying in state after her death.

They would have thought her in a dead faint had they not remembered that she had just rung for them. A few very rare tears ran from time to time down her insensible cheeks. Her women gathered from a gesture that she wanted to be put to bed.

Twice after the minister Zurla's soirée, the count had presented himself at the duchess's house. Turned away each time, he wrote that he wanted to ask her advice on his own behalf: 'Should he keep his position after the affront they had dared to show him?' The count added: 'The young man is innocent, but even were he guilty, should they have arrested him without warning me, when I am his acknowledged protector?' The duchess did not see this letter until the following day.

The count was not a moral man. One might even add that what the liberals understand by *morality* (to seek the happiness of the greatest number) seemed to him a deception. He believed himself obliged to seek before all else the happiness of Count Mosca della Rovere. But he was thoroughly honourable and perfectly sincere when he spoke of resigning. Never in his life had he told the duchess an untruth. The latter paid not the slightest attention to this letter in any case. Her course, which was a very painful one, had been decided on: to pretend to forget Fabrizio. Which effort having been made, everything else left her quite indifferent.

The next day, around noon, the count, who had called at the Palazzo Sanseverina ten times, was finally admitted. He was astounded by the duchess's appearance ... She's forty years old, he said to himself, and yesterday so dazzling, so young! ... Everyone tells me that during her long conversation with Clelia Conti, she looked just as young and far more attractive.

The duchess's voice and tone were as unfamiliar as her personal appearance. That tone, void of all enthusiasm, all human concern, all anger, caused the count to turn pale. It reminded him of the state one of his friends had been in a few months earlier, who was at the point of death and had received the last rites, but had tried to hold a conversation with him.

After a few minutes, the duchess was able to speak. She looked at him, but her eyes remained lifeless: 'Let us separate, my dear count,' she said in a weak but perfectly distinct voice, which she was struggling to make sound friendly. 'Let us separate, we must. As heaven is my witness, for these past five years my behaviour towards you has been beyond reproach. You have given me a splendid existence, instead of the tedium that would have been my dreary portion at the castle in Grianta. But for you I would have encountered old age several years sooner . . . On my side, my one preoccupation has been to try to help make you find happiness. It's because I love you that I am proposing this separation, *à l'amiable*, as they would say in France.'

The count did not understand. She was obliged to repeat herself several times. He went mortally pale and, throwing himself down on his knees beside her bed, he said everything that profound shock and then the keenest despair can inspire in a quick-thinking man who is passionately in love. Over and over he offered to give in his resignation and follow his mistress into some retreat or other a thousand leagues from Parma.

'You dare to talk to me of leaving, when Fabrizio is here!' she cried at last, half sitting up. But because she could see that Fabrizio's name had made a painful impression, she added after a moment's respite, lightly pressing the count's hand: 'No, my dear, I'm not going to tell you that I have loved you with the passion and the raptures that we no longer experience, I fancy, once past the age of thirty, and I'm already a very long way from that age. They will have told you that I loved Fabrizio, because I know that was the rumour going round that *spiteful* court.' (Her eyes shone for the first time in this conversation as she uttered the word *spiteful*.) 'I swear to you before God and on Fabrizio's life, that not the least thing has ever taken place between him and myself that wasn't fit to be witnessed by a third person. I shan't tell you either that I love him exactly as a sister would. I love him instinctively, if I can so put it. I love his courage, so simple, so perfect, which you could say he doesn't realize he has. I remember that this kind of admiration began on his return from Waterloo. He was still a child, for all his seventeen years. His great worry was to know whether he really had been present at the battle, and, were it to be "yes",

whether he could say he had fought, he never having marched
against an enemy battery or column. It was during the earnest
discussions we had together on that important topic that I
began to find him utterly charming. His great soul revealed
itself to me. What studied lies a well-brought-up young man
would have displayed in his place! Anyway, if he is not happy,
I can't be happy. There, those words describe well enough the
state of my heart. If it's not the truth, at least it's all I'm able to
see of the truth.' The count, encouraged by this note of candour
and of intimacy, tried to kiss her hand. She withdrew it with a
sort of revulsion. 'Those days are over,' she told him. 'I am a
woman of thirty-seven, I find myself on the threshold of old
age, I can already sense all its discouragements, and perhaps
I'm even close to the grave. That is a terrible moment, so it's
said, yet it seems to me that I desire it. I am experiencing the
worst symptom of old age: my heart has been extinguished by
this awful calamity, I can no longer love. I can now see in you,
dear count, only the shadow of someone who was dear to me.
I shall say further, it's gratitude and that alone which leads me
to address you in such terms.'

'What's to become of me?' the count repeated, 'when I feel I
am more passionately attached to you than in the early days,
when I used to see you at La Scala.'

'I'll make a confession, my dear, to talk about love bores me,
and seems indecent. Come on,' she said, attempting to smile
but in vain, 'take heart, be a man of spirit, a judicious man, a
resourceful man when it's called for. Be with me what you
really and truly are in the eyes of the indifferent, the cleverest
man and the greatest politician Italy has produced in centuries.'

The count got up and walked about in silence for a few
moments.

'Impossible, my dear,' he said finally. 'I am being torn apart
by the most violent passion and you ask me to question my
reason! There's no more reason for me!'

'Please, let's not speak of passion,' she said curtly. And this
was the first time, in two whole hours of conversation, that her
voice had acquired an expression of any kind. The count, in
despair himself, sought to console her.

'He deceived me,' she exclaimed, without making any sort of response to all the reasons for being hopeful that the count had been expounding. '*He* deceived me in the most cowardly fashion!' Her deathly pallor left her for an instant, but even at this moment of violent arousal, the count observed that she did not have the strength to raise her arms.

Great God, can it be possible, he thought, that she was simply unwell? But in that case it might well be the start of something very serious. Then, filled with concern, he suggested sending for the celebrated Razori,[2] the country's, and all of Italy's, leading physician.

'So you want to give a stranger the pleasure of knowing the full extent of my despair? . . . Is that the advice of a traitor or of a friend?' And she looked at him with a strange expression.

It's all over, he told himself despairingly, she no longer has any love for me! What's more, she no longer even ranks me among the common-or-garden men of honour.

'I must tell you,' the count went on, speaking with urgency, 'that I've wanted above all to obtain the details of the arrest that has made us despair, and what's peculiar is that I still don't know anything definite. I've had the policemen at the nearby police post questioned, they saw the prisoner arrive by the Castelnovo road, and got the order to follow his *sediola*. I immediately dispatched Bruno again; as you know he's as zealous as he's devoted. He has orders to work back from police post to police post to find out where and how Fabrizio was arrested.'

Hearing him utter Fabrizio's name, the duchess was seized by a slight convulsion. 'Forgive me, my dear,' she said to the count as soon as she was able to speak. 'These details are of great interest to me, give me all of them, make me understand every smallest circumstance.'

'Very well, signora,' the count resumed, trying to make light of it in order to distract her somewhat, 'I very much want to send a confidential agent to Bruno and order him to keep on going all the way to Bologna. It's there perhaps they'll have abducted our young friend. What was the date on his last letter?'

'Tuesday, five days ago.'

'Had it been opened in the post?'

'No trace of its having been opened. I have to tell you it
was written on awful paper. The address is in a woman's hand,
and that address bears the name of an old washerwoman
who's a relative of my maid. The washerwoman thinks it's all
about a love affair, and Chekina is paying her back for the
postage without adding anything extra.' The count, adopting
an altogether business-like tone, tried to discover, in discussion
with the duchess, on which day the abduction might have been
carried out in Bologna. Only now did he realize, he who was
ordinarily so very shrewd, that this was the tone he needed to
adopt. The details interested the unhappy woman and seemed
to distract her a little. If the count had not been in love this
very simple thought would have occurred to him the moment
he entered the room. The duchess sent him away so that he
could dispatch fresh orders to the faithful Bruno without delay.
Since they had concerned themselves in passing with the question of learning whether sentence had been passed before the
time when the prince had signed the letter addressed to the
duchess, the latter seized the opportunity with something like
urgency to tell the count: 'I shan't criticize you for having left
out the words *unjust proceedings* from the letter you wrote and
that he signed; it was a courtier's instinct that had you by
the throat. Without suspecting it, you preferred your master's
interests to those of your mistress. You've acted at my behest,
dear count, and for a long time now, but it's not within your
power to change your nature. You have all the attributes of a
minister, but you also have the instincts that go with that métier.
The suppression of the word *unjust* has destroyed me. But far
be it from me to criticize you in any way; instinct was to blame,
not the will.'

'Remember,' she added, altering her tone and adopting the
most imperious expression, 'that I am not too distressed by
Fabrizio's abduction, that I haven't felt the least inclination to
remove myself from this country, that I'm full of respect for the
prince. That is what you have to say, and now here's what I
wish to say to you: since I count on determining my behaviour
myself in future, I wish to separate from you *à l'amiable*, that's

to say, as a good and an old friend. Take it that I'm sixty years old. The young woman in me is dead, I can no longer go to any extremes, I can no longer love. But I should be even more unhappy than I am should I happen to compromise your destiny. It may enter into my plans to make it look like I have a young lover, and I wouldn't want to see you distressed. I can swear on Fabrizio's happiness,' whereupon she paused for half a minute, 'that I have never been unfaithful to you, not in five years. That's a very long time,' she said. She tried to smile. Her pale cheeks quivered, but her lips were unable to part. 'I swear that I never even had either the intention or the desire. Now you know, leave me.'

The count left the Palazzo Sanseverina in despair. He could see that the duchess's mind was quite made up to separate from him, yet never had he felt so hopelessly in love. This is one of the things I am obliged to come back to frequently, because they are improbable outside Italy. On returning home, he dispatched no fewer than six different individuals along the road to Castelnovo and Bologna, with letters to carry. But that's not all, the unhappy count told himself, the prince may have that unfortunate boy executed on a whim, in order to get his own back for the tone the duchess took with him on the day of that fateful letter. I felt that the duchess had overstepped a mark one should never go beyond, and it was to set matters right that I was so unbelievably stupid as to cut out the words *unjust proceedings*, the only ones that bound the sovereign ... But that's nonsense, are those sorts of people bound by anything? That was the greatest mistake of my life for sure, I put at risk everything that might make it worthwhile for me. It's a matter of making amends for that piece of thoughtlessness by using my head and being active. But if I can't achieve anything, even by sacrificing a little of my dignity, I shall give that man up. We'll see how he'll replace me, with his dreams of high politics and his ideas of making himself the constitutional king of Lombardy ... Fabio Conti is nothing but a fool, all Rassi's good for is having any man the powers that be don't like hanged.

Once firmly set on giving up the ministry if the rigours regarding Fabrizio went beyond those of a simple detention, the count told himself: if in his vanity that man who was so rashly defied costs me my happiness on some whim or other, at least I shall still have my honour ... talking of which, since I don't give a damn about my portfolio, I can allow myself any number of actions which even this morning would have seemed out of the question. For example, I'm going to attempt everything that's humanly feasible to enable Fabrizio to escape ... 'Good Lord,' the count exclaimed, breaking off, his eyes opening exaggeratedly wide as if at the sight of some unforeseen happiness, 'the duchess never mentioned an escape, can she have lacked sincerity for once in her life, and can our quarrel be simply the desire that I should betray the prince? Dammit, consider it done!'

The count's eye had recovered all its satirical sharpness. The loveable prosecutor Rassi is paid by his master for all the verdicts that dishonour us in Europe, but he's not a man to refuse being paid by me to betray his master's secrets. That creature has a mistress and a confessor, but the mistress is too common a specimen for me to be able to talk to her; the day after she'd be retailing our conversation to all the fruit sellers in the neighbourhood. Revived by this glimmer of hope, the count was already on his way to the cathedral. Surprised by how jauntily he was treading, he smiled in spite of his unhappiness. What it is not to be a minister any more, he said. The cathedral, like many Italian churches, serves as a way through from one street to the next, and the count saw in the distance one of the archbishop's vicars-general crossing the nave.

'Seeing as how I've met you,' he said, 'you'll be kind enough to spare my gout the dreadful fatigue of going all the way up to the archbishop's. I'd be most deeply obliged to him if he were willing to come down as far as the sacristy.' The archbishop was overjoyed by this message, he had a great many things to say to the minister on the subject of Fabrizio. But the minister guessed that these things were mere hot air and refused to listen.

'What sort of man is Dugnani, the vicar of San Paolo?'

'A small mind and a large ambition,' replied the archbishop, 'few scruples and extreme poverty, for we do have vices!'

'Good gracious, monsignore,' exclaimed the minister, 'you're a veritable Tacitus.' And he laughed as he took his leave. No sooner back at the ministry, he sent for Father Dugnani.

'You direct the conscience of my excellent friend, the prosecutor Rassi, might he not have something to tell me?' Then, without adding a word and without ceremony, he dismissed Dugnani.

CHAPTER 17

The count regarded himself as being out of the ministry. Let's just see, how many horses will we be able to have after my fall from favour, for that's what my withdrawal will be called. The count reckoned up his wealth: he had entered the ministry worth eighty thousand francs. To his great surprise, he discovered that, all in all, what he possessed at present did not come to five hundred thousand francs. That's twenty thousand livres a year at best, he told himself. I have to agree, I'm a complete featherbrain. There isn't a bourgeois in Parma who doesn't think I've got a hundred and fifty thousand livres a year, and, on that subject, the prince is more of a bourgeois than any of them. When they see me living in squalor, they'll say I know how to conceal my wealth. Good God, he exclaimed, if I'm minister for another three months, we shall see that fortune doubled. In this thought he saw an opportunity to write to the duchess, and grasped it avidly. But in order to apologize for a letter, given the terms they were now on, he filled this one with figures and calculations. We shall have only twenty thousand livres a year, he told her, to live all three of us in Naples, Fabrizio, you and I. Fabrizio and I will have one saddle horse between us. Hardly had the minister sent off his letter, before the chief prosecutor Rassi was announced. He received him with an arrogance that bordered on impertinence.

'So, signore,' he said, 'you have a conspirator who is under my protection abducted in Bologna, you wish moreover to cut off his head, and you tell me nothing! Do you at least know the name of my successor? Is it General Conti, or yourself?'

Rassi was thunderstruck. He was too little accustomed to the ways of good society to guess whether the count was being serious. He went very red, mumbled a few scarcely intelligible words. The count gazed at him and enjoyed his embarrassment. Suddenly, Rassi shook himself and exclaimed, perfectly relaxed but with the expression of Figaro caught in flagrante by Almaviva:[1] 'My word, signor count, I shan't beat about the bush with Your Excellency. What will you give me to answer all your questions as I would those of my confessor?'

'The cross of San Paolo (this is the order of Parma) or money, if you can provide me with an excuse for granting it to you.'

'I would prefer the cross of San Paolo, because it makes me a nobleman.'

'What, dear prosecutor, you still set some store by our poor nobility?'

'Had I been born into the nobility,' replied Rassi, with all the impudence of his métier, 'the relations of the people I have had hanged would hate me, but they wouldn't despise me.'

'All right, I shall save you from their contempt,' said the count. 'Cure me of my ignorance. What are you counting on doing with Fabrizio?'

'Well, the prince is in quite a quandary. He's afraid that, seduced by the lovely eyes of Armide,[2] forgive the somewhat colourful language, those were the sovereign's exact words, he's afraid that, seduced by those very lovely eyes which have affected him also just a little, you may leave him to his own devices, and there's only you who will do where the Lombardy business is concerned. I shall even tell you,' added Rassi, lowering his voice, 'that there's a grand opportunity here for you, well worth the cross of San Paolo you're giving me. The prince would grant you, as the nation's reward, a nice estate worth six hundred thousand francs that he would distrain from his domains, or else a consideration of three hundred thousand écus if you were willing to consent not to interfere in the fate of Fabrizio del Dongo, or at least to raise it with him only in public.'

'I was expecting better than that,' said the count. 'Not to involve myself with Fabrizio is to quarrel with the duchess.'

'Right, that's also what the prince says. The fact is, between

ourselves, he's dreadfully worked up against the signora duchess, and is afraid that, as a compensation for quarrelling with
that charming lady, now that you're a widower, you will ask
him for the hand of his cousin, the old Princess Isota, who's
only fifty.'

'He has guessed correctly,' exclaimed the count. 'Our master
is the shrewdest man in his States.'

The count had never entertained the baroque idea of marrying this old princess. Nothing could have appealed less to a
man who was bored to death by the formalities of court life.

He began playing with his snuff-box on the marble top of a
small table beside his chair. Rassi saw in this sign of embarrassment the possibility of a nice windfall. His eyes shone.

'But please, signor count,' he exclaimed, 'if His Excellency
is willing to accept, either the six-hundred-thousand-franc
estate, or the monetary consideration, I ask him not to choose
any other negotiator but myself. I will take it on myself,' he
added, lowering his voice, 'to get the sum increased or even get
quite a sizeable forest added to the estate. Were His Excellency
to condescend to tone down and temper his language a little
when talking to the prince about the young upstart who's been
put inside, the estate he will be offered by a grateful nation
might perhaps be raised into a duchy even. I repeat to His
Excellency: the prince may curse and swear about the duchess
for quarter of an hour, but he's much bothered, to the point
even where I've sometimes thought there was some secret circumstance he didn't dare confess to me. Basically, we could
have a gold mine here, I from selling you the most intimate
secrets and quite freely, because I'm thought to be your sworn
enemy. Basically, though he may rage against the duchess, he
also believes, as we all do, that you alone can bring all the
secret diplomacy in respect of the duchy of Milan to a successful
conclusion. Will Your Excellency permit me to repeat verbatim
the sovereign's own words?' said Rassi, growing excited. 'The
arrangement of the words often reveals a pattern that no translation can convey, and you may be able to see more in them
than I can.'

'I permit everything,' said the count, continuing, with a distracted air, to tap the marble table with his gold snuff-box, 'I permit everything and will show my gratitude.'

'Give me a patent of nobility that can be passed on, independently of the cross, and I shall be more than satisfied. When I talk about ennoblement to the prince, he replies: "A nobleman, a scoundrel of your sort! We'd have to shut up shop the very next day. No one in Parma would want a title any more." To get back to the duchy of Milan business, the prince was saying to me, not three days ago: "That rascal's alone in following the thread of our schemes. If I expel him or if he follows the duchess, I might just as well give up all hope of seeing myself one day as the leader of the liberals and adored throughout Italy."'

At which the count breathed more freely: Fabrizio will not die, he told himself.

Never in his life had Rassi managed to hold an intimate conversation with the first minister. He was beside himself with happiness. He saw himself on the eve of being able to give up the name of Rassi, which had become synonymous in those parts with all that is base and obsequious. The common people gave the name Rassi to rabid dogs and recently some soldiers had fought a duel because one of their comrades had called them Rassi. And then not a week went by without this wretched name being set into some appalling sonnet. His son, a young and innocent schoolboy of sixteen, had been chased away from cafés on the strength of his name.

It was the burning memory of all these advantages of his position that led him to commit an indiscretion. 'I have an estate,' he told the count, drawing his own chair up to the minister's, 'it's called Riva. I should like to be Baron Riva.'

'Why not?' said the minister. Rassi was beside himself.

'Well, signor count, I will take the liberty of being indiscreet, I shall venture to divine the object of your desires: you aspire to the hand of the Princess Isota, and that is a noble ambition. Once you are one of the family, you're protected against falling out of favour, you have your man where you want him. I shan't hide from you that he looks on this marriage with Princess Isota with horror, but if the affair were entrusted to someone both astute and *well paid*, we might not despair of success.'

'I, my dear baron, I would despair of it. I disavow in advance all the words you may bear in my name. But on the day when that illustrious alliance finally comes to fulfil all my desires and give me so very elevated a position in the State, I shall offer you, myself, three hundred thousand francs of my own money, or else advise the prince to grant you a mark of favour that you yourself prefer to that sum of money.'

The reader will find this conversation overlong. We are nevertheless sparing him the half of it: it continued for another two hours. Rassi came away from the count's ecstatically happy. The count was left with high hopes of saving Fabrizio and more determined than ever to hand in his resignation. He considered that his reputation needed to be renewed by the presence in power of men such as Rassi and General Conti. He revelled in the possibility he had just glimpsed of getting his own back on the prince. He may cause the duchess to leave, he exclaimed, but by God he must give up the hope of being the constitutional king of Lombardy. (This was an absurd fantasy. The prince was a highly intelligent man, but he had so filled his head with it, he had become hopelessly enamoured of the idea.)

The count felt no joy as he hurried to the duchess's to give her an account of his conversation with the prosecutor. He found the door closed against him. The porter hardly dared admit to this order, received from the lips of his mistress in person. The count returned sadly to the ministry building, the blow he had just experienced wholly eclipsing the delight he had derived from his conversation with the prince's confidant. No longer having the heart to occupy himself with anything, the count was wandering dismally in his picture gallery when, a quarter of an hour later, he received a letter worded as follows:

'Since it is true, my dear and good friend, that we are no longer anything more than friends, you are to come and visit me only three times a week. In a fortnight's time, we will reduce these visits, still very dear to my heart, to two a month. If you wish to please me, make this sort of breach public. If you wanted to return almost all the love that once I had for you, you would choose a new mistress. As for myself, I plan a life of great dissipation. I am reckoning on going a lot into society, perhaps I shall even find a man of spirit to make me forget my misfortunes. In your capacity as friend, the first place in my heart will surely always be reserved for you. But I no longer want it to be said that the actions I take have been dictated by your wisdom. I want it to be clearly known above all that I have lost all influence over your decisions. In a word, dear count, you must believe that you will always be my dearest friend, but never anything more. Do not, I beg you, keep any thought of coming back, it is all over and done with. You may count for ever on my affection.'

This final touch proved too much for the count's courage. He wrote a remarkable letter to the prince, resigning all his posts, and addressed it to the duchess, with a request to forward it to the palace. A moment later, he received his resignation, torn into four, and where there was a blank space, the duchess had deigned to write: 'No, a thousand times no!'

It would be hard to describe the poor minister's despair. She's right, I agree, he told himself again and again. My leaving out the words *unjust proceedings* is an awful misfortune. It will perhaps lead to Fabrizio's death, and that will lead to my own. Sick at heart, the count, who did not wish to appear at the sovereign's palace before being summoned, wrote with his own hand the *motu proprio* that appointed Rassi a knight of the order of San Paolo and conferred a hereditary title on him. To this the count attached a half-page report laying out for the prince the reasons of State that had made this step advisable. He took a sort of melancholy delight in making two fair copies of these documents, which he addressed to the duchess.

He lost himself in speculation. He was trying to guess what plan of action the woman that he loved would follow in the future. She has no idea herself, he told himself. One thing alone remains certain, which is that once I've been told of them, she's not going to depart from her resolutions at any price. What further added to his unhappiness was that he was unable to see that the duchess was to be blamed. She bestowed a favour on me by loving me, she has stopped loving me after an error, involuntary it's true, but one which may have awful consequences.

I've no right to feel sorry for myself. The following morning, the count learnt that the duchess had begun to go back into society. She had made an appearance the previous evening at all the houses that were receiving. What would have happened had he met with her in the same salon? How to talk to her? What tone to adopt when addressing her? And how not to talk to her?

The next day was funereal. The rumour was circulating generally that Fabrizio was going to be put to death; the town was stirred. It was added that the prince, having due regard for his noble birth, had deigned to decide he would be beheaded.

It's I who am killing him, the count told himself. I can't aspire to seeing the duchess ever again. Despite which simple piece of logic, he could not stop himself from going three times to her door. True, in order not to attract attention, he went to the house on foot. In his despair, he even found the courage to write to her. He had twice sent for Rassi; the prosecutor had not appeared. The scoundrel has betrayed me, the count told himself.

The next day, three important items of news set Parma society, and even the bourgeoisie, talking. The putting to death of Fabrizio was more certain than ever, and, as a very strange corollary to this report, the duchess did not seem to be in too great a despair. To all appearances, she was grieving for her young lover only in moderation. At the same time, she was taking advantage with infinite artfulness of the pallor she had acquired from a quite serious indisposition, which had come on at the time of Fabrizio's arrest. From which details the bourgeoisie were able easily to recognize the unloving heart of a great lady of the court. Out of decency, however, and as a sacrifice to the manes of the young Fabrizio, she had split up with Count Mosca. How utterly immoral! cried Parma's Jansenists.[3] But, and this could hardly be believed, the duchess already seemed willing to listen to the cajolery of the handsomest young men of the court. It was remarked, among other peculiarities, that she had been very light-hearted in a conversation with Count Baldi, Raversi's current lover, and had teased him freely about his frequent excursions to the country house in Velleja. The petty bourgeoisie and the common people were indignant at Fabrizio's death, which these good folk put down to Count Mosca's jealousy. Court society too was much taken up with the count, but only so as to make fun of him. The third great item of news that we have cited was indeed none other than that of the count's resignation. Everyone was laughing at a ridiculous lover who, at the age of fifty-six, had sacrificed a magnificent position out of vexation at being left by a woman without a heart who, for a long time past, had preferred a young man. The archbishop alone had the wit, or rather the heart, to see that honour forbade the count to remain first minister in a country where, without consulting him, they were about to cut off the head of a young man who was his protégé. The news of the count's resignation had the effect of curing General Fabio Conti's gout, as we shall recount in due course, when we speak of the manner in which poor Fabrizio was passing his time in the citadel, while the whole town was inquiring after the hour of his execution.

The following day, the count again saw Bruno, the faithful agent whom he had dispatched to Bologna. The count felt tearful at the moment the man entered his study, the sight of him recalling the happy state he had been in when he had sent him to Bologna, more or less in agreement with the duchess. Bruno had come from Bologna, where he had learnt nothing. He had been unable to find Lodovico, whom the podestà of Castelnovo had kept in the village gaol.

'I am going to send you back to Bologna,' the count told Bruno. 'The duchess will insist on the sad satisfaction of knowing the details of Fabrizio's misfortune. Go to the sergeant in charge of the police station in Castelnovo . . .

'No, wait!' exclaimed the count, breaking off; 'leave this instant for Lombardy, and hand out large quantities of money to all our correspondents. My aim is to obtain reports of the most encouraging nature from all these people.' Bruno having well understood the aim of his mission, began writing his letters of credence. As the count was giving him his final instructions, he received a letter, wholly false but very well written. It was as if a friend were writing to a friend to demand a service of him. The friend who had written was none other than the prince. Having heard speak of certain plans for retirement, he begged his friend, Count Mosca, to keep the ministry. He asked it of him in the name of their friendship and of 'the dangers facing the country'. And he ordered him to do so, as his master. He added that the king of *** had just put two ribbons of his order at his disposal, he had kept one for himself and was sending the other to his dear Count Mosca.

'That creature will be the death of me!' cried the count in fury, in front of the stupefied Bruno, 'he thinks he can suborn me by the same hypocritical phrases that we've made up together so many times to entrap some poor fool.' He turned down the order he had been offered and in his reply spoke of his state of health as leaving him with very little hope of being able to carry out the arduous tasks of the ministry for much longer. The count was furious. A moment later, the prosecutor Rassi was announced, whom he treated like a skivvy.

'Right, because I've given you a title, you're starting to play at being insolent! Why did you not come yesterday to thank me, as was your bounden duty, boor that you are, signore?'

Rassi was impervious to being insulted; this was the tone in which he was received daily by the prince. But he wanted to be a baron and he made spirited excuses. Nothing could have been simpler. 'The prince kept me tied to a desk all day yesterday, I wasn't able to leave the palace. His Highness made me copy in my bad prosecutor's handwriting a pile of diplomatic documents so fatuous and so verbose that I truly believe his one aim was to keep me prisoner. When I was finally able to take my leave, around five o'clock, dying of hunger, he ordered me to go straight home, and not to come out again that evening. Indeed, I saw two of his private spies, well known to me, patrolling in my street up until around midnight. This morning, as soon as I could, I sent for a carriage which took me as far as the doors of the cathedral. I got out of the carriage very slowly, then, breaking into a run, I came through the church and here I am. Your Excellency is at this moment the one man in all the world to whom I wish most wholeheartedly to give satisfaction.'

'And I, signor comedian, I'm not taken in by all these more or less well-constructed tales. You refused to talk about Fabrizio

two days ago. I respected your scruples and your being sworn
to secrecy, although an oath for a creature such as yourself
is nothing more at best than a means of defeat. Today I want
the truth. What are these ridiculous rumours that are having
this young man condemned to death as the murderer of the
play-actor Giletti?'

'No one better to account for these rumours to Your Excellency than myself, since it's I who've been having them put
around by order of the sovereign. And now I come to think of
it, it was perhaps in order to prevent me from letting you know
about this incident that he kept me prisoner all day yesterday.
The prince doesn't think me a fool, and could be in no doubt
that I would come and bring you my cross and beg you to fix
it in my buttonhole.'

'Keep to the facts,' cried the minister, 'and cut the fancy
phrases!'

'The prince would very much like to hold a death sentence
over M. del Dongo for sure, but as you no doubt know, he got
a sentence of only twenty years in irons, commuted by the
prince, the day after the sentence, into twelve years in the
fortress with fasting on bread and water on Fridays and other
religious carry-ons.'

'It's because I knew only about the prison sentence that I was
frightened by the rumours of an imminent execution that are
spreading round the town. I remember how cleverly you
covered up the death of Count Palanza.'

'That's when I should have had the cross!' cried Rassi, without turning a hair. 'I should have pressed the door-knob while
I had it in my hand, when that man so wanted that death. I was
simple-minded in those days and it's armed with that experience
that I venture to advise you not to imitate me today.' (The
comparison seemed in the worst possible taste to his interlocutor, who was obliged to rein himself in so as not to start kicking
Rassi.)

'In the first place,' the latter went on, with the logic of a
jurisconsult and the complete self-assurance of a man whom
no insult can offend, 'in the first place, there can be no question
of the aforesaid del Dongo being executed. The prince wouldn't

dare. Times have changed. And in any case I, a nobleman and hoping, through you, to become a baron, I would not put my hand to it. But it's only from me, as Your Excellency knows, that the executioner can receive his orders and I swear to you that the Cavaliere Rassi will never issue any against Signor del Dongo.'

'And you will be showing good sense,' said the count, measuring him severely up and down.

'Let us make a distinction,' Rassi went on with a smile. 'I myself deal only with official deaths, but if Signor del Dongo should happen to die from a colic, don't go putting it down to me! The prince is incensed, I don't know why, with Sanseverina' (three days earlier, Rassi would have said the duchess, but like the whole town, he knew of her rupture with the first minister). The count was struck by the omission of the title from such a mouth and it may be imagined how much pleasure it gave him. He cast a look of the purest hatred at Rassi. My dear angel, he then said to himself, I can show you my love only by blind obedience to your orders.

'I must confess,' he told the prosecutor, 'that I don't take all that keen an interest in the signora duchess's various whims. All the same, since she it was who introduced to me that ne'er-do-well Fabrizio, who ought certainly to have remained in Naples, and not come here and made things difficult for us, I am anxious that he should not be put to death in my time, and I'm willing to give you my word that you'll be a baron within a week of his coming out of prison.'

'In that case, signor count, I shan't be a baron before twelve years have elapsed, for the prince is furious, and his hatred of the duchess is so keen that he is seeking to conceal it.'

'His Highness is so good! Why does he need to conceal his hatred, when his first minister is no longer protecting the duchess? Only I don't want them to be able to accuse me of skulduggery or above all of jealousy. It's I who brought the duchess into this country, and if Fabrizio dies in prison, you won't be a baron but you may get a dagger stuck into you. But let us leave such trifles aside. The fact is that I have reckoned up my fortune. I found I had barely twenty thousand livres a year, wherefore I plan very humbly to submit my resignation to the sovereign. I have some hopes of being employed by the king of Naples. That great town will offer me the distractions I have need of at this moment, which I cannot find in a miserable hole like Parma. I would stay only on condition that you obtain the hand of Princess Isota for me,' etc., etc. The conversation went on for ever in this sense. As Rassi was getting up, the count said to him, with an air of complete indifference: 'You know it's been said that Fabrizio was deceiving me, in the sense that he was one of the duchess's lovers. I in no way accept that rumour, and in order to give it the lie, I would like you to convey this purse to Fabrizio.'

'But signor count,' said the terrified Rassi, looking at the purse, 'there's an enormous sum in here, and the regulations . . .'

'It may be enormous for you, my dear man,' the count went on, with an expression of supreme contempt. 'A bourgeois like yourself, sending money to his friend in prison, fancies he's ruining himself by giving him ten sequins. I *wish* Fabrizio to receive these six thousand francs, and above all that the palace should know nothing of this remittance.'

As the terrified Rassi sought to reply, the count shut the door on him impatiently. Men of that sort can see power only behind insolence, he told himself. Having said which, this great minister indulged in an action so absurd that it pains us rather to report it. He ran and took from his desk a miniature of the duchess, and covered it in passionate kisses. 'Forgive me, my darling angel,' he cried, 'if I didn't throw that boor out of the window with my own hands, who dares to speak of you with a hint of familiarity, but if I am acting with such excessive patience, it's so as to obey you, and he'll lose nothing by having to wait!'

After a long conversation with the portrait, the count, who felt his heart to be dead within his breast, thought of a ridiculous act, which he succumbed to with the eagerness of a child. He made them give him a coat with the stars of his orders on, and went to pay a call on the elderly Princess Isota. He had never in his life appeared before her except on the occasion of New

Year's Day. He found her surrounded by a number of dogs, and dressed in all her finery, with diamonds even, as if she were going to the court. The count, having evinced some fear of disturbing Her Highness's plans, she being probably about to go out, Her Highness answered the minister that a princess of Parma owed it to herself to be always thus. For the first time since his misfortune, the count felt an impulse of gaiety. I did well to put in an appearance here, he told himself, and I must make my declaration this very day. The princess had been overjoyed to find a man so renowned for his wit and a first minister coming to her apartment. The poor spinster was hardly used to such visits. The count began with an adroit preamble, referring to the immense distance that must always separate a mere gentleman from the members of a ruling family.

'A distinction must be drawn,' said the princess. 'The daughter of a king of France, for example, has no hope of ever acceding to the crown. But that's not how things are in the family of Parma. That is why we Farnese must always maintain a certain outward dignity. And I, a poor princess such as you see me, I cannot say that it is absolutely out of the question that you might one day be my first minister.'

So unexpected and baroque was this notion that the poor count enjoyed a second moment of unalloyed gaiety.

On coming away from Princess Isota, who had blushed profusely on receiving the first minister's avowal of his passion, the latter encountered one of the palace messengers: the prince was asking for him there and then.

'I'm not well,' replied the minister, delighted to be able to act dishonestly towards his prince. 'Oh, you push me too far,' he exclaimed in a fury, 'and then you expect me to serve you! But let me tell you, my prince, that to have received power from Providence is no longer enough in this century, you need a sharp mind and great character to succeed at being a despot.'

Having sent away the palace harbinger, deeply shocked by this invalid's perfect health, the count found it amusing to go to visit the two men at court who had the most influence over General Fabio Conti. What especially caused the count to shudder, and took away all his courage, was that the governor of the citadel had been accused in the old days of getting rid of a captain who was his personal enemy by means of the *aquetta* (poison) of Perugia.

The count knew that over the past week the duchess had distributed crazy amounts of money in order to be supplied with intelligence from the citadel. But, in his view, she had little hope of success; all eyes were still too wide open. We shall not retail to the reader all the attempts at corruption essayed by that unhappy woman. She was in despair, and agents of every kind and of perfect loyalty were backing her. But there is perhaps only one kind of official business that is conducted perfectly in small, despotic courts, and that is the guarding of political prisoners. The only effect that the duchess's gold had was to get eight or nine men of all ranks dismissed from the citadel.

CHAPTER 18

Wholly devoted though they were to the prisoner, the duchess and the first minister had thus only been able to do very little for him. The prince was in a temper, the court, like the public, *resented* Fabrizio and was overjoyed at seeing misfortune befall him. He had been too fortunate. Despite scattering handfuls of gold, the duchess had been unable to make any headway at all in her siege of the citadel. Not a day went by without the Marquesa Raversi or Cavaliere Riscara having some fresh piece of advice to pass on to General Fabio Conti. They were propping up his weakness.

As we have said, on the day of his imprisonment, Fabrizio was taken to 'the governor's palazzo'. This is a pretty little building constructed in the last century to the designs of Vanvitelli,[1] who set it a hundred and eighty feet up, on the platform of the huge round tower. From the windows of this small palazzo, isolated on the back of the enormous tower like a camel's hump, Fabrizio had a view of the countryside and the Alps in the far distance. At the foot of the citadel, his eye could follow the course of the Parma, a sort of torrent, which bends to the right four leagues from the town and flows into the Po. Beyond the left bank of this river, which formed as it were a succession of huge white stains in the midst of the verdant countryside, his enraptured eye could distinctly see each of the summits of the immense wall formed by the Alps in the north of Italy. These summits, still snow-covered, even in the month of August, as it now was, provide a sort of reminder of the cool in the midst of this torrid landscape. One can follow them with the eye in the smallest detail, for all that they are a good thirty leagues from the citadel of Parma. The sweeping view from the governor's pretty palazzo is interrupted towards one corner in the south by the Farnese Tower, in which a room had been hastily got ready for Fabrizio. This second tower, as the reader will perhaps recall, was erected on the platform of the big tower, in honour of a hereditary prince who, quite unlike Hippolytus, son of Theseus,[2] had not spurned the advances of a young stepmother. The princess died within a few hours. The prince's son recovered his liberty only seventeen years later, on ascending to the throne on the death of his father. This Farnese Tower, into which, three quarters of an hour later, Fabrizio was taken up, is very ugly on the outside, rises some fifty feet above the platform of the big tower and is equipped with a number of lightning conductors. The prince who, in his displeasure with his wife, had had this prison built, visible from every side, had the peculiar ambition of persuading his subjects that it dated back many years, which is why he gave it the name of the 'Farnese Tower'. It was forbidden to discuss its construction, yet from every part of the town of Parma and the neighbouring plain, the masons could be seen perfectly clearly setting in place each of the stones that form this pentagonal edifice. In order to prove its antiquity, they set above the door through which you enter, two feet wide and four high, a magnificent bas-relief showing Alessandro Farnese, the celebrated general, forcing Henri IV to withdraw from Paris.[3] This very conspicuous Farnese Tower comprises a ground floor forty paces long at least, wide in proportion and full of very squat columns, for this disproportionately huge room is no more than fifteen feet high. It is occupied by the guard and, from the middle of it there rises the staircase, which winds around one of the columns: a small iron staircase, very light, barely two feet across and constructed in filigree. By this staircase, which shook beneath the weight of the gaolers escorting him, Fabrizio came to huge rooms more than twenty feet high that formed a magnificent first storey. They had once been furnished in the utmost luxury for the young prince who spent the seventeen best years of his life there. At one end of this apartment, the new prisoner was shown a chapel of the greatest magnificence.

The walls and ceiling are faced all over in black marble. Columns, also black, of the noblest proportions, stand in rows along the black walls, without touching them, and the walls are decorated with a number of death's-heads in white marble, of colossal proportions, gracefully sculpted and set on two crossbones. That's certainly an invention of the hatred that cannot kill, Fabrizio told himself, and what a devilish idea, showing it to me!

A very light iron staircase in filigree, likewise arranged around a column, gives access to the second storey of this prison, and it is in the rooms of this second storey, some fifteen feet high, that in the past year General Fabio Conti had given proof of genius. First of all, under his direction, solid bars had been placed over the windows of the rooms once occupied by the prince's servants, which are more than thirty feet from the stone slabs forming the platform of the big round tower. These rooms, which all have two windows, are reached along an unlit corridor placed in the centre of the building, and in this very narrow corridor Fabrizio observed a series of three iron doors formed of enormous bars and going all the way up to the ceiling. It was the plans, cross-sections and elevations of all these beautiful inventions that had earnt the general an audience with his master once a week for two years. A conspirator placed in one of these rooms could not complain to public opinion of having been treated inhumanely, yet would be unable to communicate with anyone at all or make a movement without being heard. In each of the rooms, the general had had placed large oak beams, to form benches as it were, three feet high, and this was his crucial invention, the one that gave him rights to the ministry of police. On these benches he had installed a prison cell of planks, highly resonant and ten feet high, which touched the wall only on the window side. On the other three sides, there reigned a small corridor four feet wide, between the original wall of the prison, made up of enormous squared stones, and the plank walls of the cabin. These walls, formed of four double walnut-wood, oak and pine planks, were solidly joined together with iron bolts and innumerable nails.

It was into one of these rooms, constructed in the last year and General Fabio Conti's masterpiece, which had been given the beautiful name of 'Passive Obedience', that Fabrizio was shown. He ran to the windows. The view to be had from these barred windows was sublime: one single small corner of the horizon was hidden, towards the north-west, by the galleried roof of the governor's pretty palazzo, which was of only two storeys. The ground floor was occupied by the offices of the staff, and Fabrizio's eyes were first drawn to one of the windows on the second floor, where there were to be seen a large number of birds of every kind in pretty cages. Fabrizio was amused to hear them singing and watching them salute the last rays of the evening sun, as the gaolers busied themselves around him. The window of this aviary was no more than twenty-five feet from one of his own, and situated five or six feet below it, so that he was looking directly down on to the birds.

There was a moon that day, and at the time when Fabrizio entered his prison, it was rising majestically on the horizon to the right, above the chain of the Alps, towards Treviso. It was only half-past eight in the evening, and at the other extremity of the horizon, in the west, a brilliant orangey-red dusk picked out perfectly the contours of Monte Viso and the other Alpine peaks which run from Nice towards Mont Cenis and Turin. Without his misfortune even crossing his mind, Fabrizio was moved and enraptured by this sublime spectacle. So it's in this ravishing world that Clelia Conti lives! With her thoughtful and serious soul, she must enjoy this view more than anyone. Here, it's as if you're alone in the mountains a hundred leagues from Parma. It was only after spending more than two hours at the window, admiring this horizon that spoke to his soul, and frequently also letting his eyes dwell on the governor's pretty palazzo, that Fabrizio suddenly exclaimed: but can this be a prison? Is this what I so dreaded? Instead of seeing hardships and cause for bitterness at every turn, our hero allowed himself to be drawn by the attractions of prison.

All of a sudden his attention was brought violently back to reality by an alarming din: his wooden room, not unlike a cage and above all highly resonant, was being violently shaken. The barking of a dog and short, piercing cries completed this most peculiar noise. What's going on, might I be able to escape so soon? thought Fabrizio. A moment later he was laughing, as no one perhaps has ever laughed in a prison. By order of the general, an English dog had been brought up at the same time as the gaolers, very vicious and charged with guarding important prisoners; it was to spend the night in the space so ingeniously created all round Fabrizio's cage. The dog and the gaoler had to lie in the three-feet gap created between the original stone floor of the room and the wooden floor on which the prisoner could not take a single step without being heard.

Now, on Fabrizio's arrival, the room known as 'Passive Obedience' happened to be occupied by a hundred or so enormous rats, which took flight in all directions. The dog, a sort of cross between a spaniel and an English fox terrier, was by no means beautiful but in return showed itself to be very alert. It had been tied up on the stone slabs underneath the room's wooden floor, but when it sensed the rats passing close by, it made such extraordinary efforts that it managed to withdraw its head from its collar. There then occurred the admirable battle the din of which had aroused Fabrizio, lost in daydreams that were anything but unhappy. The rats that had been able to escape the first snapping of the teeth took refuge in the wooden room, and behind them came the dog, up the six steps that led from the stone floor into Fabrizio's prison cell. Then there began an even more terrifying din: the cell was shaken to its foundations. Fabrizio laughed like a madman, so hard that the tears came. The gaoler Grillo, no less amused, had closed the door. The dog, running after the rats, was not inconvenienced by any furniture because the room was absolutely bare. The only obstacle hindering the dog as it leapt about after its prey was an iron stove in one corner. Once the dog had triumphed over all its enemies, Fabrizio called it and stroked it, and succeeded in winning it over. If this one ever sees me jumping over some wall or other, he told himself, he won't bark. But this subtle strategy was a mere pretence on his part. In the state of mind in which he found himself, he took pleasure in playing with the dog. Bizarrely, though he gave it no thought, a secret joy reigned deep in his soul.

Out of breath from chasing after the dog: 'What's your name?' Fabrizio asked the gaoler.

'Grillo, at Your Excellency's service for everything that's permitted by the regulations.'

'Well, my dear Grillo, someone by the name of Giletti tried to murder me in the middle of a high road, I defended myself and I killed him. I'd kill him again if I had to. But I want some pleasure in my life all the same for as long as I'm to be your guest. Get authorization from your superiors and go and ask for a change of clothing from the Palazzo Sanseverina. In addition to which, buy me plenty of *nébieu d'Asti*.'[4]

This is rather a good sparkling wine made in Piedmont in the homeland of Alfieri[5] and greatly esteemed above all by the class of connoisseurs to which gaolers belong. Eight or nine of these gentlemen were busy transporting into Fabrizio's wooden room several items of antique and heavily gilded furniture which had been removed from the prince's apartment on the first floor. All of them had stored religiously away in their minds the favourable comment about Asti wine. Despite all their efforts, Fabrizio's establishment that first night was pitiful. But he appeared to be offended only by the absence of a bottle of the good *nébieu*. 'He seems like a good lad, that one . . .' said the gaolers as they went off, 'and there's only one thing to hope for, which is that our gentlemen let them get money to him.'

Once he was alone and recovered somewhat from all the brouhaha: is it possible that this is prison? Fabrizio asked himself, gazing at the immense horizon from Treviso to Monte Viso, the extended chain of the Alps, the snow-covered peaks, the stars, etc., and a first night in prison as well! I can imagine that Clelia Conti delights in this aerial solitude. Here, we're a thousand leagues above the pettiness and malice that preoccupy us down below. If those birds there under my window belong to her, I shall see her . . . Will she blush when she catches sight of me? It was in debating this great question that the prisoner found sleep at a very advanced hour of the night.

From the very next day following this night, the first one spent in prison, during which he did not once grow impatient, Fabrizio was reduced to making conversation with Fox, the

English dog. Grillo the gaoler still looked at him in the friendliest manner, but a fresh order had rendered him dumb, and he had brought neither linen nor *nébieu*.

Shall I see Clelia? Fabrizio asked himself on waking. But are those birds hers? The birds were beginning to let out little cries and to sing, and at this altitude it was the one sound to be heard in the air. The vast silence that reigned at this height was a sensation full of novelty and pleasure for Fabrizio. He listened enraptured to the little, broken, lively chirping with which his neighbours the birds greeted the day. If they belong to her, she will appear for a moment in the room there, underneath my window. And as he inspected the immense chain of the Alps, against the first tier of which the citadel of Parma seemed to rise up like an advanced outwork, his gaze kept constantly coming back to the magnificent lemon-wood and walnut cages which, decorated with gold wire, stood in the middle of the very airy room that served as an aviary. What Fabrizio learnt only later was that this room was the only one on the second floor of the palace that got shade from eleven to four, it being sheltered by the Farnese Tower.

How chagrined shall I be, Fabrizio told himself, if, instead of that heavenly and thoughtful countenance I am expecting, which will perhaps blush slightly if she catches sight of me, I see arriving the gross face of some very common lady's maid, charged with looking after the birds by proxy! But if I see Clelia, will she deign to notice me? I need to act indiscreetly if I'm to be noticed. My situation must have some privileges. The two of us are alone here in any case, so far away from the world. I'm a prisoner, apparently what General Conti and the other wretches of his kind call one of their subordinates . . . But she has so much spirit, or better to say so much soul, as the count supposes, that perhaps, judging by what he says, she despises her father's profession. Whence her melancholy! A noble cause of unhappiness! But after all, I'm not exactly a stranger to her. How gracefully, with what modesty, she acknowledged me yesterday evening. I remember very well that at the time of our encounter near Como I said to her: one day when I come and see your beautiful pictures of Parma, will you remember this name, Fabrizio del Dongo? Will she have forgotten it? She was so young in those days!

But come to think of it, Fabrizio said to himself in surprise, suddenly interrupting his train of thought, I'm forgetting to be angry! Can I be one of those lionhearts such as antiquity gave the world examples of? Am I a hero without suspecting it? What, I who was so afraid of prison, I'm in one and am forgetting to be unhappy! The fact is, the fear was a hundred times worse than the evil. I need to argue with myself if I'm to feel distressed at being imprisoned, which may, as Blanes says, last ten years as easily as ten months. Can it be astonishment at this new establishment that's distracting me from the hurt I should be experiencing? Perhaps this good humour which is independent of my will and none too rational will cease all of a sudden, perhaps in a moment I shall fall into the utter misery I ought to be experiencing.

At all events, it's very surprising to be in prison and to have to reason with oneself in order to feel sad! Well, I go back to what I supposed; perhaps I have a great character.

Fabrizio's musings were interrupted by the citadel's carpenter, who had come to take measurements for screens on his windows. It was the first time this prison had been used and they had omitted to finish off this essential element in it.

So, Fabrizio told himself, I'm going to be deprived of that sublime view, and he tried to feel saddened by this deprivation. 'But wait,' he suddenly exclaimed, speaking to the carpenter, 'shan't I see those pretty birds any more?'

'Oh, the signorina's birds, she's so fond of them!' the man said with a kindly expression. 'Hidden, eclipsed, abolished like all the rest.'

The carpenter had been strictly forbidden to speak, as had the gaolers, but the man took pity on the prisoner's youth. He informed him that the enormous screens, standing on the two windowsills and getting further away from the wall as they ascended, were to leave inmates with a view only of the sky. 'It's done on moral grounds,' he said, 'it's salutary for the prisoners' souls to add to their unhappiness and the wish to turn over a new leaf. The general has also had the idea of removing the window panes,' the carpenter added, 'and having them replaced by oil-paper.'

Fabrizio much liked the epigrammatical turn the conversation had taken, a rare enough event in Italy.

'I'd very much like to have a bird to pass the time, I adore them. Buy one for me off Signorina Clelia Conti's maid.'

'What, you know her, you say her name so well?' exclaimed the carpenter.

'Who hasn't heard talk of that celebrated beauty? But I have had the honour of meeting her several times at court.'

'The poor young lady is very bored here,' added the carpenter. 'She spends her life with her birds. This morning she's just bought some beautiful orange trees that have been put at the door to the tower underneath your window on her orders. If it wasn't for the ledge you'd be able to see them.' Some words in this reply were very precious to Fabrizio, and he found an obliging way of giving the carpenter some money.

'I'm committing two sins at one and the same time,' the man said. 'I'm speaking to Your Excellency and I'm receiving money. The day after tomorrow, when I come back for the screens, I'll have a bird in my pocket, and if I'm not alone, I shall pretend to let it fly off. If I can even, I'll bring you a prayer book. You must really be suffering from not being able to say the offices.'

So, Fabrizio told himself, as soon as he was alone, the birds are hers, but in two days' time I shall no longer see them. At which thought, his eyes took on a sorrowful expression. But at last, to his inexpressible joy, after so long a wait and so much watching, at around midday Clelia came to tend her birds. Fabrizio remained motionless, not breathing, he was standing against the enormous bars on the window and very close. He noticed that she did not look up at him, but her movements appeared constrained, like those of someone who senses themselves being watched. Even had she wanted, the poor girl would not have been able to forget the very delicate smile she had seen straying across the prisoner's lips the day before, at the moment when the policemen were leading him from the guardroom.

Although, to all appearances, she was keeping a very close

watch on her actions, at the moment when she approached the window of the aviary, she blushed quite visibly. Fabrizio's first thought, glued to the iron bars of his window, was to succumb to the childishness of tapping lightly on the bars with his hand, which would have produced a faint sound. Then the mere notion of this lack of delicacy horrified him. It would serve me right if for the next week she sent her maid to look after the birds. This delicate thought would not have occurred to him in Naples or Novara.

He followed her eagerly with his eyes. She's going to leave for sure, he told himself, without deigning to look up at this poor window, yet she's right opposite it. But as she returned from the far end of the room, which Fabrizio, thanks to his more elevated position, could see very clearly, Clelia could not help looking at him out of the tops of her eyes as she walked, and that was sufficient for Fabrizio to believe he was authorized to greet her. Are we not alone in the world here? he said to himself, to give himself courage. At this greeting, the young girl remained motionless and lowered her eyes. Then Fabrizio saw them raised again, very slowly. And she self-evidently forced herself to acknowledge the prisoner with the gravest and most *distant* movement, but she could not impose silence on her eyes. Probably without her knowing it, they expressed for a moment the keenest compassion. Fabrizio observed that she was reddening to the point where the pink tinge was spreading rapidly as far as the tops of her shoulders, from which the heat had just removed a black lace shawl as she arrived in the aviary. The involuntary look by which Fabrizio replied to her salutation increased the girl's agitation. How happy that poor woman would be, she said to herself, thinking of the duchess, were she able just for an instant to see him as I am seeing him!

Fabrizio had had some faint hope of saluting her a second time as she left. But in order to avoid this fresh courtesy, Clelia made an ingenious retreat in echelon, from cage to cage, as if, as she finished, she needed to tend to the birds placed nearest to the door. Finally, she went out. Fabrizio remained without moving, gazing at the door through which she had just disappeared. He was a man transformed.

From that moment on, the one object of his thoughts was to know how he might be able to go on seeing her, even once they had put in place the terrible screen in front of the window that overlooked the governor's palazzo.

The previous evening, before going to bed, he had set himself the tedious task of hiding the greater part of the gold he had with him, in several of the rat holes gracing his wooden room. This evening, I must hide my watch. Haven't I heard it said that with patience and a jagged watch spring you can cut through wood and even iron? I'll be able to saw through the screen then. The labour of hiding the watch, which lasted two full hours, did not seem long to him. He pondered the various means of achieving his end, and his abilities when it came to carpentry. If I go about it right, he told himself, I can cut a square section out from the oak plank that will form the screen, near the part that will rest on the windowsill. I'll take that piece out and put it back as circumstances allow. I shall give Grillo all I possess so that he'll be good enough not to notice this small stratagem. Fabrizio's whole happiness was henceforth linked to the possibility of carrying out this task, and he thought of nothing else. If I can only manage to see her, I shall be happy . . . No, he said to himself, she also has to see that I can see her. All through the night, his head was filled with schemes of carpentry, and it may be he did not think once about the court in Parma, the prince's anger, etc., etc. We will admit that he did not think either of the grief into which the duchess must have been plunged. He awaited the next day with impatience, but the carpenter did not reappear. Apparently, he passed for being a liberal in the prison and they were careful to send in another, rebarbative-looking one, who only ever gave an ominous grunt in reply to all the pleasant things that Fabrizio thought up to try to say to him. Several of the duchess's numerous attempts to enter into a correspondence with Fabrizio had been uncovered by the Marchesa Raversi's numerous agents, and, thanks to her, General Fabio Conti had daily been alerted, alarmed and suffered injuries to his self-esteem. Every eight hours, six soldiers of the guard were relieved in the big room of a hundred columns on the ground floor. On top of which, the governor posted a gaoler to stand guard at each of the three successive iron doors in the corridor, and poor Grillo, the only one who saw the prisoner, was condemned to leaving the Farnese Tower only once a week, at which he showed himself far from pleased. He let Fabrizio see his disgruntlement, who had the wit to answer only with the words: 'Plenty of *nébieu d'Asti*, my friend,' and to give him money.

'Well, even that, which consoles us for all our troubles,' exclaimed Grillo indignantly, in a voice raised barely sufficiently to be audible to the prisoner, 'they forbid us from receiving it and I ought to refuse. But I shall take it. Money wasted on the other hand. I can't tell you anything about anything. Come on, you must be well and truly guilty, the whole citadel's upside down because of you. The signora duchess's jolly little schemes have already got three of us the sack.'

Will the screen be ready before midday? That was the big question that gave Fabrizio's heart to pound all morning long. He counted every quarter that sounded from the citadel clock. Finally, as a quarter to twelve sounded, the screen had still not arrived. Clelia reappeared, tending to her birds. Cruel necessity had made Fabrizio a great deal bolder, and the danger of not seeing her any more seemed so much more important than anything else that he dared, as he watched Clelia, to make the motion of sawing through the screen with his finger. It is true that immediately after seeing this gesture, highly seditious in a prison, she half acknowledged it and withdrew.

What, said Fabrizio to himself in astonishment, can she be so unreasonable as to see an absurd familiarity in a gesture dictated by the most imperious necessity? I wanted to ask her always to condescend, when caring for her birds, to look now and again at the window of the prison, even when she finds it masked by an enormous wooden screen. I wanted to indicate I shall do everything humanly possible to manage to see her. Good God, is she not going to come tomorrow because of that tactless gesture? This fear, which disturbed Fabrizio's sleep, was fully borne out. The next day, Clelia had not appeared by three o'clock, when the two enormous screens were finally set up in front of Fabrizio's windows. The various sections had been hoisted up, from the esplanade of the big tower, by means of ropes and pulleys attached on the outside of the iron window bars. The fact is that, hidden behind a Persian blind in her apartment, an anguished Clelia had followed every move the workmen made. She had seen very clearly Fabrizio's mortal anxiety, but had none the less had the courage to keep the promise she had made to herself.

Clelia had been a youthful sectary of liberalism. In her early days, she had taken seriously all the liberal propositions she had heard in the company of her father, whose one thought was to make a position for himself. She had gone on from there to feel contempt and almost horror for the pliable nature of the courtier: whence her antipathy to marriage. Since the arrival of Fabrizio, she had been racked by remorse. And here, she told herself, is my unworthy heart taking the side of the people who want to betray my father! He dares to make the gesture of sawing through a door! . . . But, she at once told herself, her heart failing her, the whole town is talking about his imminent death. Tomorrow the fateful day perhaps! With the monsters we have governing us, what in the world is not possible! What gentleness, what a heroic serenity in those eyes that are perhaps going to close. Dear God, in what anguish the duchess must be. They say she's in total despair. If it were me, I'd go and stab the prince, like the heroic Charlotte Corday.[6]

All through this third day of his imprisonment, Fabrizio was beside himself with anger, but solely at not having seen Clelia reappear. My anger against hers, I should have told her I loved her, he cried, for that is the discovery he had come to. No, it's not out of greatness of soul that I'm not thinking about prison and proving Blanes's prophecy to be false, that much honour does not belong to me. Against my will, I am thinking of that gently pitying look Clelia allowed to fall on me when the policemen were leading me from the guardroom. That look has erased the whole of my past life. Who could have told me that I would find such sweet eyes in a place like this! And at a moment when my own eyes had been sullied by the features of Barbone and the signor general, the governor. Heaven appeared in among those vile creatures. And how could I not love that beauty and seek to see it again? No, it's not out of greatness of soul that I'm indifferent to all the petty vexations prison is heaping on me. Fabrizio's imagination, running rapidly through all the possibilities, arrived at that of being set free. The duchess's affection will surely achieve miracles. Well, I shall thank her for my freedom only with my lips. These aren't the sort of places you come back to. Once out of prison, in different worlds as we are, I'd hardly ever see Clelia again! And in point of fact, what harm is prison doing me? If Clelia condescended not to crush me by her anger, what would I have to ask heaven for?

On the evening of the day on which he had not seen his pretty neighbour, he had a brainwave. With the iron cross of the rosary handed out to every prisoner on entry to the prison, he began, and successfully, to cut through the screen. Perhaps it's being foolhardy, he told himself before starting. Did the carpenters not say in my hearing that as from tomorrow they'll be replaced by the painters? What will they say if they find the window screen has been cut through? But if I don't take the risk, tomorrow I shan't be able to see her. I'd go a whole day without seeing her and through my own fault! And after she became angry and left me too! Fabrizio's foolhardiness was rewarded. After toiling for fifteen hours, he saw Clelia, and to make his happiness complete, because she did not believe she could be seen by him, she remained for a long time without moving, her gaze fixed on that immense screen. He had ample time to read in her eyes the signs of the most tender compassion. Near the end of her visit she was even manifestly forgetting to attend to the needs of her birds, and remained for minutes on end motionless, contemplating the window. Her soul was profoundly troubled. She was thinking of the duchess, whose extreme misfortune had filled her with so much pity; yet she was beginning to hate her. She could not understand the deep melancholy that had taken hold of her character; she felt out of humour with herself. On two or three occasions in the course of this visit, Fabrizio tried in his impatience to shake the shutter. It seemed to him that he was not happy for as long as he was unable to let Clelia know that he could see her. Yet if she knew that I could see her so easily, he told himself, shy and reserved as she is, she would no doubt hide from my sight.

He was much happier the next day (out of what nothings does love not create its happiness!). As she gazed sadly at the huge screen, he managed to pass a small piece of wire through the opening created by the iron cross, and he made signs which she clearly understood, at least in so far as they meant 'I am here and I can see you.'

On the following days, Fabrizio was unlucky. He had wanted to remove from the colossal screen a piece of plank the size of his hand, which he would be able to replace whenever he wanted and which would enable him to see and be seen, that is to say to speak, by signs at least, of what was going on in his soul. But it happened that the noise of the very inadequate small saw that he had manufactured out of the watch spring, made jagged thanks to the cross, had worried Grillo, who came and spent long hours in the room. He thought he had noticed, it is true, that Clelia's severity seemed to diminish in proportion as the material difficulties standing in the way of any correspondence between them grew. Fabrizio had seen very clearly that she no longer affected to look down or watch her birds when he tried to indicate his presence with the help of his fragile piece of wire. He had the pleasure of discovering that she never failed to appear in the aviary at the precise moment when it was striking a quarter to twelve, and was almost presumptuous enough to believe he himself was the reason for this extreme punctuality. Why? The idea does not seem reasonable, but love observes nuances invisible to the eye of indifference, and draws endless consequences from them. For example, since Clelia had no longer been able to see the prisoner, she looked up at his window almost immediately on entering the aviary. This was during the funereal days when no one in Parma doubted but that Fabrizio would soon be put to death. He alone did not know this. But that awful thought never left Clelia, and how could she have reproached herself for the interest she was taking in Fabrizio? He was about to perish, and for the sake of freedom! For it was too absurd to put a del Dongo to death for striking down a play-actor with his sword. It is true that this likeable young man was attached to another woman! Clelia was profoundly unhappy, and without exactly admitting to herself the kind of interest she was taking in his fate. Certainly, she told herself, if he is taken off to his death, I shall escape into a convent, and never again appear in court society, it's horrible. Civilized murderers!

On the eighth day of Fabrizio's imprisonment, she had a very good reason to feel shame. She was gazing fixedly, absorbed in her unhappy thoughts, at the screen that hid the prisoner's window. That day, he had not yet given any sign of his presence. Suddenly, a small piece of screen, larger than a hand, was withdrawn. He looked at her gaily, and she could see him greeting her with his eyes. This unexpected ordeal was too much for her, she turned quickly round towards her birds and began tending them. But she was trembling to the point where she spilt the water she was giving them, and Fabrizio could see her emotion very clearly. The situation was too much for her, she chose to run off.

This was the most beautiful moment of Fabrizio's life, without any comparison. With what raptures he would have rejected his freedom, had it been offered to him at that instant!

The next day was one of the deepest despair for the duchess. Everyone held it for certain in the town that it was all up with Fabrizio. Clelia did not have the unhappy courage to display a sternness that was not in her heart; she spent an hour and a half in the aviary, watched all his signals and frequently replied, at least with an expression of the keenest and most genuine interest. She left him at moments so as to hide her tears. Her woman's coquettishness felt very keenly the inadequacy of the language employed. Had they been speaking to each other, in how many different ways would she not have tried to divine the precise nature of the feelings that Fabrizio had towards the duchess. Clelia was hardly able any longer to delude herself, she felt hatred for Signora Sanseverina.

One night, Fabrizio fell to thinking quite seriously about his aunt. He was astonished: he found it hard to recognize her image. The memory he had preserved of her had changed utterly. For him, at that moment, she was fifty years old.

Good Lord, he exclaimed enthusiastically, how inspired I was not to tell her I loved her! He was on the point of being almost unable to understand any more why he had thought her so attractive. As far as that went, little Marietta impressed him as not having altered so obviously. The fact is that he had never imagined that his soul was in any way involved in his love for Marietta, whereas he had often believed that his soul belonged in its entirety to the duchess. The Duchess of A*** and Marietta had the effect on him now of two young doves whose whole attraction lay in their weakness and innocence, whereas the sublime image of Clelia Conti, in taking possession of his whole soul, all but filled it with terror. He was all too aware that the everlasting happiness of his life was going to force him to reckon with the governor's daughter, and that she had it in her power to make him the most unhappy of men. Each day he was mortally afraid of seeing this strange and delightful kind of life that he enjoyed in her company brought to a sudden end, by some caprice against which his will could not appeal. Notwithstanding which, she had already filled the first two months of his imprisonment with felicity. This was the time when, twice a week, General Fabio Conti would tell the prince: 'I can give Your Highness my word of honour that the prisoner del Dongo does not speak to a living soul, and spends his time overcome by the deepest despair, or sleeping.'

Clelia came two or three times a day to visit her birds, sometimes only for a few moments. If Fabrizio had not been so much in love, he might easily have seen that he was loved. But he had terrible doubts in that regard. Clelia had had a piano put in the aviary. As she struck the keys, so that the sound of the instrument might give notice of her presence and occupy the attention of the sentries walking below her windows, she replied to Fabrizio's questions with her eyes. On one subject alone she never made any reply and even, on great occasions, took flight, sometimes vanishing for a whole day. This was when Fabrizio's signals indicated sentiments whose avowal it was too hard not to understand: on this point she was inexorable.

Thus, though narrowly confined within quite a small cage,

Fabrizio led a very busy life. It was employed purely and simply in seeking a solution to a most important problem: does she love me? The outcome of thousands of observations, constantly renewed but also constantly thrown into question, was this: all her voluntary gestures say no, but what is involuntary in the movement of her eyes seems to confess that she is coming to feel affection for me.

Clelia was hoping indeed never to arrive at an avowal, and it was to avert that danger that she had rejected, with an anger that was excessive, an entreaty that Fabrizio had addressed to her several times. The poverty of the resources employed by the poor prisoner should, it may seem, have inspired a greater compassion in Clelia. He wanted to correspond with her by means of characters that he drew on his hand with a piece of charcoal, a precious discovery that he had made in his stove. He would have formed the letters one by one, in succession. This invention would have greatly improved their means of communication by enabling them to say precise things. His window was some twenty-five feet away from that of Clelia. It would have been too risky to talk to one another above the heads of the sentries walking in front of the governor's palazzo. Fabrizio doubted whether he was loved. Had he had some experience of love, he would not have been left in any doubt. But no woman had ever occupied his heart. He was, moreover, quite unsuspecting of a secret which would have caused him to despair had he known it: everyone was talking about the marriage between Clelia Conti and the Marchese Crescenzi, the wealthiest man at court.

CHAPTER 19

General Fabio Conti's ambitions, raised to fever pitch by the difficulties that had come to stand in the way of the career of Mosca, the first minister, and seemed to herald his fall, had led him to have violent scenes with his daughter. He repeated to her endlessly, and angrily, that she was ruining her own prospects if she did not finally decide to make her choice. At past twenty, it was time to settle on a match. The state of cruel isolation into which her unreasonable obstinacy had plunged the general had to be brought to an end, etc., etc.

It was to remove herself from these incessant outbursts that Clelia had originally taken refuge in her aviary. It could be reached only by a small, very inconvenient wooden staircase, which the governor's gout turned into a serious impediment for him.

These past few weeks, Clelia's soul had been so disturbed, she had so little idea about what she ought to want that, without exactly giving her father her word, she had all but allowed herself to become engaged. In one of his fits of bad temper, the general had exclaimed that he would be perfectly capable of sending her off to languish in the dreariest convent in Parma and would leave her to mope there until she condescended to make a choice.

'You know that our family, although a very ancient one, can't muster six thousand livres a year, whereas the Marchese Crescenzi's fortune is as much as over a hundred thousand écus a year. Everyone at court agrees in recognizing that he has the mildest of characters. He has never given anyone cause for complaint. He's a very good-looking man, young, very well regarded by the prince, and I say you must be out of your mind to spurn his advances. Were this refusal the first, I might perhaps put up with it, but there have now been five or six parties, and from among the leading men at court, that you have turned down, like the silly little fool that you are. And what would become of you, I'd like to know, if I was put on half-pay? What a triumph for my enemies, if they saw me lodging on some second floor, I, who was always being spoken of in terms of the ministry! No, by God, my kindness has led me to play the role of Cassandra long enough. You're going to supply me with some valid objection to this poor Marchese Crescenzi, who is kind enough to be in love with you, to be willing to marry you without a dowry, and to make over a jointure of thirty thousand livres a year, with which I could at least house myself. You're going to talk reasonably to me or, by God, you will marry him two months from now! . . .'

One word alone in this entire speech had struck Clelia, which was the threat of being sent to the convent, and as a consequence removed from the citadel, and at the very moment when Fabrizio's life seemed to hang by a thread, for not a month went by without the rumour of his impending death circulating once more in the town and at court. Whatever arguments she might find, she could not resolve to run that risk. To be separated from Fabrizio, and at the moment when she feared for his life. As she saw it, that was the greatest of evils, or at any rate the most immediate.

Not that her heart could discern the prospect of happiness, even if she was not separated from Fabrizio. She believed he was loved by the duchess, and her heart was torn by a mortal jealousy. She thought ceaselessly of the advantages this woman had, who was so generally admired. The extreme reticence she had imposed on herself towards Fabrizio, the language of signs to which she had confined him, for fear of lapsing into some indiscretion, all of it seemed to be combining to deprive her of any means of elucidating how things stood with him in regard to the duchess. Thus each day, she felt more cruelly the awful misfortune of having a rival in Fabrizio's heart, and each day she ventured less to expose herself to the risk of giving him an

opportunity of speaking the whole truth of what was going on
in that heart. Yet how fascinated she would be to hear him
vouchsafe his true sentiments! What happiness for Clelia to be
able to elucidate the awful suspicions that were poisoning her
existence!

Fabrizio was unreliable. In Naples, he had had the reputation
of being quick to swap mistresses. For all the reserve imposed
on the role of a young lady, since she had become a canoness
and had gone to court, Clelia, without ever asking questions
but by paying close attention, had got to know the reputations
the succession of young men who had sought her hand had
made for themselves. Well, compared with all these young men,
Fabrizio was the one who displayed the greatest casualness in
affairs of the heart. He was in prison, he was bored, he was
paying court to the one woman he was able to speak with.
What could be simpler? What could be *more common* even? It
was this that so distressed Clelia. Even if she had learnt, by
some full disclosure, that Fabrizio no longer loved the duchess,
what confidence could she have in his words? Even if she
believed in the sincerity of what he said, what confidence had
she that his feelings would endure? And finally, to finish filling
her heart with despair, was Fabrizio not already well advanced
on an ecclesiastical career? Was he not on the verge of being
tied by everlasting vows? Did the highest offices not await him
in that mode of existence? If the least glimmer of good sense
remained to me, should I not take flight? the unhappy Clelia
asked herself. Should I not beg my father to shut me away in
some convent a long way off? And to cap it all, it is precisely
the fear of being removed from the citadel and shut away in a
convent that is guiding all my actions! It's that fear which forces
me to dissemble, forces me into the hideous and dishonourable
falsehood of pretending to accept the compliments and public
attentions of the Marchese Crescenzi.

Clelia was profoundly reasonable by nature. At no time had
she needed to reproach herself for any ill-considered action, but
her conduct in the present instance was the height of unreason.
Her suffering may be imagined! It was all the crueller in that
she was not under any illusion. She had attached herself to a

man who was loved to distraction by the most beautiful woman
of the court, a woman who was superior to her, Clelia, in so
many ways. And this same man, had he been free, was not
capable of a serious attachment, whereas she, as she was only
too well aware, would only ever have one attachment in her
life.

It was therefore with a heart troubled by the most terrible
remorse that Clelia came each day to the aviary. Borne to this
place as if in spite of herself, her anxiety changed its object and
became less cruel, her remorse vanished for a few moments.
With an indescribable pounding of the heart, she watched for
the moments when Fabrizio was able to open the vent of sorts
he had made in the huge screen that masked the window. Often,
the presence in the room of Grillo, the gaoler, prevented him
conversing in signs with his loved one.

One evening, at around eleven o'clock, Fabrizio heard sounds
of the oddest nature in the citadel. At night, by lying against
the window and putting his head out of the vent, he was able
to make out any reasonably loud noise being made on the main
staircase, the so-called 'three hundred steps', which led from
the first courtyard inside the round tower to the stone esplanade
on which they had built the governor's palazzo and the Farnese
prison in which he found himself.

Roughly midway in its ascent, at an elevation of a hundred
and eighty steps, this staircase passed from the southern side of
a vast courtyard to the northern side. Here there was a very
light, very narrow iron bridge, in the middle of which a gate-
keeper was posted. This man was relieved every six hours, and
he was obliged to get up and move his body out of the way to
allow anyone to cross the bridge he guarded, by which alone
the governor's palazzo and the Farnese Tower could be reached.
It took only two turns on a spring, the key to which the governor
carried with him, for this iron bridge to be dashed down into
the courtyard, more than a hundred feet below. This simple
precaution having been taken, since there was no other staircase anywhere in the citadel, and since every night at midnight a
warrant officer brought the ropes from all the wells to the governor, into a study entered through his bedroom, he remained

completely inaccessible in his palazzo, and it would have been equally impossible for anyone at all to get to the Farnese Tower. This was something Fabrizio had understood right away on the day he entered the citadel, and which Grillo, who, like all gaolers, liked singing the praises of his prison, had several times explained to him. Thus he had scant hopes of escaping. However, he remembered a maxim of Father Blanes's: 'The lover dreams more often of getting to his mistress than the husband of guarding his wife. The prisoner dreams more often of escaping than the gaoler of locking his door. So, whatever the obstacles, the lover and the prisoner must succeed.'

On that particular evening, Fabrizio distinctly heard a large number of men crossing the iron bridge, known as 'the bridge of the slave', because once upon a time a Dalmatian slave had succeeded in escaping by throwing the warder off the bridge and down into the courtyard.

They've come to abduct me, perhaps they're going to take me and hang me. But there may be a disturbance, I must look to take advantage. He had picked up his weapons, and was already drawing gold out from some of his hiding-places, when he suddenly paused.

What a funny creature man is, I must say, he exclaimed. What would an invisible spectator say, seeing my preparations? Do I want to escape by any chance? What would become of me the day after I'm back in Parma? Would I not do anything at all to come back to Clelia? If there's a disturbance, let's use it to slip into the governor's palazzo. Perhaps I'll be able to speak with Clelia, perhaps the disturbance will allow me to dare to kiss her hand. General Conti is deeply mistrustful by nature and no less vain, and has his palazzo guarded by five sentries, one at each corner of the building, and a fifth at the way in, but luckily it's a very dark night. Fabrizio went on tiptoe to check on what the gaoler Grillo and his dog were doing. The gaoler was fast asleep in an oxhide suspended over the floor by four ropes, and surrounded by a crude net. Fox the dog opened his eyes, got up and came quietly towards Fabrizio to nuzzle him.

Our prisoner went slowly back up the six steps leading to his wooden cell. The noise had become so loud at the foot of the

Farnese Tower, and just in front of the door, that he thought Grillo might well wake up. Fabrizio, carrying all his weapons and ready for action, thought he was destined that night for high adventure, when he suddenly began to hear the most beautiful symphony. They were serenading either the general or his daughter. He collapsed into a fit of uncontrollable laughter. And I who was imagining laying about me with my dagger! As if a serenade weren't infinitely more normal than an abduction requiring the presence of eighty people in a prison, or an uprising! The music was excellent and Fabrizio, whose soul had known no distractions for so many weeks, found it delightful. It made him shed the sweetest tears. In his rapture, he addressed the most irresistible speeches to the lovely Clelia. But the next day, at noon, he found her so sunk in melancholy, she was so pale, she directed glances at him in which he sometimes read so much anger, that he did not feel sufficiently entitled to question her about the serenade. He was afraid of being impolite.

Clelia had every reason to feel unhappy, it had been a serenade given for her by the Marchese Crescenzi. So public a step was tantamount to an official announcement of the marriage. Up until the day of the serenade, and up until nine o'clock in the evening, Clelia had put up stout resistance, but she had been weak enough to give in to the threat of being sent immediately to the convent that had been made by her father.

What, I shouldn't see him again! she had told herself tearfully. It was in vain that her reason had added: I shouldn't be seeing the person who will cause me all manner of unhappiness, I shouldn't see the duchess's lover, shouldn't see the inconstant man who had ten well-known mistresses in Naples and betrayed them all. I shouldn't be seeing the ambitious young man who, if he survives the sentence hanging over him, will take holy orders. It would be a crime for me to set eyes on him again once he is out of the citadel. And his inconstant nature will spare me the temptation, for what am I to him? A pretext for spending a few hours of each day of his imprisonment less tediously. In the midst of all these hard words, Clelia chanced to remember the smile with which he had looked at the policemen who were surrounding him when he came out of the prison office to go up into the Farnese Tower. Her eyes were bathed in tears. What would I not do for you, dear one! You will be the destruction of me, I know; such is my destiny. I am destroying myself in a ghastly fashion this evening by being present at this awful serenade. But tomorrow, at noon, I shall see your eyes again!

It was on the very next day after that when Clelia had made such great sacrifices for the young prisoner, whom she loved with such passion; the very next day after that when, while seeing all his faults, she had sacrificed her life to him, that Fabrizio was in despair at her coldness. If, employing only the very inadequate language of signs, he had done the least violence to Clelia's soul, she would probably have been unable to contain her tears, and Fabrizio would have obtained the avowal of all that she felt for him. But he was insufficiently bold, he was too mortally afraid of offending Clelia, she might impose too severe a punishment on him. In other words, Fabrizio had no experience of the kind of emotion excited by a woman whom one loves. That was a sensation he had never experienced, not even the least hint of it. He needed a week, after the day of the serenade, to get back on to the accustomed footing of good friendship with Clelia. The poor girl had armed herself with severity, scared to death of giving herself away, and it seemed to Fabrizio that day by day she looked less favourably on him.

One day, and it was now nearly three months since Fabrizio had been in prison, without having had any communication whatsoever with the outside world, yet without feeling unhappy, Grillo had stayed very late in his room that morning; Fabrizio did not know how to get rid of him, he was in despair. Finally, half past twelve had already sounded by the time he was able to open the two little foot-high hatches he had made in the fateful screen.

Clelia was standing at the window of the aviary, her eyes fixed on Fabrizio's window. Her drawn features expressed the most violent despair. Hardly had she seen Fabrizio before she signalled to him that all was lost. She dashed to her piano and, pretending to sing a recitative from a then fashionable opera, she told him, in phrases interrupted by despair and by the fear of being understood by the sentries walking underneath her window:

'Great God, you are still alive then! How great is my gratitude towards heaven! Barbone, the gaoler whose insolence you punished on the day of your entry here, had disappeared, he was no longer in the citadel. Two evenings ago he returned, and since yesterday I have reason to believe he is seeking to poison you. He goes and prowls in the private kitchen of the palazzo which supplies your meals. I know nothing for sure, but my maid believes that that ghastly face comes into the kitchens with the intention only of taking away your life. I was dying of anxiety at not seeing you appear, I believed you were dead. Abstain from all food until further notice, I shall do the impossible to get a little chocolate to you. At all events, this evening at nine, if heaven in its goodness grant that you have some string or can make a ribbon out of your linen, let it down from your window on to the orange trees, I shall attach a cord that you can pull up, and with the cord's help I shall pass you some bread and some chocolate.'

Fabrizio had preserved like a treasure the piece of charcoal he had found in the stove in his room. He hastened to take advantage of Clelia's emotion and to write on his hand a sequence of letters whose successive appearance formed the words: 'I love you, and life is precious to me only because I see you. First and foremost, send me paper and a pencil.'

Just as Fabrizio had hoped, the extreme terror that he had read on Clelia's features stopped the girl from breaking off the conversation after the bold words 'I love you'. She contented herself with evincing considerable ill humour. Fabrizio had the wit to add, 'Because it's so windy today, I didn't really hear the advice you deigned to give me by singing, the sound of the piano drowns the voice. What is the poison you spoke of, for example?'

At these words, the girl's terror reappeared in full measure. She began hastily to trace large letters in ink on the pages of a book that she tore out, and Fabrizio was in ecstasies at seeing this means of correspondence that he had been soliciting in vain finally established after three months of trying. He took good care not to abandon the little stratagem that had been so successful, he aspired to write letters and pretended all the while he could not properly grasp the words all of whose characters Clelia was displaying as he watched.

She was obliged to leave the aviary to run after her father. She feared above all that he might come looking for her. His suspicious nature would not have been happy at the closeness of the aviary window to the screen masking that of the prisoner. Clelia herself had had the idea a few minutes before, when Fabrizio's non-appearance had plunged her into such mortal anxiety, that it would be possible to throw a small stone wrapped in a piece of paper at the upper part of the screen. If chance so had it, that at that moment the gaoler responsible for guarding Fabrizio was not in his room, that would be a sure means of communication.

Our prisoner hastened to construct a ribbon of sorts out of his linen. And that evening, a little after nine o'clock, he heard very clearly a slight tapping on the boxes of the orange trees that stood underneath his window. He let his ribbon slide down and it brought him back a very long, thin cord, with the help of which he drew up, first a supply of chocolate and then, to his inexpressible satisfaction, a roll of paper and a pencil. It was in vain that he held out the cord the next time, he did not receive anything more. The sentries had obviously been approaching the orange trees. But he was wild with delight. He hastened to write Clelia an endless letter. Hardly was it finished before he had attached it to his cord and lowered it. He waited in vain for more than three hours for someone to come and collect it, and drew it back in several times to make changes to it. If Clelia doesn't see my letter this evening, he told himself, while she's still upset by her ideas about poison, perhaps tomorrow morning she'll reject out of hand the idea of receiving a letter.

The fact was that Clelia had not been able to get out of going down into the town with her father. Fabrizio had more or less concluded this when, at around half past midnight, he heard the general's carriage returning. He recognized the sound of the horses' hooves. How joyful he was when, a few minutes after having heard the general crossing the esplanade and the sentries presenting arms, he felt a tug on the cord, which he had not ceased to keep around his arm. A heavy weight was being attached to the cord, and two brief jerks gave him the signal to pull it in. He had some difficulty getting the weight he was bringing up past a ledge that stuck a long way out below his window.

The object that he had had so much difficulty pulling up was a carafe full of water wrapped in a shawl. It was with rapture that the poor young man, who had been existing for so long in the most complete solitude, covered the shawl with kisses. But we must forgo portraying his emotion when at last, after so many days of hoping in vain, he discovered a small piece of paper attached to the shawl by a pin.

'Drink only this water, live off the chocolate. Tomorrow I shall do all I can to get some bread to you, I shall mark it on every side with small ink crosses. It is a ghastly thing to have to say, but you need to know that Barbone has perhaps been charged with poisoning you. How could you not have sensed that the subject you raised in your pencilled letter was bound to displease me? So I would not be writing to you were it not for the extreme danger that you are in. I have just seen the duchess, she is well, as is the count, but she is much thinner. Do not write to me again on that subject. Do you want to make me angry?'

Writing the penultimate line of this letter was a considerable test of Clelia's virtue. In the society of the court, everyone claimed that Signora Sanseverina was becoming very friendly with Count Baldi, such a good-looking man, the former friend of the Marchesa Raversi. What was certain was that he had quarrelled in the most scandalous fashion with the marchesa, who for the last six years had been acting like a mother and had set him up in the world.

Clelia had been obliged to start this short note, written in haste, all over again, because the first draft did not altogether conceal the new love affairs that a malevolent public imputed to the duchess.

What a low creature I am! she had exclaimed, to say bad
things to Fabrizio about the woman he loves . . .

The next morning, long before it was light, Grillo came into
Fabrizio's room, set down quite a bulky package and vanished
without saying a word. This package contained a sizeable loaf,
marked on each side with small crosses drawn with a pen.
Fabrizio covered them with kisses: he was in love. Next to the
bread was a small cylinder wrapped in a great many sheets of
paper. It enclosed six thousand francs in sequins. Finally, Fabrizio found a beautiful brand-new breviary. A hand that he had
begun to recognize had traced these words in the margin:
'Poison! Watch out for the water, the wine, everything. Live off
chocolate, try to get the dog to eat the dinner you don't touch.
You must not appear suspicious, the enemy will seek other
means. Do nothing reckless, for the love of God, be serious!'

Fabrizio made haste to remove these beloved characters,
which might compromise Clelia, and to tear a great many pages
out of the breviary, with the help of which he made several
alphabets. Each letter was neatly drawn with crushed charcoal
soaked in wine. These alphabets had dried when, at a quarter
to twelve, Clelia appeared a step or two back from the window
of the aviary. The important thing now, Fabrizio told himself,
is that she should consent to use them. But happily, it turned
out that she had a great many things to tell the young prisoner
about the attempt to poison him. A dog belonging to one of
the serving girls had died from eating a dish intended for him.
Very far from raising objections to the use of the alphabets,
Clelia had prepared a magnificent one with ink. The conversation pursued by this means, somewhat awkward to start with,
lasted no less than an hour and a half, that is to say, all the
time that Clelia was able to remain in the aviary. On two or
three occasions, Fabrizio coming out with things that were
forbidden, she did not reply, but went momentarily to give her
birds the attention they required.

Fabrizio got her to agree that, in the evening, when sending
him water, she would pass across one of the alphabets she had
drawn in ink, which was far easier to see. He did not fail to
write her a very long letter in which he was careful not to insert

any expressions of affection, at least in a manner that might give offence. This means was successful; his letter was accepted.

The next day, in their conversation by alphabet, Clelia did not upbraid him. She informed him that the risk of poison had diminished. Barbone had been attacked and all but knocked senseless by the men courting the scullery maids in the governor's palazzo. He probably would not dare reappear in the kitchens. Clelia confessed that, on his behalf, she had ventured to steal an antidote to the poison from her father; she was sending it to him. The essential thing was to reject instantly any foodstuff that seemed to have an unusual taste.

Clelia had asked Don Cesare a lot of questions, without being able to discover where the six hundred sequins Fabrizio had received had originated. It was, at all events, an excellent sign: they were becoming less severe.

The episode of the poison had greatly advanced our prisoner's cause.

Notwithstanding that he could never obtain the least avowal that might resemble love, he had the happiness of living in the most intimate fashion with Clelia. Every morning, and often in the evenings, there was a long conversation with the alphabets. Every evening, at nine o'clock, Clelia would accept a long letter, and sometimes send a few words in reply. She sent him the newspaper and a few books. In the end, Grillo had been softened up to the extent of bringing Fabrizio bread and wine, which were handed to him daily by Clelia's maid. The gaoler Grillo had concluded from this that the governor was not of one mind with the people who had charged Barbone with poisoning the young monsignore, and he was only too happy about that, as were all his fellows, for a proverb had caught on in the establishment: you only needed to look Monsignor del Dongo in the face for him to give you some money.

Fabrizio had become very pale. The complete lack of exercise was damaging his health. That apart, he had never been so happy. The tone of the conversations between himself and Clelia was intimate and sometimes very light-hearted. The only moments of Clelia's life that were not beset by morbid predictions and remorse were those she spent conversing with him.

One day she was unwise enough to say to him: 'I admire your tact. Because I'm the governor's daughter, you never speak about wanting to recover your freedom.'

'That's because I'm far from having any such absurd desire,' answered Fabrizio. 'Once back in Parma, how would I see you again? Life would be unbearable for me from then on if I couldn't tell you all I'm thinking ... no, not exactly all I'm thinking, you've called me to order there. But anyway, cruel though you are, to live without seeing you every day would be a far worse torture than this prison! I have never been so happy in all my life ... Isn't it funny to find that happiness was awaiting me in prison?'

'There's a lot that might be said under that heading,' replied Clelia, with an expression that suddenly became excessively serious and almost ominous.

'What,' cried Fabrizio, greatly alarmed, 'am I at risk of losing the tiny place I've been able to win in your heart, which is my one source of joy in the world?'

'Yes,' she said, 'I have every reason to believe you lack probity towards me, although you pass elsewhere in the world for a very honourable man. But I don't want to get on to that subject today.'

This singular overture greatly inhibited their conversation and often both of them had tears in their eyes.

The prosecutor Rassi still aspired to a change of name. He was truly weary of the one he had made for himself and wanted to become Baron Riva. Count Mosca, for his part, was working, with all the skill at his command, to reinforce this venal judge's yearning for a barony, just as he was seeking to bolster the prince's crazed hopes of becoming the constitutional king of Lombardy. These were the only means he had been able to think of to delay Fabrizio's death.

The prince told Rassi: 'A fortnight of despair and a fortnight of hoping, it's by patiently following such a regimen that we shall succeed in overcoming the character of that arrogant woman. It's by being alternately gentle and severe that you succeed in breaking in the most uncontrollable horses. Apply the caustic steadily.'

And indeed, every two weeks a fresh rumour announcing
Fabrizio's imminent death arose in Parma. Such talk plunged
the unhappy duchess into the deepest despair. Faithful to her
determination not to drag the count down with her, she saw
him only twice a month. But she was punished for her cruelty
towards the poor man by the continual alternations of sombre
despair in which she spent her life. In vain did Count Mosca,
living down the cruel jealousy inspired in him by the assiduities
of Count Baldi, that very handsome man, write to the duchess
when he was unable to see her, and acquainted her with all the
information that he owed to the zealousness of the future Baron
Riva. To have been able to withstand the atrocious rumours
that circulated endlessly about Fabrizio, the duchess would
have needed to be spending her time with a man of intelligence
and feeling such as Mosca. The nullity of Baldi, leaving her to
her own thoughts, made for an intolerable existence, and the
count could not manage to convey to her his reasons for being
hopeful.

On various rather ingenious pretexts, the minister had succeeded in getting the prince to agree that the records of all the
very complicated intrigues, by means of which Ranuce-Ernest
IV nourished the ultra-absurd hope of making himself the constitutional king of Lombardy, should be lodged in a friendly
castle in the very centre of that beautiful country, in the
neighbourhood of Sarono.

More than twenty highly compromising documents were in
the prince's own hand or signed by him, and in the event of
Fabrizio's life being put seriously at risk, the count planned to
announce to His Highness that he was going to hand over
these documents to a great power from whom one word could
annihilate him.

Count Mosca felt confident of the future Baron Riva; he
feared only poison. Barbone's attempt had alarmed him greatly,
to such a degree that he had decided on a step that on the face
of it was crazy. One morning he went to the gateway of the
citadel, and made them send for General Fabio Conti, who
came down on to the bastion above the gateway. There, walking
with him in a friendly fashion, he did not hesitate to tell him,

after a brief and suitably barbed preamble: 'If Fabrizio perishes in some suspicious manner, his death may be put down to me, I shall be looked on as having been jealous, I shall be made to look abominably stupid, and I'm resolved not to accept that. So, to clear myself, if he expires from some sickness, *I shall kill you with my own hand*, you can count on it.' General Fabio Conti made some grandiloquent response and spoke of his bravery, but the count's look remained fixed in his mind.

A few days later, and as though in concert with the count, the prosecutor Rassi allowed himself a moment of rashness most unusual in such a man. The public contempt attached to his name, proverbial among the rabble, had been making him ill since he had had sound reason to hope he would be able to escape it. He sent General Fabio Conti an official copy of the sentence that had condemned Fabrizio to twelve years in the citadel. In accordance with the law, this is what should have been done the very next day following Fabrizio's entry into the prison. But what was unprecedented in Parma, that land of secret measures, was that justice should have allowed itself to take this step without the express order of the sovereign. For indeed, how to foster the hope of reviving the duchess's alarm every two weeks, and taming her proud character, as the prince had put it, once an official copy of the sentence had left the chancellery? On the eve of the day when General Fabio Conti received this official enclosure from the prosecutor Rassi, he learnt that the clerk Barbone had been assaulted when returning rather late to the citadel. From this he concluded that it was no longer a question in a certain quarter of doing away with Fabrizio, and in a flash of prudence which saved Rassi from the immediate consequences of his folly, he said not a word to the prince, at the first audience he obtained, about the official copy of the prisoner's sentence that had been passed on to him. The count had discovered, happily for the poor duchess's peace of mind, that Barbone's clumsy attempt had been only a capricious act of private vengeance, and he had the clerk given the advice mentioned earlier.

Fabrizio was very agreeably surprised when, after one hundred and thirty-five days imprisoned in a somewhat cramped cage, the worthy chaplain Don Cesare came to fetch him one Thursday to take him out for a walk on the keep of the Farnese Tower. Fabrizio had not been there ten minutes before, overcome by the fresh air, he felt unwell.

Don Cesare used this accident as an excuse to grant him half an hour's walk each day. This was foolish; these frequent excursions soon gave our hero back a vigour which he abused.

There were several serenades. The punctilious governor tolerated them only because they were committing his daughter Clelia to the Marchese Crescenzi, and her character frightened him. He dimly sensed that there was no point of contact between her and himself, and constantly feared some headstrong act on her part. She might run off to the convent, and he would be left defenceless. Besides which, the general feared that all this music, the sound of which might penetrate as far as the deepest dungeons, reserved for the blackest liberals, might contain signals. The musicians too were themselves a source of suspicion. Thus, hardly was the serenade finished before they were locked up in the big low-ceilinged rooms in the governor's palazzo, which by day served as offices for his staff, and the door was opened for them only the following morning, once it was broad daylight. It was the governor himself who, stationed on the 'bridge of the slave', had them searched in his presence and gave them their liberty, not without repeating to them several times that he would have any of them who dared undertake the slightest commission for one of the prisoners hanged on the spot. And they knew that in his fear of giving displeasure, he was a man of his word, with the result that the Marchese Crescenzi was obliged to pay three times the going rate to his musicians, much scandalized by having to spend the night in prison.

All that the duchess was able to obtain, and only with great difficulty, from the pusillanimity of one of these men, was that he would undertake to deliver a letter to the governor. The letter was addressed to Fabrizio. It deplored the mischance whereby during the more than five months he had been in prison, his friends outside had not been able to establish any communication whatsoever with him.

On entering the citadel, the musician she had bribed threw himself at General Fabio Conti's knees and confessed that a priest, not known to him, had so insisted on burdening him with a letter addressed to Signor del Dongo, that he had not dared refuse. But faithful to his duty, he had hastened to put it into the hands of His Excellency.

His Excellency was highly flattered. He knew the resources the duchess had at her command, and was much afraid of being bamboozled. In his delight, the general went and presented the letter to the prince, who was thrilled. 'So, the firmness of my administration has succeeded in avenging me! That haughty woman has been suffering for five months. But one of these days we are going to prepare a scaffold, and her wild imagination won't fail to believe that it's intended for the young del Dongo.'

CHAPTER 20

One night, at around one o'clock in the morning, Fabrizio, lying against his window, had stuck his head through the spy-hole made in the screen and was contemplating the stars and the immense horizon that is to be enjoyed from the top of the Farnese Tower. As they strayed across the countryside in the direction of the lower Po and Ferrara, his eyes chanced to remark an exceedingly small but quite bright light, which seemed to be coming from on top of a tower. That light can't be visible from the plain, Fabrizio told himself, the thickness of the tower would stop it being seen from down below. It must be some signal for a point in the distance. He suddenly noticed that this gleam came and went at very short intervals. It's some young girl talking to her lover in the nearby village. He counted nine successive appearances. That's an *I*, he said. *I* is in fact the ninth letter of the alphabet. Then, after a pause, it appeared fourteen times. That's an *N*. Then, after a pause, a single appearance: That's an *A*. The word is *Ina*.

His joy and astonishment knew no bounds once the successive appearances, always separated by short pauses, had completed the following words: GINA PENSA A TE. Obviously: Gina is thinking of you.

He replied instantly, by the successive appearances of his lamp at the vent he had created: FABRIZIO LOVES YOU!

The exchange went on until daybreak. This night was the one hundred and seventy-third of his captivity, and he learnt that they had been making these signals every night for the last four months. But they could be seen and understood by everyone. From that night on, they began to settle on abbreviations: three flashes in quick succession indicated the duchess; four the prince; two Count Mosca. Two quick flashes followed by two slow ones meant 'escape'. It was agreed they should in future follow the old *alla Monaca* alphabet, which, to prevent the inquisitive from deciphering it, alters the usual numbers of the letters and gives them arbitrary ones. *A*, for example, has the number ten, *B* the number three. That is to say, three successive eclipses of the light mean *B*, ten mean *A*, and so on. A moment of darkness marks the division between words. They fixed a rendezvous for the next day, at one hour after midnight, and the next day the duchess came to the tower, which was quarter of a league from the town. Her eyes filled with tears on seeing the signals made by the Fabrizio she had so often believed to be dead. She herself told him, via the flashes of the lamp: 'I love you, keep your spirits up, stay healthy, have hope. Build up your strength in your room, you will need strong arms.' I haven't seen him since Fausta's concert, the duchess told herself, when he appeared at the door of my salon dressed as a huntsman. Who could have told me then the fate that was awaiting us!

The duchess had signals sent that announced to Fabrizio that he would soon be freed, THANKS TO THE GOODNESS OF THE PRINCE (these signals might be understood). Then she went back to expressing her affection. She could not tear herself away from him! The remonstrations of Lodovico alone, who, because he had been of service to Fabrizio, had become her factotum, could persuade her, once it had begun to get light, to desist from sending signals that might attract the notice of some ill-wisher. The announcement, several times repeated, of his forthcoming liberation caused deep unhappiness in Fabrizio. Clelia, observing this the next day, was unwise enough to ask the reason.

'I find myself on the point of giving the duchess serious cause for displeasure.'

'And what can she demand of you that you might refuse her?' exclaimed Clelia, driven by the keenest curiosity.

'She wants me to leave here,' he answered, 'and that's something I shall never agree to do.'

Clelia was unable to reply, she looked at him and burst into tears. Had he been able to speak to her from close to, perhaps then he would have obtained the avowal of sentiments whose uncertainty had often plunged him into deep discouragement. He was keenly aware that, without Clelia's love, life for him could be only a succession of bitter heartaches or unbearable tedium. It seemed to him that life would not be worth living any more merely to rediscover the same pleasures that had seemed interesting before he had come to know love, and although suicide is not yet fashionable in Italy, he had contemplated it as a last resort, if fate separated him from Clelia.

The next day he received a very long letter from her.

'You must learn the truth, my friend. Since you have been here, it has very often been believed in Parma that your last day had come. It is true that you have been sentenced only to twelve years in the fortress. But unfortunately, it is impossible to doubt that an all-powerful hatred is set on pursuing you, and twenty times I have been fearful that poison might put an end to your days. Seize every means *possible* therefore of getting out of here. You can see that for your sake I am failing in the most sacred duties. Judge of the imminence of the danger by the things I am hazarding saying to you, which are so out of place in my mouth. If you absolutely have to, if there is no other means of salvation, escape. Each moment that you spend in this fortress may put your life in the gravest peril. Remember that there is a party at court that has never been halted in its designs by the prospect of a crime. And have you not seen all that party's schemes constantly thwarted by the superior skill of Count Mosca? Well, they have found a sure means of exiling him from Parma, and that is the duchess's despair. And are they not only too sure of bringing on that despair by the death of a young prisoner? These few words alone, to which there is no answer, should make you appreciate the situation you are in. You say that you feel affection for me. Consider first of all that insurmountable obstacles are opposed to that sentiment ever acquiring a certain permanence between us. We shall have encountered one another in our youth, we shall have held out a helping hand to one another at an unhappy moment. Fate will have put me in this cruel place in order to lighten your sufferings, but I would reproach myself everlastingly if illusions, which are not, nor ever will be, warranted, led you not to seize every possible opportunity to remove your life from so terrible a danger. My soul is no longer at peace because of the cruel and imprudent exchange of a few signs of warm friendship with you. If our childish games with alphabets lead you into such baseless illusions which may prove fatal, it would be in vain that in order to justify myself I should recall Barbone's attempt on your life. I should myself have exposed you to a much more terrible, much more certain danger by believing I was preserving you from a present danger. My rashness is for ever unforgivable if it has given rise to sentiments that may lead you to ignore the advice of the duchess. See what you have forced me to repeat: save yourself, I order you to . . .'

This letter was very long. Certain passages, such as 'I order you to', which we have just transcribed, gave Fabrizio's love delectable moments of hope. It seemed that, deep down, the sentiments were tender enough, even if the expression was re-markably cautious. At other moments, he paid the penalty for his complete ignorance of this kind of warfare. He saw only simple friendship, or even a very ordinary humanity, in this letter from Clelia.

At all events, nothing that it told him made him alter his intentions for one instant. Supposing that the dangers she had depicted were indeed real, was it too much to buy, by a few momentary dangers, the happiness of seeing her every day? What sort of life would he lead once he had again sought refuge in Bologna or in Florence? For, if he escaped from the citadel, he could not even hope for permission to live in Parma. And even were the prince to change to the extent of setting him free (which was highly unlikely, since he, Fabrizio, had become a powerful faction's means of overthrowing Count Mosca), what sort of life would he lead in Parma, separated from Clelia by all the hatred that divided the two camps? Once or twice a month, perhaps, chance would place them in the same salons. But even then, what sort of conversation could he have with her? How to rediscover the perfect intimacy that he now enjoyed for several hours each day? What would a conversation in a salon be like, compared to those they had with the alphabets? And should I need to purchase this life of delight and this one chance of happiness by a few small dangers, where is the harm in that? Would it not be one more happiness thus to find a feeble opportunity to give her proof of my love?

Fabrizio saw in Clelia's letter only the opportunity to ask for an interview. That was the sole and ceaseless object of all his desires. He had spoken to her only once, and then only for an instant, at the time of his entry into the prison, and that was now more than two hundred days ago.

A simple way of meeting Clelia offered itself: the excellent Father Don Cesare had granted Fabrizio half an hour's walk on the terrace of the Farnese Tower every Thursday, during the day. On the other days of the week, this promenade, which might have been observed by all the inhabitants of Parma and the area round about, and have seriously compromised the governor, took place only at nightfall. The only staircase that went up to the terrace of the Farnese Tower was that in the small bell tower attached to the chapel so lugubriously decorated in black-and-white marble which the reader will perhaps recall. Grillo would take Fabrizio to the chapel and unlock the small staircase in the tower. His duty would have been to follow him up, but since the evenings were beginning to get cool, the gaoler let him go up on his own, locking him into the tower that communicated with the terrace, and went back to warm himself in his room. Well, might Clelia not be able to find herself one evening in the black marble chapel, escorted by her maid?

The whole of the long letter with which Fabrizio replied to Clelia's letter was calculated in order to obtain this interview. For the rest, he confided to her with perfect sincerity, and as if it concerned someone else, all the reasons that had determined him not to leave the citadel.

'I would expose myself every day to the prospect of a thousand deaths in order to have the happiness of talking to you with the help of our alphabets, which now don't hinder us for a moment, and you want me to practise the deception of exiling myself in Parma, or perhaps in Bologna, or even Florence! You want me to go in order to distance myself from you! You must know that such an effort is out of the question for me. I should give you my word in vain, I would be unable to keep it.'

This request for a meeting resulted in Clelia's absence, which lasted for no less than five days. For five days, she came to the aviary only at those moments when she knew Fabrizio was unable to make use of the little opening he had made in the screen. Fabrizio was in despair. He concluded from this absence that, despite certain looks that had made him conceive wild hopes, he had never inspired feelings in Clelia other than those of simple friendship. In which case, he asked himself, what does life matter to me? The prince will be welcome, if he causes me to lose it. One more reason not to abandon the fortress. And it was with a feeling of profound disgust that he replied, each night, to the signals from the little lamp. The duchess thought he was completely mad when, on the bulletin of the signals that Lodovico brought her each morning, she read the strange words: 'I don't wish to escape. I wish to die here!'

During these five days, so cruel for Fabrizio, Clelia was more unhappy than he. She had had this thought, so poignant for a generous soul: my duty is to flee into a convent, far from the citadel. When Fabrizio learns I am no longer here, and I will get Grillo and all the gaolers to tell him, then he will make up his mind to attempt an escape. But to go to the convent was to give up on ever seeing Fabrizio again. And to give up on seeing him again when he had given such evident proof that the sentiments that might once have tied him to the duchess now no longer existed! What more touching proof of love could a young man give? After seven long months in prison, which had seriously affected his health, he had refused to recover his freedom. A fickle person, such as the courtiers had depicted when talking about Fabrizio, would, as Clelia saw it, have sacrificed twenty mistresses in order to get out of the citadel one day sooner. And what would he not have done to get out of a prison where every day poison might put an end to his life!

Clelia lacked courage, she made the serious mistake of not taking refuge in a convent, which would have given her at the same time a perfectly natural way of breaking with the

Marchese Crescenzi. This mistake once made, how to resist so likeable, so natural, so affectionate a young man, who was exposing his life to ghastly dangers for the simple happiness of catching sight of her from one window to the other? After five days of terrible conflict, interspersed with moments of self-contempt, Clelia made up her mind to reply to the letter in which Fabrizio had solicited the happiness of speaking with her in the black marble chapel. The truth is, she refused, and in somewhat harsh terms. But from that moment on, all peace of mind was lost, her imagination was constantly picturing Fabrizio succumbing to the effects of poison. She came to the aviary six or seven times a day, she felt an impassioned need to assure herself with her own eyes that Fabrizio was still alive.

If he's still in the fortress, she told herself, if he's exposed to all the horrors the Raversi faction are perhaps plotting against him with the aim of getting rid of Count Mosca, it's solely because I was cowardly enough not to run away to the convent! What excuse would there be for staying here once he was certain I had removed myself for good?

The girl, at once so timid and so haughty, went so far as to risk a refusal on the part of Grillo the gaoler. What was more, she laid herself open to all the comments this man might feel free to make about her strange behaviour. She demeaned herself to the extent of sending for him and telling him, in a tremulous voice that gave away her whole secret, that within a few days Fabrizio was going to obtain his freedom, that the Duchess Sanseverina was taking very active steps in that hope, that it was often necessary to have the prisoner's immediate response to certain proposals that had been made, and that she was charging him, Grillo, with allowing Fabrizio to create an opening in the screen that masked his window, so that she could convey to him by signs the advice she received several times a day from Signora Sanseverina.

Grillo smiled and assured her of his respect and his obedience. Clelia was infinitely thankful that he said nothing further. It was obvious that he knew perfectly well all that had been going on these past few months.

Hardly had the gaoler left her room before Clelia gave the

signal that had been agreed on to summon Fabrizio on important occasions. She confessed to him all that she had just done. 'You want to die by poisoning,' she added, 'I hope to have the courage one of these days to leave my father and flee into some convent a long way off. That is what I shall be obliged to you for. I hope then you will no longer resist the plans that may be proposed to get you out of here. For as long as you are here, I have awful moments of unreason. Never in my life have I contributed to anyone's ill-fortune, and it seems to me that I will be the reason for your death. Such an idea involving a total stranger would cause me to despair, so you may imagine what I feel when I set to telling myself that a friend, whose unreasonableness gives me serious cause for complaint, but who I have been seeing every day all this while, is prey at this moment to the pangs of death. Sometimes I feel the need to learn from you yourself that you are still alive.

'It is to remove myself from this awful suffering that I have just demeaned myself to the extent of asking a favour of an underling who might have refused, and who may still betray me. As it happens, I would perhaps be fortunate were he to go and denounce me to my father. I would instantly leave for the convent, I would no longer be the very unwilling accomplice of your cruel folly. But this can't last for very long, believe me, you must obey the duchess's orders. Are you satisfied, cruel friend? It is I who am urging you to betray my father! Call Grillo and make him a present.'

Fabrizio was so much in love that this simple expression of Clelia's wishes plunged him into such fear that even this strange communication did not convince him that he was loved. He called Grillo and paid him handsomely for having been obliging in the past. As for the future, he told him that for each day he permitted him to make use of the opening he had created in the screen, he would receive a sequin. Grillo was delighted by these terms.

'I'm going to speak hand on heart, monsignore. Are you willing to submit to eating your dinner cold every day? That's a very simple way of avoiding poison. But I ask for absolute discretion, a gaoler must see everything and guess at nothing, etc., etc. Instead of one dog, I shall have several, and you yourself can make them try all the dishes you're planning to eat. As for the wine, I shall give you some of mine, and you need touch only the bottles I've drunk from. But if Your Excellency wants to finish me once and for all, it'd be enough for him to entrust these details even to Signorina Clelia. Women are always women. If tomorrow she quarrels with you, the day after, to get her own back, she'll be telling her father the whole scheme, and he'd enjoy nothing more than having a reason to hang a gaoler. After Barbone, he's perhaps the most vicious person in the fortress, and that's where the real danger lies for you in your situation. He knows how to handle poison, you can be sure, and he wouldn't forgive me for the idea of having three or four small dogs.'

There was a fresh serenade. Grillo was now answering all Fabrizio's questions. He had promised himself all the same to be careful and not to give Signorina Clelia away, who, according to him, while being on the point of marrying the Marchese Crescenzi, the richest man in the States of Parma, was still making love, in so far as the walls of a prison allowed, with the amiable Monsignor del Dongo. He was answering the latter's latest questions about the serenade, when he was thoughtless enough to add: 'They think he'll be marrying her before long.' The effect of this simple remark on Fabrizio may be imagined. That night he replied to the signals from the lamp only to announce that he was unwell. The following morning, no later than ten o'clock, Clelia appeared in the aviary, and he asked her, in a tone of ceremonious politeness that was quite new between them, why she had not told him straight out that she loved the Marchese Crescenzi, and was on the point of marrying him.

'Because none of that is true,' replied Clelia, impatiently. It is the truth also that the rest of her reply was less clear-cut. Fabrizio pointed this out and took the opportunity of renewing his request for a meeting. Clelia, who found her good faith being questioned, granted it almost straight away, while remarking that she had dishonoured herself once and for all in Grillo's eyes. That evening, once it was dark, she appeared, accompanied by her maid, in the black marble chapel. She stopped in the centre, next to the sanctuary lamp. The maid and Grillo withdrew thirty paces away by the door. Clelia was trembling all over and had prepared a fine speech. Her intention was not to make any compromising avowal, but passion's logic is insistent. Its deep concern with learning the truth does not allow it to be too pointlessly circumspect, while at the same time the extreme devotion it feels towards its object removes the fear of giving offence. Fabrizio was first of all dazzled by Clelia's beauty, for nearly eight months he had seen nothing this close to except the gaolers. But his fury returned at the name of the Marchese Crescenzi, and grew when he could clearly see that Clelia was being guarded in her replies. Clelia herself realized that she was adding to his suspicions rather than dispelling them. The sensation was too cruel for her.

'Can you be really happy,' she said, with a kind of anger and with tears in her eyes, 'at having made me transgress everything that I owe to myself? Up until August the 3rd last year, I had felt only an aversion for the men who had sought to make me like them. I had a boundless and probably exaggerated scorn for the character of the courtiers, everyone who was happy at that court I disliked. I found singular qualities on the other hand in a prisoner who was brought into the citadel here on August the 3rd. I experienced, without at first realizing it, all the torments of jealousy. The attractions of a charming woman, whom I knew well, were so many daggers thrust into my heart, for I believed, and still do believe a little, that the prisoner was attached to her. The importunities of the Marchese Crescenzi, who had asked for my hand, were soon renewed. He is very rich and we have no fortune. I rejected them with a great freedom of mind, when my father pronounced the fateful word *convent*. I realized that if I left the citadel I would no longer be able to watch over the life of the prisoner whose fate concerned me. The masterpiece of my precautions had been that, up until this moment, he did not at all suspect the awful dangers that were threatening his life. I had promised myself never to betray either my father or my secret. But the admirably energetic woman, with her superior mind and terrifyingly strong will,

who protects this prisoner, offered him, as I suppose, a means
of escape, which he rejected and sought to convince me that he
refused to leave the citadel so as not to be parted from me. I
then made a great mistake, I fought for five whole days, I should
have taken refuge instantly in the convent and left the fortress.
That step offered me a very simple way of breaking with the
Marchese Crescenzi. I didn't have the courage to leave the
fortress and I'm a lost girl. I have attached myself to a man not
to be relied on. I know how he behaved in Naples, and what
reason would I have for believing he has changed his character?
Locked up in a forbidding prison, he paid court to the one
woman he was able to see, she was a distraction for him in his
boredom. Because he could talk to her only with a certain
difficulty, his amusement took on the false appearance of a
passion. The prisoner having made a name for himself in the
world by his courage, he imagines he can prove that his love is
more than a mere passing fancy, by exposing himself to quite
serious dangers in order to go on seeing the person he believes
he loves. But as soon as he finds himself in a great town,
surrounded once more by the allurements of society, he'll again
be what he has always been, a man of the world given to
dissipation, to gallantry, and his poor prison companion will
end her days in a convent, forgotten by that fickle person and
forever regretting having confessed herself to him.'

This historic speech, of which we have given only the main
burden, was, as may well be imagined, interrupted twenty times
by Fabrizio. He was hopelessly in love, and was therefore
wholly persuaded that he had never loved before he set eyes on
Clelia and that his life's destiny was to live only for her.

The reader can surely imagine the fine things he was saying
when the maid warned her mistress that it had just struck half
past eleven and that the general might return at any moment.
The parting was cruel.

'I am perhaps seeing you for the last time,' Clelia told the
prisoner. 'A measure that is in the obvious interests of the
Raversi cabal may furnish you with a cruel way of proving you
are not inconstant.' Clelia left Fabrizio stifled by sobs, and
dying of shame at not being able to conceal them entirely

from her maid or above all from the gaoler Grillo. A second conversation would be possible only once the general let it be known that he would be spending the evening in society; but since Fabrizio's imprisonment, and the interest it had prompted among the inquisitive at court, he had found it prudent to give himself an almost continual attack of gout, so that his journeys into town, subject to the requirements of a studied policy, were often decided on only at the moment of getting into his carriage.

Since the evening in the black marble chapel, Fabrizio had been constantly transported by joy. It was true that serious obstacles still seemed to stand in the way of his happiness, but for all that he had the supreme and unlooked-for joy of being loved by the celestial creature who occupied all his thoughts.

On the third day after their meeting, the signals from the lamp ended very early, somewhere around midnight. At the very instant they finished, Fabrizio almost had his head split open by a large lead ball which, having been projected against the upper section of the screen on his window, broke its paper panes and fell into the room.

This very large ball was by no means as heavy as its volume promised. Fabrizio had no difficulty in opening it and found a letter from the duchess. Thanks to the good offices of the arch-bishop, whom she had been painstakingly flattering, she had been able to bribe a soldier from the garrison in the citadel. The man, a practised troublemaker, had either tricked the soldiers posted at the corners and in the doorway of the governor's palazzo or else come to an arrangement with them.

'You must make your escape with ropes. I shudder when I offer you this strange advice, I've been hesitating for more than two whole months before giving you the word. But the official future grows darker by the day, and we can expect the worst. Incidentally, start signalling with your lamp again this instant, to show you've received this dangerous letter. Indicate *P*, *B* and *G alla monaca*, i.e., four, twelve and two. I shan't breathe freely until I've seen that signal. I'm in the tower. We shall reply with *N* and *O*, seven and five. Once you've received the reply, no more signals, concentrate on understanding my letter.'

Fabrizio hastened to obey, and gave the agreed signals, which were followed by the promised reply, then he went on reading the letter.

'We can expect the worst. That's what the three men I have the most confidence in assured me, after I'd made them swear on the Gospel to tell me the truth, however cruel it might be for me. The first of these men threatened the surgeon who gave you away in Ferrara he'd take an open knife to him. The second one told you when you came back from Belgirate that it would definitely have been a lot more sensible to have shot the footman who came through the wood singing, leading a good, rather scrawny horse by the bridle. You don't know the third one, he's a highwayman friend, a man who gets things done if ever there was one, and as courageous as yourself. That's why I asked him above all to say straight out what you should do. All three of them told me, without any of them knowing I'd consulted the other two, that it's better to risk breaking your neck rather than spending another eleven years and four months in the continual fear of very probably being poisoned.

'For a month you must practise going up and down by means of a knotted rope in your room. Then, on a public holiday, when the garrison in the citadel will have been given free wine, you must attempt your great enterprise. You will have three silk and hemp ropes, the thickness of a swan's feather, the first one eighty feet long to descend the thirty-five feet there are from your window to the orange trees, the second three hundred feet long, and there's the problem because of the weight, to descend the hundred-and-eighty-feet height of the wall of the big tower. A third one thirty feet long will get you down the ramparts. I spend my life studying the big wall to the east, i.e., on the Ferrara side. A crack caused by an earth tremor has been filled in by means of a buttress that forms an *inclined plane*. My highwayman assures me he'd guarantee to get down on that side without too much difficulty at the cost of a few grazes at most, by letting himself slide down the slope formed by the buttress. The vertical gap is only twenty-eight feet right at the bottom. That side is the least well guarded.

'However, all things considered, my robber, who has escaped from prison three times, and who you'd like if you met him, although he abominates people of your caste, my highway robber, as I say, who's as agile and quick as you are, thinks he would rather come down on the west side, exactly opposite the small palazzo occupied in the old days by Fausta, you know it well. What would make him choose that side is that the wall, although it hardly slopes, is covered almost all the way down by scrub. There are wooden twigs as thick as your little finger which may very well scratch you if you don't look out, but which are excellent too for holding on to. Only this morning, I was looking at this western side through an excellent glass. The place to choose is exactly below a brand-new stone that was set into the balustrade up above two or three years ago. Straight down from that stone, you'll first of all find a bare space of about twenty feet. You need to get to it very slowly (you can guess whether my heart is quaking giving you these terrifying instructions, but courage consists in knowing how to choose the lesser evil, however awful it may still be). After the bare space, you'll find eighty or ninety feet of quite big undergrowth, where you can see birds flying about, then a space of thirty feet where there's only grass, stocks and nettles. Then, as you get near the ground, twenty feet of undergrowth and finally twenty-five or thirty feet that have been recently patched up.

'What would make me decide on that side is that, vertically down from the new stone in the balustrade at the top, there is a wooden shed built by a soldier in his garden, which the engineer captain employed at the fortress wants to force him to demolish. It's seventeen feet high, it's covered in thatch and the roof touches the big wall of the citadel. It's the roof which tempts me. In the awful event of an accident, it would deaden your fall. Once you get there, you're inside the ring-wall of ramparts which are quite slackly guarded. Were they to stop you, fire your pistol and defend yourself for a few minutes. Your friend from Ferrara and another brave man, the one I call the highwayman, will have ladders and won't hesitate to scale the rampart, which isn't very high, and fly to your assistance.

'The rampart is only twenty-three feet high, as a tall, sloping bank. I shall be at the foot of the last wall with a good many armed men.

'I hope to get five or six letters to you by the same route as this one. I shall go on repeating the same things in different words, so that we're in full agreement. You may guess how I feel when I tell you that the *shoot-the-footman* man, who is, when all's said and done, the best of creatures and dying of remorse, thinks you'll get off with a broken arm. The highwayman, who has more experience of this sort of expedition, thinks that, if you're willing to descend very slowly, above all without hurrying, your freedom will cost you only a few scrapes. The big difficulty is getting the ropes. That's been my one thought over the two weeks during which I've been preoccupied every minute of the day with this big idea.

'I shan't respond to your foolishness, the one unintelligent thing you've ever said: "I don't want to escape!" The *shoot-the-footman* man said tedium had driven you mad. I shan't hide from you that we're dreading a very imminent danger that may perhaps bring forward the day of your escape. To announce that danger, the lamp will say several times in succession: "The castle has caught fire!" You will answer: "Were my books burnt?"'

The letter contained five or six more pages of details. It was written in microscopic characters on very thin paper.

That's all very fine and very well thought out, Fabrizio said to himself. I owe the count and duchess my everlasting gratitude. They'll perhaps think I'm afraid, but I shan't escape. Has anyone ever escaped from a place where they couldn't be happier, to go and cast themselves into a ghastly exile where they won't have anything, not even the air to breathe? What would I be doing by the end of a month if I was in Florence? I would put on a disguise to come and prowl around the gateway to this fortress, and try to espy a pair of eyes!

The next day, Fabrizio was frightened. He was at his window, at around eleven o'clock, gazing at the magnificent landscape and waiting for the blessed moment when he would be able to see Clelia, when Grillo entered the room, out of breath.

'Quick, quick, monsignore, throw yourself down on your bed, make it look as though you're sick. There are three judges coming up! They're going to interrogate you. Think carefully before you speak. They're coming to trip you up.'

Saying which, Grillo hurriedly shut the little trapdoor in the screen, pushed Fabrizio on to his bed and threw two or three coats over him.

'Say you're in a lot of pain and don't talk much, above all make them repeat the questions to give yourself time to think.'

The three judges entered. Three escaped gaolbirds, Fabrizio told himself, observing their coarse features, not three judges. They had long black robes. They bowed solemnly and, without a word, occupied the three chairs that stood in the room.

'Signor Fabrizio del Dongo,' said the eldest of them, 'we are pained by the unhappy commission we come to perform. We are here to announce to you the demise of His Excellency, Signor the Marchese del Dongo, your father, second high majordomo, major of the kingdom of Lombardy-Venice, knight grand cross of the orders of etc., etc.' Fabrizio burst into tears. The judge went on.

'The Signora Marchesa del Dongo, your mother, imparts this news to you in a letter missive. But because she has added inappropriate comments to the fact, by a decree yesterday, the court of justice has decided that her letter will be communicated to you only in the form of an extract, and it is this extract which the clerk of the court, Signor Bona, will now read to you.'

The reading over, the judge approached the still recumbent Fabrizio, and made him follow on his mother's letter the passages copies of which had just been read out. Fabrizio could see in the letter the words *unjust imprisonment*, and *cruel punishment for a crime that is not one*, and understood what had brought about the judges' visit. On the other hand, despite his contempt for magistrates who lacked probity, all he actually said were these words: 'I am sick, gentlemen, weary unto death, you will excuse me if I can't get up.'

The judges having left, Fabrizio wept freely once more, then asked himself: 'Am I a hypocrite? I fancy I never loved him.'

On that and the following days, Clelia was very unhappy. She summoned him several times, but hardly had the courage to speak a few words. On the morning of the fifth day following their first meeting, she told him that that evening she would come to the black marble chapel.

'I can address only a few words to you,' she said as she entered. She was trembling to the point where she had to lean for support on her maid. After sending her away at the entrance to the chapel: 'You're going to give me your word of honour,' she went on, in a barely intelligible voice, 'you're going to give me your word of honour that you will obey the duchess, and attempt to escape on the day she orders you to and in the manner she will indicate, or tomorrow morning I shall take refuge in a convent and I swear to you here that never again will I address a single word to you.'

Fabrizio remained mute.

'Promise,' said Clelia, with tears in her eyes and as if beside herself, 'otherwise we are talking together here for the last time. The life you have made for me is frightful, you're here because of me and each day may be the last one of your existence.' At that moment, Clelia was so weak that she was obliged to look for support from an enormous armchair that had been placed in the old days in the centre of the chapel, for the use of the princely prisoner. She was at the point of collapse.

'What must I promise?' said Fabrizio, looking downcast.

'You know.'

'I swear then to rush headlong and wittingly into a terrible calamity, and condemn myself to living far away from everything in the world I love.'

'Promise something precise.'

'I swear to obey the duchess, and to make my escape the day she wants me to and in the way she wants. And what will become of me once I'm far away from you?'

'Swear you will escape, whatever may happen.'

'What, have you decided to marry the Marchese Crescenzi as soon as I'm no longer here?'

'Dear God, can you believe that of me? . . . But swear, or my soul will never again be at peace.'

'Very well, I swear to escape from here on the day Signora Sanseverina orders me to, whatever may happen between now and then.'

His oath having been obtained, Clelia was so weak she was obliged to withdraw, after thanking Fabrizio.

'Everything was ready for my flight tomorrow morning,' she told him, 'had you insisted on staying. I would have been seeing you at this moment for the last time in my life, I had made a vow to the Madonna. Now, as soon as I am able to leave my room, I shall go and inspect the terrifying wall underneath the new stone in the balustrade.'

The next day, he found her pale to the point where it grieved him sorely. From the window of the aviary she told him: 'Let's not delude ourselves, dear friend. Because our affection is sinful, I don't doubt that some misfortune will befall us. You will be discovered when trying to escape, and lost for ever, if not something worse. All the same, human prudence has to have its due and it orders us to try anything. To get down the outside of the big tower you need a stout rope more than two hundred feet long. For all the pains I've been to since I learnt of the duchess's plan, I've only been able to get hold of ropes that together make barely fifty feet. By an order of the day from the governor, all the ropes to be found in the fortress have been burnt, and every evening they remove the ropes from the wells, which are so weak anyway that they often break bringing up their light load. But pray to God that he may forgive me, I am betraying my own father and working, unnatural daughter that I am, to cause him mortal hurt. Pray to God for me and if your life is saved, vow to devote every moment of it to his glory.

'Here is an idea I have had. A week from now I shall be leaving the citadel to attend the wedding of one of the Marchese Crescenzi's sisters. I shall return in the evening as is proper, but I shall do my very best not to return until very late, and perhaps Barbone won't dare inspect me too closely. The greatest ladies at court, and Signora Sanseverina for sure, will be present at the marchese's sister's wedding. In God's name, see that one of these ladies hands me a bundle of ropes, very tightly packed and not too big, as compact as possible. Though I were to risk death a thousand times over, I shall employ even the most dangerous means to get this bundle of ropes into the citadel, which is to disregard, alas, my duty! If my father gets to know, I shall never see you again. But whatever the fate that awaits me, I shall be happy within the limits of a sisterly affection if I can help to save you.'

That same evening, in their nocturnal communication by means of the lamp, Fabrizio gave the duchess notice of the unique opportunity there would be of getting a sufficient quantity of ropes into the citadel. But he begged her to keep it secret even from the count, which seemed bizarre. He's mad, thought the duchess, prison has changed him, he's taking the tragic view. The next day, a lead ball, hurled by the slinger, brought the prisoner news of the gravest possible danger: the person responsible for getting the ropes in, he was told, was positively and precisely saving his life. Fabrizio made haste to report this to Clelia. The lead ball also brought Fabrizio a very accurate plan of the wall on the western side down which he was to descend from the top of the big tower in the gap between the bastions. From which point it was then quite easy to make his escape, the ramparts being only twenty-three feet high and quite slackly guarded. On the back of the map was written, in a small, delicate hand, a splendid sonnet: a generous soul exhorted Fabrizio to make his escape and not to allow his soul to be debased and his body wasted by the eleven years of captivity he had still to endure.

At this point a necessary detail, which explains in part the courage the duchess was showing in counselling Fabrizio to make so very dangerous an escape, obliges us to break off from the account of this foolhardy undertaking for a moment.

Like all parties that are not in power, the Raversi party was not very united. The Cavaliere Riscara detested the prosecutor Rassi, whom he accused of having caused him to lose an important lawsuit in which, in point of fact, Riscara himself was in the wrong. Through Riscara, the prince received notice anonymously alerting him to the fact that Fabrizio's sentence had been sent on officially to the governor of the citadel. The Marchesa Raversi, that astute party leader, was exceedingly vexed by this false step, and at once gave notice of it to her friend the chief prosecutor. She found it quite easy to understand that he should want to get something from the minister Mosca, while Mosca was still in power. Rassi presented himself fearlessly at the palace, thinking that he would get off with a kicking. The prince could not do without a clever jurisconsult, and Rassi had had a judge and an advocate, the only men in the country who might have taken his place, banished as liberals.

The prince was beside himself, heaped abuse on him and advanced on him threateningly.

'Clerical absent-mindedness,' replied Rassi, quite unperturbed. 'The thing is prescribed by the law, it ought to have been done the day after Signor del Dongo was locked up in the citadel. The clerk's very zealous, he thought he'd overlooked it and made me sign the covering letter as a matter of form.'

'And you expect me to believe such barefaced lies?' cried the furious prince. 'You should rather say that you've sold out to that villainous Mosca, and that's why he gave you the cross. But dammit all, you're not going to get away with a beating. I shall have you tried, I shall dismiss you with ignominy.'

'I defy you to have me tried!' replied Rassi confidently. He knew this was a sure way of calming the prince down. 'The law is on my side and you don't have a second Rassi to be able to get round it. You won't dismiss me because there are times when your character is severe. You then thirst for blood, yet at the same time are anxious to preserve the respect of reasonable Italians. That respect is a *sine qua non* of your ambition. In short, you'll call me back the first time your character forces you to show severity, and as usual I shall procure for you a sentence that's all in order and will also satisfy your passions, handed down by timid, fairly honourable judges. Find another man in your States who's as useful as I am!'

Having said which, Rassi fled. He had got off with one firmly applied blow from a ruler and five or six kicks. On leaving the palace, he set off for his estate in Riva. He was a little afraid of being stabbed in the first flush of the prince's anger, but he did not doubt either that within a fortnight a messenger would summon him back to the capital. He used the time he spent in the country to organize a secure channel of communication with Count Mosca. He was quite besotted with the title of baron, and fancied that the prince rated that once sublime thing, nobility, too highly ever to confer it on him. Whereas the count, very proud of his own birth, respected only the nobility proved by patents from before 1400.

The prosecutor was not mistaken in his predictions. He had been on his estate for barely a week when a friend of the prince, who had come there by chance, advised him to return to Parma without delay. The prince received him with a laugh, then adopted a very serious expression and made him swear on the Gospel that he would keep what he was about to confide in him to himself. Rassi swore with great solemnity and the prince, his eyes blazing with hatred, exclaimed that he would never be master in his own house as long as Fabrizio del Dongo remained alive.

'I can neither expel the duchess nor endure her presence,' he added. 'Her looks defy me and stop me from living.'

After letting the prince explain himself at great length, Rassi, feigning extreme embarrassment, finally exclaimed: 'Your Highness will be obeyed, of course, but it's a horribly difficult business. Condemning a del Dongo to death for the murder of a Giletti goes against all probability. It's an astonishing feat as it is to have got twelve years in the citadel out of it. What's more, I suspect the duchess of having unearthed three of the peasants who were working on the excavations at Sanguigna, and who happened to be out of the trench at the time when that brigand Giletti attacked del Dongo.'

'And where are these witnesses?' asked the prince in irritation.

'Hidden in Piedmont, I imagine. It would take a conspiracy against Your Highness's life . . .'

'That method has its dangers,' said the prince, 'it puts the idea into people's minds.'

'Even so,' said Rassi, with feigned innocence, 'that's my entire official arsenal.'

'There remains poison . . .'

'But who will administer it? That imbecile Conti?'

'From what they say, it wouldn't be the first time.'

'We'd need to get him worked up,' Rassi went on. 'In any case, when he dispatched the captain, he wasn't even thirty

years old, he was in love and infinitely less pusillanimous than
he is today. Everything must yield to reasons of State of course.
But taken by surprise as I am, the only man I can think of here
and now to carry out the sovereign's orders is Barbone, the
clerk at the prison, who Monsignor del Dongo sent flying the
day he arrived.'

The prince having once been put at his ease, the conversation
was interminable. He ended it by granting his prosecutor a
month's delay. Rassi wanted two. The next day he received a
secret sweetener of a thousand sequins. For three days he
thought it over. On the fourth, he came back to his argument,
which seemed self-evident: only Count Mosca will have the
heart to stick to his word, because in making me a baron he's
not giving me anything he values; *secundo*, by warning him,
I'm probably saving myself from a crime for which I've been
more or less paid in advance; *tertio*, I shall be avenging the
first humiliating blows the Cavaliere Rassi has received. The
following night, he conveyed the whole of his conversation with
the prince to Count Mosca.

The count was paying court secretly to the duchess. True, he
still saw her at her house only once or twice a week, but nearly
every week, and whenever he was able to make an opportunity
to talk about Fabrizio, the duchess would come, accompanied
by Chekina, late in the evening, to spend a few moments in the
count's garden. She was able to deceive even her coachman,
who was devoted to her and believed she was visiting at a house
next door.

As may be imagined, the prosecutor having entrusted his
terrible secret to him, the count at once gave the duchess the
signal agreed on. Although it was the middle of the night, she
got Chekina to ask him to come round to her that instant. The
count, overjoyed as a lover by this seeming intimacy, hesitated,
however, to tell the duchess everything. He was afraid of seeing
her become distraught with grief.

Having searched for half-words with which to soften the
fateful announcement, he ended all the same by telling her
everything. It was not within his power to keep a secret that
she had asked him for. In the past nine months, her extreme

unhappiness had had a great influence on that ardent soul, had strengthened it, and the duchess did not give way to tears or lamentations.

The following evening she gave Fabrizio the signal indicating great danger.

'The castle has caught fire.'

He replied correctly.

'Were my books burnt?'

The same night she was fortunate enough to get a letter to him in a lead ball. It was one week after this that the wedding took place of the Marchese Crescenzi's sister, at which the duchess was guilty of an act of very great rashness, of which we shall give an account in its rightful place.

CHAPTER 21

It was now almost a year since, in this period of her misfortunes, the duchess had had a singular encounter. One day when she was suffering from the *luna*, as it is known in those parts, she had gone without warning, towards evening, to her country house at Sacca, situated beyond Colorno, on the hill that overlooks the Po. She took pleasure in improving this estate. She loved the vast forest that crowns the hill and abuts the house. She busied herself having paths made through it in picturesque directions.

'You'll have yourself abducted by brigands, my lovely duchess,' the prince said to her one day. 'It's not possible that a forest where they know you go walking should remain deserted.' The prince cast a glance at the count, whose jealousy he aspired to excite.

'I'm not afraid, Most Serene Highness,' replied the duchess, ingenuously, 'when I walk in my woods. I'm reassured by this thought: I've not done anyone any harm, who could hate me?' The remark was thought daring, it recalled the insults proffered by the country's liberals, who were very insolent people.

On the day of the promenade of which we are speaking, the prince's remark came back into the duchess's mind when she observed a very badly dressed man who was following her at a distance through the wood. At an unexpected detour which the duchess made while continuing her walk, the stranger found himself so close to her that she took fright. Her first impulse was to call her gamekeeper, whom she had left a thousand paces away, in the parterre of flowers close to the house. The stranger had the time to approach her and throw himself at her feet. He was young, a very good-looking man, but horribly ragged. His clothes had tears in them a foot long, but his eyes radiated the fire of an ardent soul.

'I am under sentence of death, I am the doctor Ferrante Palla, I'm dying of hunger, as are my five children.'

The duchess had remarked that he was horribly thin. But his eyes were so beautiful and filled with so tender an exaltation that they banished all thought of crime. Palagi,[1] she thought, could well have given such eyes to his St John in the desert that he has just placed in the cathedral. The thought of St John had been prompted by Ferrante's incredible thinness. The duchess gave him three sequins that she had in her purse, apologizing for offering him so little because she had just settled an account with her gardener. Ferrante thanked her effusively. 'Alas,' he said, 'I lived in towns once upon a time, I saw fashionable women. Since being sentenced to death for fulfilling my duties as a citizen, I live in the woods, and I was following you, not to ask for alms or to rob you, but like a savage enthralled by an angelic beauty. It's such a long time since I saw two beautiful white hands!'

'But get up,' said the duchess, for he had remained kneeling.

'Allow me to remain like this,' said Ferrante. 'This position proves to me that I'm not at present busy stealing, and that eases my mind. For you must know that I've been stealing in order to live since they stopped me from exercising my profession. But at this moment I am just a simple mortal worshipping sublime beauty.' The duchess realized that he was a little bit mad, but she was not afraid. She could see from the man's eyes that he had an ardent, humane soul and she did not in any case dislike people of an unusual appearance.

'I'm a doctor therefore, and I was paying court to the wife of Sarasine, the apothecary in Parma. He caught us and threw her out, along with three children that he suspected with good reason were mine and not his. I have had two since. The mother and the five children are living in the most abject poverty, inside a cabin of sorts built by my own hands a league from here in the woods. Because I need to protect myself from the police and the poor woman refuses to separate from me. I was sentenced to death and quite rightly, I was conspiring. I execrate the prince, who is a tyrant. I didn't flee, for want of money. My misfortunes have grown very much worse and I should have killed myself a thousand times over. I no longer love the unfortunate woman who gave me the five children and ruined herself for my sake. I love someone else. But if I kill myself, the five children and their mother will literally die of hunger.' The man had the ring of sincerity.

'But how do you survive?' asked the duchess, much moved.

'The children's mother spins. The oldest girl gets her board at the farm of some liberal or other, where she watches over the sheep. As for me, I hold people up along the road from Piacenza to Genoa.'

'How do you reconcile robbery with your liberal principles?'

'I keep a note of the people I rob, and if ever I have anything, I shall give them back the sums I've stolen. I adjudge that a tribune of the people such as myself is performing a task which, on account of the danger, is worth a good hundred francs a month. So I'm very careful not to take more than twelve hundred francs a year. Actually, that's wrong, I steal a small amount over and above that, because that way I can meet the costs of getting my works printed.'

'What works?'

'. . . *will she ever have a room and a budget?*'

'What,' said the duchess, in astonishment, 'that's you, signore, one of the greatest poets of the century, the famous Ferrante Palla?'

'Famous perhaps, but very unfortunate, that's for sure.'

'And a man with your talent, signore, is obliged to steal in order to live!'

'It's for that reason that I have some talent perhaps. Up until now, all our authors who have become known were people paid by the government or by the religion they were trying to undermine. I, *primo*, risk my life; *secundo*, signora, imagine the disturbing thoughts I have when I go out stealing! Am I in the right? I ask myself. Does the position of tribune perform a service truly worth a hundred francs a month? I have two shirts, the coat that you see, a few poor weapons and I'm sure to finish by the rope. I dare to think I'm disinterested. I would be happy were it not for the fatal love which lets me find only unhappiness with the mother of my children. Poverty weighs on me, it's ugly. I love fine clothes, white hands . . .'

He looked at those of the duchess in such a way that she took fright.

'Goodbye, signore,' she said. 'Is there anything I might do for you in Parma?'

'Consider this question sometimes. His role is to awaken hearts and prevent them from going to sleep in that false, purely material happiness that monarchies provide. Is the service he renders his fellow citizens worth a hundred francs a month? My misfortune is to love,' he said, with a very gentle expression, 'and for almost two years my soul has been preoccupied only with you, but up until now I had seen you without making you afraid.' And he took to his heels with a prodigious rapidity which astonished the duchess and reasssured her. The policemen would find it hard to catch up with him, she thought. He's crazy indeed.

'He's crazy,' her servants told her. 'We've all known for a long time that the poor man is in love with the signora. When the signora is here, we see him wandering in the highest parts of the woods, and as soon as the signora has gone, he doesn't fail to come and sit in the very places where she has paused. Quaintly, he picks up the flowers that may have dropped from her spray and keeps them for a long time, attached to his shabby hat.'

'And you've never spoken of this foolishness,' said the duchess, in a tone of reproach almost.

'We were afraid the signora might tell Count Mosca. Poor Ferrante's such a good fellow, he's never hurt a soul, and because he loves our Napoleon, he was sentenced to death.'

She said not a word to the minister about this encounter, and because it was the first secret she had kept from him in four years, she was obliged ten times to stop short in the middle of a sentence. She returned to Sacca with money. Ferrante did not show himself. She returned a fortnight later. Ferrante, after following her for some time, capering about in the woods a hundred paces away, swooped down on her with the rapidity of a hawk, and threw himself at her feet as on the first occasion.

'Where were you two weeks ago?'

'In the mountains beyond Novi, to rob the muleteers coming back from Milan where they'd been selling oil.'

'Take this purse.'

Ferrante opened the purse, took out a sequin which he kissed and put inside his shirt, then handed it back.

'You're giving me the purse back, yet you're a robber!'

'Of course. The rule I've set myself is never to have more than a hundred francs. Well at the moment the mother of my children has eighty francs and I have twenty-five, I'm five francs to the bad and if they hanged me at this moment I'd feel remorse. I took the sequin because it comes from you and because I love you.'

The intonation of these very simple words was perfect. He really is in love, the duchess told herself.

That day he appeared altogether at a loss. He said that there were people in Parma who owed him six hundred francs, and that with that sum he would repair his cabin where his poor children were now catching cold.

'But I will advance you the six hundred francs,' said the duchess, greatly moved.

'But could the opposition party not then defame me, me a public man, and say that I'm selling myself?'

The duchess in her compassion offered him a hiding-place in Parma if he were willing to swear that for the time being he would not exercise his magistracy in the town and above all not carry out any of the death sentences that he said he had *in petto*.

'And if they hang me as a result of my rashness,' said Ferrante solemnly, 'all those scoundrels who do the people so much harm will survive for many years, and whose fault will that be? What will my father say when he receives me up above?'

The duchess spoke to him at length about his young children, who might fall mortally sick because of the damp. He ended by accepting the offer of the hiding-place in Parma.

Duke Sanseverina, on the one half-day he had spent in Parma since his marriage, had shown the duchess a very peculiar hiding-place that exists at the southern corner of the palazzo of that name. The wall of the façade, which dates from the Middle Ages, is eight feet thick. It has been hollowed out and there inside is a hiding-place twenty feet high but only two feet across. Right beside it is the much-admired reservoir mentioned by every traveller, the famous handiwork of the twelfth century built during the siege of Parma by the Emperor Sigismondo, and later incorporated within the precincts of the Palazzo Sanseverina.

This hiding-place is entered by moving an enormous stone on an iron axle situated near the centre of the slab. The duchess was so deeply affected by Ferrante's madness and the fate of his children, for whom he had stubbornly refused any gift of value, that she gave him permission to make use of this hiding-place for some time to come. She saw him again a month later, still in the Sacca woods, and because on that particular day he was a little calmer, he recited one of his sonnets to her, which seemed to her to be the equal of or superior to the finest things written in Italy in the last two centuries. Ferrante obtained several rendezvous. But his love grew in intensity, became importunate, and the duchess realized that this passion was following the laws of every love affair where it is possible to conceive of a glimmer of hope. She sent him off into the woods and forbade him to address her. He obeyed instantly with perfect good grace. Things had reached this point when Fabrizio was arrested. Three days later, at nightfall, a Capuchin friar presented himself at the gate of the Palazzo Sanseverina. He had, he said, an important secret to convey to the mistress of the house. She was so unhappy that she made him enter. It was Ferrante. 'We have a fresh wickedness here of which the people's tribune must take cognizance,' said the besotted lover. 'Acting on the other hand as a mere private individual,' he added, 'I can offer the Signora Duchess Sanseverina only my life, which I now bring to her.'

This very genuine devotion on the part of a robber and a madman touched the duchess keenly. She spoke for a long

time with this man, who passed for being the greatest poet
in the north of Italy, and wept a great deal. Here is a man
who understands my heart, she told herself. The next day he
reappeared at the Ave Maria,[2] disguised as a servant and dressed
in livery.

'I have not been out of Parma. I heard speak of a horror that
my lips will not repeat. But here I am. Think of what you are
rejecting, signora! The person you see is not a court puppet,
but a man!' He was on his knees as he uttered these words,
with an expression emphasizing their worth. 'Yesterday I told
myself,' he added, 'she wept in my presence, so she is a little
less unhappy.'

'But, signore, think of the dangers all around you, you will
be arrested in this town!'

'The tribune will say: "Signora, what is life when duty
speaks?" The unfortunate man, who has the sorrow of no
longer feeling any passion for virtue since he was scorched by
love, will add: "Signora duchess, Fabrizio, a man of courage,
is perhaps about to perish, do not reject another man of courage
who offers himself to you. Here is a body of iron and a soul
that fears nothing in the world except your displeasure."'

'If you speak to me again of your feelings, I shall close my
door to you for good.'

The duchess had indeed had the idea, that evening, of
announcing to Ferrante that she would make a small allowance
to his children, but she was afraid he might only go and kill
himself.

Hardly had he gone before, filled with morbid presentiments,
she told herself: I too may die, and would to God it were so,
and soon, if I could find a man worthy of the name to whom I
could entrust my poor Fabrizio.

The duchess was seized by an idea. She took a piece of paper
and acknowledged, in a document into which she inserted the
few legal terms that she knew, that she had received from Sig.
Ferrante Palla the sum of twenty-five thousand francs, on the
express condition that she should pay each year a life annuity
of one thousand five hundred francs to Signora Sarasine and
her five children. The duchess added: in addition, I bequeath

an annuity of three hundred francs to each of her five children, on condition that Ferrante Palla attend on my nephew Fabrizio as a doctor and is a brother to him. I ask that he do this. She signed it, antedated it by a year and put the piece of paper away.

Two days later, Ferrante reappeared. It was at the moment when the whole town was astir with the rumour of Fabrizio's imminent execution. Would that sad ceremony take place in the citadel or under the trees on the public promenade? Several men of the people went and walked that evening in front of the gateway to the citadel, to try to see whether they were erecting a scaffold. The spectacle had affected Ferrante. He found the duchess bathed in tears and in no state to talk. She waved a hand at him and pointed to a chair. Ferrante, disguised that day as a Capuchin friar, was magnificent. Instead of sitting down he fell to his knees and prayed devoutly to God in a low voice. In a moment when the duchess appeared a little calmer, without shifting his position, he broke off from his prayer for an instant to say these words: 'Once more he offers his life.'

'Reflect on what you are saying,' exclaimed the duchess, with that haggard gaze which, after sobs, announces that anger is getting the better of compassion.

'He offers his life to be an obstacle to the fate of Fabrizio, or else to avenge him.'

'There are circumstances,' answered the duchess, 'in which I might accept the sacrifice of your life.'

She looked hard at him. His eyes flashed with joy. He stood quickly up and held out his arms to the sky. The duchess went to fetch herself a sheet of paper hidden in the secret drawer of a big walnut-wood cupboard. 'Read it,' she told Ferrante. It was the gift in favour of his children of which we have spoken.

Tears and sobs prevented Ferrante from reading to the end. He fell to his knees.

'Give me back that paper,' said the duchess, and burnt it in front of him with the candle. 'My name mustn't appear,' she added, 'if you're caught and executed, for your life is at stake.'

'My joy is to die in doing harm to a tyrant. A far greater joy to die for you. That being settled and properly understood, be so good as not to mention the detail of money again, I would find it hurtful, as though you were doubting me.'

'If you are compromised, I too may be,' the duchess returned, 'and Fabrizio after me. It's for that reason and not because I doubt your bravery that I require that the man who has pierced me to the heart be poisoned and not killed. For the same reason, which is important to me, I order you to do everything in your power to save yourself.'

'I will carry it out faithfully, to the letter and prudently. I foresee, signora duchess, that my vengeance will be mixed in with yours. Even were it otherwise, I would still obey faithfully, to the letter and prudently. I may not succeed but I shall employ all my strength as a man.'

'It involves poisoning Fabrizio's murderer.'

'I had guessed as much, and in the twenty-seven months that I've been leading this abominable life as a vagrant, I have often dreamt of such an action on my own behalf.'

'If I'm discovered and condemned as an accomplice,' the duchess continued, proudly, 'I don't want anyone to be able to impute that I seduced you. I order you not to try to see me before the time comes to take our revenge. The thing is not to put him to death before I have given you the signal. At this moment, for example, his death would be fatal for me rather than useful. His death should probably not happen for several more months, but it will happen. I demand that he die by poison, and I would prefer to let him live rather than see him shot. For considerations I am unwilling to spell out, I demand that your own life be saved.'

Ferrante was thrilled by the tone of authority the duchess had taken with him. His eyes shone with a deep joy. As we have said, he was horribly thin, but one could see that he had been very handsome in his early days, and he believed he still was what he had once been. Am I mad, he asked himself, or does the duchess want one day, once I have given her proof of my devotion, to make me the happiest of men? And indeed, why not? Am I not as good as that puppet of a Count Mosca, who on this occasion has been unable to do anything for her, not even get Monsignor Fabrizio to escape?

'I may wish for his death as from tomorrow,' the duchess continued, with the same air of authority. 'You know the huge reservoir which is at the corner of the palazzo, right next to the hiding-place you have sometimes occupied. There's a secret means of making all that water flow into the street. Well, that will be the signal for my vengeance! You'll see, if you're in Parma, or will hear people say, if you're living in the woods, that the big reservoir at the Palazzo Sanseverina has burst. Act straightaway, but by poison, and above all take as few chances with your life as possible. No one must know that I've had a hand in this affair.'

'Words are no use,' replied Ferrante, with ill-contained enthusiasm. 'I've already fixed on the means I shall employ. The life of that man becomes more hateful to me than it was, since I shan't dare to see you again while he remains alive. I shall wait for the signal of the burst reservoir in the street.' He bowed abruptly and left. The duchess watched him go.

Once he was in the next room, she called him back.

'Ferrante, you sublime man!' she cried.

He returned, as if impatient at being detained. His face was magnificent at that moment.

'What about your children?'

'Signora, they will be richer than I am. You will perhaps grant them some small allowance.'

'Here,' said the duchess, handing him a large olive-wood needlework box of sorts, 'here are all the diamonds I have left. They are worth fifty thousand francs.'

'Oh, signora, you are humiliating me!' said Ferrante, with a horror-stricken gesture; and his facial expression changed totally.

'I shall not see you again before the deed is done. Take them, I want you to,' added the duchess with a haughty expression that disconcerted Ferrante. He put the box in his pocket and left.

He had closed the door after him. Again the duchess called him back. He returned looking anxious. The duchess was standing in the middle of the room. She threw herself into his arms. After a moment, Ferrante all but fainted with happiness. The duchess freed herself from his embraces and motioned to the door with her eyes.

That is the one man who has understood me, she told herself. That is how Fabrizio would have acted, had he been able to hear me.

There were two things in the duchess's character: she continued to want what she had once wanted; she never had any second thoughts about what had been decided. She would quote in this connection a remark of her first husband's, the amiable General Pietranera: 'What insolence towards myself!' he would say. 'Why would I think I was cleverer today than when I took that decision?'

From this moment on, a sort of gaiety reappeared in the duchess's character. Before the fateful resolution, at each step her mind took, at each new thing that she saw, she had a sense of her inferiority vis-à-vis the prince, of her weakness and his deceitfulness. The prince, as she saw it, had acted like a coward and had deceived her, and Count Mosca, like the complete courtier that he was, had, if only innocently, backed the prince up. As soon as her vengeance was decided on, she felt her own strength; each step she took in her own mind made her happy. I am ready to believe that the immoral happiness that they get from taking their revenge in Italy stems from the strength of that people's imagination. In other countries, people do not forgive, strictly speaking, they forget.

The duchess saw Ferrante again only towards the final days of Fabrizio's imprisonment. As the reader may perhaps have guessed, he it was who had furnished the idea of an escape. There stood in the woods, two leagues from Sacca, a medieval tower, half in ruins, more than a hundred feet high. Before talking for a second time with the duchess about an escape, Ferrante begged her to send Lodovico, with some trustworthy men, to arrange a series of ladders next to this tower. In the duchess's presence, he climbed it by the ladders and descended down a simple knotted rope. He repeated the experiment three times, then once again went through his plan. A week later, Lodovico too tried descending the old tower by a knotted rope. It was then that the duchess passed the idea on to Fabrizio.

In the final days preceding the attempt, which might lead to the prisoner's death, and in more than one fashion, the duchess did not know a moment's repose save when she had Ferrante at her side. The courage of this man sparked her own. But it can well be imagined that she needed to hide this singular association from the count. She was afraid, not that he might protest, but that she might be upset by his objections, which would have added to her anxiety. What, to take for one's close adviser a madman recognized as such, and under a death sentence! And, added the duchess, talking to herself, a man who might, subsequently, do such strange things! Ferrante found himself in the duchess's salon at the moment when the count came to let her know about the conversation the prince had had with Rassi. And once the count had left, she had her work cut out preventing Ferrante from going off there and then to carry out the frightful design!

'Now I am strong!' the madman cried. 'I no longer doubt that the deed is lawful!'

'But, in the moment of anger that will inevitably follow, Fabrizio could be put to death!'

'But then he'd be spared the dangers of the descent. It's possible, easy even,' he added. 'But the young man lacks experience.'

The Marchese Crescenzi's sister's wedding was celebrated and it was at the festivities given for the occasion that the duchess met Clelia, and was able to talk to her without arousing the suspicions of the prying eyes of high society. The duchess herself handed Clelia the bundle of ropes in the garden, where the ladies had gone for a momentary breath of air. The ropes, made with the greatest care, half of silk and half of hemp, and knotted, were very thin and quite flexible. Lodovico had tested them for strength and throughout their length they could sustain without breaking a weight of eight quintals. They had been compressed in such a way as to form several bundles in the shape of a quarto volume. Clelia took possession of them and promised the duchess that all that was humanly possible would be achieved to get these bundles to the Farnese Tower.

'But I fear the timidity of your character. And why should

a stranger excite such interest?' the duchess went on politely.

'Signor del Dongo is unfortunate, and *I promise you that through me he will be saved*!'

But the duchess was only half relying on the presence of mind of a young person of twenty and had taken other precautions, which she was very careful not to share with the governor's daughter. As it was natural to assume, the governor was present at the festivities to celebrate the marriage of the Marchese Crescenzi's sister. The duchess told herself that, if she had him given some powerful narcotic, it might be thought at the outset that he was having an apoplectic fit, and then, instead of putting him into his carriage to take him back to the citadel, they might, if they were clever, get them to accept the idea of employing a litter, which would just happen to be found in the house where the festivities were taking place. There would also be found men of intelligence, dressed as workmen hired for the festivities, who, in the general disturbance, would obligingly offer to carry the sick man all the way up to his elevated palazzo. These men, directed by Lodovico, would be carrying a considerable quantity of ropes, neatly hidden underneath their coats. It can be seen that the duchess's mind had truly gone astray since she had been thinking seriously about Fabrizio's escape. The peril facing that beloved being was too great for her soul, and furthermore had been going on for too long. So many precautions did she take, she almost caused the escape to fail, as we are about to see. Everything was carried out as she had planned, with the one difference that the narcotic produced too powerful an effect. Everyone believed, even the medical experts, that the general had had an apoplectic fit.

Fortunately, Clelia, who was in despair, in no way suspected the duchess's very criminal enterprise. Such was the chaos at the moment when the litter on which the half-dead general was enclosed entered the citadel that Lodovico and his men passed in without being challenged. They were searched, as a formality, only at the bridge of the slave. Once they had transported the general as far as his bed, they were taken to the pantry, where the servants treated them very generously. But after the meal, which didn't end until close to morning, it was explained to them that prison custom required that, for the remainder of the night, they be locked up in the palazzo's lower rooms. The next morning at first light they would be set free by the governor's lieutenant.

The men had found a means of letting Lodovico have the ropes they were carrying, but Lodovico had great difficulty in attracting Clelia's attention for a moment. Finally, just as she was going from one room into another, he got her to see that he had set down the bundles of ropes in the unlit corner of one of the reception rooms on the first floor. Clelia was greatly struck by this strange circumstance. She at once developed awful suspicions.

'Who are you?' she asked Lodovico.

And, on the latter's very ambiguous response, she added: 'I ought to have you arrested. You or your men have poisoned my father! Confess this instant the nature of the poison you used, so that the doctor in the citadel can administer the appropriate remedies. Confess this instant, or else you and your accomplices will never leave this citadel!'

'The signorina is wrong to be alarmed,' replied Lodovico, with perfect good grace and courtesy. 'There's no question of poison. We were unwise enough to administer a dose of laudanum to the general, and it appears that the servant charged with the crime put a few drops too many into the glass. We shall be eternally remorseful. But the signorina can believe that, thank the Lord, there's no danger of any kind. The signor governor must be treated for having taken, by mistake, too strong a dose of laudanum. But, I have the honour to repeat to the signorina, the lackey charged with the crime was not using real poisons, unlike Barbone, when he sought to poison Monsignor Fabrizio. We weren't aiming to avenge the danger Monsignor Fabrizio incurred. The clumsy lackey was entrusted only with a phial containing laudanum, that I swear to the signorina! But it must be understood that, were I to be interrogated officially, I'd deny everything.

'Moreover, if the signorina mentions laudanum or poison to anyone at all, even to the excellent Don Cesare, then Fabrizio will die by the signorina's own hand. She would be making all plans for escape impossible. And the signorina knows better than I do that it isn't with mere laudanum that they want to poison monsignore. She knows also that someone has conceded a delay of one month for the crime, and that it's already more than a week since the fateful order was received. So, if she has me arrested, or if she so much as utters a word to Don Cesare or to anyone else, she is delaying all our efforts for much more than a month, and I'm correct in saying that she's killing Monsignor Fabrizio by her own hand.'

Clelia was alarmed by how strangely calm Lodovico was. So, she told herself, here I am holding an orderly dialogue with my father's poisoner, who uses such polite turns of phrase to talk with me. And it's love that has led me into all these crimes! . . .

Remorse left her with barely the strength to speak. She told Lodovico: 'I'm going to lock you in this room. I'm going to run and tell the doctor that only laudanum is involved. But, good God, how can I tell him that I learnt that myself? I shall come back then and release you.

'But,' said Clelia, coming running back from near the door, 'did Fabrizio know anything about the laudanum?'

'Good God no, signorina, he would never have agreed. And anyway, what would have been the point of confiding in him for no reason? We are acting with the strictest prudence. It's a question of saving monsignore's life, who'll be poisoned within the next three weeks. The order has been given by someone who doesn't normally find anything standing in the way of his wishes. And so as not to hide anything from the signorina, they claim it's the terrible prosecutor Rassi who received the commission.'

Clelia fled appalled. So much did she count on the perfect probity of Don Cesare, that, taking certain precautions, she ventured to tell him that the general had been given laudanum and nothing more. Without answering, without asking questions, Don Cesare hurried to the doctor.

Clelia returned to the salon, where she had locked Lodovico in with the intention of questioning him further about the laudanum. She did not find him. He had managed to escape. She saw on the table a purse filled with sequins, and a small box containing various kinds of poison. The sight of the poisons made her shudder. Who's to say, she thought, whether they gave only laudanum to my father, and whether the duchess didn't want to get her revenge for Barbone's attempt?

'Great heaven,' she cried, 'here I am in contact with my father's poisoners! And I'm letting them escape! Perhaps that man would have confessed to something other than laudanum if he'd been put to the question!'

Clelia at once fell to her knees, burst into tears and prayed fervently to the Madonna.

Meanwhile, the citadel doctor, greatly surprised by the notice he received from Don Cesare, according to which he had only laudanum to worry about, applied the appropriate remedies, which soon caused the more disquieting symptoms to vanish. The general started to come round as it was beginning to get light. His first act on returning to consciousness was to heap abuse on the colonel who was second-in-command in the citadel, who had thought to give the simplest imaginable orders while the general was unconscious.

The governor then flew into a great rage against a kitchen girl who, when bringing him some broth, thought to utter the word *apoplexy*. 'Am I of an age to be apoplectic?' he cried. 'Only my bitterest enemies could take pleasure in spreading rumours of that sort. Anyway, have I been bled, for calumny itself to dare to talk about apoplexy?'

Fabrizio, completely taken up with the preparations for his escape, could not have imagined the strange rumours that had filled the citadel at the moment when the governor was brought back in half dead. At first he had some idea that his sentence had been changed and that they had come to put him to death. Finding next that no one appeared in his room, he thought that Clelia had been betrayed, that on her return to the fortress they had taken from her the ropes she had probably been bringing back, and that in short his plans of escape were henceforth impossible. The next day, at first light, he saw a man unknown to him enter his room who, without saying a word, set down a basket of fruit. Under the fruit, the following letter was concealed:

'Filled with the keenest remorse at what has been done, not, thank heaven, with my consent, but as a consequence of an idea that I had, I have made a vow to the Blessed Virgin that if, through the effects of her holy intercession, my father is saved, I shall never raise any objection to his orders. I shall marry the marchese as soon as I am requested to do so by him, and I shall never see you again. At the same time, I believe it is my duty to finish off what has been started. Next Sunday, on my return from Mass, to which you will be taken at my request (remember to prepare your soul, you may kill yourself in your hazardous enterprise); on my return from Mass, as I say, delay returning to your room for as long as possible. There, you will find what is necessary for the enterprise you are contemplating. If you perish, my soul will be desolate! Will you be able to accuse me of having contributed to your death? Has the duchess herself not repeated to me several times that the Raversi faction is winning the battle? They are seeking to bind the prince by an act of cruelty that will separate him for ever from Count Mosca. The duchess, bursting into tears, swore that this is the one recourse remaining. You will perish if you do not make the attempt. I can no longer look at you, I have vowed not to. But if on Sunday, towards evening, you see me dressed entirely in black, at the usual window, it will be the signal that the following night, everything will have been arranged in so far as my feeble means allow. After eleven o'clock, perhaps not until midnight or one o'clock, a small lamp will appear at my window; that will be the moment of decision. Recommend yourself to your patron saint, quickly put on the priest's clothing you have been provided with and set off.

'Farewell, Fabrizio, I shall be praying, and shedding the most bitter tears, you may believe, while you are running such very great risks. If you perish, I shall not survive you. Great God, what am I saying! But if you succeed, I shall never see you again. On Sunday, after Mass, you will find in your prison money, poisons, ropes, sent by that terrible woman who loves you passionately, and who repeated to me no fewer than three times that this was the course that has to be taken. May God and the Blessed Madonna keep you safe!'

As a gaoler Fabio Conti was forever anxious, forever un-happy, forever imagining one or other of his prisoners escaping. He was abhorred by everyone in the citadel. But misfortune inspiring the same resolutions in every man, the poor prisoners, even those who were chained up in cells three feet high, three feet wide and eight feet long, in which they could neither stand upright nor sit, all the prisoners, even these ones, as I say, had the idea of getting a Te Deum sung at their expense when they learnt that the governor was out of danger. Two or three of these unfortunates wrote sonnets in honour of Fabio Conti, such was the effect on these men of their ill-fortune! May whoever faults them for that be led by their destiny to spend a year in a cell three feet high, with eight ounces of bread a day and *fasting* on Fridays.

Clelia, who left her father's room only to go and pray in the chapel, said that the governor had decided that the thanksgiving would take place only on the Sunday. On that Sunday morning, Fabrizio attended Mass and the Te Deum. In the evening there were fireworks, and in the lower rooms of the castle they distrib-uted among the soldiery four times the quantity of wine sanc-tioned by the governor. An unknown hand had even sent several barrels of brandy, which the soldiers stove in. The generosity of the soldiers who had become drunk would not allow that the five soldiers who were on guard duty around the palace should lose out by their position. As they arrived in their sentry-boxes, a trusted servant gave them wine, and it is not known by whose hand those who were placed on sentry-go at midnight and for the remainder of the night also received a glass of brandy, and each time the bottle was left behind near the sentry-box (as was proved at the trial which followed).

The disruption lasted for longer than Clelia had thought, and it was nearly one o'clock by the time Fabrizio, who more than a week earlier had sawn through two bars of his window – the one that did not overlook the aviary – began to dismantle the screen. He was working almost above the heads of the sentries guarding the governor's palazzo, but they heard nothing. He had made only a few more knots in the huge rope needed for descending the terrifying height of a hundred and eighty feet.

He arranged the rope in a bandolier around his torso. It was a considerable hindrance, such was its volume. The knots prevented it from being tightly wound, and it stuck out more than eighteen inches from his body. This is the major obstacle, Fabrizio told himself.

Having arranged the rope as best he could, Fabrizio took up the one he was relying on to descend the thirty-five feet that separated his window from the esplanade where the governor's palazzo was. But since, however drunk the sentries might be, he could not even so descend right above their heads, he left, as we have said, by the second window of his room, the one that looked out over the roof of an enormous guardhouse of sorts. On a sick man's whim, as soon as General Fabio Conti was able to speak, he had had two hundred soldiers taken up into this old guardhouse, abandoned for the last hundred years. He said that after having poisoned him, they wanted to murder him in his bed, and these two hundred men were to guard him. The effect that this unforeseen measure produced on Clelia's emotions may be imagined. That pious girl was well aware of the extent to which she was betraying her father, and a father who had just been all but poisoned for the sake of a prisoner whom she loved. She almost saw in the unforeseen arrival of these two hundred men a decree of Providence that forbade her to go any further and give Fabrizio back his freedom.

But everyone in Parma was talking about the prisoner's imminent death. They had even got on to this unhappy topic at the festivities given on the occasion of the marriage of Signora Giulia Crescenzi. Since if, for some such trifle as a clumsy sword-thrust given to an actor, a man of Fabrizio's birth, and with the protection of the first minister, had not been set free after nine months in prison, then it was because the affair involved politics. In which case, no point concerning yourself with him any longer. If it did not suit the authorities to put him to death in a public place, he would soon die from some illness. A locksmith who had been sent for to General Fabio Conti's palazzo spoke of Fabrizio as of a prisoner who had been dispatched long since, but whose death had been kept quiet for political reasons. This man's story decided Clelia.

CHAPTER 22

During the day, Fabrizio was assailed by a number of serious and unpleasant thoughts, but as he heard the hours sounding that brought him closer to the moment for action, he felt cheerful and in good heart. The duchess had written that the fresh air would take him by surprise and that barely out of his prison he would find it impossible to walk. In which event, it would be better to run the risk of being recaptured than to descend a one-hundred-and-eighty-feet wall in a hurry. If that misfortune befalls me, Fabrizio said, I shall lie down against the parapet, sleep for an hour, then start again. Because I swore an oath to Clelia, I would rather fall from on top of a rampart, however high it might be, than be forever wondering about the taste of the bread I'm eating. What terrible agonies you must go through before the end, when you're dying from poison! Fabio Conti won't stand on ceremony, he'll have me given the arsenic they use to kill the rats in the citadel.

Around midnight, one of those thick white mists that the Po sometimes throws over its banks extended first of all over the town and then reached to the esplanade and bastions in the middle of which there rises the great tower of the citadel. Fabrizio thought he could see that from the parapet of the platform you could no longer make out the small acacias that surrounded the gardens established by the soldiers at the foot of the one-hundred-and-eighty-feet wall. Excellent, he thought.

Shortly after it had sounded half past midnight, the signal from the little lamp appeared at the window of the aviary. Fabrizio was ready to act. He crossed himself then fastened to his bed the small rope intended to get him down the thirty-five feet separating him from the platform where the palazzo was. He arrived without hindrance on the roof of the guardhouse occupied since the previous day by the two hundred men sent as reinforcements, of whom we have spoken. Unfortunately, the soldiers, at a quarter to one as it now was, were not yet asleep. As he crept across the roof of big hollow tiles, Fabrizio could hear them saying that the devil was on the roof, and that they needed to try and shoot him dead. A few voices claimed that such a wish was the height of impiety, others said that if they fired without killing something, the governor would put them all in prison for having alarmed the garrison pointlessly. This whole fierce debate meant that Fabrizio went as quickly as he could across the roof, and made far more noise. Indeed, when, suspended on his rope, he passed in front of the windows, four or five feet away fortunately because of the projecting roof, they were bristling with bayonets. Some have claimed that Fabrizio, crazy as ever, had the idea of playing the role of the devil, and threw the soldiers a handful of sequins. What is certain is that he had strewn sequins across the floor of his room, and he strewed them too over the platform on crossing from the Farnese Tower to the parapet, in order to give himself a chance of distracting the soldiers who might have set off in pursuit.

Once on the platform, and surrounded by sentries, who normally shouted out a whole sentence every quarter of an hour: 'All's well around my post', he made his way towards the parapet on the western side and searched for the new stone.

What seems incredible and might make one doubt the fact if the result had not been witnessed by an entire town, is that the sentries posted along the parapet did not see and stop Fabrizio. It is true that the mist of which we have spoken was beginning to rise, and Fabrizio has said that by the time he was on the platform the mist seemed already to have reached halfway up the Farnese Tower. But this mist was not thick, and he had a clear view of the sentries, some of whom were walking about. He added that, urged on as if by some supernatural force, he went boldly and placed himself between two sentries who were quite close together. He calmly undid the big rope that he had around his body and which twice became tangled. It took him some little time to untangle it and extend it over the parapet. He could hear the soldiers talking on all sides, firmly resolved to use his dagger on the first one who might come towards him. I wasn't at all agitated, he added, it was as if I were observing a rite.

He attached his finally untangled rope to an opening created in the parapet to let water run out, climbed on to the aforesaid parapet and prayed fervently to God. Then, like a hero from the days of chivalry, he thought for a moment of Clelia. How different I am, he told himself, from the irresponsible and libertine Fabrizio who entered here nine months ago! Finally, he began to descend that astonishing height. He acted mechanically, he said, as he would have done in broad daylight, descending in front of friends, to win a wager. Around the midpoint of the drop, he suddenly felt his arms lose their strength. He believes he even let go of the rope for an instant. But he quickly took hold of it again. Perhaps, he said, he held himself back by the undergrowth he was sliding past, which was scratching him. From time to time he felt an awful pain between his shoulders, which went so far as to stop him from breathing. There was a very uncomfortable swaying motion: he was constantly being pushed back by the rope on to the undergrowth. He was brushed against by several quite large birds that he had aroused and which dashed at him as they flew off. In the early stages, he thought he might be overtaken by men descending from the citadel, by the same route as himself, in pursuit, and he made ready to defend himself. Finally, he arrived at the foot of the big tower unharmed beyond having bloodied hands. He recounted how, from the middle of the tower on, the slope that it forms proved very useful. He rubbed against the wall as he descended, and the plants growing between the stones did much to hold him back. On reaching the foot in the soldiers' gardens, he fell on an acacia which, seen from up above, had seemed to be four or five feet tall, but was in fact fifteen or twenty. A drunkard who happened to be sleeping there took him for a robber. In falling from the tree, Fabrizio almost dislocated his left arm. He started to run off towards the rampart, but, as he put it, his legs felt like cotton-wool. His strength had gone. In spite of the danger, he sat down and drank the small amount of brandy he had left. He dozed off for a few minutes, long enough for him to not know where he was. On coming to, he could not understand how, being in his room, he could see trees. Finally, the terrible truth came back to his memory. He at once walked towards the rampart. He climbed it up a broad set of steps. The sentry posted close by was snoring in his sentry-box. He found part of a cannon lying in the grass. He attached his third rope to it. It turned out to be a little too short and he fell into a muddy ditch where there was perhaps a foot of water. As he was getting to his feet and trying to get his bearings, he felt himself being grabbed by two men. He was frightened for a moment. But soon he heard, close by his ear and very sotto voce, the words: 'Oh, monsignore, monsignore!' He dimly realized that these were the duchess's men. He at once fainted clean away. Some time later, he felt himself being carried by men who were walking in silence and very rapidly. Then they stopped, which caused him great anxiety. But he lacked the strength either to speak or to open his eyes. He felt himself being tightly held. Suddenly, he recognized the scent on the duchess's clothes. That scent revived him. He opened his eyes. He was able to utter the words: 'Ah, my dear,' and then fainted clean away again.

The faithful Bruno, with a squad of policemen devoted to the count, was in reserve two hundred paces away. The count himself was hiding in a small house close to the spot where the duchess had been waiting. He would not have hesitated, had it been necessary, to take his sword in his hand, along with several half-pay officers, his close friends. He saw himself as obliged to save the life of Fabrizio, who seemed to be in serious danger, and would once have had his pardon signed by the prince, had he, Mosca, not been so foolish as to seek to spare the sovereign a piece of written foolishness.

Since midnight, the duchess, surrounded by men armed to the teeth, had been wandering in complete silence in front of the ramparts of the citadel. She could not remain in one place, she was thinking that she would have to fight to get Fabrizio away from the men who would be pursuing him. That ardent imagination had taken a hundred precautions, too lengthy to be spelt out here, and unbelievably reckless. It has been calculated that more than eighty agents were on hand that night, anticipating doing battle for something extraordinary. Fortunately, Ferrante and Lodovico were at the head of things, and the minister of police was not hostile. But the count himself observed that the duchess was not betrayed by anyone, and that as minister he heard nothing.

The duchess lost her head completely on seeing Fabrizio again. She clutched him convulsively in her arms and was then in despair at seeing him covered in blood. It was from Fabrizio's hands. She thought he had been dangerously wounded. Helped by one of her men, she had taken off his jacket to bandage him, when Lodovico, who fortunately happened to be there, took charge and put the duchess and Fabrizio into one of the small carriages that had been hidden in a garden near the town gate, and they set off hell for leather to cross the Po near Sacca. Ferrante brought up the rear, with twenty well-armed men, and had promised to halt any pursuit even if it cost him his life. The count, alone and on foot, left the vicinity of the citadel only two hours later, when he saw that no one was stirring. Here I am, guilty of high treason! he told himself, wild with delight.

Lodovico had had the excellent thought of putting into one carriage a young surgeon attached to the duchess's household who bore a marked resemblance to Fabrizio. 'Flee in the direction of Bologna,' he told him. 'Be heavy-handed, try to get yourself arrested. Then cut your answers short and finally admit that you're Fabrizio del Dongo. Above all, play for time. If you're good at being heavy-handed, you'll get away with a month in prison and the signora will give you fifty sequins.'

'Does one think about money when serving the signora?'

He left and was arrested a few hours later, which gave very great pleasure to General Fabio Conti and to Rassi who, with Fabrizio at large, could see his barony disappearing.

The escape was not known about in the citadel until around six in the morning, and only at ten did they dare to inform the prince. The duchess had been so well served that, despite

Fabrizio's deep sleep, which she mistook at first for a fatal syncope, causing her to stop the carriage on three occasions, she was crossing the Po in a boat as it struck four. There was a relay on the left bank. They covered another two leagues with extreme rapidity, and were then stopped for more than an hour while the passports were checked. The duchess had all manner of passports for herself and for Fabrizio. But she was like a madwoman that day, she saw fit to give the Austrian police clerk ten napoleons and to take him by the hand, while bursting into tears. The clerk, much alarmed, began the inspection all over again. They took the stagecoach. The duchess paid in so extravagant a fashion that she aroused general suspicion in a country where any foreigner is suspect. Lodovico again came to her assistance. He said that the signora duchess was distraught with grief because of the perpetual fever of the young Count Mosca, son of the first minister of Parma, whom she was taking with her to consult the doctors in Pavia.

Only ten leagues beyond the Po did the prisoner come fully awake; he had a sprained shoulder and a great many grazes. The duchess's manner was still so extraordinary that the landlord of a village inn, where they dined, thought he was dealing with a princess of the imperial blood and was about to render her the honours he believed were her due, when Lodovico told the man that the princess would not fail to have him put in prison if he took it into his head to have the bells rung.

Finally, at around six in the evening, they reached Piedmontese territory. Only there was Fabrizio completely safe. He was taken to a small village away from the high road. His hands were dressed and he slept for a few more hours.

It was in this village that the duchess succumbed to an action that was not only terrible from a moral point of view but also fatal to her peace of mind for the rest of her life. A few weeks before Fabrizio's escape, on a day when the whole of Parma had gone to the gateway of the citadel to try to see in the courtyard the scaffold that was being erected in his honour, the duchess had shown Lodovico, who had become her household factotum, the secret by means of which one of the stones form-

ing the bottom of the famous reservoir in the Palazzo Sanseverina, the thirteenth-century construction of which we have
spoken, could be removed from a small iron surround that was
very well concealed. While Fabrizio was asleep in the small
village trattoria, the duchess sent for Lodovico. He thought she
had gone mad, so strange were the looks she gave him.

'You must be expecting that I'm about to give you several
thousand francs,' she said. 'Well, no. I know you, you're a poet,
you'd soon squander the money. I'm giving you the small estate
of La Ricciarda, one league from Casal-Maggiore.' Lodovico
threw himself at her feet wild with delight, protesting in heartfelt tones that it was certainly not so as to make money that he
had helped to save Monsignor Fabrizio. That he had always
felt a particular fondness for him ever since he had had the
honour of once driving him in his position as the signora's third
coachman. Once this truly generous man believed he had taken
up enough of so great a lady's time, he took his leave. But she,
eyes sparkling, told him: 'Stay.'

She walked about the tavern room without saying a word,
looking at Lodovico from time to time out of eyes that were
not to be believed. Finally, seeing that this strange perambu-
lation was not coming to an end, the man thought he should
address his mistress. 'The signora has made me so extravagant
a gift, so much more than anything a poor man such as myself
might have imagined, so superior above all to the paltry services
I've had the honour of rendering, that I believe in all conscience
I cannot keep the Ricciarda estate. I have the honour of
returning that estate to the signora, and to ask her to grant me
a pension of four hundred francs.'

'How many times in your life,' she said, with a quite unsmil-
ing hauteur, 'how many times have you heard it said that I had
abandoned a project once I had made it known?'

Following which words, the duchess walked about for a few
more minutes. Then, suddenly stopping, she exclaimed: 'It's by
chance and because he managed to attract that young girl that
Fabrizio's life has been saved! If he hadn't appealed to her, he'd
have died. Can you deny that?' she said, marching on Lodovico,

her eyes blazing with the most saturnine fury. Lodovico took a few steps back and thought she was mad, which caused him great anxiety where his estate of La Ricciarda was concerned.

'All right,' the duchess resumed in the mildest, most cheerful tone, utterly transformed, 'I want the good inhabitants of Sacca to have a day of excess, one they'll remember for a long time to come. You're to return to Sacca, do you have any objection? Do you think you'll be in any danger?'

'Not seriously, signora. None of the inhabitants of Sacca will ever say that I was part of Monsignor Fabrizio's entourage. Moreover, dare I say it, signora, I can't wait to see *my* estate of La Ricciarda. It seems so comic, my being a landowner!'

'Your merriment I like. The farmer on La Ricciarda owes me three or four years' rent, I fancy. I shall make him a present of half of what he owes me and the other half of his arrears I'm giving to you, but on one condition: you will go to Sacca, you will say that the day after tomorrow is the feast-day of one of my patron saints, and on the evening following your arrival, you will have my house illuminated in the most splendid manner. Spare neither money nor trouble. Remember, the greatest happiness of my life is involved. I've been preparing those illuminations from a long way back. For more than three months, I've been assembling in the cellars of the house everything that will contribute to this noble celebration. I've left with the gardener all the fireworks you need for a magnificent display. You'll let them off on the terrace overlooking the Po. I have eighty-nine large barrels of wine in my cellars, you'll set up eighty-nine fountains of wine in my park. If the day after there's a single bottle of wine left undrunk, I shall say that you don't love Fabrizio. Once the fountains of wine, the illuminations and the fireworks are properly under way, you will slip discreetly away, for it's possible, and this is my hope, that in Parma all these fine things will look like insolence.'

'Which isn't simply possible, it's certain. Just as it's certain that the prosecutor Rassi, who signed the monsignore's sentence, will be spitting with rage. And even . . .' Lodovico went on diffidently '. . . if the signora wished to please her humble servant even more than by giving him half the arrears from La

Ricciarda, she would permit me to play a small practical joke on that Rassi . . .'

'You're a man after my own heart!' cried the duchess, in raptures. 'But I absolutely forbid you to do anything to Rassi. I plan to have him hanged in public later on. As for yourself, try not to get arrested in Sacca; everything would be spoilt if I were to lose you.'

'Me, signora! Once I've said that I'm celebrating one of the signora's patron saints, if the police were to send thirty policemen to upset things, you can be sure that before they'd got to the red cross that's in the middle of the village, not one of them would be on horseback. They think they're the cat's whiskers, the inhabitants of Sacca. All accomplished smugglers who adore the signora.'

'Finally,' the duchess resumed, wearing an oddly detached expression, 'I may give wine to my good people of Sacca, but I wish to inundate the inhabitants of Parma. On the same evening when my house is illuminated, take the best horse in my stables, hurry to my palazzo and open the reservoir.'

'Oh, what a wonderful idea, signora!' cried Lodovico, laughing like a lunatic. 'Wine for the good people of Sacca, water for the townsfolk of Parma who were so sure, the wretches, that Monsignor Fabrizio was going to be poisoned, like poor L***.'

Lodovico's delight knew no bounds. The duchess looked indulgently on at his manic laughter. He repeated ceaselessly: 'Wine for the people of Sacca and water for the ones in Parma! The signora knows better than me no doubt that when they unwisely emptied the reservoir twenty years ago, there was up to a foot of water in several of the streets in Parma.'

'And water for the people of Parma,' replied the duchess, laughing. 'The promenade in front of the citadel would have been filled with people if they'd cut Fabrizio's head off . . . Everyone calls him "the great criminal" . . . But above all, be careful how you do it, not a living soul must ever know that the flood's been caused by you, or ordered by me. Fabrizio, the count himself, mustn't know of this crazy prank . . . But I was forgetting the poor in Sacca. Go and write a letter to my steward, which I will sign. You must tell him that for the celebration of my patron saint he must distribute a hundred sequins to the poor of Sacca and obey you in everything concerning the illuminations, the fireworks and the wine. Above all, there mustn't be a full bottle left in my cellars the next day.'

'The signora's steward will find there's only one problem, in the five years she's been at the house, she hasn't left ten poor people in Sacca.'

'And water for the people of Parma!' the duchess went on, singing. 'How will you carry it out, this little joke?'

'My plan is already made. I leave Sacca at around nine o'clock, at ten-thirty my horse is at the inn of The Three Buffoons, on the road to Casal-Maggiore and *my* estate of La Ricciarda. At eleven o'clock, I'm in my room at the palazzo, and at a quarter past eleven water for the people of Parma, more than they want, to drink the health of the great criminal. Ten minutes later, I leave the town by the Bologna road. In passing, I make a deep bow to the citadel, which the courage of the monsignore and the signora's spirit have just dishonoured. I take a path I know well in the countryside and I make my entry into La Ricciarda.' Lodovico looked up at the duchess and felt alarmed: she was gazing fixedly at the bare wall six paces away, and it must be agreed, her gaze was awful. Oh, my poor estate! thought Lodovico. The fact is, she's mad! The duchess looked at him and guessed what he was thinking.

'Ah, Signor Lodovico the great poet, you want a written deed of gift. Run and fetch me a sheet of paper.' Lodovico did not need to have the order repeated, and the duchess wrote in her own hand a long acknowledgement, antedated by a year, in which she declared she had received from Lodovico San Micheli the sum of eighty thousand francs, and to have given him as a pledge the estate of La Ricciarda. If after twelve months had passed, the duchess had not repaid Lodovico the eighty thousand francs, the estate of La Ricciarda would remain as his property.

It's good, the duchess told herself, to give a faithful servitor one third, just about, of what I have left for myself.

'And now,' the duchess told Lodovico, 'after the joke with the reservoir, I'm giving you only two days to enjoy yourself in Casal-Maggiore. So that the sale may be valid, say it's a matter that goes back more than a year. Come and rejoin me in Belgirate, and without any delay. Fabrizio will perhaps go to England, where you'll follow him.'

Early the next day, the duchess and Fabrizio were in Belgirate. They installed themselves in that enchanting village. But heartbreak awaited the duchess on the beautiful lake. Fabrizio had changed utterly. From the very first moment after he awoke from his somehow lethargic sleep following his escape, the duchess had been able to see that something unusual was going on inside him. The profound sentiment that he had been working to conceal was decidedly bizarre. It was this, no less: he was in despair at being out of prison. He took good care not to reveal this source of his unhappiness, it would have led to questions he would have refused to answer.

'What,' said the duchess in astonishment, 'did it not fill you with horror, that ghastly sensation when hunger forced you to feed, so as not to collapse, off one of the loathsome dishes supplied by the prison kitchens, the sensation, does this taste peculiar, am I poisoning myself this very minute?'

'I thought about death,' answered Fabrizio, 'as I imagine soldiers think about it. It was a possibility that I certainly thought I was clever enough to avoid.'

What anxiety, what sorrow, for the duchess then! This adored being, unlike any other, full of life, original, was henceforth, as she watched, prey to a profound distraction. He preferred solitude even to the pleasure of discussing things, holding nothing back, with the best friend he had in the world. He was still kindly, eager, grateful in the duchess's presence, he would have given his life for her a hundred times over, as in the old days. But his soul was elsewhere. They often did four or five leagues on that sublime lake without exchanging a word. Others might perhaps have taken pleasure in the conversations, the dispassionate exchange of thoughts that was henceforth possible between them, but they could still remember, the duchess in particular, what their conversations had been like before the fateful combat with Giletti that had separated them. Fabrizio owed the duchess the story of the nine months spent in a terrible prison, but it turned out that all he had to say about that sojourn was a few brief, insufficient words.

This had to happen sooner or later, the unhappy duchess told herself, gloomily. Grief has aged me, or else he really is in love and I now have only second place in his heart. Demeaned and cast down by this greatest of all possible sorrows, the duchess sometimes told herself: if heaven had decreed that Ferrante should go completely mad or have lacked courage, I believe I would have been less unhappy. From that moment on, this half-remorse poisoned the respect that the duchess had had for her own character. So I'm repenting having taken a decision, she told herself bitterly. So I am no longer a del Dongo!

Heaven has so decreed, she went on. Fabrizio is in love and by what right would I wish him not to be in love? Has a single word of genuine love ever been exchanged between us?

This very reasonable thought stopped her from sleeping, and what finally demonstrated that the old age which weakens the soul had come for her, with the prospect of an illustrious revenge, was that she was a hundred times more unhappy in Belgirate than in Parma. As for the person who might be causing Fabrizio's strange distraction, it was hardly possible to have any reasonable doubts: Clelia Conti, that very pious girl, had betrayed her father since she had agreed to get the garrison drunk, and Fabrizio never made mention of Clelia! But, the duchess went on, beating her breast in despair, if the garrison hadn't been got drunk, all my schemes, all my trouble would have been no use. So it's she who saved him!

It was with extreme difficulty that the duchess obtained from Fabrizio details of that night's events, which, the duchess told herself, would once have formed the topic of a conversation that was forever being rejoined! In those happy times, he would have talked all day long and with an undying verve and gaiety about the least trifle that I thought to bring up.

Needing to guard against all eventualities, the duchess had installed Fabrizio in the port of Locarno, a Swiss town at the far end of Lake Maggiore. Every day, she would go and fetch him by boat for lengthy excursions on the lake. Well, the one time when she took it into her head to go up to his room, she found it hung with any number of views of the town of Parma that he had had sent from Milan or from Parma itself, a place he should have held in abomination. His little parlour, transformed into a studio, was cluttered with all the apparatus of a painter in watercolours, and she found him finishing off a third view of the Farnese Tower and the governor's palazzo.

'All you need to do now,' she said, wearing an aggrieved expression, 'is to paint a portrait from memory of that loveable governor who just wanted to poison you. But I've been thinking,' the duchess went on, 'you ought to write him a letter of apology for having taken the liberty of escaping and making a mockery of the citadel.'

She spoke truer than she knew. No sooner had he reached a place of safety before Fabrizio's first concern had been to write a perfectly polite and in some ways perfectly absurd letter to General Fabio Conti. He asked to be forgiven for having escaped, alleging as his excuse that he had come to believe that a certain underling in the prison had been charged with administering poison to him. It hardly mattered to him what he wrote, Fabrizio was hoping that Clelia's eyes would see this letter and his face was bathed in tears as he wrote. He ended it with a quite comical sentence: he ventured to say that, finding himself at liberty, he often found himself longing for his little room in the Farnese Tower. That was the letter's crucial thought, he hoped Clelia would understand it. In the mood for writing, and still in hopes of being read by someone, Fabrizio addressed his gratitude to Don Cesare, the kindly chaplain who had lent him books on theology. A few days later, Fabrizio commissioned the small bookseller in Locarno to make the journey to Milan, where the bookseller, who was a friend of the celebrated bibliomane Reina,[1] bought the most magnificent editions he could find of the works Don Cesare had lent. The good chaplain received the books and a splendid letter which told him that, in moments of impatience, excusable perhaps in a poor prisoner, the margins of his books had been filled with ridiculous notes. He was implored as a consequence to replace them in his library by the volumes which the most heartfelt gratitude took the liberty of offering him.

It was very good of Fabrizio to give the simple name of notes to the endless scrawls with which he had filled the margins of an in-folio copy of the works of St Jerome. In the hope that he might be able to send this book back to the worthy chaplain, and exchange it for another, he had kept day by day in the margins a very accurate record of what had happened to him in prison. The great events were none other than ecstasies of *divine love* (the word *divine* replaced another word he did not dare to write). At times, this divine love led the prisoner into a deep despair, at other times a voice heard through the air gave him back some hope and produced transports of happiness. All this, fortunately, was written in prison ink, made out of wine, chocolate and soot, and Don Cesare had done no more than glance at it when replacing the volume of St Jerome on his shelves. Had he followed the margins, he would have seen that one day the prisoner, believing he had been poisoned, congratulated himself for dying less than forty paces away from what he had loved best in this world. But an eye other than that of the good chaplain had read this page since his escape. This beautiful thought, of 'dying close by that which one loves', expressed in a hundred different ways, was followed by a sonnet in which it was found that the soul, separated, after atrocious torments, from the frail body in which it had dwelt for twenty-three years, and impelled by that instinct for happiness natural to all that has once existed, would not reascend to heaven to mingle with the angelic choirs as soon as it was set free, and in the event of the awful judgement according it forgiveness for its sins, but, happier after death than it had been in life, it would go a few steps from the prison where it had lamented for so long, to be reunited with all that it had loved in the world. And thus, the sonnet's last line went, I shall have found my paradise on earth.

Although Fabrizio was spoken of in the citadel of Parma only as a wicked traitor who had violated the most sacred duties, nevertheless the good priest Don Cesare was overjoyed at the sight of the beautiful books that a stranger had sent him. For Fabrizio had been thoughtful enough not to write until a few days after they had been sent, for fear that his name might

cause the entire package to be sent indignantly back. Don
Cesare made no mention of this courtesy to his brother, who
flew into a rage at the mere name of Fabrizio. But since the
latter's escape, he had resumed all his old intimacy with his
charming niece, and since in the old days he had taught her a
few words of Latin, he showed her the beautiful books he had
received. Such had been the traveller's hope. Clelia suddenly
blushed scarlet, she had just recognized Fabrizio's handwriting.
Large, very narrow strips of yellow paper had been inserted as
bookmarks at various places in the volume. And since it is true
to say that in the midst of the contemptible obsession with
money, and the colourless frigidity of the vulgar thoughts that
fill our lives, the actions inspired by a genuine passion seldom
fail to produce their effect. As though a propitious divinity had
taken the trouble to lead her by the hand, Clelia, guided by this
instinct and by the thought of one single object in the world,
asked her uncle to compare the old copy of St Jerome with that
he had just received. How to describe her raptures in the midst
of the gloomy sadness into which Fabrizio's absence had
plunged her, when she found in the margins of the old St Jerome
the sonnet of which we have spoken, and the account kept, day
by day, of the love that had been felt for her!

From the very first day, she knew the sonnet by heart. She
would sing it, leaning at her window, in front of the window,
henceforth solitary, where she had so often seen a small opening
being revealed in the screen. That screen had been taken down,
to be placed on the courtroom desk to serve as an exhibit in an
absurd case which Rassi was mounting against Fabrizio,
accused of the crime of having escaped or, as the prosecutor,
himself laughing, said, 'of having evaded the clemency of a
magnanimous prince!'

Every one of the actions Clelia had taken was for her the
object of an acute remorse, and now that she was unhappy her
remorse was all the more acute. She tried to allay the reproaches
she directed at herself somewhat, by recalling the vow 'never
to set eyes on Fabrizio again' that she had made to the Madonna
at the time of the general's half-poisoning and had since
renewed every day.

Fabrizio's escape had made her father ill and he had, what was more, been on the verge of losing his position, when the enraged prince sacked all the gaolers in the Farnese Tower and sent them as prisoners to the gaol in the town. The general had been saved in part by the intercession of Count Mosca, who preferred to see him shut away at the top of the citadel, rather than as an actively scheming rival in court circles.

It was during the two weeks that the uncertainty relative to the disgrace of General Fabio Conti, who was genuinely unwell, lasted that Clelia found the courage to carry out the sacrifice she had announced to Fabrizio. She had had the wit to be unwell on the day of general rejoicing, which was also that of the prisoner's escape, as the reader will perhaps recall. She was unwell the following day also and, in short, managed things so well that, with the exception of the gaoler Grillo, with his special responsibility for guarding Fabrizio, no one suspected her complicity, and Grillo kept his mouth shut.

But as soon as Clelia no longer had any anxieties on that score, she was still cruelly troubled by her justified remorse. What possible reason can mitigate the crime of a daughter who betrays her father? she asked herself.

One evening, after a day spent almost entirely in the chapel and in tears, she asked her uncle, Don Cesare, to go with her to the general's, whose outbursts of rage frightened her all the more in that at every opportunity he would mix in imprecations against Fabrizio, that abominable traitor.

Once in her father's presence, she found the courage to tell him that if she had so far refused to give her hand to the Marchese Crescenzi, it was because she felt no attraction for him, and because she was sure of not finding any happiness in the union. At which words the general flew into a rage, and Clelia found it quite hard to go on. She added that if her father, seduced by the marchese's large fortune, thought he should give her the explicit order to marry him, she was ready to obey. The general was greatly surprised by this conclusion, which he was far from expecting. He ended, however, by rejoicing. So, he said to his brother, I shan't be reduced to lodging on a second floor, if that young devil of a Fabrizio causes me to lose my place by his wicked goings-on.

Count Mosca did not fail to show himself deeply shocked by the escape of that 'bad lot' Fabrizio, and repeated on occasion the comment thought up by Rassi, about the contemptible behaviour of that after all very common young man, in having evaded the clemency of the prince. This witty comment, consecrated by high society, did not catch on among the populace. Left to their own good sense, and while believing Fabrizio to be wholly guilty, they admired the determination it had taken to launch himself down so high a wall. Not one person at court admired that courage. As for the police, greatly humiliated by their setback, they had discovered officially that a troop of twenty soldiers, won over by handouts of money from the duchess, that monster of ingratitude, whose name was no longer to be pronounced except with a sigh, had held out to Fabrizio four ladders tied together, each of them forty-five feet long. Fabrizio having held out a rope that had been tied to the ladders, his one less than heroic achievement had been to draw the ladders up. A few liberals known for their rashness, among them Doctor C***, an agent in the direct pay of the prince, added, while compromising themselves, that the police had been barbaric enough to have eight of the unfortunate soldiers who had facilitated the escape of the ungrateful Fabrizio shot. He was therefore blamed even by the genuine liberals as having by his foolhardiness caused the death of eight poor soldiers. Thus it is that petty despotisms reduce the value of public opinion to a zero.

CHAPTER 23

In the midst of this general furore, Archbishop Landriani alone showed himself loyal to the cause of his young friend. He dared to repeat, even at the princess's court, the legal maxim according to which, in any proceedings, one ear must be kept free from all prejudice in order to hear the justifications of an absent party.

On the very next day following Fabrizio's escape, several people had received a rather mediocre sonnet which celebrated that escape as one of the most beautiful actions of the century, and compared Fabrizio to an angel arriving on earth with outstretched wings. Two days later, in the evening, the whole of Parma was repeating a sublime sonnet. This was Fabrizio's monologue as he let himself slide down his rope, passing in review the various incidents of his life. This sonnet gave him a high place in public opinion thanks to two magnificent lines, in which all connoisseurs recognized the style of Ferrante Palla.

But here I would need to reach for the epic style. Where to find the colours in which to depict the torrents of indignation which suddenly submerged all bien pensant hearts when they learnt of the frightful insolence of the illuminations at the house in Sacca? All declaimed as one against the duchess. Even the true liberals decided it was putting at risk in a barbaric fashion the wretched suspects detained in the various prisons, and exasperating the sovereign's heart needlessly. Count Mosca declared that only one recourse remained to the duchess's former friends, which was to forget her. The chorus of execration was thus unanimous, a stranger passing through the town would have been struck by the vigour of public opinion. But in a land where they know how to savour the pleasures of revenge, the illuminations at Sacca and the admirable entertainment given in the grounds for more than six thousand country people were an immense success. Everyone in Parma went around saying that the duchess had had a thousand sequins distributed among her peasants. That was the explanation given for the somewhat harsh reception given to some thirty policemen that the authorities had been boneheaded enough to send to this small village, thirty-six hours after that sublime evening and the general drunkenness that had ensued. The policemen had been met by volleys of stones, had turned tail, and two of them, having fallen from their horses, had been thrown into the Po.

As for the bursting of the great reservoir in the Palazzo Sanseverina, that had gone almost unnoticed. During the night a few streets had been more or less flooded, the next day you might have said that it had been raining. Lodovico had taken care to break the panes of glass in one of the palazzo windows, so that the robbers' entry was explained.

A small ladder had even been found. Count Mosca alone recognized the genius of his mistress.

Fabrizio was fully decided to return to Parma as soon as he was able. He sent Lodovico to carry a long letter to the archbishop, and this faithful servitor returned and, at the first village inside Piedmont, Sannazaro to the west of Pavia, posted a Latin epistle that the worthy prelate had addressed to his young protégé. We shall add one circumstance which, like several others no doubt, will seem redundant in countries where precautions are no longer needed. The name of Fabrizio del Dongo was never written down. All the letters intended for him were addressed to Lodovico San Micheli, in Locarno in Switzerland, or Belgirate in Piedmont. The envelope was made from coarse paper, the seal clumsily applied, the address barely legible and sometimes adorned with recommendations worthy of a cook. All the letters were dated from Naples six days before the real date.

From the Piedmontese village of Sannazaro, near Pavia, Lodovico returned post-haste to Parma. He was charged with a mission to which Fabrizio attached the highest importance. It involved nothing less than delivering to Clelia Conti a silk handkerchief on which had been printed a sonnet by Petrarch. It is true that one word in the sonnet had been altered. Clelia found it on her table two days after receiving the thanks of the Marchese Crescenzi, who had declared himself the happiest of men, and there is no need to say what impression this token of a still constant memory produced on her heart.

Lodovico had to try to obtain as many details as possible of what was going on in the citadel. He it was who imparted to Fabrizio the sad news that the Marchese Crescenzi's marriage now seemed a foregone conclusion. Hardly a day went by without him giving an entertainment for Clelia, inside the citadel. A conclusive proof of the marriage was that the marchese, immensely rich and consequently very miserly, as is customary among the wealthy in the north of Italy, was making immense preparations, yet was marrying a girl *without a dowry*. It is true that in his vanity General Fabio Conti, greatly offended by this comment, the first that would have entered the heads of all his compatriots, had just spent more than three hundred thousand francs on an estate, and he, who had nothing, had paid cash for this estate, apparently out of the marchese's own pocket. And the general had then declared that he was giving the estate to his daughter on her marriage. But the conveyancing and other costs, amounting to more than twelve thousand francs, seemed a quite absurd expense to the Marchese Crescenzi, an eminently logical person. For his part, he was having some tapestries made in Lyon, in magnificent colours that harmonized well and were designed to please the eye, by the celebrated Pallagi, a painter from Bologna. These tapestries, each of which contained a motif taken from the arms of the Crescenzi family which, as the whole world knows, is descended from the famous Crescentius,[1] Roman consul in 985, were to furnish the seventeen reception rooms that formed the ground floor of the marchese's palazzo. The tapestries, the clocks and the lustres that were sent to Parma cost more than three hundred and fifty thousand francs. The cost of the new mirrors, additional to those that the house already possessed, came to two hundred thousand francs. With the exception of two reception

rooms, the celebrated work of Parmigiano, the greatest painter
of the region after the divine Correggio, all the rooms on the
first and second floors were now occupied by celebrated painters from Florence, Rome and Milan, who were decorating
them with frescos. Fokelberg, the great Swedish sculptor;
Tenerani from Rome; and Marchesi from Milan, had been
working for the past year on ten bas-reliefs representing the
same number of heroic deeds of Crescentius, that truly great
man. Most of the ceilings, painted with frescos, also offered
some allusion to his life. There was widespread admiration
for the ceiling on which Hayez,[2] from Milan, had represented
Crescentius being greeted in the Elysian Fields by Francisco
Sforza, Lorenzo the Magnificent, King Robert, the tribune Cola
di Rienzi, Machiavelli, Dante and the other great men of the
Middle Ages. The admiration for these elect souls is purported
to form an epigram against the people in power.

All these splendid details were the exclusive focus of attention
for the nobility and bourgeoisie of Parma, and pierced our hero
to the heart when he read of them, recounted in a long, naively
admiring letter of more than twenty pages which Lodovico had
dictated to a customs man from Casal-Maggiore.

While I, I am poor! Fabrizio told himself, four thousand
livres a year all told. It's sheer impudence on my part to dare
to be in love with Clelia Conti, for whom all these wonders are
being done.

A single item alone in Lodovico's long letter, this one written
in his own bad handwriting, announced to his master that one
evening he had encountered, in the condition of a man in hiding,
poor Grillo, his former gaoler, who had been thrown into
prison, then released. The man had asked for a sequin out of
charity, and Lodovico had given him four, in the duchess's
name. The former gaolers recently given their freedom, twelve
in number, were getting ready to hold a reception with knives (a
trattamento di coltellate) for the new gaolers, their successors,
should they ever contrive to meet them away from the citadel.
Grillo had said that there was a serenade at the fortress almost
daily, that the Signorina Clelia Conti was very pale, often
unwell, and 'other things of the sort'. This absurd phrase meant

that Lodovico received, by return of post, the order to come
back to Locarno. He returned and the details he gave face to
face were even more unhappy for Fabrizio.

It may be imagined what agreeable company the latter now
proved for the poor duchess. He would have suffered a thousand deaths rather than pronounce the name of Clelia Conti in
her presence. The duchess abhorred Parma while, for Fabrizio,
anything which recalled that town was at once sublime and
affecting.

The duchess was more than ever set on getting her revenge.
She had been so happy before the accident of Giletti's death,
and now her lot was so terrible! She lived in the anticipation of
an awful event of which she would have been very careful not
to breathe a word to Fabrizio, she who once, at the time of her
arrangement with Ferrante, thought to make Fabrizio rejoice
by informing him that he would one day be avenged.

It is now possible to form some idea of how enjoyable
Fabrizio's conversations with the duchess were. A mournful
silence almost always prevailed between them. To add to the
enjoyment of their association, the duchess had yielded to the
temptation of playing an unkind trick on this nephew of whom
she was over-fond. The count wrote to her nearly every day.
He appeared to be sending couriers as in the days of their
amours, for the letters always bore the stamp of some small
town in Switzerland. The poor man had been racking his brains
in order not to speak too openly of his affection, and to construct amusing letters. A distracted eye could hardly bring itself
to read them. How can the faithfulness of an esteemed lover
count for anything, alas, when your heart has been pierced by
the indifference of the man you prefer?

In two months, the duchess replied to him only once, and
then in order to get him to test the ground with the princess,
and see whether, despite the insolence of the fireworks, a letter
from her, the duchess, would be received with pleasure. The
letter he was to present, if he adjudged it appropriate, requested
the position of the princess's lord-in-waiting, which had recently fallen vacant, for the Marchese Crescenzi, and wished
that it be granted in recognition of his marriage. The duchess's

letter was a masterpiece, showing the fondest respect and very beautifully expressed. Not a single word whose consequences, even the most remote, might not be agreeable to the princess had been allowed to intrude on the courtier's style. And so the reply breathed an affectionate friendship, undergoing the torments of absence.

'My son and I,' said the princess, 'have not had even one tolerable evening since your so abrupt departure. My dear duchess no longer remembers, then, that it was she who made me give up my consultative vote in the appointment of my household officers? She thinks herself obliged therefore to give me reasons for the marchese's position, as if the first of reasons for me were not the desire she has expressed? The marchese will have the position, if I have any say in the matter. And there will always be one in my heart, the first, for my dear duchess. My son uses absolutely the same expressions, a little strong perhaps in the mouth of a grown-up boy of twenty-one, and asks you for specimens of the minerals from the Orta valley, close to Belgirate. You may address your letters, which I hope will be frequent, to the count, who still detests you and whom I like especially on account of those sentiments. The archbishop too has remained loyal to you. We all hope to see you again one day; remind yourself that we must. The Marchesa Ghisleri, my mistress of the bedchamber, is preparing herself to leave this world for a better. The poor woman has done me much harm. She displeases me also by her ill-timed departure. Her illness makes me think of the name I would once have had so much pleasure putting in place of hers, if, that is, I had been able to obtain the sacrifice of the independence of that unique woman who, by escaping from us, carried away with her all the joy of my little court,' etc., etc.

It was thus in the awareness of having tried to hurry along, in so far as it was within her power to do so, the marriage that was causing Fabrizio to despair, that the duchess saw him every day. And so they sometimes spent four or five hours drifting about together on the lake, without exchanging a single word. Fabrizio was the very personification of goodwill but his thoughts were elsewhere and his innocent and simple soul did not supply him with anything to say. The duchess could see this and that was what tormented her.

We have forgotten to recount in its rightful place that the duchess had taken a house in Belgirate, a charming village, which bears out all that its name promises (the view of a beautiful bend in the lake). From the french window of her salon, the duchess could step straight into her boat. She had taken a very ordinary one, for which four rowers would have sufficed. She engaged twelve and so arranged things as to have one man from each of the villages situated in the vicinity of Belgirate. The third or fourth time she found herself in the middle of the lake with all these hand-picked men, she made them stop plying their oars.

'I look on all of you as friends,' she told them, 'and I want to entrust you with a secret. My nephew Fabrizio has escaped from prison, and perhaps, through treachery, they will try to recapture him, even though he's on your lake, which has the right of sanctuary. Keep your ears open and alert me to anything you may hear. I authorize you to enter my room by day or by night.'

The rowers responded with enthusiasm. She knew how to endear herself to people. But she did not think there was any question of Fabrizio being recaptured; all these precautions were for herself, and before the fateful order to open the reservoir at the Palazzo Sanseverina she would not have dreamt of taking them.

Her prudence had also led her to take an apartment for Fabrizio in the port of Locarno. Each day he would come to visit her, or else she herself went into Switzerland. Just how agreeable their perpetual tête-à-têtes were may be judged by this detail: the marchesa and her daughters came to visit them twice and they took pleasure in the presence of these strangers. For, despite the ties of kinship, we can call someone who knows nothing of our most cherished concerns, and whom we see only once a year, a stranger.

The duchess found herself one evening in Locarno, at Fabrizio's, with the marchesa and her two daughters. The local archpriest and parish priest had come to pay their respects to these ladies. The archpriest, who had a stake in a commercial enterprise and kept his ear to the ground, saw fit to say: 'The prince of Parma is dead!'

The duchess went exceedingly pale. She barely had the courage to say: 'Have they given any details?'

'No,' replied the archpriest. 'The report says no more than that he's died, that much is certain.'

The duchess looked at Fabrizio. I have done this for him, she told herself. I'd have done a thousand times worse, and here he is in front of me, indifferent, and thinking about another woman! It was asking too much of the duchess to endure this terrible thought. She fainted. Everyone hurried to assist her, but as she came to she noticed that Fabrizio was making less effort than the archpriest and the parish priest. He was dreaming as usual.

He's thinking of going back to Parma, the duchess told herself, and perhaps of breaking off Clelia's marriage to the marchese. But I shall know how to stop him. Then, remembering the presence of the two priests, she hastened to add: 'He was a great prince who was much misrepresented. It is an immense loss for us!'

The two priests took their leave and the duchess, in order to be alone, announced that she was going to bed.

Prudence no doubt commands that I wait a month or two before returning to Parma, she told herself. But I feel I shall never have the patience. I'm suffering too much here. Fabrizio's continual reveries, his silence, are an unbearable spectacle for my heart. Who could ever have told me that I would be bored out on that charming lake, the two of us together, and at a moment when I have done more to avenge him than I'm able to tell him! After such a spectacle, death is nothing. It's now that I'm paying for the extremes of happiness and childish delight I experienced in my palazzo in Parma when I welcomed Fabrizio back from Naples. Had I said a word, all would have been over and perhaps, tied to me, he would not have thought of that young Clelia. But I found that word utterly repugnant! And now she has prevailed. What could be simpler? She's twenty years old and I, sick, careworn, I am twice her age . . . I must die, I must end it! A woman of forty is nothing any more except for the men who loved her in her youth. Now, vanity will be my one source of enjoyment, is that worth the trouble of living? One more reason for going to Parma, and amusing myself. If things were to move in a certain direction, my life would be taken from me. Well, where's the harm in that? I shall die a magnificent death, and before the end, but only then, I shall tell Fabrizio: ungrateful man, this is for you! ... Yes, I can find no occupation for the little bit of life I have left except in Parma. I shall play the great lady there. What joy if now I could be sensitive to all those distinctions which once made that Raversi woman so miserable! To see my own happiness in those days, I needed to gaze into the eyes of envy ... My vanity has one advantage: with the exception of the count, perhaps, no one will be able to guess what the event was that put an end to the life of my heart ... I shall love Fabrizio, I will be devoted to his fortunes. But he mustn't break off Clelia's marriage and end up marrying her ... No, that's not to be!

The duchess had reached this point in her unhappy monologue when she heard a lot of noise in the house. Good, she told herself, now they've come to arrest me. Ferrante will have let himself be caught, he'll have talked. Very well, so much the better. I'll have something to occupy myself with. I'm going to fight them for my head. But *primo*, I mustn't let myself be caught.

The duchess, half dressed, fled down to the end of her garden. She was already thinking of climbing over a low wall and escaping into the countryside. But she saw someone entering her room. She recognized Bruno, the count's right-hand man. He was alone with her maid. She approached the french window. The man was telling the maid about the injuries he had received. The duchess went back indoors, Bruno threw himself almost at her feet, entreating her not to tell the count the absurd hour at which he had come.

'As soon as the prince was dead,' he went on, 'the signore count gave all the post stations orders not to provide horses for subjects of the States of Parma. As a result, I went as far as the Po with the horses from the house. But on leaving the boat, my carriage overturned and was smashed, wrecked, and I was so badly bruised I couldn't get on a horse, as was my duty.'

'Right,' said the duchess, 'it's three o'clock in the morning. I'll say you got here at midday. But don't go contradicting me.'

'The signora is so good, that is her all over.'

Politics in a work of literature is a pistol-shot in the middle of a concert, something unseemly to which we nevertheless cannot fail to give our attention.

We are about to speak of very unpalatable matters on which, for more than one reason, we would like to stay silent. But we are forced to come on to events that belong in our domain, since they have for their stage the hearts of our characters.

'But good Lord, how did that great prince die?' the duchess asked Bruno.

'He was out shooting migrating birds, in the marshes along the Po, two leagues from Sacca. He fell into a hole concealed by a clump of grass. He was bathed in sweat and the cold took hold of him. He was transported to an isolated house, where he died after a few hours. Others claim that Messrs Catena and Borone are dead also and that the whole accident stemmed from the copper pans of the peasant whose house they went into, which were full of verdigris. They dined in the man's house. And the hotheads, the Jacobins, who tell you what they're hoping for, are talking of poison. I know my friend Toto, the court quartermaster, would have perished but for the generous attentions of a villager who seemed to know a lot about medicine and had some very peculiar remedies made up for him. But they're no longer talking about the prince's death. The fact is, he was a cruel man. When I left, the people were gathering in order to lynch the chief prosecutor Rassi. They wanted to go and set fire also to the gates of the citadel, in an attempt to save the prisoners. But they claimed Fabio Conti would fire the cannon. Others assured them that the gunners in the citadel had thrown water on the powder and would refuse to massacre their fellow citizens. But here's the really interesting thing: while the Sandolaro surgeon was fixing my poor arm, a man arrived from Parma, who said that the people had found Barbone in the streets, the famous clerk from the citadel, had knocked him senseless, then gone off to hang him on the promenade from the nearest tree to the citadel. The people were on their way to go and smash the beautiful statue of the prince in the gardens of the court. But the signor count took a battalion of the guard, lined them up in front of the statue, and had the people told that anyone entering the gardens wouldn't leave them alive, and the people were scared. But what's very strange, and what the man coming from Parma, who's a former policeman, repeated to me several times, is that the signor count gave General P***, the commander of the prince's guard, a kicking and had him led from the garden by two fusiliers, after tearing off his epaulettes.'

'That's the count all right,' cried the duchess in a transport of joy she could not have foreseen a minute earlier. 'He'll never stand for our princess to be insulted. As for General P***, out of devotion to his legitimate masters, he never wanted to serve the usurper, whereas the count, who's less choosy, went through all the campaigns in Spain, for which he's often been criticized at court.'

The duchess had opened the count's letter, but broke off from reading it to put a host of questions to Bruno.

The letter was very droll. The count had employed the most lugubrious language, yet the keenest delight shone out in every word. He avoided giving details on the manner of the prince's death and ended the letter with these words:

'You are surely going to come back, my darling angel, but I advise you to wait for a day or two for the messenger the princess will send you, as I hope, today or tomorrow. Your return must be as splendid as your departure was foolhardy. As for the great criminal who is with you, I am reckoning on having his case heard by twelve judges summoned from all parts of the State. But in order to have the monster punished as he deserves, I must first of all tear the first verdict, if it exists, into a thousand pieces.'

The count had reopened his letter:

'On a quite different matter: I have just had cartridges distributed to the two battalions of the guard. I am going to fight and do my best to deserve the nickname of "the Cruel" with which the liberals have been gratifying me for so long. That old mummy of a General P*** has dared to speak in the barracks of entering into talks with the people, who are half in revolt. I'm writing from the middle of the street. I'm going to the palace, which they will enter only over my dead body. Farewell! If I die, it will be adoring you *all the same*, as I have lived! Don't forget to collect the three hundred thousand francs deposited in your name at D***'s in Lyon.

'Now here's that poor devil Rassi, pale as death and sans wig. You can have no idea what he looks like! The people are dead set on hanging him. That would be doing him a great wrong; he deserves to be hung, drawn and quartered. He took refuge in my palazzo and ran after me into the street. I don't quite know what to do with him. I don't want to take him to the prince's palace, that would set off the uprising in that quarter. F*** will see whether I love him. My first words to Rassi were: I need the sentence passed on Signor del Dongo, and all the copies of it you may have, and tell all those iniquitous judges, who are the cause of this uprising, that I'll have them all hanged, and you with them, my dear friend, if they breathe a word of that sentence, which has never existed. In Fabrizio's name, I'm sending a company of grenadiers to the archbishop's palace. Farewell, dear angel. My palazzo is about to be burnt down and I shall lose the charming portraits I have of you. I'm rushing to the palace to sack that iniquitous General P***, who's up to his low tricks. He's sucking up to the people just as he once sucked up to the prince. All the generals are scared stiff. I think I'm going to have myself appointed commander-in-chief.'

The duchess was sufficiently mischievous not to have Fabrizio woken. For the count she felt a rush of admiration very much resembling love. All things considered, she told herself, I have to marry him. She wrote to him there and then and sent one of her men off. That night the duchess did not have time to be unhappy.

The next day, towards midday, she saw a boat manned by six rowers cutting rapidly through the waters of the lake. She and Fabrizio soon recognized a man wearing the livery of the prince of Parma. It was indeed one of his couriers who, before setting foot ashore, shouted to the duchess: 'The uprising's been quelled!' The courier handed her several letters from the count, an admirable letter from the princess and an ordinance from Prince Ranuce-Ernest V, on parchment, appointing her duchess of San Giovanni and mistress of the bedchamber to the dowager princess. The young prince, the expert in mineralogy whom she thought was an imbecile, had had the wit to write her a short letter. But there was love at the end. The letter began thus:

'The count says, signora duchess, that he is pleased with me. The fact is, I came under fire a few times at his side and my horse was hit. Seeing the fuss that is made about so little, I long to be present at a real battle, but it must not be against my own subjects. I owe everything to the count. All my generals, who have never been to war, behaved like hares. I believe that two or three of them have fled as far as Bologna. Since a great and lamentable event gave me power, I have signed no ordinance as agreeable as that appointing you as my mother's mistress of the bedchamber. My mother and I remembered that one day you admired the beautiful view one has from the San Giovanni *palazzetto*, which once belonged to Petrarch, or so they say. My mother wanted you to have that small estate. And I, not knowing what to give you, and not daring to offer you everything that belongs to you, I have made you a duchess in my country. I don't know if you are learned enough to know that Sanseverina is a Roman title. I have just given the great ribbon of my order to our worthy archbishop, who has displayed a firmness very uncommon in men of seventy. You will not begrudge me having recalled all the ladies who had been banished. I'm told I must no longer sign, from now on, except after writing the words "your affectionate". I am angry that they should be making me strew around an assurance which is only completely true when I write to you.

> Your affectionate
> Ranuce-Ernest.'

To judge by which language, who would not have said that the duchess was about to enjoy the highest favour? Nevertheless, she found something very peculiar in other letters from the count, which she received two hours later. Without otherwise going into any details, he advised her to delay her return to Parma by several days and to write to the princess that she was much indisposed. The duchess and Fabrizio left for Parma immediately after dinner just the same. The duchess's aim, even if she had still not admitted it to herself, was to urge on the marriage of the Marchese Crescenzi. Fabrizio, for his part, took to the road in transports of the wildest delight, which his aunt found ridiculous. He had hopes of soon seeing Clelia again. He was counting on abducting her, against her will if need be, if that were the only way of breaking off her marriage.

The duchess and her nephew's journey was very cheerful. At a post station before Parma, Fabrizio stopped for a moment to resume his ecclesiastical garb. He had been dressing as a man in mourning normally would. When he returned to the duchess's room: 'I find something ambiguous and inexplicable in the count's letters,' she said. 'If you were to trust me, you'd wait here for a few hours. I shall send you a courier as soon as I've spoken to the great minister.'

It was with great difficulty that Fabrizio yielded to this sensible advice. Outbursts of joy worthy of a child of fifteen marked the reception that the count gave the duchess, whom he called his wife. For a long time he did not want to talk politics, and when they finally came to the unhappy reason why: 'You did well to stop Fabrizio from arriving officially. The reaction's well under way here. Just guess which colleague the prince has given me as minister of justice! Rassi, my love, Rassi, whom I treated like the street beggar he is on the day of the great events. Incidentally, I must warn you that they've suppressed everything that went on here. If you read our gazette, you'll see that a clerk from the citadel by the name of Barbone died on falling from a carriage. As for the sixty or so scoundrels whom I had shot dead as they were attacking the prince's statue in the gardens, they're in perfect health, only they're travelling. Count Zurla, the interior minister, went personally to the homes of each of these unfortunate heroes and handed out fifteen sequins to their families or their friends, with an order to say that the deceased was travelling and the very

explicit threat of imprisonment if they took it into their heads
to give people to understand he'd been killed. A man from my
own ministry, foreign affairs, has been sent on a mission to the
journalists in Milan and Turin, so that they don't mention "the
unfortunate event", which is the approved phrase. The man is
to press on to Paris and London, so as to give the lie in all the
newspapers, and all but officially, to everything that may be
said about our troubles. Another agent is on his way to Bologna
and Florence. I simply shrugged.

'What's nice at my age is that I felt a moment of enthusiasm
talking to the soldiers of the guard and tearing the epaulettes
off that poltroon of a General P***. At that moment, I'd have
given my life, no two ways about it, for the prince. I admit now
that would have been a very stupid way to finish. Today, the
prince, good young man that he is, would give a hundred écus
to have me die of some sickness. He doesn't yet dare ask me
for my resignation, but we speak to one another as rarely as
possible, and I send him sheafs of short written reports, which
was my practice with the late prince, after Fabrizio's imprisonment. Incidentally, I haven't torn up the signed sentence for the
good reason that that scoundrel Rassi hasn't handed it over. So
you did very well to stop Fabrizio arriving here officially. The
sentence is still in force. I don't think, however, that Rassi
would dare have our nephew arrested today, but it's possible
he may do in a couple of weeks' time. If Fabrizio is absolutely
set on coming back into town, let him come and lodge with
me.'

'What's brought all this about?' exclaimed the duchess,
astonished.

'They've convinced the prince I've been going round like a
dictator and the saviour of the country and that I want to lead
him by the hand like a child. What's more, when speaking of
him, I'm supposed to have used the fatal words *that child*. It
may be the case, I was excited that day. I saw him as a great
man, for example, because he wasn't too afraid the first time
he'd ever heard gunfire in his life. He doesn't lack wits, he even
has a better style than his father. In fact, I can't repeat it too
often, he has a good and honest heart deep down. But that

sincere young heart clenches when he's told about some dirty trick and thinks you must have a black soul yourself to be noticing such things. Remember the education he received! . . .'

'Your Excellency should have remembered that one day he'd be the master, and put some man of intelligence at his side.'

'First of all, we have the example of the Abbé de Condillac,[3] who was sent for by the Marchese di Felino, my predecessor, and succeeded in turning his pupil into the king of the simpletons. He walked in procession, and, in 1796, was unable to negotiate with General Bonaparte, which would have tripled the extent of his States. Secondly, I never thought I'd remain a minister for ten years in a row. Now that I'm disillusioned with everything, as I have been for the past month, I want to amass a million before leaving this bear garden that I've rescued to its own devices. But for me, Parma would have been a republic for the last two months, with the poet Ferrante Palla for dictator.'

These words caused the duchess to go red. The count knew nothing.

'We're going to relapse into the normal eighteenth-century monarchy: the confessor and the mistress. Basically, the prince loves only mineralogy, and perhaps you, signora. Since his accession, his valet, whose brother I've just made a captain, the said brother having served for nine months, the valet, as I say, has gone and put it into his head that he ought to be happier than other people because his profile is going to be found on the écus. After which beautiful thought has come boredom.

'Now he needs an aide-de-camp, as a remedy for boredom. Well, even were he to offer me the famous million we would need to live well in Naples or in Paris, I wouldn't want to be his remedy for boredom, and spend four or five hours every day with His Highness. Moreover, since I've got more brains than he has, by the end of a month he'd take me for a monster.

'The late prince was spiteful and envious, but he had waged war and commanded troops, which had given him a presence. He had the right stuff in him to be a prince, and I could be a minister, for good or ill. With the son, decent man as he is, candid and genuinely good, I'm forced to be a schemer. So here I am, the rival of the humblest woman skivvy in the castle, and a very inferior rival because I shall despise a hundred essential details. Three days ago, for example, one of the women who puts out the white towels every morning in the apartments had the idea of losing the key to one of the prince's English desks. Whereupon His Highness refused to trouble himself with any of the business the papers for which happen to be in that bureau. The fact is, for twenty francs you could have the boards that form the bottom taken off, or use a skeleton key. But Ranuce-Ernest V told me that would be teaching the court locksmith bad habits.

'Up until now, he's found it quite impossible to carry on wanting the same thing three days running. If he'd been born the Signor Marchese Such-and-Such, with a fortune, this young prince would have been one of the most estimable men at his court, a sort of Louis XVI. But pious and naive as he is, how is he going to resist all the clever traps he's surrounded by? So your enemy Raversi's salon is more influential than ever. There, they've discovered that I, who had the people fired on, and was resolved to kill three thousand men if I had to, rather than let the statue of the prince who'd been my master be vandalized, that I am a fanatical liberal, that I wanted to get a constitution signed and a hundred other absurdities of the kind. The lunatics would stop us enjoying the best of monarchies by going on about a republic . . . In short, signora, you're the one person in the current liberal camp, of which my enemies make me the leader, on whose account the prince has not come out in disobliging terms. The archbishop, a thoroughly honourable man as ever, is in total disgrace for having spoken in reasonable terms of what I did on that "unhappy day".

'The day following the one that wasn't yet being called "unhappy", when it was still true that there had in fact been an uprising, the prince told the archbishop that, so that you wouldn't have to accept an inferior title by marrying me, he would make me a duke. Today I believe it's Rassi, ennobled by me at the time he was selling me the late prince's secrets, who's going to be made a count. Faced with such a promotion I shall play the role of a simpleton.'

'And the poor prince will drop himself in the mire.'

'Surely. But basically, he's the *master*, and as such, less than two weeks from now, he'll have made it no longer seem *ridiculous*. And so, dear duchess, let's do as they do at backgammon, let's *go out*.'

'But we shan't be well-off exactly.'

'Basically, neither you nor I have need of luxury. If in Naples you give me a seat in a box at the San Carlo and a horse, I shall be more than satisfied. It won't ever be how much luxury we do or don't have that will give us status, you and I, but the pleasure that the clever people locally may perhaps take in coming to have a cup of tea at your house.'

'But what would have happened,' the duchess went on, 'on the "unhappy day" if you'd stood aside, as I hope you will do in future?'

'The troops would have fraternized with the people, there'd have been three days of massacres and fires (for it'll take this country a hundred years for a republic not to be an absurdity), then a fortnight of looting, until two or three regiments supplied from abroad came to call a halt to it. Ferrante Palla was in the midst of the people, full of courage and raving as usual. He no doubt had a dozen friends acting in concert with him, which Rassi will turn into a magnificent conspiracy. What's certain is that, though his clothes may have been unbelievably ragged, he was distributing money by the handful.'

The duchess, amazed by all these reports, hastened to go and thank the princess.

As she entered the room, the mistress of the robes handed her the small gold key that is worn on the belt and is the mark of sovereign authority in that part of the palace that appertains to the princess. Clara-Paolina hastened to clear the room, and, once alone with her friend, persisted for a few moments in only half explaining herself. The duchess could not properly understand what it all meant, and was very reticent in her replies. Finally, the princess burst into tears and, throwing herself into the duchess's arms, exclaimed: 'The days of my unhappiness are about to begin again. My son will treat me worse than his father did!'

'That's something I shall prevent,' the duchess replied

sharply. 'But first,' she went on, 'I need that Your Most Serene Highness should deign to accept all my gratitude and my profound respect.'

'What do you mean?' cried the princess, filled with anxiety and fearing a resignation.

'I mean that every time Your Most Serene Highness allows me to turn the trembling chin of that magot on the mantelpiece to the right, she will permit me also to call things by their proper name.'

'Is that all, my dear duchess?' cried Clara-Paolina, getting up and running off herself to put the magot in the right position. 'Let us talk completely freely, signora mistress of the bedchamber,' she said in a charming tone of voice.

'Signora,' the latter went on, 'Your Highness has seen clearly how things stand. You and I are facing the gravest dangers. Fabrizio's conviction has not been revoked. Consequently, the day they wish to get rid of me and insult you, they will put him back in prison. Our situation is as bad as it ever was. As for me personally, I shall marry the count and we shall go and settle in Naples or in Paris. The final show of ingratitude of which the count is currently the victim has thoroughly sickened him where public affairs are concerned and, were it not for Your Most Serene Highness's own interests, I would advise him to remain in this madhouse only on condition the prince pays him an enormous sum of money. I shall ask Your Highness's permission to explain to her that the count, who had a hundred and thirty thousand francs when he arrived in office, today has barely twenty thousand livres of income. I've been urging him for a long time now to think about his fortune, but in vain. During my absence, he has picked a quarrel with the prince's tax farmers, who were scoundrels. The count has replaced them with other scoundrels who have given him eight hundred thousand francs.'

'What!' exclaimed the princess in astonishment. 'Good gracious, that makes me very angry!'

'Signora,' replied the duchess, with the utmost composure, 'must we turn the magot's nose back to the left?'

'Good gracious, no,' cried the princess, 'but I'm angry that a man of the count's character should have thought of profiting in that fashion.'

'But for that robbery, he'd have been despised by every honest person.'

'Great heaven, is that possible?'

'Signora,' replied the duchess, 'except for my friend the Marchese Crescenzi, who has three or four hundred thousand livres a year, everyone here steals. And how would they not steal in a land where gratitude for the greatest services doesn't even last for a month? There's nothing real, therefore, or which survives a fall from favour, except money. I'm about to permit myself some terrible truths, signora.'

'I will permit them,' said the princess with a deep sigh, 'yet I find them cruelly disagreeable.'

'Very well, signora, the prince your son is a perfectly decent man, but he may make you much more unhappy than his father did. The late prince had character, like everybody more or less. Our present sovereign doesn't know if he wants the same thing three days running. As a result, to be able to have confidence in him, you need to live with him continuously and not let him talk to anyone. Since this is none too hard a truth to divine, the new ultra party, directed by the two who have good heads on their shoulders, Rassi and the Marchesa Raversi, is going to try to find the prince a mistress. That mistress will be given permission to make her fortune and hand out a few junior posts. But she'll have to answer to the party for her master's firmness of purpose.

'As for myself, in order to be properly established in Your Highness's court, I need Rassi to be exiled and treated with derision. I want, in addition, Fabrizio to be tried by the most honest judges that can be found. If these gentlemen recognize, as I hope they will, that he's innocent, it will be natural to grant the signore archbishop's wish that Fabrizio should be his coadjutor and future successor. If I fail, the count and I will withdraw. In which case I would leave Her Most Serene Highness with this parting advice: she must never forgive Rassi and never leave her son's States either. From close to, that good son won't do her any serious harm.'

'I have been following your arguments with all due attention,' replied the princess with a smile. 'So must I take on the responsibility of finding my son a mistress?'

'No, signora, but see to it first of all that your salon is the only one where he enjoys himself.'

The conversation went on endlessly in this way; the scales were falling from the eyes of the innocent but quick-witted princess.

A courier from the duchess went to tell Fabrizio that he could enter the town, but to remain hidden. He was hardly to be seen: he spent his time disguised as a peasant in the wooden hut of a chestnut vendor, set up opposite the gateway to the citadel, underneath the trees on the promenade.

CHAPTER 24

The duchess organized delightful soirées at the palace, which had never seen such gaiety. Never had she been more charming than that winter, even though she was living amidst the gravest dangers. But also during that crucial season, her thoughts turned only once or twice with a certain degree of unhappiness to the strange alteration in Fabrizio. The young prince came very early to the pleasant soirées given by his mother, who always told him: 'Go away and govern then. I'll wager there are more than twenty reports on your desk awaiting a yes or a no, and I don't want Europe accusing me of turning you into a do-nothing king so I can reign in your stead.'

Such advice had the drawback of always being offered at the most inopportune moments, that is to say, when His Highness, having overcome his timidity, was taking part in some charade which much amused him. Twice a week there were excursions into the countryside to which, on the pretext of winning over to the new sovereign the affection of his people, the princess would admit the prettiest women from among the bourgeoisie. The duchess, who was the life and soul of this festive court, hoped that these beautiful commoners, who had all felt bitterly envious of the glittering success of the commoner Rassi, would retail to the prince one or other of that minister's countless acts of villainy. For, among other childish ideas, the prince aspired to having a ministry that was *moral*.

Rassi had too much good sense not to be aware how dangerous these brilliant soirées at the princess's court, overseen by his enemy, were for him. He had refused to hand the perfectly legal sentence delivered on Fabrizio over to Count Mosca. It was necessary therefore that either he or the duchess should vanish from the court.

On the day of the popular agitation, the existence of which it was now the done thing to deny, money had been distributed among the people. Rassi began from there. Even worse dressed than normal, he went up into the most wretched houses in the town and spent hours at a time in systematic conversation with their penniless inhabitants. He was well rewarded for all his pains. After a fortnight of this way of life he knew for a fact that Ferrante Palla had been the secret leader of the insurrection, and what was more, that this individual, penniless throughout his life as a great poet, had sold eight or nine diamonds in Genoa.

They cited, among others, five valuable stones that were in fact worth more than forty thousand francs but which, 'ten days before the prince's death', had been let go for thirty-five thousand francs because, it was said, 'they needed the money'.

How to describe the minister of justice's raptures at this discovery? He was aware that they poked fun at him daily at the dowager princess's court, and several times the prince, while discussing business with him, had laughed in his face with all the innocence of youth. It has to be admitted that Rassi had some singularly plebeian habits. For example, as soon as a discussion took his interest, he would cross his legs and take his shoe in his hand. If his interest grew, he would spread his red cotton handkerchief over his leg, etc., etc. The prince had laughed uproariously at the joke played by one of the prettiest of the townswomen who, knowing what was more that she had very shapely legs, had started imitating this elegant gesture of the justice minister's.

Rassi solicited an extracurricular audience and asked the prince: 'Would Your Highness be willing to give a hundred thousand francs to know precisely how his august father came to meet his death? With a sum such as that, justice would be in a position to seize the culprits, if there are any.'

The prince's response was never in any doubt.

Some time after this, Chekina warned the duchess that she had been offered a large sum to allow her mistress's diamonds to be examined by a goldsmith. She had indignantly refused. The duchess told her off for refusing. One week later, Chekina had some diamonds to show. On the day chosen for the diamonds to be exhibited, Count Mosca set two trustworthy men on each of Parma's goldsmiths, and around midnight he came to tell the duchess that the inquisitive goldsmith was none other than Rassi's brother. The duchess, who was very cheerful that evening (they were performing a commedia dell'arte at the palace, one, that is, in which each character makes up the dialogue as he goes along, the outline of the play alone being posted up in the wings); the duchess, who was taking part, had for her lover in the play Count Baldi, the former friend of the Marchesa Raversi, who was present. The prince, the shyest man in his States, but a very good-looking youth and endowed with the tenderest of hearts, was understudying the role of Count Baldi, and wanted to play it at the second performance.

'I've only got a moment,' the duchess told the count. 'I appear in the first scene of act two. Let's go into the guardroom.'

There, amidst twenty guards, all very wide awake and very attentive to the conversation of the first minister and the mistress of the bedchamber, the duchess said, laughing, to her lover: 'You always tell me off when I come out with secrets needlessly. It's thanks to me that Ernest V was called to the throne. It was a matter of avenging Fabrizio, whom I loved much more then than now, although always perfectly innocently. I know very well you don't really believe in my innocence, but it hardly matters, since you love me in spite of my crimes. Very well, here is a real crime! I gave all my diamonds to a very interesting madman of sorts called Ferrante Palla, I even embraced him so as to get him to dispose of the man who wanted to poison Fabrizio. Where's the harm?'

'Aha, so that's where Ferrante got the money for his uprising,' said the count, somewhat stunned. 'And you're telling me all this in the guardroom!'

'It's because I'm in a hurry, and now Rassi is on the track of the crime. It's the truth that I never mentioned an insurrection, because I loathe the Jacobins. Give it some thought and tell me what your view is after the play.'

'I'll tell you here and now that you must inspire love in the prince . . . but fair and above board at least!'

The duchess was being called for to go on stage, and she fled.

A few days later, the duchess received through the post a long and ridiculous letter, signed with the name of one of her former lady's maids. The woman was asking to be employed at the court, but the duchess had recognized at first glance that it was neither her handwriting nor her style. On unfolding the sheet in order to read the second page, the duchess saw fall at her feet a small miraculous image of the Madonna, folded into a printed sheet from an old book. Having glanced at the image, the duchess read a few lines of the old printed sheet. Her eyes shone: she found the following words:

'The tribune has taken a hundred francs a month, no more. With the remainder we have sought to rekindle the sacred fire in souls that found themselves frozen by egotism. The fox is on my tracks, which is why I have not tried one last time to see the adored being. I told myself, she does not love the republic, she who is superior to me as much in her mind as in her charms and her beauty. How, anyway, to create a republic without republicans? Could I be mistaken? In six months' time, I shall travel, microscope in hand, and on foot, through the small towns of America, I shall see whether I must still love the one rival you have in my heart. If you receive this letter, signora baronessa, and no profane eye has read it before you, break off one of the young ash trees planted twenty paces from the spot where I dared to speak to you for the first time. Then I shall bury, under the big box tree in the garden you observed once in my happy times, a chest in which will be some of the things that cause people who share my opinions to be traduced. You may be sure I would have taken good care not to write were the fox not on my track and able to attain to that celestial being. See the box tree in two weeks' time.'

Since he has a printing-press at his beck and call, the duchess told herself, we shall soon be getting a collection of sonnets; God knows what name he'll give me in them!

In her coquetry the duchess wanted to try an experiment. For a week she was indisposed and there were no more jolly evenings at court. The princess, greatly shocked by everything her fear of her son had obliged her to do from the very outset of her widowhood, went to spend that week in a convent attached to the church where the late prince had been interred. This interruption to the soirées left the prince with an enormous amount of leisure, and proved seriously damaging to the standing of the minister of justice. Ernest V realized the boredom which threatened him should the duchess leave the court, or simply ceased from spreading enjoyment there. The soirées began again, and the prince took more and more interest in the commedia dell'arte. He planned to take part, but did not dare confess to this ambition. One day, blushing profusely, he asked the duchess: 'Why should I not act too?'

'All of us here are Your Highness's to command. If he condescends to give the order, I shall arrange the plot of a comedy, all the brilliant scenes with Your Highness's role in will be with me, and since everyone is a little hesitant on starting out, if Your Highness will watch me closely, I will tell him the replies he must give.' It was all arranged, with infinite skill. The very shy prince was ashamed of being shy. The pains the duchess took not to let that innate shyness show made a strong impression on the young sovereign.

On the day of his debut, the performance began half an hour earlier than usual, and at the time when they went through into the theatre, there were only eight or nine elderly women in the salon. Such figures hardly intimidated the prince and, moreover, having been brought up in Munich in accordance with the true principles of a monarchy, they were constantly applauding. Exerting her authority as mistress of the bedchamber, the duchess locked the door by which the common run of courtiers would come into the performance. The prince, who had a *literary* turn of mind and a good figure, got through the opening scenes very well. He repeated intelligently the phrases he could read in the duchess's eyes or which she indicated sotto voce. At a moment when the few spectators were applauding with all their might, the duchess gave a signal, the main doors were opened and the auditorium was instantly occupied by all the pretty women of the court who, considering that the prince had an attractive figure and looked very happy, began to applaud. The prince flushed with pleasure. He was playing the role of someone in love with the duchess. Very far from having to put words in his mouth, she was soon obliged to get him to cut the scenes short. He spoke of love with an enthusiasm which frequently embarrassed the actress. His speeches lasted five minutes. The duchess was no longer the dazzling beauty of the year before. Fabrizio's imprisonment and, even more so, the stay on Lake Maggiore with a Fabrizio now turned morose and silent, had aged the lovely Gina by ten years. Her features bore the traces, they displayed more intelligence and less youthfulness.

Only very rarely now did they have the sprightliness of her early years, but on stage, with the rouge and all the aids with which artifice can provide actresses, she was still the prettiest woman at the court. The passionate declamations delivered by the prince excited the courtiers' suspicions. They all told themselves that evening: here we have the Balbi of the new reign. The count rebelled inwardly. The play having ended, the duchess said to the prince, in front of the whole court: 'Your Highness acts too well. It's going to be said you're in love with a woman of thirty-eight, which will ruin my chances with the count. So I shan't perform any more with Your Highness, unless the prince swears he will address me as he would a woman of a certain age, the Signora Marchesa Raversi, for example.'

The same play was given three times. The prince was wildly happy. But one evening, he appeared very anxious. 'Either I'm much mistaken,' the mistress of the bedchamber said to her princess, 'or Rassi is looking to play some dirty trick on us. I advise Your Highness to indicate a performance for tomorrow. The prince will perform badly and in his despair, he will tell you something.'

The prince did indeed perform very badly. He could hardly be heard and he was unable to finish his sentences. At the end of the first act, he almost had tears in his eyes. The duchess stood next to him, but was cold and unmoving. The prince, finding himself alone with her for a moment, in the actors' foyer, went and shut the door. 'I shall never be able to do the second and third acts,' he told her. 'I absolutely don't want to be applauded out of politeness. The applause they gave me this evening broke my heart. Advise me, what should I do?'

'I shall go out on to the stage, make a deep curtsy to Her Highness, another to the audience, like a real stage manager, and say that the actor who was playing the part of Lelio has suddenly been taken ill and the performance will end with a few musical excerpts. Count Rusca and the young Ghisolfi will be overjoyed at being able to show off their vinegary little voices to so brilliant a gathering.'

The prince took the duchess by the hand and kissed it rapturously.

'Why are you not a man?' he said. 'You would give me good advice. Rassi has just laid on my desk a hundred and eighty-two witness statements against the purported assassins of my father. As well as the statements, there's an indictment of more than two hundred pages. I have to read all that and, what's more, I've given my word not to breathe a word to the count. This leads straight to the scaffold. He already wants me to have Ferrante Palla, that great poet whom I so much admire, abducted in France, near Antibes. He's there under the name of Poncet.'

'The day you have a liberal hanged, Rassi will be bound to the ministry with chains of iron, and that's what he wants above all else. But Your Highness won't be able to announce an excursion two hours in advance. I shall say nothing to the princess, or to the count, about the cry of pain you have just let out. But since, in accordance with my oath, I must not have any secrets from the princess, I should be happy if Your Highness were willing to tell his mother the same things he has let slip to me.'

This thought was a distraction from the pain of the actor who has flopped, which weighed heavily on the sovereign.

'Very well, go and warn my mother, I am going to her cabinet-room.'

The prince left the wings, crossed the salon through which

the theatre was reached, gruffly dismissed the high chamberlain and duty aide-de-camp who were following him. For her part, the princess left the performance precipitately. Having got to the cabinet-room, the mistress of the bedchamber made a deep curtsy to the mother and son, and left them on their own. The stir in the court may be imagined, this being the sort of thing that makes it so amusing. At the end of an hour, the prince himself appeared at the door of the room and called for the duchess. The princess was in tears, her son's expression had changed very much for the worse.

Here are weak individuals in a bad temper, the mistress of the bedchamber told herself, and looking for an excuse to be angry with someone. At first, the mother and son competed to recount the details to the duchess, who, in her replies, took good care not to put forward any ideas. For two mortal hours, the three actors in this tedious scene did not leave off the roles we have just indicated. The prince went himself to fetch the two enormous portfolios that Rassi had laid on his desk. On leaving his mother's cabinet-room, he found the whole court waiting. 'Go away, leave me alone,' he cried, in very coarse tones they had never heard from him before. The prince did not wish to be seen carrying the two portfolios himself, a prince should never carry anything. The courtiers instantly made themselves scarce. Returning, the prince now found only the manservants snuffing the candles. He sent them away, in a fury, along with poor Fontana, the duty aide-de-camp, who, zealous as he was, had been tactless enough to remain.

'Everyone's going out of their way to irritate me this evening,' he said bad-temperedly to the duchess as he was going back into the cabinet-room. He thought her very acute and was furious that she was obviously set on not offering any advice. She for her part was determined not to say anything until such time as she was asked for her advice *quite explicitly*. A full half-hour went by before the prince, who had a sense of his own dignity, made up his mind to say: 'But you are not speaking, signora.'

'I am here to serve the princess, and to forget very quickly what is said in my presence.'

'Very well, signora,' said the prince, going bright red, 'I order you to give me your advice.'

'Crimes are punished in order to prevent them from being repeated. Was the prince poisoned? That is very doubtful. Was he poisoned by the Jacobins? That's what Rassi would certainly like to prove, for then he would become a necessary instrument for Your Highness once and for all. In which event, Your Highness, who is beginning his reign, can promise himself many evenings like this one. Your subjects generally say, which is indeed the case, that Your Highness is kind-hearted by nature. For as long as he doesn't have some liberal or other hanged, he will enjoy that reputation, and no one will think of preparing poison for him for sure.'

'Your conclusion is self-evident,' exclaimed the princess bad-temperedly. 'You don't want my husband's assassins to be punished!'

'The fact is, signora, I apparently have the most affectionate ties to them.'

The duchess could see in the prince's eyes that he thought she was in perfect agreement with his mother about dictating his plan of conduct. There was a quite rapid exchange of tart rejoinders between the two women, following which the duchess protested that she would not utter a single word more, and she stuck to her decision. But, after a long discussion with his mother, the prince ordered her once more to give her opinion.

'That's what I swear to Your Highnesses I shan't do!'

'But that's being utterly childish!' exclaimed the prince.

'I request you to speak, signora duchess,' said the princess, with a dignified expression.

'That's what I beg you to excuse me from doing, signora. But Your Highness reads French perfectly,' the duchess went on, addressing the prince. 'To soothe our troubled minds, would he read us one of La Fontaine's fables?'

The princess found the 'us' very insolent, but she appeared at once surprised and amused when the mistress of the bed-chamber, who had gone over with the greatest composure to open the bookcase, returned with a volume of La Fontaine's *Fables*. She leafed through it for a few moments, then said to

the prince, handing it to him: 'I beg that Your Highness read
the *whole* fable.'

THE GARDENER AND HIS LORD[1]

A lover of gardening
Half-bourgeois, half-peasant,
Possessed in a certain village
A neat enough garden, and the close adjoining.
He had enclosed the plot with a quickset hedge:
Sorrel grew there in profusion and lettuces,
Enough for a bunch on Margot's name-day,
A little Spanish jasmine and wild thyme in plenty.
This bliss was disturbed by a hare
Which meant that our man complained to the lord of the town.
This accursed animal comes and fills its stomach
Morning and evening, he said, and laughs at the snares;
Stones and sticks are overrated:
He's a wizard, I believe. – A wizard, I defy him!
The lord rejoined: Even were he the devil, Miraut,
In spite of his tricks, will soon catch him.
I'll get rid of him for you, my good sir, upon my life.
– And when? – No later than tomorrow, no more waiting around.
The arrangement made, he comes with his men.
– Right, let's have breakfast, he says. Are your chickens tender?
Breakfast is followed by the huntsmen coming crowding in.
   They all grow excited and prepare themselves;
The trumpets and horns make such a din
   That the good man is stunned.
The worst of it was that the poor kitchen garden
Was got into a pitiful state. Farewell beds, vegetable patches;
   Farewell chicory and leeks;
   Farewell what goes in the soup.
The good man said: These are the games princes play.
But they ignored him; and the dogs and the men
Did more damage in one hour of time
   Than all the hares in the province
   Would have done in a hundred years.

*

> Petty princes, settle your disputes among yourselves;
> You'd be quite mad to call in kings.
> Never involve them in your wars,
> *Never bring them on to your land.*

The reading was followed by a long silence. The prince walked about the room, having himself gone to put the volume back.

'Well, signora,' said the princess. 'Will you condescend to speak?'

'No, certainly not, signora, not until such time as His Highness has appointed me as a minister. By speaking now, I would be running the risk of losing my place as mistress of the bedchamber.'

A fresh silence of a full quarter of an hour. Finally, the princess remembered the role once played by Marie de Médicis, the mother of Louis XIII: on each of the preceding days, the mistress of the bedchamber had made the lectress read M. Bazin's excellent *History of Louis XIII*.[2] The princess, though greatly piqued, thought that the duchess might very well leave the country, and then Rassi, of whom she was dreadfully afraid, might very well imitate Richelieu and have her exiled by her son. At that moment, the princess would have given everything she possessed to humiliate her mistress of the bedchamber, but she was unable to do so. She stood up and came, with a somewhat exaggerated smile, and took the duchess by the hand and said: 'Come, signora, prove your friendship by speaking.'

'Very well, two words, no more! Burn in the fireplace there all the papers assembled by that viper Rassi, and never admit to him they've been burnt.'

She added sotto voce, with a familiar expression, in the princess's ear: 'Rassi may be Richelieu!'

'But for God's sake, those papers have cost me more than eighty thousand francs!' cried the prince, angrily.

'My prince,' replied the duchess, forcefully, 'that's the price you pay for employing low-born scoundrels. Would to God you might lose a million and never lend credence to the squalid ruffians who stopped your father from sleeping during the last six years of his reign.'

The term *low-born* had given extreme pleasure to the princess, who considered that the count and his mistress had too exclusive a respect for sharp wits, which were always a little too closely akin to Jacobinism.

During the brief moment of profound silence, filled with the princess's reflections, the castle clock struck three. The princess rose, made a deep curtsy to her son and said: 'My health does not permit me to prolong the discussion any further. A low-born minister? Never! You won't rid me of the idea that your Rassi has stolen from you half the money he has made you spend on espionage.' The princess took two candles from the candelabra and placed them in the fireplace, in such a way as not to extinguish them. Then, going up to her son, she added: 'La Fontaine's fable carries the day, to my way of thinking, over the just desire to avenge a husband. Will Your Highness permit me to burn these *writings*?' The prince remained motionless.

He has a really stupid expression, the duchess told herself. The count is right, the late prince wouldn't have kept us up until three in the morning before coming to a decision.

The princess, still standing, added: 'The little procurator would be very proud, if he knew how his paperwork, full of lies and arranged so as to procure his advancement, has made the two greatest personages in the State spend the night.'

The prince threw himself at one of the portfolios like a man possessed, and emptied its entire contents into the fireplace. The mass of papers was on the point of stifling the two candles. The apartment filled with smoke. The princess could see from her son's eyes that he was tempted to seize a jug and save the papers, which had cost him eighty thousand francs.

'So open the window!' she shouted at the duchess crossly. The duchess made haste to obey. All the papers immediately burst into flames at one and the same time. There was a loud noise in the chimney and it was soon evident that it had caught fire.

The prince was small of soul when it came to money. He fancied he could see his palace in flames, and all the treasures that it contained destroyed. He ran to the window and summoned the guard in an altogether different voice. The soldiers having rushed pell-mell into the courtyard at the sound of the prince's voice, he came back to the fireplace, which was drawing air in from the open window with a truly frightening noise. He grew impatient, swore, took two or three turns about the room like a man beside himself, then finally ran out.

The princess and her mistress of the bedchamber remained standing, one facing the other, preserving a profound silence. Is the anger going to begin again? the duchess asked herself; my case is won, I do believe. And she was getting ready to be highly impertinent in her replies, when she had a sudden thought. She could see that the second portfolio remained intact. No, my case is only half won! She said to the princess, somewhat coldly: 'Will the signora give me the order to burn the rest of the papers?'

'But where will you burn them?' asked the princess bad-temperedly.

'In the fireplace in the salon. There's no danger if you throw them in one after the other.'

The duchess put the portfolio stuffed with papers under her arm, picked up a candle and passed on into the salon next door. She took the time to check that this portfolio was the one with the depositions in, put five or six bundles of papers into her shawl, burnt the remainder very carefully, then vanished without taking her leave of the princess.

That was grossly impertinent, she told herself, laughing. But by affecting to be the inconsolable widow, she all but caused me to lose my head on the scaffold.

On hearing the sound of the duchess's carriage, the princess flew into a rage against her mistress of the bedchamber.

In spite of the unseemly hour, the duchess sent for the count. He was at the fire at the castle, but soon appeared with the news that it was out. 'The young prince actually showed a lot of courage, and I complimented him on it effusively.'

'Examine these statements quickly, and burn them as soon as you can.'

The count read them and turned pale. 'They came very close to the truth, I must say. The procedures have been very adroitly carried out, they're on the trail of Ferrante Palla right enough. And if he talks, we have a difficult role to play.'

'But he won't talk,' exclaimed the duchess. 'Not him, he's a
man of honour. Burn them, burn them.'

'Not yet. Allow me to take the names of twelve or thirteen
dangerous witnesses, whom I'll take the liberty of having
abducted should Rassi ever want to start up again.'

'I must remind Your Excellency that the prince gave his word
to say nothing to his minister of justice about our nocturnal
expedition.'

'Out of pusillanimity, and for fear of a scene, he'll keep it.'

'And now, my love, tonight is bringing our marriage a lot
closer. I wouldn't have wanted to bring you a criminal trial as
a dowry, let alone for a fault I was led to commit through my
concern for someone else.'

The count was in love, he took her by the hand, he exclaimed;
he had tears in his eyes.

'Before you go, give me some advice on how I should behave
towards the princess. I'm quite tired out, I've been play-acting
for an hour on the stage and five hours in the cabinet-room.'

'You've had ample revenge for the princess's tart remarks,
which were only weakness, thanks to the impertinence of your
departure. Take the tone of voice again with her tomorrow that
you had this morning. Rassi isn't in prison yet or in exile, and
we haven't yet torn up Fabrizio's sentence.

'You were asking the princess to make a decision, which
always puts princes and even first ministers in a bad mood.
Anyway, you're her mistress of the bedchamber, that's to say,
her humble servant. There'll be a reaction, there unfailingly is
with the weak; within three days Rassi will be more in favour
than ever. He's going to be looking to hang someone. So long as
he hasn't compromised the prince, he's not sure about anything.

'A man was injured at the fire this evening. It was a tailor,
who displayed remarkable intrepidity I must say. Tomorrow,
I'm going to get the prince to lean on my arm, and come with
me to pay a call on the tailor. I shall be armed to the teeth, and
keeping an eye out. This young prince isn't hated yet in any
case. I want to get him used to going out into the streets; it's a
trick I'm playing on Rassi, who is certainly going to be my
successor, and won't be able to permit any more rashness of

the sort. Coming back from the tailor's, I shall make the prince go past his father's statue. He'll notice where the rocks broke the Roman skirts that nincompoop of a statuary dolled him up in. And the prince will show a remarkable lack of nous if he doesn't come to this conclusion of his own accord: "That's what you gain by hanging Jacobins." To which I shall reply: "You need to hang ten thousand or none at all. St Bartholomew destroyed the Protestants in France."[3]

'Tomorrow, my love, before my promenade, have yourself announced to the prince and say to him: "Yesterday evening, I served you in the role of minister, I gave you advice and, on your orders, incurred the displeasure of the princess. I need to be paid." He'll be expecting a demand for money and will frown. You will leave him sunk in that unhappy thought for as long as you can. Then you will say: "I ask Your Highness to order that Fabrizio be tried *in contradittorio*[4] (which means with him present) by the twelve most highly respected judges in your States." And without wasting any time, you will present for signature a brief ordinance written in your own fair hand, which I'm going to dictate to you. I shall of course include a clause that the earlier verdict be annulled. There's only one objection to that, but if you keep up the pressure, it won't cross the prince's mind. He may say to you: "Fabrizio must give himself into custody at the citadel." To which you will answer: "He will give himself into custody at the gaol in the town" (you know that I'm the master there, your nephew will come and visit you every evening). If the prince answers: "No, his escape has besmirched the honour of my citadel and, for form's sake, I wish him to return to the room where he was," you will answer in your turn: "No, because there he'll be at the mercy of my enemy Rassi." And, in one of those womanly phrases you're so good at coming out with, you will give him to understand that, in order to sway Rassi, you may well tell him about tonight's auto-da-fé. If he insists, you will announce that you are going to spend a fortnight in your house at Sacca.

'You are going to send for Fabrizio and consult with him about this manoeuvre that may lead him into prison. So that we've foreseen everything, if, while he's under lock and key,

Rassi grows too impatient and has me poisoned, Fabrizio may be at risk. But that's not very likely. You know I've brought in a French cook, the most cheerful of men, who makes puns. And puns are incompatible with murder. I've already told our friend Fabrizio that I've discovered all the witnesses to his noble and courageous act. It was obviously Giletti who was trying to murder him. I didn't mention these witnesses, because I wanted to surprise you, but the plan failed: the prince refused to sign. I told our Fabrizio that I would certainly obtain for him some high ecclesiastical position, but I shall find that very difficult if his enemies can object in court in Rome that he has been charged with a murder.

'Do you sense, signora, that if he isn't tried in the most solemn fashion, he'll find the name of Giletti disagreeable all through his life? It would be very pusillanimous not to have yourself tried, when you're sure of your innocence. In any case, were he guilty, I'd get him acquitted. When I spoke to him, the impetuous young man didn't let me finish, he picked up the official almanac and we chose together the twelve most upright and learned judges. Having made a list, we rubbed out six names, which we replaced by six jurisconsults, my personal enemies, and since we were able to find only two enemies, we made up the numbers with four scoundrels devoted to Rassi.'

This proposal of the count's seriously worried the duchess, and not without cause. In the end, she yielded to reason and, at the minister's dictation, wrote the ordinance appointing the judges.

The count did not leave her until six o'clock in the morning. She tried to sleep, but in vain. At nine, she breakfasted with Fabrizio, whom she found with a burning desire to be tried. At ten, she was at the princess's, who was not visible. At eleven, she saw the prince, who was holding his levee and signed the ordinance without raising the least objection. The duchess sent the ordinance to the count and went to bed.

It would be droll perhaps to describe Rassi's fury, when the count forced him to countersign, in the prince's presence, the ordinance signed by the latter that morning. But events press in on us.

The count debated the merits of each of the judges, and offered to change the names. But the reader is perhaps a little weary of all these procedural details, no less than of all the intrigues at court. From all this, the moral may be drawn that the man who goes near the court is endangering his happiness, if he is happy, but in any case lets his future depend on the schemes of a lady's maid.

On the other hand, in America, in the republic, one has the day-long tedium of paying serious court to the shopkeepers in the street, and becoming as stupid as they are. And no opera there.

At her evening levee, the duchess knew a moment of acute anxiety. Fabrizio was no longer to be found. Finally, at around midnight, at the court theatre, she received a letter from him. Instead of giving himself into custody at 'the gaol in the town', where the count was master, he had gone and reoccupied his former room in the citadel, only too happy to be living a few steps away from Clelia.

This was an event heavy with consequences. In that place, he was more at risk of being poisoned than ever. This act of folly made the duchess despair. She forgave him the reason for it, his mad passion for Clelia, because in a few days' time she was definitely going to marry the wealthy Marchese Crescenzi. This madness gave Fabrizio back all the influence he had once had over the duchess's soul.

It's that accursed bit of paper I went and got signed that will bring about his death! These men are mad with their ideas of honour! As if you need to worry about honour under absolute governments, in countries where a Rassi is minister of justice. He should quite simply have accepted the pardon the prince would have signed just as readily as convoking this extracurricular court. What does it matter after all if a man of Fabrizio's birth should be more or less accused of having killed, sword in hand, a histrion such as Giletti!

No sooner had she received Fabrizio's letter than the duchess hastened to the count, whom she found deathly pale.

'Dear God, I do nothing but mismanage that boy, and you're going to hold it against me again, my love. I can prove I got the gaoler from the prison in the town to come here yesterday evening. Every day, your nephew would have come to have tea with you. What's so awful is that it's out of the question that you and I should tell the prince we fear poison, and poison administered by Rassi. That suspicion would strike him as the last word in immorality. All the same, if you require me to, I'm ready to go up to the palace. But I'm sure of the response. I shall say more. I'm offering you a means I wouldn't employ on my own account. Since I've had power in this country, I haven't brought about the death of a single man, and you know that I'm such a milksop where that's concerned that sometimes, at the end of the day, I still think about those two spies I had shot a little casually in Spain. Well, do you want me to get rid of Rassi for you? The danger he poses to Fabrizio is immeasurable. He has a sure means there of making me clear out.'

This proposal the duchess found extremely welcome. But she did not adopt it. 'I don't want you having morbid thoughts in the evenings, in our retirement, under the beautiful Naples sky,' she told the count.

'But, my love, I fancy that a choice of morbid thoughts is all we have. What would become of you, what would become of me, if Fabrizio is carried off by a sickness?'

The debate resumed all the more energetically over this idea, and the duchess ended it with these words: 'Rassi owes his life to the fact that I love you more than Fabrizio. No, I don't want to poison all the evenings we're going to spend together in our old age.'

The duchess hurried to the fortress. General Fabio Conti was delighted to be able to confront her with the formal wording of the military regulations. No one to penetrate inside a State prison without an order signed by the prince.

'But the Marchese Crescenzi and his musicians come to the citadel every day?'

'That's because I've obtained an order for them from the prince.'

The poor duchess did not know the full extent of her misfortunes. General Fabio Conti had considered himself dishonoured by Fabrizio's escape. When he saw him arrive at the citadel, he ought not to have received him, for he had no orders to that effect. But it's heaven that has sent him to me, he told himself, to restore my honour and save me from the ridicule that would be a slur on my military career. I must see I don't waste the opportunity. He's surely going to be acquitted and I've only a few days to take my revenge.

CHAPTER 25

Our hero's arrival sent Clelia into despair. Pious and sincere with herself as she was, the poor girl could not disguise the fact that there would never be any happiness for her far away from Fabrizio. But she had made a vow to the Madonna at the time of her father's half-poisoning, to make the latter the sacrifice of marrying the Marchese Crescenzi. She had made a vow not to set eyes on Fabrizio, and was already prey to the most terrible remorse, for the avowal into which she had been drawn in the letter she had written to Fabrizio on the eve of his escape. How to depict what happened in that unhappy heart when, busy melancholically watching her birds fluttering about, and raising her eyes out of habit and with fondness towards the window from which in the old days Fabrizio had watched her, she once again saw him greeting her with tender respect.

She thought it was a vision permitted by heaven in order to punish her. Then the ghastly reality appeared to her reason. They've recaptured him, she told herself, he's lost! She recalled the comments made in the fortress after the escape. The humblest gaolers adjudged themselves mortally insulted. Clelia looked at Fabrizio and, despite herself, that look portrayed in its entirety the passion that had caused her to despair.

Do you believe, she seemed to be saying to Fabrizio, that I shall find happiness in the sumptuous palazzo that is being got ready for me? My father repeats ad nauseam that you are as poor as we are, but dear God, how happy I should be to share that poverty! But alas, we must never see one another again.

Clelia did not have the strength to make use of the alphabets. Gazing at Fabrizio she felt unwell and dropped on to a chair

next to the window. Her cheek was resting on the window ledge
and, since she had wanted to carry on looking at him up until the
very last moment, her face was turned towards Fabrizio, who
could see the whole of it. When, after a few moments, she
reopened her eyes, her first glance was for Fabrizio. She saw tears
in his eyes. But these tears were the effect of extreme happiness;
he could see that his absence had not caused her to forget him.
These two poor young people remained for some while as if
spellbound by the sight of one another. Fabrizio ventured to
sing, as though he were accompanying himself on the guitar, a
few improvised words which went: '*It is in order to see you
again* that I have come back into prison. *I am going to be tried.*'

These words seemed to reawaken all of Clelia's virtue. She
quickly got to her feet, hid her eyes and, quickly gesturing, tried
to express to him that she must never see him again. She had
made a promise to the Madonna and had just looked at him
out of forgetfulness. As Fabrizio ventured to express his love
once more, Clelia fled indignantly, swearing to herself that she
would never set eyes on him again, for those were the exact
words of her vow to the Madonna: *I will never set eyes on him
again.* She had inscribed them on a small sheet of paper that
her Uncle Cesare had allowed her to burn on the altar at the
moment of the offertory, while he was saying Mass.

But despite all her oaths, Fabrizio's presence in the Farnese
Tower had sent Clelia back to her old ways. She normally spent
her days alone, in her room. Hardly had she recovered from
the unforeseen agitation into which the sight of Fabrizio had
plunged her before she began to walk about the palazzo and,
as it were, renew her acquaintance with all her friends among
the underlings. A very talkative old woman employed in the
kitchens told her, wearing a mysterious expression: 'This time,
Signor Fabrizio won't be leaving the citadel.'

'He won't make the mistake of going over the walls again,'
said Clelia, 'but he'll leave by the gate, if he's acquitted.'

'I say, and I can tell Your Excellency, that he'll only leave the
citadel feet first.'

Clelia went deathly pale, and the old woman, observing this,
cut short her eloquence. She told herself she had been unwise

to speak in that way in front of the daughter of the governor, whose duty it was going to be to tell the whole world that Fabrizio had died from a sickness. Going back up to her room, Clelia encountered the prison doctor, a timid sort of a man but honest, who told her, looking most alarmed, that Fabrizio was very sick. Clelia could barely support herself. She looked everywhere for her uncle, the good Father Don Cesare, and at last found him in the chapel, where he was praying fervently. He looked extremely upset. The bell went for dinner. At table, not a word passed between the two brothers. Only towards the end of the meal did the general address a few very sour words to his brother. The latter looked towards the servants, who went out.

'General,' Don Cesare said to the governor, 'I have the honour of warning you that I shall be leaving the citadel. I am handing in my resignation.'

'Bravo, bravissimo! So as to throw suspicion on to me . . . The reason, may I ask?'

'My conscience.'

'Oh come, you're nothing but a priest, you know nothing about honour.'

Fabrizio is dead, Clelia told herself. He was poisoned at dinner, or else it will be for tomorrow. She ran to the aviary, resolved to sing while accompanying herself on the piano. I will go to confession, she said to herself, and I shall be forgiven for having broken my vow in order to save a man's life. She was thunderstruck when, having reached the aviary, she saw that the screens had just been replaced by planks fastened to the iron bars. Distraught, she tried to alert the prisoner by a few words that were shouted rather than sung. There was no response of any kind. A deathly silence already reigned in the Farnese Tower. It's all over and done with, she told herself. She went downstairs distraught, then went back up to provide herself with the little money that she had and some small diamond earrings. She also took, as she went past, the bread left over from dinner, which had been put on a sideboard. If he's still alive, my duty is to save him. Wearing a haughty expression she made towards the small door of the tower. The door was open, and they had just posted eight soldiers in the room with the columns on the ground floor. She stared boldly at the soldiers. Clelia had counted on addressing the sergeant who must be in charge of them; the man wasn't there. Clelia flew to the small iron spiral staircase that wound round one of the pillars. The soldiers watched her open-mouthed, but, seemingly on account of her lace shawl and her hat, did not dare say anything to her. There was no one on the first floor, but on reaching the second floor, at the entrance to the corridor which, the reader may recall, was closed off by three iron-barred doors and led to Fabrizio's room, she found a warder not known to her, who said to her, looking alarmed: 'He hasn't eaten yet.'

'I know that perfectly well,' said Clelia, disdainfully. The man did not dare stop her. Twenty paces further on, Clelia found another warder, very old and very red in the face, sitting on the first of the six wooden steps that led to Fabrizio's room. He said to her determinedly: 'Signorina, do you have an order from the governor?'

'Do you not know who I am?'

At that moment, Clelia was fired with a supernatural strength, she was like a woman possessed. I am going to save my husband, she told herself.

As the old warder was crying: 'My duty doesn't allow me . . .' Clelia was rapidly mounting the six steps. She dashed at the door. There was a huge key in the lock; she needed all her strength to turn it. At that moment, the old half-drunk warder grabbed the bottom of her dress. She went quickly into the room, closed the door again, tearing her dress, and, as the warder pushed against it to enter behind her, she locked it with a bolt she found next to her hand. She looked into the room and saw Fabrizio sitting at a very small table on which was his dinner. She dashed at the table, overturned it and, seizing hold of Fabrizio's arm, said: 'Have you eaten?'

Her addressing him as *tu* enraptured Fabrizio. In her agitation, Clelia had forgotten her feminine reserve for the first time, and allowed her love to show.

Fabrizio had been about to start on the fatal meal. He took her in his arms and covered her with kisses. The dinner has been poisoned, he thought. If I tell her I haven't touched it, religion will reclaim its rights and Clelia will run off. If on the other hand she looks on me as a dying man, I shall get her to agree not to leave me. She longs to find a way to break off that loathsome marriage, and chance is offering us one. The gaolers will arrive together, they'll break down the door and there'll be such a scandal that the Marchese Crescenzi will perhaps be frightened and the marriage broken off.

During the moment's silence filled with these reflections, Fabrizio could feel that Clelia was already trying to free herself from his embraces.

'I don't feel any pains yet,' he said, 'but soon they'll have me prostrate at your feet. Help me to die.'

'Oh, my one and only friend,' she said, 'I shall die with you!' As if convulsively, she clutched him tightly in her arms.

She was so lovely, half dressed and in this state of extreme passion, that Fabrizio could not resist an almost involuntary movement. It did not meet with any resistance.

In the enthusiasm of passion and generosity that follows a moment of extreme happiness, he said to her without thinking: 'An unworthy lie mustn't be allowed to sully the first moments of our happiness. But for your courage, I should now be nothing more than a corpse, or wrestling against excruciating pains. But I was about to start eating when you entered, I haven't touched those dishes.'

Fabrizio dwelt on these awful mental pictures in order to ward off the indignation he could read in Clelia's eyes. She gazed at him for a moment or two, as two violent and opposed emotions did battle, then she threw herself into his arms. A loud noise came from the corridor, the three iron doors were being violently opened and shut, men were shouting at one another.

'Oh, if only I had a weapon!' cried Fabrizio. 'They made me give them up before I was allowed to enter. They're no doubt coming to finish me off! Farewell, my Clelia, I bless my death because it has been the occasion of my happiness.' Clelia embraced him and gave him a small dagger with an ivory handle, whose blade was hardly any longer than that of a penknife.

'Don't let yourself be killed,' she told him, 'defend yourself to the last breath. If my uncle the priest hears the noise, he's a courageous man, a good man, he will rescue you. I'm going to speak to them.' Saying which, she dashed towards the door.

'If you're not killed,' she said excitedly, her hand on the bolt and turning her head towards him, 'let yourself die of hunger rather than touch anything at all. Always carry this bread with you.' The noise came closer, Fabrizio seized her round the waist, took up his position beside the door and, opening it in a frenzy, dashed out on to the wooden staircase with its six steps. He had the little ivory-handled dagger in his hand and was on the point of sticking it into the waistcoat of General Fontana, the prince's aide-de-camp, who recoiled very quickly, crying out in terror: 'But I've come to save you, Signor del Dongo!'

Fabrizio went back up the six steps and called into the room: 'Fontana's come to save me!' Then, returning to the general on the wooden steps, he coolly explained himself. He begged him at some length to forgive him for his initial upsurge of anger. 'They wanted to poison me. The meal in front of me there has been poisoned. I had the wit not to touch it, but I'll confess that the whole business has shocked me. Hearing you coming up, I thought they'd come to finish me off with a dagger ... Signor General, I request you to order that no one should enter my room. They would remove the poison, and our good prince must be told everything.'

The general, white in the face and dumbstruck, transmitted the orders Fabrizio had indicated to the hand-picked gaolers who had been following him. The men, crestfallen at seeing the poison discovered, were in a hurry to go back down. They went ahead, seemingly so as not to hold the prince's aide-de-camp up on the narrow stairs, but in fact in order to make their escape and vanish. To General Fontana's great surprise, Fabrizio paused for a good quarter of an hour on the small iron staircase around the column on the ground floor. He wanted to give Clelia time to hide on the first floor.

It was the duchess who, after several frantic endeavours, had succeeded in getting General Fontana sent to the citadel. She achieved it by chance. On leaving Count Mosca, who was as alarmed as she was, she had hurried to the palace. The princess, who was markedly averse to any show of energy, which she considered vulgar, thought she had lost her senses, and did not seem at all disposed to attempt any unusual initiatives on her behalf. The duchess was beside herself, weeping hot tears, and able only to go on saying over and over: 'But signora, in quarter of an hour Fabrizio will be dead from poison!'

Seeing the princess's complete indifference, the duchess went mad with grief. She did not make the moral reflection, which would not have escaped a woman brought up in the religions of the north, which permit self-examination: I was the first to use poison and I am perishing by poison. In Italy, reflections of that kind, in a moment of great passion, would be seen as showing a poverty of spirit, just as making a pun in similar circumstances would in Paris.

The duchess, despairing, chanced to go into the salon, where the Marchese Crescenzi happened to be on duty that day. On the duchess's return to Parma, he had thanked her effusively for the position of lord-in-waiting, to which, but for her, he could never have aspired. Protestations of boundless devotion had not been lacking on his part. The duchess accosted him with these words: 'Rassi is going to poison Fabrizio, who is in the citadel. Take in your pocket some chocolate and a bottle of water I shall give you. Go up to the citadel, and restore me to life by telling General Fabio Conti that you will break it off with his daughter if he doesn't allow you to hand the water and chocolate to Fabrizio personally.'

The marchese went pale, and his expression, far from growing animated at these words, portrayed the most craven embarrassment. He could not believe in so awful a crime in a town as moral as Parma, reigned over by so great a prince, etc. What's more, he spoke these platitudes slowly. In short, the duchess found a decent man but an exceedingly weak one who could not make up his mind to act. After twenty phrases of the kind, interrupted by Signora Sanseverina's cries of impatience, he hit on an excellent idea: the oath he had taken as a lord-in-waiting forbade him from getting involved in manoeuvres against the government.

Who could picture to themselves the anxiety and despair of the duchess, who felt that time was flying? 'But see the governor at least, tell him I shall pursue Fabrizio's murderers to the gates of hell!'

Despair enhanced the duchess's natural eloquence, but all this heat merely further alarmed the marchese and increased his lack of resolve. At the end of an hour, he was less inclined to act than he had been at the start.

The unhappy woman, having reached the ultimate limits of despair, and feeling sure that the governor would refuse nothing to a wealthy son-in-law, went so far as to throw herself down on her knees, at which the Marchese Crescenzi's pusillanimity seemed to increase yet further. At the sight of this strange spectacle, he feared he might be compromised without knowing it. But a strange thing happened: the marchese, a well-meaning man at heart, was touched by the tears and the position, at his feet, of a woman at once so beautiful and above all so influential.

I who am so great a nobleman and so rich, he told himself, I too may one day be at the knees of some republican or other! The marchese began to weep, and at last it was agreed that the duchess, in her role of mistress of the bedchamber, would present him to the princess, who would give him permission to hand Fabrizio a small basket of whose contents he would declare himself ignorant.

The previous evening, before the duchess had learnt of Fabrizio's folly in going to the citadel, a commedia dell'arte had been performed at court, and the prince, who always reserved for himself the roles of the duchess's lovers, had been so passionate in speaking to her of his affections, that he would have seemed ridiculous if, in Italy, a passionate man or a prince could ever be so!

For all his timidity, the prince always took matters of the heart very seriously. In one of the corridors in the castle he encountered the duchess, who was dragging the greatly agitated

Marchese Crescenzi along to the princess. He was so surprised and dazzled by the beauty, filled with emotion, that her despair had lent to the mistress of the bedchamber that for the first time in his life he showed some character. With a more than imperious gesture, he sent the marchese away and started to make an entirely formal declaration of love to the duchess. The prince had no doubt planned it a long time in advance, for some things in it were almost reasonable.

'Since the proprieties of my rank forbid me from giving myself the supreme happiness of marrying you, I shall swear to you on the holy, consecrated wafer never to get married without your written permission. I am very conscious,' he went on, 'that I am causing you to lose the hand of a first minister, a man of high intelligence and most agreeable. But then, he is fifty-six and I am not yet twenty-two. I think I would be insulting you and deserving of your refusal were I to speak of the advantages of having nothing to do with love. But all who value money in my court speak admiringly of the proof of love the count has given you, by making you the trustee of everything he possesses. I would be only too happy to imitate him in that regard. You will make better use of my fortune than I, and you will have at your disposal the entire annual sum that my ministers give to the high steward of the crown. In such a way that it will be you, signora duchess, who will decide on the sums I am able to spend each month.' The duchess found all these details very long-winded; the danger to Fabrizio was piercing her to the heart.

'But do you not know then, prince,' she cried, 'that they are poisoning Fabrizio this very minute in your citadel! Save him! I believe everything you say.'

The wording of this sentence could hardly have been clumsier. At the very mention of 'poison', all the impetuosity, all the good faith that this poor, right-minded prince had brought to the conversation vanished in the blink of an eye. The duchess only appreciated how clumsy she had been once it was too late to put it right, and her despair increased, something she had thought impossible. If I hadn't mentioned poison, she told herself, he'd have granted me Fabrizio's freedom. Oh Fabrizio dear, she went on, it's written then that it's I who must pierce you to the heart by my stupidities!

It took the duchess a long time and much flirtatiousness to get the prince back on to his declarations of a passionate love. He remained deeply alarmed. It was his mind alone that spoke; his soul had been frozen, first of all by the idea of poison, and then by this other thought, as disagreeable as the first had been terrible: they are administering poison in my States, and that without telling me! So Rassi wants to dishonour me in the eyes of Europe! And God knows what I shall be reading next month in the Paris newspapers!

This very timid young man's soul suddenly falling silent, his mind arrived at an idea. 'Dear duchess, you know how attached I am to you. Your ghastly ideas about poison are without foundation, I would like to think. But they have also set me to thinking; they almost make me forget for a moment the passion I feel for you, the only one I have ever experienced in my whole life. I sense that I am not fit to be loved. I am only a child very much in love. But put me to the test.'

The prince became quite animated in speaking in such terms.

'Save Fabrizio and I will believe everything you say! I'm no doubt being carried away by the crazy fears of a mother's soul. But send to fetch Fabrizio this instant from the citadel, so that I can set eyes on him. If he is still alive, send him from the palace to the prison in the town where he can stay for months on end, if Your Highness requires it, up until his hearing.'

The duchess saw, despairingly, that instead of granting by a word something so simple, the prince had become sombre. He was very red in the face, he looked at the duchess, then dropped his eyes, and his cheeks went pale. The thought of poison, raised at exactly the wrong moment, had given him an idea worthy of his father or of Philip II; but he did not dare express it.

'Listen, signora,' he said finally, as if doing violence to his feelings and none too graciously, 'you despise me as a child and, what's more, as someone lacking in charm. Very well, I am going to say something horrible, but which has been suggested this instant by the true and profound passion I feel for you. If I had even the faintest belief in the poison, I would already have acted, my duty would have dictated that. But I see only an impassioned fantasy in your request, whose full import, I ask you to allow me to say, I cannot see. You wish me to act without consulting my ministers, I who have been reigning for three months barely. You are asking me to make a great exception to my normal course of action, which I believe to be a very reasonable one, I have to admit. It's you, signora, who are at this moment the absolute sovereign, you give me hope in the matter that means everything to me. But one hour from now, once this imaginary poison, this nightmare, has vanished, my presence will become importunate for you, and you will banish me, signora. Very well, I must have an oath. Swear, signora, that if Fabrizio is returned to you safe and sound, I shall obtain from you, within the next three months, the greatest happiness that my love can desire. You will ensure the happiness of my entire life by putting at my disposal one hour of your own, and you will be mine alone.'

At that moment, the castle clock struck two. Oh, there's no longer time perhaps, the duchess told herself.

'I swear!' she cried, her eyes staring wildly.

The prince at once became another man. He ran to the far end of the gallery where the room for his aides-de-camp was. 'General Fontana, go hell for leather to the citadel, go up as fast as you can to the room where Signor del Dongo is being kept and bring him to me, I have to speak with him within twenty minutes, or fifteen if possible.'

'And general,' cried the duchess, who had followed the prince, 'one minute may determine my life. A no doubt false report of poison has made me fear for Fabrizio. Shout to him, as soon as you're within earshot, not to eat. If he's begun on his meal, make him vomit it up, tell him it's I who wish it, employ force if you have to. Tell him I'm following close behind you, and you can believe I shall be obliged to you for the rest of my life.'

'Signora duchess, my horse is saddled, I'm known to be able to handle a horse and I shall go hell for leather, I'll be at the citadel eight minutes before you.'

'And I, signora duchess,' cried the prince, 'I ask you for four of those eight minutes.'

The aide-de-camp had vanished, he was a man whose one talent was for horsemanship. Hardly had he closed the door again before the young prince, who seemed to be showing character, seized the duchess's hand. 'Condescend to come with me to the chapel, signora,' he said passionately. The duchess, speechless for the first time in her life, followed him without saying a word. She and the prince covered the full length of the great gallery of the palace at a run, the chapel lying at the far end. Having entered the chapel, the prince fell to his knees, almost as much before the duchess as before the altar.

'Repeat the oath,' he said passionately. 'If you had been just, if this unfortunate rank of prince hadn't worked against me, you would have granted me out of compassion for my love what you now owe me because you have sworn an oath.'

'If I see Fabrizio again and he has not been poisoned, if he is still alive a week from now, if His Highness appoints him as coadjutor with the future succession to Archbishop Landriani, I shall trample my honour and my woman's dignity underfoot, and I shall be His Highness's.'

'But, *my dear*,' said the prince, with a very droll mixture of anxiety, diffidence and tenderness, 'I fear some trap that I don't understand, which might destroy my happiness. It would be the death of me. What shall I do if the archbishop raises one of those ecclesiastical objections which can mean that these affairs go on for years on end? You can see that I am acting in complete good faith. Are you going to play the Jesuit with me?'

'No, in good faith, if Fabrizio is saved, if, on your full authority, you make him coadjutor and the future archbishop, I shall dishonour myself and be yours. Your Highness must undertake to write "approved" in the margin of a request that monsignore the archbishop will present to you within the next seven days.'

'I shall sign a blank sheet of paper for you; reign over me and over my States!' cried the prince, going red with happiness and truly in his seventh heaven. He demanded a second oath. He was so emotional that he forgot the diffidence that was second nature with him, and in the chapel of the palace, where they were alone, he said in a low voice to the duchess things which, spoken three days earlier, would have altered the opinion she held of him. But in her, the despair caused by the danger to Fabrizio had given way to horror at the promise that had been wrung from her.

The duchess was devastated by what she had just done. If she had yet to feel the full terrible bitterness of the words she had uttered, it was because her attention was taken up with finding out whether General Fontana might have got to the citadel in time.

To free herself from this child's foolish endearments and change the subject somewhat, she praised a celebrated painting of Parmigianino's, which was over the high altar in the chapel.

'Be so kind as to permit me to send it to you,' said the prince.

'I accept,' the duchess went on. 'But allow me to run and meet Fabrizio.'

Looking distraught, she told her coachman to set the horses at a gallop. On the bridge over the citadel's moat, she found General Fontana and Fabrizio, who were coming out on foot.

'Have you eaten?'

'No, by a miracle.'

The duchess threw her arms around Fabrizio's neck and fell into a faint that lasted for an hour and awoke fears, first for her life and then for her reason.

The governor, Fabio Conti, had gone white with anger at the sight of General Fontana. So slow had he shown himself carrying out the prince's orders, that the aide-de-camp, who assumed that the duchess was going to occupy the position of reigning mistress, had finally become angry. The governor had reckoned on making Fabrizio's sickness last for two or three days and now, he told himself, the general, a man of the court, is going to find that insolent young devil writhing in the agony that is my revenge for his escape.

Fabio Conti, thinking hard, stopped in the guardroom on the ground floor of the Farnese Tower, from which he made haste to dismiss the soldiers. He wanted no witnesses to the scene that was coming. Five minutes later, he was petrified with astonishment at hearing Fabrizio talking and finding him, lively and alert, giving General Fontana a description of the prison. He vanished.

Fabrizio showed himself to be the *perfect gentleman* in his meeting with the prince. For one thing, he certainly did not want to seem like a child taking fright at nothing. When the prince asked him kindly how he felt: 'Like a man, Most Serene Highness, who is dying of hunger, having fortunately neither breakfasted nor dined.' Having had the honour of thanking the prince, he sought permission to visit the archbishop before going to the prison in the town. The prince had gone prodigiously pale, when the thought came into his child's head that the poison was not altogether a fantasy dreamt up by the duchess. Absorbed by this cruel thought, he did not reply at first to the request to see the archbishop that Fabrizio had addressed to him. Then he felt himself obliged to make up for his distraction by laying on the charm.

'Leave on your own, signore, go into the streets of my capital without any guard. At around ten or eleven o'clock you will go into the prison, where I hope you will not be staying long.'

On the morrow of this great day, the most remarkable of his life, the prince saw himself as a little Napoleon. He had read that that great man had been looked on favourably by several of the pretty women at his court. And having once become Napoleon where the ladies were concerned, he remembered that he had also been him when he came under fire. His heart was still enraptured by the firmness he had shown in his conduct towards the duchess. His awareness of having done something difficult made another man of him for a fortnight. Generous arguments found a response in him; he showed character.

He began that particular day by burning the letters-patent creating Rassi a count, which had been on his desk for a month. He sacked General Fabio Conti and asked Colonel Lange, his successor, for the truth about the poison. Lange, a gallant Polish soldier, frightened the gaolers and told the prince that they had sought to poison Signor del Dongo's breakfast, but that too many people would have had to be taken into their confidence. The measures taken for his dinner were more efficient and but

for the arrival of General Fontana, Signor del Dongo would
have been doomed. The prince was appalled, but since he was
truly very much in love, it was a consolation to be able to tell
himself: it seems I really did save the life of Signor del Dongo,
and the duchess won't dare break the promise she gave me. He
arrived at another thought: my job is much more difficult than
I imagined. Everyone agrees that the duchess is of the highest
intelligence, policy here accords with my heart. How heavenly
it would be if she were willing to become my first minister.

That evening, the prince was so provoked by the horrors he
had discovered that he refused to get involved in the dramatics.

'I would be only too happy,' he told the duchess, 'if you were
willing to reign over my States as you reign over my heart. To
start with, I am going to tell you how I have employed my day.'
He then gave her a very exact account: the burning of Rassi's
letters-patent, the appointment of Lange, his report on the
poisoning, etc., etc. 'I find I have very little experience for
reigning. The count humiliates me by his jokes, he jokes even
in the council, and in society he passes comments whose truthfulness you are going to challenge. He says that I'm a child
whom he can lead where he wishes. I may be a prince, signora,
but I am no less a man, and these things are upsetting. In order
to make the stories Signor Mosca may tell seem improbable,
they made me call that dangerous scoundrel Rassi into the
ministry, and now here's General Conti, who believes he's still
so powerful he doesn't dare admit whether it was he or Raversi
who undertook to put an end to your nephew. I very much
wish quite simply to send General Fabio Conti before the
courts. The judges will see whether he's guilty of an attempted
poisoning.'

'But, prince, do you have judges?'

'What!' said the prince in astonishment.

'You have learned jurisconsults who look very solemn as they
walk down the street. For the rest, they will always reach a
verdict that appeals to the dominant party in your court.'

As the young prince, shocked, uttered phrases displaying his
candour rather than his sagacity, the duchess was asking herself:
does it suit me to let Conti be dishonoured? Certainly not,

because then his daughter's marriage with that decent but dreary Marchese Crescenzi becomes impossible.

On this subject, there was an endless dialogue between the duchess and the prince. The prince was dazzled by admiration. In favour of Clelia Conti's marriage to the Marchese Crescenzi, but on this express condition, angrily stated by him to the former governor, that he was pardoning him for the attempted poisoning. But, on the duchess's advice, he banished him until the time of his daughter's wedding. The duchess believed she no longer felt love for Fabrizio, but she still passionately desired Clelia Conti's marriage to the marchese. She had the vague hope that little by little she would see Fabrizio's obsession disappear.

The prince, transported by happiness, wanted to dismiss the minister Rassi in disgrace that same evening. The duchess said to him, laughing: 'Do you know something Napoleon once said? A man standing in a high place, whom everyone is watching, should not allow himself any violent movements. It's too late this evening, let's put business off till tomorrow.'

She wanted to give herself time to consult the count, to whom she retailed very exactly the whole of that evening's exchanges, while suppressing, nevertheless, the frequent allusions the prince had made to a promise that had poisoned her life. The duchess flattered herself that she could make herself so necessary that she would be able to obtain an indefinite adjournment by saying to the prince: If you are sufficiently barbaric to want to subject me to that humiliation, for which I would never forgive you, I would leave your States the next day.

Consulted by the duchess over the fate of Rassi, the count proved very philosophical. General Fabio Conti and he went travelling in Piedmont.

A strange difficulty arose concerning Fabrizio's trial. The judges wished to acquit him by acclamation, at the very first sitting. The count had to use threats so that the case might last for at least a week and the judges take the trouble to hear all the witnesses. These people are always the same, he told himself.

On the day after his acquittal, Fabrizio del Dongo finally took up the position of the good Archbishop Landriani's vicar-general. On the same day, the prince signed the necessary dispatches for Fabrizio to be appointed coadjutor, with the future succession, and, less than two months later, he was installed in that position.

Everyone complimented the duchess on how solemn her nephew looked. The fact is, he was in despair. The very next day after his release, followed by the dismissal and banishment of General Fabio Conti, and the high favour of the duchess, Clelia had taken refuge with the Countess Contarini, her aunt, a very wealthy, very old woman, solely taken up with concern over her health. Clelia might have been able to see Fabrizio, but anyone who had known of her earlier pledges and had seen her acting now, might have thought that her love for him had come to an end now that her lover was out of danger. Not only did Fabrizio go past the Palazzo Contarini as often as he decently could, he had even succeeded, after endless trouble, in renting a small apartment facing the first-floor windows. On one occasion, Clelia, having thoughtlessly gone to the window to watch a procession go by, withdrew instantly, as if terror-stricken. She had caught sight of Fabrizio, dressed in black but like a very poor workman, who was watching her from one of the windows of this slum, which had panes of oiled paper, like his room in the Farnese Tower. Fabrizio would have much liked to be able to persuade himself that Clelia was shunning him as a consequence of her father's disgrace, which rumour in the town attributed to the duchess. But he knew all too well another reason for this estrangement, and nothing could distract him from his melancholy.

He had reacted neither to his acquittal, nor to his installation in these splendid functions, the first he had ever had to fulfil, nor to his splendid position in society, nor finally to the assiduous court paid him by all the churchmen and all the devout in the diocese. The charming apartment he had in the Palazzo Sanseverina was no longer thought to be adequate. To her extreme delight, the duchess was obliged to give up to him the whole of the second floor in her palazzo and two beautiful reception rooms on the first floor, which were always full of persons of rank awaiting the right moment to pay court to the young coadjutor. The clause concerning the future succession had had a surprising effect in the country. The firm qualities in Fabrizio's character, which had once so greatly offended the poor simple-minded courtiers, were now seen as virtues.

It was an important lesson in philosophy for Fabrizio to find himself perfectly indifferent to all these honours, and far unhappier in this magnificent apartment, with six lackeys wearing his livery, than he had been in his wooden room in the Farnese Tower, surrounded by hideous gaolers and forever fearing for his life. His mother and his sister, the Duchess V***, who came to Parma to see him in his glory, were struck by his profound sadness. The Marchesa del Dongo, nowadays the least romantic of women, was so profoundly alarmed that she thought they had made him take some slow-acting poison in the Farnese Tower. Extremely discreet though she was, she thought she should speak to him about this extraordinary sadness, but Fabrizio replied only with tears.

A host of advantages, the consequence of his brilliant position, produced no effect in him other than putting him in an ill humour. His brother, that vain soul, gangrenous with the basest egotism, wrote him an almost official letter of congratulations, to which letter was conjoined a money order for fifty thousand francs, so that he might, said the new marchese, buy horses and a carriage worthy of his name. Fabrizio sent this sum to his younger sister, who had made a bad marriage.

Count Mosca had had a fine translation made, into Italian, of the family tree of the Valserra del Dongo family, published long ago in Latin by the archbishop of Parma, Fabrizio. He had it magnificently printed with the Latin text facing it. The engravings had been translated by some superb lithographs made in Paris. The duchess had wanted a beautiful portrait of Fabrizio to be set opposite that of the old archbishop. The translation was published as being Fabrizio's own work during his first period in detention. But everything had been abolished in our hero, even the vanity so natural to man. He did not deign to read a single page of the work attributed to him. His position in the world put him under an obligation to present a magnificent bound copy to the prince, who thought he must owe him compensation for the cruel death to which he had come so close and granted him entry to his bedchamber, a favour which made him an *Excellency*.

CHAPTER 26

The only moments during which Fabrizio had some chance of escaping from his deep sadness were those he spent hidden behind a glass window-pane, with which he had replaced one of the panes of oiled paper in the window of his apartment facing the Palazzo Contarini, where, as we know, Clelia had taken refuge. On the few occasions when he had seen her since leaving the citadel, he had been deeply distressed by a striking change, which seemed to him to augur the worst. Since her lapse, Clelia's facial expression had taken on a noble, serious character that was truly remarkable; she might have been thirty years old. In this extraordinary alteration, Fabrizio saw the reflection of some firm resolve. At each moment of the day, he told himself, she is swearing to herself to be true to the vow she made to the Madonna, and never set eyes on me again.

Fabrizio had divined what Clelia's affliction was only in part. She knew that her father, fallen into deep disgrace, could return to Parma and reappear at court (something without which life was impossible for him) only on the day of her marriage to the Marchese Crescenzi; she wrote to her father that she desired this marriage. The general had at that time taken refuge in Turin, and was sick with frustration. In truth, the repercussion from this great decision had been to age her by ten years.

She had indeed discovered that Fabrizio had a window facing the Palazzo Contarini, but had had the misfortune of looking at him only once. The minute she caught sight of a facial expression or a man's attitude faintly resembling his, she instantly closed her eyes. Her deep piety and her confidence in the succour of the Madonna were from now on her sole resource. It pained her not to feel any respect for her father. The character of her future husband struck her as thoroughly dreary and as emotionally empty as any other member of high society. In short, she adored a man whom she must never see again, yet who had rights over her. It seemed to her that fate had conspired to make her perfectly unhappy and we shall confess that she was right. After her marriage, she would have needed to go and live two hundred leagues from Parma.

Fabrizio knew of Clelia's profound modesty. He knew how any unusual endeavour, apt to become the subject of gossip once it was discovered, was sure to displease her. None the less, driven to extreme lengths by his excessive melancholy and by Clelia's constantly averting her gaze from him, he tried to bribe two servants of Signora Contarini, her aunt. One day, at nightfall, Fabrizio, dressed as a bourgeois from the country, presented himself at the doors of the palazzo, where one of the servants he had bribed was waiting for him. He announced himself as arriving from Turin and having letters for Clelia from her father. The servant went to take the message and showed him up into a huge anteroom on the first floor of the palazzo. It was in this place that Fabrizio perhaps spent the most anxiety-filled quarter of an hour of his entire life. If Clelia rejected him, he could no longer hope ever to be at peace again. In order to put an end to the untimely concerns my new office burdens me with, I shall rid the Church of a bad priest and go and take refuge under an assumed name in some charterhouse. At last, the servant came and announced that Signorina Clelia was prepared to receive him. His courage quite failed our hero; he was on the point of dropping with fear as he went up the stairs to the second floor.

Clelia was sitting at a small table that bore a single candle. Hardly had she recognized Fabrizio beneath his disguise before she took flight and went and hid at the far end of the room.

'So that's how much you care about my salvation,' she cried, hiding her face in her hands. 'Yet you know that when my father was on the point of expiring as a result of the poison, I made a vow to the Madonna never to set eyes on you. I have broken that vow only on the day, the unhappiest of my life, when I thought, in all conscience, I must preserve you from death. That I should consent to hear you out, by virtue of a forced and no doubt criminal interpretation, is in itself a great concession.'

These last few words so surprised Fabrizio that it was several seconds before he started rejoicing. He had been expecting the sharpest anger and to see Clelia take flight. His presence of mind finally returned and he extinguished the solitary candle. Although he thought he had clearly understood Clelia's orders, he was shaking all over as he advanced towards the end of the room where she had taken refuge behind a settee. He did not know whether he might not offend her by kissing her hand. She was tremulous with love and threw herself into his arms.

'Dear Fabrizio,' she said, 'how long you have taken to come! I can speak to you only for an instant, because it's surely a great sin. And when I promised never to set eyes on you, I surely also meant to promise not to speak to you. But how have you been able to pursue so barbarously the idea of revenge that my poor father had? Because it was he who was almost poisoned first after all, so as to facilitate your escape. Shouldn't you have done something for me, who risked my good name like that in order to save you? And now moreover you are completely bound by your holy orders, you could no longer marry me even if I could find a way of getting rid of that odious marchese. And then how could you dare, on the evening of the procession, to hope to see me in broad daylight and so violate, in the most blatant fashion, the sacred promise I made to the Madonna?'

Fabrizio held her tightly in his arms, beside himself with surprise and happiness.

A conversation that had begun with so very many things to be said between them was not likely to end soon. Fabrizio told her the full story of her father's banishment. The duchess had not been in any way involved, for the good reason that she had not believed for a moment that the idea of poison came from General Conti. She had always thought it was an inspiration of the Raversi faction, who had wanted to see the back of Count Mosca. This true history, spelt out at length, made Clelia very happy. She had been desolate at having to hate someone who belonged to Fabrizio. Now she no longer looked on the duchess with the eye of jealousy.

The happiness established by this evening lasted for only a few days.

The excellent Don Cesare arrived from Turin and, emboldened by the perfect sincerity of his heart, he dared to present himself to the duchess. Having asked for her word that she would not abuse the confidence he was about to make, he confessed that his brother, deluded by a false point of honour, and who thought he had been defied and had his reputation destroyed by Fabrizio's escape, had thought he must take his revenge.

Don Cesare had not been speaking for two minutes before he had won his case. His perfect virtue had touched the duchess, who was not accustomed to such a spectacle. It pleased her by its novelty.

'Expedite the general's daughter's marriage with the Marchese Crescenzi, and I give you my word I'll do all in my power to see the general is received as though he were returning from a journey. I shall invite him to dinner. Are you satisfied? It'll no doubt be frosty to begin with, and the general mustn't go rushing to ask for his position as governor of the citadel. But you know that I have an affection for the marchese and I shan't harbour a grudge against his father-in-law.'

Armed with these words, Don Cesare came to tell his niece that she held her father's life in her hands, that his despair had made him ill. He had not appeared at any court for six months.

Clelia wanted to go and see her father, sheltering, under an assumed name, in a village near Turin; for he had imagined that the court in Parma would demand his extradition from that of Turin, in order to put him on trial. She found him sick and almost crazed. That same evening she wrote Fabrizio a letter breaking with him for ever. On receiving this letter, Fabrizio, who was developing a character altogether similar to that of his mistress, went into retreat in the monastery of Velleja, situated in the mountains ten leagues from Parma. Clelia wrote him a letter of ten pages. She had sworn to him in the old days never to marry the marchese without his consent; she was now asking him for it. Fabrizio granted it from the depths of his retreat at Velleja, in a letter full of the purest friendship.

On receiving this letter, whose friendly nature, it must be admitted, annoyed her, Clelia herself fixed the day for her marriage, whose celebrations enhanced yet further the splendour of the Parma court that winter.

Ranuce-Ernest V was a miser at heart. But he was head over heels in love and he hoped to make the duchess a fixture at his court. He pressed a very considerable sum of money on his mother, so that she could give entertainments. The mistress of the bedchamber knew how to take admirable advantage of this increase in wealth. The entertainments in Parma that winter recalled the heyday of the court in Milan and the amiable Prince Eugène, the viceroy of Italy, whose kindness has left so lasting a memory.

The coadjutor's duties had recalled him to Parma. But he declared that, for reasons of piety, he would continue his retreat in the small apartment that his patron, Monsignor Landriani, had forced him to take in the archbishop's palace. And he went and shut himself away there, followed by a single manservant. Thus he did not attend any of the very brilliant entertainments at court, which earnt him in Parma and in his future diocese an immense reputation for sanctity. One unlooked-for effect of this retreat, prompted in Fabrizio solely by his deep and despairing sadness, was that the good Archbishop Landriani, who had always loved him, and whose own idea, indeed, it had been to make him coadjutor, developed a certain jealousy of him. The archbishop rightly thought that he should go to all court entertainments, as is the custom in Italy. On these occasions, he wore his ceremonial costume, which was, roughly speaking, the same as that in which he was to be seen in the choir of his cathedral. The hundreds of domestics gathered in the colonnaded antechamber of the palace did not fail to come up and ask a blessing of the monsignore, who was very willing to pause and bestow it on them. It was at one of these moments of solemn silence that Monsignor Landriani heard a voice that said: 'Our archbishop goes to the ball, and Monsignor del Dongo doesn't leave his room!'

From that moment on, the immense favour that Fabrizio had enjoyed at the palazzo was at an end. But he could fly by his own wings. His whole conduct, which had been inspired only by the despair into which Clelia's marriage had plunged him, passed for being the effect of a simple and sublime piety, and the devout ladies read, as though it were some edifying text, the translation of his family's genealogy, which betrayed the most extravagant vanity. The booksellers produced an edition with a lithograph of his portrait, which was taken up within a few days, above all by the common people. The engraver, in his ignorance, had reproduced around Fabrizio's portrait several of the vestments that should be found only in portraits of bishops, and to which a coadjutor cannot aspire. The archbishop saw one of these portraits and his fury no longer knew any bounds. He sent for Fabrizio and said some exceedingly harsh things to him, in terms that his passion at times made very coarse. Fabrizio did not have to try very hard, as may well be imagined, to behave as Fénelon might have done in similar circumstances. He heard the archbishop out with all possible humility and respect. And once the prelate had ceased from speaking, he recounted the whole history of the translation of the genealogy made by Count Mosca at the time of his first imprisonment. It had been published in a worldly intention, which had always seemed somewhat improper for a man of his rank. As for the portrait, there had been no sign of it in the second edition, any more than in the first; and the bookseller having addressed twenty-four copies of this second edition to him at the palace during his retreat, he had sent his man to buy a twenty-fifth. And having learnt by this means that the portrait was selling for thirty sous, he had sent a hundred francs in payment for the twenty-four copies.

All these arguments, although expounded in the most reasonable tones by a man who had quite other reasons for feeling aggrieved in his heart, heightened the archbishop's anger almost into a frenzy. He went so far as to accuse Fabrizio of hypocrisy. This is how the common run of men are, Fabrizio told himself, even when they have some intelligence!

He had a more serious concern at that moment: this was

about the letters from his aunt, who demanded absolutely that he come and reoccupy his apartment in the Palazzo Sanseverina, or at least come and visit her sometimes. There, Fabrizio would be sure to hear about the splendid entertainments given by the Marchese Crescenzi on the occasion of his marriage, and that was what he was unsure of being able to endure without making a spectacle of himself.

When the wedding ceremony took place, Fabrizio vowed himself to the most total silence for a whole week, having ordered his manservant and those people in the archbishop's palazzo with whom he had dealings never to address him.

Having learnt of this new affectation, Archbishop Landriani sent for Fabrizio much more frequently than usual, and sought to hold very lengthy conversations with him. He even obliged him to confer with certain canons from the countryside, who had complained that the palace had been acting against their privileges. Fabrizio took all this with the complete indifference of a man whose thoughts are elsewhere. I would do better to become a Carthusian, he told himself, I would suffer less among the rocks of Velleja.

He went to visit his aunt and could not hold back his tears as he embraced her. She found him so greatly altered, his eyes, made even bigger by his extreme thinness, seemed so to protrude from his head, and he himself appeared so sickly and unhappy, with his little threadbare simple priest's black coat, that at the outset the duchess too could not hold back her tears. But a moment later, once she had told herself that the alteration in this handsome young man's appearance had been brought about by Clelia's marriage, her feelings were almost equally vehement as those of the archbishop, though more skilfully contained. She was cruel enough to dwell at length on certain colourful details that had marked the charming entertainments given by the Marchese Crescenzi. Fabrizio did not respond. But his eyes half closed as if from a nervous tic and he grew even paler than he had been, which would at first have seemed impossible. At these moments of acute pain, his pallor took on a greenish tinge.

Count Mosca appeared and what he saw, which he found

incredible, finally cured him once and for all of the jealousy that Fabrizio had never ceased to excite in him. This astute man employed the most ingenious and tactful turns of phrase to try to give Fabrizio back some interest in the things of this world. The count had always had great respect and considerable affection for him. That affection, being no longer counter-balanced by jealousy, became at this moment almost devoted. He has certainly paid a price for his good fortune, he told himself, casting his mind back over his troubles. On the pretext of showing him the painting by Parmigiano that the prince had sent to the duchess, the count drew Fabrizio aside: 'Well now, my friend, let's talk as men. Can I do anything for you? You mustn't be afraid of questions on my part. But would some money be useful, can my influence be of service? Speak, I'm yours to command. If you prefer to write, write.'

Fabrizio embraced him tenderly and talked about the painting.

'Your conduct is masterful, politics at its shrewdest,' said the count, reverting to a light conversational tone. 'You are contriving a very agreeable future for yourself; the prince respects you, the people venerate you, your little threadbare black coat keeps Monsignor Landriani awake at night. I have some experience of affairs and I can swear I wouldn't know what advice to give you to improve on what I see. You take your first step in the world at twenty-five and you attain perfection. There's much talk of you at court. And do you know to what you owe that distinction, which is unique at your age? That little threadbare black coat. The duchess and I have the use, as you know, of Petrarch's[1] former house on that beautiful hill in the middle of the forest, in the vicinity of the Po. If ever you grow weary of the nasty, petty machinations of the envious, I thought that you might be Petrarch's successor, whose fame will enhance your own.' The count racked his brains to produce a smile on that anchorite's face, but he did not succeed. What made the alteration so striking was that up until recently, if Fabrizio's features had a fault, it was that of sometimes displaying an inappropriate expression of sensuality and amusement.

The count did not let him leave without telling him that, for all that he was in a state of retreat, it would be an affectation perhaps not to appear at court on the following Saturday which was the princess's birthday. The words were like a dagger in Fabrizio's heart. Dear God, he thought, what was I doing coming to the palace! He could not think without shuddering of the encounter he might have at the court. This idea absorbed every other. He thought that the one recourse remaining to him was to arrive at the palace at the precise moment when the doors to the reception rooms were being opened.

And indeed, the name of Monsignor del Dongo was one of the first to be announced at the gala evening, and the princess received him with the utmost distinction. Fabrizio's eyes were fixed on the clock and, at the moment it marked the twentieth minute of his presence in the room, he was getting up to take his leave, when the prince came in to his mother's. Having paid his respects to him for a moment or two, Fabrizio was manoeuvring himself skilfully closer to the door, when one of those tiny eventualities of a court, which the mistress of the bedchamber was so good at arranging, suddenly arose at his expense. The duty chamberlain ran after him to tell him that he had been designated to join the prince at whist. In Parma this is a signal honour and far above the rank that the coadjutor occupied in the world. The whist table was an honour of moment even for the archbishop. At the chamberlain's words, Fabrizio felt himself pierced to the heart, and although he was utterly opposed to making a scene in public, he was on the point of saying that he had suddenly come over dizzy. But he reflected that he would be open to questions and condolences even more unbearable than the game. That day he shrank from talking.

Fortunately, the general of the Minorites happened to be numbered among the great personages who had come to pay their respects to the princess. This very learned monk, a worthy emulator of the Fontanas and the Duvoisins,[2] had placed himself in a distant corner of the room. Fabrizio took up his position standing in front of him so as not to be able to see the door and talked theology to him. But he could not avoid his ear hearing the Signor Marchese and Signora Marchesa Crescenzi being announced. Against his expectations, Fabrizio felt a violent impulse of anger.

Were I Borso Valserra, he told himself (this was one of the first Sforza's generals), I would go and stab that dreary marchese, with the selfsame ivory-handled dagger that Clelia gave me on that blessed day, and teach him a lesson for having the insolence to appear with the marchesa in a place where I am!

So much did his features change that the general of the Minorites said: 'Is Your Excellency perhaps not feeling himself?'

'I've a terrible headache ... the lights are making me ill ... and I'm only staying because I've been named to play whist with the prince.'

At this, the general of the Minorites, who was a commoner, was so taken aback that, no longer knowing what to do, he began bowing to Fabrizio, who, for his part, far more troubled than the general of the Minorites, began talking with a strange volubility. He could hear that it had gone very silent behind him and refused to look. Suddenly, a bow tapped on a music desk. They were playing a ritornello and the celebrated Signora P*** sang the aria from Cimarosa that was at one time so celebrated: 'Quelle pupille tenere!'[3]

Fabrizio held firm during the opening bars but soon his anger vanished and he felt an extreme need to shed tears. Dear God, he said to himself ... what a ridiculous scene, and dressed as I am! He thought it wiser to explain himself. 'These overpowering headaches, when I fight against them, like this evening,' he told the general of the Minorites, 'end in fits of tears that might set tongues wagging in a man of our profession. So I ask Your Most Illustrious Reverence to permit me to weep as I look at him but not otherwise to give it a thought.'

'Our father-provincial in Catanzara is similarly afflicted,' said the general of the Minorites. And he began quietly on an interminable history.

The absurdity of this history, which brought in details of the father-provincial's evening meals, caused Fabrizio to smile, something that had not happened to him for a long time. But soon he stopped listening to the general of the Minorites. Signora P*** was singing, with a divine talent, an aria by

Pergolesi[4] (the princess liked music that was passé). There was a slight sound a few paces away from Fabrizio; for the first time that evening, he turned his eyes away. The chair that had just occasioned this slight scrape on the floor was occupied by the Marchesa Crescenzi, whose tear-filled eyes met directly with those of Fabrizio, which were hardly in any better state. The marchesa lowered her head. Fabrizio continued to look at her for a few seconds. He was familiarizing himself with that head laden with diamonds. But his look expressed anger and disdain. Then, telling himself: 'And my eyes will never look at you,' he turned towards his father-general and said: 'And now my trouble's coming on worse than ever.'

Indeed, Fabrizio wept hot tears for more than half an hour. Luckily, a Mozart symphony, horribly botched, as is the custom in Italy, came to his aid and helped him to dry his tears.

He held firm and did not turn his eyes towards the Marchesa Crescenzi. But Signora P*** sang once more and Fabrizio's soul, relieved by the tears, arrived at a state of perfect repose. Life then appeared to him in a new light. Am I claiming to be able to forget her completely from the very start? he asked himself. Would that be possible? He arrived at this thought: can I be more unhappy than I have been for the past two months? And if nothing can heighten my anguish, why resist the pleasure of seeing her? She has forgotten her oaths. She is fickle; aren't all women? But who could deny her a celestial beauty? She has a look which sends me into raptures, whereas I have to force myself to look at the women who pass for being the most beautiful! Very well, why not let myself be enraptured? That at least would be a moment of respite.

Fabrizio had some knowledge of men but no experience of the passions, but for which he might have told himself that this momentary pleasure, to which he was about to yield, would undo all the efforts he had been making for the past two months to forget Clelia.

The poor woman had come to the entertainment only when forced to by her husband. She had wanted at least to withdraw after half an hour, on the pretext of her health, but the marchese declared that, to have her carriage brought forward in order to leave, when many carriages were still arriving, would break altogether with custom, and might even be interpreted as an indirect slur on the entertainment given by the princess.

'In my capacity as lord-in-waiting,' the marchese added, 'I have to remain in the room under the princess's orders, until everyone has left. There may be, there no doubt will be, orders to give to her people, they're so slack. And do you want one of the princess's mere equerries to usurp that honour?'

Clelia resigned herself. She had not seen Fabrizio. She was still hoping he might not have come to the entertainment. But just as the concert was about to start, the princess having given the ladies permission to sit down, Clelia, who was far from alert in such matters, allowed the best seats next to the princess to be taken from her and was obliged to come and look for a chair at the end of the room, all the way to the distant corner where Fabrizio had taken refuge. On arriving at her chair, the costume, peculiar in this setting, of the general of the Minorites arrested her gaze and she did not at first remark the thin man dressed in a simple black coat who was talking to him. Nevertheless, a certain secret movement drew her gaze to this man. Everyone here has a uniform or a richly embroidered coat; who can that young man be in such a simple black coat? She was giving him her full attention when a lady, coming to take up her place, caused her chair to move. Fabrizio turned his head. She did not recognize him, so altered was he. At first she said to herself: this is someone who looks like him, it could be his older brother. But I thought he was only a few years older and this is a man of forty. Suddenly, she recognized him from a movement of the mouth.

The poor man, how he has suffered! she said to herself, and she lowered her head, overcome by grief, and not so as to be faithful to her vow. Her heart was overwhelmed by compassion. That was not at all how he had looked after nine months in prison! She was no longer watching him, but without exactly turning her eyes away, she could see all his movements.

After the concert, she saw him approach the prince's card table, placed a few paces from the throne. She breathed freely once Fabrizio was thus some way off.

The Marchese Crescenzi, however, had been greatly irritated at finding his wife relegated so far from the throne. He had been busy all evening persuading a lady whose husband was under a financial obligation to him, and was sitting three chairs away from the princess, that she would do well to change places with the marchesa. The poor woman objecting, as was natural, he went in search of the indebted husband, who made his better half listen to the dreary voice of reason, and the marchese finally had the pleasure of consummating the exchange; he went to fetch his wife.

'You will always be too modest,' he told her. 'Why do you walk looking down like that? You could be mistaken for one of those bourgeois women who are utterly astonished to find themselves here, and whom everyone is astonished to see here. That's typical of that madwoman of a mistress of the bed-chamber! And they talk of slowing down the progress of Jacobinism! Remember that your husband occupies the leading male position at the princess's court. And even if the republicans were to succeed in suppressing the court and even the nobility, your husband would still be the wealthiest man in the State. That's something you should bear in mind more often.'

The chair in which the marchese had the pleasure of installing his wife was only six paces from the prince's card table. She could see Fabrizio only in profile, but she found him so much thinner, he had the look above all of someone so far above anything that might happen in this world, he who in the old days never let the least incident pass without commenting on it, that she finally came to this terrible conclusion: Fabrizio had changed altogether, he had forgotten her. If he was so much thinner, it was the effect of the severe fasting to which his piety was subjecting him. Clelia was confirmed in this unhappy thought by the conversation of all her neighbours. The name of the coadjutor was on everyone's lips. They were searching for the reason for the signal favour of which they could see he was the object. He, so young, to be admitted to the prince's card game! They admired the polite indifference and haughty expression with which he threw down his cards, even when he was trumping His Highness.

'It's unbelievable,' exclaimed the old courtiers, 'his aunt's favour has quite gone to his head. It won't last, thank heaven. Our sovereign doesn't like people putting on those superior airs and graces.' The duchess approached the prince. The courtiers, who had remained at a very respectful distance from the table, with the result that they could pick up only the odd word of the prince's conversation, noticed that Fabrizio had gone very red. His aunt will have been lecturing him, they told themselves, for looking so very uninterested. Fabrizio had just heard Clelia's voice, she was replying to the princess who, as she went around the ball, had addressed a word to the wife of her lord-in-waiting. The moment came for Fabrizio to have to change places at the whist table. He now found himself directly facing Clelia, and he gave himself up several times to the pleasure of gazing at her. The poor marchesa, sensing she was being looked at, quite lost countenance. She several times forgot her obligation to her vow. In her desire to divine what was going on in Fabrizio's heart, she fixed her eyes on him.

The prince's game having ended, the ladies rose to go into the supper room. There was something of a mêlée. Fabrizio found himself right next to Clelia. He was still very determined, but he happened to recognize a very faint perfume which she put on her dresses. This sensation undid everything he had promised himself. He went up to her and spoke, in a low voice and as if talking to himself, two lines from the Petrarch sonnet he had sent her from Lake Maggiore, printed on a silk handkerchief: 'How happy I was when the common crowd thought me unhappy, and now how my lot has changed!'

No, he hasn't forgotten me, Clelia told herself, in a transport of joy. That beautiful soul is not inconstant.

> No, you will never see me change
> Lovely eyes which have taught me to love.

Clelia dared to repeat to herself these two lines from Petrarch.[5]

The princess withdrew straight after the supper. The prince had followed her as far as her apartment, and did not reappear in the reception rooms. As soon as this was known, everyone wanted to leave at once. There was total disorder in the ante-rooms. Clelia found herself right next to Fabrizio. The profound unhappiness depicted on his features filled her with compassion. 'Let us forget the past,' she said, 'and preserve the memory of our *friendship*.' On saying which words, she laid down her fan in such a way that he might pick it up.

Everything changed in Fabrizio's eyes; in an instant he was a different man. From the very next day he declared that his retreat was ended, and he returned to take up his magnificent apartment in the Palazzo Sanseverina. The archbishop said and believed that the favour the prince had done him by admitting him to his card table had caused the new saint to completely lose his head. The duchess could see that he had come to an agreement with Clelia. This thought, serving to renew the unhappiness produced in her by her fateful promise, finally decided her to absent herself. Her folly was marvelled at. What, remove herself from the court at the very moment when the favour of which she was the object appeared without limit! The count, perfectly happy now that he could see there was no love between Fabrizio and the duchess, told his mistress: 'This new prince is virtue incarnate, but I called him "that child". Will he ever forgive me? I can see only one means of really making it up with him, and that's absence. I'm going to show myself full of respect and good grace, after which I shall be unwell and ask for leave of absence. You'll allow me that, since Fabrizio's future is assured. But will you make the immense sacrifice,' he went on, laughing, 'of changing the sublime title of duchess for another much inferior one? In order to amuse myself, I shall be leaving affairs here in an inextricable tangle. I had five or six hard workers in my various ministries, I had them pensioned off two months ago, because they read the French newspapers. And I've replaced them with inconceivable nincompoops.

'After our departure, the prince will find himself in such a pickle that, appalled though he is by Rassi's character, I don't doubt he'll be obliged to recall him, and I shall be waiting only

for an order from the tyrant who disposes of my fate, to write
a letter of fond friendship to my friend Rassi and tell him that
I have every reason to hope that his talents will soon receive
their just reward.'

CHAPTER 27

This serious conversation took place on the day following Fabrizio's return to the Palazzo Sanseverina. The duchess had still not got over the joy that shone forth in every one of Fabrizio's actions. So that pious young woman has deceived me! she told herself. She wasn't able to resist her lover for three months even.

The certainty of a happy outcome had given the young prince, pusillanimous creature that he was, the courage to love. He had some knowledge of the preparations for departure that were being made at the Palazzo Sanseverina, and his French valet, who was no great believer in the virtue of great ladies, gave him courage in respect of the duchess. Ernest V permitted himself to take a step which was severely criticized by the princess and everyone of good sense in the court. The common people saw it as a mark of the astonishing favour that the duchess enjoyed. The prince went to visit her in her palazzo.

'You're going,' he said in a serious tone that the duchess found odious. 'You're going. You're going to betray me and break your promises! Yet, if I'd delayed by ten minutes granting you Fabrizio's pardon, he'd have been dead. You leave me unhappy. But for your promises, I'd never have had the courage to love you as I do! You are without honour then.'

'Give it your mature consideration, prince. Has there been an interval of time in all your life equal in happiness to the four months that have just elapsed? Your renown as a sovereign, and, I dare to believe, your happiness as an amiable man, have never risen to so high a point. Here is the compact I propose:

if you condescend to agree, I shall not be your mistress for a
fleeting moment and by virtue of an oath extorted by fear, but
I shall devote every second of my life to your felicity; I shall
always be what I have been these past four months, and perhaps
love will come to crown affection. I would not swear to the
contrary.'

'Very well,' said the prince, enraptured. 'Take a different
role, be more besides, reign both over me and my States, be my
first minister. I offer you a marriage such as is permitted by the
unhappy proprieties of my rank. We have an example close at
hand: the king of Naples has just married the duchess of Part-
ana. I offer you all I am able to do, a marriage of the same
kind. And I shall add a sad political thought to prove to you
I'm no longer a child and that I've thought about everything. I
shan't make too much of the condition I'm imposing on myself
of being the last sovereign of my line, the vexation of seeing in
my lifetime the great powers disposing of my succession. I bless
these very real disadvantages because they offer me one more
means of proving to you my esteem and my passion.'

The duchess did not hesitate for a moment. The prince bored
her and she found the count thoroughly amiable. There was
only one man in the world she could have preferred to him.
Moreover, she reigned over the count, and the prince, dominated by the exigencies of his rank, would more or less have
reigned over her. And then, too, he might become unfaithful
and take mistresses. Within a few years, the age difference
would seem to give him the right.

From the very first moment, the prospect of being bored had
decided everything. Nevertheless, the duchess, who wanted to
be charming, asked for permission to reflect on it.

It would take too long to report here the almost tender turns
of phrase and infinitely gracious terms in which she was able
to cloak her refusal. The prince became angry. He could see his
whole happiness escaping from him. What would become of
him once the duchess had left his court? What a humiliation,
moreover, to be refused! What is my French valet going to say
when I tell him the story of my defeat?

The duchess had the art of calming the prince down, and

bringing him gradually back to the negotiation of her real terms. 'If Your Highness condescends to agree not to insist on the effect of a fateful promise, which fills me with horror, as it leads me to feel contempt for myself, I will spend my life at his court, and that court will always be what it has been this winter. All my moments will be devoted to contributing to his happiness as a man, and his renown as a sovereign. If he requires that I should obey my oath, he will have blighted the rest of my life and will see me instantly abandoning his States never to return. The day when I lose my honour will also be the last day that I shall set eyes on you.'

But the prince had the obstinacy of the pusillanimous. His pride both as a sovereign and as a man had been provoked moreover by the refusal of his hand. He had been pondering all the difficulties he would have had to surmount to get that marriage accepted, yet which he was resolved to overcome.

For three whole hours, the same arguments were repeated on either side, often mixed in with very forthright language. The prince exclaimed: 'So you want to make me believe, signora, that you lack honour? Had I hesitated this long on the day when General Fabio Conti was giving Fabrizio poison, you'd be occupying yourself today with erecting a tomb for him in one of the churches of Parma.'

'Certainly not in Parma, this land of poisoners.'

'Very well, leave, signora duchess,' the prince went on, angrily. 'And you will take my contempt with you.'

As he was going out, the duchess said to him quietly: 'All right, present yourself here at ten o'clock this evening, in the strictest incognito, and you will strike a bad bargain. You will have seen me for the last time, and I would have devoted my life to making you as happy as an absolute prince can be in this Jacobin century. And remember what your court will be like when I'm no longer there to haul it forcibly out from its natural dreariness and spite.'

'On your side, you are refusing the crown of Parma, and better than the crown, for you would not have been a vulgar princess, married for political reasons and who isn't loved. My heart is yours entirely, and you would have found yourself once and for all the absolute mistress of my actions as of my government.'

'Yes, but the princess your mother would have had the right to despise me as a vile intriguer.'

'Well, I would have banished the princess with an allowance.'

The cutting rejoinders went on for another three quarters of an hour. The prince, who had a delicate soul, could not resolve either to exert his right or to let the duchess leave. He had been told that the first advance having been made, by whatever means, women always come back.

Having been dismissed by the indignant duchess, he ventured to reappear, trembling all over and most unhappy, at three minutes to ten. At ten-thirty, the duchess got into a carriage and left for Bologna. She wrote to the count the minute she was outside the prince's States:

'The sacrifice is made. Don't ask me to be cheerful for the next month. I shan't see Fabrizio again. I shall wait for you in Bologna, and whenever you like, I shall be the Countess Mosca. I ask only one thing of you: don't ever force me to reappear in the country I am leaving, and always remember that instead of an income of a hundred and fifty thousand livres, you're going to have thirty or forty thousand at most. All the fools will gaze at you open-mouthed and you will be thought well of only in so far as you are willing to lower yourself to understand all their petty notions. *Tu l'as voulu, Georges Dandin!*'[1]

One week later, the marriage was celebrated in Perugia, in a church where the count's ancestors have their tombs. The prince was in despair. The duchess had received three or four couriers from him, and had not failed to send his letters back to him, unopened. Ernest V had treated the count extremely handsomely and given Fabrizio the great ribbon of his order.

'That's what I liked above all about his farewells. We parted,' the count told the new Countess Mosca della Rovere, 'the best friends imaginable. He gave me a great Spanish order, and diamonds worth fully as much as the order. He told me he would make me a duke, were it not that he wanted to hold on to that means of summoning you back into his States. I am therefore charged with declaring to you, a fine commission for a husband, that if you condescend to return to Parma, be it only for one month, I would be made a duke, under a name chosen by you, and you would have a fine estate.'

Which was what the duchess rejected, with a sort of disgust.

After the scene that had taken place at the court ball, which had seemed quite decisive, Clelia appeared no longer to remember the love that she had seemed for an instant to share. The most violent remorse had seized hold of that virtuous and believing soul. Fabrizio understood this very well, and despite all the hopes that he strove to give himself, a gloomy wretchedness had nevertheless taken possession of his soul. This time, however, unhappiness did not lead him into a retreat, as on the occasion of Clelia's marriage.

The count had asked 'his nephew' to give him an exact account of what had been going on at court, and Fabrizio, who was beginning to realize how much he owed him, had promised to fulfil this commission scrupulously.

Like the town and the court, Fabrizio did not doubt but that his friend was planning to return to the ministry, and with more power than he had ever had. The count's predictions were not long in coming true. Less than six weeks after his departure, Rassi was first minister, Fabio Conti minister of war, and the prisons, which the count had all but emptied, were filling up again. By putting these men into power, the prince believed he was getting his revenge on the duchess. He was madly in love and hated Count Mosca above all as his rival.

Fabrizio had a lot of official business. Monsignor Landriani, at the age of seventy-two, had lapsed into a state of great languor and since he seldom emerged from the palace, it was up to the coadjutor to carry out almost all his functions.

The Marchesa Crescenzi, overcome by remorse, and frightened by her director of conscience, had found an excellent way of keeping out of Fabrizio's sight.

Using as a pretext the end of a first pregnancy, she had turned her own palazzo into a prison. But the palazzo had a huge garden. Fabrizio knew how to get into it and along the path that Clelia liked the best he laid flowers arranged in bouquets, and ordered in such a way as to spell out a message, as once she had sent them to him every evening in the final days of his imprisonment in the Farnese Tower.

The marchesa was greatly irritated by this venture. The impulses of her soul were governed now by remorse and now by passion. For several months she did not allow herself to go down once into the garden of her palazzo. She even made a point of not looking out at it.

Fabrizio was beginning to think that he had been parted from her for ever, and despair was beginning to take possession of his soul. The society in which he spent his life he found thoroughly disagreeable, and had he not been convinced deep down that the count could not find peace of mind outside the ministry, he would have retreated into his small apartment in the arch-bishop's palace. It would have been consoling to live entirely with his own thoughts, and to hear a human voice only in the official exercise of his functions.

But, he told himself, I owe it to the Count and Countess Mosca not to be replaced.

The prince continued to treat him with a distinction which set him in the first rank at court, a favour which he owed in large part to himself. The extreme reserve which, in Fabrizio, stemmed from an indifference bordering on disgust for all the affections or petty enthusiasms which filled men's lives, had pricked the young prince's vanity. He often said that Fabrizio had all his aunt's spirit. The prince's candid soul had half glimpsed a truth, which was that no one approached him with the same emotional disposition as Fabrizio. What even the common run of courtiers could not fail to see was that the consideration which Fabrizio had obtained was not that of a mere coadjutor, but outweighed even the regard that the sovereign showed the archbishop. Fabrizio wrote to the count that if ever the prince had the wit to realize the mess the ministers, Rassi, Fabio Conti, Zurla and others of the same calibre, were making of affairs, he, Fabrizio, would be the natural channel through which he could take action, without compromising overmuch his self-respect.

But for the memory of the fateful words 'that child', he told Countess Mosca, applied by a man of genius to an august personage, the august personage would already have cried: 'Come back quickly and rid me of this beggarly crew.' Were the man of genius's wife to deign here and now to make a move, however slight, the count would be recalled in delight. But he will return through a much better door if he's willing to wait until the fruit be ripe. For the rest, they're bored to their heart's content in the princess's salon, all they have to amuse them is the foolishness of Rassi, who since he became a count has developed a mania for nobility. Strict orders have just been given that anyone who can't prove eight quarters of nobility 'shall not venture' to present himself at the princess's soirées (those are the terms of the rescript). All the men entitled to enter the great gallery in the morning, and find themselves along the sovereign's route to Mass, will continue to enjoy this privilege. But newcomers will have to give proof of the eight quarters. From which, they say, you can easily tell that Rassi has no quarters.

It may be imagined that letters of this sort were not entrusted to the post. Countess Mosca replied from Naples: 'We have a concert every Thursday, and conversation every Sunday. You can't move in our salons. The count is thrilled by his excavations, he devotes a thousand francs a month to them and has just had workmen brought in from the Abruzzi mountains, who cost him only twenty-three sous a day. You really should come and visit us. It's now more than twenty times I've sent you a summons, ungrateful sir.'

Fabrizio had no intention of obeying; he found the simple letter he wrote to the count or countess each day an almost intolerable drudgery. He will be forgiven once it is known that a whole year went by in this fashion, without his being able to address a single word to the marchesa. All his attempts at establishing some form of correspondence had been rejected with horror. The habitual silence which, out of a weariness with life, Fabrizio everywhere maintained, save in the exercise of his duties and at court, combined with the perfect purity of his behaviour, had led to him being venerated to such an extraordinary extent that he finally determined to follow his aunt's advice.

'The prince has such veneration for you,' she wrote, 'that you must expect before long to fall from favour. He will lavish marks of neglect on you, and the awful contempt of the courtiers will follow his. These petty despots, however honourable they may be, are as changeable as fashion and for the same reason: boredom. You can find strength against the sovereign's whims only in preaching. You improvise so well in verse! Try to speak for half an hour about religion. You'll come out with heresies to start with, but pay a learned and discreet theologian who'll come to your sermons and alert you to your errors, you can put them right the next day.'

The kind of unhappiness which a frustrated love produces in the soul means that anything demanding attention or action becomes an awful drudgery. But Fabrizio told himself that his reputation with the people, should he acquire one, might one day be useful to his aunt and to the count, for whom his veneration increased day by day, as public affairs taught him to recognize how spiteful humankind was. He made up his mind to preach, and his success, prepared for by his gaunt appearance and his threadbare clothes, was unprecedented. People detected a flavour of profound sadness in his oratory, which, allied to his attractive looks and stories of the high favour he enjoyed at court, won over every woman's heart. They made out that he had been one of the bravest captains in Napoleon's army and soon this absurd exploit was not in any doubt. People reserved seats in the churches where he was due to preach. The poor installed themselves there speculatively from five in the morning.

His success was such that Fabrizio at last had the thought, which altered everything in his soul, that, even if only out of simple curiosity, the Marchesa Crescenzi might very well one day come and attend one of his sermons. The enraptured public suddenly saw his talent increase. When he was moved, he permitted himself images whose boldness would have caused more practised orators to shudder. At times, forgetting himself, he yielded to moments of impassioned inspiration and the entire audience burst into tears. But it was in vain that his *aggrottato*[2] eye searched among all the faces turned towards the pulpit for the one whose presence would for him have been so great an event.

But if ever I have that good fortune, he told himself, either I shall be taken ill or I shall remain absolutely tongue-tied. To guard against this latter disaster, he had composed a sort of tender and impassioned prayer which he always placed in his pulpit, on a stool. His plan was to start reading this composition should the presence of the marchesa ever render him incapable of uttering a word.

He learnt one day, from those of the marchese's servants who were in his pay, that orders had been given for the Casa Crescenzi's box to be got ready at the grand theatre for the following day. It was a year since the marchesa had appeared at a performance, and it was a tenor who was all the rage and filling the auditorium every evening who had made her depart from her habits. Fabrizio's first reaction was an extreme joy. At last I shall be able to see her for a whole evening! They say she's very pale. And he sought to picture to himself what that enchanting face might be like, with its colours half erased by the struggles of the soul.

His friend Lodovico, altogether disconcerted by what he called his master's folly, found, if with great difficulty, a box in the fourth tier, almost opposite that of the marchesa. An idea occurred to Fabrizio: I hope to give her the idea of coming to my sermon, and I shall pick a very small church, so as to be in a position to see her properly. Fabrizio normally preached at three o'clock. On the morning of the day the marchesa was due to go to the theatre, he had it given out that, since he would be detained the whole day in the archbishop's palace on official business, he would preach just this once at eight-thirty in the evening, in the small church of Santa Maria della Visitazione, situated exactly opposite one wing of the Palazzo Crescenzi. For his part, Lodovico offered the nuns of the Visitazione an enormous quantity of candles, with a request that the church be as bright as day. He had a whole company of grenadiers from the guard, and a sentry was placed, with a fixed bayonet, in front of every chapel, to prevent theft.

Although the sermon had been announced for eight-thirty,

by two o'clock the church was completely full and the din in
the lonely street, dominated by the noble architecture of the
Palazzo Crescenzi, may be imagined. Fabrizio had had it given
out that in honour of Our Lady of Pity, he would preach on
the pity that a generous soul must feel for an unfortunate, even
were he a guilty man.

Disguised with all possible care, Fabrizio got to his box in
the theatre just as the doors were opening and there was as
yet no illumination. The performance began at around eight
o'clock, and a few minutes later he experienced the joy that no
mind can imagine that has not felt it: he saw the door to the
Crescenzi box open. Shortly afterwards, the marchesa entered.
He had not had so clear a sight of her since the day she had
given him her fan. Fabrizio thought he might suffocate from
joy. He felt such extraordinary impulses that he told himself:
perhaps I'm about to die! What a charming way to end this
unhappy existence! Perhaps I'm going to collapse in this box.
The faithful gathered at the Visitazione won't see me arrive and
tomorrow they'll learn that their future archbishop has taken
leave of his senses in a box at the opera, disguised as a servant
moreover and clad in livery! Farewell to my entire reputation.
But what does my reputation matter!

Nevertheless, around a quarter to nine, Fabrizio regained
control of himself. He left his fourth-tier box and had the
utmost difficulty reaching, on foot, the place where he was to
take off his semi-livery and put on something more appropriate.
Only around nine o'clock did he arrive at the Visitazione, in so
pale and feeble a state that the rumour spread in the church
that the signore coadjutor would not be able to preach that
evening. One may well imagine the attentions the nuns lavished
on him, at the railings of their inner parlour, where he had
taken refuge. The ladies talked a lot. Fabrizio asked to be alone
for a moment or two, then hurried to his pulpit. One of his aides-
de-camp had informed him, at around three o'clock, that the
church of the Visitazione was completely full, but with people
belonging to the lower orders, attracted seemingly by the spectacle of the illuminations. On entering the pulpit, Fabrizio was

agreeably surprised to find all the chairs occupied by young people of fashion and personages of the highest distinction.

A few phrases of apology began his sermon and were received with suppressed cries of admiration. Next came the impassioned description of the unfortunate man for whom pity must be felt in order to do fitting honour to the Madonna of Pity, who had herself suffered so greatly on Earth. The orator was very emotional. There were moments when he could scarcely pronounce the words in such a fashion as to be heard in every part of the small church. In the eyes of all the women and a fair number of the men, he looked himself like the unfortunate man who must be pitied, so extreme was his pallor. A few minutes after the words of apology with which he had begun his discourse, it could be seen that he was not his usual self. That evening, they detected in him a tenderer, more profound sadness than usual. Once, they saw tears in his eyes, at which instant there arose a general sobbing in the audience so loud that the sermon was broken off altogether.

This first interruption was followed by ten more. People let out cries of admiration, there were outbursts of tears. At every moment, shouts could be heard, such as 'Oh, holy Madonna', 'Oh, great God!' So general and so invincible was the emotion among this elite audience that no one was ashamed to let out a cry and those who got carried away did not seem at all ridiculous to their neighbours.

During the break that it is customary to take in the middle of a sermon, Fabrizio was told that absolutely no one was left in the theatre. One lady alone could be seen still in her box, the Marchesa Crescenzi. During this momentary respite, a lot of noise was suddenly to be heard in the audience; it was the faithful voting a statue to the signor coadjutor. His success in the second part of his address was so wild and so worldly, the eruptions of Christian contrition constantly giving way to altogether profane shouts of admiration, that he thought he should address a reprimand of sorts to his hearers as he left the pulpit. Whereupon, everyone went out at once, moving in a manner that had something strange and formal about it, and on reaching the street they all started to applaud furiously and shout: 'E viva del Dongo!'

Fabrizio hurriedly consulted his watch, and ran to a small barred window which lit the narrow organ passage inside the convent. As a courtesy to the incredible, unprecedented crowd that filled the street, the doorman at the Palazzo Crescenzi had set a dozen torches in the iron hands to be seen projecting from the façades of palazzi built in the Middle Ages. After a few minutes, and long before the shouting had ceased, the event that Fabrizio had been awaiting so anxiously transpired; the marchesa's carriage, returning from the theatre, appeared in the street. The coachman was obliged to stop and it was only at the gentlest of trots, and by dint of shouting, that the carriage was able to reach the door.

The marchesa had been affected by the sublime music, as the hearts of the unhappy are, but far more by her perfect solitude at the performance once she had learnt its reason. In the middle of the second act, with the admirable tenor on stage, even the people in the pit had suddenly abandoned their places to go and tempt fortune and try to get inside the church of the Visitazione. The marchesa, finding herself stopped by the crowd in front of her door, burst into tears. I did not make the wrong choice, she told herself.

But precisely because of this moment of tenderness, she stood firmly out against the entreaties of the marchese and all the friends of the family, who could not imagine that she should not go and see so astonishing a preacher. He has even prevailed over the finest tenor in Italy, they said. If I see him, I'm lost! the marchesa told herself.

In vain did Fabrizio, whose talent seemed more dazzling by the day, preach several more times in this same small church next door to the Palazzo Crescenzi, he never caught sight of Clelia, who finally became indignant even at this affectation of coming to disturb her lonely street, after she had already expelled him from her garden.

Looking round the faces of the women who were listening to him, Fabrizio had been noticing for quite some time a small, dark, very pretty face, whose eyes flashed fire. These magnificent eyes were normally bathed in tears after the ninth or tenth sentence of the sermon. Whenever Fabrizio was obliged to say things at length that he himself found tedious, he was quite ready to rest his gaze on that face, whose youthfulness appealed to him. He learnt that this young person's name was Anetta Marini, the only daughter and heir of the wealthiest cloth merchant in Parma, who had died a few months before.

Soon, the name of this Anetta Marini, the draper's daughter, was on everyone's lips. She had fallen madly in love with Fabrizio. At the time the famous sermons began, it had been settled that she should marry Giacomo Rassi, the elder son of the minister of justice, whom she did not find unattractive. But no sooner had she twice heard Monsignor Fabrizio and she was declaring she no longer wished to marry. And when she was asked the reason for this singular volte-face, she replied that it was not right for an honest girl to marry a man when she felt hopelessly smitten with another. Her family searched unsuccessfully to start with for who this other man might be.

But the burning tears that Anetta had shed at the sermon set them on the right track. Her mother and uncles having asked her whether she loved Monsignor Fabrizio, she answered boldly that, since they had uncovered the truth, she would not demean herself by a falsehood. She added that, having no hope of marrying the man whom she adored, she wanted at least to be spared having to look at the ridiculous face of the *contino*[3] Rassi. Within two days, this ridiculing of the son of the man who was an object of envy for the entire bourgeoisie became the talk of the town. Anetta's answer was thought charming and everyone repeated it. It was cited at the Palazzo Crescenzi as it was cited everywhere.

Clelia took good care not to open her mouth on such a topic in her own salon. But she put questions to her maid and, the following Sunday, having heard Mass in the chapel in the palazzo, she made her maid get into her carriage and went in search of a second Mass in Signorina Marini's parish church. She found all the town beaux gathered, drawn by the same motive. These gentlemen were standing by the door. Soon, from the great stir there was among them, the marchesa realized that

Signorina Marini was entering the church. She found herself very well placed to observe her and, despite her piety, paid scarcely any attention to the Mass. Clelia saw in this bourgeois beauty a determined expression that, in her view, might have suited at most a woman who had been married for several years. For the rest, she had a very shapely small figure and her eyes, as they say in Lombardy, seemed to engage in conversation with the objects they were observing. The marchesa made her escape before the Mass ended.

The very next day, the friends of the Crescenzi ménage, who came to spend every evening, recounted a new piece of absurdity on the part of Anetta Marini. Because her mother, fearing some foolishness on her part, allowed her only a very little money to spend, Anetta had gone to offer a magnificent diamond ring, a present from her father, to the celebrated Hayez, in Parma at that time for the reception rooms of the Palazzo Crescenzi, and asked him for the portrait of Signor del Dongo. But she wanted the portrait to be dressed simply in black, not in a priest's costume. And now, the day before, the young Anetta's mother had been greatly surprised and even more shocked to find in her daughter's bedroom a magnificent portrait of Fabrizio del Dongo, set in the finest frame to have been gilded in Parma these last twenty years.

CHAPTER 28

Swept along by events, we have not had time to sketch in the comic race of courtiers who pullulate at the court of Parma and passed droll comments on the events we have been recounting. What, in those parts, makes a minor member of the nobility, equipped with three or four thousand livres a year, worthy of figuring, in black stockings, at the prince's levee, is first of all never to have read Voltaire and Rousseau. This condition is none too difficult to fulfil. They needed next to be able to talk sympathetically about the sovereign's cold, or the last box of minerals he had received from Saxe. If after that you did not fail to attend Mass one single day in the year, and could number two or three overweight monks among your close friends, the prince would deign to address you once in the year, a fortnight before or a fortnight after the 1st of January, which gave you considerable standing in your parish, and the collector of taxes did not dare to be too hard on you if you were behind with the annual sum of a hundred francs that you were taxed on your small properties.

Signor Gonzo was one poor devil of the sort, very much a nobleman, who, apart from possessing some small substance, had obtained, thanks to the influence of the Marchese Crescenzi, a magnificent position, bringing in fifteen hundred francs a year. This man could have dined at home but he had one passion: he was at his ease and happy only once he found himself in the salon of some great personage who might say to him from time to time: 'Shut up, Gonzo, you're nothing but a fool.' This verdict was dictated by ill humour, for Gonzo was nearly always more intelligent than the great personage. He could talk about anything and rather gracefully. He was moreover ready to change his opinion at a grimace from the master of the house. Truth to tell, although highly astute where his own interests were concerned, he had no ideas at all, and when the prince did not have a cold he was sometimes at a loss when entering a salon.

What had earnt Gonzo a reputation in Parma was a magnificent tricorn hat, adorned with a somewhat moth-eaten black plume which he put on even when in a frock-coat. But one needed to see the manner in which he carried this plume, whether on his head or in his hand. That was where his talent and his importance lay. He inquired with genuine anxiety into the state of health of the marchesa's small dog, and had the Palazzo Crescenzi caught fire, he would have risked his life to save one of the beautiful chairs in gold brocade, which for so many years past had caught on his black silk breeches whenever on the off-chance he dared to sit down for a moment.

Seven or eight personages of this sort arrived every evening at seven o'clock in the Marchesa Crescenzi's salon. Hardly were they seated before a lackey, magnificently clad in a daffodil-yellow livery covered all over in silver braid, as well as a red jacket to round it off magnificently, came to take these poor devils' hats and sticks. He was at once followed by a footman bringing a minute cup of coffee, supported by a filigree silver stand. And every half an hour, a maître d'hôtel, wearing a sword and a magnificent coat in the French style, would come and hand round ice creams.

Half an hour after the little threadbare courtiers, five or six officers would be seen to arrive, talking in loud voices and with a very military air, and usually arguing about the number and kind of buttons that a soldier's uniform should have in order for the commander-in-chief to be able to win victories. It would not have been wise to quote a French newspaper in this salon, for even if the news item happened to be of the most pleasing kind, that fifty liberals had been shot in Spain, for example, the narrator would still have been convicted of having read a French newspaper. The master stroke of all these people was to obtain every ten years an increase in their pension of a hundred and fifty francs. Thus it is that the prince shares with his nobility the pleasure of reigning over the peasantry and the bourgeoisie.

The principal personage in the Crescenzi salon, without question, was the Cavaliere Foscarini, a perfectly worthy man, which meant that he had been in and out of prison under every regime. He had been a member of that famous chamber of deputies which, in Milan, rejected the registration law introduced by Napoleon, a rare enough gesture in history. Having been for twenty years the friend of the marchese's mother, the Cavaliere Foscarini had remained the man of influence in the household. He always had some amusing tale to tell, but nothing escaped his shrewd eye; and the young marchesa, who felt guilty deep in her heart, trembled before him.

Since Gonzo had a veritable passion for this great nobleman, who said rude things to him and made him cry once or twice a year, his obsession was to seek to do him small favours. And had he not been paralysed by the habits of an extreme poverty, he might now and again have succeeded, for he was not without a certain element of finesse and a much larger one of effrontery.

Gonzo, such as we know him, somewhat despised the Marchesa Crescenzi, for never once had she addressed an impolite word to him. But then she was the wife of the famous Marchese Crescenzi, the princess's lord-in-waiting, who, once or twice a month, would say to Gonzo, 'Shut up, Gonzo, you're nothing but a fool.'

Gonzo observed that everything that was said about the young Anetta Marini drew the marchesa out for a moment from the dreamily inattentive state in which she customarily remained sunk until such time as it struck eleven, when she would make the tea and offer some to every man present, calling him by his name. After which, at the moment of returning to her own apartment, she seemed to know a moment of gaiety, which was when they chose to recite satirical sonnets to her.

They make up excellent ones in Italy, it is the one literary genre which retains a certain vitality. True, it is not subject to censorship, and the courtiers at the Casa Crescenzi always introduced their sonnet with the words: 'Will the Signora Marchesa permit me to recite a very bad sonnet to her?' And once the sonnet had raised a laugh and been repeated two or three times, one of the officers would not fail to exclaim: 'The signor minister of police should certainly get busy hanging the authors of such infamous things.' In bourgeois company, on the contrary, they welcome these sonnets with the most open admiration, and lawyers' clerks sell copies of them.

The kind of curiosity displayed by the marchesa gave Gonzo to suppose that she had heard the young Marini's beauty being praised too often in her presence, a girl who was worth a million moreover, and that she was jealous of her. Since, with his perpetual smile and wholesale insolence towards anyone not from the nobility, Gonzo got everywhere, the very next day he arrived, carrying his plumed hat with a certain air of triumph, in the marchesa's salon, where he was hardly to be seen more than once or twice a year, when the prince had said to him: 'Goodbye Gonzo.'

Having bowed respectfully to the marchesa, Gonzo did not move away as usual, to go and take up his position on the chair that had just been brought forward for him. He set himself in the middle of the circle and exclaimed brutally: 'I've seen Monsignor del Dongo's portrait.' Clelia was so taken aback she was obliged to lean on the arm of her chair. She tried to weather the storm but was soon obliged to abandon the salon.

'It must be agreed, my poor Gonzo, that you are uncommonly tactless,' exclaimed haughtily one of the officers who was finishing his fourth ice cream. 'How could you not have known that the coadjutor, who was one of Napoleon's army's very bravest colonels, once played an abominable trick on the marchesa's father, by leaving the citadel which General Conti commanded, as though he were leaving the Steccata?' (The principal church of Parma.)

'There are indeed many things I don't know, my dear captain, I'm a poor imbecile who commits gaffes all day long.'

This retort, very much in the Italian style, brought a laugh at the brilliant officer's expense. The marchesa soon returned. She had plucked up courage and was not without some vague hope of being able herself to admire the portrait of Fabrizio, which was said to be excellent. She extolled the talents of Hayez, who had made it. Without realizing, she directed winning smiles at Gonzo, who was looking slyly at the officer. Since all the other family courtiers were indulging in the same pleasure, the officer took flight, not without having vowed an undying hatred of Gonzo. The latter had triumphed and that evening, as he took his leave, he was engaged to dine the next day.

'And here's something even better!' exclaimed Gonzo the following day, after dinner and once the servants had gone out. 'Hasn't our coadjutor now gone and fallen in love with the young Marini!'

The agitation that arose in Clelia's heart on hearing so extra-ordinary a remark may be imagined. The marchese himself was moved. 'But, Gonzo, my friend, you're raving as usual and you ought to show a little restraint when speaking of a person who's had the honour of playing whist with His Highness eleven times!'

'Well, signor marchese,' replied Gonzo, with the coarseness of men of his kind, 'I can swear to you that he'd be just as keen on playing with little Marini. But it's enough that you don't like these details. They no longer exist so far as I'm concerned, I wish above all not to offend my adorable marchese.'

After dinner, the marchese always retired to have a siesta. He was careful not to do so on this particular day. Gonzo would rather have cut out his own tongue than say another word about the young Marini, but he was constantly launching out on a conversation calculated to make the marchese hope he was about to revert to the young town girl's amours. Gonzo had in full measure that Italian form of wit where they delight in delaying coming out with what people want to hear. The poor marchese, dying of curiosity, was obliged to take the lead. He told Gonzo that whenever he had the pleasure of dining with him, he ate twice as much. Gonzo did not understand and began to describe a magnificent gallery of pictures that the Marchesa Balbi, the late prince's mistress, had been creating. He cited Hayez three or four times, in the very deliberate tones of the highest admiration. The marchese said to himself: good, he's finally going to get on to the portrait commissioned by the young Marini! But that was what Gonzo was careful not to do.

Five o'clock struck, which put the marchese in a very bad mood, he being accustomed to getting into his carriage at half past five, after his siesta, to go to the Corso.

'That's you all over, you and your idiocies,' he said roughly to Gonzo. 'You'll have me getting to the Corso after the princess, whose lord-in-waiting I am, and she may have orders to give me. Come on, get a move on, tell me in a few words, if you can, what is this supposed love affair of the monsignor coadjutor's?'

But Gonzo meant to keep the account of that for the ear of the marchesa, who had invited him to dinner. He *dispatched* the story that was being asked for therefore in a very few words, and the marchese, half asleep, hurried off to take his siesta. Gonzo adopted a quite different manner with the poor marchesa. She had remained so young and innocent in the midst of her high fortune, that she thought she should make amends for the rudeness with which the marchese had just addressed Gonzo. Charmed by this success, the latter rediscovered all his eloquence and found it as much a pleasure as his duty to enter into endless detail with her.

The young Anetta Marini had paid up to a sequin for the place that was reserved for her at the sermon. She always arrived with two of her aunts and her father's former cashier. The places, which she had had reserved from the previous day, had generally been chosen almost facing the pulpit, but a little to one side of the high altar, for she had noticed that the coadjutor often turned towards the altar. Now, what the audience had remarked also was that, *not infrequently*, the very expressive eyes of the young preacher were pleased to pause on the young, strikingly beautiful heiress; and seemingly with some emotion for, the moment his eyes were fixed on her, his sermon became learned, the quotations abounded and there were none of those impulses that come from the heart. The ladies, who had almost straight away lost interest, began to look at the Marini girl and to defame her.

Clelia made him repeat all these singular details up to three times. The third time, she became very thoughtful. She worked out that it was just fourteen months since she had set eyes on

Fabrizio. Would there be any great harm, she asked herself, if she spent an hour in a church, not in order to see Fabrizio but in order to hear a celebrated preacher? I would anyway place myself a long way away from the pulpit and would look at Fabrizio only once on entering and again at the end of the sermon ... No, Clelia told herself, it's not Fabrizio I'm going to see, I'm going to hear the astonishing preacher! Amid all this reasoning, the marchesa felt remorse. She had behaved so well these past fourteen months! Anyway, she said to herself, to find some peace with herself, if the first woman who comes here this evening has been to hear Monsignor del Dongo preach, I shall go too. If she hasn't been, I shall stay away.

The decision having been taken, the marchesa delighted Gonzo by saying: 'Try to find out which day the coadjutor will be preaching, and in which church? This evening, before you leave, I may perhaps have an errand for you.'

Hardly had Gonzo left for the Corso before Clelia went to take the air in the garden of her palazzo. She did not raise the objection with herself that she had not set foot there in the last six months. She was lively, animated; she had colour in her cheeks. That evening, her heart throbbed with emotion as each of the bores entered her salon. Finally, Gonzo was announced, who, from the first glance, could see that he was going to be indispensable for the next seven days. The marchesa is jealous of the young Marini, and, my word, what a comedy that would be to put on, in which the marchesa would play the lead, little Anetta the soubrette, and Monsignor del Dongo the lover! My word, two francs for admission would be cheap at the price. He was beside himself with delight and kept interrupting people the whole evening and telling the most preposterous anecdotes (the celebrated actress and the Marquis de Pequigny, for example, which he had learnt the day before from a French traveller). The marchesa, for her part, could not remain still. She walked about the room, she went into a gallery next door, to which the marchese had admitted only pictures each costing more than twenty thousand francs. So clear was the language of these pictures that evening that the marchesa's heart became wearied by emotion. At last, she heard the double doors opening, she hurried into the salon: it was the Marchesa Raversi! But as she paid her the customary respects, Clelia felt her voice fail. The marchesa made her repeat her question twice: 'What do you think of the preacher who is all the rage?' which she had not at first understood.

'I had looked on him as a little schemer, a very worthy nephew of the illustrious Countess Mosca. But the last time he preached, I have to say, at the church of the Visitazione, opposite you, he was so sublime all my hatred went and I now look on him as the most eloquent man I have ever heard.'

'So you were at one of his sermons?' asked Clelia, trembling all over with happiness.

'What,' said the marchesa, laughing, 'so weren't you listening? I wouldn't miss him for anything. They say he's got a weak chest, and that soon he won't be preaching any more!'

Hardly had the marchesa left before Clelia summoned Gonzo into the gallery. 'I am almost decided,' she said, 'to hear this preacher who gets so much praise. When will he be preaching?'

'Next Monday, in three days' time, that's to say. And it's as if he'd guessed what Your Excellency is planning, because he's coming to preach at the church of the Visitazione.'

Not everything had been explained, but Clelia had lost the power of speech. She took five or six turns round the gallery, without adding a word. Gonzo told himself: it's revenge that's eating away at her. How can anyone be so insolent as to escape from a prison, especially when they have the honour of being guarded by a hero such as General Fabio Conti!

'Anyway, you need to hurry,' he added, with a hint of irony. 'His chest's affected. I heard Doctor Rambo say he's not got a year to live. God is punishing him for having broken his ban by escaping treacherously from the citadel.'

The marchesa sat down on the divan in the gallery, and gestured Gonzo to do the same. After a few moments, she handed him a small purse into which she had earlier put a few sequins. 'Reserve four places for me.'

'Will poor Gonzo be allowed to slip in in Your Excellency's train?'

'Of course. Reserve five places . . . I'm not in the least anxious to be close to the pulpit,' she added, 'but I'd like to see Signorina Marini, who's said to be so pretty.'

The marchesa did not live during the three days separating her from the famous Monday, the day of the sermon. Gonzo, for whom it was a signal honour to be seen in public in the entourage of so great a lady, was flaunting his French coat with sword. Nor was that all; taking advantage of its closeness to the palazzo, he had a magnificent gilded armchair carried into the church, intended for the marchesa, which the bourgeoisie considered the height of insolence. The poor marchesa's feelings may be imagined when she caught sight of the chair, which had been placed exactly facing the pulpit. Clelia was so embarrassed, lowering her gaze and cowering in a corner of the immense chair, that she did not even have the courage to look at the young Marini, whom Gonzo pointed out with his hand, with a shamelessness she found shocking. Any human being not from the nobility was nothing at all in the eyes of the courtier.

Fabrizio appeared in the pulpit. He was so emaciated, so pale, so *worn away*, that Clelia's eyes instantly filled with tears. Fabrizio spoke a few words then stopped, as if his voice had suddenly failed him. He tried in vain to begin a few phrases. He turned round and picked up a sheet of paper with writing on it.

'My brothers,' he said, 'an unhappy soul, well deserving of your pity, engages you, through my voice, to pray for an end to his torments, which will cease only with his life itself.'

Fabrizio read the rest of his paper very slowly, but such was the expression of his voice that by the middle of the prayer, everyone was in tears, even Gonzo. 'At least I shan't be noticed,' the marchesa told herself, bursting into tears.

As he read from the paper, Fabrizio hit upon two or three thoughts on the state of the unhappy man for whom he had come to solicit the prayers of the faithful. Soon, the thoughts came crowding in. While appearing to address the audience, he was speaking only to the marchesa. He finished his discourse a little sooner than usual, because, despite all his efforts, the tears had overcome him to such an extent he could no longer

pronounce the words intelligibly. Sound judges found the sermon strange, but the equal at least, where pathos was concerned, of the famous sermon preached under the lights. As for
Clelia, hardly had she heard the first ten lines of the prayer
Fabrizio was reading out than she saw it as a dreadful crime to
have been able to go fourteen months without seeing him. On
returning home, she went to bed so as to be able to think of
Fabrizio in complete freedom. And the following day, quite
early, Fabrizio received a letter couched as follows:

'Your honour is being counted on. Find four *brave men* of
whose discretion you can be certain and tomorrow, just as it is
striking midnight at the Steccata, find yourself near a small
door bearing the number 19, in the via San Paolo. Remember
that you may be attacked, do not come alone.'

On recognizing these heavenly characters, Fabrizio fell to his
knees and burst into tears. At last, he cried, after fourteen
months and one week! No more sermons.

It would take too long to describe all the kinds of foolishness
to which, on that day, the hearts of Fabrizio and Clelia were
prey. The small door indicated in the letter was none other than
that of the orangery at the Palazzo Crescenzi, and ten times
during the day Fabrizio found a way of setting eyes on it. He
armed himself, and alone, a little before midnight, he was going
rapidly past this door when, to his inexpressible joy, he heard
a well-known voice saying, very quietly: 'Come in, friend of my
heart.'

Fabrizio entered cautiously and found himself indeed in the
orangery, but facing a heavily barred window raised three or
four feet above the ground. The darkness was total. Fabrizio
had heard a sound in the window and was reconnoitring the
bars with his hand when he felt a hand that had been passed
through the bars take his and carry it to lips that bestowed a
kiss on it. 'It's me,' said a beloved voice, 'I've come here to tell
you I love you, and to ask you if you're willing to obey me.'

The reply, the joy, Fabrizio's astonishment, may be imagined.
The first transports over, Clelia said to him: 'I have made a vow
to the Madonna, as you know, never to set eyes on you, that is
why I am receiving you in total darkness. I want you to know

that, were you to force me to look at you in broad daylight, everything would be over between us. But first of all, I don't want you to preach in front of Anetta Marini, and don't go thinking that it was I who was foolish enough to have a chair carried into the house of God.'

'My darling angel, I shan't preach any more in front of anyone. I preached only in the hope that I would one day see you.'

'Don't say that, remember that it is not permitted for me on my side to see you.'

Here, we ask for permission to pass, without saying a single word about them, over a gap of three years.

At the time when our narrative resumes, Count Mosca had already been long back in Parma, as first minister, more powerful than ever.

After these three years of heavenly happiness, Fabrizio's soul experienced a caprice of tenderness that changed everything. The marchesa had a charming two-year-old boy, Sandrino, who was his mother's joy. He was always with her or on the lap of the Marchese Crescenzi. Fabrizio, on the other hand, hardly ever saw him. He did not want him to become accustomed to cherishing another father. He conceived the design of abducting the child before he had any very distinct memories.

During the long hours of each day when the marchesa was unable to see her lover, Sandrino's presence consoled her. For we have to confess to something that will seem bizarre north of the Alps: despite her lapses, she had remained faithful to her vow. She had promised the Madonna, it will perhaps be recalled, *never to set eyes on* Fabrizio. Those had been her exact words. As a consequence, she received him only at night and there was never any light in the apartment.

But he was received by his mistress every evening, and what is to be admired, in the midst of a court devoured by curiosity and boredom, is that Fabrizio's precautions had been so cleverly thought out that this *amicizia*, as they say in Lombardy, was not even suspected. Their love was too intense for there not to be quarrels. Clelia was very liable to jealousy, but the quarrels almost always arose for a different reason. Fabrizio had abused some public ceremony or other in order to find himself in the same place as the marchesa and to look at her, and she had then seized on an excuse to leave in great haste, and had banished her lover for a long time.

They were astonished in the court of Parma not to know of any amorous intrigues involving a woman so remarkable for her beauty and for her high-mindedness. She gave rise to passions that inspired many acts of folly, and Fabrizio too was often jealous.

The good Archbishop Landriani had long since died. Fabrizio's piety, his exemplary morals and his eloquence had caused him to be forgotten. His older brother had died and all the family's wealth had come down to him. From this time on, he distributed each year the hundred and some odd thousand francs that the archbishopric of Parma brought him in among the vicars and parish priests of the diocese.

It would have been hard to think of a life more honoured, more honourable and more useful than that which Fabrizio had made for himself, when the whole thing was disturbed by this unfortunate caprice of a father's affection.

'In accordance with the vow, which I respect, yet which blights my life since you refuse to see me by day,' he told Clelia one day, 'I'm obliged to live constantly alone, having no other distraction but work. And even work is lacking. In the midst of this dreary and austere fashion of passing the long hours of each day, an idea has occurred to me which is tormenting me and which I have been combating in vain for the last six months. My son will never love me; he never hears me named. Raised amidst the agreeable luxury of the Palazzo Crescenzi, he scarcely knows me. On the few occasions when I see him, I am thinking of his mother, of whose celestial beauty he reminds me yet whom I can't look at, and he must think I look very solemn, which, for a child, means unhappy.'

'Well,' said the marchesa, 'your words alarm me, what are they leading up to?'

'To having my son back. I want him to live with me. I want to see him every day, I want him to become accustomed to loving me. I want to love him myself at my leisure. Since a fatality like no other in the world decrees that I am deprived of the happiness that so many tender souls enjoy, and that I don't spend my life with all that I adore, I at least want to have beside me someone who recalls you to my heart, who in some sense takes your place. Men and affairs are a burden on me in my enforced solitude. You know that ambition has always been an empty word for me, since the moment when I had the good fortune of being locked up by Barbone, and everything that is not a sensation of the soul I find absurd in the melancholy which overwhelms me when I am far away from you.'

It is easy to understand the acute pain with which her lover's unhappiness filled poor Clelia's soul. Her sadness was all the more profound because she felt that Fabrizio was not entirely in the wrong. She went so far as to question whether she should not attempt to break her vow. Then she could have received Fabrizio by day like any other person in society, and her reputation for discretion was too well established for anyone to speak ill of her. She told herself that with a great deal of money she might have herself released from her vow. But she sensed also that this purely worldly arrangement would not appease her conscience, and heaven in its irritation would perhaps punish this fresh crime.

On the other hand, if she consented to accede to Fabrizio's very natural desire, if she sought not to inflict misery on that tender soul that she knew so well, whose tranquillity had been so strangely endangered by her peculiar vow, what was the likelihood of abducting the only son of one of the greatest noblemen in Italy without the deception being discovered? The Marchese Crescenzi would expend enormous sums, would himself take charge of the search and sooner or later the abduction would be known about. There was only one way of warding off that danger, the child had to be sent a long way off, to Edinburgh, for example, or Paris, but that was something to which a mother's affection could never make up its mind. The other and in fact more reasonable method proposed by Fabrizio had something ominous about it, something even more awful in the eyes of this distraught mother. They had, Fabrizio said, to feign an illness. The child would grow worse and worse and finally come to die, at a time when the Marchese Crescenzi was absent.

A repugnance which, in Clelia, went almost as far as terror, caused a breach which could not last.

Clelia claimed that they must not tempt God, that this beloved son was the fruit of a crime and that if divine anger was aroused again, God would not fail to take him to himself. Fabrizio spoke again of his singular destiny. The rank which chance has bestowed on me, he told Clelia, and my love oblige me to an everlasting solitude, I cannot, unlike most of my confrères, enjoy the comforts of intimacy, since you are willing to receive me only in the dark, which reduces the part of my life that I can spend with you to mere moments, so to speak.

Many tears were shed. Clelia fell ill. But she loved Fabrizio too much to carry on refusing the terrible sacrifice he was asking of her. Sandrino appeared to fall ill. The marchese hastened to summon the most celebrated doctors, and Clelia at once encountered a terrible difficulty she had not foreseen: this adored child had to be prevented from taking any of the remedies prescribed by the doctors. This was no small matter.

The child, kept in bed more than was good for his health, became genuinely unwell. How to tell the doctors the cause of this sickness? Torn between two contrary and heartfelt interests, Clelia was on the verge of going out of her mind. Must she consent to an apparent cure and so sacrifice all the fruits of a long and arduous pretence? Fabrizio, on his side, could neither forgive himself for the violence he was doing to his mistress's heart, nor give up on his plan. He had found a means of being let in each night to be with the sick child, which had led to a further complication. The marchesa came to nurse her child and Fabrizio was obliged at times to see her by the light of the candles, which seemed to Clelia's poor sick heart an awful sin, presaging Sandrino's death. In vain did the most celebrated casuists, consulted about the observance of her vow, in the event of its fulfilment being patently harmful, reply that the vow could not be seen as having been broken in a criminal fashion so long as the person bound by a promise to the Deity abstained, not for some vain satisfaction of the senses but in order not to cause an obvious harm. The marchesa was in despair none the less, and Fabrizio could see the time coming when his bizarre notion would lead to the death of Clelia and that of his son.

He had recourse to his close friend, Count Mosca, who, ageing minister though he was, was moved by this story of a love of which he was largely ignorant. 'I will secure the marchese's absence for five or six days at least. When do you want it to be?'

Some time later, Fabrizio came to tell the count that everything was ready for them to be able to take advantage of his absence.

Two days later, as the marchese was returning on horseback from one of his estates in the vicinity of Mantua, some brigands, seemingly hired in pursuance of some private act of revenge, abducted him, without maltreating him in any way, and put him into a boat, which took three days to descend the Po and make the same journey that Fabrizio had once effected after the famous Giletti affair. On the fourth day, the brigands set the marchese down on an uninhabited island in the Po, after taking the trouble to rob him of everything he had, leaving him neither money nor any personal effects of any value. It was two whole days before the marchese was able to get back to his palazzo in Parma. He found it draped in black and all his staff heartbroken.

This abduction, very neatly carried out, had a most unhappy outcome. Having been installed secretly in a large and beautiful house where the marchesa came to see him almost every day, Sandrino died at the end of a few months. Clelia imagined that she had been struck by a just punishment for having been unfaithful to her vow to the Madonna. She had seen Fabrizio so often in the light, twice even in broad daylight, and with such transports of tenderness, during Sandrino's illness. She survived this beloved son for only a few months, but she had the comfort of dying in the arms of her lover.

Fabrizio was too much in love and too much of a believer to resort to suicide. He hoped to find Clelia again in a better world, but he was too intelligent not to feel that he had much to atone for.

A few days after Clelia's death, he signed several documents by which he guaranteed a pension of a thousand francs to each of his domestic servants, reserving for himself a pension of the same amount. He gave land, worth roughly a hundred thousand livres a year, to Countess Mosca; a similar sum to the Marchesa del Dongo, his mother, and what might remain of his paternal fortune to one of his sisters, who had made a bad marriage. The next day, having submitted his resignation from his archbishopric and all the positions that had been heaped on him through the favour of Ernest V and the friendship of the first minister to the appropriate quarter, he retired into the Charterhouse of Parma, situated in the woods close to the Po, two leagues from Sacca.

Countess Mosca had strongly approved, with time, that her husband should resume the ministry, but she had never been willing to return to the States of Ernest V. She held court in Vignano, a quarter of a league from Casal-Maggiore, on the left bank of the Po and consequently within the States of Austria. In the magnificent palazzo of Vignano, which the count had had built for her, she received the whole of Parma's high society every Thursday, and her numerous friends every day. Fabrizio would not fail to come to Vignano one day. In a word, the countess had conjoined all the appearances of happiness, but she survived Fabrizio for only a very short time, the Fabrizio whom she had adored and who spent only one year in his charterhouse.

The prisons of Parma were empty, the count was immensely rich and Ernest V was adored by his subjects, who compared his government to that of the grand dukes of Tuscany.

TO THE HAPPY FEW[1]

Notes

PART I

EPIGRAPH

1. *Ariosto*: Ludovico Ariosto (1474–1533), poet and dramatist, read and remembered, above all, for his great epic poem, the *Orlando Furioso* (1516–32), which was translated into English in 1591 by Sir John Harrington.

FOREWORD

1. *This short novel was written in ... 1830*: The *Charterhouse* was in fact written in 1838 and is by no means short, but at the time Stendhal had also been writing a series of short historical novels based on manuscripts he had discovered in Italy. For all its nineteenth-century setting, this much longer novel may be thought of as belonging to that series (see Introduction).
2. *Caffè Pedroti*: The café's actual name was Pedrocchi and was much liked by Stendhal.
3. *puntiglio*: Point of honour.

CHAPTER 1

1. *His Imperial and Royal Majesty*: That is, the Austrian Emperor.
2. *cicisbeo*: An old Italian word for a married woman's acknowledged lover, an alternative term to 'cavaliere servente'.
3. *Charles V and Philip II*: Charles V (1500–1558) and Philip II (1527–98), successive rulers of the widespread Spanish possessions, which included Milan, in the sixteenth century.
4. *Encyclopédie ... Voltaire*: The *Encyclopédie, ou Dictionnaire*

raisonné des sciences, des arts et des métiers, was published in
thirty-five volumes between 1751 and 1772. Most of the great
figures of the French Enlightenment contributed to it. Stendhal
was astonished that his reactionary father should have subscribed
to this profoundly radical and profoundly secular publication.
Voltaire was the name under which François Marie Arouet
(1694–1778) became known throughout Europe as tragedian,
historian, novelist, essayist, poet and, above all, campaigning
political force against clericalism and injustice.

5. *the archduke*: Francis II (1768–1835) was the last Holy Roman
   Emperor (1792–1806), first Emperor of Austria, as Francis I
   (1804–35), and king of Bohemia and Hungary (1792–1835).

6. *Gros*: Antoine Gros (1771–1835), an artist who began by painting romantic subjects and ended up painting classical ones. His
   lack of success led to his suicide.

7. *the Monferina, the Sauteuse*: The 'monferina' is a Piedmontese
   country dance; the 'sauteuse' ('saltarella' in Italian) a lively dance
   in triple time. Both are still danced today.

8. *voltigeur*: A light-infantryman in the French army, here func-
   tioning as an officer's batman.

9. *Salome by Leonardo da Vinci*: The painting Stendhal had in
   mind is in fact by Bernardo Luini, and is in the Uffizi in Florence.

10. *assignats*: Promissory notes first issued by the French Revolution-
    ary government in 1790.

11. *aunes*: A measure of cloth, a little under two metres.

12. *the Viscontis and the Sforzas*: The Visconti family ruled Milan
    from the thirteenth century until the middle of the fifteenth; the
    Sforzas, notably Ludovico Sforza, wealthy patron of Leonardo
    da Vinci, ruled Milan from 1450 to 1535.

13. *Italian legion*: A regiment founded by Napoleon and recruited
    from among Italians favourable to the French.

14. *Directory in Paris*: The Directory ruled France from October
    1795 until Napoleon's coup d'état in November 1799.

15. *Marengo*: A village in Piedmont near which Napoleon defeated
    the Austrians in June 1800.

16. *Mamelukes in Egypt*: The Mamelukes were the dominant warrior
    class in Egypt at the time of Napoleon's expedition to that
    country in 1798.

17. *Bocche di Cattaro*: An inlet on the Dalmatian coast used for a
    penal settlement.

18. *many serious authors*: A reference to Laurence Sterne's *Tristram
    Shandy*, a comic novel very much admired in France, in which

the eponymous first-person hero never quite reaches the point of being born.

19. *General Bonaparte ... came down from Mont Saint-Bernard*: And Stendhal eventually along with him, as a young soldier (see Introduction).

20. *Prince Eugène, the viceroy of Italy*: Eugène de Beauharnais (1781–1824) was Napoleon's son-in-law and became viceroy of Italy aged twenty-three.

CHAPTER 2

1. *RONSARD*: Pierre de Ronsard (1524–85) was the finest of the French Renaissance poets and the leader of the group known as the Pléiade.

2. *(1813)*: That is, the thirteenth year of the century would see the prophecy fulfilled.

3. *disasters at the Beresina!*: A river, now in Belorussia, crossed with terrible losses by Napoleon's Grande Armée on its retreat from Moscow.

4. *Jacobins*: The most extreme of the democratic factions during the French Revolution, the supporters, above all, of Robespierre and the Terror.

5. *Count Prina ... assaulted in the streets*: Count Joseph Prina (1768–1814), finance minister of the Italian Republic under the French, was assassinated in Milan on 20 April 1814.

6. *General Bubna*: Ferdinand, Count Bubna Littiz (1772–1825), became military governor of Lombardy in 1818.

7. *Cisalpine Republic*: That part of northern Italy under French occupation.

8. *Tasso ... Ariosto*: Torquato Tasso (1544–95), a pastoral and epic poet, whose best-known work is *Jerusalem Delivered*. For Ariosto, see Epigraph, note 1.

9. *Cagnola ... Marchesi*: Louis Cagnola (1702–33), an Italian classical architect; Pompeo Marchesi (1790–1858), a neoclassical sculptor.

10. *Vigano*: Salvatore Vigano (1769–1821), a dancer and choreographer, and the nephew of the composer Boccherini.

11. *Napoleon ... landed in the Golfe de Juan*: Napoleon's return from exile in Elba marked the start of the Hundred Days, which ended with his final defeat at the battle of Waterloo.

12. *Monti*: Vincenzo Monti (1754–1828), Italian poet best known for his translation of Homer's *Iliad*.

13. *Ligny*: A small Belgian town where, two days before the battle of Waterloo, Napoleon defeated a Prussian army coming to join up with Wellington.

CHAPTER 3

1. *the four brothers Aymon*: The name sometimes given to a celebrated twelfth-century romance of chivalry, in which the Emperor Charlemagne does battle with the four sons of Duc Aymes, whose horse, Bayard, is capable of leaping prodigious heights and distances.
2. *Marshal Ney*: Michel Ney (1769–1815) distinguished himself on numerous occasions during the Napoleonic Wars. After Napoleon's exile, he rallied to King Louis XVIII under the Restoration, before rejoining Napoleon during the Hundred Days. He fought heroically at Waterloo and after the defeat was executed for treason.
3. *prince of Moskova, the bravest of the brave*: Two of the nicknames by which Ney was known.
4. *Jerusalem Delivered*: See Chapter 2, note 8.

CHAPTER 4

1. *Bourbons*: The Bourbon dynasty had ruled France up until the Revolution, and would rule it again, briefly, after 1815.
2. *Fénelon*: François de Salignac de la Mothe Fénelon (1651–1715), writer and churchman, formerly tutor to Louis XIV's grandson, was banished from Versailles and turned increasingly to mysticism. He became archbishop of Cambrai in 1695.
3. *The Cossacks!*: There were no Cossacks at Waterloo, but they were the Russian mounted troops the French most feared, following the catastrophe of the 1812–13 Russian campaign.

CHAPTER 5

1. *the allies*: The English and Prussians, following the battle of Waterloo, together with Russian forces.
2. *M. Pellico*: Silvio Pellico (1789–1854), an Italian writer, liberal and patriot who fell foul of the Austrians and spent eight years as a prisoner in the Spielberg fortress between 1822 and 1830.
3. *Andryane*: Alexandre Andryane (1797–1863), a Frenchman by birth, became an active supporter of the liberal conspirators in

Milan. He was arrested by the Austrians in 1823 and sent to the Spielberg fortress. His *Memoirs of a Prisoner of State* were published in 1838–9.

4. *Emperor Francis II*: See Chapter 1, note 5.

5. *Bayard*: Pierre Terrail, Seigneur de Bayard (1476–1524), fought with great valour for the French in northern Italy under King Francis I. He became a historical legend as 'Le chevalier sans peur et sans reproche' ('The knight without fear and beyond reproach').

6. *seccatore*: An Italian word for a bore.

7. *Correggio*: The Italian painter whom Stendhal admired the most. His real name was Antonio Allegri (1494–1534), he came from near Parma and he painted some remarkable frescos in the dome of the cathedral there. Stendhal particularly admired his very sensual handling of female figures.

8. *Marini, Gherardi, Ruga, Aresi, Pietragrua*: These are the names of real women, the fashionable beauties whom Stendhal came across on his first visit to Milan in 1800. Eleven years later, Angela Pietragrua became his mistress (see Introduction).

9. *San Micheli*: Michele Sanmichele (1484–1559), architect and engineer. Much of his best work is in Verona.

10. *Spielberg*: The Spielberg fortress in Brno, in what is now the Czech Republic, was for a long time the most notorious political prison in the Austro-Hungarian Empire.

11. *the Constitutionnel*: A liberal Paris newspaper founded in 1815, which finally closed in 1914.

CHAPTER 6

1. *Gouvion-Saint-Cyr*: Laurent, Marquis de Saint-Cyr (1764–1830), a highly successful field commander under Napoleon, who became a marshal and a reforming war minister under the Restoration.

2. *'93*: 1793 was the year in which King Louis XVI was executed and in which the Revolutionary Terror began in earnest.

3. *Canova*: Antonio Canova (1757–1822), the leading Italian sculptor of the age, a neoclassicist.

4. *tabouret*: A folding stool on which those of a certain rank were entitled to sit in the presence of the French king.

5. *petit coucher*: A sovereign's ceremonial retirement to bed: another Louis XIV touch.

6. *General Lafayette*: The Marquis de Lafayette (1757–1834).

Having fought for the American rebels in the war of independence against England, he returned to France and was for a time a moderating influence on Revolutionary excess. In 1792, however, he emigrated, to return only in 1800, once Napoleon had seized power. Politically speaking, he remained a liberal and was admired by Stendhal, who frequented his salon in the 1820s.

7. *Fronde*: Between 1648 and 1652, when Louis XIV was still a minor, there were two 'frondes', or armed uprisings, against the power of the Crown, the first known as the 'fronde of the Parlements', the second as the 'fronde of the princes'. Both failed and the monarchy emerged stronger than before.

8. *transparencies*: These were panels lit from behind which displayed the names and coats of arms of distinguished guests.

9. *This tower, built ... by the Farnese ... around the beginning of the sixteenth century*: Better known now as the Castel Sant' Angelo, the fortress in which, when he was still Cardinal Alexander Farnese, Pope Paul III was at one time imprisoned by Pope Innocent VIII.

10. *Diderot, Raynal ... two chambers*: Denis Diderot (1713–84), a bohemian and erratic figure, was perhaps the most radical of all the French Enlightenment thinkers and the prime mover behind the great *Encyclopédie* (see Chapter 1, note 4); the Abbé Guillaume Raynal (1713–96) was a leading anti-colonialist and, despite his holy orders, anti-clerical. The 'two chambers' here stand for a system of representative government such as Restoration France established.

CHAPTER 7

1. *edit the Moniteur, like the San-Felice woman once did in Naples!*: The *Moniteur universel*, started in 1789, was the official newspaper of French governments from 1799 to 1848. Louise San Felice (1768–1800) conspired against the French in Naples and was indeed hanged.

2. *Tartufe*: A consummate hypocrite and the central figure in the comedy of that name by Molière.

3. *Emperor Decius ... suffer martyrdom like Poliuto in the opera*: Decius was the Roman Emperor from 248 to 251, and a persecutor of Christians. Polyeuctus was a Roman officer, converted to Christianity, who died a martyr's death in Armenia around 250. The opera is presumably Donizetti's *Poliuto*, written, though not performed, in 1838.

4.   *Joseph ... Potiphar*: Joseph was imprisoned by Potiphar, the
     Egyptian officer he served, after Potiphar's wife accused him,
     falsely, of having made sexual advances to her. See Genesis 39.

CHAPTER 8

1.   *Goldoni's La Locandiera*: Carlo Goldoni (1707–93), a predomi-
     nantly comic dramatist and the author of some 250 works. *La
     Locandiera* was first performed in 1753.
2.   *Come face al mancar dell'alimento*: The line comes from a poem
     by Monti (see Chapter 2, note 12).

CHAPTER 9

1.   *mortaretti*: A 'mortaretto' is a sort of squib.
2.   *Mercadante*: Saverio Mercadante (1795–1870), a Neapolitan
     composer who wrote some sixty operas, widely performed
     throughout the nineteenth century.

CHAPTER 10

1.   *saw themselves as so many Brutuses*: Although he took part in
     the plot to assassinate Julius Caesar, Brutus has often been
     regarded as a man of high principle, acting in the best interests
     of the Roman State.
2.   *Themistocles*: (*c.* 525–462 BC), Athenian statesman and naval
     commander, largely responsible for the great victory over the
     Persians at Salamis in 480. He was later exiled and ultimately
     lived in Persia.
3.   *siege of Tarragona*: Tarragona was captured by the French after
     a siege in 1811.

CHAPTER 11

1.   *'Pius VII ... letter as the "citizen cardinal Chiaramonti" in
     favour of the Cisalpine Republic'*: Luigi Barnaba Chiaramonti
     was Pope, as Pius VII, from 1800 to 1823. The 'pastoral letter'
     was a Christmas homily issued in 1797, urging acceptance of the
     Cisalpine Republic, instituted in northern Italy by Napoleon. As
     Pope, he first signed a concordat with Napoleon, then crowned
     him as Emperor in 1804, and finally broke with him, being held
     prisoner for a time in France as a consequence.

CHAPTER 12

1. *Madonna of Cimabue*: There is no Madonna by Cimabue in San Petronio.
2. *baiocchi*: An old papal coin of minimal value.

CHAPTER 13

1. *Bouffes in Paris*: A theatre where comedies were put on; 'bouffes' deriving from the Italian 'buffo', meaning 'comic'.
2. *Tancred*: A French knight (d. 1112) who distinguished himself on the First Crusade and is one of the heroes of Tasso's epic poem, *Jerusalem Delivered*.
3. *Burati*: Pietro Buratti (1772–1832), a poet who wrote in Venetian dialect.
4. *into what Circe long ago turned the companions of Ulysses*: They were turned into swine, in a famous episode in the *Odyssey*.
5. *the travel guide of a Mrs Starke*: Mariana Starke (1762?–1838), a dramatist and travel writer who was living in northern Italy during the years of the Napoleonic conquest. Stendhal is probably referring to her *Information and Directions for Travellers on the Continent*, which was translated into French in 1826.
6. *sbirri*: Italian police officers.

PART II

CHAPTER 14

1. *podestàs*: The rough equivalent of a mayor, exercising power in a town or locality.
2. *Parmigiano*: Or else Parmigianino, real name Francesco Mazzola (1503–40), a painter and etcher in the Mannerist style who came from Parma, as his adopted name implies.
3. *'Intelligenti pauca!'*: Literally 'Men of little intelligence', but figuratively the equivalent of 'Need I say more?'

CHAPTER 15

1. *Barbone*: The nickname given to Antonio Gasbarone, a celebrated Italian brigand in Stendhal's day.
2. *Guido Reni*: A painter (1575–1642) from Bologna, greatly

admired in the seventeenth and eighteenth centuries, but less so since, his work now being thought over-sentimental.

CHAPTER 16

1. *Judith*: A beautiful Jewish widow who enters the camp of Nebuchadnezzar's besieging army, then seduces and decapitates its general, Holofernes. See the Book of Judith in the Apocrypha.
2. *Razori*: Giovanni Rasori (1766–1837), a pro-French doctor whom Stendhal had known in Milan.

CHAPTER 17

1. *Figaro caught in flagrante by Almaviva*: In the last act of Beaumarchais's comedy *The Marriage of Figaro*, Count Almaviva comes upon Figaro apparently making love to his (the count's) wife, although the supposed countess is in fact the maid Susanna, dressed up.
2. *Armide*: One of the heroines of Tasso's *Jerusalem Delivered*. She uses her charms to prevent the knight Rinaldo from joining the Crusader army.
3. *Jansenists*: An especially rigorous Christian sect in France in the second half of the seventeenth century. Stendhal uses the name to characterize all bigoted moralizers.

CHAPTER 18

1. *Vanvitelli*: Luigi Vanvitelli (1700–1773), a Neapolitan painter, writer and architect who built in the classical style.
2. *Hippolytus, son of Theseus*: Hippolytus rejected the advances of his stepmother, Phaedra, who then claimed he had raped her and hanged herself. His father, Theseus, having prayed to Poseidon that his son be punished, Hippolytus was dragged to his death by his own horses.
3. *Alessandro Farnese . . . forcing Henri IV to withdraw from Paris*: Alessandro Farnese (1545–92) was sent by Philip II of Spain to the assistance of French Catholics against the Protestant King Henri IV. He forced Henri to raise the siege of Paris in 1590.
4. *nébieu d'Asti*: 'Nebbiolo' is the best-known grape variety in the wine-growing region around Asti.
5. *Alfieri*: Conte Vittorio Alfieri (1749–1803), adventurer, lover, poet, tragedian and an early Italian nationalist who lived with

and may eventually have married the Countess of Albany, wife, then widow of the Young Pretender to the British throne.

6.   *Charlotte Corday*: Charlotte de Corday d'Armont (1768–93) stabbed the extremist Marat in his bath, in the hope of stemming the Revolutionary violence, and was guillotined.

CHAPTER 21

1.   *Palagi*: Pelagio Palagi (1775–1860), a Bolognese painter.
2.   *he reappeared at the Ave Maria*: That is, at sunset, when the angelus is rung.

CHAPTER 22

1.   *Reina*: Francisco Reina (1770–1826) was also a prominent liberal, imprisoned by the Austrians.

CHAPTER 23

1.   *Crescentius*: A Roman patrician whose dates are uncertain; he tried to have the reigning Pope strangled and to restore the Roman Republic.
2.   *Fokelberg ... Tenerani ... Hayez*: Bengt Erland Fogelberg (1786–1854) and Pietro Tenerani (*c.*1789–1869) were both well-known neoclassical sculptors; Federico Hayez (1791–1882) was a Venetian painter of mainly Romantic subjects.
3.   *Abbé de Condillac*: Étienne Bonnot de Condillac (1715–80), a philosopher much influenced by Locke, believing that all knowledge was derived from sense data. He was tutor to the duke of Parma from 1758 to 1767.

CHAPTER 24

1.   THE GARDENER AND HIS LORD: This is in fact an abridged version of a poem from Book IV of La Fontaine's *Fables*.
2.   *Marie de Médicis ... Bazin's excellent History of Louis XIII*: Marie de Médicis (1573–1642), born into the great Florentine Medici family, became queen of France as the wife of King Henri IV. Following his assassination, in 1610, she had herself declared regent on behalf of her son, Louis XIII. He later had her imprisoned and she took up arms against him. A reconciliation was negotiated by the effective ruler of France, Cardinal

Richelieu, but she was finally forced into exile in Germany. Anaïs de Bazin's *Histoire de France sous Louis XIII* was first published in 1842, the year of Stendhal's death.

3. *St Bartholomew destroyed the Protestants in France*: On the night of 23–4 August 1572, some three thousand French Protestants were slaughtered on the orders of King Charles IX; the massacre led to a resumption of the religious wars between Catholics and Protestants.

4. *in contradittorio*: That is, in adversarial proceedings, with the case for the defence being put to the court.

CHAPTER 26

1. *Petrarch's*: Francesco Petrarca (1304–74), one of Italy's greatest poets, celebrated for the sonnets written in the vernacular and dedicated to Laura, a girl with whom he fell platonically in love in Avignon. Stendhal admired him not least as a (very) early forerunner of the movement to unify Italy.

2. *the Minorites . . . the Fontanas and the Duvoisins*: The Minorites were a strict order of Franciscan monks. Francesco Luigi Fontana (1750–1822), a Barnabite friar, later a cardinal, who drew up Napoleon's excommunication for Pope Pius VI in 1809. Jean Baptiste Duvoisin (1744–1813) was Napoleon's ecclesiastical adviser.

3. *Cimarosa . . . 'Quelle pupille tenere!'*: Domenico Cimarosa (1749–1801) was one of Stendhal's favourite composers. He wrote some eighty operas, notably *The Secret Marriage*. The aria comes from an opera called *Gli Orazi e Curiazi*; its English title would be 'Those Tender Pupils'.

4. *Pergolesi*: Giovanni Batista Pergolesi (1710–36), a Neapolitan composer whose best-known opera is *La Serva padrona* (*The Maid as Mistress*).

5. *two lines from Petrarch*: Not in fact from Petrarch but from Pietro Metastasio (1698–1782), poet and librettist.

CHAPTER 27

1. *Tu l'as voulu, Georges Dandin!*: A proverbial line from Molière's comedy *Georges Dandin ou le Mari confondu* (*George Dandin or the Husband Confounded*), in which Dandin, a rich peasant, marries above himself and finds his wife being unfaithful with an aristocrat. The words mean 'You asked for it, George Dandin!'

2.   *aggrottato*: Literally, 'frowning'.
3.   *contino*: Or 'contadino', meaning 'peasant'.

CHAPTER 28

1.   *TO THE HAPPY FEW*: This dedication is in English in the original. Stendhal cites the phrase at least three times in different places in his oeuvre.

PENGUIN CLASSICS

THÉRÈSE RAQUIN
EMILE ZOLA

'It was like a lightning flash of passion, swift, blinding, across a leaden sky'

In a dingy apartment on the Passage du Pont Neuf in Paris, Thérèse Raquin is trapped in a loveless marriage to her sickly cousin Camille. The numbing tedium of her life is suddenly shattered when she embarks on a turbulent affair with her husband's earthy friend Laurent, but their animal passion for each other soon compels the lovers to commit a crime that will haunt them forever. *Thérèse Raquin* caused a scandal when it appeared in 1867 and brought its twenty-seven-year-old author a notoriety that followed him throughout his life. Zola's novel is not only an uninhibited portrayal of adultery, madness and ghostly revenge, but is also a devastating exploration of the darkest aspects of human existence.

Robin Buss's new translation superbly conveys Zola's fearlessly honest and matter of fact style. In his introduction, he discusses Zola's life and literary career, and the influence of art, literature and science on his writing. This edition also includes the preface to the second edition of 1868, a chronology, further reading and notes.

Translated with an introduction and notes by Robin Buss

Penguin Classics

THREE TALES
GUSTAVE FLAUBERT

'When she went to church, she would sit gazing at the picture of the Holy Spirit and it struck her that it looked rather like her parrot'

First published in 1877, the *Three Tales*, dominated by questions of doubt, love, loneliness and religious experience, form Flaubert's final great work. 'A Simple Heart' relates the story of Félicité – an uneducated serving-woman who retains her Catholic faith despite a life of desolation and loss. 'The Legend of Saint Julian Hospitator', inspired by a stained-glass window in Rouen cathedral, describes the fate of Julian, a sadistic hunter destined to murder his own parents. The blend of faith and cruelty that dominates this story may also be found in 'Herodias' – a reworking of the tale of Salome and John the Baptist. Rich with a combination of desire, sorrow and faith, these three diverse works are a triumphant conclusion to Flaubert's creative life.

Roger Whitehouse's vibrant new translation captures the exquisite style of the original prose. Geoffrey Wall's introduction considers the inspiration for the tales in the context of Flaubert's life and other work. This edition includes a further reading list and detailed notes.

Translated by Roger Whitehouse

Edited with an introduction by Geoffrey Wall

PENGUIN CLASSICS

OLD GORIOT   HONORE DE BALZAC

'His blue eyes, formerly so lively, seemed to have turned a sad leaden grey
. . . People either pitied him or were shocked by him'

Monsieur Goriot is one of a select group of lodgers at Madame Vauquer's
Parisian boarding house. At first his wealth inspires respect, but as his
circumstances are reduced he becomes shunned by those around him, and
soon his only remaining visitors are two beautiful, mysterious young
women. Goriot claims that they are his daughters, but his fellow boarders,
including master criminal Vautrin, have other ideas. And when Eugene
Rastignac, a poor but ambitious law student, learns the truth, he decides
to turn it to his advantage. *Old Goriot* is one of the key novels of Balzac's
Comédie Humaine series, and a compelling examination of two
obsessions, love and money. Witty and brilliantly detailed, it is a superb
study of the bourgeoisie in the years following the French Revolution.

M. A. Crawford's fine translation is accompanied by an introduction
discussing Balzac's creation of distinctive characters from all levels of
society, and his ability to transform the lives of ordinary people into
profound tragedy.

Translated with an introduction by M. A. Crawford

PENGUIN CLASSICS

THE COUNT OF MONTE CRISTO
ALEXANDRE DUMAS

'On what slender threads do life and fortune hang'

Thrown in prison for a crime he has not committed, Edmond Dantes is confined to the grim fortress of If. There he learns of a great hoard of treasure hidden on the Isle of Monte Cristo and he becomes determined not only to escape, but also to unearth the treasure and use it to plot the destruction of the three men responsible for his incarceration. Dumas's epic tale of suffering and retribution, inspired by a real-life case of wrongful imprisonment, was a huge popular success when it was first serialized in the 1840s.

Robin Buss's lively English translation is complete and unabridged, and remains faithful to the style of Dumas's original. This edition includes an introduction, explanatory notes and suggestions for further reading.

'Robin Buss broke new ground with a fresh version of *Monte Cristo* for Penguin' *Oxford Guide to Literature in English Translation*

Translated with an introduction by Robin Buss

PENGUIN CLASSICS

MADAME BOVARY GUSTAVE FLAUBERT

'Oh, why, dear God, did I marry him?'

Emma Bovary is beautiful and bored, trapped in her marriage to a
mediocre doctor and stifled by the banality of provincial life. An ardent
devourer of sentimental novels, she longs for passion and seeks escape in
fantasies of high romance, in voracious spending and, eventually, in
adultery. But even her affairs bring her disappointment, and when real life
continues to fail to live up to her romantic expectations the consequences
are devastating. Flaubert's erotically charged and psychologically acute
portrayal of Emma Bovary caused a moral outcry on its publication in
1857. It was deemed so lifelike that many women claimed they were the
model for his heroine; but Flaubert insisted: 'Madame Bovary, c'est moi'.

This modern translation by Flaubert's biographer, Geoffrey Wall, retains
all the delicacy and precision of the French original. This edition also
contains a preface by the novelist Michèle Roberts.

'A masterpiece' Julian Barnes

'A supremely beautiful novel' Michèle Roberts

Translated and edited with an introduction by Geoffrey Wall
With a Preface by Michèle Roberts

PENGUIN CLASSICS

SENTIMENTAL EDUCATION   GUSTAVE FLAUBERT

'He loved her without reservation, without hope, unconditionally'

Frederic Moreau is a law student returning home to Normandy from Paris when he first notices Madame Arnoux, a slender, dark woman several years older than himself. It is the beginning of an infatuation that will last a lifetime. He befriends her husband, an influential businessman, and their paths cross and re-cross over the years. Through financial upheaval, political turmoil and countless affairs, Madame Arnoux remains the constant, unattainable love of Moreau's life. Flaubert described his sweeping story of a young man's passions, ambitions and amours as 'the moral history of the men of my generation'. Based on his own youthful passion for an older woman, *Sentimental Education* blends love story, historical authenticity and satire to create one of the greatest French novels of the nineteenth century.

Geoffrey Wall's fresh revision of Robert Baldick's original translation is accompanied by an insightful new introduction discussing the personal and historical influences on Flaubert's writing. This edition also contains a new chronology, further reading and explanatory notes.

Translated with an introduction by Robert Baldick
Revised and edited by Geoffrey Wall

PENGUIN CLASSICS

NOTRE-DAME DE PARIS   VICTOR HUGO

'He was like a giant broken in pieces and badly reassembled'

In the vaulted Gothic towers of Notre-Dame lives Quasimodo, the hunchbacked bellringer. Mocked and shunned for his appearance, he is pitied only by Esmerelda, a beautiful gypsy dancer to whom he becomes completely devoted. Esmerelda, however, has also attracted the attention of the sinister archdeacon Claude Frollo, and when she rejects his lecherous approaches, Frollo hatches a plot to destroy her that only Quasimodo can prevent. Victor Hugo's sensational, evocative novel brings life to the medieval Paris he loved, and mourns its passing in one of the greatest historical romances of the nineteenth century.

John Sturrock's clear, contemporary translation is accompanied by an introduction discussing it as a passionate novel of ideas, written in defence of Gothic architecture and of a burgeoning democracy, and demonstrating that an ugly exterior can conceal moral beauty. This revised edition also includes further reading and a chronology of Hugo's life.

Translated with an introduction by John Sturrock

PENGUIN CLASSICS

GERMINAL   ÉMILE ZOLA

'Buried like moles beneath the crushing weight of the earth, and without a breath of fresh air in their burning lungs, they simply went on tapping'

Etienne Lantier, an unemployed railway worker, is a clever but uneducated young man with a dangerous temper. Compelled to take a back-breaking job at the Le Voreux mine when he cannot get other work, he discovers that his fellow miners are ill, hungry and in debt, unable to feed and clothe their families. When conditions in the mining community deteriorate even further, Lantier finds himself leading a strike that could mean starvation or salvation for all. The thirteenth novel in Zola's great Rougon-Macquart sequence, *Germinal* expresses outrage at the exploitation of the many by the few, but also shows humanity's capacity for compassion and hope.

Roger Pearson's lively and modern new translation is accompanied by an introduction that examines the social and political background to Zola's masterpiece, in particular the changing relationship between labour and capital. This edition also contains a filmography, chronology and notes.

Translated and edited by Roger Pearson

THE STORY OF PENGUIN CLASSICS

Before 1946 ... 'Classics' are mainly the domain of academics and students, without readable editions for everyone else. This all changes when a little-known classicist, E. V. Rieu, presents Penguin founder Allen Lane with the translation of Homer's *Odyssey* that he has been working on and reading to his wife Nelly in his spare time.

1946 *The Odyssey* becomes the first Penguin Classic published, and promptly sells three million copies. Suddenly, classic books are no longer for the privileged few.

1950s Rieu, now series editor, turns to professional writers for the best modern, readable translations, including Dorothy L. Sayers's *Inferno* and Robert Graves's *The Twelve Caesars*, which revives the salacious original.

1960s The Classics are given the distinctive black jackets that have remained a constant throughout the series's various looks. Rieu retires in 1964, hailing the Penguin Classics list as 'the greatest educative force of the 20th century'.

1970s A new generation of translators arrives to swell the Penguin Classics ranks, and the list grows to encompass more philosophy, religion, science, history and politics.

1980s The Penguin American Library joins the Classics stable, with titles such as *The Last of the Mohicans* safeguarded. Penguin Classics now offers the most comprehensive library of world literature available.

1990s The launch of Penguin Audiobooks brings the classics to a listening audience for the first time, and in 1999 the launch of the Penguin Classics website takes them online to a larger global readership than ever before.

The 21st Century Penguin Classics are rejacketed for the first time in nearly twenty years. This world famous series now consists of more than 1300 titles, making the widest range of the best books ever written available to millions – and constantly redefining the meaning of what makes a 'classic'.

The Odyssey continues ...

The best books ever written

PENGUIN (🐧) CLASSICS

SINCE 1946

Find out more at www.penguinclassics.com